WALCZYK

A NOVEL BY
TELLIS K. COOLONG

Published by Telly Productions
P.O. Box 4, Milford, ME 04461-0004

For information address Telly Productions
P.O. Box 4, Milford, ME 04461-0004 or e-mail at
tellyproductions@gmail.com

ISBN – 13: 978-1-484-83848-8
ISBN – 10:   1-484-83848-3

Second printing February 2014

Cover photography by Logan Tripp
Cover design by Tellis K. Coolong

Printed in the U.S.A.

For Mum and Dad,

Who Lived This Journey With Me

WALCZYK

PROLOGUE

The invention of the cellular telephone was truly a miraculous creation, one that proved that it is possible to bring almost the entire planet together with one simple, portable piece of technology.

It was also the world's biggest pain in the ass.

Peter Walczyk felt this most strongly as his dragged him out of a much needed, long overdue sleep and into a world where the sun had barely begun to creep up over the horizon. He flipped his phone open, not looking at the display to see who was calling.

It didn't matter who it was.

They were fired.

"What," he grumbled into the phone, making the question sound like an answer.

"Where the hell are you?" came the husky voice of his twenty-three year old assistant, April Donovan. Despite being hired to assist him (hence her title of *assistant*), April was more like his mother. A mother almost ten years his junior, with a mouth like a sailor and a knack for getting what she needed out of people by simply alternating sweet and sour tones.

"April?" he slowly asked, realizing that the alarm clock was on his wife Sara's side of the bed, "What time is it?"

"It's almost six. Where the hell are you?"

"In bed," he replied a bit put off. "Where are you?"

"Outside! For three hours now! You changed your security code and didn't tell me! Again!"

"Oh, yeah," Walczyk said, remembering that Sara had changed it when she fired Oliver, her most recent assistant. Oliver was an overly dramatic young man with better hair than Walczyk's wife. Hearing Sara moan, he rolled over, sliding a hand over her stomach, caressing her bare navel.

"Would you kindly get a robe on and come let me in!"

Walczyk sat up, seeing that he was not going to be able to multi-task this morning. "April, you sound more agitated than usual. Is everything okay?"

"I don't think so," she said, her voice cracking. April was not a woman to cry. She was emotional, certainly. She could be compassionate. Empathetic. But she never cried. Never in his presence. Never in the presence of any of their vast number of shared acquaintances. "Can you come let me in?"

"I'm on my way," Walczyk said, worried. Without a goodbye (April never said goodbye), the line went dead. Walczyk slid his phone onto the nightstand, leaned over to kiss his wife on the cheek, and picked his pants up from the floor.

What were you thinking? Walczyk asked himself as he slid down the stairs into his living room. *Sleeping in on your first day off in four months. Bah!* He was exhausted; there was no doubt about that. The past fourteen weeks of production on his series, *Ordinary World*, had been grueling, made more so by contract disputes with Cate Davis, who was being wooed away by NBC to do a *Law & Order* spin-off set in Chicago. Oh, and there was also the threat of yet another strike, this time by the Directors Guild.

On top of all of that, things with Sara hadn't been great. Their marriage was important to Walczyk, even though it was far from perfect. She complained that he was never around. He complained that she was never around. The marriage, five years old now, was the victim of his moodiness: the frequent depressive spells that drained him of everything, and the highly excited periods. Both extremes separated them, emotionally and physically. Sara spent most nights of the week in the city, coming home occasionally to check on Walczyk and sleep in her own bed. With this arrangement, Walczyk was able to cycle through his crazy moods and keep the scripts coming, and Sara could focus on her own work.

When he met her, Sara was a dancer with the famed Kitty Kat Girls burlesque troupe. Following the dissolution of the troupe, Sara embarked on a fairly successful career as an actress, appearing in episodes of *Grey's Anatomy, True Blood, Justified,* one of the *CSI* fleet of series, and, of course, *Ordinary World*, where she'd been cast, not by Walczyk, but by his producing partner, Ian Maeder, as the sex-addicted relationship counselor Dr. Elizabeth Lovsky. It was about the time when things between them started becoming uncomfortable that Sara started flirting with the notion of writing a film of her own. Walczyk had set her up with Ella Marsters, the lead actresses from *Ordinary World*, and a talented writer in her own right.

Walczyk opened the front door to his Laurel Canyon home. Sitting on the doorstep was April, wearing a dirty, torn, grass-stained dress. Walczyk quietly sat down beside her. "So, what's up?"

April's response was to flop over onto Walczyk's lap, bury her face in her hands, and sob. Walczyk was pretty sure what had happened. He was also pretty sure that she was still drunk, evidenced by the near-empty bottle lying on the step beside her. Walczyk gently stroked the back of her head, pulling her hair back out of her face. The sun rose behind the house and cast its radiant orange glow onto everything around them as April cried. Finally, she sat up, eyes red and puffy, her nose glistening with mucus. She gave a weak laugh and wiped her nose with the back of her hand, which she then wiped on her dress. "I am such a retard."

"April, don't say that."

"Well, I am," she insisted.

"I know. But it's offensive." Acting on that hunch, he launched right into assessment mode. "So who ended it?"

April looked up at him, her eyebrows tilted up like an inverse "V" over her eyes. "I did."

Walczyk nodded, picked April up from his lap, and leaned her against his shoulder. They sat in silence, April sniffing intermittently and Walczyk listening to nature wake up around him.

"So why'd you end it?" Walczyk gently asked.

"Because," she said, not following the thought up with a reason, but with a chug from her bottle of scotch.

"Good reason," Walczyk said, snatching the bottle away and

watching the morning sun glow stretch down towards the thicket of trees that were creeping up the hill towards his house.

She crashed against him, burying her wet face in his shirt. "Because he said it."

"Said *it*?"

"He told me he loved me."

"Aah," he said, nodding. "So you dumped him." Walczyk knew that April was unpredictable, and that she never acted after careful thought. She was the Alpha in any situation, a mindset that had cost her several relationships. But that take-charge attitude also got April her job with Walczyk after she forced her way into his office in the middle of a meeting with Joss Whedon. Seeing her like this, Walczyk's heart broke for her. "Listen to me," he said, picking her head up from his pant leg. "You panicked. Derrick made a very big move last night, saying he loved you. If I'd been seeing Sara for four months, and she said she loved me, I'd tweak too." His mind flashed back to another life, when he had also freaked out at hearing those three little words.

"But you wouldn't dump her."

"We're not far from the converse of that now, if that makes you feel any better."

"The slow, drawn-out implosion of your marriage does nothing to make me feel better," she said, pulling herself up into a seated position.

"But you do love him, right?"

"Yeah," she said, sounding quite unsure.

"April, this is important. Do you love him?"

"I think so," she said, swaying. "I wouldn't have spent four months with him if I didn't, would I?"

"Do you want to know what I think?"

"Let me have it," she said, lurching forward for her bottle. Walczyk caught her and steadied her.

He held the bottle back. "I think you love the *idea* of Derrick, but the jury's still out on whether or not you love the actual item. I think you're feeling what I was feeling at your age – that need to start settling down."

"I don't need anyone," she slurred.

"Bullshit," Walczyk countered. "Everybody needs somebody."

"Then why the hell did I dump him?"

"Same reason you're now going to pieces over losing Derrick, who, if I may say so, is nothing *that* special. Not enough so to go wandering around Los Angeles in the middle of the night."

"Lust?"

"Not quite."

"Insanity?"

"Closer."

"What then?"

Walczyk held up the bottle. "Because you're filthy, stinking drunk."

April leaned over for the bottle, losing her balance. Walczyk set the bottle down on the stone step and steadied April once more, keeping his arm around her.

"I have to know something, April."

"What's that, Boss?"

"Just what the hell did you do to that dress?"

She looked down at the dress, holding the hem up. Black smudges and grass stains decorated the hem of the light blue, torn dress.

"You wouldn't believe me if I told you."

"Try me."

"Well, I couldn't get in. The code was changed."

"Sorry. It's two-six-seven-two-six."

"Lot of help that is now. Well, I wasn't going to pass out on the street and get carted off by the po-po. So I did what I had to do."

"You scaled the gate," Walczyk said, grinning.

"I scaled the gate," she nodded. "And on my way over, snagged my dress on one of the sharp pointy thingies. And the rest..."

"Peter?"

Walczyk turned around. Standing in the doorway wearing Walczyk's dress shirt from last night, was Sara. Behind him, April's phone went off.

"Hey, Hun. I'll be right in," Walczyk said, loving the indecent way Sara always looked with her incredible dancer's legs sticking out from under one of his shirts.

"Peter, we need to talk," Sara said urgently.

"Okay. I'll be right in."

"No, Peter, it's really important."

"Then why don't you go get dressed? We'll go out and get

some breakfast and talk about it. How's the Griddle Café on Sunset Boulevard sound?"

"Peter, shut up and listen. You have to hear what I have to say before the…"

April grabbed Walczyk's arm. "Boss…"

"I swear, Peter, I didn't want it to go down like this–"

"Walz, look!" April said, tugging again on Walczyk like a petulant child.

"Just a minute!" He turned back to Sara. "Didn't want what to go down like this?"

"Walczyk, you have to look at this!"

"Peter, you have to listen to me!"

Walczyk finally turned to April. "April, will you give me a damned minute! My wife is trying to talk to me!" He returned his attention to Sara. "Sorry, Hun. Now what's so–"

Walczyk's field of vision was suddenly obscured by a shaky video playing on April's iPhone, which had been shoved in his face. He turned to April, confused. "What's this?"

"Peter," Sara begged, stepping down onto the pavement, putting a hand on his shoulder. "Listen to me. Before you see that. I have to tell you. Last night, at the wrap party…"

Walczyk grabbed the cell phone and looked at it, squinting to make out the dark video.

"… someone must've had a camera…"

Walczyk was able to discern that the video, which had the logo of the Paparazz-Eye celebrity gossip network stamped on the lower left-hand corner, was of two people making out in a dark corner of what looked like a parking garage.

"I never meant for it to go this far…"

The clip zoomed in on the two people kissing in the corner. Walczyk could now make out the distinct signage from the parking garage across the street from the Four Seasons Los Angeles at Beverly Hills, where the *Ordinary World* wrap party was held last night.

"You were being so distant. I thought maybe you weren't in love with me anymore–"

Walczyk realized the two kissers were both women, and his heart sank as he recognized them.

"I never meant to fall in love with her, but I did."

The video froze at a point where the two women broke their

clinch for a moment. One of the women on April's phone was Ella Marsters.

The other woman was Sara. Walczyk suddenly remembered Sara saying she was going to leave early. She said she had a headache and someone was going to take her home. He'd never asked who.

"Peter, I'm in love with Ella."

Walczyk slumped in stunned silence, watching the video start over from the beginning. Watching Sara run her hands all over Ella. Watching the two women open their mouths to one another. Watching his wife embrace someone else. And it happened over and over again.

"Peter, say something," Sara pleaded.

"Boss," April asked, putting a hand on his shoulder, "are you all right?"

Answering both women, Walczyk stood, stepped down two steps, and threw up in the hydrangea bush. Slowly, he turned, wiping his mouth on his arm. He gave April back her phone, carefully, as though it were an egg.

"Peter..." Sara began.

He silently paced the yard in front of his home. He breathed in deeply, the sound of the air sucking in through his nose filling the silence. His head felt thick, like he was in the midst of a really good drunk. April stood by, watching helplessly, fearing the worst. Walczyk stared at the ground for several moments, before turning to his bedraggled assistant. Amidst the soft morning sounds of the birds, crickets, and traffic, another sound softly clicked in the background.

"Boss–"

"Peter–"

Walczyk held up a finger to silence both women and carefully listened. There was a murmur of voices. The clicking of cameras.

They already knew.

"Sara, get in the house."

"Peter, please..." Sara pleaded

"Now!" Sara glanced from her husband to April, turned, and slipped back into the house.

"You," Walczyk said, calmly turning to April, "go home."

She stared at him incredulously. "Go home? How the hell am I supposed to go home? I dumped my ride home."

Walczyk stepped inside, retrieved the keys to his silver Jaguar from the ceramic dish by the door, and tossed them to April. "Go home, April. Clean up. Pack a bag. A week, ten days worth of stuff and be back here in an hour and a half."

"Why?" April asked warily as she descended the stairs to Walczyk's home.

"Because I can't deal with this," he breathed, his lungs unwilling to hold air. "The paparazzi are already circling. I... I've got... I've got to get out of this place. Now go. Please. And be quick."

"Where are we going?" she asked, reaching the last of the stone steps leading to Walczyk's front door.

"I have no idea."

CHAPTER ONE
THREE MONTHS LATER...

Peter Walczyk sat in his writer's nook, which was the café section of the Bronze Lantern book store on Cole Island's bustling Main Street, sipping at a raspberry Italian soda. He wondered if putting a shot of raspberry flavoring into tonic water was what made his Italian soda truly *Italian*. His eyes scanned the room. He saw customers making a mess out of ordering a flavored coffee. He saw Garry Olsen, the Lantern's owner and manager, zipping around making sure everything was perfect. He looked back at his empty computer screen, with its cursor blinking at him, daring him to write something. *Come on. Do it. I dare you. Be productive today. Show them all!*

After a few moments staring at a blank screen, Walczyk let his eyes wander back to the counter, where an exceptionally round man with thick glasses, flabby arms, and a Voltron T-shirt was trying to convince Alicia, the poor girl stuck at the cash register for the afternoon shift, that he *always* got extra *whipcream* on his mocha-loca-choca-whatever, and that this extra portion of *whipcream* was always free. The human snowman's disagreement rose to a volume that attracted the attention of the overly eager-to-please Garry Olsen. Garry stopped his task of picking up magazines and proceeded to the counter. Walczyk was rather thankful for the timing of the incident, since the magazine Garry had been about to pick up was a copy of *Paparazz-Eye Weekly*. This popular piece of pulp was printed by the Paparazz-Eye Media Network, a denigrating "news" machine dedicated to the sole purpose of taking the lives of the famous – public and private – and making them the world's business. This particular issue had that tired, overly-published image of Sara locked in that damned kiss with Ella in the parking garage adjacent to the Four Seasons hotel. The headline 'Did He Drive Them To It?' was printed beneath the photograph, and in a small circle to the left of the text was a picture of Walczyk, making a particularly sour looking face, which was no doubt snapped on the red carpet at some film premiere without warning. They loved that, these paparazzi rat bastards. The worse a person looks in one of their pictures, the more they get paid for it. That seems to be the general rule of thumb in the paparazzi business. And the un-famous say that such attention is the price one paid for being famous. An uninformed opinion, Walczyk felt, as these people didn't have photographers dogging their every move, following them to the grocery store or the Laundromat. They surely didn't get to enjoy the cacophony of whirrs and clicks and pops as cameras snapped pictures at breakneck speed, their operators screaming out at you, trying to get you to look in their direction while flash bulbs went off in a massive, strobing wall of bright light. There was a reason people like Jack Nicholson always wear sunglasses.

But the magazine was only part of the reason Walczyk dreaded having Garry working around in the café. Garry was very eager to please. *Too* eager, at times. Walczyk valued his privacy and space, and he did not mesh too well with the star-struck owner of the Bronze Lantern, who had made it his goal in life, since Walczyk had walked into his store three months ago, to make sure that he was pleased and satisfied and comfortable at all times. Walczyk was completely pleased and satisfied with the service he got from the teenage girls working the counter, and that they didn't know who the hell he was. But Garry, in his enthusiastic efforts to ensure that Walczyk was comfortable, kept him constantly on guard with his constant barrage of inane questions. "Whatcha writing? The next season of that little TV show of yours?" or "Why didn't your wife come with you on your little vacation?" Most recently, the question that drove him to Walczyk's corner was, "You see that trash they published about you in the *Snooper*? As if your wife's really a lezzie! What nonsense!" Garry meant well, bless his little heart (as his mother would say whenever Walczyk complained about the retailer). After all, as Walczyk's mother constantly reminded him, he *was* the first resident of Cole Island to go off after graduation and become an Academy Award winner. Every time one of his movies played at the Nickelodeon in Portland, his face graced the cover of a magazine, or an ad for *Ordinary World* ran on basic cable, it was a reminder that a local boy had done good.

Beside him, he noticed the balding man in the pastel yellow T-shirt scowling in his direction, no doubt angry that Walczyk had commandeered a small end table that sat between two overstuffed leather chairs and was using it as a work table. Whenever Walczyk would catch the man's eye, he'd just smile and nod, as though they were casual acquaintances. Every day, there was something different that Walczyk, or someone else seemed to do that pissed off "Ol' Yeller," as April had taken to calling him. One day it was the indecency of a mother nursing her crying baby. Another time, Ol' Yeller spent an entire afternoon barking at a table of teenagers who were working on some kind of writing project, laughing while enjoying their mocha shakes. "The café is a place for silent pursuits," he kept repeating, like some anal retentive mantra. But the worst thing this miserable goat did was a quiet little sin he committed every single day – read the newspaper. A newspaper he never paid for. A newspaper he would tear apart, devour, fold and refold, and completely disorganize over the course of an afternoon, destroying a perfectly salable newspaper. *Without paying for it.*

"Get... that... *thing*... out... of... here!" the Man in the Yellow Shirt barked on this particular day, making each word its own nasty, snide little sentence.

The entire café turned to look at Ol' Yeller, born one Todd Miller according to Walczyk's mother, was pointing, accusingly, at a beautiful almost pure white beagle, tethered to a leash connected to Walczyk's assistant, April, who was wearing cut-offs and a bikini top. Garry Olsen rushed over to the dog, immediately petting it, along with two young children, whose faces were alight with joy at the antics of the puppy.

"Oh, what's the matter, Todd?" Garry asked, not standing up. "Someone move your end table on you again?"

"It's that *thing*, Garry!" Ol' Yeller snapped, pointing at the little beagle. "Don't you know–?"

"Oh, shut up and read your damned newspaper," April interrupted.

"April," Walczyk hissed, growing weary of reminding April that people talked differently on Cole Island than they did in Los Angeles.

April waved him off, as she always did, and took the dog over to the counter, where she ordered an Italian soda and an iced coffee from Alicia and asked her to deliver them to Walczyk's table. She then proceeded to parade the dog past Ol' Yeller and sat at the table with Walczyk.

"So, April, what's the deal with Sparky here?" Walczyk asked, eyeing the beagle, whose tail was whapping back and forth in the air, making a swishing noise that he hoped was setting Ol' Yeller's teeth on edge.

She handed the leash to Walczyk as Alicia arrived at the table with the drinks. "His name is Dexter, and you'd better be nice to me, or I won't let you sleep with him."

"That's your dog?"

"Yeah."

"And you named him 'Dexter?'"

"Yes, I did. Why? What's wrong with Dexter?"

"Nothing. Except that it really isn't a dog's name."

"Neither are Brownie and Cocoa, but it worked for your parents."

"My parents own two *chocolate*-colored dachshunds: Brownie and Cocoa. And, while I admit they are cloyingly sweet names, they are appropriate names for two brown wiener dogs. Dexter, on the other hand," he said, staring the dog in the eye, "says nothing about a white beagle. Now *Snowball*, that would've been an appropriate name. *Flurry*, *Blizzard*, all great names for a *white* dog. Hell, even *Whitey* would've made more sense than Dexter."

"Dexter was my grandfather's name, and he had white hair," she said, her mouth verging on a frown.

"Your grandfather's name is Leopold, and he's still alive."

"I don't care if he was named Julio Igleseas," Ol' Yeller complained from behind his wrinkled paper. "Just get him out of here!"

Taking the upper road and ignoring the man, Walczyk steered the conversation in a slightly different direction. "Dexter is kinda cute, though. It could grow on me, if this really were your dog. Come on, now, whose is he?"

"Oh, he's my dog. *Our* dog. The house dog."

"April, we live in a cramped room at a prissy B&B. I doubt management will let us have a dog in the room."

"Hey, what management doesn't know–"

"April, we can't–" Walczyk paused as Dexter gave his hand a big lick. Walczyk looked down to see Dexter looking up at him, the canine equivalent of a smile crossing his fuzzy face.

"And I suppose you're now going to tell me that *all* the experts say that pets are a great form of therapy."

"Exactly!" she said, stabbing a finger into his chest. "And don't worry about piddles and poopies. He'll sleep in his crate, and Melissa said that dogs seldom mess in their crates."

"Piddles and poopies?"

"You know. Their messes."

"I gathered," Walczyk said, half surprised, half pleased April hadn't said pisses and shits. "And this Melissa is–?""

"The girl who owns the pet shop across the street. Auggie and Lando's Pet Emporium. She said that animals tend not to mess in confined spaces. She didn't know why, but she said it's true."

"And is Melissa prepared to take Dexter back after he makes a snack out of one of your Manolo Blahniks? Or makes piddles or poopies on your iPhone?"

"Why don't you want a dog, Boss?"

"It's not that I don't want him. It's that we don't have room for him. April, we live out of a hotel room. There's barely enough room for the two of us. How the hell are we going to fit a dog into that living situation?"

She thought a moment, finally smirking and replying, simply, "Carefully?"

Apparently, April pondered as she helped lug their seven suitcases out to her Jeep Liberty, Sissy LeVasseur and the courteous staff at the Spruce Nettle Inn weren't animal lovers. To their credit, though, it did take them two days to find the nerve to ask Walczyk and April (and Dexter) to leave the B&B. "This is most certainly going to be on the Paparazz-Eye website by the end of the day," Walczyk mused as they packed. "*Hollywood Recluse and Dog Booted from New England Inn.* I've hit a new low."

Walczyk had inquired at the Hummingbird Inn, the Seaside Hotel and the Independence Inn, while April had checked out the Chestnut Thistle, the Overlook, and the Brass Tack. None of these fine establishments wanted to host Walczyk, April, and more importantly, baby Dexter, during Walczyk's ever-extending homelessness. It was as she'd said when Walczyk gave her the grand tour of Cole Island: "These fancy little touristy joints seem to have been named by people trying too hard to be sophisticated. I mean, what the hell's a 'spruce nettle', anyway?"

April found herself wishing her new address *was* the Brass Tack when she first saw the Meadowbrook Motel and its proprietor, a bullfrog-looking man parked out front in a cheap aluminum folding lawn chair, smoking a Tiparillo and scratching his bulging stomach through a dirty red tank top. Watching from the front seat of the Jeep as Walczyk settled the arrangements with the bullfrog man, April knew that it would be imperative that she break out "The Kit" upon checking in.

Sure enough, April was not surprised when she and Dexter crossed the threshold into Walczyk's room, Number 15, which was on the back side of the motel. Thankfully, her room was only a few doors down, Number 12. While Walczyk's room didn't stink of old cheese (as hers had), old feet (as hers had), or old people (again, as hers had), it was your standard discount motel room: two twin beds covered in chintzy floral bedspreads. Between them was a cheap flea market simulated oak bedside table. April wondered to herself where the hotelier had stolen the nightstand Bible from. A tarnished brass lamp hung over each bed, no doubt dim enough to hide the worst of the stains on the mottled, almond-colored carpet covering the floor.

While Walczyk juggled his three pieces of luggage and Dexter's leash, April had brought the two large rolling suitcases and matching shoulder bag that comprised "The Kit." She opened the front pocket of the shoulder bag and removed one of those large, black plastic leaf collecting bags and a pair of thick yellow rubber gloves. Walczyk grabbed Dexter and pulled the twitchy beagle up into his lap to keep him out of April's pursuit of cleanliness.

"What are you doing?" she asked, pulling on the rubber gloves.

"Holding the dog," Walczyk said, scanning the room for the remote control.

"I thought you didn't like Dexter."

"The jury's still out on ol' Dex. But *you* like him, so we're keeping him regardless of how I feel. I figure I'd better make an effort to get to know him."

Finding the remote in the top dresser drawer, Walczyk snapped the television on and stroked the dog's head. April, meanwhile, stripped the bed down, being careful not to let the bedclothes touch her bare arms. She shoved the motel bedding, complete with pillows, into the garbage bag.

"You know, you could get your shit unpacked," April said, tossing the large leaf bag into the far corner of the room near the bathroom.

"And you could ask nicely," Walczyk suggested, a wry smile crossing his boyish face.

"You're right, I could," she said. Walczyk rolled his eyes, but he placed Dexter carefully on the floor and went to work, removing a DVD player and a set of RCA cables from one of his own suitcases. He then proceeded to hook the machine up to the motel's decrepit television.

April gracelessly tipped the larger of the suitcases, a red monstrosity larger than herself, onto the floor. She leaned down, unzipped the case, and opened it up. Inside was a vast supply of bedding, folded and sealed in vacuum storage bags. She reached for two of them, unzipping them one at a time, removing the pillows that were compressed within them and allowing them to regain their normal, plump size. Behind her, the opening chords to the theme song from *All in the Family* played, telling her that Walczyk had succeeded in hooking his DVD player up.

"Flannel or cotton sheets?" April asked, bending back down into the large suitcase.

"Cotton," Walczyk replied, returning to his armchair and picking Dexter back up. April pulled a set of green cotton sheets from the vacuum bag and made Walczyk's bed, sure to leave all sheets and blankets untucked at the ends. She stuffed each of the re-inflated pillows into cases, and tossed them onto the bed. She stowed the empty vacuum bags into the suitcase, along with a still-sealed selection of sheets and pillow cases and wheeled the suitcase to the door.

"You need the bathroom before I start?" she asked, peeling her shirt off.

Walczyk shook his head, picking up the remote and switching the TV off. "Go for it. I'll be with Dex out on the veranda, such as it is."

April stepped out of her shorts and zipped open the shoulder bag. "Do *not* take him outside without his leash!"

"Yes, dear," Walczyk said as April removed a disposable painter's jumpsuit and a filter mask from the bag. Walczyk untied the leash from the table leg and sat at the foot of the bed, coaxing Dexter over so he could attach the leash to his little pink collar.

"Really, April? Pink?" Walczyk asked over his shoulder. "Don't you think the poor thing's going to be messed up enough as it is, having you for a mom and me for a crazy uncle?"

April pulled up the painter's jumpsuit and zipped it up to her throat. "Pink was all they had in his size in stock. Melissa promised me a black collar as soon as they come in–"

"On Tuesday?" he finished.

"How'd you–?"

"On Cole Island," he said, standing up and leading the dog to the door, "everything comes on Tuesday."

"Well, then, it'll be in on Tuesday." She dragged the other suitcase over to the bathroom, unzipping it and revealing a bevy of cleaning supplies. "Last chance to go before I get to work."

"If the mood strikes, I'll just pick a tree opposite Dexter," he said, smirking as he followed the impatient dog out of the room.

Despite its deficiencies – and there were many – the Meadowbrook Motel had one thing going for it: behind the shitty looking strip motel, there was a beautiful, undisturbed stretch of land. Walczyk unfolded the canvas camp chair he'd snagged from April's Jeep and plopped down, tying Dexter's leash to the leg. He leaned back, letting the crisp aroma of east coast air waft into his nose. He'd been to several beaches on the west coast with Sara, but he was still convinced that the air at the beaches along the coast of Maine smelled different than it did off the coast of California. Was it logical? No. Was it scientific? No, he'd long ago decided. But that was just the way it was.

Walczyk pulled out a legal pad and began to scribble notes on it for a story. It was incomplete, but it had also never yet gone down on paper, and Walczyk wanted to record it while he still had an interest in the idea. He wasn't sure if this would be his next movie or his first foray into novel writing. He just knew that it was *not* going to be a television series. He missed the "one and done" philosophy that filmmaking had. Not that that was even true anymore, what with the majority of the industry's prize projects being sequels, prequels, adaptations, or remakes of existing properties.

After fifteen minutes or so of writing, Walczyk stopped and looked down at the pad. He didn't know where to go with his creation. Questions tumbled around in his head as he sat there, staring up at the clouds through his cheap gas station sunglasses. He had never seen the logic in paying large sums of money for sunglasses, an item you always end up losing eventually. A wet sensation crossed his calf and he looked down to see Dexter staring up at him with dark chestnut eyes and a look of want on his face.

"What?" he asked, knowing there would be no reply.

"*I'm bored, you jackass,*" Dexter replied wordlessly.

"You can't be bored. Look at all this grass to play in."

"*Ooh. Playing in the grass. How dignified!*"

"Well, life as a dog isn't meant to be dignified."

"*Where the hell have you been the past, oh, I don't know, span of existence? The pets of the rich, famous, and powerful are treated better than the servants of the rich, famous, and powerful. Now apologize.*"

Walczyk shook his head, doubting his own sanity. "I can't believe I'm talking to a dog."

"*Probably the most intelligent conversation you've had all week.*"

Walczyk returned his attention to the notes and blurbs he'd scribbled onto his notepad and turned to a fresh page and started another idea. His train of thought was interrupted by the rhythmic slapping of Dexter's tail against his leg. He put down the notepad and pulled Dexter up into his lap. Dexter put his front paws on Walczyk's chest and began licking at the scruffy beard growth that had been forming on Walczyk's face. Walczyk pushed the dog away and reached for his notepad again. The dog bounded back up onto his chest and ran his tongue over the entirety of Walczyk's mouth. Walczyk, his eyes clamped shut, gave in and let the dog ravage him, laughing the entire time.

"Hey, you two!" April bellowed out the open window. "Ten

minutes and you have to come in!"

"Aw, Mom!" Walczyk called back, grinning.

"I mean it. Ten minutes and you need to come in and clean up. We're going to your parents' for supper tonight."

"Oh," he said, his joy deflated as quickly as it had inflated. Sensing his mood, Dexter jumped back down to the grass.

Twenty minutes later, with April cleaning her own room, Walczyk stepped into his freshly-scrubbed shower and let the cool water cascade down on him. The smell of lemon-scented cleansers permeated the entire bathroom, even with the windows open. He thought about the stories he'd attempted to write that afternoon and realized they were utter shit.

Knowing how April laid out a bathroom, he reached blindly for his bar of Zest, the same soap his Grammie Reynolds used to use when she would scrub his face as a child. As Walczyk washed, his mind wandered from random topic to random topic: maybe a visit with his old best friend, Vic Gordon. A day at the beach with Dexter. Grocery shopping. These thoughts began to coalesce into one general question: *where do I go from here?*

Walczyk washed his face, scrubbing deep into his skin with the pale green bar of soap. He wondered, as he moved on to his underarms, just how long he could hide from his life here in Maine. How long could he deny the fact that, waiting for him in California, was a career, a horde of fans, an army of paparazzi, and his wife, with her new girly plaything.

Walczyk dreaded dinner. Not because he disliked his parents. Quite the opposite. Henry and Diane were the kind of parents every child wished they had. They were fair and giving, understanding and willing to love unconditionally. But like all parents, they lacked one simple capability: they could not mind their own business. And he knew that, just like the past five Friday nights he'd had dinner with his parents, they would use dinner as their opportunity to put their weekly questions to him: What was he going to do? What was his plan? Was he staying in Maine for good? Was he returning to Los Angeles anytime soon?

Standing naked in a cold shower, streams of water trickling down his face and onto the shower floor, Walczyk suddenly felt hollow. Happiness seemed years away. He couldn't even clearly remember what it had felt like to roll around with Dexter. He remembered laughing, but he was outside of his body, watching another Peter Walczyk wrestling with the beagle. It was all something he'd only witnessed, nothing he'd actually done himself. The thought of laughing, of happiness, seemed alien to him. Looking at his haggard reflection in the shaving mirror April had hung by suction cups to the smooth ceramic tile of the shower, he wondered just what his purpose in life was. Was it to be Hollywood's golden boy? To go down in a blaze of glory at the peak of his career? Or was he meant to just vanish from the public eye, like Salinger, to enjoy a reclusive retirement on his own terms.

Why not just smash your head through the bathroom mirror?

He shook his head, trying to toss the random thought from his mind. These thoughts were coming more and more often lately, and they were getting more and more graphic. He'd always had these racing thoughts, as Sara's therapist called them, but it was only recently – in the past four or five months – that they been focused on hurting himself. Like the voice of an evil demon taunting him from within his head. But he had always been able to shake them, at first easily, but lately with actual effort. He didn't know why he had these thoughts – he didn't want to hurt himself. He couldn't bear the idea of his parents finding him lying unconscious on the floor. He couldn't bear the notion of breaking their hearts. But lately, that little voice seemed to be offering a solution that would put an end to all those questions his parents had been posing to him. All the questions April had been putting to him. And all the questions he was asking himself. His jaw clenched as he pictured himself lying on the floor, shards of a shattered mirror sticking out of his face and bleeding to death.

He shook his head hard again, eyes screwed shut, willing the thoughts from his mind. He didn't know why he had these disturbing images. He didn't know how to stop them. He only knew that he didn't want to go to Friday night dinner.

He didn't want to go anywhere.

"You made the *Snooper*," April said, breaking the ice as she climbed into the Jeep with a six-pack of Twisted Teas. She glanced into the back seat to check on Dexter before strapping herself back in. The drive from town to Walczyk's parents' house always seemed to take forever, even though April was becoming familiar with the eight-mile trip out of town. Walczyk sat in the passenger seat, having asked her to drive, silently staring out the window. He certainly wasn't the laughing man who had been playing with a dog a few hours ago. He stared at the sky, an inscrutable look of either anger or sadness masking his face.

"What'd they say?" Walczyk finally asked just as they were passing the last of Walker Street's hotels.

"Have a look," she said, fishing a crumpled copy of the *Snooper* from her over-sized purse. She passed it to him. He scanned the headline, reading it aloud: "'Walczyk Divorce Drama – Did She Drive Him Out of Hollywood?'"

April chuckled. "Where do they come up with this shit?"

"'Divorce drama?' We're not getting a divorce. We're just… not speaking." He tore the paper open, examining the story. A long-distance photograph of Sara and Ella walking down the street together, hand-in-hand, was blown-up to grainy proportions on page four.

From the back seat, Dexter gave a weak groan. The poor little guy was not enjoying the drive to Grammie and Grampie Walczyk's house. Walczyk turned to look at the carsick dog. "It's okay, Buddy. I hear you," Walczyk half-heartedly joked to the miserable canine.

April grabbed the paper back and continued reading as she drove, occasionally glancing up at the road. She finally found the spot she was looking for. She folded the paper in half and tossed it back to Walczyk, her finger on a paragraph. "There! Read there! Doesn't that just burn your ass? Who buys this shit?"

"*You* buy it," Walczyk countered, giving the paper a cursory glance.

"Of course *I* buy it! We have to know what they're saying."

"And they're saying what?" he asked, humoring her. "That I drove Sara to a life of lesbianism?" He nodded. "Probably. That it's my fault my marriage fell apart? Undoubtedly."

April snatched the paper back, cramming it into her bag. "You really don't care what they print, do you?"

"No. I really don't care."

"They're printing lies and bullshit about you, making money doing it, and you don't care?"

"April, I learned long ago not to get upset over what those rags print. Tabloid gossip begets depression, which begets alcohol, which begets alcoholism, which begets tabloid gossip. See the pattern?"

"Still. They're saying here that Sara *drove* you out of Hollywood? That's ludicrous!"

"It is. I know it is, you know it is, and she knows it is. Anyone else, I don't care. Let them print whatever they want. Let them say I'm getting a sex change so I can be with her. Let them say I'm hooking up with that fifteen-year-old Goth girl from Papal Indulgencies, or... I don't know, some hot, young actor who looks good without his shirt on."

"Brandt Talbot?"

"Who?"

"That kid who plays the werewolf on *Phases*?" April remembered meeting Brandt at a premiere party for some shitty Michael Bay film. Charming kid. Simple as dirt, but charming.

"Yeah, whatever," Walczyk said. "The point is, it doesn't matter. As long as they stay away from my family, I don't care what they print. I don't like it, but there's nothing I can do to stop it. I'd rather spend my time thinking about the problems I can or might be able to fix."

"Such as?"

"Such as whether or not Duane McGraw would notice if I moved a better TV into my room." Walczyk gave a half-hearted smile and pulled the rumpled *Snooper* from April's bag and began to read the article.

Friday night dinner with the Walczyks had quickly become a tradition for Walczyk and April since arriving on Cole Island. April had first met Mr. and Mrs. Walczyk – or Henry and Diane, as she quickly came to call them – about three months into her employment as Walczyk's assistant, almost five years ago. Henry and Diane had taken a rare week-long journey to Los Angeles to catch up with their son and daughter-in-law and attend the premiere of *Aaron Lawrence Is Dead*, Walczyk's first studio picture. Diane was horrified by the premise of the movie, fearing that Aaron *Lambert*, the "real" Aaron Lawrence, would not appreciate having an alcoholic jerk named for him in a major motion picture. However, they had enjoyed the film thoroughly and were proud of their son's accomplishment.

And while April enjoyed her time with both of Walczyk's parents, it was his father that she'd formed a rather close bond with. Perhaps it was his no bullshit attitude, or perhaps the fact that Henry was the kind of father she always imagined fathers should be: stern but loving, cool-headed but passionate. The fact was, she'd fallen in love with Walczyk's parents.

Henry and Diane Walczyk lived in a comfortable home situated on the shore of Cole Island's west side, known locally as the Back Nine. Their location, looking out over the Atlantic Ocean, gave them the perfect view of the sunset. From April's first trip through the house, she was struck by the "lived in" feel of the place. It was a little bit worn around the edges, but it was apparent that two very lively children (and their very lively friends) had passed through its many rooms. Henry proudly pointed out the defects in the house: the patching that covered the kitchen drywall where a young Peter had launched a He-Man figure during an especially rowdy session of Masters of the Universe with childhood friends Vic Gordon and Dougie Olsen. The burn on the carpet in front of his recliner, where Melanie had been ironing decals onto T-shirts with her friends Glenda and Dawn for Spirit Week their junior year at Cole Island High. His pride and joy, however, was a cigarette burn on the arm of the couch. The burn had been mended with superglue, but it remained a visible reminder of Walczyk and Melanie's first (and last) house party.

April loved homes. Houses were a dime a dozen, but *homes* were lived in. Homes had memories. Homes had scars and bumps and character. Having lived her life in a string of apartments and hotel rooms that had experienced very little real living, a visit to the Walczyk home reminded her that real families imprint their souls on the walls surrounding them.

What April loved the most, though, was that moment when the front door opened each Friday night, with the smell of a home cooked meal engulfing her and the scratch of Henry's five o'clock shadow against her face, the smell of his Old Spice (Henry was one of the few men on whom, April thought, Old Spice was not a creepy scent), and the strength in his arms. These were the qualities of a dad. She regretted never having had one in her life, a fact she shared with very few people.

"So, April tells me you're working on a new project," Walczyk's mother said during one of the many lulls in the dinner conversation. "What's it about?"

Walczyk sighed, not really ready to share the story. "It's nothing."

"Nothing?" His father looked up from his steak. "I hear you spent most of the afternoon working. Is it the next season of *Ordinary*

World already?"

"No, I'm not working on *Ordinary World* yet." Walczyk was very mindful of his tone, making sure he wasn't short with his father. He turned to his mother. "Mum, can you please pass the steak sauce?" She passed the sauce, a piquant blend of horseradish and mayonnaise that she'd developed on her own.

"So what is it?" Dad asked again, genuinely eager to hear.

"I'm telling you," Walczyk said, growing exasperated, "it's nothing." Still aware of the anxious looks of his parents, he tipped his head back, exhaling. "This guy clones his ex-girlfriend when she leaves him, and the clone turns out to be a psychopath."

He saw his mother's eyes meet his father's, uncertain and concerned. His mother forced a smile onto her face. His father's look was inscrutable. "So when do you go back to work on *Ordinary World*?" Mum posed that question every week, and every week, after he told her he didn't know, she would seem disappointed and change the subject, instead discussing some distant relative who had "the cancer" or gout or sciatica on both sides.

"They've got to finish cutting this season's episodes," April said in an effort to save Walczyk from repeating his weekly response. "Work will probably resume–"

"I don't think I'm going back to *Ordinary World*," Walczyk found himself saying, suddenly and bluntly, not looking up from his baked potato. The clinking of silverware ceased. There was no more chewing. No more sipping. No more breathing.

"What?" was the response that came at him in three different voices.

Walczyk huffed, shifting his gaze to his dining companions, then back to his half-eaten steak. But he did not feel like eating the well-done meat. He did not want to drink his Twisted Tea. He didn't want to be sitting at this table. And he certainly didn't want to deal with the fall-out from what he'd just said.

"I said I don't think I'm going back," he reiterated, finally looking up. In the silence, he saw his parents look, in turn, from each other to April, and back to him again. He saw the horror crease their faces. The shock. The disappointment.

"What's Ian think about all this?" April finally asked. Ian Maeder was Walczyk's close friend from Hofstra and, more recently, producing partner on *Ordinary World*.

"I haven't talked to him about it. Haven't really talked to anyone about it."

"Why do you want to leave?" his father managed to get out, finally.

He simply shrugged his shoulders. "I don't know. I just don't... I don't enjoy it anymore. I don't want to be there. I don't want to see those people. I just... I want it to be done."

"Is this about Sara and Ella?" his mother carefully asked.

"No, it's got nothing to do with Sara and Ella. I've been thinking about it for a long time now. Long before all that bullshit."

His mother opened her mouth, looking like she was going to object to his language, but seemed to reconsider and sat back in her chair, instead asking, "What'll they do without you?"

"They'll get by. They'll hire a new showrunner."

"What's a showrunner?" his mother asked.

"A showrunner is a producer who sees to the day-to-day operations of a TV series," April explained. "Right now, Walczyk... Peter... does that."

"How are they going to make the show without you as the show... the showrunner?"

"I'd assume they'll hire another of these showrunners," his father said. "What'll you do now?"

Again, Walczyk responded by shaking his head. "I don't know." Walczyk looked around the table at the three panic-stricken faces, rolled his eyes, and said, "Relax. I'm just thinking about it. Nothing's set in stone." He then picked up his fork and went back to his dinner, cutting off a bite-sized piece of steak and dipping it in his mother's special steak sauce before popping it into his mouth.

April felt like a lazy *schnorrer*. It happened every week as soon as dinner was over: Walczyk would disappear into the kitchen to aid his mother in doing the dishes, leaving April to sit with Henry either in the living room, or, as they did tonight, out on the back porch. Tonight, as they watched the sun begin its dip below the horizon, they enjoyed cigars. April wanted to help out in the kitchen, but it seemed to be her contribution to keep Henry company watching Cocoa and Brownie wrestle in the back yard, while Dexter ran circles around them, yipping at anyone, canine or human, who would give him attention.

"Saw in one of those scandal rags that they think Peter's getting divorced," Henry said, puffing a cloud of toxins out into the evening air. The cigars had initially been an idea of April's to keep Maine's notorious mosquitoes away, but soon turned into one of those guilty pleasures that you know is bad for you, but you don't care, like drive-through milk shakes or cheese soaked nacho chips at a ballgame.

"Those magazines don't know their ass from a hole in the ground," April grunted, rubbing her full belly. "They'd print that Elvis joined the Scientologists if they thought it'd sell a few thousand issues."

"So you think it *is* garbage?"

"The divorce rumors? Look, Henry, I've been with your son every day since he left California. I've not heard him talk to her once. And he's never mentioned divorce to me."

"But you didn't figure he'd ever leave *Ordinary World* either, did you?" Henry asked, aiming a mouthful of cigar smoke at a passing black fly, the fiercest of Maine wildlife.

"Your boy is full of surprises," April said, wishing she'd had some warning on this matter before being floored over dinner with the idea of Walczyk not finishing out *Ordinary World*'s run.

"Does he hate her?" Henry asked softly.

"Sara? I don't think so. Why?" April countered.

"That story he's writing. The psychotic ex-girlfriend clone thing. You have to admit, in the hands of the right psychotherapist..."

"Yeah," April said, puffing her cigar, "but it might be healthy for him to get it all out on paper. You know he's never said one word about it – not one – since we left L.A."

Silence enveloped the two as they puffed away at their cigars, watching the evening sky turn from light blue to a deep plum, trimmed with orange at the horizon. The dogs had returned to drop exhausted at their feet. Behind them, the faint 'click' of the yard light turning on caught Dexter's attention. He perked up a moment and looked around, then dropped his head back down onto April's toes.

"You remember that show *Livingstone* that used to be on HBO?"

"Yeah, I remember it. What about it?"

"I loved that thing. Why'd HBO take it off?"

"Henry, the demise of *Livingstone* is a long, conflicting story about contracts, temperamental creative geniuses, and an executive producer who, to paraphrase the series' lead character, just went fucking crazy."

Henry looked at her, smiled, and returned his cigar to his lips, taking another deep puff, enjoying the silence with April as his dark chocolate dogs began to vanish from sight in the back yard.

"It happens, I guess," Henry said. "You know, people going crazy for no reason all the time. It just… happens."

"Where does this casserole dish go?" Walczyk asked, wiping the warm glass vessel with a blue checkered dish wiper.

"Which casserole dish?" his mother asked.

"The one I just dried," Walczyk said, holding up the square glass dish.

"On the top shelf of the bottom cupboard, left of the stove." Diane Walczyk was a very "particular" woman. She never allowed her children to call her "anal retentive," because she felt that term sounded kind of dirty. She would, however, cop to being compulsively organized.

About three years ago, tired of their aging kitchen with its boring wood paneling, his parents had the entire room gutted, creating a more user-friendly arrangement of cupboard and closet space and painting everything light blue. The result was a beautiful, yet functional kitchen. Walczyk's only complaint was that now he couldn't find anything in the kitchen. His exodus from California was the first time he'd been home to visit since the remodeling three years ago, and the change was a bit much to take at first. He had memories of building gigantic kingdoms with his Masters of the Universe toys and any kitchen items his imaginative mind could turn into mountain spires, bridges, or enemy strongholds. He remembered hearing from his friend Vic Gordon that there was no Santa Claus in that kitchen and, more importantly, that the stork had nothing to do with the creation of a baby. The family ate meals in there. He and his sister were pressed into servitude over the old, scratched stainless steel sink with the broken spray hose and the pipe that leaked if you dumped too much water down the drain all at once. He remembered that Dad had kept a bottle of whiskey above the fridge, in those cupboards that Mum always said just held Gram's gold-plated silverware. Rainy Saturday mornings watching Mum make ground ham sandwiches for somebody's funeral. Hot summer evenings listening to Dad and Sis play cribbage while he and his mother sat and read, sharing a large bowl of popcorn. But he was sure there were plenty of new stories about this kitchen. Kids who came Trick-or-Treating and got to choose their own candy apple. Hot summer evenings where Henry and Diane sat playing Skip-Bo and talking about their children.

"Remind me, again, where does the colander go?"

His mother pointed a sudsy finger across the room at wide closet situated in the corner of the room. "Second shelf of the closet," she said, returning her attention to the dishpan as she saw Walczyk find the proper shelf. "You never did tell me what you thought of our new kitchen."

"I like it."

"No, you don't."

"Well, there's nowhere to create a large mountain for Castle Grayskull to be built on, and no way to make the long, narrow bridge that extends across the Pit of Despair."

She passed him a large frying pan, which he wiped and went around his mother to put under the cupboard. "Nope," she called out, stopping him as he moved to put it away. "Pots and pans are on the shelf beneath the colanders and bread pans."

Walczyk stood back up, moving towards the closet, where he saw a long row of sauce pans, frying pans, Dutch Ovens, and those really tiny little sauce pans he used to make packaged gravy in. He returned to the sink, an awkward silence hanging in the air as his mother washed and rinsed and he wiped.

"So, are you seeing anyone?"

"I don't need a shrink," he said, feeling more annoyed than usual with the questions.

"No, I mean are you seeing *someone*?"

He chuckled. "If by someone you mean a girl, then, no, I'm not seeing *someone*."

"You don't have to answer me like I'm an idiot. I was just asking. I mean, you spend a lot of time with April."

"She's my assistant. We share a vehicle. She runs my life."

"Your *professional* life. Not your personal life."

"No," he said thoughtfully. "She pretty much runs that too. She's why you get to feed me every Friday night."

"Well, is there anything going on there?"

"Is there anything going on where?"

"Don't make me spell it out."

"Why don't you try?"

"Fine," his mother said, exasperated. "Are you two sleeping together?"

"Mum!"

"What?"

"That is none of your business."

"Peter, it's nothing to get defensive over. I think she's–"

"Mum," he said, putting his hands on her shoulders, looking into her gray eyes, "anything going on between April and I is merely the goings-on of two very close friends."

"You mean you two have one of those friends with benefits relationships like I heard about on *Dr. Phil*."

"No. Meaning there's a lot about my life I've shared with April that I've shared with no one else. And vice versa."

"Except that you're quitting your show."

"I said it was just a thought."

"At least be honest with your mother: it's more than just a passing thought." He looked up, glaring at her. She resolutely returned her attention to the dishpan, industriously scrubbing the roaster. If Walczyk didn't know his mother as well as he did, he would've sworn she was pouting. He opened his mouth to speak, but closed it, erring on the side of caution. Then his mother asked her next question in a sort of fake casual tone. "Have you seen Hannah Cooper yet?"

Boy, do you know how to pick topics, he thought to himself. "No, I haven't," he replied flatly. "How is she?"

"Good." His mother returned to the dishes. The kitchen was silent, aside from the sloshing of dish water. Finally, as if unable to cope with sweet, blissful silence, she blurted out, "You know, your father adores her. Says she's an excellent teacher."

"She always was a smart kid. I'm glad he likes her."

"You should look her up some time. I'm sure she'd love to see you."

"No, I think she's had all the Peter Walczyk she can handle for one lifetime."

"Peter, that was almost twenty years ago. I doubt she's still angry with you."

"I doubt she *was* ever angry; that's what hurts. I treated her like shit and she kept sending me birthday cards."

"So you *are* talking?"

"I wouldn't call it *talking*. We exchange cards," Walczyk responded, exasperated with this line of questioning. "Christmas... sometimes birthdays. A message or two on Facebook once in a while. I wouldn't call it a repaired friendship."

"So, you need to get in touch with her. I'm sure she wouldn't mind if your father gave you her number." She passed Walczyk the roaster, eyeballing him carefully. "So, Peter, it's been three months. Your father and I are wondering – mind you, we're not being nosy. It's just... we just... we love you, Peter, and we want to know..."

"... what the deal with Sara and me is," Walczyk said, finishing his mother's sentence. She nodded, a hint of guilt flashing across her face as she smiled somewhat sheepishly.

Walczyk picked up a cover and began wiping. "The truth is, I don't know what's going on there. I don't hate her. I don't hate Ella."

"Peter, you know it is okay if you do hate her." Walczyk turned to his mother, who was throwing her wash cloth into the water. "After all, she sneaked around behind your back, lied to you and cheated on you! Your wife! The woman whose career you made, the woman who promised – and I was there to witness it – promised to love, honor, and obey you for all the days of her life cheated on you. With a friend of yours. It would be understandable for you to hate her."

"It would. But I don't."

"I'm proud of you, Peter. It takes a big man to forgive what you've had to deal with."

"Don't get too carried away," Walczyk said, dryly. "I never said I forgive her. But I just can't hate her. I've tried. God knows I tried, but in the end, I learned that I just can't. She's still one of my–"

A cough behind them caught their attention. They turned to see April, standing in the doorway, looking rather unhappy.

"April. What's up?" Walczyk asked, releasing his mother.

April held out her hand. In it was Walczyk's open cell phone. "It's for you."

"Who is it?" he asked, knowing the answer.

"The missus," April said cautiously.

Walczyk's stomach dropped and he suddenly felt his mood grow darker. "I'm not taking it," he mumbled, turning around to wipe the last of the dishes.

"You need to," his mother said, pulling him away from the

dishes and towards her. "You at least need to talk to her about what happened. Who knows, maybe you can fix it."

"Or, at the very least," April suggested, "find out where things went sour."

"I know where it went sour," Walczyk said, inhaling deeply. He turned to his mother. "And there's nothing to talk about, nothing to fix."

April thrust the phone at him. "Boss, quit being such a pussy!"

"April!" Walczyk barked at her, tilting his head in his mother's direction.

"What?" his mother asked, feeling all eyes on her. "She's right. Peter, you *are* being a… a wimp. Now answer it!"

Walczyk stared at his mother, then turned to April, taking the phone. "You've corrupted her, you know."

Walczyk put the phone up to his ear, and started out of the kitchen.

"Hello," he said solemnly.

The cold water lapped at Walczyk's feet as the moon shimmered on its surface. Standing in his boxers and a T-shirt, Walczyk stared out across the miles and miles of water. The swishing of the water against the shore was the only sound that could be heard, aside from his own breathing.

The call had been short, its outcome inevitable. Sara still loved him. But it would never work. She was sorry, but she wanted a divorce.

Walczyk turned to sit on a large rock near the shore. The rock had been painted by two pre-adolescent artists and showed the ravages of time and the constant change of seasons, but the masterpiece was not entirely lost. A bright blue sea, appearing purple in the moonlight, covered the bottom half of the rock. Painted above the "sea line" was a grassy patch, with four crude figures, rendered in greater detail than those stick figure bumper stickers that yuppie families put on the rear hatch windows of their SUVs. This set of figures depicted the entire Walczyk family, including Stomper, the family dog. The two taller ones, one in a shirt and tie and the other in pants and a pink shirt, stood with their arms around the two shorter figures. One of the shorter figures was clearly Walczyk's sister Melanie, with her long hair and short legs. Peter was recognizable by the Ghostbusters emblem on his T-shirt and a pen and notepad in his hand. Painted in the background was a crude representation of the Walczyk home, and a light blue sky covered the top of the rock.

A pen and paper. And a smiling face. Life had been so much easier back then. There were no worries, aside from how he was going to convince his parents that he just *had* to have that new He-Man or Transformers figure in Merrow's Department Store window. There were no studios demanding results. No agents nagging him for more material. And no wives to break his heart. The smile had yet to leave his face, as he looked at the icon of himself. A pen and paper. That was Peter Walczyk, age eight.

"She makes me wrap that old rock with a tarp and clothesline rope every winter, you know."

Walczyk turned around to see his father standing at the foot of the grassy slope leading down to the water, also clad in his shorts and a t-shirt. Behind him, a lone light shone from the kitchen.

"I wondered how it stood up so well to time and the elements," Walczyk said, turning back to the mural.

"I think she touched it up the summer after you graduated high school," his father said, stepping closer, dew glistening on his sandals. "What's up?"

"Couldn't sleep," Walczyk offered, turning around again to look out over the black waters.

"Body probably doesn't need it," his father said, obviously being careful not to chastise him for sleeping all day. "April says you've been doing a lot of sleeping lately."

Walczyk stood, looking out across the water, his eyes straining to see the lights from the mainland. He honestly couldn't remember if the cityscape across the water was visible five miles away. He doubted it.

"Peter, can we talk?"

Walczyk's shoulders hitched up subtly, quickly. "What about?" he asked moments later.

"You. Me. Sara. Anything."

Walczyk said nothing. It wasn't that he didn't want to talk to his father. Quite the opposite, he wanted to grab his father, hold onto him, and just unload everything that was weighing him down. He wanted to take that weight bearing down on his chest and ask his father to lift it for him. He wanted to unburden himself on his father, tell him everything.

He wanted to walk into the kitchen. Top drawer by the sink. The big knife with the chipped, stained wooden handle. Two or three swift plunges into his chest should be all it'd take. Then things would be easier.

Walczyk shook off the disturbing image, turning to his father. "I don't want to talk about Sara."

"Fair enough." Walczyk's father stepped forward, taking his hand.

Tears stung Walczyk's eyes as he looked back into his father's steely eyes. His father reached out and pulled him close, cupping the back of his head with his hand. Walczyk suddenly began sobbing into his father's shoulder. Henry held his son, tears rolling down his own cheeks. Walczyk tried speaking, but nothing coherent broke through the sobs that racked his body, forcing him to almost convulse with each wave of crying. He felt himself crumble down, but could do nothing to stop it. The grass was wet beneath his bare legs as he knelt there, supported by his father, crying into the night.

It could've been five minutes later, or it could've been five hours later – neither would be able to tell – when Walczyk finally straightened up, wiping his running nose with the back of his hand. His father dabbed at his own eyes.

"Hmmm," Walczyk finally murmured, breathless. "Where the fuck did that come from?" He quickly looked to his father, who never tolerated such April-like language growing up. His father, however, simply waved a hand, a wry smirk across his face. They sat on the dew-soaked grass several more minutes, staring up at the stars. Walczyk's mind raced, pictures of himself approaching the kitchen drawer interspersed with the young, painted icon Peter playing in the back yard with young Vic and their mutual friend, Walczyk's neighbor Max Leavitt. The premiere of *Aaron Lawrence Is Dead* in L.A. with the family, a newly hired April. His wedding, Vic at his side, giving his best friend's newly wedded wife a kiss. Signing his contract at HBO for *Ordinary World* with Ian. Sara's smiling face, gazing out at him from across the bed, the sun shining onto her delicate skin, lighting up her hair, casting a glowing aura around her. She was an angel.

"She wants a divorce," he mechanically said after a while.

"That was to be expected," his father said softly, giving Walczyk's hand a squeeze.

"She ruined my life, Dad."

"I know."

"She gutted me," Walczyk said. "Humiliated me. Dragged my name through the mud and..."

"And?"

"And... and I think I hate her for it."

He felt a chip in the boulder upon his heart fall away, leaving the load just that much lighter.

"Oh, I hope not," his father said. "Hate is an awful powerful, awful absolute thing to feel."

"I know. But still," Walczyk said, lying down on the wet grass. "And I... I don't know what to do now. I can't be what everyone expects me to be. I can't do it anymore."

"What do *you* want to do?" his father asked him.

"You don't know how bad part of me wants April to abandon me here, a neurotic mess, and return to her life in L.A., where she can climb the industry ladder and realize her dream of becoming an agent herself. How bad part of me wants you and Mum to wash your hands of me. Sometimes, I want... I want you and Mum to do what Sara's done – just write me off. Be done with me."

"Why should we write you off?"

To give me that final excuse to do what I know I have to do, Walczyk wanted to say.

"I don't know. I guess I'm just feeling self-destructive. I want to prick myself just to make sure I can still bleed."

His father was quiet a good long time. Walczyk watched the blinking lights of a plane, probably a 747, cross the sky, no doubt en-route to Bangor International Airport with a load of happy passengers. Or maybe it was carrying a load of passengers who were as weary of life as he was.

"You're quite depressed, aren't you?"

Walczyk said nothing.

"Since you returned to Maine?"

"A fair assessment," he conceded.

"You're not suicidal, are you?" his father asked, his voice steady and calm.

"No," Walczyk replied, carefully wording his response: "I don't *want* to kill myself."

"But you think about it."

Walczyk avoided his father's eyes. He didn't *want* to do

anything, but sometimes it felt like the only solution. He just couldn't bear to tell his father about all of those... intrusive thoughts.

"Have you considered going to see someone?"

"Absolutely not," Walczyk said. "On top of everything else, I don't need the paparazzi snapping shots of me going into a shrink's office."

"What if I guaranteed you'd never be discovered?"

"And how would you do that?"

"Angela Cariou."

"Who's Angela Cariou?"

"She's the school's counselor. We've discussed it. She's offered to talk with you."

Walczyk thought about it. It might be nice to talk to someone who wasn't a Walczyk or connected to the celebrity machine. Someone who he could just unload on. Get all the hate out on. Someone who could tell him he wasn't crazy, just angry.

"Well..."

"Well?"

"Well, do you think it's a good idea?" Walczyk asked, feeling very unsure.

"I do. What do you say?"

"Well, I guess I'm gonna see a shrink," Walczyk said, rolling the idea over aloud.

His father reached over and touched his son's leg. They sat there under the sky, both men smiling, shorts getting wet from the grass, not caring in the least bit.

CHAPTER TWO
THE CLASS OF 1996

It had been three days since the call, and Walczyk had not traveled farther than the distance from the Jeep to his room at the Meadowbrook Motel. April knew the phone call had been difficult for Walczyk. When she sniffed around as to details of the conversation, all he would volunteer was that they would be getting divorced. April pushed Walczyk to get in touch with his agent, Elias Gaul, a mutual friend of both Walczyk and Sara. But when Walczyk said he didn't want to talk to Eli, April couldn't fathom it; Walczyk was quite close with Eli. They shared lunch together several times a week. Now, as far as April knew – and she spent almost every waking moment near Walczyk – Walczyk hadn't reached out to his friend since leaving Los Angeles three months ago.

April, however, *had* been in touch with Eli. He was happy to hear that Walczyk was writing again, even if he didn't think there was a market for a story about a man who clones his ex, nor that it was a project worthy of the caliber of artist that Walczyk was. Eli was quite frank that he wanted Walczyk to return to *Ordinary World*, and he even asked April to "see to it" that Walczyk reorder his priorities. There was plenty Walczyk could do from Maine if he didn't want to return to L.A. right away. Eli's biggest fear, however, was that Walczyk would return to old, destructive patterns that he often clung to when he found himself depressed or unbalanced: sleeping all day, watching TV all night, never leaving his bed, and drinking, alone and to excess. Walczyk's parents had expressed the same fear.

Thankfully, Walczyk didn't sleep all day, nor did he stay up all night watching television. And he didn't drink anything more than three or four hard iced teas a night when he sat down to work. He'd written fifty-some pages in his screenplay, which was tentatively titled *The Next One*. April was very happy that he was working, and working so diligently. There were none of the sharp mood swings that she and Walczyk's parents had feared. Diane, being a mother, was happy that her little boy was happy, but Henry voiced his concerns that it was just a matter of time. April, too, tended to err on the side of caution. The one thing that did concern everyone, though, was Walczyk's seclusion. But all three could justify, by different means, just why Walczyk would be shutting himself away at this time. April and Diane had agreed that, for the time being, they'd leave him be, as long as he wasn't showing signs of becoming seriously depressed. Henry, however, kept pushing all of them to take his seclusion as a symptom of a much bigger problem.

However, by the fifth day, April had had all she could take. There were only so many things to watch on sixty-two channels: news, talk shows, reality shows, old faded sitcoms, sports, religious programming, country music videos, and more reality shows. April threw the remote on the bed, bored. Walczyk had told her to feel free to take off, but she really didn't feel comfortable doing so. She'd tried to get Walczyk to let her read this big script, but he never shared his rough drafts. *Never*. He likened seeing his rough drafts to seeing him standing bare-ass naked. And her reminding him that she had seen him in such a state, on several occasions, didn't even help sway him.

"Let's go." She said, hopping up from the bed, an idea forming in her head.

"Where?" Walczyk responded, not looking up from his laptop.

"I don't know. That bookstore, the Blazing Lantern?"

"The *Bronze* Lantern."

"Whatever. Let's go!"

"I'm fine where I am."

"No, you're not."

"April, I'm busy. I'm writing."

"You can write there too," she said, a hint of pleading in her voice. "And I can read. Or we could go to the beach."

"Still writing," he said, not looking up.

"Bring pen and paper! It'd be great. It's sunny out, a beautiful day to spend outside. God knows a little Vitamin D would do wonders for your moods."

He looked up at her, glaring.

"And Dexter can get some long-overdue exercise!"

"You take him for walks."

"To shit and piss, yeah. Not a real work-out for our little boy here."

"I've told you before, feel free. But I'm on a roll right now."

"So you're not just locking yourself away from the world so you won't have to face your impending divorce? You're working?"

He looked up, cold anger in his face. She regretted resorting to such tactics to pull him away from his work.

"What page are you on?"

"I don't keep track."

"The computer does. What page?"

A pause. "Fifty-seven."

"You've been working for almost a week on this thing and you've only accomplished fifty-seven pages?"

She leaned forward and grabbed the laptop from the table, turning it around and reading the screen's contents. Walczyk calmly reached out, extricated the computer from her clutches, and replaced it on the table with far more care than she'd exercised when picking it up. Wordlessly, she walked over to the dresser and started removing clothes from it.

"What are you doing?" Walczyk asked, following her around the room with his head.

"Packing a bag."

Walczyk looked up from his laptop, eyes rolling. "For what?"

She turned around, removing a pair of his swim trunks from the dresser drawer. "We are going out for the day."

"People are staring," Walczyk grumbled, his hands hovering over April's pale, naked back.

"You *wish* people were staring," April said, feeling the sun energizing her as it radiated through her pores. In her hands, she had a rolled up screenplay, just one of many that Eli had overnighted to Maine last week for Walczyk's consideration.

"Just what I need, every magazine in the country showing me slathering my assistant in suntan lotion. 'Walczyk Moves On.'"

"Hey, I offered to do you first," she said. Walczyk finished her back and stood up, getting back into his fold-up lounge chair. "So," April asked, not looking up from her screenplay, "what's the plan?"

"You tell me. This is your big day out. I had my day planned already."

"No, I mean the *plan*. When are we going back to L.A.?"

"I don't know," he said, pulling a legal pad and pen from April's beach bag.

"How long are we going to live out of that shithole motel room?"

"I don't know."

"Have you considered seeing someone?"

"April, I'm not even divorced yet!"

"I mean a professional!" she hissed. "You know... a psychiatrist. A psychologist. A therapist. A counselor. A shrink. A–"

"I get the idea," he said, holding up a hand to stall her from continuing.

"Good, because those are all the synonyms I can think of."

"If you must know, my father and I have already had this discussion."

"And–?" April pressed.

"And... I'm going to the bathroom."

Walczyk got up from his camp chair and slid his sandals on, trotting across the beach towards a string of rest rooms at the foot of the hill which led up to the roadside from the beach. April returned her attention to her scripts. *Great Minds* was a horror movie about fraternal twins who could swap bodies, the guy into the girl and vice versa. It was rather silly, but it was markedly better than the three vampire erotica scripts she'd just endured. Still, she found it hard to keep focused on the work at hand. Just as she allowed the urge to nap to take over her body, she could feel a presence above her blotting out the sun.

"Excuse me, is this your dog?"

April opened her eyes and craned her head up to see a handsome man in his early thirties standing over her, his wet swim trunks clinging to his cut, tanned body. In his right hand, he was holding Dexter's leash, with Dexter standing beside him, his tail whapping excitedly against the stranger's leg. She quickly looked from the handsome man holding her dog to Walczyk's chair, to which she'd leashed him. The chair, without Walczyk in it, was now tipped over. A smile crossed her face as she got up from her blanket. "He is," she said, brushing her hair from her face. "Where the hell'd you find him?"

"Down by the shore, trying to join me for a dip in the ocean."

"You were swimming in *that*?"

"Oh, yeah," the man said, pushing his mop of brown hair back. "It's a great workout."

"But it's so fricking cold."

"You get used to it when you grow up in it."

April reached out for Dexter's leash. "Well, thank you for finding him. I'm new to puppy care, and he's new to... not running away."

The handsome guy smiled, handing the leash back. "No prob."

"Vic?" cried out Walczyk's voice from behind April. She turned to see Walczyk standing in the sand, a big, stupid smile on his face.

"Walczyk!" The stranger cried, his face breaking out in a huge smile. "Son of a bitch, I heard you were back!"

Walczyk grinned. The two men reached out and grappled onto each other in a massive bear hug.

"Damn, I missed you, Vic," Walczyk mumbled into Vic's shoulder. Walczyk let go and looked at his old best friend. "Look at you. You really let yourself go," he joked, his smile beaming impossibly wide.

"How the hell are you, Walz?"

"Not bad. You know... all things considered."

"Yeah. Shit, Peter, I saw about Sara on the news. I'm sorry. I'd have never guessed it would go down like that."

"Who could've? What about you? Still working at the family business and chasing Ingrid Connary, no doubt."

"Well, I'm *running* the restaurant now," he said, smiling. "And my troubles are nothing compared to yours. My biggest concerns are old ladies bitching about a fifteen cent raise on coffee, fighting with the cook – baby brother Andrew – and keeping Uncle Donny in line."

"Is he still tending bar?" Walczyk asked.

"And hanging on to the job like the Pope."

"April," Walczyk said, bringing April forward. "This is my friend Vic Gordon. Vic, April Donovan."

"I've heard a lot about you," she said offering her hand.

"Only good things, I hope," Vic said, taking April's hand.

April smiled. "So this restaurant you're talking about... please tell me it's not the one with the surf board tables."

"No," Vic laughed, "not the Moondoggy." Vic turned and pointed at the building on the bluff above the beach. "That's the Barrelhead." The Barrelhead was a large white structure with a balcony that looked out over the ocean and the bridge spanning across the Atlantic back to the shore of Maine. April remembered seeing it from the bridge coming to Cole Island and thought it would've made a hell of a view for a hotel's luxury suite. Vic looked down to see Dexter licking water from his legs. Vic scooched down and rubbed Dexter's wet head. "He really is a good boy."

"Dexter or Walczyk?" April asked, grinning.

Vic grinned, simply saying "Yes." He rose and, checking a watch that wasn't there on his wrist and asked Walczyk, "You got the time, Walz?"

Walczyk fished his cell phone from his shorts' pocket. "Three fifty-two."

"Shit! I told Andrew I'd be in at four! Listen, you guys, come in tonight. You'll have dinner and we'll catch up."

"Plan on it," Walczyk said, grinning.

"A pleasure, April," Vic said, smiling at her before taking off at a full run across the beach.

Now why couldn't I have met him three months ago? April asked herself, renewing her grip on Dexter's leash.

"So this son of a bitch, he's had a few, he decides the only way to get rid of the kid is to call the kid's mother!"

April laughed, slopping beer on the table. "No way!"

"Yeah way," Walczyk said. "Vic tracks down a phone book, slips into an empty bedroom, and proceeds to call Mrs. Lambert."

"What'd you say?" April asked Vic.

Vic shifted his position, stooping over a bit, and putting a "phone" up to his ear. "Hello? Mrs. Lambert? Do you have a son named Aaron? You do? Well, this is a concerned third party. Your son is at a house party out on the Dover Road, and he's quite inebriated.

I'm afraid he could be a risk to himself and to others."

A roar of laughter and profanity could be heard emanating from their booth in the far corner of the Barrelhead. Sitting across from each other were Walczyk and April. Vic sat in a backwards chair which had been pulled up from an adjacent table.

"You didn't," April said between fits of laughter.

"He did," Walczyk said deadpan, sipping at his rum and Coke.

"Seriously," April said as she turned to Vic, staring into his deep blue eyes. "Moment of truth, Vic: did you call this Aaron kid's mother? Honestly."

"Honestly?" Vic said, pausing. "Honestly, I don't remember who called. But I do remember Helen Lambert showing up in her bathrobe and slippers. Grabbed Aaron by his ear and *dragged* him out of that house. And he wasn't at school Monday, so either his old man beat him till he had to sleep standing up, or he just couldn't force himself to face the music in front of all of us."

April broke out laughing, grabbing Vic by the arm. "So who was the bigger asshole? Aaron or Vic?"

"Oh, Aaron, by a mile," Walczyk said. "Vic calling his old lady – and *you* called Mrs. Lambert, Victor, own up to it after fifteen years – was not just a prank. It was a public service to those of us at that party trying to get laid."

"And this Aaron Lambert… he's the inspiration for Aaron Lawrence? Of *Aaron Lawrence Is Dead*?"

"It is but it isn't. Brandon Albert was the kid whose funeral no one wanted to go to, but everyone was forced to go. But he was more a loner than a public annoyance. Aaron *Lambert*, however, was the perpetrator of the nasty, evil things that the Aaron *Lawrence* character does in the film, leading up to his death. Including pissing himself when he'd pass out."

"So does this real Aaron Lambert live around here? I'd love to meet him."

Walczyk turned to Vic. "Yeah, does he? I'd love to give catch up. Maybe get him to sign my *Aaron Lawrence* DVD."

"You'll have to mail it to his office. He passed the bar and is a lawyer in Jersey."

"Some big shot Mafia lawyer?"

"Come on, Walz," Vic snorted. "You know there's no such thing as the Mafia."

"So I've got the dirt on you, Vic, and while I've quite enjoyed it," April said, smiling at the finally happy Walczyk, "I came here to get the dirt on Hollywood's premiere writer-slash-director."

"He was an incredible jerk-slash-loser," Vic said, grinning.

"The hell I was!" Walczyk cried out indignantly.

"The hell you *weren't*! This kid," Vic said to April, his arm around Walczyk's shoulders, "never looked up from his camcorder long enough to notice the world spinning around him. Don't get me wrong, I'm glad he learned all that movie stuff, because now I have a silent investor in this place if I ever need a bail out, but he should've been getting laid instead of making movies."

"I got laid," Walczyk said defensively.

"In high school?" Vic asked.

"Yes, in high school!"

"No, my friend, I'm sorry, but that was graduation night. You left high school a virgin."

"Did not!"

"Did too! You and Hannah got it on at the Graduation party at the Lambert's camp," Vic clarified. "Technically – and we are getting technical here – that's *after* graduation."

"Your graduation party was at the camp of a kid no one liked?" April asked in astonishment.

"Aaron was a douche," Walczyk said.

"Still is," Vic added.

"But you have to remember, he was – no doubt still is – a douche with rich douche parents."

"Didn't hurt that Mrs. Lambert disliked wearing clothing and had a figure like Cindy Crawford, eh, Walz?"

"Cindy Crawford's body, yes. But Judge Judy's face."

"You guys were assholes," April said, emptying her glass. She leaned in to them. "And I think I like you both just a little bit more for it, too."

"I'll drink to that," Vic said, draining his drink. "And that's all I'll drink to. My ass has to get back to work."

"Gotta go general manage?" Walczyk quipped.

"Hey, I'll bet I 'general manage' just as good as you 'executive produce!' And to prove that, I'm gonna go general manage my ass off!" Vic rose from the table, his chest puffed out.

"Yeah?" Walczyk asked, challenging Vic. "And just what does

a general manager manage?"

"Right now? Payroll, all of the ordering, the hiring and firing, keeping up on the restaurant and liquor licenses, customer service and complaints. Plus I'm the executive chef on Tuesday nights."

"Vic, why don't you just 'general manage' the decision to hire some help?" April asked.

"Vic has always had a problem with sharing responsibility," Walczyk said.

"No, it's not that," he barked over April's head. "It's just that it's just easier to do it all myself than it is to explain it to two or three people, check up on them, and turn around and do it the right way when they don't."

"Sounds like a certain auteur I know," April remarked, picking up hers and Vic's glasses from the table.

"What the hell are you doing?" Vic snapped.

"What?" April asked, adding Walczyk's rocks glass to her collection.

"*That*," he said, pointing to her hands, filled with glasses. "I've got waitresses for that. Chelsea!"

"Yeah, but I want them refilled tonight," she teased. "Another rum and Coke, boss?"

"You know it," Walczyk said. "Another beer, Vic? My round."

"You guys aren't getting a check, so it doesn't matter whose round it is."

"Oh, no, I'm paying," Walczyk said, reaching for his wallet.

"Oh, no, you're not," Vic replied.

This back-and-forth continued until Vic threatened to tell the press that Walczyk was a bed wetter, and that he had the photographs to prove his point. "April, sit down. *I'll* get the drinks. A girl looking like you, you'd never survive my Uncle Donny."

"I don't know," Walczyk said, smirking. "I'd kinda like to see her going *tête-à-tête* with Cole Island's favorite barkeep. "

"What's he, some eighty-year old letch? Like Hollywood's not full of them. I'll be fine." She took the glasses from him and walked away. Vic sat back down in the booth.

"You know, you have a nice thing going here, Vic," Walczyk said. "The old man must be proud."

"On the good days he is," Vic said wistfully.

"How is John?" Walczyk softly asked.

"When he's good... it's great. We laugh, talk, tease each other; we discuss the business, the world, the Red Sox..."

"And the not-so-good days?"

Vic drew in a deep breath through his nose, inflating his body to an erect posture. "They're there. And more frequently, lately, but..." Vic never finished that sentiment. He stared out through the window at the moonlit surf down the hill from the restaurant.

A deep, hearty laugh came from the bar, breaking the solemn mood. Vic turned back to Walczyk, a ghost of a smile on his face, and asked, "So, have you seen Hannah yet?"

Walczyk glared at Vic. "Did my mother put you up to that?"

"What? I'm asking a simple question. Did one classmate run into another classmate yet?"

"No, one classmate hasn't run into another classmate yet."

"One classmate should, you know," Vic said, cocking an eyebrow. "Another classmate who knows one classmate's back is starting to feel left out." Vic paused a moment, then turned confidentially to Walczyk. "She does know you're back, you know."

"I should hope she'd know," Walczyk said. "I'm the first celebrity since John Travolta to set foot on this island in a good ten years." Walczyk looked over in the direction of the bar, where April was telling a joke to the large, white-haired bartender. "Looks like she's holding her own over there."

Uncle Donny roared a loud laugh from across the room. April grabbed the rail of the bar as she doubled over, laughing and taking the Lord's name in vain.

"Guess I was wrong about her," Vic said.

"Told ya."

April returned to the table, laughing. "Boss, I've got a joke for you. This guy walks into an ice cream shop. On the counter is a guarantee: 'We serve every flavor of ice cream imaginable! If we can't find what you want, you get free ice cream for life.' So the guy walks up to the counter and says–"

"Hate to burst your bubble," Walczyk said, "but Donny told me that one when I was ten. But I can't wait to see you tell it to Redford when we go to Sundance."

"Well, guys," Vic said, helping April distribute the drinks, then taking the tray, "I seriously need to return to work. Gimme a call, Walz. We'll hang together. My place, of course, not the Meadowbrook

Motel."

"Deal," April cut in.

"And it was nice to meet you again, April," Vic said, shaking April's hand. "And Walz, I'm serious. Find Hannah. She wants to see you."

"I will," he said, digging into his drink.

"Night, guys," Vic said, waving as he walked out to the kitchen.

"Nice guy," April said.

"Sure is," Walczyk said. "Best friend a guy could ask for. I just wish I'd been a better friend over the years."

"How so?" April asked.

"His father."

"What about him?"

"John Gordon was a brilliant man. Charming. Smart. Bought this place with Vic's mom in the early eighties. It was a shit heap, I guess. And they turned it into what you see. Well, around eighty-five, eighty-six, Cassandra – that's Vic's mother – up and leaves town, leaving John to raise eight-year-old Vic, ten-year-old Angie – she lives in Seattle now – and six-year-old Andrew; he's the one Vic said is the cook. Vic's Uncle Donny was pissed. He was Cassandra's brother, but he wrote her off when she left. He helped John raise the kids."

"What a bitch!"

"From what Dad says, they were better off without her. Well, a month after Vic graduates, John starts acting weird. Two months later, they find out it's the early stages of Alzheimer's. He finds himself slipping. Vic starts helping him run things."

"So Vic was being serious when he said that he inherited the family business?"

"John saw to that as soon as he got his diagnosis. So if Vic seems reluctant to talk about his family..."

"Yeah..." April drank quietly. "Wow. I never *knew* my father. I suppose that's easier than–"

"Than watching him lose his mind?" Walczyk finished.

April nodded and took a drink. "So what's the deal with this ex-girlfriend, Heather? Why are you avoiding her like the plague?"

"*Hannah*," Walczyk said matter-of-factly after taking a drink, "and it's... complicated."

"Not really," April retorted. "Your old man told me. You guys were the *It* couple of your time."

Walczyk grinned. "Seems so silly now. But the entire town was caught up on us. We were destined to be together. When we got together, everyone rejoiced. Then–"

"Then you tweaked out when the thought of being long distance finally dawned on you, and you dumped her. In a letter that you left in a book she gave you for graduation."

"Sounds so cold when you say it like that," Walczyk remarked. "Henry really filled you in."

"Warts and all."

"Then you can appreciate why it's awkward for me to keep in touch."

"Have you?"

"Sort of. She sent me a beautiful letter after *Aaron Lawrence* premiered. We Facebook every now and then." Walczyk downed the last third of his drink. "We're friendly."

"But you've been here almost three months and you've not laid eyes on her."

"No, I've seen her," he said casually.

"Where?"

"The Lantern. Once, shortly after we got here."

"And you didn't go over and talk to her?"

"I got up, walked out, and threw up in the bathroom at Things Past next door."

"Threw up?" April said appreciatively. "Well, well, well, Mr. Walczyk, I do declare you might not be over this young woman."

"Shut up," he snapped, holding up his empty glass as their waitress passed by.

April grinned and asked, "Is that the reason why you're dodging her?"

"Look, it didn't end well. We're friendly only by a fluke in the laws of the nature. I find it best to just leave it alone! I wish everyone else could too."

"It's because you were an asshole to her, isn't it?" April asked, dumping the remains of her old scotch into her new one.

"I give up," Walczyk said miserably.

April reached out and put her hand on his arm. "Walz, you were eighteen. It was decades ago. I doubt she's harboring any grudges."

"Oh, I doubt she's ever really held a grudge. That's the kind of person she is."

"That's the problem, isn't it?" April asked, getting it. "You've always been your own worst enemy, Walz, as long as I've known you. You refuse to forgive yourself. You take the minor, shitty things you've done in your life, blow them up out of proportion, and refuse to let them go, instead torturing yourself and imagining worst case scenarios as a form of penance."

"Wow," Walczyk said, stunned. "Been holding that in long?"

April reached out, grabbed her scotch, and took a healthy drink from the glass. "How many years have I worked for you?"

Behind April, the front door opened and laughter and cursing filled the restaurant. Two women and a young man, all of them in their early thirties came in. One girl was a blonde in a very revealing tank top and skirt, and the other was a brunette in a tight purple t-shirt and jeans. The young man wore an eye patch and a Hawaiian shirt.

"What the hell happened to him?" Walczyk muttered aloud.

April turned to see the trio cross over to the bar. "Who, the pirate?"

"Dougie Olsen," Walczyk said. "His father is Garry Olsen, who owns the Bronze Lantern. What the hell happened to his eye?"

"That's the perfect question to ask this Hannah chick when you track her down tomorrow."

"*If* I track her down," Walczyk clarified.

"No, *when* you track her down," April re-clarified. "As in tomorrow," April re-re-clarified. "So who's the entourage?"

"The girl in purple's Mia Walker. She and Dougie have been a couple since our freshman year of high school. I don't know for sure, but I think I remember Mum telling me that they got married a few years ago. Be on the look-out for a ring."

"And the skank?"

"That's Ingrid Connary."

"As in Vic's ex," April sputtered.

"Yeah," he said noncommittally. "Nice girl. A bit *too* nice in some regards. She and Vic... well, they're Cole Island's other 'It couple'. Very on-again/off-again, those two."

"Vic didn't say anything about a girlfriend," April remarked, eyeing Ingrid.

"Then we're catching him in the off again phase."

"Oh," April said, sounding about as dejected as April was capable of sounding. She quickly shook it off with the remainder of her scotch. "So, what's the plan?"

"Plan?"

"Well, while I do love it here… I mean the sights are gorgeous and the locals are wonderful, but we do need to head back to Los Angeles soon. Just a guess? Something I can give Eli as a rough estimate so he'll stop chewing his nails and crying himself to sleep at night? You know how he is."

"I don't know as though we're leaving anytime soon."

"What do you mean? You've got post to do on this season. Then there's pre-production for next season, even if you're not going to write, and–"

"What I mean is that I'm not so sure I want to leave. There's no reason Ian can't supervise post for the rest of season three. And if I decide to write, I can do the final season from here."

"So it *is* the final season?" April asked.

"Yeah. There's no need to keep dragging this thing out. Four seasons. Forty-eight episodes. That's enough."

"So what you said at dinner the other night…" She took a heavy slug of scotch. "You know you can't hide here forever."

"Why not?" Walczyk asked frankly.

"Because after a while, just like with this Hannah girl, you'll have to deal with Sara. You'll have to man up, return to the scene of the crime, and let the chips fall where they may."

"There's nothing left for me in L.A."

"Except friends, a job, and a beautiful house you already own."

"I don't want those things anymore."

"You don't want to see your friends again? Eli? Ian?"

"I don't know. I'm just… burnt out on the whole deal. Every script is the same, variations on a theme, all of them. There are no more original ideas. None. Did Eli tell you that Fox has been after me to write a film reboot of *M*A*S*H* for them? Why remake that? What's wrong with Robert Altman's original?"

"Walz, that's human nature. We're a population that is stuck in nostalgia. The audience doesn't want thought-provoking. They want remakes that they know will satisfy them. That will take them back to simpler times."

"Maybe, but that's not what the *artists* want. Anyway, it's a moot point."

"Another thing," April said, pressing forward with her own agenda. "You can't live out of the Meadowbrook Motel forever. Eventually you'll come down with something."

"Can we change the subject?"

"No, we can't. We've been changing the subject for too long now."

"April, if you want to go back west, go. I can take care of myself."

"I'm not so sure about that. But regardless, you're my boss. I'm your assistant. You want to stay in Maine, I'll order a winter jacket. You want to go back to Los Angeles and face the heat, I'll be right behind you, telling you just what to say to the *Enquirer*."

"It's good to know that," he said genuinely. "Thank you."

Vic returned to the table, with Ingrid, Mia, and Dougie in tow. "I think you know these guys."

One-eyed Dougie Olsen smiled and advanced, hand out to shake. "Peter, how the hell are you, buddy?"

Walczyk put on a broad grin, grimacing at the use of his first name by anyone other than family or close, close friends. He'd shed the use of his first name when he went to college, finding it a good enough time to start simply going by "Walczyk," which he preferred to his rather phallic-sounding first name.

"Douglas, how've you been?" Walczyk asked, knowing the answer would be–

"Peachy, brother. Just peachy. You?"

"Oh, you know. Made a few movies… the wife cheated on me," Walczyk thoughtlessly blurted out.

Vic broke out in forced laughter, killing the silence. He walked around the crowd and put his arm around April. "And this lady, this is April Donovan, the woman who keeps Walczyk in line. April, this is Dougie Olsen and Ingrid Connary, Cole Island High Class of 1996, and Mia Walker, Class of '98."

April greeted each in turn as Walczyk was pulled in for hugs from the girls.

"What brings you guys in tonight?" Walczyk asked, reaching back desperately for his rum and Coke.

"Vic texted us and told us you were here," Ingrid said, fixing a red bra strap beneath her tank top. "We were just out tooling around in the truck and figured what the frig, let's go see Peter Walczyk, the Portugal son."

"*Prodigal* son," Mia said as she stepped forward and hugged Walczyk. "Peter, I don't think I've seen you since that party at Vic's uncle's camp right before you left town."

That party, held at Vic's Uncle Donny's camp on Sebago Lake, had been a defining moment in Walczyk's life. It was at that party that Hannah told Walczyk she loved him. It was the last time they'd ever make love.

"Yep, that sounds about right," Walczyk said, trying hard not to let his racing mind slip down a road of regret and sorrow.

Vic motioned towards a table in the middle of the room. "Let's all sit down over here," he said. "We'll be a lot more comfortable." He looked from Walczyk to April, asking "the same?" Both nodded, and he looked at Dougie, Mia, and Ingrid. "The usual?" They all nodded. Vic turned to the bar, where his uncle stood, leaning against the bar, reading a boating magazine. "Uncle Donny!"

"Yo!" the heavyset bartender barked back, not turning away from the baseball game he was watching with a group of men at the bar who Walczyk remembered as Stumpy McGillicuddy, Gibby Perkins, and Tommy Howes.

"The usual for Doug, Mia and Ingrid, a rum and Coke for Walz and scotch, neat, for April. I'll just have a Corona."

"Sure thing," Donny said, snapping to. He reached up over the bar and began whipping out different sized glasses.

"So, Peter," Ingrid said as Vic sat down at the table with them, "what brings you back here?"

Walczyk was very happy they'd left Dexter with his folks when he staggered into Room 15 at almost three in the morning. April staggered behind him, like Boris Karloff in *Frankenstein*. They both collapsed on Walczyk's bed.

"You know what, Boss?"

"What's that, April?"

"I'm pretty freaking drunk," April observed, with a little giggle.

"No, April... there's nothing pretty about it," Walczyk said.

"Yeah," she muttered, resting her head against Walczyk's hip.

"So did you find out how that one eyed guy lost h

Walczyk picked his head up to look at ╱   52

noticed her statement made no sense at all. "

focusing his energy into completing that thought. "Buı ╷

rest assured that Vic isn't banging Ingrid Connary."

"Good," April said. "I don't like her. She's a slut."

"Yep," Walczyk agreed, "she hasn't changed much in fifteen years."

"I tried to beat up a girl that acted like her once," April rambled.

"Yeah?"

"Yeah. She said that if I wanted to start some stuff then I had some stuff that had to get started."

Walczyk grinned. He loved April when she was drunk. As much as he loved her sober, "Drunk April" was much more fun. She seldom made sense when she talked, was even less coordinated on her feet, and generally let her guard down and gave Walczyk a look at the real April, and her real feelings.

"Walczyk?" she called out.

"Yes, April?" Walczyk replied.

"I love you."

"I love you too. Always will. Hey, you know how you said we can't live in this dump forever?"

"I said that?"

"Yeah, earlier."

"Wow. That sounds very smart."

"Well, I was thinking…"

"You know, I love your Dad. He's such a sweetie. I wish he was my Dad."

Walczyk didn't know what to say. April rarely talked about her lack of a father sober, and never drunk. For her to bring the subject up, and to say that she wished his father was her father, that said a lot about the kind of man Henry Walczyk was. Walczyk reached down and stroked April's hair, his head comfortably numb. "He'd love to have another daughter."

"So let's live with them now and leave here and leave the ugly toad man here."

"Actually, I was thinking that I'd buy a house. The old Merry place is for sale. It's a nice house. I'd like living there."

"That's good. I think I love Vic."

"You just met him."

"I know. Girly of me, isn't it?"

April murmured another ten or fifteen minutes about Vic, Ingrid, and Henry before passing out, hugging Walczyk's left leg. Walczyk went to sleep with a smile on his face, having a plan finally. He was going to get a house. He was going to make it a home. He was going to start over. He was going to feel better.

He just wished he wasn't so afraid of seeing Hannah Cooper again.

Cole Island High School had changed quite a bit since Peter Walczyk was a student there in the mid-1990s. Then it was an illogically laid out mess, where you'd have to go through Stella Lyons's room just to get into Mrs. Robinson's room, through Mr. Duffy's room in order to get to crazy old Mr. Taylor's room, and so-on. In 2001, a grant was given to the school by an anonymous former alumnus (Walczyk vowed up and down it wasn't him, as he'd liked the bass-ackwards mess that the school was), and the interior of Cole Island High School was gutted, down to the last portable wall and janitor-hung door, and the school was redesigned in a more sensible manner. Seeing the final result, Walczyk found it hard to believe this was the same Cole Island High School that he'd graduated from.

Walczyk stood staring up at a large glossy framed one-sheet poster from *Aaron Lawrence Is Dead* hanging in the office of the principal of Cole Island High School. On one side of the poster was a framed five-by-seven photograph of Walczyk and his parents, standing in front of Grauman's Chinese Theatre at the premiere of *Aaron Lawrence*. Another photo taken at the premiere included a smiling Sara clinging to his father's side. A third picture featured just Walczyk, on the set of *Ordinary World*, leaning forward in his director's chair, glasses up on his forehead and his hands rubbing the bridge of his nose. Walczyk remembered that staged shot, which appeared in an issue of *Rolling Stone,* was Sara's idea. A fourth picture flanking the large, glossy poster was a teenage Walczyk, holding a homemade sound clapper, the only worthwhile product of his semester in wood shop class. In the photo, Walczyk peered out through the spread sticks, *Intolerance* scribbled on the front in chalk.

"Quite the shrine, isn't it?"

Walczyk turned around. Standing in the doorway to his father's office, wearing denim shorts and a tank top, was Hannah Cooper, ginger hair cascading down past her shoulders. It had been nine years since they had last seen each other. Two days before Christmas 1999, outside of Ferguson's Market down on O'Connor Street, and somehow she had changed very little. Hannah had finally decided she wanted to embrace her destiny and teach. Walczyk had decided, but not yet told his parents, that he was going to abandon his studies at Hofstra, having decided with his roommate, Ian Maeder, to go west in pursuit of jobs at a small production company in Burbank that one of Ian's friends worked at.

Hannah's right eye squinted slightly as she smiled and pushed a tuft of hair back behind her ear. The thin-strapped tank top exposed the birthmark on the front side of her left shoulder. She smiled, her thin pink lips tugging wide across her soft, pale skin. She reached back, putting a hand behind her long, slender neck. It was remarkable, Walczyk thought as he soaked her in, that as much as she'd changed, she'd still stayed the same skinny, awkward girl he and Vic both eventually fell in love with.

"Han," he said, stepping toward her as she entered the office. He still stood several inches over her, something he rather enjoyed, having an irrational attraction to shorter women. She dropped the stack of books she was carrying on a nearby table. Walczyk just shook his head. He searched quickly for something to say, but Hannah lurched toward him and took him into a surprisingly tight hug, given her petite frame. She put her head against his chest, and he breathed in the smell of vanilla shampoo, a scent it had taken him years to identify. She pulled back, still holding him.

"Hey, Peter," she said, again flashing what was called "Prettiest Smile" in the 1996 edition of *The Islander*, Cole Island High's yearbook. "How's my favorite director?"

He fought the urge to be honest. "Couldn't be better. How's the best thing to happen to Cole Island High since high-speed internet access?"

"Taking exactly two weeks off – principal's orders – before I start in on my lesson plans hardcore," she said, letting go of him. "You're looking trim," she said abruptly. She reached over and toyed with his hairline. "A little too trim in some places, but that was always your biggest fear, wasn't it?"

"That and world peace," he remarked, smirking.

"I'm going to ask two questions."

"Okay."

"And you need only answer one."

"Sounds fair."

"One: what are you doing back in Cole Island?"

Walczyk had thought long and hard about this, having no real reason for returning to his childhood home. He had no real reason when his mother asked him, when his father asked him, and when a million other friends, family, and various locals asked him. He inhaled deeply through his nose, straightening up. "What would you say if I asked what the second question was?"

She smiled wryly. "Okay, then. Two: why has it taken three months for our paths to cross?"

Without thinking, he blurted out the first thing that came to him: "In response to your first question: my wife left me for another woman, and I'm pretty sure I'm in the midst of a nervous breakdown."

There was silence between them. He realized what he'd said, and the ramifications of that statement, even in a presumably private conversation. He opened his mouth, ready to suffer through a really rough, embarrassing explanation. Then Hannah burst into laughter. She shook her head, the hair behind her pink ears shaking loose and falling back around her shoulders. She stifled the laughter, red faced from embarrassment. "I'm sorry, Peter." She might have been sorry, but it hadn't stopped her from laughing. She swallowed a breath of air, calming herself. She grabbed his arm, caressing it as she centered herself. "I'm *so* sorry. It's not funny."

"I suppose it could be, if you looked at it from the right perspective," Walczyk said. "But the long and the short of it is... when that video of Sara and Ella broke, I panicked. I just couldn't... I didn't want to talk to the press."

"Can't say as I blame you," Hannah said, regaining her composure.

"So in about three seconds, I ordered my assistant April–"

"The pretty little blonde you brought with you?

"Yeah. I told her to pack a bag and we headed out with no destination in mind."

"So what made you decide that Cole Island was the place to be?"

"Would you believe me if I told you it was a shitty little bar just outside of Cleveland, Ohio?"

"You're having a nervous breakdown, so yeah, I'll buy that your epiphany came in a shitty little bar outside of Cleveland." She sidled up next to him, her eyes narrowing to almonds, the corners of her mouth tightening as they did when she was purposely being sultry. "Didn't happen to bring any as yet to air episodes with you, did you?"

He leaned in close to her, and whispered, "And that answers one of *my* questions."

"Which is?"

"Why, exactly, are you still talking to me?"

She stretched her hand out and took his, stroking her thumb over the top of it, just as she used to when they held hands beneath the lunch table senior year. "The answer to that is, honestly, I don't know."

He studied her face, then challenged her with, "A lie."

"Okay. Ask me later," she said, breaking eye contact. "I might have a real answer for you. For now, I've got to go down to my room and get some books unpacked."

"Before you go... can you tell me about Angela Cariou."

Hannah's face screwed up. "The school therapist?"

"Yeah."

"Well, she does a good job getting through to students who might otherwise be reticent to see a therapist."

"Aah," Walczyk said, then noticed the confusion on Hannah's face. He guessed he owed it to her to bring her up to speed. He explained briefly, without as much explicit detail as he had with his father, his feelings concerning Sara, the divorce, and his general dissatisfaction with life. Throughout his discourse, he noticed the growing look of shock on Hannah's face. He finished with a recap of his discussion a week and a half ago with his father on the dewy grass in the middle of the night.

"Oh, my God," she said under her breath, reaching out for her friend and pulling him into another hug. "I'm so sorry. The press..." she began, then broke off, opting for silence. After a warm embrace, she gently let go of him, still holding onto his arms. "I think your father is right. That you need to talk to a professional, but I don't think Angela Cariou is quite the right person. But that's just me. You do whatever you think you should do. Maybe you could–"

"I'm *not* seeing anyone on the Island," Walczyk said,

forestalling the inevitable mention of Sherman Cottle or Dr. Troy down on Marina Street.

"So Angela is what brings you here today?" Hannah hesitantly asked.

"In part. Dad's bringing her in to get to know me. If it works, then yeah, I'll start seeing her every week, here at the school to keep the press off my trail. So," he began, changing the subject, "you're one of those teachers who empties their classroom every June fifteenth or whatever and moves it all back in every August fifteenth or so."

"Not everything. Just the books I don't have copies of at home."

Walczyk shook his head, smiling. "So I guess it's true what Henry says about you."

"Oh, and what's that?"

"That you're one of the most dedicated teachers he has working for him."

Hannah's cheeks reddened. "Your father's too kind." Hannah stepped forward, taking Walczyk's hand in hers. She turned it palm up, and removed a Sharpie marker from her back pocket, and began to scrawl on Walczyk's hand. She finished, curled his hand back up, and patted it. "Give me a call some time. There's no reason why we shouldn't have dinner some night this week." With that, she smiled, turned, and walked out of the office, leaving Walczyk alone with his father's leather-bound books and a funny feeling in his stomach.

Walczyk continued along the wall. At the far side of the room, on a small reading table, were three framed pictures. The first was Walczyk, his parents, and sister Melanie in 1992, Melanie wearing her cap and gown from graduation. Next to the family picture was a photo of the family from Melanie's wedding in the summer of 1996: Melanie looking amazing in a white lace dress and her husband Adam cutting quite a figure in his tuxedo, his parents dressed quite nicely as the parents of the bride, and Walczyk in a short-sleeved shirt and a tie, Hannah clinging to his arm, a floral print sundress falling modestly about her. Walczyk reached out, picked up the third picture, and admired it. In it, his father wore another black suit and his mother wore a cream-colored dress that cost more than she wished it had. A very pregnant Melanie clutched her husband with one arm, her stomach with another. Standing front-and-center in the photo, Walczyk wore a charcoal tuxedo and Sara was beautiful in a snug-fitting floor-length white wedding gown.

"Sorry. Should've taken that one down by now," his father's voice called out from behind him. Walczyk turned around, startled to see his father in his office wearing shorts and a camp shirt. A bold look for Henry Walczyk, a man who was never seen in the school in anything less than freshly pressed shirt and pants and a tie.

Walczyk looked once more at the photo, smiled wistfully, and replaced it on the table where he'd found it. "It's okay," he said, crossing over to his father's desk. "It's a great picture. We're all actually smiling in it."

"I hear you had company." Walczyk's father walked into the office, his arms filled with books.

"Yeah, you sent her to the right room," Walczyk said, sitting behind the desk. "Your idea or Angela Cariou's?"

"So how is Hannah?" Henry said, evading the question and setting the stack of books and legal pads on the corner of his desk.

"Great," Walczyk said, getting up. He crossed the room to the *Aaron Lawrence* poster, and pointed. "Why right across from your desk?"

"As a reminder that if you put your mind and heart into it, you can accomplish anything."

"Wow," Walczyk said, touched. "Tell me this, though: where would you put the *First Date* poster?"

His father smiled. "Right beside the *Aaron Lawrence* one."

"Why? You, and most of America, hated that movie."

"To remind us that just because we can do a thing, it does not necessarily mean we must do that thing."

"If you ever decide to retire, let me know. You'd make a hell of a business manager."

"So, do you have any big plans for the weekend?"

"I do now," Walczyk said, holding his hand up, showing the magic-markered phone number off to his father, who grinned at the sight of it.

There was a knock at the door. Walczyk turned to see a rather attractive woman in her fifties, slender, her dark brown hair piled on top of her head, seemingly held in place by a yellow Number 2 pencil. She wore light blue sweat pants and a blue T-shirt. She looked across the room over a pair of eyeglasses. "Well, this must be Peter Walczyk," she said smiling, her voice husky from too many years of smoking.

Walczyk's father rose from his desk and crossed the room. "He is indeed," he said, smiling. "Thank you so much, Angela," he began.

The woman smiled, turning to Walczyk. "Hello, Peter. I'm Angela Cariou."

"Nice to meet you," Walczyk said uneasily, suddenly awash with a cold sweat. Angela reached out and he shook her hand.

"I recognize you from the photos here in your father's office," she said, gesturing around the room. "So, you ready to get down to business?"

Walczyk followed Angela into a small office that had been the senior lounge in his Cole Island High days.

"You look scared shitless," Angela said, gesturing for Walczyk to go inside her office. The room was a small, cluttered affair, with photographs, motivational posters, framed diplomas and degrees covering the walls. A brown chestnut bookcase was filled with books of various titles and topics, from psychology and education to a lovingly worn hardcover collection of the Harry Potter books. At the rear of the room sat a very cluttered, very disorganized desk, with stacks of papers and books covering every inch not being used by the antiquated computer sitting atop it.

"A bit extreme," Walczyk said, standing in front of the desk, "but you're on the right path."

Angela beckoned him to sit down in an overstuffed chair, which currently held two crocheted pillows, a jacket, and one of those incredibly racist looking sock monkey dolls that Walczyk felt trod too close to resembling minstrel show performers and not actual simians. "Just dig a hole," Angela said, coming out from behind her desk dragging her rolling office chair. Walczyk draped the coat over an adjacent chair, also laden with books, and parted the pillows, digging a hole for himself.

"Oh, I'll take Frasier," she said, reaching out for the sock monkey. She grabbed the toy and tossed him into the other chair atop the books. "So, what can I do for you?"

"You're seeing a shrink?!?" Vic blurted out from across the table in the back corner of the Barrelhead, by the kitchen.

"You want to shut the hell up?" April hissed, elbowing Vic. "We're trying to keep this on the down-low!"

Walczyk shook his head. "Thank you, April, but at the same time, let's not create a bigger scene in covering it up." He then turned to Vic. "And, yes, Vic, I'm seeing someone."

"Who, Doc Cottle?"

"No, I'm not seeing Dr. Cottle," Walczyk said, his voice showing his deep disdain for the Island's resident general practitioner. As a physician, you couldn't ask for a more adept man than Sherman Cottle. Honoring doctor-patient confidentiality, however, was not one of Dr. Cottle's strong suits, as he tended to ramble a bit after his evening brandy to his wife Helena, an unabashed gossip.

"What's that on your hand?" April asked, reaching out and grabbing Walczyk's hand. She overturned it in her own tiny hand and examined the writing on his palm. "207 201 0626? What is that?" April asked.

"Holy shit," Vic said, grinning.

"What?" April snapped, growing impatient. "What is it?"

"It's a phone number," Vic cooed, giving Walczyk a punch in the arm.

"No shit it's a phone number!" She turned to Walczyk. "But *whose* phone number?"

"If I tell you, will you promise not to go nuts over it and start reading more into it than is necessary?"

"Promise." She nodded. Walczyk turned to Vic.

"No way. I know what it is! You were at the school today, weren't you?"

"Yes," Walczyk said wearily, "I was."

"And so was *she*, wasn't she?"

"Yes, *she* was there."

Then it dawned on April, who smacked herself in the head. "Of course! The *It* couple, together again!"

Walczyk yanked his hand back from April and put it back in his lap, drinking his rum-and-coke with his left. "Yes, it's Hannah's number."

"Did you put it in your phone yet?" April asked quickly.

"No," Walczyk said. "I've been busy."

"With this teacher shrink person," Vic surmised.

"My meeting with *Angela* was about an hour long. I also set up Dad's new laptop on the school network, helped Mum pick up groceries at Ferguson's, and e-mailed Eli."

"You e-mailed Eli?" April asked, excitedly. "What'd he say?"

"He told me about a couple dozen offers that have come streaming in for me."

"That *Mission: Impossible*-esque spy series set in the 1960s?" she asked, stoked.

"Yes," Walczyk replied, less than stoked.

"The movie about the body-swapping twins? Because I got a copy of that too."

"*Great Minds*? Yep," Walczyk replied, unenthusiastically. "I got 'em all: the movie about a woman who gets hired out to destroy failing relationships, and that stupid ape sitcom."

"Ape sitcom?" Vic asked.

"Yeah. It's kind of inspired by *Planet of the Apes*, but set in a modern setting, with ape offices, ape janitors, ape teachers, ape everythings."

"So?" April asked eagerly. "What'd you say?"

"I told him not to hold his breath."

"Walczyk!" April shrieked, attracting some unwanted attention to their table. "Some top talent is attached to those projects! Lacey Chabert has supposedly talked to them about exec producing and starring in *Great Minds*."

"Please! Lacey Chabert wouldn't do that dog shit if her house was being foreclosed on."

"Okay, so that one's a loser. But you can't deny that the one about the professional couple-breaker-upper has some potential."

"Yeah, why don't we cast Ella in the lead?" Walczyk snapped.

"Okay…" Vic said, slowly getting up, "I think they need me in the kitchen." With that, he bolted for the back of the restaurant.

"Sorry," Walczyk said. "I know you and Eli are trying, but those ideas… they're rehashes of other projects, or they're half-baked, harebrained shock comedies. I swear, Eli's just taking everything they offer and passing it along to me."

"Of course he is! That's his *job*!"

"No, his *job* is to filter through the crap and give me the good stuff."

"Well…" she paused, considering her next words carefully. "Maybe there *is* no good stuff."

"Thank you," Walczyk said, nodding at her. "Thank you for confirming what I've been saying all along. This is an industry that has run out of original ideas!"

"But you've got to do something."

"No, I don't. I've worked hard my entire career so that when I don't feel the urge to work, I don't have to."

"But your career."

"Screw my career! I won't do garbage. Not again!"

A waitress whose name tag said she was McKenzie arrived with a tray bearing drinks for Walczyk and April. She handed a fresh rum and Coke to Walczyk, and a Michelob light to April.

"Do you want to save any of this?" she asked, reaching for the remnants of Walczyk's chicken parmesan.

"No, I'm all set, McKenzie, thanks."

"And you?" she asked April, indicating the half a steak left on April's plate.

"No, thanks."

"Anything wrong with it?" McKenzie asked.

"Just that my eyes are bigger than my belly," she said. "Thanks, though. Tell Vic it was great."

McKenzie smiled, collected the plates, and trucked off for the kitchen.

"So," April began, sipping at her beer. "Tell me more about 207 201 0626."

"Her name is Hannah, and there are no *plans*. She just gave me her number so we could keep in touch. She's a big fan of the show."

"Aah," she said. "Your parents will be glad you've finally patched things up with her."

"There wasn't really much to patch up."

"So things are good with you guys?"

"I think so. Hannah was never one to carry a grudge. Besides, that was all a hundred years or so ago. If she's still clinging onto that…"

April rose and craned her neck, looking past Walczyk for a moment, then sat back in her seat. "She's not a psycho, is she?"

"No," Walczyk replied, confused. "No, she's not a psycho."

"Not a stalker?"

"No, not a stalker."

"Not sitting four tables down from us, staring and pointing."

Walczyk turned around. In the corner table by the door, he saw a couple seated, having drinks. The man, who he didn't recognize, was a few years older than he, with thinning brown hair and a round build, wearing a Hawaiian shirt and thick black glasses. But the girl was unforgettable, sitting there in a simple, flowered sundress.

207 201 0626 was sipping at a margarita and pointing over at Walczyk.

"That's him," Hannah said, pointing across the room, tugging on Cameron Burke's Hawaiian-print sleeve. "That's Peter."

"*That's* Peter Walczyk?" he asked.

"Yeah. Don't you know who he is?"

"Between you and Henry and the rest of this island, how could I *not*. It's just..."

"What?"

"Well, he looks shorter."

"Well, he's sitting down, silly." Suddenly, Peter turned around, staring right at them. "Damn," she said, slouching down in her seat and dragging Cameron down by the shirt with her.

"What?" Cameron hissed.

"I can't believe he saw us," she said, picking up her menu.

"I can't believe you're having such a cartoony reaction to being caught red-handed gawking across a crowded restaurant. After all, you two are friends, aren't you?"

"I don't know if we're still friends or not," she said.

"Why wouldn't you be?"

"Because. It's been a long time. Feelings change."

"But you said you hear from him every Christmas."

"I get a Christmas card with a few lines of message. Not exactly a close, emotional bond."

"I'm sure that he's still your friend. You said things were good at the school today when you met up with him."

"He could've just been being polite."

"Will you knock it off?" Cameron urged, forcing her hand from his shirt.

"Why should I?"

"Because he's on his way over here."

Hannah looked up. Peter was moving across the room, smiling.

"Hey, Hannah," he said, approaching the table. He seemed to be in a better mood than he'd been in when they first met up in Henry's office. *Must've been his meeting with Angela Cariou,* she thought to herself.

"Hey, Peter," she said.

"Long time no see," he chuckled.

"Indeed."

"Don't let me keep you from your drinks. I just spotted you from across the room and thought I'd come say hello."

"Peter," she said, indicating Cameron, "This is Cameron Burke. He also teaches English at Cole Island High."

Cameron stood. "Mr. Walczyk, it's a pleasure," he said, holding his hand out.

Peter shook Cameron's hand. "*Mr.* Walczyk is your boss, Cameron. I'm just Walczyk."

"Well, it's a pleasure... *Walczyk.* And if you don't mind my saying, *R.U.R.* was some of the finest material I've ever seen on television."

Peter smiled. "Thank you, Cameron. I appreciate it. I'm especially proud of the work we did on that miniseries." He turned to look back at his table, where his drink had arrived. "Are you guys eating tonight or just having drinks?"

"Just drinks. We're thinking of catching the Friday night movie down in the park."

"Movie in the park?" Walczyk asked.

"You've been back almost three months and you didn't know about Friday night movies in the park?" Hannah asked.

"We've kept our heads pretty much down since getting back," Peter said.

"*We?*" Cameron asked.

He quickly turned back to his table. April was on her phone. He turned back. "Yeah, I'm here in Maine with my assistant. Listen, since you guys are just having drinks, why don't you join us? We've finished dinner and I'm sure April would love to meet the infamous 207 201 0626."

"You refer to me by my phone number?" Hannah asked warily.

"She and Vic have been giving me a ribbing about the Sharpie'd digits," Peter said, holding his hand up to display Hannah's phone number. "Come on. Join us."

Hannah and Cameron exchanged looks before Hannah stood,

smoothing out her dress. "Sounds like fun." She picked up her margarita and stepped out of the booth. Cameron grabbed his Guinness and they followed Walczyk across the restaurant to his table, where his assistant was animatedly talking into her iPhone.

"... and, for the love of God, please tell David E. Kelley that we're *still* not interested in just being a script factory for his next legal dramedy. Got it?" April looked up, noticing Hannah and Cameron, and turned her attention back to the phone. "Just pass it along, Elias, all right? Look, I've got to go. Bye." She slid it back into her purse and stood up. "You must be Hannah Cooper," she said, her demeanor turning on a dime. "I'm April Donovan. Nice to finally meet you. I've heard quite a bit about you."

"I hope that some of it was at least good," Hannah said, laughing.

"According to anyone named Walczyk or Gordon, you're nothing short of an angel." April turned her attention to Cameron. "Who's this?"

"Cameron Burke. I teach English at the high school with Hannah."

"Please, sit," Peter said, sliding into the booth next to April. Hannah and Cameron slid in on the other side, putting their drinks on the table. "Cameron was just telling me that they show movies in the park downtown every Friday night."

"Yeah," April said, sipping at her beer. "You didn't know that?"

"No," Peter said, surprised. "Why didn't you mention it to me?"

"Because Friday nights are dinner night with your folks, and usually the movie is well underway by the time we get back to the motel."

"Listen to her," Peter said, throwing a thumb in April's direction. "Makes it sound like we're an old married couple or something."

Cameron laughed. "It's all too easy for these friendships to turn into that, isn't it?" Hannah cast him a dirty look. "I don't even *plan* to do laundry without checking with this one first."

"So what's tonight's movie?" April asked.

"*Mad Love*," Hannah said.

"The old Peter Lorre film?" Peter asked.

"What's *Mad Love?*" April asked.

"Oh, it's a gem," Cameron said excitedly. "Peter Lorre is this mad scientist who falls in love with this actress performing in a cheesy little Grand Guignol theatre in Paris. She's married to this piano maestro. Well, there's this train accident and the husband's hands – he's Colin Clive, the guy who played Dr. Frankenstein – his hands are destroyed and Peter Lorre steps in as the good guy and offers to perform surgery to give maestro new hands."

"And?" April asked, hooked.

"And he gives them to him. But they're the hands of a knife-chucking murderer."

"Kinda like that script Eli was trying to get you to polish up a few years back," April said.

"Kinda," Peter replied, "except that this is nothing like that."

"What time's the movie start?" April asked.

"Sundown," Hannah said. "But I thought your father said you guys usually have dinner with Henry and Diane on Friday nights?"

"Henry took Diane out for her birthday," April said.

"But if we want to get a good spot," Cameron added, finishing his Guinness, "we should get there around eight thirty."

April turned to Peter. "What do you say, kid? Wanna go to a movie?"

Peter shrugged. "Why not?"

"You better bring some lawn chairs or something, though," Cameron warned, "The few folding chairs they set up always get taken by the oldies."

"We'll see if Vic has anything," Peter said, then returned his attention to his rum and Coke.

Any attempts at stealthily slipping into his parents' house at a quarter to one were quashed by the barking of two little dachshunds and a beagle puppy, their nails clipping along the hard wood floors. April instantly scurried towards the dogs, scooching low to pet them, hoping to calm them down. "Such good little guard dogs," she cooed, scratching the Mohawk tuft of hair running down Cocoa's neck. "Such good dogs!" The barking ceased.

"I know what you boys want," Walczyk said, reaching under a cupboard and pulling out three dog biscuits. He doled them out, effectively silencing the dogs. "So, what'd you think of the movie?"

"You know, for the 1930s, that was one screwed-up movie," April whispered, slipping Dexter's pink collar around his snowy neck.

"Cameron told me it was one of the last overtly violent horror pictures to play in England for a few decades," Walczyk said, slipping his sandals off. "But I meant what'd you think of Hannah."

April stood. "I think that it's too soon for you to be asking me what I think about Hannah."

"I don't mean what do you think of her like *that*. I just mean what do you think of her?"

"I think she's incredibly friendly," April said, walking over to the dining room table, where she found Dexter's leash. "She's sweet and fun to talk to and has a great sense of humor. I can certainly see what you saw in her all those years ago. And I can see what Cameron Burke sees in her now."

"She's not with Cameron," Walczyk said, brushing April's comments off.

"Yeah, she is," April said, attaching the leash. "It's obvious. They're either a couple or he's gay, and I don't get a gay vibe from him."

Walczyk considered this for a moment. April was right: Hannah and Cameron made a great couple. They complemented each other nicely. Hell, if he thought back about it, he could've sworn that she finished a couple of his sentences. But still… Hannah and Cameron? It didn't make sense. They never touched each other. They never made any overtly "couple" gestures. And Walczyk noted no sexual tension between them.

"Did I hear someone mention Hannah Cooper?" Walczyk's mother stood in the doorway to the kitchen wearing her bathrobe, her eyes looking so small without her glasses on.

"Shit! We woke you. I'm sorry," Walczyk put a hand on his mother's shoulder. "We'll just get Dexter and take off."

"Forget about it," she said, smiling. "I'm up almost on the hour anyway. The result of getting old. Now what were you saying about Hannah Cooper?"

"I was just saying that–"

"Because your father said that you two saw each other at the school today. How'd that go?"

"I'm gonna take Dexter out to pee," April said, slipping out of the kitchen. She patted Walczyk's mother on the arm. "Good night,

Diane."

"So? How'd things go with Hannah?" Diane eagerly asked.

"Mum, don't get excited. Nothing is going to happen between me and Hannah."

"Who said it would?" she asked innocently, moving for the sink. Walczyk stepped back, letting her through. "So, how did things go?"

"Fine," Walczyk said, not really knowing what his mother wanted to hear. "We talked. We laughed. We came to an understanding about the past."

"Did you apologize?"

"No," Walczyk said. "We kind of agreed that it was many, many years ago."

"Still, Peter, you need you to apologize."

"Oh? And did she share this with Dad at some staff meeting?"

"No, but any woman would want the man who *Dear John'ed* her to apologize. It's just the polite thing to do."

"I don't know," Walczyk said. "Besides, considering she was packing a date, I'm sure that she's gotten over me by now."

"A date? You mean Cameron Burke?"

"Yeah," Walczyk said. "The two of them looked friendly enough. I don't want to step on any toes."

"Peter, they're just co-workers. If I remember right, they did have a little something a few years ago, but that's just that – a few years ago. In the past. She's as single as you and April." She reached into the cabinet and pulled down a small glass tumbler, then filled it with water as Walczyk explained how they'd all met up at the Barrelhead, then gone to the downtown movie. Diane took some pills from an orange plastic bottle on the sideboard and turned to her son. "How was your talk with Angela?"

"Okay," he said. "Just a basic getting-to-know-you deal. I gave her some history on me, on me and Sara, and on me and my work. Told her about the trip cross-country and the hopping from B&B-to-motel."

"And?"

"And," he began, reading his mother's mind, "I'm going to see her again next week."

A smile erupted across Diane's face. At night, with her hair fluffed up and without her glasses, in a thin house coat and barefoot, she was so small and fragile, a tiny little person who scarcely resembled the strong woman who had raised him. Walczyk reached out and gave her a big hug, careful not to squeeze her too hard. He felt his mother's dry lips on his scruffy cheek. "I'm proud of you," she said, then turned around and walked back to her bedroom.

Walczyk looked down at the dogs, who were licking his feet, and smiled. He shut the kitchen light off and walked to the front door. He stopped, looking out the window over the sink at the waters of the Atlantic Ocean. There was the same rippling black surface, the same scattered reflection of the moon, and the same purple tint to everything. But it all looked so different this time. This was a vista he could get used to.

Then it hit him. The solution to all of his problems.

CHAPTER THREE
THE OLD MERRY PLACE

Walczyk stared out at the Atlantic crashing against the shore down the hill from the building that had been known for decades on Cole Island as the Old Merry Place, named for the building's original inhabitants, Duane and Lynn Merry, back in 1971. The Merrys hadn't lived there as long as some of the property's other residents, like the Leavitts or the Wilcoxes, but the name 'The Old Merry Place" had stuck.

Walczyk had never set foot in the house until the late eighties, when he would visit Max Leavitt. The two eight-year-olds would sketch out movies they'd never make. Max would play the part of FBI agent/ninja Max Joseph, taking down the kidnappers of the President's daughter. Walczyk would be a teen who found a secret room behind his closet door. Walczyk still had those old stories in a notebook at the bottom of the green army chest his Grandfather Walczyk had given him when he went off to college (along with a warning not to lend any money to 'those hobos' he'd be living with).

The layout of the house was simple and straight-forward. The first floor held the kitchen, which opened out into the living room. A bedroom and bathroom were at the other end of the house. Upstairs was the master bedroom (and its attached master bath) and a second room.

The master bedroom also held the house's *pièce de résistance:* a sliding glass door that led out onto a long balcony that stretched the entire width of the top story. The balcony looked out over the back lawn, with its rolling hills of dense green grass waving in the breeze down over a steep embankment to the edge of the Atlantic Ocean. It was a beautiful piece of property, both when he'd visited it years ago, and now, with only a few improvements made.

Walczyk turned around to face Vic and April, who were standing side-by-side on the balcony. "Well, what do you think?" he eagerly asked. While he knew April was no proponent of spending any more time in Maine than they had to, she seemed eager to finally close the deal on a place, this being their third day of house hunting and the fourth house they'd looked at this morning, as she reminded them frequently.

"You know what he'll say," April dubiously said to Walczyk.

Vic crossed his arms, scowled, and in a near perfect approximation of Henry Walczyk, said, "She's a lot of space, Peter. A lot of space."

Vic, Walczyk, and April laughed, standing on the balcony looking over the back yard.

"That's pretty good," April said, leaning over the railing. "When did you perfect that little act of mimicry?"

"Sixth grade," Walczyk cut in. "We were the old man's last sixth grade class before his big move to the principal's office."

"And you were the worst sixth grade ever," Vic growled, his arms crossed again as Mr. Walczyk.

"Were you really?" April asked, imagining a pre-pubescent Walczyk and Vic raising hell for a younger Henry Walczyk.

"Hard to tell," Vic said.

"How's that?"

"As far back as 1979, the year he started teaching, he'd been telling his sixth grade classes that they were the worst sixth grade he'd ever had."

"*Your* father? Bullshit!"

"The man you've met is far from the strict disciplinarian that stalks the halls of Cole Island High School."

"I'm sure you're exaggerating," April said, patting Walczyk's arm reassuringly. "Anyway, I'm sure he'll like it."

"Thanks," Walczyk said. "But Vic, what do you think? You've

actually built one of these damned things."

"Built? I turned an upstairs loft in my uncle's garage into an apartment."

"You built your apartment?" April asked, sounding impressed.

"I slapped up some walls, hired a plumber and an electrician, and told Ingrid to pick out some paint that wouldn't look too fruity."

"*Fruity?*" April said. "And just where does that shade fall in the Sherwin Williams color palette?"

The sound of two sets of feet coming up the stairs turned their heads to the doorway. Walczyk's father stepped into the room a few moments later, Dexter following close behind him. All eyes were on him when he entered the room. He looked around, from April to Walczyk and his mother, to Vic. Dexter bolted for April, who dropped to one knee to pet the loyal dog.

"What?" Dad asked. "She's a lot of space." He walked over to Walczyk, putting his hand on his son's shoulder. "But it's a beautiful space."

"Does that mean we're moving again, boss?" April asked.

"Yeah, boss, does it?" Vic asked, child-like excitement in his voice.

"Yeah. It means we're moving, kids." Walczyk turned and looked out over the back balcony once more, the sun glittering on the water. He was home. Again.

The house was already beginning to feel like it was a home as the smell of charcoal briquettes burning filled the air. The sound of dogs yipping as they played in the back yard and the sound of Walczyk's mother fussing over whether or not the mayonnaise had "turned" in the fifteen minute trip from her kitchen to "the Old Merry Place" finished the Norman Rockwell scene forming in Walczyk's mind.

It had been much to Walczyk's initial chagrin that Vic had insisted on throwing him a housewarming party the very night he signed the paperwork at the York Real Estate offices in town. Susie York, the agent who had shown them the house earlier that day, had been quite excited to have such a no-fuss sale in a month when sales had been rather low.

"When a party comes to you, no strings attached, you welcome it and you attend it," his mother told him. The woman, of course, would clearly have freaked out if she'd been told that a party was being thrown at *her* home without advance warning.

Walczyk sat on the porch in one of the red wooden camp chairs his father brought over from his own cellar, puffing on a cheap cigar to keep the flies away. What no one probably understood was why Walczyk felt the urge to immediately begin living in the house, without electricity or running water. Those amenities had already been arranged for: the power guy would be there the day-after-tomorrow, then the Hunter boys would get the water running. Walczyk was just anxious – very anxious – to get on with his life, and he saw nothing wrong with moving in right away. The sooner he could move in, the sooner he could be normal again. To be himself – just Walkzyk.

To that end, Vic had returned from a trip to the Walczyk homestead with a truck loaded down with loaner furniture: two kitchen tables, three identical folding red canvas camp chairs for the porch, a set of mismatched TV trays, a garbage bag filled with towels, wash cloths, dish towels, and a queen-sized inflatable mattress.

Now, Vic stood behind a folding card table that had various bottles of spices, dressings, and oils strewn messily around a large plastic salad bowl filled with raw hamburger. Beside him, Walczyk's mother, who had long ago surrendered the kitchen to April and her chopped salad from hell, dutifully followed directions as Vic taught her his father's secret recipe for the Barrelhead's famous Cole Island Bourbon Burger. Down the hill a stretch, Henry tossed a plastic Frisbee for Dexter and the dachshunds to chase after. It felt like the fourth of July, with citronella candles burning and the easy sound of 1970s southern rock echoing from Vic's truck stereo. And Walczyk just sat there, puffing at his cigar, his head still spinning from the whirlwind purchase of his house.

Down the hill, by the road, a cloud of dust began to rise in the air. A little white station wagon made its way up the gravel path to the front door. Walczyk rose to his feet, squinting through the bright sun. He stepped down off the steps from the porch and walked to the edge of the yard, where the grass gave way to the gravel driveway. Only when the station wagon came to a stop and the dust cleared was Walczyk able identify the driver.

Hannah Cooper got out of the car, a broad smile across her face. She gave a big wave before reaching into the back seat and pulling out what looked like an ice cream cake from Ferguson's

Market. "I know, I know," she said, bringing the ice cream cake up the walk, "I remembered half-way here that you don't have any power yet."

"We'll just have to eat desert first, then," Diane called from next to Vic at the card table, elbow deep in Cole Island Bourbon Burger meat, a silly smile spread across her face. Walczyk's mother was infamous for her love of ice cream.

Walczyk was baffled. While Hannah was a welcome sight, balancing an ice cream cake in one hand while fending off the dogs with the other, he was surprised by her presence at the impromptu barbecue. He then began to smell outside influence. Someone had called her and told her to come. He knew that this wasn't April's doing – her suggestion, perhaps maybe, but not her doing, as she lacked the networking skills to contact Hannah.

"Hannah! Bring *that* right over here!" Vic bellowed, yanking a handful of Wet Ones from the plastic dispenser and wiping down his hands and arms, leaving a string of pink pre-moistened towelettes on the table before taking the cake from Hannah to present it to Diane. With the cake out of his hands, Vic picked the little redhead up in a big embrace. Hannah laughed as Vic spun her around, holding her up with one arm.

Finally, after much protesting from Hannah, Vic put her down on the ground. She turned around to greet her boss. "Henry," she called out, arms open wide. She gave him a hug, laughing. "Not much longer now, is it?"

Walczyk shook his head, smiling. His father's Hannah grin was back. A simple thin-lipped half-smile that crossed Henry's face only when he saw Hannah. Walczyk suspected that there would always be a very, very special spot in his father's heart for Hannah Cooper.

"Since these guys were here when I picked out the house," Walczyk said, stepping towards the grill, smiling at Hannah, "I think it's safe to say that you are my first official house guest."

She laughed, reached out, and pulled Walczyk into a hug. She pulled back, an arm still wrapped around him. "So you're not leasing?" Hannah asked.

"Nope, I bought it outright," Walczyk said, a hint of pride in his voice. "Why? Where'd you hear I was leasing?"

"Where *didn't* I hear it? Weezie's, the post office, half of Commerce Street, paparazz-eye.com–"

"You visit paparazz-eye.com?" Walczyk asked.

"Word gets around fast, doesn't it?" April said, extricating Dexter from Hannah's leg.

"So what brings you over?" Vic asked, digging back into the mixing bowl of hamburger.

"Had to see if the town rumors were true. If Peter Walczyk planning on setting down roots for a while."

Walczyk grinned. "Truth is, I don't know what I'm doing. I got sick of living out of the Meadowbrook. That, and this place was within my means."

Hannah laughed. "Cole Island is going to have to get used to Peter Walczyk all over again." She put an arm around his waist, leaning her head against his shoulder.

"No," Walczyk said, "Peter Walczyk's going to have to get used to Cole Island all over again."

Walczyk leaned back in his red camp chair, cigar in mouth and a rum and Coke in his right hand, gazing out across the sprawling green lawn beneath him. The thin red sliver of a Frisbee in flight bounced back and forth between Vic and April, always over Dexter's head. The hum of the crickets at the water's edge gave accompaniment to the Lynyrd Skynyrd pouring out from Vic's truck. Beside Walczyk, Hannah sat, sipping at a glass of wine. Vic had made a special run into town after the *grown-ups* had left to pick up some alcohol for the four friends, so they could properly celebrate the purchase of the new house into the wee small hours of the morning.

"It's quite a view from up here," Hannah commented.

"It's what sold me on the house, actually," Walczyk replied.

"It'll be the perfect place to write from."

"Exactly my thinking," Walczyk said, putting his cigar in the ashtray resting on the TV tray between the camp chairs.

"So," Hannah asked, picking the cigar up and taking a puff, "what are you working on now?"

"Not much. Next week I have to crack down and start watching the season we're set to air in January. Ian, my showrunner and executive producer, is insisting that I sign off on what he's done in my stead. On top of that, I've also got my agent e-mailing me projects left and right."

"Exciting," she said.

"Yeah, but they're all crap. But that doesn't matter, because I think it's all a build-up to a rumor I'm hearing."

"What would that be?"

"Eclipse Entertainment wants me to do a remake of *A Christmas Carol* starring Ian McKellen."

She lay back in her chair. "One of the best Christmas movies of all time, you always said."

"That's why I'm reluctant to do it," he said, picking up the cigar. "There have been so many remakes of that poor thing. Each one a click or two away from what the original was."

"Replicative fading," Hannah said assuredly. Walczyk shook his head, wordlessly, not knowing what she was taking about. She smiled and explained: "You make a copy of a copy of a copy too many times, each generation of copies is just that much farther from the integrity of the original."

Walczyk studied her a moment, locking eyes with her. She was trying to hide it, but not very well. A grin threatened to erupt from her serious face. Walczyk sat up in his seat and coolly remarked, "You're quoting *Star Trek* to me again, aren't you?"

She maintained her serious composure for only a few seconds before bursting into laughter. Walczyk shook his head, chuckling. "How could you tell?" Hannah asked.

"*Replicative fading*? Please!"

"Actually, the theory is quite sound. Say I had a TV show on video tape."

"Perhaps the *Star Trek* episode you're citing?"

"*Star Trek: The Next Generation,* but yes, a VHS. Now say I copied it for you. That leaves you with a second generation tape."

"A second generation tape of *The* Next *Generation*?"

"Don't confuse me," she said, laughing. "Now you use your second generation copy to make a copy for Vic. His is a third generation. And he copies it for April..."

"Giving April a fourth generation copy," Walczyk said, beginning to understand.

"Right. April's copy, now, is four generations more degraded than mine is."

"But with digital technology out there, why are we all using analog video tapes?"

"To make a point!" she shouted, almost spilling her wine.

"Each remake of *A Christmas Carol* loses a little more of what the original movie was. And you don't want to be behind the version where you can barely tell it's zombies attacking everyone."

Walczyk slowly nodded, taking a drink. "Chalk another one up to *Star Trek*," he said.

Hannah held her hand out and accepted the cigar from Walczyk. "I thought you were writing a script of your own."

"Eh, I'm stuck on it right now. But you'll get a kick out it. It's about this guy who gets his ex-girlfriend cloned and it goes horribly wrong."

"Is there any way it could go wonderfully right in that scenario?"

"I don't think so, which works great for my story," Walczyk said.

"Interesting." Hannah handed the cigar back to Walczyk. "So you're considering cloning Sara?"

"Let's not talk about Sara," Walczyk said, more bluntly than he should have.

"Sorry," Hannah said sheepishly, returning to her wine.

"I'm sorry," Walczyk said after a moment, looking over at his old friend. "It's just... *Ordinary World* and Sara and my plans for the future seem to be all anyone wants to talk to me about anymore. But I shouldn't have snapped at you. I'm–"

"No, it's quite understandable," Hannah said. "So what's the story with April? She seems like a real spitfire."

"Believe it or not, she's actually mellowed since coming to Maine." He paused, taking a drink, and following the thought up with, "I think I might have ruined her."

"Ruined her?"

"She used to be real hard core," Walczyk explained. "Now she's adopting dogs and swapping recipes with my mother and–"

"–and falling for your best friend."

Walczyk shook his head, chuckling. "You noticed that too, huh?"

"I don't know her well, but it's safe to say that subtlety isn't one of her long suits," Hannah said. "All the same, good for her. Vic needs someone to get him out of his rut."

"He's bumming about a girl too?"

"Far from it. You know his cycle: Vic meets a great girl, Vic loses a great girl, Vic starts sleeping with Ingrid Connary, rinse and repeat."

"He's still doing that, eh?"

"Ingrid? Yeah." Walczyk studied her a moment before bursting out laughing. "And to make matters worse, he spends most of his time hanging with Dougie Olsen and that bunch."

"Yeah, we ran into them the night I hooked up with Vic at the Barrelhead. Not exactly a meeting of the minds going on there."

"No, that bunch hasn't done a whole heck of a lot with their lives since graduation that hasn't come from a can or been rolled in tiny little papers."

"Too bad," Walczyk mused. "But, hey, Dougie lost his eye. That's something."

"Yes," Hannah conceded. "He did at that.

Walczyk took a puff off the cigar, sitting up in his chair. "And how the hell did that happen?"

"No one really knows," Hannah said, taking the cigar from Walczyk. "There are stories, of course, but they're just that: stories."

"Such as?"

"Well, the morning crew at Weezie's says Greg Walker chased him out of the house in the middle of the night, after catching Doug with his daughter while she was still in high school, and he fell face-first onto a garden rake."

Walczyk winced in horror.

"Carroll Bates–"

"The first, second, or third?"

"Second. He says at the hardware store that Mia put her thumb..."

"Enough! Enough!" Walczyk took a drink. "These stories all seem to follow a certain trend, don't they?" Hannah nodded. "And which one do you subscribe to?"

"Well, I know Mia was involved – she's involved in all the stories, so it's hard to rule her out. And I know it's gone. The eye, that is. Andrew Tang at the medical center confirmed that one for me."

"What about you?" Walczyk asked. "I've heard very few stories about you."

"I find that hard to believe," Hannah replied, giving the cigar a puff. "Given the constant updates about you that I get from your father."

"Oh, Henry's very sweet on you, that much is for sure. But as for sharing stories, he hasn't. And neither has Mum. They're of the mind I should've gotten out of the car when I got here, tracked you down, and picked up where we left off."

Hannah laughed. "Well, not much has changed. I've been teaching English at the school since 2001. I love having your father as my principal. In the summers I work on lesson plans and try to get a novel off the ground, to no avail."

"Why do you think I stick to script writing? There, you only have to write the dialogue. The rest is someone else's job." Walczyk stubbed out the butt of the cigar. "So what's the story with you and Cameron Blake?'

"It's *Burke*," Hannah said, laughing. "And what do you mean, 'what's the story?'"

"That's got to be his car you're driving, says 'BURKE-2' on the plates. What's the story?"

She smiled. "Story is he's a great friend."

"Is that all? I could've sworn he wanted to put his arm around you during that movie."

"I imagine he did. He's still quite taken with me."

"Still?"

"We might have dated for a little while. But in the end, we realized that we had the romantic and sexual chemistry of your parents' dogs."

"I don't know," Walczyk said. "I think I caught Cocoa sniffing around Brownie's naughty spot last week."

"But was Brownie interested?" she retorted, smirking.

"I don't know," Walczyk laughed. "I had better things to do than watch two dogs sniff each other in the junk."

"Like finish up the upcoming season of *Ordinary World*."

"Han..."

"Sorry. You don't want to discuss *Ordinary World*," she said, the look on her face resembling that of a scolded child.

"It's not that. It's just..."

"Yeah?"

"I don't think you want to see it."

"Of course I do!"

"It's not that good."

"I'm sure it is."

"I'm sure it isn't," Walczyk said.

"What did you do, let someone else run the show for the rest of the year?"

"Yes and no. We finished shooting. But usually I oversee the final cut of each episode. I left that job in Ian's hands."

"And you didn't want to finish those episodes? See them through?"

"Not really. I don't know... I just... I lost my sense of direction."

"You always have been your own worst critic, Peter Walczyk." She picked up her wine glass. "Don't worry. I won't badger you about it." Silence settled between them for a moment. Far below them, on the lawn, the laughter of Vic and April as they played Frisbee in the relative dark cut into the night air. Walczyk could imagine the back lawn after he'd finished with it: the two oak trees down by the river bank would have a hammock strung up between them. An in-ground barbeque pit would be dug, perfect for toasting S'mores or hot dogs, or just providing warmth as he and his friends sat around the fire, watching day drift lazily into night.

"Tell you what," Walczyk said. "Give me a hand. April leaves Monday for L.A."

"She's moving back?"

"No, she's living in Maine. For now, at least. I do pay her rather well to do nothing, after all. But, no, we talked about it tonight. She's going out there to clean up the house, get it ready for renters, get my stuff out of it, and so forth. She'll be gone most of the week."

"So what am I going to do for you while April's gone?"

"Keep me company? Make sure I don't accidentally kill Dexter? Mainly, it's not while she's gone that I really need you, it's when she gets back. Labor Day weekend. We're going to Portland to pick her up, do some furniture shopping, get some electronics."

"But I have school the following Tuesday."

"And I can't get that taken care of?" Walczyk saw Hannah consider it, but it ended in her shaking her head and looking down. "Seriously, though, we'd have you home in plenty of time. April gets in on Friday, we shop Saturday and Sunday, get up Monday morning and drive back, April's Jeep loaded with goodies."

"Peter, I don't know. It's only the sixth day of school. I need to be on the ball. It's been a hectic summer."

"I'm hearing that a lot lately. What happened? You get dumped too?"

"Not quite." Hannah sat back in her chair, suddenly quiet. She sipped at her wine, not saying much of anything for what felt like years.

Breaking the silence, April bounded through the doorway onto the balcony. "Vic's taking me to his place. He says he's got a motorized pump for the mattress."

"Sounds good. Tell Vic I'll swing by tomorrow."

"Will do, Boss." April turned to Hannah. "Nice seeing you again. I'm sure we'll be seeing a lot of each other."

Hannah smiled at April. "I'm sure of it." The moon was casting an eerie blue beam onto the back lawn, its light flickering off the rippling ocean just beyond the lawn.

"I'll do it on one condition."

"Name it," Walczyk said, offering her the cigar.

Hannah took the cigar, puffed, and through her exhale, said, "Tell me, friend to friend, what happened to your marriage."

Walczyk took the cigar back, taking a deep drag from it, wondering where to begin.

"Well, it went down like this..."

"Found it!" Vic's voice boomed at the far end of the darkened garage. April looked around for the source of the voice, seeing only old Christmas decorations and what looked like it used to be a moose's head on a plaque. Her skin crawled the longer she stayed in the garage. Not because it was dirty; on the contrary, it was rather clean. But because it was disorganized. Cluttered. An untidy mess if ever she saw one.

"Great," she called out, stepping on a box marked "X-Mas Lites," causing the contents to give a crackle of broken glass as she crushed the box. "Sorry! My bad!"

"The lights?" Vic asked, looking up from the box he was sifting through.

"The lights," she confirmed.

"Don't sweat it," Vic said, standing up straight, a small black device that must have been the electric air pump clutched in his hand.

"You know," April said, "it'd only take a day, two days tops, to get this mess cleaned up and organized."

"No, we can't go doing that," Vic joked, tripping over a box of old toys.

"You okay?" April asked, reaching out across the room impulsively.

"Fine," Vic said, regaining his balance. "Just some old Ninja Turtles that I can't believe I still have."

"Ninja Turtles were cool when I was of a toy-playing age, and you have ten years on me. That means, when you were playing with Teenage Mutant Ninja Turtles toys, you were… how old?"

"Okay, now," Vic said, finally reaching April. He thrust the small, albeit heavy pump at her. "Let's not start calculating ages."

She smiled and led the way out of the cluttered garage. Above it, a modest little apartment unit sat. Vic lived up there with his brother Andrew. According to Walczyk, it was quite the party spot during their last few years of high school. The apartment had been built after Vic's mother had abandoned her family and the Gordon home was sold to keep the restaurant afloat.

"So," Vic said, pulling the limp mattress from out of the back of April's Jeep, "is *this* what you expected when you signed on to be Peter Walczyk's assistant? Hiding out in motel rooms? Playing house off the Maine coast?"

"I braced myself for the unexpected when I hitched my horse to his crazy wagon." She looked down at the pump. "So this is it? This little thing is going to blow this mattress up?"

"And keep it blown up, if you fill it every night before you go to bed."

"By all means, show me how to run this son-of-a-bitch. Unless you want to come blow my mattress up every night."

"I wouldn't mind," Vic said, smiling. "But listen, it's simple. Step one: stick the nozzle into the air valve. Step two: switch on pump." Vic flicked a small switch on the top of the pump. Nothing happened. He flipped the switch back and forth several times. Still, nothing.

"Simple, eh?" April asked, grinning.

Vic rolled his eyes at her, and pulled the air pump from the mattress. He popped the bottom cap off. Four D-cell batteries were clipped into the machine, a thick layer of bronze-green crust on them.

"Step three: Make sure batteries are from this century," April said, smirking. Seeing Vic wasn't amused, she gave a quick smile.

"You happen to know of a place that sells D-batteries at whatever-the-hell-o'clock it is."

"There's an all-night gas station down past the Spruce Nettle Inn. They'll have batteries. They'll cost you, of course."

"Of course."

April closed the back hatch of her Jeep and turned to Vic. "Well, come on, Squanto."

"Squanto?"

"He was a Native American guide for the pilgrims."

Vic shook his head, amused. "The shit you learn on a quest for batteries." He piled into the Jeep, shutting the door with a loud slam and April headed out onto the main road, asking left or right before taking off down the road.

"April, there's been something I've been wanting to ask you," Vic said as they drove.

"Oh, really, now," April said, smugly. "I wondered when this was coming."

"It has to do with Walczyk."

"I figured it was."

"Then you know what I'm going to ask you," Vic said.

"I have a fairly good idea."

"Okay, then, I don't have to ask you. Let's just have the answer, then."

"We had sex a handful of times. All of it early on, right after he hired me. He wasn't with Sara yet. It was good, but it was what it was: stress release."

"Fascinating. But I was going to ask how Peter is doing."

"Peter?"

Vic rolled his eyes. "Peter? Walczyk? Walz? Whoever. How is he?"

April opened her mouth to say that Walczyk was fine, then stopped before the words left her mouth. She shut her mouth, stared at the road highlighted in her headlights, and mumbled something she'd never told anyone before about Walczyk: "He's sick."

The humming of the Jeep's motor continued on as the tires rumbled under the uneven pavement.

"What kind of sick?" Vic asked after a moment's silence.

"I think he's cracking up," April said, hesitantly. "I mean, one week he won't leave that shithole motel we were living out of. The next, he's buying a damned house. He's been running hot and cold with great frequency lately."

"And this makes him sick how?" Vic asked, looking over at her.

"I have no idea. But I think he's having some sort of... I don't know what to call it. *Quarter life crisis?*"

"Walczyk's always been a very moody guy. You had to have picked up on that rather early."

"I did."

"Add that to all the shit that's coming from Sara leaving him, and I think it's understandable he'd be pretty low. But that doesn't explain those highs he has, when he stays up all night and talks a mile a minute at you."

The Jeep pulled up in front of the all-night gas station/convenience store, the blindingly bright fluorescent lights casting a deathly glow onto everything in the yard. As April turned the key, shutting the motor off, Vic turned in his seat and reached out, taking April's hand in his. "Can I tell you what I think?"

"Please," April said. "You're his oldest friend. You know him better than I do." She couldn't put her finger on it, but there was something about this guy – this simple townie – that made her feel safe, as her mother had when she was a little girl, scared of the wind.

"I think..." There was a long pause as Vic summoned up the strength to say it. Finally, he sunk back in his seat.

"What?" April asked.

"Nothing. It's stupid. Just forget it. Let's go get you some batteries."

It would take April a long time to *just forget it*.

Walczyk was lying on his stomach, pecking away at the laptop on the floor. He was following up on a note from Ian, trying to figure out just how to get the first episode of season three of *Ordinary World* to segue smoothly into the second. There was something missing in the transition from his episode 301 to Jonathan Frakes's episode 302.

April stomped into the living room in a pair of shorts and a tank top, carrying a small maroon toiletry case and a nasty look plastered across her face. "I can't live like this!" She stormed over to the kitchen table and fished through her purse, scrambling for her iPhone. "This is beyond primitive. There were flies buzzing around my lantern while I brushed my teeth and put on my mask. Flies, Walczyk! *Flies!*"

"April, do you remember if we ever shot that scene where Kara has that fantasy about having sex with the guy from her gym?"

"Yes, good evening," April said into her phone, putting on her business voice. "I'm calling to see if you have any vacancies."

"I know it's impossible," Walczyk said, gazing out a nearby window, "but she really hasn't aged a day since I last saw her."

"Well, the sooner the better," April snapped into the phone. "I can be there in ten minutes if you have something."

"And I don't know how, or why, but she doesn't seem to be carrying a grudge. I don't have to tell you I was a real dick about ending things."

"Well, how soon can I get something? Any size, smoking or non. I'll take the janitor's closet at this point."

Walczyk turned back to his laptop. "She laughed at me when I asked her about her and that Cameron guy."

"Some help you are!" April screamed into her phone before shutting her phone off. Walczyk clicked "save." They looked at each other. "Progress?" she asked.

"I'd like to think so," he said, closing the lid on the laptop. "You going to be okay here? I can call the folks and see if you can stay in Sis's old room."

She shook her head, dropping down onto the inflatable mattress. "No, I'll be fine. I'm just cranky." She squirmed on the mattress, trying to get comfortable. She added, "And I want a real bed."

Walczyk chuckled as he rolled over on his side.

"Walz?"

"Yeah?" he replied, his eyes starting to droop.

"What do you know about Vic's parents?"

"His father has Alzheimer's and his mother was a bitch," he said flatly. "Why?"

April leaned over, turning off the lantern. "Nothing. Just... nothing." The moon shone in through the window over their head. "Walz?" she asked in the dark.

"Yeah," he said.

"You bought a house."

"Yeah," he said to the back of her head. "I bought a house."

"In Maine."

"Yeah. In Maine."

"Do you think that was such a good idea? I'm not being critical. It's just..."

"Just what?"

"You... you tend to do stuff, jump in on things, without really thinking it through."

"What do you mean?"

She rolled over, finding herself nose-to-nose with him. "This house. You bought a damned house. In Maine. On the other side of the country."

"Everyone has summer homes," he countered. "Travolta, Barbara Walters, Martha Stewart... they all have summer homes right here in Maine."

"Your dad is under the impression this is something more than just a summer home. That this is something a bit more permanent."

"It is what it is, April: a refuge." With the rhythmic chop of the ocean lulling him to sleep, he thought about the house, and what he wanted to do with it, and wondered how long it would take before people started referring to it as "The New Walczyk Place."

CHAPTER FOUR
LEARNING CURVE

"He *what*?!?" Elias Gaul shrieked from his office in Los Angeles.

"He bought a house," April calmly repeated, sipping at her coffee. The airport was busy for a Monday morning in Maine, but April had found a relatively quiet corner in which to make a call to Walczyk's panicking agent. April leaned back, comfortable in her cushy chair, her laptop in front of her.

"That's what I thought you said. Is he insane?" Eli gave a second's pause before answering his own question and saying, "Better yet, are *you* insane?"

"What's my ebbing sanity have to do with any of this?"

"You're supposed to be keeping an eye on him!"

"And I am, Eli. For the first time in weeks, he's happy. For the first time in weeks, he's gone a day without mentioning Sara, Ella, lesbians, or *Paparazz-Eye*. I think he's finally moving on."

"Is he seeing anyone? A shrink? A therapist? A psychiatrist?"

"I highly doubt it," she lied. Telling Eli that Walczyk was seeing a high school guidance counselor for psychiatric counseling was not advisable, especially alone over a cell phone and in a very public place. "Eli, why can't you just accept the fact that he's happy for once?"

"Because his *happiness* is counter-acting his need to get his ass out here and get back to work. He's got a deadline with HBO looming – a deadline he can't get out of, since they're locked in on this season premiere's airdate – and no work is getting done on the series."

"Eli, you know that Ian is overseeing production of the rest of the season."

"And Ian says there are episodes that still need his sign-off, and they're stacking up."

"Well, they've got to face the fact that they just might not be getting his seal of approval before they air. And that'll just have to be the way it is."

"April!"

"Eli! Look, what do you want me to do? I'm easily terminable. And, remember this, my friend, so are you. I'm not his boss, I'm not his nurse, and I'm not his wife. And neither are you!"

"No, I'm just his friend, and as his friend, I'm scared shitless that he's not taking care of himself."

"Look, Elias, he just doesn't care. His wife *left him*! It's only been four months. Let him come to grips with all this, okay?"

"But he still needs to be working on something. And so far, there's nothing."

"I think he's still working on *The Next One*."

"Is that wife-clone thing?"

"It is."

"Yeah. Like that'll fly."

"It's got as good a chance as the shit you've been sending him lately."

"That *shit* has support from studios, networks, and people with names bigger than his."

"That's good to know, because he thought maybe a bunch of mentally deranged fourth graders had churned it out. Especially *Monkey Business*."

"*Monkey Business*? What the hell's that?"

"It's just what Vic started calling the one about the apes."

"Well, as long as *Vic* is consulting on projects now, I suppose we're in good shape. God knows what we were lacking in this operation was a fucking greasy spoon owner's opinion."

"Hey!" she barked. "That's a cheap shot."

"Look, April, don't treat me like I'm the bad guy here. I love you both, and I want the best for you both. I really do. But if Walczyk doesn't get his ass back out here, or at least start working on something sellable in this new house of his, he's very likely going to ruin his credibility."

"Will I do?"

"What?"

"A body in L.A. You can't get Walczyk in California. Not for a while. But I'm coming."

"When?"

"Today."

"Today? What the hell for?"

"He's selling the house, as I know you know. He wants me to represent him in the divvying up the property, to sign off on papers and whatnot. And I've also got to pack up my place."

"You're giving up your apartment?" Eli asked skeptically.

"Yeah," she said, suddenly realizing that with that one statement, she was admitting to herself, for the first time, that she might not be going back to Los Angeles, to stay at least, for quite some time. And suddenly she felt a little panicky.

The free-for-all that was the bell between second and third period was sheer chaos. The ten minute interval gave the four hundred and sixty-seven students at Cole Island High School precious little time to use the facilities (and get caught smoking in said facilities), touch base with friends in other classes, exchange books from one subject to another, get some PDA time with their significant other, and get to their next class. Hence, the rush between classes was a maddening one, and one during which anything could happen.

"Jason! Olivia!" Principal Henry Walczyk barked across the hall, pointing a finger at a large boy in a Patriots jersey who had been giving upright CPR to a tiny, underfed blond girl in an incredibly short skirt.

"Hey, what's up, Mr. Walczyk?" Jason asked, casually, offering Henry his right hand while his left rested comfortably on Olivia's bottom.

Henry shook the boy's hand, forcing a smile. "Jason, can you do me a favor?"

"Sure thing, Mr. W," Jason said. Jason Pike was a good kid.

He pumped Henry's gas at his father's Citgo station. He was a decent student. Not the brightest, nor the best, but at least he honestly tried at his studies. In addition to working for his father, Jason was on the school's lacrosse team. He was a good kid.

"I know you're a senior, and that by this time next year, Miss Turner will still be here and you'll be away at college. I understand that time is limited for the two of you to be together, and you want to spend every moment you can with each other. But, please, consider giving yourselves some breathing room. At least during school hours."

"What?"

"Your hands, Mr. Pike," Henry sighed. "Please keep them in plain sight."

Jason caught the hint and removed his hand from Olivia's backside. Henry thanked him and continued down the corridor. On his way, he managed to collect three cell phones, suggest that the punch line to the joke about the little boy, his daddy, and a penguin was *not* a punch line that should be repeated in school, and confiscate a *Penthouse* magazine from three burly shop kids who, he had to admit, had at least listened to his prior advice to try reading more.

From the door to her classroom, short, fiery little Stella Lyons sidled up next to him. Her face was tight with frustration. "Well, well, well… day one, two hours in, and you're carrying a handful of cell phones, a pornographic magazine, and wearing a scowl. Things going that bad?"

"I'm not scowling," Henry said, wiping the scowl from his face. Stella was up to something. He could tell just by her tone. She was not normally one to chit-chat.

"Let me offer you this tidbit of advice, Henry: pick your battles, don't let your battles pick you." She offered that same bit of advice on a bi-weekly basis. Too bad she didn't follow her own advice.

"What can I help you with, Stella?" Henry asked, dreading the answer.

"It's those kids."

"This school has four hundred and sixty-seven kids, Stella. Which ones are you referring to?"

The screwed-up face Stella now wore made Henry sure that he'd not said that using picture-perfect grammar, and that Stella was trying to decide whether or not to correct him on it. "*Those* kids," she hissed pointing across the hall. Hannah Cooper and Cameron Burke were standing outside of Mr. Burke's classroom, which was directly across the hall from Hannah's.

"Stella..." Henry struggled to keep his voice even. The little woman crossed her arms across her chest. "Let me guess... summer reading?"

"'A joke.' That's what Mr. Burke called it. And Miss Cooper, she said there's no need for it."

"They have a point, Stella," Henry admitted. "The kids never do it."

"So we let them get away with not doing their homework instead of enforcing the rules?"

"Would you believe that Miss Cooper voiced her concerns over the summer reading curriculum earlier today?"

"I would," Stella huffed. "And she probably made a case for dissolving it. But I personally think there's something to be said for expecting students to–"

"Stella, I'm sick of refereeing these little fights you get into with Hannah and Cameron. So, if I'm going to make a ruling, once and for all, you're going to abide by it. Deal?"

She mulled it over a moment or two before muttering her assent. "Deal."

"Each teacher is in charge of his or her own classroom and its curriculum. If you want to assign summer reading, assign it to the students you'll be having in the fall, not to Mr. Burke or Miss Cooper's. Satisfied?"

Stella gave a grunt, turned on her heel, and stalked off down the hallway towards a group of laughing girls.

Pick your battles, he reminded himself as he walked away. *Don't let your battles pick you.*

The din of eighteen overlapping voices decreased by only a few decibels as Hannah Cooper entered her classroom, putting the maroon ceramic coffee mug on her desk. She rarely drank coffee in front of students, still able to recall the putrid stench of stale coffee and Pep-o-mint Life Savers on the breath of one too many teachers when she was on the other side of the big desk, only some twelve or thirteen years ago. She raised the mug to her lips, sucking down some more of the vile black caffeinated water. But, coffee breath or no coffee breath, today was going to have to be the exception. A weekend-long marathon of *The Twilight Zone* that stretched until almost two in the morning had left her without energy, expecting to see a monochromatic Rod Serling standing just around every corner. Period one had gone rather well, she thought, despite only a handful of students being prepared to take Stella Lyons' quiz over her assigned summer reading material, *Silas Marner*. Upon learning the work had not been done, she had simply handed out the well worn copies of *The Catcher in the Rye* she had stacked up front as she introduced herself, which half-way through struck her as more of a traditional formality than a necessity, considering she'd babysat four of her new students, went to school with the siblings of a good seven or eight, and knew a majority of the rest of them just from living in a tight knit town alongside them.

It had almost been more torture than relief for Hannah to have a free period next. She resisted the urge to sneak off-campus and run down to Been's, Cole Island's only drive-through coffee shop, for a real cup of coffee. She'd planned on stopping by Been's and picking up a cup en-route, but the line was out the door. She was now contemplating giving up teaching and opening a competing coffee shop. She gave up on her little fantasy when she found herself unable to come up with a clever, quirky name for her coffee shop. She blamed Peter entirely for her lack of energy and concentration.

Hannah picked her dog eared copy of Shakespeare's *The Taming of the Shrew* up from her desk and hugged it to her chest. "Welcome back, guys," she called out, and the class quieted down, with the exception of Lisa and Marie, who were oblivious to the fact the class and teacher were staring at them until one of them sensed total silence in the room. They turned, embarrassed, and faced forward. "So, any excitement this summer?"

Stories of projects and hobbies, softball games, vacations and a few gripes about working all summer spilled from almost every student in the class. Surprisingly quiet was one of the school's more outspoken, more lively students, Taylor Hodges. Based on his calm, quiet comportment and his low-hanging head, Hannah was happy to assume Taylor, too, had stayed up too late watching *The Twilight Zone* and didn't press the issue. "It certainly sounds like everyone had a productive, enjoyable summer in one way or another. As you know, first quarter we tackle the big guy, William Shakes–"

"Excuse me, Miss Cooper?" Hannah's eyes darted over to Taylor, suddenly all smiles and looking straight up at her.

"Yes, Taylor?"

"You used to date Peter Walczyk, right?"

The class fell silent. Hannah directed her glare at the shaggy-headed, wide-eyed student filmmaker sitting across the room from her in what had to have been a homemade t-shirt featuring Peter Finch from the movie *Network*, with the caption "I'm as mad as hell and I'm not going to take this anymore!" Hannah knew this was the moment Taylor, the school's resident film buff, had been waiting for all summer: to talk about Peter Walczyk, one of his personal heroes. Not to gossip, but to discuss, and maybe gush a little. He wanted to know the man, not the celebrity, as he'd told her numerous times already. Taylor pushed his chestnut brown bangs back with his hand, just like Peter used to, and edged toward the corner of his chair. "Has he dropped any hints to you about what's happening with the next season of *Ordinary World*?"

"I wouldn't know, Taylor. And I'd rather not discuss my personal life with my students. Ever," Hannah wearily replied.

"Then what's he working on?" Sasha Connary asked, leaning forward almost exactly over Taylor's shoulder. "I've seen him writing at the Bronze Lantern almost every day since he arrived on the Island." Sasha looked nothing like her older sister or her mother, acted nothing like her older sister or her mother, and had very little to do with either. Deep down, Hannah admired Sasha: here is a young woman who, despite the home she came from and the role models in her life, possessed an intellect and character that strengthened the production team she was part of. Such self-respect was something Hannah only learned during the latter part of her college years.

"I wouldn't know, Sasha," Hannah replied, equally guarded. "And, before anyone asks any more questions, I will *not* discuss—"

"Is it true that his wife left him for another woman?" Corinne MacArthur asked flatly.

"What an ignorant question," Taylor spat across the room. "Damn it, Corinne, don't you know any—"

"Taylor! Language!"

"I'm sorry, but it *is* a bit insensitive to ask questions like that about your ex, don't you think? Could you tell me, though, just what the hell he's doing back in Maine?"

"Second warning for your language, Taylor," she snapped, feeling weaker.

"Sorry," Taylor said quickly.

"I heard he had a falling out with the principal during his senior year," Dustin Harris offered from his seat behind Taylor. "Are they still not talking?"

"Is this *really* the last season of *Ordinary World*?" Lisa Sommers asked.

"Have you seen any of it?" Marie Chase piped in.

"Who's that drop-dead gorgeous gutter-mouth he's shacked up with?" Ryan Bates asked.

But it was innocent, sweet, unassuming Sasha Connary who crossed the line, no doubt without even realizing it: "Do you think you two will patch things back up and get back together?"

"As you all remember," Hannah said, turning back for her desk, filled with self-loathing over what she was about to do, "Mrs. Lyons assigned some summer reading for you, in the form of *Fahrenheit 451*. I know most of you have been able to tackle the material, so let's have a little pop quiz over the book." She laid *The Taming of the Shrew* back down on her desk and picked up the stack of green quiz sheets that had been waiting for her on her desk first thing this morning.

Peter Walczyk sat on the kitchen counter, lost in the dancing of the particles of dust in the thin shaft of light that cut through the spotted glass window just over his shoulder. The scent of artificial lemons permeated the house and the sounds of soap operas took Walczyk back to his childhood for a moment. School vacation. His mother had just removed him from the universe of He-Man and Skeletor and had temporarily separated his sister from her magazines and her Walkman. For the day, Peter and Melanie were Mom's cleaning assistants. The absolute worst job ever. First off, they had to put on old clothes: sweat pants and T-shirts too tattered to be worn in public. Each kid was issued a roll of paper towel and they shared a bottle of Windex. Working in tandem, they dusted the shelves, top to bottom. Then it was on to all the knick-knacks that were housed on them. All those rinky-dink tchotchkes had to be picked up and dusted and returned to their exact spot. Then Walczyk did the television, back first then, with a clean towel, the screen, while Melanie dusted the bookshelf and the well abused collection of Funk and Wagnall's encyclopedias. Mom, meanwhile, was on a rickety green metal stepstool, stretching far beyond her normal reach to banish cobwebs form the corners of the ceiling. Melanie would fetch the vacuum cleaner and vacuum the furniture while Walczyk dusted the lower tiers of the entertainment center and swept out any dust bunnies or toys that made their way under the couch.

Once all was put in order, the children were sent to their rooms, to return to their pastimes. If they wanted to leave, they had to put on clean socks, as their mother would have gotten on her hands and knees and scrubbed the floor. Afternoons pitting Man-at-Arms against Tri-Klops with the smell of Pine-Sol filling the air were a fond memory, despite the manual labor that preceded them.

"Peter!"

Walczyk shook his head, the walls of his parents' house replaced by the empty walls of his own, still rather Spartan house. He followed the sound of the television into the living room, where he found his mother on the floor, a damp cloth in her hand.

"Hey, Mum, what's up?"

"Are you okay, Peter?" she asked.

"Fine," he said, feeling as though he'd just woken up from a long nap.

"Are you sure? You seem distracted."

"I'm just tired, that's all. You know me. My sleep schedule gets thrown out of whack and I'm another person. What should I do now?"

"Did you finish washing the kitchen walls?"

"Yeah. The cupboards are done and the stovetop is scrubbed down too."

"Good. I'll just continue on in there. Go outside while I finish. I don't want your dirty feet tracking up my clean floor."

The more things change, Walczyk mused as he ambled out the kitchen door. He plopped back down on the hanging glider his parents had bought him as a housewarming gift and gave a sharp push with his foot before pulling his leg up onto the cushion. He lay there, rocking, his mind a million miles away. Well, 3,165 miles away at least. Lately, he found his mind drifting into areas he'd never given much consideration to. At this time last year, at this time of day, he was probably still in a production meeting for any given episode of *Ordinary World*, ironing out issues such as locations, sets, costuming, the number of extras they'd need for the restaurant scene, and obtaining the legal clearances necessary for Ella, as Danielle, to sing "Someone to Watch Over Me" to Ethan, played by Christopher Westmore, as they fell asleep in each other's arms following Ethan's emergency appendectomy. And, of course, the end of the script would still need to be written. Walczyk's chest tightened as his mind went from that meeting to the set, where grips and assistant directors and camera operators all rushed about, getting every little detail just right for when filming began. He saw himself calling action. Saw Danielle singing to Ethan in his bedroom. He heard Marvin the D.P. cursing about the aperture; the script supervisor correcting Ella's recitation of the lyrics. He saw himself coaching Ella how he wanted her to rub the back of Chris's neck as she sang. Sara always loved it when he rubbed the back of her neck. His breath shortened. He called for action. Danielle/Ella sang to Ethan/Chris. Walczyk would have nodded; she had finally gotten those lyrics right. Ella stroked the back of Sara's neck. She leaned in and kissed Sara gently on the lips. When they finished, Sara turned to him and spoke:

"Peter!"

Walczyk bolted upright in the porch swing, his breath short, his chest tight. His mother reached out and grabbed his shoulder, steadying both him and the porch swing. He looked up at his mother, still shaking off the vivid image.

"Yeah?"

"Let's go get started on the upstairs bathroom."

He slowly got to his feet and stepped back into the house, wishing he'd listened to April and just hired a cleaning crew.

The shattering crash of dishes in the kitchen only intensified the mounting headache that was slowly amassing behind Vic Gordon's eyes as he entered the Bronze Lantern. With about twenty minutes to open, there were napkins and silverware strewn all over Uncle Donny's bar, cases of supplies sitting on the floor instead of beneath the waitresses' station, and there wasn't a wet floor sign to be seen anywhere on the freshly mopped floor. Vic peeked over the

Vic made his way over to the kitchen, where he found Phil Watson kneeling down to help Ingrid Connary pick up what used to be a tray of what used to be water glasses. Ingrid was one of his best waitresses. As opening neared, she generally took for granted that people might be on the other side of the swinging double café doors.

Phil, on the other hand, was just an imbecile. Hannah had tried to remind Vic, ad nauseam, that this was not a very nice way to describe Phil, who had struggled to make it through school, relying on Hannah to serve as his tutor and salvation. One of the few non-student new hires at the start of the summer, Phil's only talents were in ruining dishes, getting in the way of the cooks, and making the waitresses uneasy with his long, lingering stares directly into their eyes. Sure, Phil was a nice enough guy but clearly he wasn't destined for anything beyond the menial labor that Cole Island could offer him.

Vic looked down at the carnage and sighed. Ingrid looked up to see Vic staring down at her. She opened her mouth to speak, but Vic held up a hand, staving off a machine-gun-fire of words that would do nothing to remedy things.

"Who into who?" was all Vic asked, rubbing the bridge of his nose. Ingrid again got ready to launch into a long, blabbering explanation, but Vic shot her a silent glance, and she clammed up, lowering her eyes back to the mess on the floor. Phil, to his credit, had not stopped picking up the broken water glasses and alcohol bottles. Vic turned over the cardboard box that now contained only a single bottle of vodka. He turned around and headed back through the kitchen, stopping by the pass. On the other side of the four tiered heat lamp holding area for finished hot dishes, Vic's younger brother Andrew was staging his station for the small, but steady lunch rush that would last from roughly 11:15 to 1:30, or so. Andrew held a finger up, continuing his count of the contents of the small fridge under the counter. When Andrew had finished, he stood up, looked at his brother and said, "Phil into Ingrid." Vic shook his head and swore under his breath. "What are you going to do, Vic?" Andrew asked, putting metal scoops into the stainless steel pans in the cold station. "Douche bag's a nuisance. I warned you about that day one."

Vic thought long and hard about what he was about to say. For years now, he'd wanted to say it to his brother. To force Andrew to face up to the fact that he, too, had a part in this family business, and that he wasn't towing the cable, so to speak.

"Andrew, I have two favors I need, one somewhat now, one somewhat later."

"What's somewhat now?" Andrew asked, dropping a basket of fries he knew he'd need upon seeing Mary Caroline McPherson and her husband, Alec, lumber through the doors, early for their patty melt and no-salt fries.

"Somewhat now is sparing me one of the dish boys to go to Ferguson's, maybe George's Liquor Store, to see if someone can spare us the Smirnoff, two red wines, and the Bacardi that numb nuts just turned into mop water."

Andrew quickly looked around. "You can have Alex. I need Kevin here. And I want him back in twenty; he's covering for Chris."

"Where the hell's Chris?" Vic asked, quickly looking around for the large, bearded second-in-command Andrew relied on.

"Jury duty." Andrew waited for a reaction from Vic, but got none. "Victor, we both told you. Where the hell have you been? Seriously, man," he said, pulling the basket of fries and lightly tossing them, getting rid of the excess oil. "That agent of Walczyk's has got your head so damned addled—"

"Oh, shut up!" Vic barked.

"Face it: you need to start delegating. Don't try to run this place by yourself!"

"And that, Little Brother, brings me to the somewhat later favor."

"What?"

"In all actuality, it's more of a demand than it is a favor."

"Will you get on with it? We've got a dinner rush at five."

"Fine, "Vic said, reaching over to the basket and pulled out a hot handful of homemade fries, dropping them into a glass bowl. "You're now the assistant manager of this place. And your first order of business is simple: get rid of Phil Watson by the end of the week. End of the day would be preferable."

"Any other orders, oh Grand Sultan?"

"Yeah, after you fire Phil, go find us a new, not so stupid Phil."

Vic started for the back office, snacking on the few piping hot fries. From behind him, Andrew called out, "And what if I refuse?"

Vic yelled back, smiling. "I'll call Sis."

Once his mother had left, Walczyk walked back into the house, into the bathroom, and shut the door behind him. He dropped to his knees on the towel spread across the front of the tub and curled up in a ball, sobbing. His body rocked with the grief that flowed out of him in a feral, pained wail. He swung his head back, bouncing it off the cabinet. It hurt, but it was a feeling other than misery and grief. He recoiled, breath failing him, and slammed his head back again. His eyes burned at the onslaught of tears streaming from them. Snot filled his nose and his head grew thick and plugged as he lay on the floor, banging the back of his head against the cabinet.

CHAPTER FIVE
WABBIT SEASON

"You're lucky Kiefer Sutherland is so fast with a sick bag," Elias Gaul commended, dragging April's luggage with one hand and April with the other. "Just how the hell did you get your hands on that much airline booze?"

"Carefully," she said, grimacing as a lance of pain pierced through the frontal lobe of her brain and she stopped. She reached up, grabbing her forehead. Eli reached out to steady her, but she held up a hand in protest, hiked up the strap of her carry-on, and continued walking. "He is a nice guy, though. Kiefer."

"I've heard as much. How's Walczyk?"

April grimaced. "Well, he won't talk about Sara. Or Ella. Or the marriage, the break-up, the divorce, coming back to L.A., finishing up *Ordinary World*."

"Sounds completely well adjusted."

"It's weird, Elias – on the surface, he's *not* doing all that bad. Not all the time. He has his spells where he's miserable, and I try to push him, since that's what he hired me for, to motivate him. Then there are other times when he's a completely different person. No sorrow, no regret, no crushed heart. He's a man of limitless energy then. Vic thinks there's something wrong with him."

"So do you think Walczyk's making Maine his new home?"

"Home? No, I don't think so. This'll just be a summer home for him. He's just sorting everything out." Uneasily, she added, "He'll be back."

"Well, I hope so. His up-and-leaving reminded me just how few friends I actually have around here."

They stepped out onto the sidewalk, a cool breeze ruffling April's hair. She inhaled deeply. The air was dirty and stale. The sounds of cars zooming up and down the freeway, drivers honking horns, and the sound of a million voices all on their cell phones at the same time.

God, she had missed Los Angeles.

"So, are you nervous?"

"About what?" Walczyk asked, reaching for the glass of iced milk his mother had waiting for him when he showed up for breakfast that morning. Growing up, breakfast was a Sunday morning thing. During the week, it was cereal and toast or a piece of fruit. Saturdays were another of Mum's famous "Fix your own" affairs. But Sunday, the stops were pulled out and a smorgasbord was set out: scrambled eggs, ham, bacon, sausage, French toast on the third Sunday of the month and Belgian waffles on the first. But since he'd returned to Cole Island, he'd had breakfast with his mother almost every morning. It was a nice time for him to get to talk to his mother without the distraction of April or his mother's flitting about trying to get meals ready.

"About seeing Angela again?"

"No. Why?"

"You're not saying much."

"There's not much to say, really."

"You *do* like Angela, don't you?"

"She's a good person."

"But as a therapist?"

"As a therapist... she's not all that hot."

Walczyk's mother looked surprised. "Why not?"

"Because... I don't know. There's just something about her I don't like."

"I'm sorry to hear that. It has meant a lot to your father that you're seeing someone. He worries about you, you know."

"I know," Walczyk said, remembering that night down by the shore. "And it's for him that I'm sticking with it."

"You mean–?"

"I mean if it weren't for Dad's vested interest in me seeing this woman, I'd probably already have quit."

"Peter, if you're not getting anything out of your sessions–"

"But you just said that he–"

"That it means a lot to him? Well, it does. But after forty-one years of marriage, I think I know your father pretty well, and he wouldn't want you doing something you weren't getting any benefit from."

Walczyk considered the option for a moment. He didn't know what he'd do for therapy if he quit seeing Angela. There was no one else on the Island that he felt comfortable seeing, and he wasn't about to travel to the mainland every week to get his head examined. But he did promise his father…

"What don't you like about it?" his mother asked, taking a drink from her decaf. "If I'm not being too nosy, that is."

"No," Walczyk said, shaking his head, "you're fine. I just… Angela has these little activities that she likes to try out on me."

"'Try out on you?'"

"Yeah. Like last week, she had me write a letter about my disappointments in life and the things that got me down."

"I do that myself from time to time," his mother confessed. "It's not that uncommon to address issues in letter form. When I quit that horrible job as a secretary in Dr. Houston's office, I wrote him the worst letter, telling him exactly what I thought of him."

"And I see how that's therapeutic. But this letter Angela had me writing was to my unborn child."

Walczyk's mother almost dropped her coffee cup. "Unborn child? You mean… you and Sara… you lost a baby?"

"No," Walczyk said, reaching out to take his mother's hand. "I mean the unborn child we'd never have together."

"I see how that could be weird. And you're right, it doesn't make any sense."

"The week before, she wanted me to pretend Frasier was Sara and let him… her… it… have it."

"Frasier?"

"Frasier is one of those sock monkey dolls. Angela keeps it in her office."

"It must be…" Walczyk's mother was slow in responding to that one. He figured she was trying to figure out how to not be negative or pejorative. Finally, she spoke. "She probably figures…" Again, she stopped and thought long and carefully about what she was going to say. When that failed her, she said what seemed to be the first thing on her mind: "That's just weird."

As they laughed about the response, Walczyk's phone rang. He looked at the display. "It's April."

Walczyk's mother sprang to her feet, putting her coffee cup in the sink. "You two talk. I've got to put some laundry in anyway."

"Mum, this is *your* house. Your don't have to leave the room just because–"

"You'd better hurry up and answer it," his mother told him, then disappeared into the other room. Walczyk tapped the screen and put the phone up to his ear. "Hello?"

"Walczyk, what's going on?" April already sounded re-energized by Los Angeles,

"Just finishing up breakfast with Mum."

"You're not home? Good!"

"You say that like you want the house to yourself."

"I say that like I'm glad you're out and about. You have your weekly with Angela this morning, right?"

"Yeah." Something was bothering Walczyk. "April, what time is it?"

"Nine forty-five."

"I know what time it is here. What time is it in L.A.?"

"Six forty-five."

"You're up at six forty-five in the morning?"

"Yeah."

"What in God's name for?"

"To–"

"I swear, if you say you're checking up on me–!" The line was silent. "You were, weren't you?" More silence. "Damn it, April, I'm a grown man. I can take care of myself for a freaking week!"

"I know," she said, uncharacteristically calm.

"Then why are you calling at the ass crack of dawn?"

"Actually, I'm just getting back from my jog."

"You went running at six in the morning?"

"I couldn't sleep. My body still thinks it's nine forty-five."

"And you're not going to make any effort to adjust to local time?"

"Why bother? I'll be back in Maine in a week and then I'll have to just readjust to eastern standard time."

That actually made sense, though he couldn't imagine April cutting short her L.A. hobnobbing at nine o'clock because it was bedtime in Maine.

"So you're out and about," April observed. "That's good."

"Well, enjoy it," Walczyk said, "because I don't plan on leaving Rancho Walczyk at all tomorrow."

"Boss!"

"What?"

"For the love of God," April said, "promise me that you're not going to lock yourself up in there and not leave the house for a week."

"Never gonna happen," Walczyk said, getting up to put his empty glass of milk-coated ice cubes into the sink.

"Never say never," she warned.

"Your friend April is absolutely right," Angela Cariou said, her office looking messier than when Walczyk last visited it, if that was even possible. "Routine is good for good mental health."

"Please don't tell her that," Walczyk said. "Might go straight to her head."

Angela smiled. "You're making jokes, Peter."

"Sorry," he said, fighting the urge not to lower his eyes to the floor.

"Don't be. It's a good thing. It may mean that you're starting to come out of your funk."

"*Funk*. Is that the clinical term for what I've got?"

"It *is* in the DSM-IV," Angela said. "So, tell me, have you talked to Sara lately?"

"No," Walczyk said, this time allowing his eyes to fall to the gray industrial carpeting covering the floor of Angela's office.

"I thought we agreed that you were going to give her a call. That's what you told me last time."

"What is this desire of yours – of everyone's – to have me call that woman? What do you all think it will accomplish?"

"What do *you* think it would accomplish?" she asked in return.

"You know, I hate when you shrinks just reword your questions and throw them back at you. Now, honestly, what would me calling Sara accomplish? What could it accomplish? What would be the final outcome of that conversation?"

"Are you worried it'll turn into a coast-to-coast screaming match?"

"Oh, no," he said, looking up from the floor. "Quite the opposite. Everything will be ever-so-polite. Ever-so-restrained. We'd avoid talking about anything of consequence and go out of our way to show each other that we're unaffected by this entire damned affair."

Angela shifted in her chair. "But clearly, you *are* affected by what has happened with Sara. And you won't truly feel better until you have a frank conversation with her."

"No offense, Angela, but if I wanted to have a conversation with my wife, I'd call her, not visit the guidance counselor at my father's school."

"My technical title is 'school therapist'," she clarified. "And, no offense, Peter, but I'm beginning to seriously doubt you'd call her."

"Why's that?" Walczyk demanded.

"Because you're afraid."

He laughed. "Afraid of my wife? "

"In a sense, yes. But to be more precise, I think you're afraid of what would happen in that conversation."

"What do you mean, *What would happen in that conversation?*"

"What I'm trying to get across here is this: would it – or could it – be any more disturbing to deal with whatever comes out in that conversation than what you're going through now?"

Suddenly it dawned on Walczyk. Exactly what Angela was aiming it. He felt like such a simpleton for having almost fallen for it. "You're trying to Duck Season/Wabbit Season me, aren't you?"

"Duck Season/Wabbit Season?"

"A scenario from a trilogy of Looney Tunes cartoons. You see, its duck season and Elmer Fudd's out hunting. Daffy, not wanting to have his beak blown off for the three thousandth time, convinces Elmer that it's wabbit season and Bugs Bunny becomes the target. At one point, Bugs and Daffy have this long back-and-forth at the point of Elmer's gun, Daffy moving the barrel of the rifle towards Bugs and shouting 'Wabbit season', then Bugs moving the gun to Daffy and shouting 'Duck season'. Eventually, employing that age-old, tried-and-true reverse psychology that even certified therapists use, Bugs keeps the gun pointed at himself and says, 'Wabbit season', tricking Daffy into aiming the shotgun at himself and screaming 'Duck season! Fire!' Elmer obliges and blows Daffy's beak clear around the back of his head."

"So you're saying you're afraid of getting your beak blown off?"

"No, what I am saying is that I don't appreciate your attempts to use reverse psychology to convince me to call my wife."

"Okay, Peter. I won't use reverse psychology to make you do anything against your will."

"Are you saying that to try and use it again on me?"

"No, I am not."

"Why not?"

"Because of the fact that duck season, wabbit season logic wouldn't work unless you had made that decision yourself. But, in my professional opinion, I do think that having a conversation with Sara could do more to bring you back to a better frame of mind than other therapy options."

"And just what would those other options be?"

"Hypnosis."

"Get out of here."

"Role-playing, then."

"Forget it."

Angela sat there quietly. The sight of the woman, slouched in her chair, made Walczyk feel a flash of remorse. He certainly wasn't helping her help him. But the sheer notion of hypnosis gave him the heebie-jeebies, and he was equally put off by the notion of Angela role playing as Sara. She didn't know Sara. She couldn't possibly engage in a realistic conversation with him. And Walczyk would know in an instant that he wasn't really talking to the real Sara Danielle Collins. So how could that possibly be therapeutic?

"Let's change our focus here, Peter," Angela said abruptly.

"Oh, please, let's," he said, wondering what she was thinking now.

"Do you think your recent depression is a result of your marital problems?" Angela asked.

"No," he blurted out without thinking.

"How so?" Angela inquired.

"Because my depression *caused* my marital problems."

"Care to expand upon that?"

"Well, I was getting pretty hard to live with. One day I'd be fine, everything was great, I felt like I could conquer the world. When I was like that, I'd put in sixteen hour days on the set, or crank out entire episodes on my laptop. Of course, with a schedule like that, there wasn't much time for a wife." Walczyk said. "Then, right out of the blue, my mood would do a three-sixty and I could hardly get out of bed. I'd be grumpy, irritable, even downright nasty. I can see why Sara wouldn't want to spend time with me when I was like that."

Angela sat in silence for a long while, studying him, studying her notes. She'd even laid her hand on the spine of a thick text book titled *Common Psychological Disorders*, but then let go of the book. She continued to study him as she dug at her chin with the cap of her pen.

"Peter, I have to apologize," Angela finally said. "It seems I might have jumped to an incorrect conclusion concerning your depression and its connection to your marital problems."

"How so?" Walczyk asked, confused. He had never heard of the shrink apologizing to the patient.

"Well, while I still believe that talking to Sara might be beneficial to you, I fear that you have a lot more to deal with here than a divorce, as bad as that is." She paused, reached for a pen and a Post-It note, and began scribbling away on it. As she wrote, she continued. "I honestly don't think a high school therapist is the best resource for you at this point, although it was flattering that your father thought I could help you."

"You mean you're dumping me?"

"I'm admitting that there is nothing more I can do for you as a therapist. This isn't a rejection of you, Peter. It's simply a rejection of the notion that I am capable of providing you with the necessary treatment to overcome your psychological disturbances." She handed him the note.

"What's this?" he asked.

"Those are the names of three excellent psychiatrists. Two of them have practices in Bangor, and one works out of Augusta. I would suggest that you make an appointment with one of them immediately."

Walczyk was shocked, then suddenly angry. What was it with this woman? First she went on and on about how a conversation with Sara would solve all his problems, and now she's telling him she can't help him. Well, he decided that he'd had it with her, and he'd be damned if he was going to make an appointment in Bangor or Augusta or anywhere else, for that matter, with some med school crackpot who would ask him stupid questions or want to hypnotize him or do some silly role-playing thing. Whatever was wrong with him, he'd deal with it himself, in his own way.

CHAPTER SIX
ENCOUNTERS

Walczyk awoke around nine on a cool Thursday morning. A glance out the window was comforting as he took in the lazy feeling of a drizzly day. Not all that comforting, however, was the inflatable mattress he'd been sleeping on. It had lost its air, leaving only a limp piece of vinyl between him and the hardwood floor. The boundless energy that had overtaken his entire body two weeks ago was back. He'd stayed up until roughly four the night before and finished the second act of *The Next One*. Paradoxically, he thought, the further along in the script he got, the more the concept began to fall apart, and the further his interest in it began to wane. The writing of this screenplay – or any he attempted – seemed to mirror his mood. When he found himself in a good mood, the script went forward at an even, fruitful pace. The material was good. When he was in a bad mood, however, it took what seemed like months to push out a single scene. In these moods, completing acts were a chore that left him exhausted and bitter. But when he was energized, it was as if someone else – some genius – were writing the script. Everything was pure gold, ready to go straight to screen as is. He loved to write as super happy Walczyk, was content to write when he was in a good mood, and was rarely seen at his computer when he was in a bad mood, unless there was a deadline looming overhead. He'd searched for years to find the cause of super happy, but when alcohol, drugs, sex, and risk-taking failed to activate that rare, special mood, he'd heeded Eli's advice to leave well enough alone. "Don't tinker with yourself," Eli warned one night over dinner. "You've got a good thing going sixty-six-point-six percent of the time. Don't question it. Just enjoy it."

The sudden sound of his cell phone dragged him out of his early morning drowsiness. The singing of the three hundred dollar tether shook him out of his reminiscence, and he got to his feet, making his way to his phone, which he'd left on the TV tray under the east window. He flipped it open, answering "Peter Walczyk" in a deep, clipped manner.

"Good morning, Peter Walczyk," the voice of his mother said. "How'd you make out last night?"

He smiled. Diane Reynolds Walczyk been calling to ask how he'd been *making out* every day since he moved into his home. His mother had wanted him and April to stay at their house while they properly cleaned and outfitted the house, but Walczyk insisted they could get more done if they stayed in the house while working. So his mother had to resort to a daily phone call to keep tabs on her son. "I am surviving without April, thank you very much, Mum."

"I didn't mean anything bad by it. I was just asking—"

"Things are fine, Mum, thanks. What's going on around the corner this morning?"

"Nothing much. I didn't wake you, did I?"

"No, I was up," he lied.

"Want to come over for breakfast? I don't have to go to work today."

Walczyk thought about it for a moment, then chided himself for thinking he had any other plans at all. His breakfast plan was some Cap'n Crunch in an old Cool Whip tub and half a bottle of apple juice. "I'd love to."

"Great. Get ready and I'll come pick you up."

"You don't have to. I've got April's Jeep."

"And you leave it right where it is. You don't want to do anything to that car."

His mother saw any person behind the wheel of any vehicle not legally licensed to said person as an invitation to doom and disaster. Walczyk's father confided that it drove her crazy thinking of April and himself taking turns driving April's Jeep from California to Maine. "I'll be over around, oh, I don't know, quarter to ten?"

"Sounds good," Walczyk said, dropping the argument. "If I don't answer the door, just let yourself in. I'm going to take a shower. See you then." As usual, the call ended not with a prompt benediction, but a long, protracted silence that would continue until one of them gave in and said good-bye first.

Fifteen minutes later, just as Walczyk lathered his hair, a loud knock sounded from the entry way, telling him that his mother was both early and had forgotten his instructions. A second knock let him know it wasn't the postman, as postmen only knock twice for Lana Turner.

"Come in!" he bellowed from the curtainless shower. Shower curtains were on his list of important things he needed to buy for the house. Number two on the list, to be exact, right after an intercom system so he could tell his mother to quit beating on the damned door and come in.

"Come in!" he yelled again, rinsing his hair out quickly. He stepped out of the fiber glass tub, dripping onto the white tile floor of the downstairs bathroom. He'd yet to christen any of the facilities upstairs, although he did look forward to getting moved in upstairs and cleaning up that beautiful claw-foot bathtub in what would be his private bathroom, and taking a long, quiet soak. Some of the world's best thinkers enjoyed a good bath. Mike Myers practiced *Saturday Night Live* sketches in the bath. Gargantuan US President William Howard Taft carried his around with him. Popcorn magnate Orville Redenbacher died in his bath. Winston Churchill conducted diplomatic matters from the tub. And, by gum, if being smart in the bath was good enough for good ol' eccentric Winny, it was good enough for good ol' eccentric Walczyk. Grabbing his towel from the sink, Walczyk wrapped himself and stormed out of the room as the third knock resonated through the empty house, prepared to give his mother a quick tutorial on just what to do when someone says "Come in."

Rounding the corner that led from the hallway to the front door, Walczyk instantly saw the reason for his mother's awkwardness in entering.

It wasn't his mother standing in the foyer. It was three handsome, clean cut, smiling young people: two boys wearing off-the-rack suits and what might have been their grandfathers' ties and a young woman in her teens wearing what looked like one of Lucille Ball's old dresses. They stood in the doorway, their faces registering the shock and embarrassment of seeing a half-naked man.

And there were Bibles clutched in their hands. Bibles and leaflets.

A loud, deafening groan echoed inside Walczyk's head as he took in the solicitors. He was happy, at least, that April, a proud yet not entirely devout Jew, was not there to challenge the youthful trio to a religious debate.

The girl, blonde with virtually no make-up on her thin lips stepped forward. "Good morning, sir," she eagerly said. The boys stepped forward as well, effectively blocking her line of sight to the towel-clad Walczyk. Walczyk would have paid anything to see the girl peeking at him through the tight purity shield they'd formed between her and the sopping wet heathen dripping on the hardwood floor. Turning on their Crest White Strip smiles again, the visitors pressed intrepidly onward.

"How are you today, sir?" the young man on the left asked, his head slightly cocked to the side.

His mind screamed at him, a cacophony of voices all giving him precise directions: *Don't say anything! Don't say anything! Tell them you're not interested! Whatever you do, don't say anything!!!*

"I'm super, thanks for asking," he shot out, unable to control himself. "And you?"

"I'm great, thank you, Mr..."

"Gaul," he said, spitting out the first name that came to mind. "Elias Gaul." He knew that if whatever sect they were from did a Google search on the name "Elias Gaul," they'd either find the 1886 serial killer in Montana, who fed his victims to the pigs of a Chinese butcher in the infamous Deadwood mining camp, or the homosexual working for the prestigious Schueller Talent Agency.

"We thought Mr. Peter Walczyk lived here," the shorter boy said.

"Nope," Walczyk groped. "Just me."

"Well, Mr. Gaul," the taller youth said, nary a strand of his blonde hair moving in the light morning breeze that began to nip at Walczyk's cold, semi-dry legs. "We're just going around today to see how people are dealing with the turbulent times in our world."

There was no chance for Walczyk to interject, perhaps to tell them he had to get back to the ritualistic animal sacrifice he and his voodoo Wicca coven were conducting in the dirt-floored basement, sacrificing three virgins and a sheep to AlMaHaKalekkalan, the dark underlord of the Brotherhood of Omicron Persei, and that such a delay would only cause AlMaHaKalekkalan to rain down upon the Earth with fire, then ice, then fire of a second kind. The three teens quickly launched into their well-rehearsed message of redemption while Walczyk just kept nodding, grunting a 'yeah' or a 'nope' when he felt he was being asked a question. The concept of a script based on a group of aliens called the Brotherhood of Omicron Persei had nudged his creative mind to consider it further. "Now that's a novel idea," he remarked under his breath.

"It is indeed, sir," the girl said, still crouched behind her suited protectors. "Now you understand why it is important for us, as Christians – now more than ever – to stand behind the Bible and use it as a weapon, to destroy the evil influences that are–"

Never before had the sound of the theme from *Bewitched* been such a beautiful sound. That simple, catchy theme was his immediate redemption. Walczyk cocked his thumb in the direction of the other room. "Excuse me. I'm going to have to be rude and go answer that. Could be work. I'll be right back." They smiled and nodded, and he turned around and slid into the kitchen, desperately hoping that whoever was calling wouldn't hang up before he got to them. He flipped his phone open, greeting the caller with, "Thank you, thank you, thank you, whoever you are!"

His mother's voice came from the other end of the line. "I'm not coming up that drive-way with those people there."

"You have to," he hissed. "Mother, I haven't even gotten dressed yet!"

"I will not get lured into this sick game you play with these people."

"This is no game, trust me!"

"Who'd you tell them you were?"

Walczyk hesitated a moment before replying, "Elias Gaul."

"Your agent?"

"Yeah."

"All right. I'm going home. You can drive over in April's Jeep. *Slowly.*" She followed up quickly with, "And be nice to those people. They're being true to their faith, after all," before hanging up.

Walczyk continued to keep the now-silent phone pressed to his ear and strolled back down the hallway to the small foyer.

"I know, sweetie, but I don't think that they're ready for that." He gave a "just a minute" signal to the three visitors, and returned his attention to the dead phone. "Well, you tell your father in your own way and I'll tell mine in my own way." Walczyk again turned to the three on-lookers, saying "My fiancé. We're eloping because no one can agree on the wedding."

"Oh, congratulations," the girl said, smiling. The two boys turned and glared at her.

"Oh, just some kids at the door," Walczyk said to his imaginary friend. "They send along their blessings." There, Walczyk thought. The bait was set. Now to spring the trap. "I love you too, Mark." He closed the phone and returned his attention to the three travelling evangelists. "So you were saying something about sin in our society?"

It was eleven by the time Walczyk extricated himself from his visitors. When he finally arrived at his mother's house, breakfast was a cup of coffee for his mother and an egg and cheese breakfast sandwich with a glass of iced milk for him. Walczyk had always demanded his milk be served over ice, ever since an unfortunate gastrointestinal episode involving a restaurant in Brunswick, an absent minded waitress, and a luke warm glass of milk being served to a ten-year-old Peter Walczyk. For a year and a half, he completely refused milk as a beverage. Then, slowly, he began to reacquire a taste for it, but only under strict conditions. At home, he kept a glass beer stein in the freezer, so he could have ice cold milk at a moment's notice. When out in public, however, he demanded it be served over ice, perplexing far too many waitresses over the years to account for.

Walczyk ate in silence and his mother picked up a book she was reading. His mother, for as long as he could remember, had always carried a book around with her. In the car on family trips. Before, during, and after supper. In the doctor's office, and even in the bath. It seemed that a book was always attached to Diane Walczyk's hand.

"So what are you reading?" he asked, nodding towards the book.

"Dean Koontz. *Mr. Murder*."

"Dean Koontz?" Walczyk asked, astonished.

"Yes, why?" Diane asked, not looking up.

"Nothing. I just find it strange that you read Dean Koontz."

"I started reading mysteries and thrillers years ago. Your sister got me into them."

"It's not that."

"What is it, then?"

"It's just, well, this state *raised* Stephen King. He's ours. Maine hasn't much. He's a natural resource, like lobster and pine trees. You mean to tell me you sat two tables away from him in the dining commons at the University of Maine, and you read Dean Koontz?"

"Koontz doesn't creep me out."

"What?"

"Stephen King always gave me the willies."

"Steve's a great guy," Walczyk said indignantly. "I've never, not once, found him to be creepy."

"Okay, maybe 'creepy' is the wrong word," she backpedaled.

"No, you have always called him creepy. You said he was creepy when I was in fourth grade and wanted to watch *Carrie*."

"So I said he's creepy once! You make it sound like I ran around screaming creepy anytime his name comes up."

"Please! 1989. Sixth grade. I bring home a copy of *Misery* from the library. You take it from me and inform the library staff that they're not to let me check out anything by King because he's *too creepy*."

"How do you remember these things?"

"You and Dad teamed up on me after supper. You said, 'I don't want you reading him. That book is too old for you and he's creepy', and all Dad said was, 'You're too young to read a book like that. Your mother thinks he's creepy,' and you said, 'Well, he *is*!'"

"He just... he would hang around with all those... creepy war protestors at the Union. He was the ringleader. He had long hair and a beard and–"

"And only creepy men wear long hair and beards? How about Jesus Christ? Is he creepy?"

Walczyk's mother was suddenly very upset. She shook his finger at him. "You watch your mouth. You need to be careful what you joke about. You come close to blasphemy a lot, Peter. The way you and your friends use 'G-D' this and 'J-C' that. That's a sin."

He didn't reply. Nothing he said would do any good, so he kept his mouth shut. But silence didn't stop her. She was on a roll now.

"And I really wish you'd have them tone down the language on your show. Your Grandmother would *love* to watch it, but your father won't show it to her because he doesn't want to listen to her complain about the language."

"Funny, she doesn't complain about the sex, nudity, and occasional violence," he said with a smirk. "It's the language that gets her."

Diane scowled at him. "Can't you just, I don't know, edit out the swear words and mail her a video tape?"

Walczyk decided to leave the reference to video tapes alone, knowing damned well that his parents, and Grandmother Walczyk were still using VHS on a daily basis. "What do you, want me to just have them shoot two versions?" he quipped. "The regular broadcast version and then a special *Grammy Walczyk* edition with softer language, but the same amount of breasts and fisticuffs."

"If I thought you were being serious, I would think that was a wonderful idea and a very respectful thing to do. Look, I'm just asking that you leave out the A-, B-, C-, D-, F-, G-D, H-, J-C, K-, M-, N-, P-, S-, and T-words."

When Walczyk wondered what the K-word was, his mother insisted that it existed, that he'd used it once as a child, and that she'd never utter it herself. She then firmly stated that not *all* young people talk that way. Perhaps she was right. Maybe all young people *didn't* talk that way. He decided that the three kids on his door step this morning (who come to think of it should have been in school) would be unable to come up with the long-hand version of the A-, D-, S- and K-words.

Walczyk remembered when he won a playwriting scholarship for a one-act play he'd written as an assignment during his first year at UMaine. The play was called *The Porch*. It was a fictional re-creation of any given afternoon or evening spent in his Grandfather Walczyk's sunroom up in Patten, listening to his Grampie Walczyk, his uncles, and his father all trade stories about the woods, the way life used to be, the local goings-on in town, and whatnot. For the sake of literary integrity, Walczyk kept all of the colorful language and racial slurs, only changing the names of people being discussed. His parents had praised it, saying they were proud of their son. However, not long after the adoration began to die down, a letter from his mother came, asking him to rewrite the play so Gram could read it without being scandalized. Walczyk commented that it shouldn't scandalize her. After all, she'd spent sixty-odd years listening to Grampie talk like that.

Now, more than ten years later, Walczyk and his mother were still discussing "language." Tired of trying to one-up his mother, Walczyk changed the subject. "I need a bed. I'm tired of that piece of S-word air mattress."

"You can have the twin bed in your old room," his mother offered.

"Mum," he began, knowing it would be hard for his mother to part with the furniture, a memory of the past. "A thirty-five year old divorcee with millions at his disposal shouldn't have to steal his childhood bed out from under his parents' roof."

"We don't mind," she said, probably lying, but clearly wanting to help out her son. She prided herself, after all, on keeping that room as he'd left it the day he ran away from home in the summer of 1996.

"All the same, I think my days of sleeping in a twin bed are over. So where should we start?" Walczyk asked. "Gilbert's?"

"They closed down last fall," his mother replied.

"I saw it when we drove through town. It's open."

"They kept the name, but it's no longer a furniture store and it's no longer run by Marsh and Emma. Now it's one of those junk shops that sells cheap plastic toys and gags and T-shirts with dirty sayings on them."

"Huh," Walczyk said, wishing such a shop had been open when he was growing up, because he had never felt his childhood was complete given he didn't own rubber dog poop. "What about Drew's?"

"Drew's might have some dressers and things, maybe a bed frame, but no mattresses. Now, Cunningham's, they might have mattresses, but we'd need to take measurements of the mattresses, then go buy the frame, then go back to Cunningham's and buy the mattresses."

Walczyk's eyes crossed. He forgot that locally owned businesses can only carry about a third of what you want. "Why don't I just grab Vic sometime and go to Augusta?"

She shook her head. "Why go all that way when we can find most of it here?"

"I know, I know. Just sounds like a lot of fu–" He blessedly caught himself. "–frigging around to do," he said. "It'll take all day."

"And you've got something better to do today?" Mum asked,

smiling at him.

She had him there. His plans for today included some *Mario Kart*, maybe another vain attempt to turn something palatable out *The Next One*. Then there were the three latest scripts Eli had mailed him, which he didn't even want to look at, knowing that one of them was a live-action version of the board game *Stratego*.

"Then let's start at Cunningham's," Walczyk said. He dug his phone out and began to text away. "We won't be able to fit it all in the Jeep. I'll call Vic to borrow his truck."

"Oh, no," his mother protested. "You're not borrowing *another* vehicle!"

"April Donovan, look at you!" Sara exclaimed, arms outstretched, as she walked into the home she used to share with Walczyk. She took April into her arms and gave her a tight hug. Sara let go, and put her hands on April's face and kissed her on both cheeks. "You look incredible. Life seems to be agreeing with you back there in Maine."

"Well, it *is* the Vacationland," April said. Then, forcing some politeness into her voice, she turned to Sara's assistant. "Hello, Cora." They had history, but April didn't feel it was worth reliving at this specific point in time.

"I see you've been busy laying claim to everything," Cora said coolly, scanning the room, taking in the Post-It notes. She dropped her personal organizer onto one of the chairs in the living room. "Let's just make one thing clear. He created this situation, so he's entitled to–"

"Cora," Sara said firmly.

Cora turned to Sara. "Yes?"

"Play nice," Sara said. Cora scowled like a scolded child and picked her organizer back up, burying her nose in it. "Sorry about that," Sara said sweetly. "She's under the impression that Peter wants to screw me one last time."

"Actually, that couldn't be further from the truth. He's not all that caught up in this," April said, picking her things up from an end table.

"Cora's right, though   you *have* been busy," Sara commented, looking around at the Post-Its hanging from just about everything in the room. "So what's the system?"

"Well, the items with the yellow Post-Its are the stuff that belongs to Walczyk. Blue is your stuff. Pink, Walz just doesn't want, and green is the stuff–"

"Let's make this simple, shall we?" Sara said, breezily. She snatched the pad of blue Post-Its from April, tagged two or three items, and gave her a smile. "Done. Next room?"

The kitchen was been a breeze – Sara wanted none of it. Everything in the den was all stuff that belonged outright to Walczyk, except for a few DVDs that Sara pulled and placed in a stack on an end table she'd debated back-and-forth about before tagging blue.

In the bedroom, Sara found considerably more items to tag blue. "So how is he?" Sara asked, sticking blue Post-Its on some of the furniture that April had marked with pink "Walz just doesn't want" tags.

"He's good." April felt very conflicted. She genuinely liked Sara. She was a good person, with a big heart. Her only real flaw was that she was a two-timing tramp, and that was something that April knew, with time, she could find herself working around. On the other hand, it was her boss – that miserable lump of a man on the east coast no doubt spending his day playing Wii and eating animal crackers – who was the direct result of that indiscretion. Had Sara just gone about it the right way – hell, had Sara just been smart enough not to make out with Ella at a party in part thrown for her husband, with cameras and strange people around – the damage would have been less. The humiliation could have been circumvented.

"So what do you think of Henry Walczyk?" Sara asked, tagging some picture frames decorating the bedroom. "Isn't he the most adorable thing ever?"

"He's… " April considered giving her a smart-ass, snappy reply. But, instead, she found herself unable to be snarky about the man. "Henry's fantastic. Already adopted me into the family."

"He show you where the spare key is hidden?"

"Day three," April said, still remembering the smile on Henry's face as he showed her the key, hidden on a nail behind a slate placard that read *Bless This House*. "I hope you know he still thinks the world of you."

"Still? Well, that means a lot," Sara said, smiling wistfully, pawing through a dresser. April began to pull clothes from Walczyk's dresser, folding them and putting them into boxes. She didn't even know if he wanted them anymore or not, but the past three months had been taxing on his limited wardrobe, and the ten outfits he'd brought with him on this little sojourn were slowly beginning to show their wear.

"Oh, no!" Sara cried out, now on her knees and reaching under the bed.

"What is it?" Cora asked, rushing to Sara's side. Sara emerged from beneath the bed with a photo album. A white photo album, decorated with ribbon. The wedding album.

"Oh, no," April echoed. She watched as Sara opened the album and looked down at herself, elegant in a custom made white lace dress. The casual smile that her face had borne all day as she tagged her belongings vanished, and the true Sara was finally revealed: a pained, conflicted woman.

"Well, she obviously doesn't want this," Cora said, reaching for the album and slamming the cover shut.

"Cora, go wait in the car." Sara was careful not to let her assistant see that tears were forming in her eyes. After Cora was gone, she wiped her eyes and looked over to April. "She *is* right; I can't take this. Do you think–?"

"I don't think Peter could take it," April said, pulling out her iPhone. "But I'll find out for sure." She typed furiously into the little device.

Sara flipped through a few more pages before shutting the book, tears leaking down her cheeks. "I didn't want this, you know," she said, wiping her face. "I never meant this to happen. It's just–"

"Sara, you don't owe me an explanation," April said carefully. In all truth, April didn't *want* to know why Sara had cheated on Walczyk. Why she had chosen to do so with his friend, an actress on his own show. Why she was suddenly remorseful. It wasn't going to change the damage that had been done to Peter or the price of tea in China. She didn't want to get involved. She'd never spoken ill of Sara, aside from a few snarky comments about her suddenly becoming a lesbian. She never trash-talked Sara or put her down, especially not in front of Walczyk. She behaved herself in this regard because of two very important factors. One: anything you say gets back to you and bites you in the ass. Guaranteed. And two: she had enough going on in her life, professional and personal, without needing to wonder why a dancer-turned-actress found it necessary to leave her husband for someone else. She just didn't have the time to let it be personal to her.

"I owe someone an explanation," Sara said after a moment.

"Sara," April said, careful not to put too much meaning into this, "that person's not here."

"No," she said, looking down at the cover of the album. "No, he isn't."

"Why haven't you told him?" April asked.

"It's not the kind of thing a person gets into over the phone."

"You told him you were filing for divorce over the phone."

"Ella's idea, and I hate myself for that. Besides, cold as it sounds, that was business. As to all the hows and whys. Well, those are personal. I owe him enough not to get into that over the phone."

"You may never get to unload all of that, then," April said. "Because the west coast is the last place Walczyk plans on being anytime soon, in the foreseeable future and beyond."

"That's a shame," Sara said. "I have a lot I still need to tell him."

Furniture shopping with his mother had been a novel experience for Walczyk. But it had been fun, and Walczyk couldn't remember the last time he had actually had *fun* with his mother. Thanksgiving was always a nice reunion for the family, but catching up was the focus of their attention. Christmas was a hectic mess of making sure they were at such-and-such's house by such-and-such a time, and that they didn't stay too long, or they'd never get to another such-and-such's house by such-and-such a time. This was different. Walczyk and his mother were laughing together, with and at each other, making chit-chat – something they hadn't done in over eight or nine years. It pained him to think that, over the years, Hannah and Vic probably had more in common with his parents than he had.

At Cunningham's, Walczyk's mother found a nightstand and bureau for the master bedroom, as well as a very nice, understated bed frame for Walczyk's room (turns out they did, in fact, sell bed frames). At Drew's, Walczyk picked out an oak table that he decided would serve nicely as the desk for his upstairs office, and a bed frame for April's room and mattresses for his and April's beds. When they had finished, Walczyk and his mother returned to Cunningham's, where he helped Pat Cunningham's grandson Josh wrestle the smaller purchases into the bed of Vic's pick-up truck and was promised same-day delivery of the mattresses, bed frames and bureau.

At another little antique shop in town, they found a fascinating little coffee table that, according to Walczyk's mother, would be "cute, with some work." Uninterested in "cute, with some work," Walczyk instead purchased an old 1940's-era typewriter, ignoring the shopkeeper's warnings that it wasn't totally functional, and a tall pedestal-like table to put the typewriter on.

It wasn't until the drive home that Walczyk realized he was no longer enjoying himself. He switched the radio on to fill the silence in the truck and gritted his teeth together, his jaw tight, as he drove. All he wanted to do now was get his new bed set up so he could spend the rest of the day in it. A tightness grew inside him, pushing its way around his ribs, constricting them. His eyes tingled and burned, and he felt moisture collecting in the corners of them. He looked over at his mother, who was no doubt going over in her head exactly how much money they'd spent while staring at her book. Walczyk couldn't understand her reluctance for him to buy things; he *needed* these things. He couldn't keep sleeping on an air mattress that needed to be refilled every morning. He couldn't entertain friends in an empty house, couldn't work in a barely occupied shell. He was selfish. He wanted things. *His* things: a bed, a shower curtain, and his seventy inch, 1080p high-definition LED flat-panel TV, 3D Blu-ray player and Dolby 7.1 surround sound home theater system.

They pulled into his parents' driveway and Walczyk shifted the pick-up into park. His mother opened the door and got out, but Walczyk couldn't make himself move. He felt as though he were part of the seat he was sitting on. More than that, he didn't *want* to move. He had no desire to go into that empty house and occupy himself. What was the point?

"Peter?" his mother asked, reaching across the seat to touch his arm. "Are you all right?"

He looked up at her, tears running down his cheeks. "No," was all he could push past that black mass, which had now moved to his throat. The word sounded like it came from a six-year-old. A six year old who didn't want to go to school, but who had no good reason to stay home. Walczyk's mother tentatively reached over to caress her son's arm.

"Peter, what's wrong?" It was the voice of the mother of a frightened six-year-old, who fought her every instinct to keep her baby home, away from whatever it was about school that was scaring him.

He opened his mouth a crack, taking a breath in, looking for the words. Shaking his head, he gave her the only answer he had: "I don't know."

"So, how was it?" Eli Gaul, leaning back in his chair, hands clasped behind his head.

"She cried."

"Sara Collins cried?" he asked sarcastically.

"Don't say it like that," April said, crossing her legs. "It sounds catty."

"How should I say it?"

"I don't know... surprised?"

"Why should I be surprised?"

"I don't know, I guess... I guess I had been thinking she was happy with how things turned out."

"No, she's been far from happy," Eli said. "She hates herself for what she's done to Walczyk."

"Why is this the first I'm hearing of this?"

"Because I figured you were busy spewing anti-Sara venom around Cold Island."

"*Cole* Island, and no, I've not. Thanks for thinking I could be big about all this."

"So," Eli said, getting off the subject, "everything's taken care of at the house?"

"I'll be at the house to meet the movers at nine tomorrow morning to start packing up the stuff going to Maine, then Sara's mover will show up around noon to pack her share, and the remainder is getting hauled off for charity."

"A rather clean split, as far as Hollywood romances go," Eli said. "Paparazz-Eye will be disappointed."

"Paparazz-Eye can kiss my ass."

"Speaking of ass, you've got that big night out with Ian tonight, don't you?"

"Don't you start! It's strictly platonic."

"Many of Ian's sordid rendezvous start out as 'strictly platonic.'"

April was finding herself growing weary of defending her dinner date with Ian. Aly had grilled her about it for an hour when they did lunch during a break over on the Warner's lot. She, too, warned

April by citing Ian's track record for bedding any female willing to get dressed up and join him in a public place.

"Two colleagues are getting together for dinner and a few drinks. There's nothing more to be read into it. Period. End of story." She shifted in her chair. "Now talk to me about upcoming projects?"

"As in what?"

"As in have you found any?"

"Well, there's this zombie thing Marathon Pictures is doing."

"Which zombie thing?" April asked. "There have to be at least three dozen zombie projects floating around the town right now and Marathon is responsible for a third of them."

"Anthony Severance wants Walczyk to remake *Night of the Living Dead* for them. Taylor Lautner and Emma Watson are ready to sign, given its Walczyk who at least provides the script."

"I don't know," April said wearily. "Remaking *Night of the Living Dead*? He'll see it as sacrilege. He's always going on about how it's the best horror movie ever made."

"You don't have to agree with the idea, April – you just have to pitch it to him. Personally, I think it's a great project comeback for him. And, as you said, he loves that movie."

"Tell me more about it tomorrow over breakfast," April said. "And I'll bring it to him when I get home and settled in."

"Sounds great. So when's Mr. Maeder picking you up?"

"He said to be in the hotel lobby at six," April said.

"Well, my dear, have fun. And behave."

"Eli," she warned.

"And, for the love of God, use a condom!"

"Bite me," she said, kicking his desk.

Eli's desk phone rang. He tapped a few buttons. *"Mr. Gaul? Your three o'clock is here."*

"Send him in," Eli said. "Hate to kick you out, but–"

"But you're kicking me out."

"Exactly," Eli said. Call me tomorrow morning?"

"Will do." April rose and walked over to Eli, giving him a big kiss and a hug.

"This feels so good," Eli confessed, squeezing her tight.

"I've missed you, you old queen."

"I've missed you too, you uppity bitch." They released each other and stepped away. Eli smiled. "I've got to hand it to you, April."

"What's that?" she asked, picking up her bag from the floor beside her chair.

"Sticking with him like this. I mean, let's face it, you're a California girl. Your heart is here. I just can't picture you in Mayberry, Maine."

She suddenly felt about three inches tall. She smiled, blew Eli a kiss, and walked out of his office, her chest feeling tight. She wondered if this was what panic attacks felt like as she stepped into the elevator, those four words rattling around in her fried brain.

Your heart is here.

CHAPTER SEVEN
MICK-A-PALOOZA

After a short talk about his bad mood with his mother, Walczyk returned to his place, beaten there by the furniture truck, which had already dropped off the beds, mattresses, and bureau. He dragged everything inside and left it propped up against the rear wall of the living room, except for his mattress, which he dropped on the floor. He put on a DVD of *Looney Tunes* shorts and drifted off to sleep before the first "That's All Folks" splashed across the screen.

It wasn't until someone nudged him with a foot that he woke up.

"What the hell?" Walczyk grunted, rolling over to see the owner of the foot – Vic Gordon. "What are you doing here? I thought you weren't done work until seven."

"You're right. It's eight," Vic said, smiling.

Walczyk bolted upright on the mattress, first staring out the window, where the sky had begun to darken, then at the clock on the wall, which actually read five past eight. Walczyk hopped to his feet. "Shit. I got back here around four and figured I'd just take a half-hour nap before sorting this stuff out."

"Seems like you needed more than a half hour," Vic said, setting a brown paper bag on the kitchen table that was still on loan from the Barrelhead. "Ready to do some video gaming on my Wii?"

"Look, if you want to take it back to your place..." Walczyk began. He felt bad that everyone had loaned him stuff and he was taking so long getting it back to them. A Wii and games, a TV, the kitchen table, and a few other odds-and-ends from Vic, furniture from his parents, and some kitchen stuff from Hannah. He felt like a complete leech, but felt assuaged by the fact that, this weekend, during the great excursion to Portland, he'd be able to buy all new stuff and give everyone back their belongings.

"Will you shut up about it?" Vic urged. "I never play alone anyway. I hope you haven't eaten," Vic said, going through the paper bag he'd put on the counter and removing two foil take away containers. "Because I brought over a shitload of fried chicken from the Moondoggy."

Walczyk's mouth watered. "Do they still make it the same way?"

"Guy hasn't changed his recipe in thirty-two years," Vic said, prying the lid off of one of the containers and pulling out a drumstick. Walczyk followed suit.

Vic was right. As a child, Friday nights were special because they were take-out nights in the Walczyk home. They would order pizzas at Mama Rosa's or get Chinese food from Rosen's (Ira Rosen was Jewish, while his Chinese wife, Jae, was not). But Walczyk's favorite take-away nights were the third Friday of the month, when Henry would bring home fried chicken from the Moondoggy (Diner, not Surf Shop). Guy Martin was very secretive about his 13 original herbs and spices that he used in his fried chicken, though he'd let probably half of them, including paprika, garlic salt, and oregano, slip over the years while bragging about the chicken. It was so crunchy and crispy, yet juicy and tender at the same time. All of those Friday nights, eating take-out chicken around the dinner table with his family, flooded back to him with his first bite of that drumstick. He groaned in approval as he continued eating.

"And," Vic announced, reaching into the brown paper bag again, pulling out two glasses and a bottle of Glenlivet scotch that no doubt came from the store room at the restaurant. "Now we have ourselves a good, old-fashioned Mick-a-Palooza."

"Very nice," Walczyk said, picking the bottle up and examining it. It was still sealed. He tore away the wrapping around the neck of the bottle and opened it up, taking a deep sniff of the liquor. "You invite Hannah over?"

"Hannah sends her love, but she says that scotch, Guy Martin's fried chicken, and ultra violent video games are just too much for her on a school night."

"Bullshit," Walczyk said, pouring healthy measures of scotch into each of the glasses. "She could've passed on the fried chicken."

Vic grinned, taking another bite of his drumstick. "All you remembered it to be?"

"You know, Vic," Walczyk said, passing his friend a glass of scotch, "all of the eating I did in California – real Italian pizzerias, Chinese-run Chinese restaurants, fried chicken from around the world – and there's nothing that beats the cooking back here." He shook his drumstick for effect, briefly, before stripping the last of the meat from it. "I don't know what it is."

"That's because this, my friend, is soul food," Vic said, thumping the top of the foil take-out container with the bone of his drumstick. "It's ingrained in your psyche."

"Well, thank God for that," Walczyk said. He looked back inside the container. "Did you just get breasts and legs?"

"I don't like thighs or wings. You?"

"No. You did good, boy. You did good." Walczyk walked over to Vic, glass raised in his hand. "To the things that never change in life: friends, family, and Guy Martin's fried chicken."

"Skoal," Vic said, clinking glasses with Walczyk before taking a hearty slug of the scotch.

"Skoal." Walczyk took a drink of scotch. He rarely drank straight alcohol. Rum and Coke was his drink of choice, and that tasted best when either he could only taste the Coke, or the rum was so strong that the sweetness of it went down easily. Scotch, he found, he could only handle in small sips, as he'd never been a huge fan of malt drinks. It reminded him a bit too much of beer or champagne, two other drinks he generally sipped at. This Scotch, however, went down more smoothly than he'd remembered, though he could feel it in his mouth and throat a few moments after he'd drunk it. He looked up to see Vic smirking at him.

"Still not a Scotch drinker, are you?" Vic said.

Walczyk took another sip to prove Vic wrong. It slightly burned going down, and left what he could only describe as the vapor of scotch inside his mouth.

"Here," Vic said, reaching into the bag, and pulling out a bottle of Captain Morgan's Spiced Rum. "The Cap" had been Walczyk's favorite brand since 1995. Since the first time he and Vic first declared what they un-PC-ly referred to as "Mick-a-Palooza," or, more commonly, St. Patrick's Day. Over the years, Mick-a-Palooza shifted from only being held on St. Paddy's Day to being any time Vic and Walczyk got together to drink, watch movies, and talk about life, love, and the pursuit of happiness. What Walczyk loved the most about the made-up holiday was that one didn't "plan" Mick-a-Palooza in order to celebrate it; one "declared" it. And it was through a text message two days ago that Vic "declared" Mick-a-Palooza. The last one Walczyk could remember was in 1999, when Vic hopped a Greyhound to New York just to declare Mick-a-Palooza in the dead of winter. The name of the holiday had, of course, offended some of Walczyk's friends, who didn't care that Vic himself was Irish when they voiced their disgust at the racial epithet.

"You playing bartender tonight or something?" Walczyk asked, examining the bottle of Captain Morgan's.

"Or something. I provide the poison, but it's your job to off yourself with it."

Walczyk grabbed a bottle of Coke from Vic and put it in the freezer to quickly chill it. "So, whatcha wanna do first?"

"Drink and eat chicken," Vic said. "Put whatever you want on TV and I'll watch." Vic dumped several pieces of chicken on one of the paper plates he'd brought with him. He reached into the fridge and removed a can of Budweiser from the thirty pack (he had always, vehemently refused to call it a "thirty rack") he kept living there. "So what were you watching before seepy-byes?"

Walczyk rolled his eyes, picking the mattress back up and leaning it against the wall. "Looney Tunes."

"Well, crank up some of that, at least 'til we get good and buzzed," Vic said, plopping down in one of the folding camp chairs.

Walczyk turned the TV on and grabbed the remote for the DVD player, starting the disc up. "I'm so glad you declared Mick-a-Palooza," Walczyk said. "I really needed it."

"Me too, buddy," Vic said, his mouth full of fried chicken, "Me too."

Hannah was lying on her bed, correcting the last of Stella's cursed summer reading quizzes, which were abysmal. When asked the significance of the title of the book *Fahrenheit 451*, Dustin Harris responded, "Feran Heights 451 is the address where the star of the books lives." Hannah snickered to herself. At least no one had mistaken *Fahrenheit 451* for the protagonist's name this year. Hannah wondered, as she sloughed through the exams, if this was how the students had felt over the summer. Thinking of places they'd rather be and people they'd rather be with, but instead stuck with Stella Lyons' summer reading. Henry had told her numerous times before that it really was her own fault. Hannah had been intimidated by Stella Lyons back when she and Peter and Vic had the woman as an English teacher when they were in high school. There was no rationale behind it, Hannah knew this. But that five-foot-four woman, with her wasp's nest of salt-and-pepper hair wrapped tightly around the top of her head in a slanting beehive and her moth ball smelling clothes, intimidated her to no end. When Hannah graduated high school, she had no intention of becoming a teacher, let alone becoming a teacher at her old alma mater.

Question two asked, "Using complete sentences, explain, in depth, what *Fahrenheit 451* is about." The given response, "Fahrenheit 451 is about 176 pages." This time, Hannah allowed herself to laugh aloud. Scanning up to the top of the paper, she saw it was Taylor Hodges' exam. She guessed that he probably was familiar enough with the material, but was giving his smart-aleck answers just to get under Stella's skin. Hannah appreciated this, but unfortunately had to write an F on the page.

It was only when her phone chirped, telling her she had a text, that she realized it was well past ten and only half of her correcting had been finished. She picked her cell phone up and flipped it open.

FROM: WALCZYK   TIME: 10:04PM
MESSAGE: YOU SHOULD BE AT MCIKAPALOOZE
YOU TEACHERS PET!

Hannah rolled her eyes, having expected the drunken texting to start earlier. She quickly messaged back, asking what the boys were up to and put her phone away, determined to get her odious task finished. She picked up the next exam and began to go over it. It was at least a little more promising, since the student, Sasha Connary, knew that the significance of the title *Fahrenheit 451* and that it was an appropriate title since the novel is about book burning. Her answer to question two was weaker, as she simply wrote, "*Fahrenheit 451* is about censorship" when asked what the book was about. Hannah shrugged and gave her full credit, wishing she could've given Taylor credit for his reply to that particular question. The remainder of Sasha's exam was competent, but she had expected no less from the young woman.

Hannah's phone chirped at her again. It was a poorly typed, but nonetheless meaningful set of Bon Jovi song lyrics. The lyrics took her back to a much simpler time. It had been a cold winter night, in the back seat of Henry Walczyk's Chevy Celebrity, on the way home from a high school dance, when Peter had put his hand on her leg. It was a subtle gesture, but for Hannah, it was earth-shattering. It was proof that Peter actually liked her. In the dark, petrified that Henry would see, she slipped her own hand over Peter's and they sat in the back seat, in silence, listening to what from that moment on was "their song."

Hannah began typing back to Walczyk, quoting the next few lines of the song even though they were not particularly appropriate to the moment. She hit send, and picked the sheaf of papers back up. The next quiz belonged to Troy Dexter, one of her more intellectually challenged students, who had simply filled in every answer alternating "don't know" with "don't care." While appreciating Troy's honesty, she was forced to draw an F at the top of the page. She knew that Stella would be severely disappointed in the results of these exams, and that she would blame Hannah and Cameron for not impressing up on the students just how important the summer reading was.

As she plowed through more exams from more students who hadn't touched Bradbury's novel, Hannah couldn't help but dwell on why Stella treated her as she did. She didn't treat Cameron this way. Of course, Cameron was a graduate of Houlton High School up in Aroostook county, had never had to deal with the woman as a student. Cameron also stood up to Stella early on in his career, telling her in no uncertain terms that she had no say as to what went on in his classroom, what he taught, or how he taught it. This was something that Hannah, who still felt the sting of being constantly mocked her for being the only girl in class to enjoy reading science fiction and fantasy, had never had the nerve to do.

Hannah's phone chirped again. She eagerly scooped it up and flipped it open, reading more song lyrics. She smiled and, for a brief, brief moment, considered scooping all of those darned quizzes up and throwing them away. But she thought better of it, having played an entire argument with Stella in her mind in a few seconds, and went back to grading.

Marie Chase's exam was blank, except for her name. *Good for you, Marie*, she thought to herself as she moved on.

Los Angeles was filled with dozens upon dozens of restaurants, some of them shit holes, like the Dim Sung Orchid on Channing's, or the notoriously pompous and disgusting Nüance, perhaps operated by folks who had spent too many years as kids licking batteries. But the Dim Sum and Nüance only managed to stay alive because they *were* the worst restaurants in town. Novelty items, providing the patrons with horror stories they could tell for the rest of their lives about the worst dining experience of their lives.

April was an amateur foodie. Always had been. She loved fine dining. She'd enjoyed gourmet meals at LaMarchand in Woodland Hills, had breathtaking desserts at Divinity in Laurel Canyon, and eaten authentic homemade pasta at the little Italian bistro right in her own neighborhood, where the owners knew her by name. And then there were her Friday afternoon strolls with Walczyk down North La Brea Ave, to Pink's Hot Dog Stand, perhaps the most famous hot dog stand in the world.

She noticed Ian was wearing his best Armani, the one he only dusted off for studio parties, celebrity weddings and funerals. This told her they weren't going to Pink's. Ian took a right off West Hollywood Boulevard, onto North St. Vincente, and April's heart began to patter as he pulled up to the curb and put the car in park. She grabbed his arm. "You didn't!"

He nodded. "Walczyk said you might like it."

A smile spread across her face, much like the smiles on the faces of kids upon entering Disney Land. April got out of the car and looked up at the Union Jack flapping in the breeze. She had loved driving by this place when she first arrived in L.A., she had dreamed of sneaking inside and just to smell the food, but a long waiting list kept her from even that. Ian handed the keys to the valet and looked at her, smiling. "You deserve nothing less for your last night in town." Ian proffered his arm, and April took it. Two doormen opened the double doors and April stepped inside Gordon Ramsay at the London, in West Hollywood.

The Beef Wellington had been exquisite, and aside from not

having spied Chef Gordon Ramsay himself in the restaurant, the evening had been perfect. It wasn't until her fourth glass of wine that things got serious.

"Are you okay?" Ian asked.

"Fine, why?" she lied.

"I don't know," he said. "You just seem distracted."

"Well, you did take me to the nicest restaurant in town," April said. "I guess I'm just a little awestruck. That and I'm still looking around to see if Chef Ramsay is here tonight."

"I'll buy that," Ian said, returning to his own wine. "But you've been distracted for quite some time now."

April shook her head, trying to clear it. "It's nothing. Personal shit, that's all."

"Since when have you kept secrets from me?"

"Ian, I said drop it."

As soon as she'd said it, she felt bad for being so sharp with Ian. As impervious to her frequent nastiness as he was, she sometimes had to wonder if Ian was ever hurt by her brusqueness. Then his foot crept across the floor under the table and the tip of his shoe caressed her ankle. She couldn't help but smile. It had been Abel Gleason in the seventh grade who was the last person to play footsie with her. She nuzzled his foot back with her stocking-clad foot, having shed her shoes a half hour ago.

"So what the hell are you still doing with Peter Walczyk?"

"Um, working?" April said, equal parts confused and angered by the question, which she'd been fielding ever since her plane touched down at LAX.

"Tell yourself that, if you like, but don't try to pass that bullshit off on me."

"Bullshit?" April asked heatedly.

"Bullshit," Ian clarified. "Bullshit because the April Donovan I knew would have never settled for this life. I asked you once before why you'd hitched your horse to Walczyk's wagon. You told me that you wanted a fast ride to the top, and working for someone like Walczyk would get you there."

"Ian, if you have a point," April retorted, pulling her foot back to her side of the table, "you'd better hurry up and make it, because you're pissing me off!"

"My point," Ian said, leaning forward and clasping April's

hands in his own, "is that you're so much more than just a personal assistant, and you know it."

"What do you want me to say, huh? *What do you want me to say?* Tell me, because I don't know what I can say that will get you to shut the fuck up!"

The restaurant quieted down around them. April felt every eye in the place on her. She slowly, cautiously sunk back into her seat and, mercifully, the din of the restaurant resumed.

"How long has it been since you've done that?"

"Done what?" she asked, wishing she had more wine.

"Blown up like that. Created a scene that got people staring in a public place. Let your true feelings out."

'If you think I'm holding something back..."

"I think you are. And I don't think you're happy in Maine."

"I'm enjoying Maine a lot, actually. Cole Island is beautiful, I've met some great new friends, and..." She trailed off, struggling to find a third thing about Maine she was enjoying.

"And–?" Ian prompted.

But she found herself coming up empty handed. She'd enjoyed getting to know Hannah and Vic. A lot. They were great people, even if Vic was a unabashed, libidinous manwhore on the same level as Ian. And the Island was great. Such a small, tight-knit community, yet big enough to let everyone be themselves. It was a miraculous microcosm of the world, albeit with a limited exposure to the world outside. But that was it: a few nice people and a great place to visit.

"You're saying I don't belong on Cole Island."

"Peter Walczyk is a brilliant man, who has been struck a tremendous blow. Few in this town actually fall in love. But he did. And now that the fairy tale is over, he's questioning the world. He's seeking solace in the arms of the only thing that hasn't betrayed him: his hometown. And I think that's wonderful. For him, but it's not for you."

"So what you're saying is–"

"I'm not saying. I'm asking. Leave Walczyk and move back out here."

"And do what? My job's in Maine right now, working for Walczyk."

"Well, maybe you could work for me."

"What?"

"Come to work for me, April." Ian leaned in, confidentially. "You can be my assistant." She snorted. "Fine. I'll make you a producer on *Ordinary World*. You can work with me in development. Anything you want."

"So you're poaching me from your best friend to be *your* assistant," April said, a scowl on her face.

"In a manner of speaking, yes. April, you've got so much going for you. I just feel it's being wasted in small town Maine, filling grocery orders and making medical appointments."

April looked down at her plate again, avoiding Ian's piercing eyes. She loved Cole Island. But Ian was right: she was no longer herself. She wasn't the fiery creature who once told Steven Spielberg to piss off because he was offended when she said she didn't care for his last *Indiana Jones* movie. She was no longer using her looks and her intelligence to wheedle things out of people. But most important, most glaring, was her reaction to that miserable bastard who almost always wore a faded, worn out yellow polo shirt and who tore apart the newspapers at the bookstore: she couldn't recall if she'd even verbally abused him for being such a tightwad.

"This whole exodus to Maine… it's changed me," April finally said, her voice shaking.

"I know it has, but, April, for as much as you love Cole Island and everyone you've met there, you know, deep down inside, that your heart is here."

April mulled the offer over all throughout the evening. Ian had let the subject drop, though he came close to bringing it all up again when he asked her if she'd fallen in love with Walczyk (which, she assured him, she hadn't). She let the thought of Ian's offer tumble around in her mind, like a lone sock in a clothes dryer – not the assistant offer, but the producer position – and the more she thought about it, the more it made sense, and the more it made other things make sense. And the more it all scared the hell out of her.

Walczyk and Vic were lying on the mattress on the floor, staring up at the ceiling. The cheesy-ass horror movie they'd been watching, *Teenagers from Outer Space*, had ended, and the menu screen was still displayed on the TV, casting an eerie glow over the room. At Walczyk's side was a defrosted freezer mug filled with warm rum and Coke; at Vic's side, a bottle of scotch.

"So," Vic said, devoid of energy, "whatcha wanna do?"

Walczyk didn't move. "Another movie?"

The unintelligible noise Vic made in reply gave Walczyk the impression that a movie wasn't quite in order. "We could call Hannah," Vic finally suggested.

"She'd kill us," Walczyk said. "She's got school tomorrow."

"I could call us a couple of girls," Vic said. "Ingrid's got this friend, Jade. She's a cutie. They'd probably get over here in about five minutes."

"Nah," Walczyk said. "I don't think I need a cutie named Jade. And really I don't think you need an Ingrid."

"I'll have you know," Vic said, almost in defense of himself, "that I haven't slept with Ingrid Connary in almost five months. Now *that's* saying something."

"It certainly is," Walczyk offered.

"Seriously," Vic said after a long belch, "you should get to know this Jade girl. She's not really like Ingrid at all."

"Meaning...?"

"Meaning..." Vic began, pausing to think, "You know... that she's not... well... easy."

"Oh," Walczyk said. "Thanks, but no thanks."

"Just thought I'd throw it out there."

"That's mighty fine of you."

Vic chuckled. Walczyk turned to look at him. Vic explained his laughter: "How would you win her back?"

"What?"

"Supposing you could win Sara back with one big romantic gesture. What would you do?"

"Vic..."

"Hey, it's just us, we're pissed drunk, and there's no one else around. If you could win her back with one last romantic gesture what would it be?" Walczyk said nothing. "Come on, Peter, what would you do? Skywriting? Put her picture up on some Jumbotron at a Lakers game? Take out an ad in *Variety* or some shit? If you were guaranteed that making some big, last-ditch romantic gesture would get her back–"

"I'd sing."

"Sing?"

"She's always wanted to hear me sing."

"You're married however long you were married and you

never sang to your wife?"

"Never."

"Why not?"

"Because I can't sing! You've heard me. I'm not musically inclined."

"Not musically inclined? Walz, Buddy, you play the piano!"

"But that doesn't mean I can sing. It just means I can play the piano."

"Still. This is your wife. The woman you vowed to spend the rest of your life with. The woman who's seen every inch of you naked, from every imaginable angle. Who's seen you in sickness and in health. Who's probably seen you take a dump. And you never sang in front of her?"

"Nope," was Walczyk's reply before lying back on the mattress. They lay in silence, staring at the ceiling, for some time. "Yeah. I'd sing for her."

"Do you talk to her any?" Vic asked.

Walczyk rolled over to look at Vic. "Who?"

"Sara."

"Oh. Nope," he replied, rolling back onto his back.

"So it is over," Vic clarified.

"I don't know."

"Do you want it to be?"

Walczyk sat up, downing the remainder of his warm rum and Coke, flopped back down. "In many ways, many, many ways, yes, I wish it was all over. That I was done with her, and that we could become whatever we're going to become next. She wants to keep it friends," Walczyk said, belching. "I don't know. I don't know if I want to keep it friends. Don't know if I *can* keep it friends. There's no doubt about it, Vic: I'm still in love with her. I wish so bad we could erase this whole damned video thing and just get back to what we had. I've had a lot of failures in my life, Vic. Movies. Scripts. Like this thing I'm writing about the guy who cloned his wife. I've been very disappointed with a lot of what I've done. *Ordinary World* has turned into a joke, as far as I'm concerned. An exercise in mediocrity. Everyone's asking how I could walk away from it. It's simple: I hate it. I think it's shit, and I hate it. And, quite frankly, I'm a phone call away from officially turning the whole show over to Ian for good and walking totally away, because there's gonna be a next season, even without me, don't you doubt that for a second, Victor John Gordon. But you want to know what I think my biggest failure is? It's the women in my life. I had a queen; a beautiful, smart, intelligent, caring woman, and I let our relationship sour. I let it self-destruct. I let it crumble up and blow away in the wind like so much dust. I never treated her right. Never. Never gave her the attention she deserved. Never said I'm sorry – and I *am* sorry – for acting the way I did. But that's that, and the cards have fallen where they're going to, and that love is gone, and I'm too stupid to see that I'm one lucky S.O.B. to at least have a friendship with her, because I don't deserve it. I don't." He paused. Vic didn't say anything, so he continued. "I just wish Hannah still loved me. There. I said it. To another living, breathing human being." There was no response. Just silence. "Vic?"

Walczyk rolled over. Vic was lying, passed out, his mouth hanging open, dead to the world.

April hated waking up in a strange bed. Perhaps it was her unerring need to have the home court advantage in every situation. Perhaps it was that pang of guilt that was in her stomach the first handful of times she woke up in someone else's bed, like she'd done something wrong. Or perhaps it was not remembering where she'd left her panties. Any way you roll it, April felt at odds when the day greeted her in Ian Maeder's bedroom. She looked around the room, hoping to find her clothes within arm's reach. Sure enough, in a chair by the door, was the red dress she'd worn to Gordon Ramsay's the night before, neatly folded up for her. She wondered if all of the girls Ian slept with got this treatment.

The door leading to the bathroom opened and Ian walked out, his nude body glistening with the remnants of his shower. His hair was combed straight back.

"Morning," April said from the bed, tugging the covers up under her chin.

"Morning," Ian said, crossing to the dresser on the other side of the room. "Didn't know you were awake."

"Big plans today?" April asked, looking away as Ian slid into a pair of boxers.

"Getting my cuts of episodes five and six ready to send to Walz. Then I have a production meeting at eleven with Sarah Jordan Miller and the suits at Paramount, then it's back to the studio to start in on seven and eight." As he talked, Ian crisscrossed the room, assembling his clothing for the day from a deep closet by the bathroom door to the dresser and back again. He stood, barefoot, in a pair of black dress pants, a deep blue long-sleeved shirt, and a thin pair of black socks in his hand. He moved across to the bed and leaned in, his mouth puckering up as it neared April's. She allowed him to kiss her, then backed away.

"Ian, don't be getting the wrong impression about this."

Ian sat on the side of the bed, taking April's hand in his. "April, since the very first moment I saw you, the day Walczyk hired you, I wanted you. You had it all: you were stunning, intelligent and sassy, and you could appreciate a good *Godzilla* movie."

"Ian..."

"And did I mention modest?" Ian asked, smiling.

"Look," she said, warningly, "last night was–"

"Mind-blowing?" Ian suggested.

April smiled. "And you're–"

"Oh, so very good at what I do?"

None of this was making things any easier for April. She was fully aware of Ian's infatuation with her. The longing glances at cast parties, the thinly veiled sexual innuendo whenever they'd get together. His inability to hold together a serious relationship. April knew that all of this was because Ian was, somewhere deep inside himself, in love with her. He had to be. There was a month and a half where the first thing he said to her and the last thing he said to her whenever they'd bump into one another was that he loved her. April knew that this needed to be handled carefully.

"Listen, I'm trying to be serious," she said.

Ian wiped a hand down his face, removing the smile from his lips, replacing it with a very forced-looking "serious face." April elbowed him, aware of the sheets slipping a little from her chest.

"Please," she pleaded. "Just let me say what I have to say."

Ian's posture changed, and his face straightened out. "Okay, April. What is it?"

"There's been a lot of build-up to what happened last night. A great deal has been made about it in the past." April tried not to listen to herself as she spoke, because she knew it was making little to no sense whatsoever. "Now don't get me wrong, you're a dear, dear friend, and I will always love you for that. And last night, that was something I've needed. For about five months now. But..." she paused, hoping he'd interrupt with the remainder of her sentence. No such luck. "But this," she said, gesturing between them, "this can't go on. Aside from the fact we're currently on two different coasts, there's Walczyk. And if we get involved, we'll end up splitting up eventually. Our own pasts have shown that to be the inevitable outcome of any relationship. And if we give up our friendship for a purely sexual relationship, I'll have lost a good friend, and I can't bear to do that."

April stopped. Ian looked at her for a long moment, digesting what he'd just heard. A smile crossed his lips and he leaned forward and kissed April gently on the mouth. "April, I don't know what else you thought last night was, other than a little intoxicated stress relief."

She felt like such an ass. But despite that, she still couldn't escape what Eli had told her: her heart was here, in L.A.

CHAPTER EIGHT
BANGOR

Vic Gordon turned the Jeep's satellite radio up, blaring out the sounds of Hootie & the Blowfish. He rolled down the window and lit up a cigarette. "I swear to God, Vic, April will *end* me if she knows I let people smoke in here."

Vic exhaled. "Relax, Walz. You can't live your entire life in fear of your assistant, can you?"

"I most certainly can – and will. Watch me."

"Gimme that," Hannah said from the back seat as she slid a pair of hip-hugging jeans up under the floral print skirt she had worn to school.

"Hannah!" Walczyk barked into the back seat as the slender redhead snatched the lit cigarette. "Since when do you smoke?"

"Since seventh period English. Jake Dyer and Eric Bettencourt might just be the death of me yet." She took one more, long drag, then gave the cigarette to Walczyk. "And as far as anyone outside this Jeep is concerned," she exhaled, "I don't smoke."

Walczyk looked around him and smiled, glad to be sharing this road trip with his two best friends. It had been about seventeen years ago that they'd undertaken their first road trip to Bangor: a rendezvous with Hannah's cousin Amber and a showing of *Ace Ventura: When Nature Calls* at the Bangor Mall cinemas in 1995. As predicted, Vic was instantly drawn to Hannah's cousin, which suited Walczyk just fine: it gave him the chance to contemplate making a move on Hannah.

"Look at this," Walczyk said, smiling as he held the smoldering cigarette. "A tradition reborn." He took a drag from the cigarette and offered it to Vic.

"You're not going to get sentimental, take pictures, and cry, are you?" Vic asked.

"No, I'm just saying... We're finally old enough to get into Geddy's in Orono without getting ID'd."

"It's called the Elysium Ultra Lounge now," Hannah said, "and, from what I've heard, it's changed considerably."

"They still serve booze?" Walczyk asked.

"Probably, yeah," Hannah replied.

"Then we'll make a go of it! Anyhow, for nostalgia's sake, there's always the morning after breakfast at the Oronoka."

"The 'Noka closed years ago," Vic said, glumly, taking the cigarette.

"Well, shit, son, what's left up there?"

"There's a Denny's on Hogan Road."

"I didn't leave L.A. to go to Denny's."

"What *did* you leave L.A. for?" Hannah asked. Walczyk ignored the question, leaning his head against the vibrating glass.

"So when does April's flight get in?" Vic inquired, tossing the stub of a cigarette out the window.

"Eleven," Walczyk replied. "And she is pissed. I don't think she's all too keen to return to Maine. Eli said L.A. kind of got to her."

"You're not *making* her stay here, are you?" Hannah asked.

"Of course not. But I *am* paying her, and that's one and the same as far as April's concerned. That, and between a layover in Washington D.C. and asking her to change her final destination from Portland to Bangor so we could go reminiscing... I just don't think she's a happy camper."

"I'm guessing, from your foreshadowing," Hannah remarked, "that a wooden shoe was thrown into the gears of that machine."

"Indeed," Walczyk said. "And, adding insult to injury, we couldn't find anything non-stop to Bangor. So, she had to swallow her pride and fly on the cheap. This, for the girl who says that it's 'first class or kiss my ass.'"

"On the cheap? Like in one of those pontoon planes like Skinner does those Island tours in?"

"On the cheap as in she had to fly coach, though they call it *'consumer class'* now to make it sound fancier. She was at the airport at seven this morning, and has layovers in St. Louis, Atlanta, and D.C. before finally landing in Bangor late at 9:15 tonight."

"So, what's the agenda," Vic asked.

"Well, I need to check on some living room furniture at Dorsey's."

"We should stop at Bull Moose."

"What's Bull Moose?"

"This awesome store that opened up after you left Maine. They've got kick-ass deals on movies, music, books, you name it."

"Okay. Dorsey's, dinner, then this Bull Moose place."

"Well, there's an hour spent," Hannah said. "Please tell me you have other plans."

"Well, I was going to treat you all to dinner at the Oronoka..."

"We could always go to Tesoro's," Hannah suggested, and the primal, approving grunts from Vic and Walczyk let her know that they'd be dining *Italiano* this evening.

"After dinner, I definitely want to go to Dirty Del's," Walczyk said, smirking. Dirty Del's was formally known as Del's Video Store, one of those dusty convenience stores that rented well-worn VHS tapes and sold lottery tickets and overpriced twenty ounce bottles of soda. But that was just the legitimate side of the store. Behind a plaid flannel sheet was a magical, unbelievable, unfathomable three stories of pornographic movies and magazines, condoms of every size, color, flavor, scent, and texture; a wide array of marital aides. The store's front display windows had always featured plain white mannequins dressed in sexy little outfits. No trip to Bangor had ever been complete for the gang unless they stopped by Dirty Del's and dragged poor Hannah through three stories of sheer filth and moral decadence.

"If we're going to Dirty Del's..." Hannah began.

"Which," Vic interrupted, "I read is now called Del's Erotic Supermarket..."

A roar of laughter erupted inside the Jeep at the absurd attempt to make the crotchless panty and sex toy emporium sound like a respectable business. "If we go to Del's..."

"Say it," Vic insisted.

Hannah sighed. "If we go to *Del's Erotic Supermarket*, I'd prefer to go after supper. There's something about those red ball gag thingies that soon before supper that... well, it's just not right."

They all laughed, the words "Erotic Supermarket" spewing out of Walczyk between chuckles.

"Okay, so Dorsey's, dinner, Bull Moose, Dirty Del's–"

"Erotic Supermarket," Vic said in a clipped, low tone.

"Erotic Supermarket," Walczyk corrected, "then on to Tesoro's. And maybe that really rough-looking bar next to the bus station. Or if Han's up for it, maybe Bella's?"

"Eh, you might want to hold off on Bella's," Vic warily.

"Why? It's Bangor Boobs," he proclaimed, remembering his and Vic's shorthand for the topless bar. "Or are they now Bella's Sensual Laundromat?"

"No, they're still Bangor Boobs," Vic said. "It's just that said boobs are covered up now."

"What the hell happened to this damned town?" Walczyk cried. "First, no Oronoka! Then, no Geddy's! Now, Dirty Del's is an Erotic Supermarket and Bella's boobs are covered! Who even heard of a topless bar that didn't go topless? It's absurd!"

"Actually, it's a layer of colored liquid latex painted over the nipples," Hannah said. The boys turned to Hannah.

"Someone's done her home work," Vic said, cautiously eyeing Hannah through the rear-view mirror. "You apply there for a summer job?"

She frowned, disapprovingly, at Vic. "You know the newspaper? That big sheet of white paper with all the words on it? *You* use it to make impressions of the comics on your Silly Putty, Vic. *I*, on the other hand, read it, and it tells me things. Things like that the city of Bangor passed an ordinance prohibiting nudity in a place where alcohol is served."

"The place is dry?" Walczyk complained.

"Nope," Vic picked up. "Instead, the girls all wear booty shorts and, according to Hannah, our expert on nudography, vulcanized nipples."

"You can barely tell the difference." Hannah quickly grimaced.

"Now, how the hell would *you* know *that*, Hannah?" Vic asked.

"Never mind," Hannah said, slinking back in her seat. "I just–"

"You just what?" the boys said in unison, staring at her in the rearview mirror.

She sighed, then relented. "I was there one night."

A screech of tires, a jostling of people, and the Jeep veered to the side of the highway. Vic slammed the Jeep into park, unhooked his seatbelt, and turned around, meeting Hannah's eyes. Walczyk had done the same. The boys sat there, shoulder to shoulder, as stunned as if they'd just learned their mutual ex-girlfriend was not really a demure, intelligent girl from small-town Maine, but a British secret agent, under cover, forced to reveal her identity to the boys to save their lives from a Lithuanian hit man named Itzmek or something.

"What?" she said, sliding as far back into her seat as its construction would allow. She got no answer.

"What is it with the women in my life turning into lesbians?" Walczyk asked, apparently to no one in particular.

"Don't tell me they put the rubber nipples part in your newspaper," Vic said.

Vic and Walczyk looked at each other a moment, unsure how to continue. Vic nodded at Walczyk, prompting him to go first. He turned back to Hannah, no longer the redheaded innocent with whom he had always been embarrassed to watch movies with nudity in them around. A different woman sat in the back seat of the Jeep; a fiery ginger with piercing green eyes and secrets man should perhaps never learn.

"You," Vic began, with pauses between each word, "went to Bella's?"

"Yes," she replied, matter-of-factly.

"For the purpose of seeing the breasts and the bottoms of other girls?" Walczyk finished, being painstakingly clear about what he was saying.

"Yes," she repeated, sounding a bit weary of this line of question. "I was at Bella's. *Once*," she reiterated, as though this were absolutely natural for a conservative, heterosexual woman. "A bunch of us went."

The plot thickened. "Define 'a bunch'," Walczyk demanded.

She rolled her eyes. "This is ridiculous. I went to Bella's two years ago. Me and Ingrid Connary,"

"Yummy," Vic muttered under his breath. Seeing Hannah glare at him, he got serious again. "Continue."

"Ingrid, Jen Provencher, Kat Dennis, Libby Stern, and Kendra Draken," she said, listing off six of their high school classmates. While Walczyk tried to make the connection, Vic gave a loud "aah," indicating that he had put it all together.

"What?" Walczyk asked Vic, who had gone from astonished to amused, the corners of his mouth twitching as he forced himself not to laugh. "Vic, what the hell's so funny?" Walczyk demanded. Vic's only response was a snort of laughter, something unintelligible, and his pulling the Jeep back onto I-95, building up speed to his previous cruising velocity of eighty-five m.p.h. Once Vic locked the cruise back in, Walczyk turned back to Hannah. "Are you going to tell me?" he asked.

"We went to Bella's for bachelorette party."

Vic laughed again.

"I don't see why that's so funny," Walczyk said, looking from Hannah's general direction to Vic, now shaking his head in amusement.

His laughing subsided, Vic said, "Hannah and that lot at a nudie bar? That's not weird?"

"Weird that it's girls at a bachelor party, yes, but not that they'd go to a nudie bar to celebrate."

Vic continued to snicker. "Go ahead and ask her whose bachelor party it was."

Walczyk turned back to April. "Well?"

"Casey German," Hannah finally said.

"Casey German!" Vic chimed in from the front seat, his eyes still on the road.

"Casey German," Hannah clarified, "is a good friend of mine."

"And Casey German is also a lesbo," Vic snickered.

"Casey German is a *lesbian*, yes," Hannah stated, matter-of-factly. "She came out our sophomore year of college. She met a girl, they were perfect for each other, and when Vermont legalized same-sex unions, they decided to get married."

"Lesbionical Matrimony," Vic said, still laughing.

"Actually, Vic," Walczyk said, "it's not so strange. Women are marrying women. Men are marrying men. Lesbian weddings are becoming more and more commonplace. Hell, *I* married a lesbian."

Vic fell silent, remorse filling his eyes. He mouthed, "Oh, God," as though he'd just made fun of a recently deceased loved one. "Jeez, Walz, I am so, so… all those lesbo jokes…"

A peal of laughter came from the back seat. Walczyk turned in his seat to look at Hannah. She slapped two hands over her mouth, no doubt mortified that she'd laughed at Walczyk's marital troubles.

Turning back around, Walczyk smiled, the man that he was now the polar opposite of the man who had confessed his severe depression to his mother not thirty-six hours ago, banging his head against the wall in the midst of a panic attack to silence the racing thoughts in his mind.

Walczyk stared out the window of his room, where he had a spectacular view of the back parking lot. They had made good time, considering their brief roadside interrogation of Hannah. Having made no reservations, Walczyk considered it a mitzvah that he was able to find four single rooms when he walked into the Birch Point Inn, a cozy little B&B right at the intersection of Hogan Road and Stillwater Avenue.

It had been agreed upon between Vic, Walczyk and April that they'd take a half-hour nap, meeting in Walczyk's room around four o'clock to go furniture shopping and out for dinner. Walczyk shook his head, trying to get rid of the distracting thoughts that he found were coming more and more frequently lately. He turned his attention back to the laptop in front of him, and clicked "play" on the media player, filling the small room with the familiar, haunting theme song from *Ordinary World*. Walczyk looked at the monitor, his hand stroking the beard that had started growing the day he told April they were leaving Los Angeles. The episode began, taking him back to the day they'd shot this scene. Just the crew, Ella, and a sea of extras. It had been an exciting day.

A couple of thoughts came to Walczyk and he jotted them down on a yellow legal pad beside the laptop. A knock at the door interrupted him. He stopped playback and walked over to the door, asking along the way, "Who is it?"

"Meg Haskell, *Bangor Daily News*. Mr. Walczyk, is it true you've returned to Maine to open a topless donut shop?"

He yanked the door open. Hannah stood in front of him,

smiling, bouncing on the balls of her feet. "Why? You looking for a job?"

Hannah frowned and entered the room, shutting the door behind her. She flopped onto Walczyk's bed, lying on her chest. "I'm bored."

He smiled. "Funny, I'd have never guessed." He returned to the table in the corner, where he had set up his laptop.

"What are you working on?" she asked. "Your psycho clone wife story?"

He looked at her, suspiciously. "No, that's on the backburner for now."

"So, what is it?" She peered around him, catching a glimpse of the paused video on the laptop. It was a frozen image of Ella, in padding, as a very pregnant Danielle. "Oh! My! God! Is that what I think it is?"

"Yes," he snapped, slamming the laptop shut more forcibly than he'd intended. "But it's top secret. Me, Ian, and our editor, Ray, are the only ones who have seen this, and I intend to keep it that way."

"Fine," she pouted, skulking around the table. She looked out the window and gasped, pointing, "Oh, my God, is that a unicorn!"

For absolutely no good reason, Walczyk leaped up from the table, crying out, "What?!" As soon as he reached the window, he knew he had fallen for the oldest trick in the book. Behind him, Hannah snagged the laptop and ran across the room with it. Walczyk leaped and tackled her on the bed, carefully wrestling the laptop from her as he lay on top of her, keeping her pinned. "What would you have done if you'd broken this, Miss Cooper?"

She considered the question, looking up at him as he pinned her arms to the bed. "Run?"

He laughed, looking into her eyes. He suddenly saw her, eighteen years old, lying in the grass under the thick oak tree at Donny Sullivan's camp. Walczyk was on top of her, holding her hands down, laughing. "I love you, Peter," she had said to him, the purest, most truthful phrase ever uttered on this earth. He stared into her eyes, a lump in his chest cutting off his wind.

"Peter, are you okay?"

The mass cleared, and he automatically sucked in a deep breath of air. When he looked down at her, he realized they were in a motel room, it was fifteen years later, and he had never forgiven

himself for leaving her. He shook his head. "Sorry. Just, uh," he
climbed off her, taking his laptop and walking across the room as she
turned onto her side to watch him. He looked back at her and realized
she still wanted an answer. He improvised with, "Guess I'm just out of
shape."

She sat up, cross-legged, on the bed. "Fine. I can respect your
not wanting me to see the episode until it's a final cut. Can you just tell
me one thing?" He nodded. "What is the deal with Ethan? He's acting
weird. All the panic attacks and memory lapses. And why is he so
angry all the time? What's going on?"

"First of all, that was more than one little question," he said.
He paused, then continued. "Season three is a season about change.
These guys, the core characters, think they've finally got it made. I
think you'll agree, that's part of the illusion when you leave college
and settle into that first job. It's so easy. Things just fall into place. But
there's always that moment, that blink of an eye, when things change
like *that*," and he snapped his fingers for effect. "You wake up one
morning, and it's all different. You don't know who you are, what you
are doing, or why you're doing it. Well, this season opens with the
gang, they're starting to realize things are turning to shit. Season two
ended with the big fight between Ethan and Brad Stone, and Kara
having to bail Ethan out of jail for fighting over another woman. So
that relationship is on the rocks. Danielle took the pregnancy test. I will
tell you that it's positive, and she realizes her life is over, as she sees it.

"Oh, my God," Hannah said her hand over her mouth.
"Danielle's pregnant?"

Walczyk pressed on. "Sis gets the job offer in Ohio, but Eric is
clear about wanting to stay in Maine, so she's deciding if she wants to
stay or go. In all these stories, they're facing decisions that really mean
deciding what they want in life."

"And what do they want?" she asked, curious.

Walczyk shook his head. "That's the problem. We've filmed
the season finale, had the cast party, and neither of us are still unsure as
to what they wanted."

They sat in silence, the unopened laptop in Walczyk's hands,
his eyes on the floor, for several minutes. The silence was finally
broken by a knock on the door, then the shrill announcement,
"Housekeepings. Do youse need fresh towel? Turn down? Meents on
peelow? Sensual massage?"

Hannah bounded across the room and tore the door open. Vic stood in the hall, proud of himself. "Oh, I sorry. Only one per customer."

"Vic, what's up?" Walczyk called out from across the room, locking access to his laptop.

Vic dropped into the overstuffed armchair wedged in between the bed and the table. "I'm bored, Walz," he complained. "That's what's up."

"I think that makes three of us," Walczyk said, closing the lid to his laptop.

The search for furniture was fruitful, with Walczyk finding the perfect recliner with heat and massage, a living room set, a six chair dining room set, and a matching oak desk and bookshelf. A near-hysterical salesman, having recognized Walczyk, promised next-day delivery – despite the next day being a Saturday – and practically wept when he tallied up the bill for Walczyk.

Finding a place to eat, however, had proven more difficult, though. There was a thirty-minute wait at Tesoro's, and most of their old favorite eateries near the hotel were gone; Miller's famous all-you-can-eat buffet was now a McDonald's, Paul's Restaurant was now an Outback Steakhouse, and the rest of Stillwater Avenue was made up of chain restaurants, looking identical to their counterparts across the country, down to the amount of salt put on French fries. It was somehow saddening to Walczyk to see the small, unique Maine businesses being swallowed up and spit out as a giant corporate empire. But all was not lost, when Walczyk recalled his favorite college haunt, a homegrown restaurant in the downtown section of neighboring Orono called Pat's Pizza.

"Who needs Miller's anyway?" Vic asked, his mouth full of hot pizza. "I've always said that Pat's makes the best pizza in Maine. Well, if you can't get Mama Rosa's, that is," he added, making sure to give proper credit to Cole Island's premiere pizzeria.

A small smile crept across Hannah's face, and she leaned over to Walczyk, whispering in his ear. "You see those two guys over there?" She gave a quick point with her nose in the direction of two young men, one portly with a shaved head and glasses, the other skinny with sharp, pointy facial features and a thick mop of dark brown hair.

"You mean Abbott and Costello over there that have been staring at me all night and trying to decide if I'm really me?" Walczyk asked, enjoying the rum and Coke he had before him.

"Yeah, those two," Hannah whispered.

"What about them?"

"Just makes me feel important, you know. Eating dinner with someone that people are staring at."

"People stared at you all the time when you dated Kevin Gellar," Vic said, his mouth full.

"Then let me rephrase: It makes me feel important that I'm eating dinner with someone that people are staring at, and we're not in a filthy pick-up truck eating our dinner from cardboard baskets lined with paper towels. And I didn't date Kevin, Vic! I went on *a* date with him."

"Hannah, it's now fifteen years later," Vic said, pushing his plate aside. "I think we're due an explanation. Just what in the name of blazing hell were you doing on a date with Kevin Gellar?"

"Victor," she hissed.

"No, Vic's right, Han," Walczyk interjected. "What *were* you doing, in a truck, dressed up nice, with Kevin Gellar, who was no doubt wearing that dingy gray 'Coed-Naked Hunting' t-shirt and that deer piss-smelling red and black plaid flannel hunting jacket."

"Kevin was not a bad guy," she said in defense of the boy. "He just came from the wrong side of the tracks."

"You mean the *under*side of the tracks," Walczyk quipped.

"Peter," she scolded.

"Okay, truth time, there, girlie," Vic said, finishing the draft beer in front of him. "What was it with you and those hard luck cases? Kevin Gellar. Shawn Rush. Oh, and let us not forget the infamous Clifford Robinson?"

Walczyk burst into laughter. "Oh, damn," he wheezed between laughs, "I forgot about Eggie Robinson."

Vic had lost it, too, joining Walczyk in a restaurant-disturbing laugh at the expense of Hannah, who glowered from the corner of the booth.

"That was an awful nickname for poor Cliff," she said.

"The man swallowed four boiled eggs, whole," Walczyk said.

"After you offered him forty dollars to do it," she scowled. "And after he did it, you had Thomas Lyons whack him in the stomach with that Wiffle ball bat and make him throw up."

"Throw up what?" Vic said, slowly and clearly. She refused to speak. They poked her. She continued to refuse.

"I'll give you forty dollars to say it," Walczyk said, and Hannah lost her composure, laughing loudly.

"He threw up the eggs."

"I believe the man wants to know what condition were they in?" Vic asked.

"They were whole," she said between giggles. "Whole hard boiled eggs!"

"Hard boiled eggs aside," Walczyk said, fishing out his wallet. "Just why *did* you go on all those dates with all those losers?"

She peered up, keeping her chin tucked to her chest. "Promise not to laugh?"

"No way," Vic said. "I can't, in all good conscience, promise that."

"I went out with them because... well, they were... social misfits. People didn't like them because they were poor or stank or–"

"Or swallowed hard boiled eggs and puked them up whole," Vic said.

"Now wait a minute, Victor. I think there's more to it than that," Walczyk said, challenging her. "What else is there, Han? What's the real secret behind you and your romantic evenings with the Shrek brothers?"

"My mother felt bad for them," she said carefully. "Really bad. So she would ask me to go on dates with them, to make them feel better."

"And you being the decent, up-standing pushover that you are," Vic continued, "got all done up, wore enough perfume to drown their own various stenches out, and showed them one night out with a girl who didn't pronounce the word 'pisketti.'"

"In an obscenely inaccurate nutshell, yes, Victor."

Vic was satisfied, and sat back, pulling out his wallet as the waitress handed out the checks. Hannah started looking for her wallet inside her purse.

"And?" Walczyk asked, not moving.

They looked up at him, Vic confused, Hannah worried. "And what?" she tentatively asked him.

"And what else?" Walczyk asked, tapping the tips of his fingers in a cascading rhythm on the wooden tabletop.

"There *is* nothing else," she said, shaking her head and

returning to her purse.

"But it doesn't fit, Hannah," Walczyk said, leaning forward. "Outside of Vic, and myself, you *rarely* dated in high school. Yet you made time for these rejects from the Island of Misfit Toys. What are you leaving out?"

She looked at him in dismay. A combined look of recognition and horror crossed her face. "No," she pleaded. "Please, Peter, I don't know how you found out, but please, don't tell him."

Vic perked up like a cat hearing a can opener going off. "Please don't tell him what?"

She looked back and forth between the two of them, unable to climb over Walczyk to escape. She looked at him, pleading. "No," she whimpered.

"I'm not going to say a word," Walczyk said, leaning back.

"Oh, thank God!"

"No, I want to hear you say it," he said, taking the checks from Vic and Hannah. "Say it, and we can leave."

"Fine. But before I do, I just want to say that I was still doing a good thing for those poor boys."

"Say it," Walczyk pushed.

"It wasn't my idea. It was my mother's," she wheedled.

"Say it," Vic chimed in.

"She paid me!"

Walczyk stared at Hannah, aghast, shaking his head.

"What the shit did you just say?" Vic asked, stunned.

She sighed. "My mother would give me money to go out with them. I'm not proud of it, but that's what it is.'

"You harlot," Vic whispered, the ghost of a grin growing on his face.

"You Good Will tramp," Walczyk said, still shaking his head.

"What are you so surprised about?" Hannah demanded to know. "You said you knew already."

"No, I didn't," he said. "I made you *think* I knew something because, Class of '96's Most Gullible Girl, I knew you'd spill your guts rather than let someone else do it and not do it properly, with all the backpedaling, assignation of blame, and declarations of purity."

Walczyk got up from the booth and walked down to the large cash register on the counter, which was still invariably manned by the white-haired Bruce, the son of the restaurant's founder.

"Did Eggie throw anything else up?" Vic asked in a hushed tone, leaning across the table.

Hannah, not dignifying that question with a remark, brushed past Vic and started for the counter.

"Do you think that Hannah ever got paid to go out with us?" Vic asked, approaching the counter.

"I'm telling myself she did," Walczyk said, handing his check over to the white-haired man behind the register. "Makes me feel extra dirty, considering all the stuff we did."

"Good call," Vic said.

"Do you think we went too far, though?" Walczyk asked. "You know. Pushing her to spill the beans like that."

"Probably," Vic said.

"Oh, Peter," Hannah called out from behind them. Walczyk collected his change and pocketed it, turning around to see Hannah standing at the table of a pair of twenty-somethings with laptops and notebooks strewn about the table in front of them.

"What's up?"

"Oh, God," a voice called out. It finally dawned on Walczyk who he was looking at: Abbott and Costello who'd been staring at him all through dinner..

"Wow," the fat one uttered. "It's..."

Walczyk shot a look of malice at Hannah. Payback for Clifford Robinson, he knew.

"Look, I know you guys hate getting asked this," the big guy prefaced his request with, "but are you really–?"

Walczyk looked at Hannah, who sheepishly grinned. Walczyk put on his best "public smile" and replied, "I sure am."

The energy level in the booth went up even higher, as the larger boy, clad in a garish Hawaiian print shirt and khaki cargo shorts, despite the cool autumnal weather outside, stuck his hand out. Walczyk shook it. "I'm Kemp Harris," the young man said, eagerly pumping Walczyk's hand.

The skinnier lad, considerably cooler in demeanor than his friend, extended a steady hand, saying "I'm John Sirois."

In the wide eyes of these two guys, probably freshmen or sophomores at the nearby University of Maine, Walczyk couldn't help but see himself and Ian Maeder at that age, bidding goodbye to Hofstra in hopes of striking it big in Los Angeles.

"So, whatcha working on?" Walczyk asked politely, nudging the corner of a sheet of green copier paper with a screenplay printed on it.

They exchanged glances, asking each other through flickers of the eye, if they should. "We're trying to get something going on a horror movie John came up with," Kemp said, picking up some papers. "But we're stuck."

"Yeah, that writer's block can be a bitch, can't it?" Walczyk sympathized, turning to leave. Hannah grabbed him and turned him around.

"Peter, we've got an hour before we have to go get April at the airport. I'm sure that's more than enough time to give them a nudge in the right direction." She turned to the two young guys. "Walczyk's kind of stuck on the upcoming season of *Ordinary World*. You see–"

"What are we looking at?" Walczyk interrupted, picking up one of the bound copies.

"Well, I had this idea for a horror movie," John said, opening his own copy of the thin screenplay. "This guy gets married, and driving to their honeymoon, the car leaves the road and his wife dies."

"Okay," Walczyk said, leafing through the script. "So what happens to this guy then?"

The students exchanged looks, grinning, not really believing this themselves. "Well," John continued, "Bill, that's the widower, he gets approached by this mad scientist who wants to bring Bill's wife, Sally, back to life."

"Let me guess," Walczyk said, shifting his weight, "you're doing this straight." It wasn't a question. It was a statement. And, judging from the nervous glances between John and Kemp, an accurate one.

"Yeah," Kemp meekly replied.

"Well," Walczyk said, closing the script and putting it down on the table, "as a *Saw* meets Zack Snyder's version of *Dawn of the Dead*, modern-age torture porn movie kind of thing, it sucks." Hannah elbowed Walczyk in the ribs, hard. The boys' faces drained of color as they no doubt contemplated their life's work being shredded by those two little words. "But," Walczyk added, picking up the script again, "with a different approach, you might have something."

"What kind of approach?" John asked.

"Well, and trust me on this, you don't want to take a modern approach to a horror movie."

"Why not?" Vic asked from behind him.

"Because modern horror movies suck. Now, two bits of advice," Walczyk said, flipping quickly through the script. "One: don't take yourselves too seriously; that's where you're screwing this whole thing up. Remember that, other than a plus sign on a pregnancy test, there are no more new scares to be had. You can either ignore that fact, try, and fail, or you can acknowledge it, work around it, point it out, or make it work to your advantage, and wind up with a good picture."

"Uh," John asked, "what's number two?"

"For the love of God, change that title. Who the hell's going to see a picture called *Where the Dead Walk*." He opened the script he'd been thumbing through, scribbling his e-mail on the inside cover, and tossed it back to Kemp. "When you've done your fourth draft, shoot me an e-mail. I'd like to see what you've come up with." Walczyk turned to Vic and Hannah, and the three walked out of Pat's Pizza into the brisk October night.

"Oceanic Airlines is pleased to announce the arrival of its flight 9678, Philadelphia to Bangor. Passengers will be disembarking the plane at Gate Four."

It had been a long time since he'd been to Bangor International Airport, as his flights generally flew into Portland. Being in the terminal, regardless of the changes made to it since his 2005 visit home, still reminded him of Grammie Reynolds' death, and his hasty return to Maine with his then-fiancée, Sara, to be with his family. They had arrived late and the terminal was partially darkened, as it was now.

He tried shaking himself out of the difficult memory, one where he cursed himself for not visiting his grandmother more before dementia muddled her mind for the last nine months of life. He found Hannah reading a travel magazine she'd found on a bench, published by one of the airlines, that gave tips for expediting your trip through security. Vic was on his phone, getting a rundown of the day's business from a very harried chef-turned-assistant manager Andrew, filling the silences with the token "yeps," "uh-huhs," and "nopes" that made up roughly seventy-five percent of Vic's telephone vocabulary.

Walczyk was wondering if the Red Baron Bar and Lounge was still upstairs, where he would sit during his freshman year of college, back when a person could wander into an airport and sit around for hours without a government screening. He would spend weekends watching people traveling back and forth through the terminal, hastily writing character sketches of the commuters, fantasizing about what they were really like. He looked around the terminal. An old man in the suede jacket, he was an English professor at St. Michael's College in Vermont, slipping up to Maine for a quick romp with his girlfriend, a former grad student who was now teaching at John Bapst High School. A woman in jeans and a Bangor High sweatshirt was not happy about having to pick up her mother-in-law, who was arriving from Massachusetts for an extended visit. These character sketches, pure conjectures and admittedly having little chance of being accurate, were actually quite useful in creating and filling out several of the characters in his student films.

A murmur of excitement filled the downstairs of the airport, as the first passengers started flowing down the two escalators, flying into the arms of loved ones or finding a quiet corner to stand in silence until their luggage had come through. Walczyk began scanning the passengers, guessing where they'd come from, what they did, and why they were in Maine.

The twenty-something mother with the baby carrier: she was coming home from her parents' place in Detroit, introducing them to her newborn son, and missing her investment banker husband badly. Her name was Shauna Bradley.

The scrawny, bearded student in the green army surplus jacket: he's an earth sciences student at Husson, returning from New York where he had gone to celebrate his one year anniversary with his girlfriend, one of those patchwork skirt-wearing hippie girls. His name was Phil Rush.

The well-dressed young woman with the scowl on her face: she's an assistant to someone very important. Possibly someone famous. Her boss made her move to Maine, then sent her back to California to clean his house out. Her name was April Donovan.

And April Donovan pushed her way through Shauna (and Baby) Bradley, Phil Rush, a butcher, a baker, and a candlestick maker. She was dragging a very large carry-on bag.

"Welcome back, kid!" Walczyk said, reaching out to give her a hug.

She did not budge, did not take her eyes from him, and certainly did not give him a return hug. She barely moved her mouth as she said, in measured tones, "Let's go."

Without waiting for anyone else to say hello, or even agree that they were ready to go, for that matter, April started for the door, shoving the rather heavy, clanging carry-on into Vic's arms. "And the award goes to..."

"What about your bags?" Hannah called out to April, who had already triggered the automatic door.

"They'll send them to Cole Island when they find them." She walked out of the terminal.

Walczyk turned to find Vic pawing through the contents of the carry-on April had thrust at him. His hand came out of the bag, clutching a towel-wrapped statue. Vic unwound the towel, and seeing what it was, nearly dropped it.

"Vic, be careful with my Oscar," Walczyk called out. "I don't know when I'll win another one."

No one, not even April in her foul travel mood, felt much like sitting around the hotel after getting back from the airport. After April showered and changed into clothes she'd borrowed from Hannah, Walczyk swung by Best Buy to make a few essential purchases – that seventy inch flat panel TV for the living room he'd been dreaming of, three thirty-two inch TVs for the bedrooms and his office, an X-Box 360, a PlayStation 3 and a Wii (He and Vic couldn't decide which console to go with), Blu-ray players to go with all of the TVs, and a surround sound set-up for the living room, which Vic promised he could install himself, saving Paul the salesman the worry of figuring out how to get to Cole Island and back during a business day.

After the purchases had been set aside in Best Buy's stock room for pick-up Sunday, it was April who decided that a night of drinking and merriment was in order, and that found them all at the Blue Moon in downtown Bangor, a trendy little nightspot that seemed to cater to all types. A half-hour later, all worries were forgotten...

"My friends, they're the best friends!" Walczyk announced, his glass in the air. Smiles of recognition crossed the faces of Vic and Hannah as they looked at to their happy friend across the table from them.

"Loyal, willing, and able!" Hannah recited, raising her pear martini.

"Now let's get to drinking!" Vic chimed in, lifting his pint of dark, thick Guinness to his friends.

"All glasses off the table!" Walczyk, Vic and Hannah shouted, each draining their glass immediately. Vic was the first done, slamming his empty pint glass on the table, a thin tendril of foam sliding down the inside of the glass. Hannah was next, surprisingly, clanging her martini glass against the table, gasping for breath as she laughed. Then Walczyk put his glass on the table, ice and a lime all that remained of his Bacardi and Coke.

"What the hell was that?" April asked, her untouched Kamikaze still in her hand.

"That," Walczyk said, already looking around for their petite waitress, who had either been checking out Hannah or himself most of the night, "was my Uncle Leroy's trademark toast. Never mattered what the holiday or occasion was – Thanksgiving, Christmas, New Years, weddings, funerals, and boat christenings, he didn't have a drink without reciting it, and he never recited it alone."

"Don't forget Fourth of July barbecues," Vic piped in. "He'd set it to music on the Fourth."

"And Fourth of July barbecues, of course," Walczyk said. "I taught that toast to these guys the summer before we started high school. After God knows how many months of pleading, begging, washing dishes – without being asked – and other brown nosery, we managed to talk our parents into letting us go on a camping trip together, unchaperoned, down on this beach clearing just off the main road that cuts through the Back Nine."

"And Victor," Hannah butted in, "thought that, since we were now adults, that we needed to start acting it."

"So," Walczyk said, waving the waitress back over to their table, "Vic steals this bottle of Johnnie Walker from–"

"Black Label," Vic said, laughing. "Johnnie Walker *Black Label*."

"I think it's just called 'Black Label,'" April said, sipping at her drink.

"Doesn't matter," Walczyk said, grinning. "Vic wouldn't let us call it just 'Johnnie Walker'. It had to be Johnnie Walker *Black Label*."

"It's what the bottle said," Vic insisted, defending that decades-old decision. Turning to the waitress, asked, "Could we get another round, Hun?"

"So, he steals this bottle of Johnnie Walker Black Label,"

Walczyk specified, getting a nod of approval from Vic, "from his old man's store room. The first weekend in August, the three of us load up our backpacks and hit the road, embarking on an epic four and a half mile pilgrimage from my house to that little clearing near the beach. That's when we realized two very important things."

"What's that?" April asked, interested.

"You can't pitch a pup tent on the beach," Vic said, shaking his head. "Just doesn't work."

"And?" April asked, edging out of the way as the waitress weaved around the table, collecting empty glasses and dropping off fresh ones wordlessly.

"That three soon-to-be high school freshman, hormones in full bloom," Hannah said, showcasing a trait of over-enunciating the first word in each sentence, a trait that only emerged when she drank, "can have a hell of a time with a bonfire, three sleeping bags, and a bottle of Johnnie Walker."

"Johnnie Walker *Black Label*," Vic corrected before taking a hard swig of his beer.

"So, anyway," Walczyk continued, "we set up camp, build a fire, and enjoy some baked beans, straight from the can," Walczyk said. "Vic and I wanted to get into the booze right off the bat, but Hannah said that only winos, alcoholics, and low class people drink before seven."

"And I still believe that," she said, poking the table top with her finger, a generous portion of her second pear martini already gone.

"So, we wait till seven – on the dot – and we break out the hooch," Vic said. "We make Hannah take the first sip, you know, in case our parents were hiding in the bushes, waiting for alcohol to pass our lips and turn us into sinners. Then we began a wholesome evening of playing *Never Have I Ever* and making fun of Alfred Rooney because he didn't have a mommy."

"That's awful!" April said, astonished.

"Why? You never played *Never, Have I Ever* when you were a kid?"

She glared across the table at him, taking notice of the fascinating shade of blue his eyes were. "No, that you made fun of this Alfred kid for not having a mother. You didn't have a mother!"

"Yeah, but people *liked* me. I didn't come to school smelling of deer piss."

"You mean he… did a deer actually piss on him?"

"It was buck lure, but whatever," Walczyk clarified, taking another drink. "Boy stank!"

"So three drunk teenagers, on a beach, with no supervision," April began. "Who got naked first?"

"No one got naked," Hannah said, defensively. "We might have all slept in our underwear, but that was it."

"Why your underwear?"

Vic belched. "Because Hannah's a prude."

"Vic," April hissed, elbowing him.

"I gotta go pee," Hannah said, quickly leaping up from the table. As she stepped away from the table, she stopped behind April's chair. Eventually, April looked up. "Oh, right. Girl has to go pee. Other girl goes with her. Forgot. My bad."

April dragged herself to her feet and trotted off to the bathrooms with Hannah.

"Wanna check out the upstairs?" Vic asked, picking up his glass.

"Why not?" Walczyk said, grabbing his Bacardi and Coke. They started toward the back of the bar, where the stairwell was.

"So, what's the deal with April?" Vic asked, as they mounted the stairs at the rear of the bar, curious as to what lay above the narrow strip that was the first floor, a bar on one side and a line of booths and high tables on the other.

Walczyk turned to Vic, giving him a curious glance. "You mean the *deal* deal, right?"

Vic nodded as they turned and headed up another short stretch of stairs. "I mean, if you don't mind. After all, she is a woman in your employee."

"Don't make me sound like her pimp, Vic," Walczyk said, stepping into the second floor bar. "But seriously. When she's not on the job–"

"–you don't care if she's *on the job*," Vic said, grinning and elbowing Walczyk.

Walczyk reached out, putting his hands on Vic's shoulders. "Victor, if a decent, clean cut, restaurant managing good ol' boy from Maine can wine and dine the Donna Karan pants off a born in the city/die in the city woman like April Donovan, then I wish him the best of luck."

The boys looked around the upper level of the Blue Moon, and found themselves feeling as though they had entered an entirely different joint. A row of tables dotted the wall opposite another bar, which this time was a real bar, solid oak top, mirror decorated with postcards and photos, bottles of anything you could ever want to inebriate yourself with. Deciding against making their way through the thick wall of people standing between them and what looked like a pool table, Vic and Walczyk instead bellied up to the bar, hoisting themselves onto padded wooden stools.

The bartender, while deftly spinning multiple bottles at once, looked harried as he tried to get drink orders out before he forgot them. While the downstairs area was a relaxing lounge, it was clear that the upstairs division was a serious good, old fashioned bar, with booze, NESN on the TV, and a standing-room-only atmosphere. Seeing Vic and Walczyk sit, the bartender gave them a silent "just a second" finger, then went back to work.

Vic's "no worries" went unheard over the din of the partying masses drowning him down to a merely audible murmur.

"So, since you brought it up," Walczyk said, resuming the subject, "what are your intentions towards my assistant?"

"Well, sex comes to mind," Vic said bluntly.

"Sex always comes to mind," Walczyk said.

"True," Vic conceded. "But honestly, I don't know. She's mouthy, bitchy, rude, inconsiderate, conceited, self-centered, cutthroat, manipulative, impatient… did I mention rude?"

"Possibly," Walczyk said.

"Well, it bears repeating. Rude, unappreciative, confusing, alluring, seductive, large breasted, and hot damn does she fill out a bikini properly."

"Well, that just about covers it, doesn't it?"

The bartender finally made his way down to their end of the bar, tired but putting on a good face. "What can I get you?" he screamed, his increased volume sounding like a mumble over the noise.

Vic and Walczyk exchanged looks before Vic yelled out, "Two Johnnie Walkers!"

"Black Label!" Walczyk quickly added, and the bartender nodded and turned away.

"So, what do you think?" Vic asked.

"April? She's different," Walczyk said, choosing his words

carefully.

"How different?"

"That list you rattled off? Rude to stacked and everything in between?" Vic nodded. "Well, problem is, she's well aware of all of it. She's a powerful woman, and a difficult one to sum up."

The bartender delivered the two drinks, and Vic slipped him a twenty before Walczyk could reach for his wallet. "This one's mine, kid," Vic said, grinning. "You were saying?"

"April's a formidable woman, to say the least. I've seen her make A-list stars – and I'm talking celebs of the internet sex tape, foreign baby adoption, or head butting gay fashion designers variety – into rethinking their accepting or passing on a picture. I stood by, dumbfounded, as she tore into a certain CGI-obsessed writer/director at the premiere of the final installment of his galactic space opera, because he simply asked her afterwards what she thought. This is the girl, Victor, whose break-up with a certain brooding, James Dean-esque actor sent said actor over the edge and into the Horizons rehab facility for two months."

"Come on!" Vic said, clearly not buying it. "April did not send anyone to rehab and she certainly didn't make what's-his-face cry."

"Suit yourself," Walczyk shrugged, enjoying the familiar taste of Black Label. "But she *did* land Alyson Hannigan for *Things People Do*."

"Yeah, but she and Alyson Hannigan are best friends," Vic countered. "But point taken. She's a strong, persuasive woman. It'll be damned-near impossible to trick her into any sort of... conjugation, improbable to sufficiently impress her enough to make her throw herself at me, and unlikely that my dumb Maine hick charm will reduce her to a quivering mass of something that wants to see my cramped bedroom."

"Actually, being your plain, simple, uncomplicated self will get you very far with her."

"Really?"

"Well, that and lots of alcohol." Vic gave him a look. "Trust me on this, Victor, I have knowledge – don't ask what kind, or how – but I have knowledge that might help you, but only if she's already somewhat interested."

"Because you banged her already, right?" Vic asked.

Walczyk turned, shocked. "How did you–?"

"Please! You two have it written all over yourselves!"

"How so?"

"You eat, sleep, and breathe together and there is no sexual tension? You're at ease around each other; the kind of ease that exists between two people only after they've slept together and have managed to keep intact whatever relationship existed before said fornication."

"So, like you and Hannah," Walczyk said, finishing his Black Label.

"Exactly." Vic dryly replied.

A cheer erupted from the crowd, and Walczyk and Vic turned to see the game winning home-run in last night's World Series game being replayed on *Sports Center*.

"How'd you figure it out? Hannah tell you?" Vic asked.

"Second time we got together to catch up. But to her credit, she never said a word. Not with her mouth."

"'Never said a word not with her mouth?'"

"It was her eyes."

Vic nodded. "Sorry about that. I haven't exactly felt great about keeping it from you myself."

"I don't see why you guys are so bothered by it. I'd left her, and not in a good way. I'd gotten married and moved on. I'd hoped she'd moved on. Frankly, I'm glad it was you and not someone like Dougie Olsen or Alfred Rooney."

"Why's that? Roon the Goon's not that bad a guy."

"No, it's because whether or not things panned out for you two, I know you'd have still been her friend in the end."

"And that's exactly what we are now. Friends."

"Just like me and April," Walczyk said, finding his head feeling thick as he nodded.

"Exactly. Like you and April. Like me and Hannah. There's no sexual tension there, what-so-ever. No physical attraction. And no necessity for being anything other than what you really are – really, really good friends. None. Because we've done it. We've each of us reached the highest plateau of friendship that can ever exist in a relationship. A pure, worry free, pretense free friendship," Vic said, swaying on his stool, "with no sexual tension at all. You and Hannah and me and April."

"Yeah," Walczyk said, lips feeling thick, his mind thicker. "No sexual tension at all."

"So," Hannah said, enjoying the chance to spend time with the woman who probably knew Peter better than anyone else on the planet, "you said you visited some friends while you were in L.A."

Silences were uncomfortable enough for her just between people she knew well, let alone between people she'd just met. But she'd quickly learned that silences were to be expected with April. She figured it was because April was actually comfortable with these periods of awkward noiselessness.

"Yeah," April finally said after a long silence. "I thought about hooking up with this guy I'd been seeing before I left. Derrick." She pointed to an empty table in the corner and Hannah followed her, sitting opposite her.

"Nice," Hannah said, genuinely pleased for April.

"But I decided not to. Too much back story there."

"Oh," Hannah said. "What does Derrick do?"

"He's a graphic artist. Works in advertising."

"What'll you have?" their waitress asked, slipping up to the table unseen.

"Pear martini," Hannah said, feeling silly drinking such a childish drink.

"Scotch and soda," April ordered. The waitress disappeared.

"So he's a graphic artist. That's so neat. Has he worked on anything I'd have seen?"

"He designed the print ad campaigns for *Ordinary World*," April said, flagging down the waitress. "Posters, billboards, bus signs, newspaper and magazine ads."

"Nice. So this Derrick... he was your boyfriend"

"I never use that word. But if I did, the answer would be yes. He was. Until I left L.A."

"Oh. I'm sorry."

"Don't be. I ended it."

"Why? Did he cheat on you? Because so many of them cheat on you now. It's disgusting."

"No, he didn't cheat on me. He... he treated me the best I'd been treated in a long while."

"Then what?"

"The night Walczyk found out... about Sara... Derrick told me he loved me."

Hannah stared dumbly at April, unable to articulate her confusion. "Never heard of it working that way. Usually it's..."

The waitress returned, dropping off the drinks. April handed over her credit card. "Start a tab? Both of us?" The waitress nodded, and took off.

"April, you didn't have to do that."

"I'm sure, by the time I've left Cole Island, I'll have received the same favor from you."

That clenched it for Hannah. They were best friends now. She smiled, her mouth feeling a bit numb. "So, will he do the next season of *Ordinary World*? I mean, considering what happened to you two–?"

"I hope he does. He's a brilliant artist."

"That must be so much fun," Hannah said. "Being around of all those famous people."

"Eh, it has its up and downs," she said, taking a generous sip from her glass.

Hannah's head jerked as she tasted the bitter drink April had ordered for her. "Do you have any family out that way?"

"What family I have is spread across the country."

"I can't imagine. Everyone in my immediate family lives within a forty mile radius. My folks moved to Boothbay Harbor shortly after I started teaching. My only living grandparent, my Grammie Allen, lives at the Silver Pines Retirement Community just this side of the Back Nine. I'm an only child, and my mother was an only child, so I don't have any aunts, uncles, or cousins."

"Guess you need to make sure you have a lot of kids," April said.

"So who else did you see? Anyone famous?"

"Sorry, Han, but I don't name drop."

"Oh. Sorry." Hannah was rather disappointed, not that April didn't want to talk celebrities, but that she'd just barely established a rapport with her. "I crossed a line. Sorry."

"Okay. Hannah," April said, taking Hannah's hand in hers. "Listen to me: I snap at everyone. If you pull up into your shell and stare at the floor every time I'm abrupt with you, we're going to have a hard time being friends."

Hannah laughed, having a hard time thinking of what she needed to say. "I want to dance," was the great revelation she'd landed upon.

April laughed. "With anyone in particular?"

"I don't know," she said, not opposed to finding Peter. "Maybe."

April got up and grabbed Hannah's arm, dragging her along as they walked towards the stairs at the rear of the downstairs section. "I wondered what the deal with that was," April said, having a hard time controlling Hannah and the two Kamikazes as she steered the lightweight towards the stairs. "All these years, all that sexual tension building up. He's a damned sexy man, Hannah. If I could, I'd be tempted to give you a run for your money."

"No, you wouldn't," Hannah said, poking April in the chest with a finger. "You're my best friend now. You'll just have to take the other one!"

"You don't drink often, do you?"

"Not at all," she said. "I can't. I'm a teacher. I can't have the kids knowing I drink. They'd be disappointed that I'm like them." Then she burst out laughing.

April turned away, scanning the room for Walczyk and Vic, but it was her inebriated friend who tracked them down first.

"Peter Henry Walczyk!" Hannah shrieked across the room, jumping up and down and waving her arms.

April pushed Hannah's waving arm down, shushing her. Folks near her turned, looked, and pointed, and began talking excitedly amongst themselves. Vic and Walczyk got up from the bar, Vic apparently in no better shape than Hannah.

"See those two girls?" Vic said, pointing to two sundress-wearing girls who were watching Vic and Walczyk as he spoke. "They're college girls."

"I'd never have guessed," April said dryly.

"Want a drink, April?" Walczyk said, staggering over to April and putting his arm around her. Without waiting for a reply, he screamed at the bartender, "Evan! Evan!" The bartender looked in Walczyk's direction. "She wants a Kamikaze. Me too. Two Kamikazes!" The bartender nodded, and Walczyk grabbed the girls by the hand, dragging them through the throng of people to a table way in the back, tucked in the corner across from the pool table.

"So how's it going?" Walczyk slurred, April pushing his arm off of her shoulders.

"Really good," Hannah said, throwing her arm around April's

shoulder. "April and I are officially BFFs. She said so downstairs."

"Where the hell are those damned drinks?" April muttered, removing Hannah's arm.

"She told me was sleeping with the guy who made that pictures for your show," Hannah told Walczyk, slumping into his shoulder. "I bet they made a cute couple. But that they're not a couple like you and me were."

Walczyk laughed. "No one was a couple like you and I were."

Vic emerged from the wall of bodies, two drinks in hand. Behind him, Marika, one of the waitresses, brought the other two -- all Kamikazes. Vic thanked her, giving her a tip, and sat down in the empty chair in the corner beside April.

"My best friends, they *are* my bestest friends," Hannah said, teetering between Walczyk and April.

"Loyal! Willing! And able!" Vic chanted, banging his glass on the table between words.

Walczyk emptied about half of his glass, before continuing, "Now let's get to drinking!"

All eyes were on April, who shook her head once before raising her glass. "Now get your asses off the table?"

Walczyk slammed against the door of his hotel room, his balance thrown off by the sheer volume of alcohol in his system and the weight of Hannah crashing into him. He gave her a stern shush, which only resulted in an even louder "You shush!" from Hannah.

Walczyk finally got Hannah on the bed, where she could do no damage, and staggered to his laptop. He knew he couldn't reply to e-mails like this, but he could read them. He knew if he went to bed in the state he was in right now, he'd never get to sleep and he'd probably get sick from Hannah tossing and twitching on the bed.

The TV snapped on behind him and he listened. A complete circuit through the channels only confirmed his memory that there was never anything on television after two in the morning.

His inbox had a few random e-mails from HBO suits about the show, four different e-mails from Eli marked "Production Opportunity: Read," and an e-mail from Sara that he'd probably delete.

"Hey, you're on TV!" Hannah squealed. Walczyk turned, and saw an episode of *Ordinary World* rerunning on HBO Signature. He got up, lumbered over to the bed, and sat beside Hannah, who was lying on her stomach, her feet tapping the headboard.

Hannah leaned her head against his thigh, and he looked down. She'd rolled over onto her back, looking up at him, smiling. He smiled back, letting those green eyes suck him back in to memories of sharing her with Vic as a prom date. Skipping school senior year and going to that water park in Trenton, still able to smell the sea air and see the sun glinting off the water cascading down the curves of the blue and pink flower print bikini she was wearing. Her hugging his arm on the beach the morning after the Johnnie Walker Black Label night.

The memories vanished into an amber-colored as she rolled over again to continue watching the episode, her long, fragrant red hair filling his field of vision.

On TV, Kara tore up the letter she'd left on the counter and walked out of Ethan's life with no notice. Eric and Alyssa enjoyed their weekly cross-country phone call. Ethan showed up at Danielle's apartment, and the camera faded out on their backwards stumble, kissing, into her bedroom. The camera tracked into the bathroom. On the top of the trash can, a pregnancy test. Positive. Fade out.

Hannah rolled back over, butting Walczyk's leg with her head. "What then?"

"Then," Walczyk said, "Hannah Cooper went to bed."

"Aw!"

"Seriously. You've had a long night, Buttercup."

He reached out for her hand. She took his hand, and tugged, somehow assuming her small frame could tug his large body onto the bed. He tugged back, pulling her partway up from the bed. She let go of his hand, giddily crashing back down against the mattress. He reached out again. She refused to take his hand, repeating, "Then what?"

"'Then what' what?"

"Then what *happens*, silly," she snapped, smirking. "I wanna see the new episode!"

"Sorry, Hun," he said. "Can't."

"Come on! It's on your computer."

"A rough cut is, yeah."

"Well, then give me that. I want to be the first girl in the world to ever see it! I want to be special."

"Trust me, Han: you're special," he said. Those green eyes wouldn't break away from his. Finally, he breathed out, knowing what he had to go. He got up and moved for the table. He picked up his laptop and, kicking his shoes off, climbed onto the bed beside Hannah, propping himself up with one of the hotel pillows and his own, personal pillow, getting comfy. Hannah rolled over, climbing up onto her hands and knees, and fixed the other hotel-issue pillow beside Walczyk, and unbuttoned her shirt, peeling it off and leaving her in a white cotton camisole. She made a deal out of kicking her shoes off, landing one in the small grey plastic trash can beside the dresser and the other on top of Walczyk's canvas sneakers.

"Are you quite ready now?" he asked, watching her as she obsessively smoothed out her skirt over her thin, pale legs.

"Quite," she replied, leaning back against Walczyk.

With a few clicks of the mouse, a caption came on the laptop screen: "Six Months Later." Walczyk nervously watched Hannah, not the monitor, as the scene faded in on a vast maze of phone sales cubicles. Agents talked into headsets, their customers unheard as the camera panned through the aisles. After four or five cubicles, and snippets of their conversations, the camera stopped at Danielle Travers, the character played by the infamous Ella Marsters. Danielle was on a call. As she talked, she stood, stretching. It was clear that she was around six months pregnant.

Walczyk looked down, expecting to see a shocked Hannah. Instead, he saw a passed out Hannah, her face nestled into his shoulder. He closed the laptop carefully and let his head loll back, spent but satisfied. He kissed her gently on the top of her red head and reached over, snapping off the nightstand light.

Seventeen rooms down the hall, April awoke with a start, the mental image of herself driving over a cliff in her Jeep stamped into her still cloudy brain. She slid out of bed and walked noiselessly across the room to the bathroom. Snapping on the light, the loud mechanical "whrrr" of the overhead fan and the reflection of naked herself staring back at her in the mirror jumped her. She shook off the shock, unwrapped one of the shrink wrapped plastic cups left on the countertop, and filled it with cold water. She drank the cup down quickly, and half of another before dumping the remains. She shut the light off and walked back to bed.

She slid under the crisp covers, knowing they weren't ones she'd had Walczyk pack ahead of time in her emergency kit, but she was too tired to complain as they slid along her bare body. Resting on her side, she shut her eyes again, hoping to gain unconsciousness as easily as she had mere hours ago.

Behind her, Vic Gordon's hand slid over her bare stomach, tugging her towards his body. "You okay?" he asked, his lips brushing the microscopic hairs on her ear.

She most certainly was not okay.

CHAPTER NINE
WHAT HAPPENS IN BANGOR...

Hannah Cooper awoke early Saturday morning to the sound of a shower thrumming within the bathroom behind her. The TV had already been turned on and was tuned to some cable news channel (which side they leaned towards, Hannah couldn't tell). Coffee dripped from the small in-room coffee maker. Hannah shuffled her legs in bed. She quite enjoyed the feel of the crisp hotel sheets. She sat up, reaching instinctively for her glasses, but soon noticed a stiff, gunky feeling in her eyes that meant she'd slept with her contacts in. She blinked repeatedly, trying to clear her field of vision. Then reality returned to her: she wasn't in her room, nor was she alone.

Details of the events of the previous evening were a blur to her. She remembered the Blue Moon and the Johnnie Walker (*Black Label*) that she shared with Peter and Vic and April, the first time she'd had it in years. She vaguely remembered talking with April about boys. She had the feeling that the two had finally broken through that barrier of awkwardness that kept them from being friends. It was the trip to the upstairs part of the bar that served as the point at which she stopped remembering anything but snapshots of events. She remembered a cab ride somewhere. And there was breakfast, possibly at a Denny's, but she was unable to differentiate whether or not that was a memory from this trip or a road trip to Portland with Cameron for a *Star Trek* convention.

She shrugged off the confusion, chalking it up to a fun night that could be over and done with, with no ill consequences, and slid out of bed. She crossed the room, moving over to the table and pouring herself a cup of coffee. Walczyk's laptop sat open on the table by the window. She took a curious glance at it, awakening another memory from her drunken last night: Walczyk had shown her the first episode of the new season. She remembered none of it. A legal pad beside the computer had a string of notes scribbled incomprehensibly in the margins.

Across the room, on one of the bedside tables, her phone began ringing. She rushed to the phone, picked it up, and flipped it open.

"Hello?"

"Morning, Han," the cheerful voice of Cameron Burke called out.

"Hey, Cameron. What's up?"

"You, apparently."

"Why wouldn't I be up."

"Well, I figured with all the drinking and partying..."

"What drinking and partying?" She was beginning to grow curious about the nature of Cameron's call.

"The drinking and partying that I'm looking at right now."

"Cameron, you're not making any sense. I'm in..." she stopped herself. She knew that nothing happened in Peter's hotel room, and Peter knew that nothing happened in Peter's hotel room, but the rest of the world might not be so willing to give her the benefit of the doubt. Even a good friend like Cameron Burke. "I'm in the hotel still."

"But you weren't at twelve-thirty last night."

"No, I was out with Peter, Vic, and April."

"Don't I know it."

"If you have a point to make, Cameron, please make it. I've still got to get packed and see when everyone else wants to take off."

"It's paparazz-eye.com. Just check it out."

"How? I don't have a computer with me."

"You'll find one," he assured her. "See you when you get back, Kid!"

"See you, Cam," she said, shaking her head as she shut the

phone and tossed it onto the rumpled bed. She spied Walczyk's computer and wondered if he'd mind her borrowing it for a moment, to check out this mysterious e-mail. She rapped softly on the bathroom door. "Peter?"

There was no response.

"Peter, it's Hannah. Is it okay if I use your computer to check my e-mail?"

"Sure," is what the response sounded like. Wondering why all of the men in her life had to be so darned weird, she crept across the hotel's carpeted floor and sat down behind the laptop. She lifted the lid up, revealing the screen. She clicked a few buttons and got the web browser up. She went to her e-mail account and read the one-sentence e-mail from Cameron. It was a web link. She clicked it and a video began.

Thankfully, the video had been short. Taken with a shaky cell phone, it lasted only two minutes, forty-five seconds.

But Hannah had to speak to Peter. Now. She rushed across the room to the bathroom door and knocked again. "Peter."

Again, there was no reply.

"Peter, can you open up? I need to talk to you."

Nothing.

"Peter!"

Again nothing. It wasn't like Peter to ignore someone knocking at a door, even if he was busy. Flashes of worst case scenarios flew through her brain. Images of her friend lying in a pool of his own blood in the bathtub, his head cracked open. Hesitantly, she reached down and tried the handle. It opened without resistance. "Peter?" she called as she slowly pushed the bathroom door open. A blanket of steam wafted toward her. The shower was running. *Lying in a pool of his own blood in the bathtub, his head cracked open…*

"Peter?" she called again, beginning to be very, very worried.

She slowly crept toward the bathtub.

She slowly reached forward and touched the shower curtain. It fluttered under her fingers. She swallowed hard, grabbed it, and yanked it open.

On the floor of the bathtub, steaming water pelting down at his pale skin, Peter Walczyk lie, curled up in a ball, his head banging softly against the side of the tub.

"Peter!" Hannah cried out, reaching for him. He didn't

respond. He simply continued banging his head against the wall of the tub. "Peter!" she called out a second time. Nothing. Without a second thought, Hannah climbed into the tub, wrapping her arms around her friend. She hugged him tight, the water cascading down on her, soaking the white cotton camisole and silk skirt she was wearing.

"Peter, what–?"

He looked up at her with wide, blood-shot eyes, snot running down his face, and said only one word.

"Help."

"So, what do you want to do for breakfast?" Vic asked, sitting up in the bed. He hadn't slept this good in ages.

"Knock it off," April barked, slipping into the pants she'd borrowed from Hannah.

"What? It's a perfectly acceptable, non-intrusive question that doesn't give away the fact that we just had some mighty fine sex. What do you want to do for breakfast? I was thinking we pack our bags, get Walczyk's TV and shit at Best Buy, and start south. There's this great restaurant in–"

April spun around, the blouse Hannah had also lent her still unbuttoned and flapping open, giving him another look at her magnificent boobs. "I want you to *swear* that this isn't going to get out."

Vic laughed. "And what if it does?"

April leapt onto the bed, straddling Vic's body, her hand tightly grasping his right ear. "You are going to promise me this isn't going to get out, or you're not walking out of this room."

Vic winced as her nails dug in. "Fine! Fine! I promise! I promise! Now get off me, you psychopath!"

Her hand didn't leave his ear. "You promise what?"

"I promise I won't tell anyone that you're good in bed."

She wrenched his ear.

"Aah! All right! I swear I won't tell anyone we slept together."

Satisfied, April climbed off, slid her shoes on, and started for the door.

"You know, that really hurt, you lunatic!" Vic cried out, rubbing his ear. He pulled his hand away and looked down at it, half expecting blood.

"Good. Then you'll remember what you just swore to."

As she neared the door, the room phone rang. It was one of those loud, bell-clanging rings that would wake the dead.

"Whatever you say, I'm not here," April hissed as Vic reached for the phone.

"Fine."

"I'm serious," she said, stepping back into the room. "I. Am. Not. Here."

Vic answered the phone. "Hello?"

"Vic. It's Hannah."

"Oh, hey, Han. What's up?"

"Is April with you?"

Vic looked across the room. It was as though April had heard what Hannah had just asked. "Er... no, she's not. Why would you think–"

"She's not answering her cell or her room phone. If you... see her... tell her Peter isn't feeling well and that he wants to get going as soon as possible."

"Deal," Vic said. "Is everything–"

"I've got to go. Just... if you see her–"

"Sure, Hannah," Vic said, getting a very, very odd vibe. Without a goodbye, Hannah ended the call. Vic put the phone back on the cradle and turned to April.

"What'd she want?"

"She was looking for you."

"Me?"

"You. Walz wants to get underway ASAP."

"Why?"

"She said he wasn't feeling well."

"What is it?"

"Didn't say."

"And why'd she come calling here looking for me?"

"Because you weren't in your room and you weren't answering your phone."

"Shit!" she said, fishing it out of her purse. "I must've shut the ringer off last night after you got me drunk."

"After *I* got *you* drunk?," Vic said innocently enough. "I seem to remember the girls finding the boys upstairs with quite a load on."

"Whatever," April barked. "She knows, doesn't she?" April said.

"So what if she does? It's Hannah, for crying out loud. She's our friend. She'll be happy for us."

"What's there be happy for?" April asked, fiddling with her iPhone.

"Well, two of her friends have gotten together."

"We're not *together*, Vic. We screwed. That's it."

"I'm not so sure, April. I definitely felt..."

April left the room, looking at the screen of her iPhone and muttering.

"–something."

"Will you leave me alone?" Walczyk said, gently pushing Hannah's hands away. She had always been a very hands-on person, not knowing boundaries with familiars. Her mouth turned down, into a pout, as it always did whenever she'd been reprimanded or scolded, and she backed away, handing Walczyk's shirt to him. He looked at her, feeling even worse than he had in the shower. But what could he do, let her dress him? He remembered, albeit through a fog, asking for her help, but not *that* kind of help. He breathed out, straightening up.

"You should go to back to your room," Walczyk said, looking at his bedraggled friend. "Clean up. Put on some fresh clothes. Get packed."

"Not before we talk," Hannah said, sitting down on Walczyk's bed.

Walczyk, for a moment, had considered playing dumb, asking "About what?," but thought better of insulting Hannah's intelligence and testing the limits of his own acting abilities. "The panic attacks have been going on for about two months now, with varying degrees of severity. What you saw, that was about a seven. Hope you know it took great effort to keep this one quiet so you wouldn't hear me. I had no idea you'd blast your way into the bathroom and catch me... well, in the act, as it were."

"Does anyone else know?"

"Angela Cariou. Dad knows. Mum to an extent."

"To an extent?"

"She doesn't know about the head-banging. I... I just couldn't pile all of that on her at once."

"The woman's battled breast cancer, Peter. I think she can handle more than you give her credit for."

"Fair enough. So now you know. What's the next step?"

"Exactly what I was going to ask you. Are you getting help?"

"I was until your precious Angela Cariou fired me as a client."

"She told me you were uncooperative, reluctant to share, and that you didn't take the sessions seriously. You'd come every other week, then every third week. You would just sit there, challenge her, and make no effort to discuss anything."

"To each her own," Walczyk said, shrugging. Had he really been that much of an asshole to the high school guidance counselor? He doubted it. He also knew that the woman, by her own admission, was not qualified to treat him. But Walczyk also knew that this wasn't the time to get into a fight with Hannah about the psychological merits of her colleague.

"Was that Vic or April you were on the phone with?" he asked. He'd heard her talking to someone, trying ever-so-hard to be quiet, while he dressed in the bathroom in clothes she'd picked out for him: a pair of Dockers, the *All in the Family* T-shirt Ian had given him for his birthday a few years back, and a striped oxford shirt. He wondered if it was by design or accident that the boxer shorts she'd picked out for him employed the same color scheme as the oxford.

"Vic," she said cautiously. "But I think April was there with him."

"No doubt," Walczyk said. Much of last night was a blur, but during the round of that annoyingly catchy "500 Miles" song that Hannah and he had led a group of patrons of the Blue Moon through, he seemed to remember Vic and April sharing a kiss beneath the TV in the far rear corner of the bar's upstairs section. "And they're on their way over."

"Your friends need to know about this."

"My friends know all they need to know."

"No. We do not. Peter, you've been banging your head into walls for two months now, suffering extreme panic attacks. You're not seeking any sort of psychological treatment, you're not taking any kind of medication, and you're harboring secrets. This has to end. I'm not going to stand by and watch you turn into some–"

A knock at the door cut her off. Walczyk got up from the bed and opened the door. Standing there, together, were Vic and April. April was back in her own clothes, with Hannah's in her hands, piled up neatly.

"Thanks, Hannah. I woke up to a phone call that my bags had arrived from the airport."

"You're welcome, April."

"Morning, boss," April said wearily, plopping down on the bed.

"Morning," Walczyk said back. They came into the room, Vic stopping to pat Walczyk on the arm. Walczyk shut the door.

"So what's up?" April asked. "Vic said you sounded like something important was up."

"Yeah," Vic said. "That's what I told April when I found her in–"

"The both of you are the shittiest damned liars I've ever come across," Walczyk said, shaking his head.

"Yeah," Vic said, looking down at the carpet.

"This means nothing," April snapped. "He and I are *not* getting together."

"Never said it looked that way," Walczyk said.

"So what's the big emergency?" Vic asked.

"Yeah," April asked.

"Well, some shit's been going on for a while now," Walczyk began after staring at Hannah for several seconds, "and Hannah thinks it's time that I come clean with you all."

"Did you two get together?" Vic asked, curiously.

"Hell, no," Hannah spat out quickly and callously. A wince crossed her face, drawing a smile from Walczyk.

"No. I've been having–"

"Trouble sleeping," Hannah blurted out.

"Trouble sleeping?" April asked, looking as though this was news to her.

"Yeah, He told me this morning that he's... that he's been having these freaky dreams. About Sara. Disturbing ones."

"Like murdering her dreams?" Vic asked.

"Vic!" Hannah snapped.

"No, it's a legit question," April said, turning to Walczyk. "Weird like that?"

Walczyk shook his head, completely thrown by Hannah's sudden, and surprisingly convincing lie. "Well, no. More like... sex dreams."

"And you dragged us all out of bed to tell us that?" April

groused.

Fearful that they weren't buying it, Hannah's mind raced, looking for something. Anything to –

Then it hit her. She rushed to Walczyk's computer and sat down, typing away at the keyboard. "And there's this!"

Curious as to what she was up to, he followed Hannah to the computer. Vic and April followed suit, a considerable distance between them.

Once they'd all circled the computer, Hannah cued up the video. It started with Walczyk stumbling out of the Blue Moon downtown. With him, also drunk, was April, hanging from the arm of Vic, who kept threatening to jump in a nearby fountain. They staggered about, laughing, telling jokes, and cursing loudly. Then, a fourth person, a familiar, thin redheaded woman in her mid-thirties, rushed up behind them and jumped up on Walczyk's back. He staggered around with Hannah clinging to his back, trying to catch his balance. After a minute of random foolishness, a voice from the unseen crowd of onlookers – possibly the photographer – called out: "Hey, Walczyk! Where's your wife?"

There was about five seconds of silence. Looks are exchanged between the members of Walczyk's entourage. A murmur falls over the audience outside of the Blue Moon.

"To hell with her," Walczyk responded. "We're over."

Then Hannah leaned forward, whispered something into his ear, and kissed the side of his neck.

"And the rest is history," Hannah said, closing the lid to the laptop.

"Is this the first you've seen of this?" Walczyk asked April.

"Sure is," she said, looking bewildered.

"I've never seen it before," Vic said.

"How could you?" April asked, elbowing him.

"Just saying, this is news to me."

"Where'd you find this?" Walczyk asked Hannah.

"Cameron called me this morning and told me about it." She rose and touched Walczyk's arm. "Peter, I'm so sorry. I know this kind of thing could ruin you."

"It's nothing," April said in the background.

"That these videos have a way of haunting people for–"

"But nothing. It's already been buried in the latest news cycle.

Old news."

"What's the new news?" Vic asked.

"You know that show *Sister Mother*?"

"The one about the nun with the teenage daughter," Walczyk clarified.

"Yeah. I got a text from Eli: the nun, Daniella Miral, just got busted for a laundry list of drugs. Pot, coke, bath salts... she won't be back in her habit for a long time coming."

"And that's good news?" Hannah asked, looking to be on the verge of tears.

"It's wonderful news for you," April said, pushing Hannah's hand away. "You dodged a PR bullet!"

"Oh," Hannah said, lightening up.

"So, crisis averted," Walczyk said.

"So," Walczyk said, looking over the breakfast menu. He figured it had to be at least fifteen years since he'd last set foot in Dysart's Truck Stop in Hampden, Maine.

"So," April parroted back.

"You and Vic."

"You and Hannah."

"No me and Hannah," Walczyk corrected.

"But you said she spent the night in your room."

"But nothing happened."

A smile crossed April's face. "Nothing?"

"Nothing. What about you and Vic?"

The smile vanished. "Nothing."

"Nothing?" Walczyk asked, returning to his menu.

"Nothing," April looked over her menu, ending the conversation. Just as the silence enveloping them became comfortable, April broke it with, "So she knows about the panic attacks?"

Walczyk put his menu down. "How the hell did *you* know about the panic attacks?"

"Everyone knows about the panic attacks."

"My parents," Walczyk deduced, cursing them in his mind for being so loose-lipped with his secrets.

"Henry and Diane have said nothing," April said, hands up in her own defense. "But you don't live under the same roof with someone and not know when he's having a panic attack."

"Well, thank you for keeping it to yourself."

"Oh, I didn't keep it to myself. Just turns out that your parents already knew."

"Get over here, you son of a bitch!"

When Hannah came out of the ladies' room, she found Vic Gordon off to one side, playing an electronic buck hunting arcade game, cursing the computer-generated wildlife.

"Any luck?" she asked, peeking over his shoulder.

"Not really," Vic said, slamming the blaze orange prop rifle into the gun rack mounted below the coin slots. "Feel better?"

Anyone else, and the question would have been too personal; too intrusive. But this was Vic and there were no boundaries as far as Vic Gordon was concerned. She hugged his arm as they walked through the maze of connecting rooms on their way back to the dining room.

"So, something's wrong with Walczyk, you know," Vic said as they meandered around, looking amongst the burly truckers, grizzled loggers, and bleary-eyed college students for their friends.

"I know," she said, wishing so bad she could tell Vic what was going on."

"And you're not going to tell me, are you?"

"I can't," she said, letting go of his arm. "I'm sorry, Vic."

"It's okay. He'll tell me when he's ready." Vic turned from the game, draping his arm across Hannah's shoulders and steering her back towards the dining room. "You know, I think I'm in love with April."

Hannah stopped dead in her tracks, causing Vic to come to a complete stop, forcing the waitress behind her to curse and find an alternate route around them, her tray laden with food. Unable to stop it, a smile crept across Hannah's face.

"Knock it off," Vic said, giving Hannah a light shove. "You've known I was in love with her for a while now, haven't you?"

"Well, it doesn't take a *wIgh* to figure that one out."

"A *wIgh*?"

She grimaced. "It's Klingon for 'genius.'"

Vic leaned down and kissed her forehead, smiling. "Only you, my friend. Only you."

"I think it's a terrible idea," Walczyk said from the back seat of the Jeep. Despite the awkward chemistry between them, Vic and April occupied the front of the vehicle. "Anthony Severance wants *me* to write it?"

"What's the problem?" Vic asked. "They know you're a fan of the original."

Walczyk made a disgusted noise as he shook his head slowly. "Me remake *Night of the Living Dead*? Ugh."

"Is 'ugh' in reaction to the number of zeroes attached to the price tag for just a rough draft and two rewrites, or to the idea of rewriting a personal favorite?"

"What do you think?" Walczyk snapped.

"Sweetie," April said, "look at it this way: they're going to remake the thing, with or without you. With you, you have the chance to turn the movie into what you want a remake of *Night of the Living Dead* to turn out like. Without you, some hack gets his greasy mitts on the material, completely destroys it, and renders a completely unwatchable remake of one of the greatest motion pictures ever captured on thirty-five millimeter film."

"Good call on the thirty-five millimeter," Walczyk said, exhaling. He looked over to Hannah. Were she awake, no doubt, she would have chimed in by now, offering sound advice as to whether or not to proceed with the project or to back away from it slowly. April's argument was sound, though: the movie *was* going to get made, with or without Walczyk. All he could do now was either help making something worth watching, or do nothing, and watch an abomination bubble forth.

"Fine," Walczyk said, leaning back in his seat. "But I won't direct. Rough and two revisions. And I get final say."

"I don't know about final say," April said.

"I do," Walczyk said, closing his eyes.

CHAPTER TEN
ZOLOFT NATION

The New Walczyk Place came together nicely, and quickly. His parents had been over in his stead to watch Dexter and had taken it up on themselves to move the existing furniture into the proper bedrooms (though they did give April's bed to Walczyk and vice-versa). And, true to their Saturday delivery promise, Dorsey's van arrived just as they'd arrived home, depositing the remainder of the furniture, and on Tuesday the FedEx truck dropped off the home video equipment they'd picked out at Best Buy. But Walczyk was consumed with the impending deadline of November ninth to deliver the first draft of *Night*. The title he loathed, mainly for its simplicity, but kept in an effort to play nice with Anthony Severance, a very touchy, territorial producer. Many a time, as he bent his head down to begin work on the project, he wished he'd kept his damned mouth shut and let April glare at him the entire trip home from Bangor to Cole Island.

Across the Island, fall began to set in. The stores had their yearly clearance events, and began closing down one by one. Guy Martin boarded up the windows to the Moondoggy Surf Shop, but kept the Moondoggy Diner open. According to Hannah, Melissa at Lando and Auggie's Pet Shop had let her inventory dwindle down, taking the two remaining cats home with her for the winter when she hung up the

"Closed" sign. It had been after a great deal of consideration, and his wish not to leave Walczyk and April without their favorite eatery, that Vic decided to hold off on closing down the Barrelhead for the off-season. Business-wise, it was a smart move, too, as traffic in and out of the restaurant was steady enough to keep the bills paid (he said he had nothing better to do anyway, except maybe drink and play PlayStation with Walczyk). The Bronze Lantern, as always, stayed open, but reduced its hours, closing at seven instead of ten. Cole Island wasn't a large community, and when the weather turned and the tourists went home or headed south, it grew much, much smaller.

"There just ain't enough to bring people here! We'll never make money if we don't attract people!" Harley Mildger loudly complained as Ingrid Connary filled his coffee cup at the Barrelhead one quiet Saturday afternoon.

"Does that old bastard ever shut up?" April grumbled, spooling linguine onto her fork three tables behind Harley.

"He doesn't necessarily shut up," Vic said, squeezed into the booth beside April. "But he does change the tune of his song. Just wait for this summer. He'll be saying, 'Jumped up Moses, there's too many damn outta townas around here. Gettin' so I got to lock my doors at night!'" April laughed. Vic turned to Walczyk, who was poking at his turkey and stuffing with his fork. "Am I right, Walz?"

Walczyk didn't look up from his plate. Vic leaned in and whispered something in April's ear.

"What are you talking about?" Walczyk said, finally looking up from his meal.

"Nothing," Vic replied, and went back to April's ear.

Walczyk reached for his Diet Coke. "If it's plans to hook up, it's your turn to host, Vic."

Vic slowly backed away from April's ear. "What are you, keeping track of our little sleepovers?"

"I'm tellin' ya, Leroy," Harley groaned loudly, "we was better off with all them annoying hippies roaming around with their fancy cameras and them battery-driven cars!"

April laughed, prompting Vic to start in. When they both looked to Walczyk for his reaction, he humored them with a smile, which quickly vanished as he returned to his lunch.

"Loves the sound of his own voice, doesn't he?" April commented, breaking the welcome silence.

"Well, in many ways, Harley Mildger isn't your typical Cole Islander," Vic said. "All he does is piss and moan. He'd complain to you that he's always thirsty and never has a bottle of water. But give him a bottle of water, and he'd just complain that you gave him a bottle of water. 'God, just eight ounces? Shoulda just saved your money.' Or 'Aw, Dasani? I only drink that there Portland Springs.'"

"I thought it was *Poland* Springs," April remarked.

"It is, but that doesn't stop old Harley. He gets it all wrong. Portland Springs water. Dingley Moore beef stew. My favorite is his most common physical ailment."

"I'm almost afraid to ask," April said, smirking.

"His 'sacroiliatica'," Vic said. "Bothers him something awful in the cold."

"'Sacroliatica'? That's just too funny to be real."

"I swear to you," Vic said, sliding an arm around April. "But, on the other hand, Harley *is* your typical Cole Islander."

"How so?" April asked, nodding to Lynn Bates, the short blonde beautician she saw every month for a pampered afternoon of nails, hair, and gossip. Lynn was with one of the other women from the salon, being escorted to a table by Ingrid Connary.

"Because all he does is piss and moan," Walczyk quipped, coldly. "He just takes it to a level not many around here can achieve."

"Sounds to me like you ought to put them all on an iceberg, Harley, Leroy, the Bronze Lantern's Saturday morning Bingo club, and Stella Lyons, and push them out to sea to cannibalize each other or fall into the Arctic waters."

Walczyk half-heartedly chuckled. Vic and April exchanged concerned looks, then a crash came booming from the kitchen. At Harley's table, applause broke out. Vic hopped up and took off.

"Better go see what's going on in there, Gordon!" Harley called after him. April just wanted to pop the little old man's head off.

Walczyk touched very little of his lunch and decided to take none of it with him. After April had finished, they left the car at the Barrelhead and walked up into town, having planned to spend the afternoon writing and reading at the Bronze Lantern.

As they entered, the sound level coming from the store was almost overpowering. The first sight they saw was a frazzled Garry Olsen rushing from the cash registers to the book search computer he'd set up at the back of the store. He barely shook out a wave as he jogged by, evidently not making his first trip like this. April and Walczyk turned the corner past the magazines and looked into the café area. There were seven or eight kids, the eldest no more than eight or nine, drawing on scrap paper and slopping food all over the large oak table April had become accustomed to considering "her table." Walczyk was walking the perimeter of the café, looking at the wall beneath each table for an electrical outlet.

"This is horse shit!" April barked. "That's our table!" She stuck out a finger at the children, who had moved on from paper to the table top itself with their Crayola masterpieces.

Walczyk put a hand on April's arm. "It's okay," he replied quietly. "We don't need a wall table. I can work off the battery."

She turned and sat at a nearby table, staring with daggers in her eyes at the group of kids defacing their table. "If they were teenagers, we could hit their fingers with rulers or baseball bats or something. But because they're only seven or eight—"

"They don't know any better," Walczyk said, a bit more sharply than he'd intended.

April, being April with her thick, diamond-proof skin, didn't even bat an eyelash at Walczyk. "Well, they should've been *taught* to know better before they're turned loose on a store and its tables."

"It's hot chocolate and crayons, April, not hydrochloric acid and indelible ink. Now relax and go get your magazines." He flipped open his laptop and began staring at the screen, scowling.

"What's up with you?" she asked, sharply.

"Nothing," Walczyk snapped. "I just don't feel like listening to any more bitching and moaning than I have to. So there are kids at the table we always sit at. It's not *our* table anyway. It's the place's table. They just got there first."

"What's up with you? For real this time."

"*Nothing.* I just didn't sleep all that well last night."

"More like the last four nights. I know you've been up all night watching *Futurama* and playing video games."

"You keeping tabs on me now?" Walczyk asked sharply.

"No. But the living room isn't that far from my bedroom," April snapped back. "Are the panic attacks getting worse?"

"I'm fine. I'm just not… I'm not feeling myself lately."

"Anything I can do?"

Walczyk looked down at his keyboard and hissed, "No, I'm

fine. I just need to ride it out."

"Okay," she said, getting up to collect some magazines from the racks. Walczyk began checking his e-mail. He had a message from Anthony Severance at Marathon Pictures welcoming him aboard the *Night* project. He skimmed the e-mail and moved it to a new folder he'd created, called *Night* (naturally). There was a lengthy e-mail from Sis that he decided to read later, at home, and the usual monthly array of e-mails from various television networks and home video companies, confirming the deposit of his royalties for his films and television programs. The last was a very short e-mail from his mother, no doubt passing along some little poem that she'd no doubt gotten from someone who'd gotten it from someone who'd gotten it from someone who'd gotten it from someone.

```
To: Peter Walczyk pwalczyk07@gmail.com)
From: Mum (hdwalczyk72@ciwifi. net)
Subject: Thinking of you


Dear Peter:

I've noticed you've been down in the
dumps again lately. I wish I could
help, but I also know that you know
yourself best, and that you'll find a
way out of it. Please know that your
father and I are praying for you every
night. God will get you through this.
We just need faith.

I found this while going through some
old cards and letters in my hope chest.
It was from your Grampie Reynolds, hand
written inside of a get well card he
gave me when I was diagnosed with
breast cancer:

"If I gave everything I have to the
poor and even sacrificed my body, I
could boast about it; but if I didn't
love you, I would have gained nothing.
Love is patient and kind. Love is not
jealous or boastful or proud or rude.
It does not demand its own way. It is
not irritable, and it keeps no record
of being wronged. It does not rejoice
about injustice, but rejoices whenever
```

```
the truth wins out. Love never gives
up, never loses faith, is always
hopeful, and endures through every
circumstance. Prophecy and speaking in
unknown language and special knowledge
will become useless. But love will last
forever!" (1 Corinthians 13, 3-8)

Peter, I don't care how many awards you
have or how many DVDs of your movies
there are - you will always be that
little boy who went to go to school in
his pajamas in the first grade. PLEASE
call us if you need anything.

My love will last forever!
Mum
```

Walczyk hadn't even realized April had returned to the table when he shut the lid on his laptop. He sat staring at the closed computer for several minutes before April broke the silence.

"Boss?"

Walczyk looked up to see April's concerned face. His eyes burning and he wanted to speak, but the lump forming in his throat just wouldn't let the words pass. He managed to squeeze out "I need to get some air" before dashing for the front door.

Walczyk turned a sharp left as he left the Bronze Lantern, not knowing where he was going, aside from anywhere near that computer and that book store. However, Hannah apparently had a different idea. As she stepped into the street from the door to her upstairs apartment, she was sideswiped by Walczyk, who knocked her back into the wall, from where she slid to the cold cobblestone sidewalk.

"Hannah!" he called out, reaching out to her. "You okay?"

She took his hand and pulled herself to her feet. "Fine, thanks. You've looked better, though. What's wrong?"

"If I say 'nothing', will you let it go?"

Her hands still in his, she squeezed gently and said, "Sure."

He scanned her eyes for deceit. He'd never seen it there before, and he didn't see it there now.

April came bolting out of the Bronze Lantern, looking frantically around as she hit the sidewalk, crying out, "Walczyk?"

Finally, she turned her head in the right direction, seeing Walczyk still holding Hannah's hands. Walczyk's hands fell back to his sides. "Walczyk, are you all right?"

"It's nothing, April. Just a little fender bender," Hannah said, wearing a false smiling.

"As long as you're not–" April's thought was interrupted as she glanced through the plate-glass window into the café. "Son of a bitch! There's someone at our table!" April dashed back inside, ready for war.

"She's something else," Hannah said. "So how's it going?"

"Okay," Walczyk said, his eyes on the sidewalk.

"How are things going with–"

"The panic attacks are what they are," Walczyk said.

"Take a little friendly advice?"

"I'll listen."

"Get to a doctor. Do it now. While you can."

"Because I don't know what the hell I'm doing."

Hannah's face drained of color. "No, Peter. I never said that–"

"I am so sick and fucking tired of everyone thinking they know what's best for me!"

"Peter Henry Walczyk, you will *not* speak to me like that!"

It then registered to him what he had, in fact, said to his friend. His breath shortened. "I'm so sorry," he said, shaking his head. "It's just… I'm not… I don't feel–"

"Peter, you need to get help. Please. Make an appointment. Dr. Troy is an excellent therapist. I've heard great things about her from many people. People who you wouldn't even know were in therapy."

Walczyk's eyesight became weaker. His breathing more strained. His chest hurt. He couldn't do this. He *wouldn't* do this. Not now. Not on Main Street. Not in front of Hannah. As his chest constricted, he felt this innate the need to get away from everyone. He needed to be alone. He was not going to break down in the streets.

The weekend had come and gone without a single call from Peter. As he hadn't made plans to come over to watch *Star Trek* on Saturday night, as they almost always did, Hannah carried on without him, doing a double feature by herself that had Kirk and McCoy trapped in a haunted castle and Spock putting his life on the line to save his estranged father. But the viewing did not make her feel any happier.

Mercifully, school kept her busy during the week, and time flew. She wondered if she was paranoid, or if Henry really was avoiding her, as they shared very little time together over the course of the week. As Friday rolled around, she was so angry with Peter she considered asking Cameron over for *Trek* and saying to heck with Peter. Adding to the frustration was the fact that her day wasn't going as planned at all. The time she'd allotted for her first period class to work on their book reports had turned into a fifty-minute gab session, which she found herself not really in the mood to either address or break up. Period two, her free period, ended up being filled with a Stella Lyons rant over "the filth" that was passing for literature these days. Mercifully, her third period junior English class chose to use their project preparation time more maturely, and were surprisingly calm and quiet as they worked on their assignments. The ease of the remainder of her classes ebbed and flowed, leaving her with a mostly positive day.

In no mood to wait around after school, she collected her papers and started for the front door, saying goodnights to Jack Duncan and Joann Benes along the way. However, things went from uncomfortable to more uncomfortable for her when she stepped out the front door to the school and saw, parked in the school bus loading zone, April's maroon Jeep Liberty, with Peter Walczyk behind the wheel.

"Hop in, Teacher Woman."

"No thanks. I'll walk." She wasn't in the mood for any of Peter's grandiose gestures today.

"Han," he pleaded, leaning over to open the passenger side door for her. She huffed, tightened her clutch on her books, and got in. As she sat, however, she felt something under her. She reached down and pulled out orange pill bottle. It rattled in her hand as she rolled it around, searching for the label.

The label read *Peter Walczyk*. She looked over at her friend, a smile plastered on his face. "You saw someone."

"Yep."

She looked down at the bottle again. "Given your feelings about Dr. Cottle, I figured if you went for the pharmaceutical route, you'd at least go see Dr. Troy."

"I'm not interested in talking. I'm interested in getting better. No offense to this Troy woman, but Dr. Cottle works faster. Less talk about himself. More pharmaceuticals to dig me out of this God forsaken slump."

"And Dr. Cottle thinks that," she skeptically asked, reaching out for the thin plastic bottle, scanning the label, "Zoloft is the answer?"

"He seems to think it'll do more good than seeing the high school shrink."

"*Therapist*," Hannah said, correcting him as she always did when Walczyk called Angela a shrink. "You really didn't enjoy it, did you?"

"Not in the least."

Hannah held the bottle up. "How long have you been on this?" she asked, pointing her pen at the prescription bottle.

"Five days, counting today. Why?"

"Zoloft doesn't waste any time, then, does it."

"What makes you say that?"

"Well, that's the first smile I've seen you crack in a long time."

"Listen, I've got something on my chest and I need to get it off."

"Shoot."

"The other day. In front of the Bronze Lantern. I treated you like shit."

"You did," Hannah replied.

"And I'm sorry about that. No matter how bad I'm feeling, it's no excuse to take it out on the only friends I have."

She looked up at him. He was being genuine. She smiled. "Then you are forgiven. So, what are you doing tonight?"

"Nothing big. Friday night dinner was Wednesday this week. What's up?"

"Why don't you come over? You can catch up on the *Star Trek* you missed out on. Spock is reunited with his estranged father and Kirk and Bones are trapped in a haunted castle."

"Sounds educational and entertaining all around."

"Well? What do you say?"

"I say it's a date."

Walczyk stood in front of the bathroom mirror, scratching the growth of beard on his face. He rather liked the looks of a beard on himself. And it was a known fact that the more successful directors all had beards. Francis Ford Coppola. Steven Spielberg. George Lucas. (Sharing this with April garnered the response, "Well, two out of three ain't bad.")

Hannah had also commented on the beard he'd begun growing the night he began taking Zoloft, two weeks ago. That, he felt, was all the approval he needed to justify keeping what his mother had taken to calling a "scratchy mess." April, on the other hand, was a proponent of Walczyk shaving. "You look like a complete and utter homeless," she sniped one night over dinner at Walczyk's parents' house. "Worse than that yellow-shirted creepy bastard at the bookstore." Walczyk's father just stayed out of it.

Walczyk grabbed his toothbrush and loaded it down with a strip of green toothpaste from a battered, twisted tube he'd removed from the medicine cabinet. As he brushed his lower teeth, he considered how far he'd come in just two short weeks. This new euphoria was brilliant. For the first time in ages – at least since the first season of *Ordinary World* – Walczyk was truly happy.

Even better, he found himself consumed by a boundless energy. Walczyk pulled Ian's rough cuts of episodes three through six of *Ordinary World* out of the waste paper basket in his office and tore into them, sending long, note-filled e-mails. He was actually enjoying dinners with his parents again, and, much to the delight of April and Eli, he started in on the screen play for *Night*.

Walczyk spit a gob of whitish-green foam into the sink and returned the toothbrush to his mouth, scrubbing his upper teeth and gums. Dr. Cottle had warned him to be on the lookout for side effects. Innocuous things, really. Cottle mentioned sleepiness, nervousness, insomnia, dizziness, nausea, skin rash, headache, diarrhea and upset stomach. Some of the side effects, like loss of appetite and weight loss, didn't strike Walczyk as all that bad. One of the side effects that did give him concern was that, from time to time, his stomach would roil, as though it were vibrating within his body. Like butterflies, but without the predicted nervousness. Walczyk's mother suggested this could be the "upset stomach" that could be predicted, but Walczyk dismissed that. He'd had upset stomach before; this wasn't it.

Walczyk spit one more time, then filled the small, slender water glass setting on the bathroom counter from the tap. Another side effect Walczyk noticed from taking Zoloft was that he sometimes found himself rambling on about things from time to time. He'd talked Garry Olsen's ear off one day about the post-production process on an episode of *Ordinary World*. He spent almost an hour describing his first date with Sara to his father one night after supper. And Hannah actually had asked him to quiet down as he talked his way through the Joan Collins episode of *Star Trek*. And, while he realized he was a bit more excited than usual, he felt it a good thing – at least he was finally excited about things, and what the hell could be wrong with that?

Walczyk finished rinsing his mouth and spit the remainder of the cold tap water into the sink, then rinsed the basin out, removing all remnants of toothpaste. He opened his medicine cabinet and replaced the toothpaste, dropped his brush into the water glass, and removed the prescription bottle from the cupboard, shaking a Zoloft pill into his hand. He swallowed the pill, then closed the medicine cabinet and admired his beard once again. As he scratched his throat, he smiled. It was a good time to be Peter Walczyk.

CHAPTER ELEVEN
AT THE BEEP

Restless. He felt restless. He paced through the house, his chest heaving. Tight. Panicked. The note said, "We'll be back sometime." "Sometime." He had no idea when "sometime" was.

He just couldn't do it, and he needed to tell her. But she wasn't there. What good was having an assistant if she wasn't there?

She was with Vic. They had become more and more open about their romance since Bangor. It was going to be a mess. Walczyk could tell. It would be a mess before all was said and done. Someone would go home crying, and they'd come straight to him for consolation. He flipped open his phone and speed-dialed April again. Just as before. Just like it had been all day. Four rings and straight to, "This is the personal line of April Donovan. At the tone, leave name, number and brief message. Thank you."

Walczyk left no message. The message hadn't changed since the fifth time he'd called. He needed to speak to her.

Night was a nightmare. He hadn't been able to come up with anything. He was tapped out. He'd awakened around ten in the morning, taken a couple Zoloft, and started working on his treatment for the film. But nothing came to him. He'd bang out several mismatched sentences, maybe a solid paragraph or two, get up to go fix a snack or use the bathroom, sit back down, and what he'd written would have turned to shit. His latest attempt at updating the story of *Night of the Living Dead* was as banal as it was clichéd. Walczyk looked at the screen for several moments, bothered by one thing in particular. It wasn't the fact that, up until two weeks ago, he had been convinced it was ridiculous even to do a remake of the horror classic. No, what really bothered him now was that his efforts were almost shot-for-shot identical to the opening of original *Night of the Living Dead*. Walczyk pressed down on the "delete" key, clearing the screen. However, he found he could not start again.

His entire day had been like this. He'd get the first scene up to the first zombie attack written, then scrap it. It was shit. All of it. Uninspired, not frightening, and certainly not original. He found himself despairing. Would he ever be able to get this project started? Would he ever get going on it, or would he have to give up on it, costing himself an easy paycheck?

He glanced at the clock on the wall. It was only quarter to two. Hannah wouldn't be out of school for some time now. He couldn't talk to her about it. His father would also be at the school until about four. He couldn't hash it all out with his Dad. He tried calling the house, hoping his mother would pick up, only to hear his own voice greet him back. He'd recorded that greeting back in 2008, when he and Sara had bought the folks a new digital answering machine following the demise of old their tape-based machine. He'd recorded the message himself to show them how to do it, but they had found nothing wrong with the message and, apparently had kept it. Again, he did not leave a message.

He tried to settle himself down, taking another Zoloft and plopping down in front of the downstairs TV for an afternoon of the antics of the Three Stooges. But nothing was funny. Not the eye-pokes, the face slaps, the whacks in the head, Curly's "whoop whoop whoops," Moe's "you knuckleheads" or Larry's gag about the burnt toast, rotten eggs, and the tapeworm, which had been Walczyk's favorite. Walczyk had hoped that, if the Stooges couldn't improve his mood, they would at least put him out for a while. It had been three days since he'd had a full night's sleep, and the time had certainly dragged on, without anything coming out in the form of writing. He'd tried revisiting *The Next One*, to no avail. And he found that banging out an outline for season four of *Ordinary World* was out of the question. He couldn't maintain focus long enough to move from one episode to the next.

After two hours of the Stooges, he shut the TV off, fixed himself a fresh rum and Coke, and returned to his writing. He stared at the blank screen, but nothing was new. Variations on a theme. It had all happened before, and it would happen again. Walczyk retried April's cell, hanging up this time after "This is the personal line of April Donovan."

He tried another number. "You have reached Vic Gordon, owner of the Barrelhead Restaurant. I am unable to take your call at this time. Please leave a message with your name and number and I'll get back to you as soon as possible. Thanks, and have a nice day."

And another dial. "Hi, this is Hannah. I'm not available right now, but when I am, I'll call you back if you'll leave me your name and phone number. Thanks!"

Another dial. "Good morning. Schueller Agency."

A live person!

"Yes, is Elias Gaul in?"

"May I ask who is calling?"

"It's Peter Walczyk."

A pause. "I'll put you through to his extension, Mr. Walczyk."

Another pause. He could talk to Eli, of course. Eli would listen. Eli would understand that this was just not a writable project. Eli could–

"You have reached Elias Gaul at the Schueller Agency. Leave your name, number and a brief message at the tone and I'll get back to you as soon as possible."

Walczyk hung up and redialed.

"You have reached the home of Henry and Diane Walczyk," Walczyk's voice greeted. "No one's able to take your call right now. Leave a message and we'll get back to you."

He had to get through to someone. Anyone. They had to know he couldn't write this. That it was impossible to write this. That it just could not be done.

"You have reached Vic Gordon, owner of the Barrelhead Rest–"

"Hi, this is Hannah. I'm not available right now, but when I am, I'll call you–"

"This is the personal line of April Donovan–"

"You have reached Elias Gaul at the Schueller Agency–"

"This is the personal line of April Donovan–"

"You have reached the home of Henry and Diane–"

"You have reached the extension of Henry Walczyk, principal of Cole Island High School. At the beep–"

"I'm sorry, Mr. Walczyk, Angela is not in today."

"This is Ian Maeder at WalzIan Productions. Leave it at the tone."

His chest was pumping. His heart raced. His eyes burned. The world seemed to be clinging to him. He could not move his body. He tore at his shirt, peeling it away, and felt his chest move once again. A voice at the far side of the room called out to him, unintelligible. He moved towards the voice, stepping around the plush armchair. The voice spoke again.

They think you're crazy.

He stared at the couch. The voice wasn't coming from the couch. He knew that. He wasn't crazy. He knew it. And he didn't care if they didn't know it. He was going to tell them all that, too.

He was not crazy!

He flipped open his phone and began speed-dialing again. Hannah. Vic. April. His parent's house. Eli. His father's office. No one available. No one answering.

"This is Hannah. I'm not–"

"You have reached Vic Gordon–"

"This is the personal line of April–"

"This is Han–"

"You have reached Vic–"

"This is the personal–"

They're planning how to get rid of you!

Bullshit! He thought to himself, awash with a cold sweat. They couldn't all be against him. Not Sara. Sara still loved him. She said so. She just wasn't *in* love with him anymore. She still loved him. She'd take his call.

"Hi. You've reached Sara Collins-Walczyk. Sorry I can't take your call at–"

They're going to get you!

He closed the phone and squeezed it hard in his hand, feeling it begin to crack.

He wasn't going to let them get him.

CHAPTER TWELVE
POLAR ECLIPSE

"He's probably pissed off about us going on a trip without him," Vic said over the phone while April juggled the bags in her hands, groping for her house keys that were in her pocket.

"That doesn't explain him ignoring his phone," April said, concerned. She slid the key into the lock, turned and opened the door. She deposited the keys back in her pocket and stepped over the threshold.

"Sure it does," Vic's voice said. "You're getting the silent treatment for ignoring his seventeen calls."

April stepped inside. Silence greeted her. "Walczyk?" she called into the darkened house. There was no reply.

"Not home?" Vic asked.

"Boss!" she cried out. Again, there was no answer. "Vic, something isn't right here."

"Will you relax?" Vic laughed. "He's probably over watching *Star Trek* with Hannah."

"You really think he'd walk to town?" April rounded the corner into the kitchen. As she stepped in to turn on the light, a crunch came from beneath her foot. She flipped on the light and bent down to pick up one of the many broken pieces of black plastic scattered about the floor. It bore the LG logo. It used to be a cell phone. "Is this–?" April asked aloud, fingering the shard of plastic.

"'Is this' what?" Vic asked, sounding confused. "April, what the hell's going on?"

Vic never got his clarification. A noise broke the silence. A soft, low noise, but a noise nonetheless. It was coming from the living room.

April slowly made her way into the darkened living room, her foot brushing through something. She stooped low and picked up one of Walczyk's movie poster T-shirts. He turned and looked around the room. Nothing seemed out of place. There were no doors ajar. No broken windows. Just the shattered phone.

"April?" Vic's voice called out from across town.

Then she heard it again. A banging sound, coming from the living room. It was too rhythmic to be a fluke. Her heart racing, April scanned the room. There *was* something out-of-place, now that she looked hard enough. It took her a minute to put two and two together: it was the sofa. It wasn't resting flat against the wall.

The banging was coming from behind the sofa. April slowly crept up onto the couch and looked down over the top. Her voice tightened in her throat.

"Vic–"

"April, get out of there. Wait in the Jeep. I'll be right over."

"No, Vic… you need to go to the school. Find Henry. Get him over here."

April had not taken her eyes away from what she saw behind the couch. Curled up in a ball on the floor, naked, was a pathetic, frightened, feral-looking man, banging the back of his head against the wall.

"April! What's going on?"

"Just get Henry over here! Now!"

The demented eyes of Peter Walczyk stared up at April in fright and terror.

CHAPTER THIRTEEN
DIRIGO

Peter Walczyk sat across from the TV, staring off into nothingness. His mind raced with images of what he'd rather be doing. Enjoying a cold drink at home with Vic and April. Devouring another DVD of *Star Trek* episodes with Hannah. Making love to his Sara. Anything but sitting on the stiff foam of an institutional couch, staring at a bookshelf loaded with puzzles in taped-together boxes, volumes of Reader's Digest condensed books, and dog-eared VHS copies of *Cheaper By the Dozen* and *Patch Adams*. The occasional bang of elbows against the plexi-glass separating him from the patients in the hallway on the other side of the wall reminded Walczyk that he wasn't in Kansas anymore.

Three thoughts struck him: 1) He had videos to return to the video store; 2) The chicken cutlets in the fridge were going to spoil; and 3) Someone had to feed Dexter. Three thoughts about three things he was unable to do anything about at the current moment.

Walczyk turned as a slender, angry-looking man wearing a large white baseball cap, sweat pants, a white undershirt, and a tattered baby blue terrycloth robe was escorted into the room. The man quietly sat down at the table in the back of the room. Walczyk nodded at him, then returned his attention to a second book shelf in the small, antiseptic room. There was an absurdly immense collection of grocery store romance novels, a smattering of *National Geographic* magazines (with all the native women's' breasts colored over in black Sharpie marker), and a chess set with mismatched pieces.

Walczyk sat, staring at the worn institutional carpeting on the floor, knowing his fate was being discussed by a square-shaped intake nurse, his parents, and April in another room. And he didn't care. He just wanted to lie down. He was so tired. Tired of feeling like utter shit all the time. Tired of being worn out. Tired of having the world sitting on one shoulder and a small version of himself that only said, "to hell with it all" on the other. He was tired of making decisions. Tired of putting on a good front. Tired of pretending to enjoy his work when he wanted, more than anything, to quit it.

He was tired of having to fight to be normal.

That thought raced through his head ahead of all others. He'd push it down for a second, then it would come back, two-fold. It continued to multiply every time he tried to quash it. It obsessed him. It pushed every other single, solitary thought from his mind.

Except for *that* one. The green dragon sitting on his doorstep.

You should just hang yourself, Peter. Then you won't have to deal with any of it. Ever. Again.

A feeling of dread engulfed him. It would be a while before he left the Dirigo Psychiatric Hospital.

"Tell me," the doctor said, leaning back in his office chair with a foot propped up on an open desk drawer, "what do you remember?" The doctor was an impossibly big man, both in height and girth. When he stepped into the room, Walczyk had him pegged at six-four, weighing about three hundred some pounds. He was dressed nappily in brown corduroy pants, a moss green sweater vest and a collared shirt peeking out from under it. He had unkempt salt-and-pepper hair, poking up in varying directions, and a large, bent nose. But when the doctor smiled, a warm light appeared in his eyes, putting Walczyk at ease.

Walczyk sat back in his chair. What had gone down was still a blur. One long, winding blur, broken up by the occasional solid image. The doctor's office was not all that unlike the office of Angela Cariou back on Cole Island. This doctor – Dr. Jonathan S. Lentz, according to the diplomas on the wall – had amassed quite a unique collection of decorations for his office: taped to the wall were a postcard with a picture of Hugh Laurie from the TV show *House*, several newspaper clippings, most of them from the comics section, and a *New York Times* crossword puzzle, completely filled in and marked "FINISHED" in red pen across the grid, with a date of April 6, 2002 scribbled beneath it. A Batman Pez dispenser and one of those hotplates to keep coffee mugs warm sat on his desk.

"Not much," Walczyk offered up, still trying to decipher the blur of images rattling through his head. Almost out-of-body, he saw himself peeling off his shirt, smacking his head against the baseboards of the wall behind the sofa, calling people over and over again.

"That's not surprising," Dr. Lentz said. "You were in quite a state of shock when you were taken to the hospital. How about we start from the beginning? What do you remember at your home on Cole Island?"

"I remember feeling very scared. Everyone was planning something. Plotting against me." He looked up from the floor into Dr. Lentz's gray eyes. "They were going to get me put away."

"Away where?"

Walczyk thought a moment before replying, "Here."

"You do know this was not a plan by your friends and family, right?" Dr. Lentz asked, fingering the tag from the tea bag coming out of his plastic travel mug. "To have you committed?"

"No, but, it was… it was so real though. Like that voice in the back of my head. My voice. Myself telling me that–"

"That they were going to have you put away," Lentz calmly said.

"Yeah."

"Do you remember anything after…" He consulted his clipboard before continuing. "…April found you?"

He thought for a moment. It came to him. "I remember her washing my face. Then Vic and my Dad were there… helping me to my feet. Vic gave me some clothes. Then…"

And then it was gone. It was frustrating. As he did whenever he was frustrated, Walczyk slid his hands over from his forehead to the back of his neck. But as soon as his hands reached the back of his head, he felt a large lump, and lightning bolts of pain blasted through his skull. He gritted his teeth and squeezed his eyes shut, trying in vain to force an image to the front of his mind's eye.

"Be careful," Dr. Lentz said, leaning forward. "You've still quite the welt on the back of your head. Now, let's skip ahead to the next thing that you do remember."

Walczyk relaxed himself and continued. "I was on a hospital bed. But I... they don't have hospital beds at the health center. I... I don't remember where I was."

"You weren't taken to the medical center on Cole Island. Your parents drove you to the emergency room in Augusta for treatment."

"Oh," Walczyk said, none of this making any sense. "Well, I remember... lying in a hallway on one of those rolling beds, under a thin blanket. There were people staring at me. Pointing. So cold. I remember the cold. And a... homeless guy? Staring at me from his bed across the hall. At least I think he was homeless. I just remember I didn't like the way he was staring at me. Like he wanted to kill me. I remember shouting for help, telling the man to quit staring at me. Then... I'm in a machine."

"Yes, they performed a C.A.T. scan on you, given the injury to your head," Dr. Lentz provided.

"And after that... I remember this really plain looking room. There were people screaming on the other side of the wall. My parents and April were in the room with me. I think Dad had been crying. My head was starting to ache. I reached up to touch it." He stopped himself from touching the back of his head this time, not wanting a repeat of the tidal wave of pain that he'd experienced before. "What happened to my head?"

"Your friend April said you were banging your head against the wall when she found you."

Walczyk nodded, remembering the incident in the bathtub at the hotel in Bangor. The day Hannah found him. "I remember my Dad was getting antsy. He stood up and sat down a lot. Then there was this guy in scrubs, maybe he was the doctor. He said there was nothing they could do there. They said they could try to 'get me a bed' at another hospital."

"Not bad. And where are you now?"

He thought long and hard. His headache prevented him from concentrating on anything other than the pulsating sensation at the back of his skull. "I don't know."

"You're at the Dirigo Psychiatric Hospital in Bangor," Dr. Lentz stated.

"The mental hospital?" Walczyk asked, confused.

"The preferred term is *psychiatric* hospital, but I believe you get the gist of it," Dr. Lentz said. "We specialize in hospital and community-based treatment programs for mental illness and substance abuse. This ward, Three-North, is a psychiatric ward, meaning that you'll be with other psychiatric patients. The chemical dependency patients are housed in another ward."

"Okay," Walczyk said, rolling the term "mental illness" over and over in his foggy head, trying to make sense of his being in a hospital specializing in mental illness.

"I remember that I didn't want to go to a mental, er, psychiatric hospital," Walczyk stated. The memories were starting to get a little clearer to him. "Mum started crying. April told the doctor and my parents that I couldn't, under any circumstances, be admitted to any damn mental hospital – her words. She said I'd have to get in-home treatment back on Cole Island from a private provider, or that I'd have to go elsewhere. It was Dad who told me that this was the best solution."

"And how did you feel about that?"

"I didn't trust him. It was like before all over again. He was out to put me away. They'd gotten to him, and they wanted him to convince April and Mum."

"Who are *they*?" Dr. Lentz asked.

"I don't know. I just had this feeling someone wanted me gone. Well, April wasn't having it. I remember Dad taking her outside. When they came back, she was crying. She sat down on my bed and started talking to me. Telling me that they didn't know what was wrong and that I needed specialized care. Finally, I just gave up. Figured they were going to have their way one way or the other. Then there was this mad rush to get stuff done and I woke up here."

"It's not surprising that you don't remember the trip from Augusta to here. You were on a heavy dose of Lorazepam when the hospital in Augusta discharged you into your parents' care," Dr. Lentz said, referring to his clipboard.

"The only thing I remember about the trip was lying in the back seat. Smelling McDonald's. Wanting it, but not being able to ask for it. I remember my folks talking really quietly. I remember my head in April's lap, her stroking my hair. Then, they're getting me out of the car. I fell down. April and Dad picked me up. Mum got me a wheelchair.

"Then I was in a little, cold office. Mum and Dad and April were with me. I remember clipboards being shoved at me. One of those blood pressure things. Mum stripping the shoe laces out of my sneakers. April taking all the stuff out of my pockets. A lot of talking and me signing a bunch of papers later, and it was time to get me checked in. That's when..." Walczyk's eyes stung. Tears began to drip out. "That's when they all left me."

Dr. Lentz passed Walczyk a box of tissues. Walczyk took the box and placed it on an end table beside the chair he was sitting in, taking a few to wipe his eyes and nose.

"Mum and Dad and April left, and the next thing I remember was waking up in my room."

"That was about an hour ago," Dr. Lentz said calmly.

Walczyk looked around the room. "What time is it?"

"It's almost noon now."

"Noon?" Walczyk asked, searching for a clock. "But it was three when I started calling people."

"That was yesterday. Thursday. Today is Friday."

"Friday?" Walczyk couldn't believe it. He'd lost almost an entire day somehow. An entire day, of which he only had vague snippets and fuzzy memories of.

"I imagine it must be very disconcerting," Dr. Lentz said. "It's bad enough when we lose days and aren't hopped up on Lorazepam."

"What is this Lorazepam?"

"A heavy sedative commonly called 'Ativan'. You'd grown rather agitated while waiting to be seen at the hospital, so they administered it to calm you down."

"So what's going to happen to me now?" Walczyk asked, fidgeting with the hood of his sweatshirt, which was currently up over his head.

"Well, for the time being, you're going to be our guest. We'll talk with you, review your medical history, your prescriptions. We'll try to figure out why you went off the deep end like you did. And we'll see what we can do to make sure it doesn't happen again. How's that sound?"

"Like I'm going to be here for a while," Walczyk replied, a cold wave of dread washing over him.

A tray of food had been brought up for Walczyk around five on Friday night. On it was a rectangular slice of pepperoni pizza, some niblet corn, a banana, and a thing of two-percent milk. The entire meal reminded Walczyk of high school, except that the tray was round and had a dome cover on it. Walczyk picked at the pizza, eating the pepperoni and molten mozzarella cheese before passing out again.

When he next awoke, he didn't know how long he'd been out. It was dark outside. The desk lamp had been clicked on, and sitting at the foot of his bed were April and his mother. His father was pacing behind them.

"Hey," he said, feebly, sitting up.

"How are you doing?" Mum said in a shaky voice.

"Okay," he said. "Dopey."

They talked for a few minutes, Walczyk recounting what he could of the trip, and getting some holes filled in by April and his parents.

"We brought you a few things," Mum said, clearly mustering up as much cheer as she could in her bloodshot eyes.

"But don't get your hopes up; they're being picky about what they'll let you have," April said.

"Well," Dad said behind her, "I suppose they have to be careful about potentially dangerous items."

"Your laptop's out of the question," April said.

"Good," Walczyk said.

"We bought you some clothes at Walmart," Mum said, reaching down for a bag on the floor." April assures us that we got your sizes right."

"They told us you couldn't have drawstrings or laces or belts," April added, "So don't expect high fashion here."

Walczyk looked through the bag. There were several T-shirts that were nice, but he'd have never picked out for himself. One that stood out in particular was a brown T-shirt with a cartoon monkey in a 1950's-inspired space helmet on it, the words "Space Monkey" written beneath the picture. Two pair of flannel pajama pants with the drawstrings removed, some underwear and a pair of navy blue slippers were in the bag. Also in the bag were a couple of paperback books, one being 'Salem's Lot by Stephen King (Walczyk really hoped his mother picked that one out) and The Strange Case of Dr. Jekyll and Mr. Hyde by Robert Louis Stevenson.

"I picked that one out," his father said, almost proudly. "Don't know if you've read it or not, but I've always enjoyed it." Walczyk looked down at the cover – a simple painting of a man's face, half in the light, half in the darkness. The half in darkness looked pensive, thoughtful, and the light half was snarled and feral looking. There was something about the artwork, about that half-calm, half-maniacal man, that piqued Walczyk's curiosity. In a second bag were a couple of thick notebooks, a package of the exact same black gel pens Walczyk insisted on writing exclusively with, and a miniature radio with headphones.

"I made a case with your doctors," April said as Walczyk examined the credit card-sized radio. "I told them that you couldn't sleep without some kind of sound, and since moving a TV was out of the question, they did say that you could have a small music player at nights."

"We also brought you a beard trimmer and a shaving kit," his mother informed him. "In case you get the urge."

"It's at the front desk with your name on it," his father clarified.

"Are you guys all coming back tomorrow?" Walczyk asked, hoping.

"Visiting hours," his father began, "are from seven to eight. We'll be by every night."

"You can't keep driving back and forth," Walczyk began, not knowing why he was arguing their promise to visit every night.

"No, we can't," his mother said. "That's why we're staying at a hotel here in Bangor for the week."

"Mum, you don't have to–"

"Yes, we do. We *want* to. We want to be here for you, Peter."

A badly spray-tanned woman in Tinkerbell scrubs stopped by the door, looking in on the gathering with a scowl on her face. "It's eight o'clock," she informed them, thoroughly unenthused. "Visiting hours are over. You can all come back tomorrow." The nurse then left. April shot her a dirty look.

Walczyk shakily got out of bed and held on to his father, who was starting to cry. He kissed his father and thanked him for taking care of him.

"Of course," Henry whispered. "I love you."

"I love you too," Walczyk said. He let go and moved down the line to his mother, taking her in his arms and holding tightly to her.

"The nurses at the desk have our hotel number and April's cell phone number if there's *anything* that you need," his mother said before telling him, "I love you."

"I love you too, Mum." His mother stepped back and April rose from the bed, giving Walczyk a tight hug.

"This is so weird," she said.

"We'll muddle through," Walczyk said, taking April in his arms. "I'm so sorry I put you through all of this," he added, kissing her cheek.

They showed themselves out. Not long after, Walczyk made his way to the door, shutting out the light and stowing the bags from his parents in his closet. He lay down on the bed, popping the batteries into his radio. He ran his thumb up and down the dial, until he locked in on a station playing "the best of the seventies, eighties, and today." Walczyk lay down in his bed, curled up in a ball, and fought the urge to cry as he pondered the notion that he was all alone in this strange place, surrounded by strange people, with no chance for early parole.

CHAPTER FOURTEEN
SURVIVOR'S GUILT

"We have to tell the press what happened," April said, pacing in front of the bed in Henry and Diane's hotel room at the Birch Point Inn.

"April," Diane said in protest, weakly shaking her head.

"Diane, we need to say something," April restated.

"Why?" Diane asked. "It's none of their business what Peter's going through. Haven't they done enough to him already?"

"Diane, please listen to what I'm saying," April began.

"No, you listen to me! We are *not* going to put it in every newspaper and magazine and all over the internet that my little boy is in a mental hospital!"

"Diane," Henry said softly.

"Why, Henry? Why do we have to do this?" She turned to April. "Why do you want to do it? What's the benefit, in the end, of doing this? Of making him a spectacle?"

April sat down on the bed beside Diane and reached out, holding her hands. "Diane, if we don't release some kind of statement, then once the press gets a hold of the story – and they will get a hold of this story, I promise you that –they'll twist it and shape it into the industry's next great rehab story. 'Peter Walczyk ODs!' 'Peter

Walczyk Goes Off the Deep End!'"

"But that's just it!'" Diane shrieked. "He *did* go off the deep end! April, if we let this get out, they'll eat him alive!" April opened her mouth to reassure her that things would be all right when her phone rang. She huffed and dug the phone out from her pocket. She knew who it was before she even glanced at the caller ID.

"We're working on it," she said into the phone, turning to mouth the name "Eli" to Henry and Diane.

"April, I need details," Eli urged. "I need to make a public statement to get the tabloids off my ass."

"Look, I'm with Henry and Diane right now. We're discussing—"

"What's to discuss? All you need to do is tell me what happened so I can tell the press something! They're chomping at the bit, April. You know how it goes. Word got out that he tweaked at the hospital in Augusta. Now we need to say something, sooner rather than later, to shut them up."

"Eli, they're not so sure—"

"Put me on speaker."

"Eli, I don't think now's the time to—"

"Put me on speaker," he commanded, enunciating each word.

April pressed a button and laid the iPhone down on the bed. "All right, Eli. You're on with Henry and Diane Walczyk. And so help me God, you'd better be nice!"

"Good evening, Mr. and Mrs. Walczyk," Eli said across the country. "You might remember me from your son's wedding. I'm Elias Gaul."

"Peter's agent, yes," Henry said. "Hello, Elias."

"Mr. and Mrs. Walczyk, I know this is a very delicate subject for you both, and I can appreciate your not wanting to make any decisions concerning Peter without his input, but quite frankly, we need to move on this in his stead, as he's in no condition to be doing this himself."

"April said something to that effect," Henry said. "She said you needed to make some kind of statement to the press about Peter's health."

"Exactly. You see, word got out about his upset at the hospital in Augusta, and now they're beginning to make up their own stories. If I can get out there now with something – with the truth – then we can head off most of the rumors and speculation. Bear in mind, I'm not planning on telling them everything. In fact, the tighter we can keep it, the better for all involved."

There was a tense pause as Henry and Diane exchanged looks. Finally, Diane leaned in toward the phone. "He's staying at the Dirigo Psychiatric Hospital in Bangor, Maine."

"Okay, thank you, Mrs. Walczyk," Eli said. "Now, do you have any idea what's wrong?"

"We don't know yet," Henry said. "April found Peter in an agitated state and had Peter's best friend, Vic Gordon, track us down. Then April, Diane, and I rushed him to the hospital in Augusta."

"Cole Island doesn't have a hospital?"

Diane cleared her throat. "April thought – and I agree, now that I've had time to think it over – that it might turn into a press nightmare if it had gotten out that he was rushed to the health center. Small town, and all."

"What are his doctors saying happened?"

"They don't know yet," Henry said. "They're keeping him for several days to evaluate him. They've taken him off his current medications."

"Current meds?" Eli asked.

"He was taking an antidepressant prescribed by his doctor on Cole Island," April clarified. "Zoloft."

"Okay," Eli said, taking a moment to collect his thoughts. "Is there anything special you want me to say in the press release?"

"Just that we're praying for him," Diane said.

"Of course," Eli said. "Well, that's about all I need to draft a statement to the press. Do you want to look it over before I make it public?"

"No," Henry said. "If Peter and April trust you, Elias–"

"Don't you worry, Mr. Walczyk. I plan on saying just enough to get the wolves away from the door. If you or Mrs. Walczyk have any questions, or need anything, April has my number. *Do not* hesitate to call."

"Thank you, Elias," Diane said.

"Well, I won't keep you any longer. Thank you for the information, Mr. and Mrs. Walczyk. Try to get some rest. April–?"

April picked the phone up and deactivated the speaker function. She turned to Henry and Diane. "I'm just going next door for a second. I'll be right back over." They nodded to her, Diane on the verge of tears. April left the room. "Is that all you need?" she asked Eli.

"That's all his manager needs," Eli said. "As for his friend, however... April, what the hell happened?"

While she let herself into her own room, April launched into a retelling of the entire story, from Cole Island and the couch to Augusta and Walczyk's freak-out in the hallway, wrapping up with Walczyk's admittance to Dirigo.

"My God," Eli said. "And they really don't know why this all happened?"

"Not yet," she replied. "As soon as I know anything..."

"Well, you've had a hell of a day or two," Eli said. "I'll let you go for now. Keep in touch, April. Let the big guy know that I love him and that everything will be taken care of for him."

"Will do," April said.

"I love you, Girly."

"I love you too, Eli," she said, shutting the phone off. April sank down to the floor, taking a deep breath as she sat. She fought the urge to cry, having promised herself that she wasn't going to fall apart. She picked the phone back up and flipped through the numbers stored. She selected Ian Maeder's number and dialed.

"Hello, you," Ian answered.

"Hi, Ian," she meekly replied.

"Listen, I was a real asshole not calling you back a couple of weeks ago after... well, you remember. I hope–"

"Ian, are you alone?"

"Yes," Ian replied. "Why? What's the matter?"

"Sit down," April said. "I have to tell you about Walczyk."

"Hit me again," Hannah said, sliding the now-empty beer bottle across the coffee table.

Rising from the couch, Vic picked the bottle up. "I think you've reached your limit, Missy."

"Well you can shit in one hand and think in the other and see which one you fill up first," Hannah said, slumping down on the rust brown sectional couch that had been in Vic Gordon's over-the-garage apartment as far back as she could remember.

"Here, try this instead," Vic said, pulling a clear plastic bottle of water from the fridge and bringing it back to Hannah in the living room.

Hannah looked up at Vic with sad, puppy dog eyes, not at all unlike the eyes of Dexter, who was quietly curled up on another clumping of sectional pieces on the other side of the living room. "That's not what I had in mind."

"Well, it's what *I* had in mind. And you'll take it, and you'll like it, and you'll drink it. Then you'll fall on your knees thanking me tomorrow morning that I cut you off when I did. Because, Hannah Louise Cooper, you still can't hold your liquor."

"I don't care." She cracked open the bottled water, taking a healthy swig of it.

"Atta girl," Vic said. "I want you to drink that whole thing before you go to bed."

"Why?"

"Because I'm taking care of you, that's why." Vic flipped through the channels, unable to settle on any one TV show. There was nothing on Friday nights.

"How do you think he is?" Hannah asked, lying down, the arms and legs on her left side dangling over the edge of the couch.

"April said they've got him heavily sedated right now. It looked like he was going to pass out as soon as they left."

"And we can go see him?"

"Yeah. April's staying with Henry and Diane at the hotel. I'm swinging by the house tomorrow to get some stuff for April. She's spending the week in Bangor with him."

It felt so strange, talking about him like this, Vic thought. He was in the hospital. A patient. And it wasn't the kind of hospital where you wear one of those backless johnnies. At least he didn't think they wore johnnies. In the nursing homes he'd been in, checking them out trying to find one for his old man, they let the people wear regular clothes. Of course, they had people helping them dress.

Vic's phone rang. He reached out quickly and grabbed it, his heart stopping. Ever since April had called yesterday afternoon, Vic couldn't stand the sound of his own ringtone. It reminded him too much of that phone call from April that they were committing Peter. He'd have to change it in the morning.

Vic was relieved to see the display screen read "Incoming Call: Dougie Olsen." "Hey, Doug, what's up?"

"Hey, man, what's crack-a-lacking?" Dougie was stoned. He

only used the word "crack-a-lacking" when he was high.

"Nothing much," Vic said, having decided earlier that day to tell no one of what had happened with Walczyk. He wasn't going to be responsible for starting that rumor mill churning.

"Chilling with Mr. Wal-zack no doubt." Before Vic could answer, Dougie jumped to the next topic. "You really hitting it with that manager of his?"

"She's his *assistant*, and we're *dating*," Vic said. When they were both drunk or stoned, Dougie was a great guy to be around. Funny, generous, and never an asshole. But as Vic talked to him tonight, sober, he realized that there just wasn't much to Dougie Olsen.

"Why don't you guys come over? We've got some great shit. You'll love it."

"No, thanks," Vic said. "April's pretty tired and I've got an early day tomorrow."

"But you never come over any more. The girls miss you, man!"

"I miss everyone, too. And I promise, some weekend, I'll take Saturday off and I'll come over, maybe bring April, and we'll party with you."

"Now, that, Mr. Gordon, is a plan."

"Good. Well, I won't keep you guys. Have a good night. Stay safe."

Dougie mumbled something and ended the call. Vic stared at the phone, the phrase "stay safe" bouncing around inside his empty mind. First he's cutting Hannah off for being tipsy, then he's telling Dougie and company to "stay safe" while smoking up. When the hell had be become the responsible one?

"Who was that?" Hannah asked.

"Dougie Olsen," Vic said, getting up from the floor. "Tell me, Han, what did I *ever* see in hanging out with that bunch?"

"Well, you were sleeping with Ingrid at the time."

"Besides that."

"Well," she said, pulling herself upright, "he's a funny guy. When he's messed up."

"True."

"And he's gets his hands on the best weed on Cole Island."

Vic slowly turned to Hannah, stunned at what he'd just heard. "And how the hell would you know that?"

She smiled at him. "Hang out with me more and you'll learn more about me."

Vic smiled at her frankness. "So what time do you want to leave tomorrow?"

"Well, you said visiting hours are at seven."

"Yeah, but April said if we showed up in the afternoon or something they'd let us in to see him. They don't have any classes or anything on the weekend."

"Let's be realistic, now," Hannah said, sitting up slowly. "You're not going to sleep tonight and I'm probably not, because I only sleep in my own bed and I'm not going home tonight. We might as well go over to his house first thing tomorrow and pack the stuff that April said to get and leave right after."

"Okay," Vic said, returning to the couch with a beer for himself. He plunked down next to Hannah, who toppled over against him as soon as he sat down.

"How did we let this happen?" Vic asked. "I mean, we're his friends. You'd think we'd be the first to have noticed something change in his behavior. Of course, now that I think about it, it's all there. When he first got back, I thought he was awful moody, but then I remembered that he's always been like that. So I let it go. I mean, his wife had dumped him. Of course he's gonna be depressed. But that's just depression. Everyone gets depressed. Hell, I guess you could say I've been depressed for a while now. I mean, my life has turned out way different from what I'd expected. I'm almost thirty-five, and I still live with my brother. I'm still at the restaurant. I'm still single. Still no kids. Still no huge successes. And then there's the old man... I'm not blaming him, though. I made the decisions I made because I wanted to make them. It's just... if I had the chance to do everything over again..." He mulled it over a moment. "Does that make me a bad son?"

Hannah did not reply.

"Hannah?"

Vic looked down at Hannah, who was slumped up against him, passed out, a faint snore coming from her open mouth.

"That's my Hannah," Vic said, leaning down to kiss her forehead, "always there when I need you."

PETER WALCZYK ENTERS TREATMENT FACILITY
A Paparazz-Eye Exclusive

"Ordinary World" writer/director/producer Peter Walczyk has checked himself into an undisclosed psychiatric facility in his native Maine, a rep for the 35-year-old auteur announced this morning.

Walczyk's rep, Elias Gaul, told Paparazzi-Eye, "With the counsel of family and friends, Peter has decided to check himself into a facility to deal with emotional issues he's been coping with for a while now. He graciously asks for your respect and privacy as he takes the necessary steps toward recovery." Gaul's statement confirmed that Walczyk is not seeking treatment for drug use.

This is the latest in a string of surprising turns for the "Ordinary World" showrunner, who split from his wife, actress Sara Collins-Walczyk, in August following the highly publicized discovery of Collins' relationship with "Ordinary World" star Ella Marsters.

CHAPTER FIFTEEN
A NEW CAST OF CHARACTERS

Walczyk returned to the world of the living not gently, but with a loud, obnoxious order: "Up and at 'em, Pete!"

He slowly sat up in bed, fighting what felt like a massive hangover. Standing in the doorway was a tall, burly woman with close-cropped hair and a pair of huge glasses. She was wearing wind pants (bet they let her keep the drawstring in hers) and a cream colored T-shirt.

"Breakfast time, Peter," she said cheerily. "C'mon. Get up! Everyone else is already in the cafeteria. We don't have all morning."

Walczyk rolled back over. "I'm not hungry."

"You will be," Nurse Wind Pants said. "Come on. You're not doing yourself any good lying in your bed moping about being here."

Walczyk responded with silence.

"In case you're wondering, being a moody loner isn't going to get you out of here any sooner. And enjoying yourself while you're here isn't going to confirm that you belong here long-term. Trust me."

Walczyk rolled over. "Look, being social and making friends, that was my wife's bit."

"Oh, you're married?"

"I was," Walczyk said, running his thumb over his wedding

ring. He still hadn't taken it off. No one had ever mentioned it to him. In fact, he'd almost forgotten he was still wearing it. He considered, for a moment, taking it off and handing it over to Nurse Wind Pants to put into storage with his personal effects. He took his fingers off the gold band and looked up. "Look, I just want to be left alone in here until I see Dr. Lentz again."

"There will be time for that later," the nurse said, stepping into the room. "As for now, I suggest you get your butt out of that bed and come down to breakfast with me. And do it quick, will you? I'm getting hungry."

Walczyk considered lying back down, but something told him that this Nurse Wind Pants was not a woman who gave up easily. He got up, slid on the dark blue slippers his parents had brought him, pulled on his hoodie, and moped down the hall behind the nurse. Chairs and benches lined both sides of the hallway, and he remembered this was where the majority of the patients were congregated. Walczyk noticed that, even if there were people in the rooms, still in bed or just pacing, the doors to all of the rooms were open. The ward held about twenty rooms, all double occupancy. At the far end, away from the main areas and the hub of excitement, was a little room, lined with windows. It looked like a nice, quiet spot to take a book and get away from the insanity.

Flanking the nurses' desk were two common rooms, each containing an old color television. The left room contained a small kitchenette, with a fridge stocked with juice and water and popsicles. Along the walls were several tables, which were covered with newspapers, magazines with the address boxes cut off, and half-finished jigsaw puzzles.

"My name's Susan, by the way," the nurse said as they neared the large double door that stood across from the nurse's station, locked at all times. To the right of that door was the small nurses' office where Walczyk vaguely remembered being checked into the hospital. The nurses' station was a large area with three computers and a long series of desk drawers, which the nurses were constantly unlocking and locking to retrieve items.

Tucked away in a corner across from the nurses' station was a white door. As they passed it, Walczyk peeked in through the small, circular window in the door. Inside was a padded room, with a mattress and pillow on the floor. And nothing else.

To the left of the large, locked door were three pay phones, divided from each other by heavily graffiti-ridden partitions. A dog-eared phonebook missing pieces from its cover sat under the middle phone. A short, plump woman with bad grammar and a mass of frizzy gray hair was on one of the phones, crying that the nurses were mistreating her.

"Hope, two going down to the caf," Susan yelled over the reception desk. Another nurse, roughly Walczyk's age, with curly red hair and blue-and-white striped scrubs, came out of a private office and did a double take.

"Name?" she asked.

"Peter Walczyk," Susan told Hope.

Nurse Hope did a double take and suppressed a smile, put her clipboard down, and pressed a red button on the wall. A motorized whirr and click sounded from the door. Susan opened the door and the two of them walked into another hallway. The door shut quickly behind them, with another whirr and click. He turned and looked back. Behind the reception desk, Hope had been joined by another nurse, probably in her forties with streaks of grey running through her short hair. The pair were talking animatedly, occasionally casting glances at the door that had just locked. Walczyk flipped his hood up.

"I take it you're some sort of big deal," Susan said as they walked through the corridor. "The nurses are all talking about you. What are you, an actor?"

"I created a TV show that airs on HBO," Walczyk said, trying to sound humble about the whole deal.

"Oh, yeah?" Susan asked. "What's it called?"

"*Ordinary World.*"

"Aah," Susan said, edified, as they stopped in front of an elevator. She punched a button. "I don't get HBO."

Susan led Walczyk down the hall to an elevator and they got in. A quick ride from the third to the first floor and they were deposited within hearing distance of the cafeteria. Susan escorted Walczyk down a corridor and into the yellow-walled cafeteria, where Walczyk got into line. There was a fruit bar set up, with apples, oranges, bananas, grapefruit, and even some cut-up pineapple. He picked up a cube of lemon Jell-o on a Styrofoam plate, considered grabbing an apple, and stepped up to the steam table, where three hair-netted women were standing in transparent plastic aprons.

"Eggs, three strips of bacon and two sausages, please," Walczyk said to the cafeteria worker standing behind the Plexiglas sneeze guard. He was thrust back to his high school days, standing in line with a tray, asking for what he wanted for a meal. Not even the studio commissaries were set up like this anymore. Susan had made a big to-do about the "Belgium" waffles that were served on Saturday mornings, but there was only one waffle left, and it looked rather steam-logged. Walczyk opted not to deprive the woman of her "Belgium" waffle.

The woman behind the line shook her head. Walczyk grew confused. "You have to pick one. Sausage or bacon."

Portion control. Now Walczyk really was back in high school. He opted for the sausage, getting two shriveled little links alongside a clump of bright yellow eggs that retained the shape of the corner of the metal pan they were in. Walczyk looked around the area. Closely supervised, two patients were spreading peanut butter onto plain bagels with plastic knives. It wasn't the presence of plastic cutlery, even non-serrated cutlery, that surprised Walczyk, but the toaster. He considered the damage a hand down a toaster could do as he picked up a plastic tumbler and dispensed himself some apple juice. There was a woman at a cash register, sitting on a stool, reading a section of the *Bangor Daily News* weekend edition. She looked up from her reading, and picked up her clipboard.

"Name?"

"Peter Walczyk."

The woman looked up from the clipboard, scrutinizing Walczyk's face for a moment, and then returned to her clipboard, finding his name and making a mark by it.

"Good to go, dear," she said. Walczyk turned to see Susan dig some wrinkled bills from her wind pants' pocket and pay for her own meal. She shoved the change back in her pocket, uncounted, and stepped up behind Walczyk.

"Sit wherever you like," she said, then headed off for a table staffed by individuals who were clearly wardens and not inmates – the wardens all wore ID badges on lanyards around their necks and wore scrubs. Walczyk found himself wondering why they wore scrubs. He got that nurses and doctors in regular hospitals wore scrubs, as they were comfortable and easy to move in, but so are regular clothes. And unlike with regular doctors and nurses, the chances of blood or other bodily fluids getting onto their clothing at a mental hospital was slight. Yet everyone was wearing scrubs, like regular nurses. Walczyk also noticed that the staff were the only people in the room with shoe laces.

Walczyk found a secluded table off to the side and sat down. He was hungry after all, he learned, as he began to eat. He didn't remember eating much over the past couple of days, aside from the pepperoni on the pizza that was sent up last night. He took a bite of the scrambled eggs and found they were devoid of anything resembling a taste. Abandoning them after only two bites, he tried the sausage. That, he decided, at least tasted like it used to be sausage. Walczyk got up to dump his tray when he found his way blocked by a tall, round fellow with wavy sandy brown hair and a day's beard growth.

"Don't dump your tray," the man told Walczyk.

"Why not? I'm done with it."

"Nurses have to look at it. Make sure you ate enough."

"Oh," Walczyk said, sitting back down.

"You don't like them eggs neither, huh?" the stranger asked, joining him.

"No," Walczyk said wearily. "Not really."

"My name's Richard," the man said, thrusting a hand out at him. "You're my roommate."

"Oh. Hello," Walczyk mumbled back. Walczyk sat back down at his table and took a sip of his apple juice. Richard sat down beside him.

"What's your name?" Richard asked, giving Walczyk the impression that he couldn't stand silence.

Walczyk considered giving him a fake name for a moment or two. Deciding to play nice, in case it got back to the nurses that he was giving out assumed names, Walczyk gave Richard an answer: "Peter."

"So what's wrong with you, Peter?"

Walczyk stared at Richard, stunned at the intimacy of the question. "I'm tired," he replied, a bit pissy.

"Oh, it's okay. Don't worry none, Peter," Richard said, leaning in. "We all talk about our problems. But talking about it is the only way to get better. Me, I hear voices."

"Oh," Walczyk said, at a loss for conversation. "They don't know what's wrong with me yet."

"They'll figure you out, Peter. Don't you worry none." Richard thought hard, no doubt looking for something else to ask the new guy. "So you didn't know I was your roommate?"

"No, I didn't."

"Well, you *was* pretty doped up yesterday."

"Yeah, I don't remember seeing you in the room when I was awake."

"That's because I stayed away when your family and your girlfriend was here so you could talk to them."

"She's just... just a friend. And thank you. That was nice of you."

"I don't like being in the room anyway. It's too quiet. I like being in the hall with the other guys."

And like a cattle call, one of the nurses – a tall, slender man with a long grey ponytail and thick salt-and-pepper stubble – announced it was time to leave the cafeteria. Susan Windpants strolled over to Walczyk's table. "Richard, go get your tray," she said, then turned her attention to Walczyk's tray. "You need to make an effort to eat more, Peter. You're not going to do yourself any favors starving yourself."

"I'm not a breakfast person," he said.

"Well, you'd better become one, because if we don't think you're getting proper nutrition, you'll get put on a meal program and your meals will be prescribed by a nutritionist."

Walczyk nodded and dumped his tray at the back of the cafeteria, growing to dislike Susan the more he dealt with her. This was going to be a long weekend.

The water was lukewarm, and it barely trickled out of the shower head, but it felt good to be taking a shower. One of the few things Walczyk had been aware of over the past several days was that it had been three days since he'd taken a shower. This particular shower was a rather curious experience for Walczyk. When he asked at the reception desk for soap and shampoo, he was told it was already in the shower. However, all he found when he stepped into the bathroom was a soft soap dispenser bolted to the wall off to the side of the shower knob. He pumped the handle several times, dispensing a small dab of opalescent soap. He worked the milky goop into his hair, then turned away from the shower head, lathering his body with it, generously applying it to his underarms, which were ripe.   He leaned against the rear wall, letting the water cascade down his back. He was still trying to make sense of it all. He, Emmy and Academy Award-winning writer Peter Walczyk, the man responsible for one of television's hottest commodities since *The Sopranos* or *Seinfeld*, had been committed to a mental hospital. The man the press plagued when he appeared in public with his friends. The man now known as Patient number 655321.

Prisoner 655321 felt more like it.

The door to the bathroom opened and Richard poked his head in. "You better hurry up. We got group at nine."

Walczyk turned and began to rinse his hair. *Yep*, he thought. *That was it. Prisoner 655321.*

Around nine o'clock, word thundered through the ward that it was morning meeting time. Walczyk stepped out of the bathroom wrapped in the only clean towel left. The large pile of sopping wet towels on the floor by the door tipped Walczyk off that Richard had taken his shower before breakfast. Richard was buttoning up a green and black plaid flannel shirt as Walczyk dressed in the monkey T-shirt his mother had bought him and a pair of flannel pajama pants. As he slipped on his slippers, Richard called over, "Ready for morning meeting, Peter?"

"What *is* this morning meeting?" The way Richard was going on about it, Walczyk half-expected one of those overly exuberant talk-show hosts to be there, hiding car keys under chairs to surprise everyone if they behaved.

"It's..." Richard thought a moment. "It's a meeting we have to go to. They're not long. Maybe a hour or so."

Walczyk rolled his eyes. Just what he wanted – to spend an hour (or so) with Richard and the other inmates. It seemed he was not fated to spend his time at the Dirigo Psychiatric Hospital alone. *I wonder what I have to do to get into that solitary confinement room*, he thought to himself as he pulled on his hoodie, flipping the hood up over his still tender head.

"I'm good," Walczyk said, plopping down on his bed, snagging *Dr. Jekyll and Mr. Hyde* from the desk beside his bed. "Thanks for letting me know, though."

Richard looked at Walczyk with worry in his watery eyes. "But you got to go. They make us."

"I said I'm good," Walczyk repeated, propping himself up against his pillow.

A tall, thin, blonde woman stepped in behind Richard. *Warden*, Walczyk instantly surmised. She just gave off the vibe of a person who would be running the place.

"Good morning, Richard," she said cheerily.

"Good morning, Emily," Richard said with greater cheeriness.

"Why aren't you on your way to the TV room for morning meeting?"

Richard became somewhat panicked. "I was. I swear it. I was just telling the new guy..." Richard screwed his face up, hard, thinking. He finally looked up, defeated. "What's your name again?"

"Peter," Walczyk said before burying his face in his book.

"Oh, yeah. Peter. I was just telling Peter about the morning meeting."

"Well, thank you, Richard. That was very courteous of you," Emily said, putting a hand on the man's arm. "Why don't you go on ahead? We'll catch up."

Richard nodded and took off down the hall at quite a clip. Emily turned back to Walczyk and looked him over, smiling. "You don't belong here," she said.

Walczyk looked up from his book, surprised to hear such a thing from a member of the staff. He couldn't say that he didn't agree with her. This place was filled with people who couldn't help themselves. Who were ghosts of their former selves. Walczyk just had a little dip off the deep end. He really didn't belong here. "What makes you say that?" he asked.

She shrugged. "It's obvious. You don't need anyone's help. You just need some meds to get your head straight and you'll be fine."

He remembered this act from Angela Cariou's office. "Tell me, does everyone in the mental health industry believe that 'Duck Season/Wabbit Season' logic will get them what they want?"

She stepped into the room and shrugged. "What can I say? You'd be surprised how often that works. But I *am* right; you don't belong here." Walczyk looked at her, trying to figure out her angle. She seemed serious. She sat down at the end of Richard's bed, which set perpendicular to Walczyk's. "You don't belong tucked away in a mental hospital in Bangor, Maine. You should be at some fancy clinic somewhere in California, where you have your own personal doctor on-call twenty-four hours a day, catered meals, and all the privacy you want."

"Wabbit season."

"Duck season. What do you need, Peter Walczyk?"

"I'm not getting into this." He returned his attention to his book. "Besides, you've got a group to get to."

"That's the beauty of running group," Emily said. "They can't start without me." Walczyk would have sworn she was flirting with him, but informing Dr. Lentz of that would probably get him another week of close observation.

Giving up, Walczyk put his book down. "All right. I'll listen. What do you want?"

"I just want to know what you want to get out of your treatment."

"I want to quit feeling miserable," Walczyk said.

"Okay," Emily said back. "What's making you miserable?"

"I'm pretty sure you know," he replied.

"Your wife? She did leave you. She humiliated you. She drove you out of your home and back here. Am I close?"

"She didn't *drive* me anywhere. Coming to Maine, that was my bright idea."

"You're being sarcastic when you talk about coming home to Maine. Why'd you come back here?"

Walczyk sighed. Apparently Emily wasn't going to be satisfied with just one open, honest answer. "It seemed like a good idea while we were on the road."

A voice bellowed Emily's name from out in the hallway. "Yeah," she yelled back, turning her head toward the open doorway. "I'll be right down." She turned back to Walczyk. "Well, you're right: I do have a group to run. And my adoring public awaits," she said, smiling. "Would you do me a favor?"

"What?" Walczyk asked, cautiously.

"Would you come to group? I won't make you speak if you don't want to." Walczyk knew, as she turned on that pretty, white smile, that she had no intention of living up to that promise.

He followed Emily down the hall and into the larger of the two group rooms that were on either side of the main desk. As Emily got set up and fielded "hellos" from a half dozen over-eager patients, Walczyk found a chair near the back of the common room, next to the refrigerator, and slipped his book out from his front pocket and opened it up.

"Good morning, everyone," an overly cheery man in his early twenties said. He was dressed in khakis and a button-down shirt. He had an ID badge clipped to his waistband. Beside him, Emily was digging out a clear plastic clipboard.

"How is everyone today?" Emily cheerily asked, hugging her clipboard. After a smattering of responses from Richard and several of the female patients, she threw a glance towards the back of the room, making the briefest of eye contact with Walczyk. "We have some new people, so we're going to start by introducing ourselves. Using your first names only, tell us who you are and, today, tell us something you want to have happen this weekend. I'll start. My name is Emily and I want to get my house cleaned by the end of the weekend."

There was a smattering of laughter from the room, mostly from the women. The young man with Emily leaned forward. "Hi. I'm Rick, and I've got some writing to get done on my novel this weekend."

The woman in front of Walczyk, a forty-something blonde with a wide, yellow, toothy smile, turned around in her chair. "He been writin' that for months now. Some kinda book. Won't tell no one what it's about."

Walczyk offered a half smile, nodding, and leaned back in his chair. One by one, everyone introduced themselves, turning to look right at Walczyk as they spoke.

"I'm Bill, and I want to get to see my kids this weekend," said a very tall, gaunt-faced man chewing a toothpick.

"I'm Louise, and I want to get a day pass to go with my mother and sister to the flea markets this weekend."

"My name's David, and I want to get the hell out of here," a young man in his mid-twenties mumbled from his chair in the corner near the door, his oversized white baseball cap jammed down over his eyes.

"I'm Richard Daigle," Richard said, waving. "You know. Your roommate!"

"No last names, Richard. Remember?" Rick reminded him.

"Oh, sorry," Richard said reflexively. "And what I want to do is... oh, I don't know what I want to do this weekend."

"What do you mean, you don't know?" Emily pressed, leaning forward, speaking as if to a child.

"I don't know," Richard repeated, helplessly. A barrage of

suggestions flooded in from the other patients. Richard finally, after careful consideration, decided, by himself, that he'd like to eat some Chinese food this weekend. Neither Emily nor Rick seemed thrilled with the reply, but accepted it and moved on to the next person.

Dean, a chubby man with black slicked-back hair, a pockmarked face, and no sleeves on his t-shirt, wanted to talk to his wife, whom he hadn't spoken to in a month. Patty, a plump little woman in a wheelchair wearing a faded Minnie Mouse T-shirt didn't answer. She just dug at the floor with one of her slipper-clad feet. The woman in front of Walczyk with the big smile identified herself as Elaine. "And for what I want to do this weekend, I want to have my kids come take me home." She broke down in tears.

Walczyk noticed that whenever someone had mentioned leaving the facility, either on a day pass or for good, Emily or Rick were careful not to say that it could happen. Walczyk guessed that was probably because these folks weren't leaving for a while now.

"Okay," Rick said, standing up. "It's time for our new guy to introduce himself."

New guy... way to not *make me stand out.* After some coaxing from Rick, Emily, and Richard, Walczyk put up a hand. "I'm Peter."

A half-cheery, half-bleary chorus of "Hi, Peter" came from the room. Richard was waving excitedly back at Walczyk. Walczyk managed to scrape up a half-smile for Richard.

"Ain't you the guy off the TV?" Elaine asked, jabbing a chubby pink digit at him. "The one with the wife who–"

This was why he didn't want to attend any morning groups and introduce himself.

"Excuse me," Emily said, quelling the hubbub that had erupted. "I'm going to ask that we not talk about that part of Peter's life. We need to respect his privacy."

Rick stood beside Emily. "That's right. Remember how we talked about respecting people's privacy a few weeks ago?"

"But he's famous," David said, sneering at Walczyk as he readjusted his hat. "He's used to not getting privacy."

"All the more reason that we need to respect his privacy here," Emily pressed, a bit more firmly. "How would you feel if we started sharing things about your life that you didn't want shared?"

"But I'm not some big shot movie star slumming it in Crazy Town for a week or two to get off the pep pills."

"David, that's enough." Rick's voice was the closest Walczyk had heard anyone sound angry in this place so far.

"No, it's all right," Walczyk said. "Everyone gets an opinion."

"But no one wants to listen to David's," Dean piped in, taking his toothpick out. "Just leave the guy alone, David."

"Kiss my ass, G.I. Joe!" David snapped, hopping to his feet.

"David!" Emily shouted. "That's your last warning. If you can't control yourself, you'll have to leave."

"Sounds good to me," he grunted, charging from the back of the room to the door. As he passed Walczyk, he gave a shove, knocking him out of his chair.

"David!" Rick shouted, following him out of the room. Emily rushed to Walczyk's side, and along with Dean, the two helped him up. Walczyk shook off their hands.

"Are you okay?" Emily asked.

"A lot better than that maniac," Walczyk grunted. "Somebody better adjust his meds."

"Peter, I understand why you're angry," Emily said as Dean uprighted Walczyk's chair, "but we don't talk like that here." When she returned to the front of the room, Emily retrained her focus on Walczyk. "All right, Peter, we were on you. Would you like to continue?" Emily said once everybody had settled down.

"Not necessarily," he said. After a few moments of taking in the staring, expectant faces of his fellow inmates, he breathed out a loud sigh. "My name is Peter. *That* Peter, for those of you wondering. And like my roommate, I don't know what I want to do this weekend."

I don't want to kill myself was all he could think of, but he certainly didn't want to share that with anyone in the room.

The meeting continued on, with the group discussing positive coping skills. Walczyk tuned the discussion out for the most part, letting his mind wander. How did he get here? He couldn't put his finger on it. He had been doing so well after Dr. Cottle had prescribed the Zoloft. He had been improving, he thought. He felt better. He had more energy. Hell, even his libido was starting to return, thanks to a rather erotic dream he'd had about Linda, one of the production assistants on *Ordinary World* who, he was told, had quite the crush on him. He was being more social. He was hanging out with Vic and Hannah, both at his place and in public. He was even enjoying Friday night dinners with his parents, and not shrugging off their questions about his status with Sara.

But then, somehow, the bottom fell out of it all. He got moody again. He couldn't shake the darkness that began to cascade down around him. And once it covered him, it tightened its grip on him, squeezing the hope out of him.

He'd begun reliving the last day he spent at his home when he was shaken out of his reminiscence by Emily.

"There. That wasn't so bad, was it?" she asked, sitting next to him, hugging her clipboard to her chest.

"Aside from getting used as a human tackling dummy? Yeah, it went fine."

"I'm so sorry about that. David has… well, let's just say he's a very angry young man."

"I'll say," Walczyk replied.

"That being said, don't be afraid of him. He'll be over it in a few hours, if he's not already."

"Good for him," Walczyk said. The kid was a young punk, trying his damndest to seem tough and menacing. But Walczyk, admittedly, was an out-of-shape cream puff, spoiled by years of Hollywood catering. Mr. Tough Guy could probably soundly kick his ass if he'd wanted to.

"I have a surprise for you."

"What's that? More tackling practice?" Walczyk asked cautiously.

She ignored his sarcasm. "Dr. Lentz came in to see you today. He didn't want to just dump you here without meeting with you a couple of times. Why don't we head down to his office?"

"You don't have to escort me," Walczyk said, getting up.

"Oh? You remember where it is?"

Walczyk thought back. He remembered being in Dr. Lentz' office yesterday, but he couldn't remember how he got there, or how he got back to his room.

"Fine," he said, resignedly. "Show me the way."

What do you want to accomplish today? The question rattled around the inside of Walczyk's head as he was escorted to the overstuffed chair opposite Dr. Lentz's desk. The good doctor was certainly dressed down today, wearing a plaid short-sleeved shirt and khakis instead of dress cords and a sweater.

"You look, to me, to be a man with something heavy on his

mind," Lentz said, his plastic travel mug filled with tea still at his side. "Why don't we discuss it."

"It's just... in group today, Emily asked what I want to accomplish. What did I want to do?" He sat in silence, hearing the second hand of the clock above his head tick away. "I know. It's such a simple concept. But I've got to tell you, it's also a foreign concept to me at the moment."

"Peter. don't beat yourself up over it. Your goals needn't be lofty. Not right now. We're simply trying to focus your brain on the little things. Give you something to accomplish so you can thrive on that feeling of accomplishment. Reading a book. Writing something. That sort of thing."

"But that's just it – I have no goals I want to meet. No obstacles I'm dying to overcome. No milestones worth passing. I just want to make it through the day and go to bed, so I can get to the next day, and the next after that."

Dr. Lentz took in a deep breath before speaking. "You're a writer; why not start something new while you're here? Maybe write about your troubles. Your reaction to being in a psychiatric hospital. Who knows, you could make us all famous," Dr. Lentz said. "Just remember, 'Lentz' is spelt with a Z."

Walczyk stared at the navy blue slippers on his feet for a few moments, thinking. Finally, he looked up. "I suppose I could start on something."

"Or, you don't have to write. I see you have a book with you." Lentz's eyes were on the copy of *Dr. Jekyll and Mr. Hyde* that lie on the floor next to Walczyk's foot. "Fascinating book," Lentz said. "Have you read it before?"

"No, though I think I might have seen a movie version of it once, a long time ago. Sara was – is – an admitted fan of old black-and-white horror films." He gave a soft laugh. "It's one of the things that had initially attracted me to her."

"Why not make it your goal to read a certain portion of it?" Lentz suggested.

"Fine," Walczyk said, growing weary of the entire concept of finding a goal to accomplish. "I'll tell you all about it Monday."

"No, it's not like that. You're on the honor system to read it. I don't need a book report. It's just a goal you set for yourself. The world won't end if you don't meet it." Lentz took a sip of his tea. "Now, today I'd like to spend some time talking about you. Your past history. Your work habits. Your life."

"Okay," Walczyk said, not necessarily knowing where this was going.

For the next hour, Walczyk and Dr. Lentz went over Walczyk's life with a fine-tooth comb, dissecting the insignificant and making it profound. They talked about everything from Walczyk's work schedule to the last time he felt happy to his sex life, which Walczyk said was non-existent at this point.

"So, is it safe to say," Dr. Lentz began, making notes on his iPad, "that you do have moods in which you are highly productive?"

"Yeah," Walczyk replied. "It's like nothing can stop me. I'm just... in the groove. My fingers fly over the keyboard. Nothing can stop me."

"Isn't it great?" Dr. Lentz commented, as though he knew exactly what Walczyk was talking about. "Then, you say, there are times when the creativity flows like molasses."

"Yeah. I can't get out of bed in the morning. I have to force myself to get five or ten pages written, and then they're usually shit at that."

"How was your relationship with your friends, your wife, your co-workers when you were in this super-productive state?"

"Great," Walczyk said, feeling himself rising a little. "They called it 'The Old Walczyk' in the office or on-set. We'd burn though rewrites like nothing. My prep work on the episodes I was directing seemed to fly by. Shooting... well, the crew couldn't keep up with me sometimes. I was always getting what I wanted in the first take or two, then flying into the next set-up. Then I'd go home and start writing or re-writing, into the early hours of the morning. I'd crash for an hour or two, then get right back at it."

"And when you were in your less-than-productive state of mind?"

"Episode 204. 'The Best of Both Worlds.' I shot day's worth of material, went home feeling fine, woke up the next morning feeling utterly despondent. I dumped the whole thing in the lap of my co-producer and best friend, Ian. I didn't even call him myself – I made Sara call him. This was all last minute, mind you. Ian had zero lead time to get his prep work done. Eventually, he had to trash everything I'd done and start over, filming an eight-day episode in six days. He won the Emmy for that one. Damn well earned it, too."

"So, I take it that sort of thing is–"

"Not cool. A director needs lead-in time to set up his camera angles, to chart the course of the episode, make decisions about certain character threads. And I dumped all of that on Ian because I couldn't get out of bed. He threatened to quit after that episode."

"But this Ian, he's still your friend, right? And he's still on the show?"

"He's running it in my absence."

"Meaning?"

"Meaning he's in charge of the day-to-day operation of the series."

Dr. Lentz thought for a moment. "Let's talk about life after Hollywood, shall we? What would you say your mood has been like since you've come to Maine?"

"I don't know," Walczyk said. "Okay, I guess. I get depressed, then I snap out of it. I get really antsy and I snap out of it. Nothing unusual."

"Would you say you spend more time in a depressive state than you do a hyperactive state?"

"Yeah," Walczyk said.

"But given what you've been though, that's not surprising. Tell me, and be honest now, do you have any suicidal thoughts?"

"I don't know if you'd call them suicidal," Walczyk began cautiously. "But yeah, I have spent a lot of time lately thinking how easy life would be if I were to just... you know."

"Yes," Lentz said. "Did you ever try to act on those feelings?"

"No."

"Ever form a plan of action?"

"No," Walczyk said, thinking back. "Mainly, I just think about how much easier life would be if I weren't around."

Dr. Lentz considered this a moment. What was he thinking? Was he going to put Walczyk on suicide watch? Have Nurse Susan sit on him so that he couldn't do anything? "In the future, any thoughts of that kind, or urges, or voices telling you to harm or kill yourself that you might have, need to be reported to one of the staff immediately, day or night. Increased suicidal ideation is one of the side effects of Zoloft in some patients." Dr. Lentz looked at the clock behind Walczyk's head. "And our hour is up for now. I'd like to meet with you again this afternoon."

"Okay," Walczyk said, thankful that he wasn't going to have to fill the entire day by himself.

"Your parents are staying in town a while, aren't they?"

"Yeah," Walczyk said after thinking back on his visit with them last night, which was a bit foggy in his memory. "They're staying with my assistant April, just down the road."

"Would it be all right if I contacted your parents and asked them to join us?"

"What for?" Walczyk asked.

"Well, honestly, they know you better than I do. They might be able to help me figure out what's going on with you. I was thinking of getting together with the three of you around, say, two o'clock. So, is that all right with you?"

"Sure," Walczyk said, still confused as to why his parents were being brought in, why Dr. Lentz was playing these frustrating waiting games, and why no one had told him what was the matter with him yet.

After his session with Dr. Lentz, Walczyk just wanted to curl up on his bed and read in peace and quiet. However, when he returned to his room, he found Richard there, reading aloud from the stack of comic books he had strewn across his bed. Walczyk knew the moment he entered the room that possibility of reading in there was over and done with. Instead, he took his copy of *Dr. Jekyll and Mr. Hyde* and wandered down the corridor, heading for that nice, quiet little area at the end of the hall.

"Where are you headed, Peter?" Emily called out from behind him.

"I saw this room down at the end of the hall this morning. I figured I'd go in there and do some reading." He held the book up to prove he was off to read.

"Sorry, Peter, but that room's closed right now. They're doing one-on-one evaluations in there."

"Then I guess I'm off to my room to *try* to read," he said, disappointed, knowing that he'd not be able to get into his book with Richard in there.

"Why don't you read out here with the rest of the residents?" Emily suggested.

"Because I want to be alone."

"You don't want to have much to do with the others, do you?"

Emily asked, challenging him.

"Look, I just need quiet to read, and there's a TV in each of the other rooms."

"Then why don't you forget about the book? I know that the other residents would like to get to know you a little better."

"I'd rather read," Walczyk wearily said, not understanding why it was so unforgivable to want to have some peace and quiet to read his book.

After a moment or two of their silent stand-off, Emily smiled. "That's okay, then. But sometime this afternoon, maybe before your next meeting with Dr. Lentz, you and I can make a date to sit down and start setting some goals for you."

"Fine," he said, trying very hard not to snap. He turned and walked into his room. Walczyk soon learned that had been right in his early assessment of his chances of reading with Richard in the room. Before he'd even gotten to his bed, Richard started to tell him how the different colors of Green Lantern rings give that Lantern different powers (Walczyk had assumed that the Green Lantern's ring was, naturally, green). Walczyk lay back and shut his eyes as Richard rambled on about Sinestro and Kilowog and Oa. Just as Walczyk managed to tune Richard out, he heard his name called out. He rolled over and looked. Rick stood in the doorway.

"Peter, you have a visitor."

Walczyk wasn't expecting anyone. His folks probably weren't showing up until their big group meeting with Dr. Lentz at two, and Vic and Hannah probably weren't going to get here until visiting hours at seven. Walczyk got up off his bed, slipped his slippers back on, and stepped out into the hallway.

"Who is it?" Walczyk asked.

Rick was uncharacteristically quiet. "She's down by the nurse's station."

She? He reasoned that it must be April, checking in because she's bored. Walczyk walked quickly toward the main desk, but his heart stopped when he saw who his visitor was.

Sara was standing in front of him, red-eyed, clutching her purse.

"Hello, Peter," she said, breathless.

"Sara," he said, stunned. She reached out and latched onto him, hugging him tightly. Walczyk squeezed her for all he was worth, unable to believe she was in his arms again.

"What are you doing here?" he whispered into her ear.

"You don't think my husband's going to be hospitalized and I'm not going to come visit," Sara said back.

Getting the feeling he was being watched, Walczyk let go of Sara. His suspicions were confirmed as he saw Emily, Rick, Hope, and several of the patients staring at them.

"Let's go down to my room," Walczyk said awkwardly.

They walked through the hall in silence. Oddly enough, there was no one around. No one watching TV in the common rooms. No one in the quiet room at the end of the hall. No one hanging out in the corridor, leaning against the scratched-up plexi-glass.

"Let me tell you," Walczyk told her after they'd settled in and Sara asked what his first impressions were, "you've not really lived life until you've showered in the bathroom of a mental hospital. It's truly a new experience."

"How so?" Sara asked, sitting at the foot of Richard's bed. Richard was surprisingly absent from the room and his comic books were cleaned up and put away.

"Well, first of all, forget locking the door when you go to the bathroom. The only things around here that have locks have nurses carrying keys to them."

"Peter..." she trailed off for a moment, as if summoning her courage. "What happened?"

"We don't know yet. I think they're suspecting the Zoloft I was on, though. They haven't given any of it to me since I got in here."

"Zoloft?"

"It's an anti-depressant."

"You're on meds?" She reached out for him. "Oh, baby–"

He held his hands up. "Please, don't–"

"Sorry," she said, covering her mouth. "I'm just used to calling you that. Guess it slipped out."

"No. Don't feel bad for me," Walczyk said. "Don't feel bad for me and don't blame yourself."

"Peter, I don't blame myself," she said unconvincingly.

"Not yet," he retorted. "But I know you. You will."

There was a knock at the door. An unnecessary knock, since the door opened not long after the rapping on the other side. It was Emily.

"Sorry," she said. "But we don't allow closed doors on the ward." She smiled meekly, her attention on Sara.

"Oh," Walczyk said. "Sorry."

"It's okay. You probably didn't know." Emily waved and popped her head back out of the room, leaving the door wide open behind her. Sara shook her head, smiling broadly.

"What?" Walczyk asked.

"I can't believe it."

"What?" he repeated.

"She wants you." She shook her head, laughing to herself.

"You mean Emily the nurse?"

"Yeah. Why's that such an absurd notion?" she asked.

"Well, because I'm a mental patient and she's my nurse?"

"You're *not* a mental patient," Sara said. "And you don't belong here. You're not like some of these others."

"How do we know? They're still checking me out."

"But you're normal," she said, making sure no one was within earshot.

"Kid, I'm far from normal."

Sara smiled, lowering her eyes to the floor. Eventually, she peeked up. There were tears in her eyes. Walczyk's smile faded. He leaned forward to take her hand. She pushed it away.

"What'd I say?"

"Nothing." Sara got up and moved to the other bed, sitting down beside Walczyk. She took his hand in hers, interlacing their fingers. "It's just... well, no one else calls me 'Kid.' It took me back." She leaned her head on his shoulder, staring out into the hall. Patients were walking back-and-forth, or being pushed in wheelchairs or aided with walkers. Every once in a while, a peal of laughter would come from down towards the reception desk, where Walczyk presumed everyone hung out.

"You do know that I still love you, right?" She looked up at her husband. Her eyes filling with tears. "Baby, I never meant to hurt you." She took his unshaven face in her hands, stroking his beard. "I didn't want this to happen. It just... Ella makes me feel..." She shook her head, at a loss for words. "It's no denigration of you or our marriage. You were a terrific husband. I never wanted for anything in our home. I just... she completed me in a way you never did. In a way you never could."

Tears slid down both their cheeks. It was hard to tell who moved first, but soon, their lips met. It was remarkable. There she was, after so many dreams and after so much remembering – there she was! She still smelled like Sara. Still felt like Sara. She still–

"Peter!"

The world of the Dirigo Psychiatric Hospital crashed back down in around him, and Walczyk found himself sitting upright on his bed, alone. It was gone. All of it. He slowly turned toward the door. Richard was standing there. Once Walczyk made eye-contact with Richard, the announcement came: "It's time for lunch, Peter."

"Thank you, Richard," he snapped, finding it hard to feel sympathy for, or be polite to, the forty-year-old child he was rooming with.

CHAPTER SIXTEEN
A TASTE OF HOME

Walczyk sat down to his lunch, which was not the chicken alfredo he'd heard everyone talking about upstairs, but hamburgers. Very small hamburgers. However, they tasted remarkably good. Good enough that Walczyk was rather pissed he could only get one of them.

Walczyk had just slid *Dr. Jekyll and Mr. Hyde* out from inside his hoodie and cracked it when a rattling of dishes-on-a-tray caught his attention. He looked up to see a very skinny, very short young woman with black hair and freckled cheeks. She had to be in her early twenties. She had a barrage of holes in her ears, where she once wore a multitude of earrings, as well as tell-tale holes in her eyebrows, nose, lower lip and labret. She was dressed in a ratty black T-shirt with the sleeves torn off, equally distressed blue jeans and heavy black eye make-up.

"I won't bug you, but can I sit here? David's planning a revolution if he can't get out for a cigarette today." The young woman's ensemble was topped off by a pair of elbow-length black gloves with no fingers, displaying chipped bright green fingernail polish.

Walczyk first considered it a trap, but he felt sorry for the girl, whose tray was wider across than she was. "Go for it," he said, pushing her chair out with his foot. She placed her tray on the table and sat.

"Thanks," she said.

Walczyk returned to the book, but found himself feeling incredibly rude just sitting there, not speaking to the girl. He looked over the top of his book. She was picking at her tossed salad, arranging the ingredients in straight columns. A column of cucumber. A column of cherry tomatoes. A column of baby carrots. He fought the urge to ask if the croutons went in a circle around the outer rim of the plate. It was a very curious little preparation of the salad, but she seemed to know what she was doing. The girl tore open the first of three salad dressing packets she had on her tray and ran strips of ranch up and down over the cucumbers, drowning them. She then picked up a packet of Italian dressing and did the same with the tomatoes, going a little easier on them with the dressing. The third packet, an orange dressing that had to have been either Catalina or French, was drizzled over the carrots. When she was done, she picked her fork up, speared a cucumber and ate it. Looking up from her salad, she saw she was being watched and her cheeks flushed red.

"Sorry," Walczyk said, returning to his hamburger.

"No, it's okay. I know I'm weird."

"Never said that," Walczyk said, pretending to resume his book.

"Well, I'm saying it, because no one else will. I am weird."

Walczyk put his book down, not out of frustration, but out of curiosity. "Why do you... do that thing with your salad?"

She finished chewing another cucumber and wiped her mouth with her napkin. "I'm OCD. Can't stand the idea of my food being mixed together. It's among my multitude of sins."

Walczyk returned to his book, but only for a moment before his mind told him that he was being watched. He poked his head up over the book again. The young woman was watching him intently. "What's up?"

She broke her stare, again flushing. "Sorry. Didn't mean to stare. It's just–"

"Yeah," he said. "If I were in here with Steven Spielberg or Martin Scorsese, I'd probably react the same way."

"What do you mean?"

"I mean," Walczyk said, putting his hamburger down, "I'm aware that it's got to be odd, getting treatment in a place where there's a celebrity as a patient."

"Oh, you're a celebrity?" It was half-question, half-statement. The young woman returned to her salad, starting in on the row of cherry tomatoes.

"I'm Peter," he said, giving a half wave.

"Kaley," she said. "And what I was staring at was this." She tapped the cover of his book.

"You know *Dr. Jekyll and Mr. Hyde?*" Walczyk asked, looking down at the book's cover.

"Well, everyone knows the story to some extent," she said. "Dude has two halves. A gentle, polite, likeable side and a wicked, lascivious, violent side. But no, I was looking at the cover. That's a pretty sick painting."

Walczyk re-examined the cover painting, the man with his face half-submerged in darkness, half illuminated in light. He stared into the eyes of the man, and realized for the first time that the man in the painting had his hazel eyes, just like his.

"So what are you in for?" Kaley asked conversationally, moving into the heart of the salad.

"No idea," Walczyk said. "We're meeting with my family at two, though."

"We?"

"Dr. Lentz."

"Lentz is a cool shit. A lot better than Berenbaum. She can be a real bitch." Kaley meekly looked down. "Sorry."

"It's okay."

"She really doesn't have a clue as to what she's doing, though. Which is apparent just talking to her. But they give her all the vegetables, so it's not like they're going to complain." Kaley finished the row of tomatoes. "You okay? You seem kind of, I don't know, out of it. Not that I know what you're normally like, Peter."

"No, I'm not all right," Walczyk confessed. "I had this... this dream before I got here. It was a little too real."

"Those are the worst kind. Mind me asking what it was about?"

"My wife. Well, my ex. My ex-wife."

"So it was about Sara Collins-Walczyk," Kaley surmised.

Walczyk looked up from his meal. "I thought you didn't know who I was."

"Never said that," Kaley said, smirking devilishly. "I just

never encouraged you to drone on and on about being famous."

"So you know about Sara and me and–"

"The British chick? Oh yeah. Hard not to, really. The press ran that one into the ground."

"Yes, they certainly did," Walczyk said.

"So in this dream, were you here or in California?"

"She flew to Maine to see me. Here at the hospital."

"When's the last time you talked to her?" Kaley asked. "In the waking world, I mean."

"A month ago. She called to tell me she was filing for divorce."

"Shit," Kaley winced. "How'd the dream reunion go down?"

Walczyk shrugged. "She kissed me."

Kaley leaned away from him. "This didn't turn out to be some twisted sex dream did it?"

"No. She just kissed me."

"Then what happened?"

"Then, Richard walked in."

"You dreamed Richard walked in on you and your wife making out?"

"No. In real life. He walked in and woke me up for lunch."

A schlubby blonde nurse with large square-shaped glasses and greasy hair strolled up to their table. He was wearing a name badge that identified him as "Roger," He checked Kaley's tray. "You ought to get a little more than just salad next time, Kaley, if you ever want to get over your eating disorder." He turned to Walczyk. "And you must be *the* Peter Walczyk."

"Must be," Walczyk said, instantly hating this guy. He was so cocky. It was evident in the way he strutted around with his clipboard and his belt loaded down with keys. Big deal. Everyone he'd seen here so far had a clipboard. Walczyk would've wagered that even the janitor had a clipboard, somewhere on his cart. Probably tucked away between the lemon Pledge and the Windex.

Roger checked over Walczyk's tray. "Okay. You two can go dump your trays and line up to go back upstairs." Roger, his head thrown back (probably to keep those huge glasses on his oily face), moved onto the long rectangular table in the middle of the room where the majority of the patients ate their meals.

"What was that?" Walczyk asked, getting to his feet.

"That was Roger," Kaley said, standing. She picked up her tray, and looked at Walczyk. "And be careful of Roger."

"Why?"

"Because Roger's a dick."

The dream, the kiss, and his willingness to open up to Kaley about it were still rumbling through Walczyk's head when he sat down in the quiet room with Emily. "Do you mind if we shut the door?" Emily asked. "It tends to get a bit noisy out there after lunch. Lots of bottled up energy."

"Fine by me," Walczyk said.

"So, how was your morning?"

"Confusing."

"The first morning usually is. Remember in our morning meeting how we were talking about picking a goal? Something that we wanted to accomplish?"

"Yeah," Walczyk said.

"Well, you'll also remember that you were one of the folks who had a hard time coming up with a goal for the weekend."

"I remember," Walczyk said, growing weary of the pussy-footing.

"Well, this is generally a workshop I do during the week, and with a group of people, but I think this might help you get through the weekend a bit easier. What we're going to talk about is something we call positive planning." She waited, possibly for Walczyk to say something. He didn't. "Positive planning is a way of structuring your day, so that you have little goals to accomplish and things to look forward to. It also puts the responsibility of what happens in the course of your day in your hands."

"You're going to teach me how to plan things," Walczyk clarified, unable to believe something so simple warranted its own workshop.

"I'm going to *help* you to structure your day better. A busy day is a day where we dwell less on ourselves and more on the things we have to get done."

Walczyk resigned himself to the fact that he was going to make a "plan for the day." He didn't want to – he wanted to sit in his room and read or nap – but he also found he didn't want to be argumentative or difficult with Emily. Nothing good could come of his being difficult.

Walczyk grabbed a pen from the table. "All right, Where do we start?"

Emily smiled at him, a twinkle in her eyes. She handed Walczyk a sheet of paper. It was titled "Weekend Planning" and had blanks at the top for his name and the date. He filled them in, feeling like a sixth grader getting ready for a pop quiz over the capitals of the U.S. Beneath the title was the heading "3 Things I Must Accomplish This Weekend," accompanied by more blanks.

"I suppose it's counter-productive to write 'get out of here' for number one," Walczyk said.

Emily frowned. "Make these things you *know* you can accomplish. You're a writer. You must have a project you're working on."

Instantly, several ideas came to the forefront of Walczyk's mind. His cloned wife/psycho story that he'd abandoned. He dismissed that. He'd given up on it. It was crap. If he was lucky, he could sell the treatment to a studio and someone else could write it. Then the obvious choice came to mind: *Ordinary World*. He'd not yet officially quit, and he supposed he could be working on an outline for the direction of season four to give to Ian. But he felt wrong doing that without the other writers on the show. Then it struck him: "Well, there's *Night*."

"What's *Night*?"

Walczyk smiled dismissively. "It's this remake of *Night of the Living Dead* that Marathon Pictures wants me to write for them."

"That's exciting," she said. "Sounds scary," she added, sounding more like a kindergarten teacher than ever. So you've got your movie script to write, but you'll never get the whole thing written in one weekend."

"I've seen it happen before," Walczyk said. "But I doubt I can get a bottle of scotch, some clove cigarettes, and absolute privacy in here."

"No," she said cautiously. "No, that's highly unlikely. So, what is a good, realistic goal to set for yourself? Fifteen pages of your script?"

"I won't be writing the script yet. I'll start with what we call a treatment." The term was lost on her. "It's basically a story version of the script. Short on details, heavy on just getting the story out there. It'll be a blueprint to follow for writing the first draft of the screenplay."

"So let's just say," she began, "'Get a start on... what'd you call it again? Your treaty?"

"*Treatment*," Walczyk clarified.

"Treatment," she repeated. "How many pages do you want to get done?"

"I'm supposed to keep these goals easy or challenge myself?" Walczyk asked.

"Well, the goal should be something you can achieve if you're willing to put a reasonable amount of effort into it."

"Let's say, then, that I need to finish Act I by the end of the weekend."

"Okay," Emily said. "Write it down." He obeyed and, together, Walczyk and Emily came up with two other weekend goals: one was to call Ian and let him know he was okay. He hadn't spoken to Ian since the wrap party the night before he left L.A. The third thing on his list was to make a list of things he needed to talk to Sara about. These were business things and personal things. Stuff he'd been putting off since they split up.

After making plans for healthier nutrition and exercise and for being social (which Walczyk had balked at initially), and ways he would actually have fun, they came to the final section of the sheet: "Three coping skills I can use to tolerate distress are..." As he had tuned out Emily's morning discussion, Walczyk wasn't completely aware of what "coping skills" were, so Emily had to give him a quick recap of what he'd missed.

"Coping skills are just things we do to deal with the depression, confusion and distress in our lives. They can be as simple as listening to music, reading a book or watching a movie or your favorite TV show, or as involved as browsing in your favorite store, taking a scenic drive to a beautiful place, or buying yourself something that you can afford."

"Well, I've already got a thirty-two inch flat panel TV in my bedroom that I haven't even taken out of the box yet," he said with a wry smile on his face.

Emily tried to stay serious, but allowed a grin to escape across her face after a struggle. "I'm happy to see you're starting to warm up a little."

"Well," Walczyk said, shrugging, "as I see it, I can either try to be pleasant and admit that I need help, or make myself miserable trying to prove that I don't belong here."

"So you do admit that you belong here?" Emily asked.

"Would it destroy that sense of accomplishment you're feeling if I said I was still on the fence?"

"I'd feel a sense of accomplishment if I got you to finish this worksheet."

"Look," Walczyk said, picking the paper up. "I've got three goals picked out for myself, I've outlined how I'm going to take care of myself, and even committed to making friends with one of my fellow inmates."

"*Patients*, please," Emily asked.

"Fellow patients, then. I think we've got a good plan in place for me. I should have nothing to complain about this weekend."

Shortly thereafter, while they went over his plan for seeking help if he found himself in a dangerous situation, Rick arrived to escort Walczyk to Dr. Lentz's office. "So, how was your weekend planning session?" Rick asked as they walked down the corridor. What few patients were in their rooms were reading or napping, or as was the case with one little old lady who had to be in her seventies or eighties, just staring up at the ceiling.

Rick and Walczyk stopped in the middle of the corridor, where a plain door marked "Jonathan S. Lentz, MD" stood ajar. Walczyk stepped into the room and found his parents sitting at the desk opposite Dr. Lentz. His mother looked relatively relaxed, compared to her last visit, while his father looked a bit tenser. They rose from their chairs when they saw Walczyk enter the room and surged toward him, enveloping him in a large three-person hug.

"Thank you, Rick," Dr. Lentz softly said across the room. Rick closed the door behind him as he left.

"How are you doing?" Walczyk's mother whispered into his ear.

"Fine," he said. "How'd you guys fare at the hotel?" Walczyk knew his mother *hated* sleeping anywhere but home, so it was a great sacrifice for her to spend the night in a hotel, in a strange bed, with strange pillows, watching a strange TV, without Cocoa and Brownie in her lap keeping her company.

"It was good," his father said softly. Walczyk gave his father an extra squeeze around the waist, then let go of his parents. The three

Walczyks sat down in the various chairs spread around the room.

"How's April?" Walczyk asked.

"Good," Mum quickly, but unconvincingly, said. "She's back at the hotel sleeping. She'll be by later."

"She feels like she's got a lot on her back right now," Dad said.

"She does," Walczyk said, feeling guilty. Of course, in the five years she'd worked for him, they'd gone over what needed to be done in the case of an emergency, but they'd always assumed that Sara would be there to take over some of the responsibility. As it stood, there was a lot of public relations stuff to be done that his parents couldn't help with.

"Did she and Eli release a statement to the press?" Walczyk asked.

"It's all taken care of. And so far, they paparazzi are giving you your privacy," Dad said.

Walczyk looked over to see Dr. Lentz sitting at his desk, feet up and resting on an open drawer. "Your Mum and Dad and I were talking a bit before you got here. Just bringing them up to speed on your current pharmacological status, the sorts of activities you will be engaging in on Monday, and what not." Dr. Lentz turned to Walczyk's parents. "Do you have any questions?"

They turned to one another before responding to Dr. Lentz that they were in full understanding.

The doctor turned to Walczyk. "And do you understand your treatment plan as I've outlined it to you over the past day or so? I know you weren't entirely with it yesterday, so if you have any questions, stop me anytime. Okay?" Walczyk nodded. "All right," Dr. Lentz said, taking his feet down and leaning forward in his squeaky chair. "I've talked with Peter briefly yesterday and earlier today and have gotten a better understanding as to how he generally operates. According to Peter, at times he's one person: a manic, productive fellow who lives on an emotional high. Spends big. Loves big. Lives big – he's invincible and nothing will stop him. This Peter is prone to making grandiose plans and has what we clinically call 'racing thoughts' – his brain just can't keep up with him sometimes. Then there's the other person: depressed, withdrawn, reclusive. He's excessively tired, but cannot sleep. Susceptible to emotional outbursts. All for no reason. These incidents of depression are not necessarily spurred on by a trigger."

"Are you saying he's got some multiple-personality disorder?" Walczyk's father asked cautiously.

"No, not at all. It's always the same person, just in two vastly different moods. No, I think it's more accurate to say that Peter suffers from what we call bipolar disorder."

The room was quiet. No one looked at Walczyk for the longest time. Finally, feebly, Walczyk's mother spoke up. "Isn't that what insane criminals have?"

"Oh, no. No, not at all," Dr. Lentz said calmly. "In fact, a great number of high-functioning people have been diagnosed bipolar."

"I've heard of it before," Walczyk said. "Not too long ago, Catherine Zeta-Jones came out about her struggles with it."

"Carrie Fisher, from the *Star Wars* films, has been quite vocal about her experiences with bipolarity," Dr. Lentz shared. "And the list goes on-and-on. Many people with bipolar disorder are very creative and highly successful."

"So it's treatable?" Walczyk asked.

"It's manageable. In fact, we're going to start today. In most cases, lithium carbonate is prescribed in a controlled dosage."

"And how will this lithium carbonite help?" Dad asked.

"*Carbonate*," Dr. Lentz stressed. "And, well, Henry... it's all rather mysterious. But for some time now, lithium salts have been proven to stabilize mood swings, like the types present in bipolar disorder. In fact, it's the most common treatment for the disorder."

"Is this a new treatment?" Walczyk's mother asked.

"Actually, its ages old, though the blokes had no idea what they were prescribing at the time." Dr. Lentz chuckled. His laughter did not spread. "You see, in ancient times, doctors would have their mentally ill patients drink from certain alkali springs. The doctors never knew it, but their patients were ingesting quantities of lithium which were in abundance in these springs."

"So this lithium works?" Walczyk asked.

"It will most likely work – I say *most likely* because there are always exceptions, which we can address when and if they arise. But you will need to take it as prescribed."

"So," he pulled his book from his pocket, "I'm like Jekyll and Hyde? Two sides of a coin."

"In a sense," Dr. Lentz said, leaning forward in Walczyk's

direction. "But even with bipolar disorder, you're still always the entity we know as Peter Walczyk. Sometimes you are manic and do things like buy an expensive car or a house or stay up for days on end. Sometimes you are depressed and you feel hopeless and despondent or even emotionally distraught. But you are still Peter Walczyk. *You* don't change. Your *mood* changes. Everyone has mood swings. Yours are just more extreme... and more obvious to yourself and to others."

"Is there any sort of middle-ground," Mum asked, "or will Peter constantly be either manic or depressed?"

"Our aim is for Peter to have a great, vast middle-ground to exist within." Dr. Lentz turned once again to Walczyk. "But let me be absolutely clear – this will not be an easy process. The pharmacology behind this is not an exact science, as every person tolerates these drugs in different ways. Until we find a good level to keep you at, your moods will continue to fluctuate. You will probably have more depressed episodes than hypomanic episodes. And even after we get you straightened out, you'll constantly be doing blood work to make sure the levels of lithium in your bloodstream aren't toxic. You'll most likely put on weight. Depending on what other drugs you'll be on, your sex drive may decrease and your physical potency will be affected as well." Lentz looked from a worried-looking Walczyk to his worried-looking parents, smiling mischievously. "I don't expect you to remember any of this right now, outside of maybe bipolar disorder, hypomania, and impotence." Walczyk smiled in spite of himself. "Tonight you'll begin taking lithium. As soon as we're done here, and don't worry, I'll give you a little more time with your parents, we'll do a blood draw so we have a baseline. Down the road, once you get a better idea how you're going to tolerate the lithium, you can have your own doctor, Dr. Cottle can prescribe an–"

"No," Walczyk said, grabbing the arms of his chair. "That lunatic's not coming anywhere near me!"

Walczyk felt his father's hand on his shoulder, firm but calming. "Dr. Cottle's the general practitioner on Cole Island who put Peter on Zoloft in the first place," his father explained, then looked at Walczyk. "It's okay, Peter. We can get you someone else."

"Peter," Dr. Lentz said knowingly. "I wouldn't say your man Cottle's a lunatic. But I am willing to bet he's out of his depths when it comes to diagnosing psychiatric disorders."

"Why *did* the Zoloft make him so sick?" Walczyk's mother

asked quietly.

"God only knows," Dr. Lentz said, taking off his glasses. "Some manic depressives just don't tolerate SSRIs well."

"What are SSRIs?" Mum asked.

"They're the family of drugs that Zoloft belongs to. That's no denigration of the product – it's a great drug, and has been shown to be quite helpful for some bipolar patients. Like I said, this isn't an exact science."

"So, the $64,000 question, I guess," Walczyk's father asked, shifting in his chair, "is how long can Peter expect to be in here?"

"Well," Dr. Lentz said. "I'm thinking no longer than a week or two. I want to see the lithium take effect, and that sometimes takes anywhere from a week to several weeks. I know that this isn't an ideal setting, especially when privacy is at a premium. But I am not discharging him until I'm confident that, with the help of his family and his friends, he can take care of himself. And bear in mind, we *are* dealing with more than just bipolarity."

Walczyk felt all eyes fall on him. In particular, on the welt on the back of his head. "That wasn't a suicide attempt."

"No, it most certainly was not," Dr. Lentz said. "But you have seen people in here with scars and marks that are not necessarily the result of a suicidal attempt. Self-harming tendencies such as those you exhibited Thursday afternoon do warrant concern, though."

Walczyk's stomach sank. *Well, that does it,* he thought. *You're not getting out of here Monday morning.*

Hours later, when the cattle call for supper came, Walczyk was told that he could stay behind; he had guests coming. With his pick of abandoned common rooms, Walczyk chose the smaller one, which had no windows, to work in.

He stared at the blank page for several minutes before his brain sparked and his body filled with energy. He briefly questioned whether or not it was a hypomanic episode, but decided if it was, bully for him. It was better than the depressive state he'd been living in since arriving here. He picked up his pen and wrote. As he neared the exposure of the first real, gnarly, nasty zombie, a knock on the glass behind Walczyk shook him out of his creativity. He turned. One of the night nurses, whose name he wanted to say was Mary, was standing in the doorway, smiling. Flanking her were Vic, April, and Hannah. Walczyk felt his eyes burning as he got up. Before they even got through the door, Hannah let slip a sob and rushed out, pulling him into her arms and planting a wet, tear-stained kiss on his cheek. She stroked the back of his head, mumbling "Oh, my God, Peter... Oh, my God...." After a while, Walczyk stepped back from her, keeping his arms wrapped around her.

"Hey, hey, now. We'll have none of that." Walczyk leaned in and, in a confidential tone, said, "Besides, you cry too much, they'll give you a room and take away your shoe laces."

She laughed, wiping her eyes then fetching a tissue from a large box on the reception desk. Walczyk turned to Vic, who set two large paper bags down on the counter at the nurses' station. He reached out for Walczyk, pulling him in for a tight hug. The two men stood still, embracing for a while, before letting go of each other. Walczyk then turned to April and was somewhat surprised to see tears in her eyes. He figured she'd have gotten it all out of her system last night. He kissed her cheek and told her it was good to see her again, then let go and stepped back.

"So, what's in the bags?" Walczyk asked, craning his neck to get a better look at the two bags behind Vic.

"We can't have the obligatory alcohol," Vic said, grinning, "but I'm declaring an emergency Mick-a-Palooza."

Walczyk laughed with delight as Vic reached into the bag and pulled out a foil container. Before he had the chance to explain, Walczyk exclaimed, "You didn't!"

Vic pulled back the cover to the container and showed it to Walczyk. "Guy Martin's fried chicken, anyone?"

"So Vic comes into the gas station's restaurant part," Walczyk said, waving a drumstick in the air, "and he says, 'Guys, we gotta get the hell out of here!' So I start arguing with him about how I'm not done my French onion soup. And he's like, 'Seriously, Walz, we gotta get going. Now!' Then Dougie Olsen pops in, and they have this incredibly long, incredibly silly whisper conversation that ends with both saying 'Duuuuude' to the other. Then Olsen is dragging me up out of my booth and out the door. I barely had a chance to throw my five bucks on the table for the soup and Coke before they've got me out the door and shoved into the front seat of Olsen's blue Ford LTD. Twenty miles later, I find out that I was being used to keep the diner staff busy while Olsen pre-occupied the front counter girl and Vic snuck in through the unlocked back door and stole two thirty-packs of beer."

"Victor John Gordon!" Hannah gasped, grabbing Vic's arm.

"We were seventeen!" Vic said. "We didn't know any better."

"You didn't know, at seventeen, that stealing beer out of the back of a store was a crime?" April scoffed.

"I just want to know where me eating soup fit into the grand scheme of things," Walczyk said.

"Easy. You kept the restaurant employee busy preparing your meal while Olsen distracted the lady in the front with his trying to buy a *Penthouse* without a valid ID."

"What I don't get," April said, "is why, with a father who had a storeroom full of alcohol, you didn't just rip off your Dad's place?"

"While Dad did, indeed, have a storeroom full of alcohol and a mind that wasn't as keen as it used to be, he also had a foot that fit all-too perfectly up my ass when I got caught stealing booze from said storeroom."

"My question," Hannah said, frowning, "is how you can still get fuel from that gas station and not feel a twinge of guilt, all these years later."

"Oh, that's the best part of the story," Vic said.

"And what's that?" April asked.

"Well, the word all over town the next day was how someone broke into the back of the Citgo and took those two thirty-packs. The cops came and investigated. Sheriff Kyle got word out on the streets that he knew who was responsible, and that he was keeping his eye on them. So, our unwitting patsy, Precious Peter over here, felt so guilty when he found out what he'd been a part of, mailed forty bucks to the gas station in a plain envelope with no return address and no stamps."

"You what?" April asked incredulously.

"Peter, I'm proud of you," Hannah said, reaching over to pat his knee. "That couldn't have been easy."

"So Vic and ol' One Eye commit the crime," April clarified, "and you pay the penalty."

"That's how most of my childhood with Vic went," Walczyk admitted.

"Hey, Walz, I forget, were you with me the day old Brad Folmer was walking along the side of the road in his white jeans and his white jeans jacket?"

"Don't think so."

"Yeah, he's walking and trying to thumb a ride. I'm pretty sure you and Big Tom Lyons were with me." Vic turned to Hannah and April. "Anyhow, so I pull up beside him–"

"You didn't splash poor Brad," Hannah said, horrified.

"No, I didn't splash poor Brad," Vic said, annoyed. "That was another guy, another time."

April hauled off and elbowed him, hard, in the ribs. "Ow, damn it," he grunted, then got on with his story. "Anyhow, Brad's walking down the road, thumbing for a ride, and I pull up next to him. Lyons rolls the window down, just a crack, and I say something like, 'Hey, Folmer, tired of walking?' He nods and says 'Yeah', and starts pulling at the handle on the door. That's when Lyons says, 'Why don't you try running for a while, then?' and we floor it!"

Walczyk and Vic laughed heartily, while April tried to suppress a chuckle and Hannah looked at the three of them mortified.

"That's awful. Brad Folmer was a great guy."

The laughter died when the door to the little room opened and Theresa, an unpleasant nurse with a particularly bad spray-on tan, came in.

"Will you *please* keep it down in here?" she asked, scowling. "I've got people sleeping in some of these rooms." Theresa had a very unpleasant, almost sneering face, overly made-up with blue eye shadow and shiny, glittery lip-gloss. She wore a set of hospital scrubs decorated with little Snoopy drawings. April would no doubt suggest that this nurse was trying too hard, with her make-up and tan and piss-poor attitude, to hide the fact she was about fifty pounds overweight and not exactly easy on the eyes.

"Sure," Walczyk said, suddenly anxious for the evening to end. "Sorry."

"Sorry," Vic and Hannah mumbled. April said nothing.

As if she thought they were up to something, the nurse scrutinized Walczyk and the others in the room. "Visiting hours are over in fifteen minutes. You should start cleaning that stuff up," she said, pointing a pudgy, ring-covered finger at the table. "And you're not throwing any of it away here. Take it with you."

"Sounds good," Walczyk said, watching with great relief as Theresa left the room without another word.

"What a bitch," Hannah said, rather bluntly.

"Hannah!" Walczyk and Vic gasped.

"Well, Hannah's right," April said, coming to her defense. "She *is* a bitch. There's no reason to treat people like that in a hospital."

While he did feel she might have been over-reacting a bit, Walczyk was happy to see April back to her old self. Her L.A. self, who didn't put up with anyone's crap. Everyone got up at the same time and start picking things up. "So, tell me again," Hannah said, dumping empty chicken containers into one of the paper bags, "what's this bipolar disorder mean? Science was never my strong suit."

"It's basically that you have these mood swings for no real reason," Vic offered quickly.

"Yeah," Walczyk said, surprised. "The moods aren't necessarily triggered by anything except changes in body chemistry."

"And this lithium shit they're putting you on," April said, wiping the table down with some wet naps, "It should stop the mood swings?"

"It should stabilize them. Make them less frequent and more manageable."

"So there's no cure," Hannah said.

"No. There's not."

The room fell silent. April squeezed a couple of soda bottles into the top of one of the bags and stood next to Vic, leaning her head against his arm.

"So," Walczyk said, trying to forestall the goodbyes, "you guys heading back tomorrow?"

"Actually, Hannah and I are going back tonight," Vic said. "We were going to spend the night, but the hotel your folks and April are at is full-up and we didn't feel like spending the afternoon looking around for a room."

"Besides," Hannah said, "we figured that we'll sleep better in our own beds."

"That and someone should feed the dogs and let Andrew have a day off this week," April said, giving Vic a playful elbow to the ribs.

"I'm afraid that means we won't be back until Monday or Tuesday," Hannah said, looking like she was ready to break down again. "I'm so sorry, Peter, but–"

Walczyk took her hands in his. "Don't. I'll be fine. The doctor says I'll be out soon enough. You guys focus on your regular lives. I'll be fine."

"Your parents and I will be back tomorrow afternoon," April said, slinging her purse over her shoulder, reminding Walczyk that they would all soon be gone and it'd be just him, the other patients and Nurse Spray Tan.

"Well," Vic said, "we should hit the road if we want to see Cole Island by midnight."

"Oh!" Hannah cried out. "I almost forgot!" She dashed over to her chair and pulled a box, which was wrapped in the colored funnies from the weekend paper, from a plastic bag and handed it to Walczyk. "Here. This should help with some of the boredom."

"I think you'll be able to guess who picked it out," Vic said.

"If it's *Star Trek* DVDs, I certainly will." Walczyk placed the box on the table.

"Aren't you going to open it?" Hannah asked, impatiently.

"Oh, you want me to do it now?" Walczyk asked playfully, picking the box back up.

"Of course!" Hannah said, clearly excited.

Walczyk picked the package up again. He tore at the paper, letting it fall to the floor as he unwrapped the box. Once it was unwrapped, he could do nothing but stand there and grin. It was a *Star Wars*-themed Lego kit for building a model of Luke Skywalker's X-Wing fighter. Walczyk looked up from the box to Hannah, who was smiling broadly.

"They don't make *Star Trek* Legos, or I'd have gotten you the *Enterprise*."

"That's okay," Walczyk said, turning the box over and over in his hands. "I might have time to figure it out on my own."

April was the first to give Walczyk a hug. "You gonna be okay?" she asked.

"Kinda have to be," Walczyk said.

"I'm going to start researching this bipolar thing tonight. We'll get a handle on it. I promise."

Walczyk smiled. "With you on the case, I have no worries."

Vic was next to say his goodbyes. The two men held each other for a long time, not moving or speaking, just holding onto each other tightly.

"I love you, buddy," Vic said softly.

Vic let go of Walczyk and immediately turned away. Walczyk

smiled at Hannah, who was shying away from him.

"Come on," Walczyk said, holding his arms out to her. She gently put her arms around his neck and rocked with him, from foot to foot. Walczyk inhaled deeply, drawing in that ever-so-familiar scent of vanilla shampoo as he held onto Hannah. She cried. His own eyes stung as he fought back the tears. He'd promised himself he wasn't going to let his visitors see him cry.

"I don't want to rush things," April said after several minutes of Walczyk holding onto Hannah, "but it's past eight, and Nurse Pleasant will surely be back to make sure we've gotten everything cleaned up."

Hannah kissed Walczyk again and wiped her eyes. "I promise I'll be back," she said.

"I promise *I'll* be back," Walczyk replied. "Thank you all so much. This was amazing."

The tears threatened to overwhelm him. "Drive safely, Vic. And thanks for the Legos, Hannah."

With one final hug apiece, Hannah, Vic, and April filed out of the quiet room, taking with them almost every trace that they'd been there, save for the brightly colored box of Legos. Walczyk walked over to the table and picked up the box and a couple of soda bottles that Vic and April had forgotten on the table, and walked to the trash can with them. He held them up, smiling at the entire situation. His best friends had brought him supper. In a mental hospital. It made absolutely no sense whatsoever.

Walczyk sank into one of the plush armchairs and pulled his knees tight to his face. He wanted to focus on anything right now other than the emotional distress he was feeling.

The soft sounds of someone coming into the room caught his attention. Walczyk looked up, tears streaming down his face, and saw Kaley standing in the doorway, clutching a worn book from the ward library.

"Oh, I'm sorry," she said. "I'll leave you alone."

"No," Walczyk called out. "I'd rather have some company, if you don't mind."

"Sure," Kaley said, smiling faintly as she shut the door behind her and sat down in the chair opposite Walczyk. The same chair Hannah had occupied not ten minutes ago.

"Who were those guys with all the chicken? Family?"

"You could say that. They're my friends from home, Vic and Hannah. And my assistant, April. How'd you know we had chicken?"

"The whole ward smells like KFC." She paused, flipping her book open, then looked back at him. "And what the hell do you need an assistant for?"

"Well, I used to need one," Walczyk said. After a few moments of silence, Kaley opened her book again and started reading. Walczyk looked out the window, watching a blinking light slip across the black sky. No doubt a plane either approaching or departing Bangor International Airport. He looked away from the window and his attention turned to that large box on the table. He walked over to the table and sat, examining the back side of the box, which gave photographs of various configurations of the Lego pieces inside.

"What's that?" Kaley asked, her book in her lap. "Legos?"

Walczyk laughed. "Yeah. A present from my friend Hannah. I imagine they'll want to keep them at the main desk, since there are small parts and whatnot."

"Doesn't mean we can't play with them before they take them."

Walczyk looked from the box to Kaley, who was smiling. The first genuine smile he'd seen on her face since he had met her.

"Why not?" Walczyk asked, carefully opening the end of the box and sliding out a cardboard tray filled with Lego bricks.

"So what's it supposed to be?" she asked, sliding her chair over to the table.

"Ever watch *Star Wars*?"

"Who hasn't?" she retorted.

"It's Luke's X-Wing," Walczyk said. "I think it even comes with a little Luke Skywalker figure."

"Most of them do," she said, reaching in and grabbing a handful of Legos, the sound of tiny bits of plastic filling the room. "So I hear Lentz came in to see you today. Did he have any news for you?"

"I've got bipolar disorder," Walczyk said, not recognizing his own voice as he spoke the words.

"Welcome to the club," she said, giving him a light punch to the shoulder.

"You mean–?"

"It's amongst my many sins," she said. "OCD. Bipolar. Seasonal affective disorder." She indicated her forearms, covered by fingerless black gloves. "Self-injury and suicidal tendencies. I think that's about it, unless you count my eating disorder."

"My God," Walczyk said. Here he'd been pitying himself because he had one mental disorder, which was treatable. Imagining the hell that Kaley must have gone through boggled his mind and broke his heart.

"Well, He has helped. You should've seen me before."

"Before treatment?"

"Before God. I can't imagine facing all of this without knowing that He's got my back." Walczyk was surprised. This frail, skinny girl with her black-and-red hair and her extreme make-up and her black clothes was preaching the power of prayer. It truly was an interesting combination. "Sorry," she said. "I try not to get too preachy, but I can't help myself sometimes. I just would have never made it if I didn't know that He was looking out for me."

"If God's got your back," Walczyk said, careful not to come across as crass or mocking, "then how come He let you get so sick?"

"Maybe so that I could be here for you when you needed it."

Walczyk sat back in his chair. "Now *that's* is a concept."

"Mind blowing, isn't it?" she asked, sorting the Lego bricks out by color.

"So, you mind if I pick your brain about bipolar disorder?" Walczyk asked, trying to figure out what Kaley was building on her side of the table.

"Please do," she said, picking up a black brick.

"Dr. Lentz, he said that lithium's not a permanent cure."

"No, it's just a symptom manager. You'll always be bipolar."

"Are you on lithium?"

"Am now. I started out on a drug called Depakote. It did the trick when I'd take it, but I stopped taking it."

"Why? Did it stop working?"

"No. Just expensive as hell. It was either pay my rent or take my meds. I chose rent. Then I went manic and chose a laptop and clothes and a couple tattoos and a scumbag named Dennis who liked to hit me. Looking back, I think I was with him because I liked that he hit me. Saved me the effort of hurting myself and gave me a much better scapegoat."

"What happened then? Sounds like you were in a pretty dangerous situation, what with the mania and the beatings."

"I came here for my first time. And they switched me off the Depakote and onto lithium, which is loads cheaper. Unfortunately, Dr. Berenbaum, the woman who put me on the lithium, forgot to tell me about one major side effect."

"What's that?" Walczyk asked, beginning to see what Kaley's Lego structure was going to be.

"What might happen if you cold turkey off the lithium, like I did when I finally left Danny."

"Michael?"

"Another boyfriend I'd started living with. Anyhow, cold turkey off lithium and you can get incredibly, incredibly suicidal."

"Could you describe 'incredibly, incredibly'?" Walczyk asked warily.

"'Incredibly, incredibly' is locking yourself in a garage and turning the car on."

"Holy shit," Walczyk said.

"Yeah. My little brother Blake found me. He's seven."

The room grew so deafeningly quiet that Walczyk could hear the humming of the fluorescent lighting fixtures.

Kaley held up her Lego creation – a very rudimentary human-like figure. "What do you think? It's Robot Kaley."

"I can tell by the black-and-red hair," Walczyk said. The door opened and Mary, the more pleasant of the two duty nurses on duty, came in.

"I see you couldn't wait to get into your Legos. It was awful sweet of your friend to bring those for you."

"That's Hannah," Walczyk said, feeling his face smile.

"Well, I hate to ask you to do this, but can you start packing things up? It's nine and everyone's back in their rooms."

"Sure thing, Mary," Kaley said, starting to pull Robot-Kaley apart.

"Thanks," Walczyk said. Mary left the door open behind her when she left.

"So, did they give you a time table on when they're springing you?" Kaley asked, picking up Legos and putting them in the cardboard tray.

"Lentz just said soon."

"Lentz is good about letting people go if they've got stable homes to go back to. And it looks like you've got that."

Walczyk thought about it. Compared to what Kaley had described, he had to guess that he did come from a stable home, even if he did live with his assistant while his wife lived with her girlfriend on the other side of the country. With everything packed up, Walczyk stood, grabbed the box of Legos, and turned to Kaley.

"Well, it's been a fun hour," she said. "Though I didn't get much read."

"What *are* you reading?"

"*Dracula* by Bram Stoker."

"I've always liked the structure of that book," Walczyk said, moving for the door. "It being a collection of journal entries and whatnot."

"I just found it on the shelf in the TV room and thought it's got to be better than outdated *People* magazines with stories about your wife in them."

Walczyk snorted a laugh. "Have a good night."

"You too, Peter," she said.

"Hey," he said, turning back to her, "call me Walczyk."

Kaley nodded. "Fine, Walczyk, but you have to promise never to call me 'Richardson,' okay?"

"It's a deal," he said, extending his hand. She took his hand in hers, small and fragile, and shook it with a surprising amount of force, then turned and squeezed through the doorway past him, disappearing down into the hall. Walczyk snapped the light off and shut the door behind him.

CHAPTER SEVENTEEN
HOPE AND PRAYER

Again on Sunday, breakfast was a bleak affair. Walczyk had the fluorescent eggs and the withered sausage and he sat at his table off to the side, reading his book. He was about twenty pages into it, but knew nothing of what was happening. He consumed the words, but they did not linger long in his mind. He was on his third glass of juice, trying to wash the taste of the quick-dissolving lithium out of his mouth.

"You got any friends coming today?" Richard asked from across the table, loading his eggs up with ketchup.

"My parents," Walczyk said, "and my friend April. What about you?"

"No," Richard said glumly. "My parents don't have the money to drive down here from Caribou a lot. I have a brother who lives in Levant, but he don't like me."

"Oh," Walczyk said, wishing he hadn't asked. He couldn't fathom being in this place without anyone coming to visit. After breakfast, Walczyk left *Dr. Jekyll and Mr. Hyde* in his room and tried socializing in the hallway. He found he had very little to say on the topics of discussion: cigarettes, NASCAR and the sad state of country's financial stability. He did learn, though, that Theresa, the spray-tanned nurse with the bad attitude, was on the outs with her boyfriend, and that's why she was being more miserable than usual with the patients.

Just as the conversation turned back to the economy, Hope, the red-headed nurse Walczyk could have sworn was gossiping about him his first morning there, walked over.

"Good morning, Peter."

"Morning," he replied.

"You have a phone call."

Walczyk tried to guess who would be calling him on a Sunday morning as he walked to the phone. It couldn't have been April or his folks, as they were right down the road and coming by to visit later. Walczyk reached the pay phone in the corner of the reception area and picked it up from the table. "Hello?" he said into the receiver.

"Hey there, little brother!" It was his sister, Melanie. She sounded a little nervous. In the background, the sounds of her two children, Rodney and Esther, filled the silence. "How've you been?" The question was followed by an explosion of tears. Walczyk tried to calm his sister over the phone. He was slowly getting used to people getting emotional when they talked to him for the first time since his committal. After a moment or two, and some calming words from the voice of his brother-in-law Adam on the other end of the line, Melanie resumed speaking. "Sorry about that."

"No worries," Walczyk said. "So, I take it Mum and Dad filled you in on what's been happening."

"Daddy called Thursday night," Melanie managed to get out before being overcome with tears again. Once she finally collected herself, she repeated, "Sorry about the crying."

"Hey, knock that off," Walczyk said. "I'm sure *I'd* be the emotional wreck if the tables were turned and my big sister were in the nut house."

"Peter, I wish I could come see you."

"Don't worry about it, Sis."

"It's just... Adam can't–"

"Flying to Maine would do no good anyway," Walczyk said, cutting his sister off. "I only get guests for an hour in the evening. You'd spend the rest of the day with Mum and Dad and my assistant April in a hotel room going stir crazy."

Melanie sniffled. "You're sure you don't want me to come to Maine?"

"Not right now," Walczyk said. "I don't want the kids to see me in here. You can come sometime when you can bring the whole family. You can tell the kids that crazy Uncle Peter bought a house with a huge back yard and that his friend April has a dog dying to be played with. Plus there's a Wii hooked up to the big screen in the living room, perfect for Uncle Peter to get thrashed at *Mario Kart* on."

"Yeah, I heard about the Old Merry Place," Melanie said. "Or are you calling it the New Walczyk Place?"

"I tried changing it, but let's be honest; it'll forever be the Old Merry Place. I'm thinking about getting it painted on a shingle to hang by the door."

Melanie laughed weakly. "So, Mum says they think they know what's going on."

"For the moment, yeah," Walczyk said. "Sis, it's weird."

"What's that?"

"Walking around, feeling physically fine. Yeah, I'm pretty tired, but there's no gimping, nothing sore – besides the back of my head – no physical impairment. Yet they're telling me I'm sick."

"I can't imagine what it's like, feeling okay but knowing that somewhere inside you, you've got this disease. It's… weird."

"Of course, now that I know the symptoms, I can look back at my life and pinpoint manic episodes or depressive episodes that I thought were just moodiness. Going all the way back to when we were kids."

"I always thought you were just ADHD. I never thought you would be hypermanic."

"*Hypo*manic," Walczyk heard his brother-in-law correct in the background.

"Sorry. *Hypo*manic. Did they give you any idea when you can expect to be out of there?"

Walczyk shrugged. "That's the question everyone's been asking. Dr. Lentz just keeps saying 'soon'. He said they'd like to keep me a week, to evaluate how I tolerate the Lithium and the Wellbutrin. And I'm sure I need to be able to prove to them I'm not going to go bouncing my head off anything again."

The line went silent again, this time even the sound of the playing children gone. Finally, there was a loud sniff, followed by, "Damn it, Peter, why didn't you tell any of us?"

Walczyk considered this for a moment. Why *hadn't* he shared any of his turmoil with his family. That wasn't like him, to keep things bottled up inside like that. But his marriage was collapsing, and that *was* personal. It was his own failure as a husband that brought it all on. He didn't want to burden anyone with it.

"I've not been a success when it comes to communicating with the people who care about me," Walczyk offered.

"No shit, Sherlock," Melanie snapped. It had been years since Walczyk had seen (or heard) his sister angry at him. But he knew he deserved it. "Why did I have to find out about you and Sara from a tabloid at the supermarket? Why didn't you call me?" Walczyk offered nothing in the way of a defense. "I thought we were close, Peter. We were each other's best friend growing up. We told each other everything. *Everything*. Even after I left for college."

"*Especially* after you left for college," Walczyk carefully inserted, remembering a phone call with his sister in which she confessed to a night of taking ecstasy and doing body shots with Alrich, the German grad student who taught her Freshman English class.

"Exactly my point! I told you stuff that would make Mum and Dad's hair turn white and fall out. And you've told me some crazy stories. Hell, Peter, we became closer confidants after we both left Cole Island."

"That we did," Walczyk said, remembering it was Melanie he first told about the night he spent with Sara in 2005, having just met her after her Kitty Kat Girls performance at Millennium. "Look, I've got no excuse. No rationale. I just..." He searched his brain for the right words, the right reasoning. "I just didn't want to disappoint anyone. Sara was my wife. We'd been talking about starting a family. Then that whole thing with she and Ella and the video blew up and I got embarrassed."

"Too embarrassed to talk to your big sister about it?"

"Yes," Walczyk said. "Mel, you aren't alone. Remember Ian Maeder?"

"Your best man," Melanie answered.

"Yeah. My best man. My best friend. Did you know that the last time I talked to him was the day before I left L.A. He's supposed to be my best friend – my producing partner – and I never told him a thing. I barely communicate with my agent. Hell, I only talk to my assistant because she lives with me and drags me out of bed every morning. Mum and Dad, hell, they're only in the loop because it'd be hard to avoid them. Cole Island isn't that big any more. It took me almost four months to get back in touch with Vic and Hannah, and Hannah and I *still* haven't discussed the break-up. So, you see, it's not just you."

Melanie was quiet, no doubt considering all of these thin excuses. "Okay, I'll accept that for now, but you'll have to do some soul searching or talk about it with your doctor or something, because I want a better answer as to why you hit rock bottom and didn't tell one single person that you felt so miserable you wanted to kill yourself."

Walczyk sat stunned. Hearing the words "you wanted to kill yourself" spoken aloud made him realize just how dark things had gotten for him. "Well, Henry and Diane didn't keep anything from you, did they?"

"No, they didn't. There have been too many secrets for too long," Melanie said.

"Then, in that spirit, I should probably tell you something else," Walczyk said.

"What's that?" Melanie asked, sounding like she was bracing herself.

"Vic used to steal your panties." Melanie laughed. "He'd decorate the inside of his closet with them. He thought it'd piss me off." Now both of the Walczyk children had broken out in laughter. Walczyk quickly realized the volume of his own laugher, catching a glance from one of the nurses at the nurses' station. He gave an embarrassed nod and returned his attention to his sister. "So how are Adam and the kids?"

"Good," Melanie said. "Adam's between projects right now, so he's been taking care of the kids so I can get some peace and quiet."

A loud wail cut through the pause in the conversation, followed by the tearful call for "Mumma."

"Sounds like somebody took a tumble," Walczyk said.

"Oh, that'll be Stanley. He's learning to walk and–"

"Stanley's already walking now?" Walczyk asked, amazed.

"He's eleven months old." Melanie said, the pride in her voice unmistakable. "He usually grabs the coffee table, but he's taken his first steps on his own."

"Sis, that's incredible," Walczyk said.

An incoherent murmur came from somewhere on Melanie's

side of the phone. The phone jostled, and the crying of a baby became noticeable on the other end of the line.

"Peter, I'm so sorry, but–"

"Don't apologize for being a mother. Besides, I'll be out of here soon enough."

"I'll call you later this week. Some day after I put the kids down for a nap."

"Sounds good."

"Now you listen to me. Don't try anything stupid."

"I won't," Walczyk said, recognizing his older sister's no-nonsense, take charge tone of voice from their childhood.

"I love you, Baby Brother," she said.

"I love you, Big Sister," Walczyk said. "Kiss the kids and tell Adam I said hello."

"Will do. Talk to you soon."

"Bye," Walczyk said, then hung up the phone. He stayed seated for a moment, pulling himself back together. It had never struck him before that his depression, and ultimately his break-down, would have such an effect on his family. That his self-destructive tendencies would scare anyone but himself. He was still rolling Melanie's words over in his mind: "You wanted to die." He couldn't deny that the statement was accurate. Sadly, it was all too accurate. True, he didn't have a plan, but it was still what Dr. Lentz called a "suicidal ideation."

"Hey, Peter!" It was Richard, who seemed out of breath. Not a real stretch, considering Richard was quite overweight and no doubt physically inactive.

"What's up, Richard?" Walczyk asked, getting up from the phone.

"Morning meeting time," he excitedly told Walczyk.

"Thanks," Walczyk said, unenthusiastically, and started toward the common room.

"Think I can sit with you today?" Richard asked. Why this kid (at forty-something, was he really a kid?) idolized him the way he did, Walczyk couldn't figure out. Richard was certainly not up on the comings and goings of the Hollywood elite, so his fascination was with the person Peter Walczyk, not the public figurehead.

"Sure," Walczyk said, getting up.

"I get to see my doctor tomorrow," Richard said, filling the lull in conversation as they walked to the common room.

"Oh? How is he?" Walczyk said, choosing a table off to the side.

"*She*. And she's good," Richard said, pulling a Rubik's cube from his pocket and fiddling with it. "She don't always believe the stuff I tell her, but that's okay. Sometimes I get stuff wrong."

"Richard, if you don't think you're being listened to, you need to speak up."

"It's okay, Peter," he said, sliding his thumbnail under the corner of a red square, peeling the sticker back. "It's just the thing with my skin. That's all."

"What thing?" Walczyk asked, turning to look at Richard, who pointed to his forehead. A trail of pinkish-red blotches, dry around the edges, spread across his forehead. Richard scratched at it, and a shower of microscopic white flakes sprinkled down.

"Don't touch it," Walczyk gently said, looking at Richard's nose. "This looks serious. You need to have this looked at. Who have you told about it?"

"Theresa."

"Yeah, I'm sure she'd gone out of her way to get this taken care of. Did you talk to anyone else?"

"My doctor," Richard said.

"And what's your doctor's name?" Walczyk asked.

"Dr. Berenbaum."

"We're batting a thousand here," Walczyk said, sitting upright. "Don't worry. I'll get this taken care of. In the meantime, don't touch it. You don't want to risk spreading it around, okay?"

"Okay," Richard said, engrossed with his Rubik's cube.

"Well, well, well," a voice from behind them said. "This must be the cool kids' table."

Richard and Walczyk craned their necks around to see Kaley standing behind them. Walczyk gave her a smile. She put her hand on Richard's shoulder.

"The cool kids' table," Richard repeated, laughing to himself.

"Richard, can I sit with you and Walczyk?"

"Who?"

"Peter," she clarified, giving Walczyk a faint smile. "Can I sit with you and Peter?"

"Sure," Richard said, picking at another sticker on the Rubik's cube. Kaley sat down on the other side of Walczyk, leaning against the window.

"And how's Walczyk this morning?" Kaley asked.

"Not bad," Walczyk said. "You're in a good mood this morning.

"Enjoy it while it lasts. I'm feeling a bit manic and when it gets out, they'll dope the hell out of me."

Walczyk smiled. "Your secret's safe with us." He turned to check on Richard, who was now moving stickers around on his Rubik's cube. He turned back to Kaley, saying, "You ever take a look at this skin rash he's got going on with his forehead?"

Kaley's entire posture shifted, and her pleasant, cheery mania disappeared. "Those red, dry patches? Yeah, I've seen it. He's got it on his arms and legs too. Eczema, I think"

"At least he's told someone competent about it," Walczyk said. "Too bad the inmates aren't running the asylum, he might get some medication for it."

Kaley sighed in disgust. "I told him–"

"I'm going to talk to Lentz about it tomorrow," Walczyk said. "If that doesn't work, I'll have April get someone in to look at it."

Hope came through the double doors at the front of the room. "As you might or might not know, Rick and Emily are off on Sundays, which means you're stuck with me." A smattering of laughter and commentary filled the room.

"I don't think I've met all of you," she said, looking at an older woman at the back of the room that Walczyk just noticed for the first time. "My name's Hope. I help lead the morning meetings when they need an extra hand. Now, this'll be a short one today, so that Mr. Johnson can get set up for worship. This morning we're going to talk about self-esteem. Who can tell me what self-esteem is?"

The room fell quiet. Richard peeled a red sticker from his Rubik's cube and stuck it to the edge of the table.

"Anyone?" Hope asked.

"Isn't it liking yourself?" Elaine asked, half-raising her hand as she spoke.

"Absolutely," Hope said, overflowing with positivity. "Self-esteem is your own mental picture of yourself."

"It's how you see yourself?" a woman in the corner meekly said, not very sure of herself.

"Exactly, Rita," Hope said. "Self esteem is a collection of your beliefs and judgments about your personality and your strengths and weaknesses. Now, who in here has trouble with self-esteem? A show of hands?" A few hands went up. "Just three of you have low self-esteem?" A few more hands went up. Beside him, Kaley meekly raised her hand. On the other side of him, Richard took the red sticker and stuck it back on the Rubik's cube. Walczyk rolled the question around in his mind. Did he have low self-esteem? He certainly didn't think so. Then again, he was the man who blamed himself for his wife's philandering. The man who opted not to share his illness with his friends and family for fear that they'd run screaming for the hills.

"Okay, thank you. Now, suppose you do have low self-esteem. Is it fixable? Is there anything you can do to raise your self-esteem?"

A murmur went across the room, consisting mainly of yeses.

"Okay," Hope said. "I'm going to go around the room and ask if you can give me a way to raise your self-esteem if it's low." She uncapped a black dry erase marker and pulled an easel forward bearing a white board.

"Dean," she said, pointing across the room. "Why don't you start us off? What's something you can do to raise your self-esteem?"

"Don't put yourself down," Dean said.

Hope wrote Dean's answer on the marker board and continued around the room, collecting answers and either putting them up on the board or working them into a correct answer.

"Richard? What about you?" He did not look up. "Richard, do you want to help us out this morning?"

"What's the question?" he asked, looking up from the now mish-mashed Rubik's cube.

"What's something you can do to raise your self-esteem?"

"Make a friend," he said, looking up.

Hope's expression showed that she didn't know where Richard was going. But she continued with him. "How does making a friend increase your self-esteem?"

"Because I made a new friend and my self-esteen feels really good.

"*Esteem*," Hope said, stressing the M. "But, Richard, there's a lot more to increasing your self-esteem than just making yourself feel better. Do you think you could come up with another thing you could do that would raise your self-esteem?"

Richard's attention had already returned to his Rubik's Cube.

"Peter?" Hope asked, moving on.

"Yes?" Walczyk replied, loving how the nurses pretended that they didn't know who he was, even though he was on the cover of their gossip mags.

"What's something you can do to increase your self-esteem?"

"Well, I had an answer, but someone took it."

"Oh? What was that?"

"I was going to say make a new friend."

Richard looked up from the cube, smiling. "So I'll just have to go with my number two answer, and that's to give yourself credit for your successes."

"That's an excellent one," Hope said, writing Walczyk's second answer on the board. "We accomplish a lot, if we break our day down and look at it. How about you, Kaley?"

Walczyk turned to look at Kaley, who was reddening at being called out. "Treat yourself kindly?" she suggested.

"Right," Hope said. "How can we possibly expect to feel better about ourselves if we don't treat ourselves with respect and kindness?"

After Hope had finished her circuit around the room, she circulated a sheet of paper listing several other ways to increase your self-esteem and reviewed the suggestions on the marker board.

"So, next time you find yourself feeling down in the dumps and low in the self-esteem department, remember there's a lot you can do to raise that old self-esteem right up." Hope looked out into the hallway. A man in his forties with a close-cut white beard was standing outside, talking to one of the other nurses. "Well, I see Mr. Johnson waiting outside, so we're going to break for today. Anyone who wants to gather for Sunday worship stick around. If that's not something you want to do, the other common room is open. We just ask that if you're going to sit in the hall that you be respectful of the people in here."

Hope collected her notes, wiped down the marker board, and left the room.

"So, what's the plan now?" Walczyk asked.

"More open time," Kaley said. "Why don't you stick around, though."

"For what?"

"Worship."

"Church? Yeah, I'm all set," Walczyk said, getting up. On the other side of him, Richard had all of the stickers back on his Rubik's cube, though he still didn't have the thing solved.

"No, it's not really church, in the general sense of the word. It's more like a Bible study and..." She scowled. "I'm not doing it justice. Just stick around. I'm sure you'll like it."

"I don't know," Walczyk said. "God and I went our own separate ways years ago, and we've both been happy about that arrangement ever since. Besides, I've got way too many skeletons in my closet to start... whatever this is."

"Okay. Save me a seat at lunch, then?"

"That's it?" Walczyk asked. "No big sales pitch on how my salvation lies in the hands of God?"

"It does," she said. At the head of the room, Mr. Johnson, wearing a Maine Black Bears T-shirt and jeans, was setting up. "But you have to put it there."

"Finished!" Richard announced, triumphantly. Walczyk turned to see Richard turning the cube in his hand, several of the stickers missing. But he did have the cube "solved"; all six sides were bearing only one color.

"Good job," Kaley said. Walczyk liked the way she spoke to Richard. She was never patronizing, but she always made sure she was understood. Richard walked over to Rita, who was staring at a newspaper.

"You're seriously sticking around for this?" Walczyk asked, turning back to Kaley.

"Why not? You don't think that a suicidal, self-mutilating metal head would want anything to do with God?"

"No, it's not that. It's just... after all you've been through, how can you still have faith in God?"

"It's *because* of what I've survived that I have faith in God," Kaley said. "Look, I'm not going to strong-arm you into staying. If you want to stick around, spend an hour of your life without your nose buried in that book you're making no headway with, you're more than welcome. If not, enjoy your reading and I'll catch you in the caf afterwards." She got up and moved closer to the front of the room, pulling a couple of chairs from the tables into a circle. Some of the other patients also pulled chairs from the tables into the circle. Dean walked to the back of the room and wheeled Patty, the nonresponsive woman in the wheelchair, to the circle.

Walczyk followed Kaley to the front of the room, dragged a

chair over, and sat down beside her. "Look, Kaley, I'm sorry if I offended you back there."

"Don't worry. You didn't."

"It's just… like I said, I'm not sure if I belong here."

"Why don't you?" she asked.

"Well, because I don't believe in God."

"What better place for you to learn more about Him, then," she said, smiling. "Walczyk, you think I was a perfect little angel when I decided it was time to bring God into my life? Hell, I've still got a lot of growing to do, spiritually. He doesn't expect us to come to him clean and untarnished. If we waited until we were, we'd be forever waiting to come before Him."

"But it's not that I think I'm a sinner. Well, I guess am, but I… I just don't believe."

"Then what do you have to lose, besides sixty minutes?"

"Good morning," Mr. Johnson said at the head of the room.

"Good morning," the collected eight or so people gathered in the room responded exuberantly.

He settled into a chair in the circle. "I see a few new faces today, so I'll introduce myself. My name's Bruce Johnson. I'm a missionary for the U.S. Center for World Mission. I also lead a number of local at-home churches in the area and facilitate Bible study groups with student athletes and student military officers at the University. Let's just quickly go around the room and introduce ourselves. Just say your name and tell me… tell me something you like about fall. Kaley, why don't you start us off?"

She reddened a little, as Walczyk noticed she generally did when called upon for an answer. "I'm Kaley, and I like the color of the leaves in the fall." Kaley turned to Walczyk.

"I'm Peter, and I guess my favorite part of fall is Halloween."

There was laughter around the room. Bruce smiled and nodded his head in Walczyk's direction. "Thank you, Peter. Next?"

"My name's Ken and I like how it gets cooler, but not too cold."

"My name's Elaine, and I like two things. First, I like the colors too, but more importantly, my birthday's at the end of September."

Patty said nothing and just stared at the floor.

"I'm Rita," a middle-aged woman with frizzy hair said.

Walczyk recognized her from his first day on the ward, crying while talking on the phone. "And I like hunting with my brother-in-law and my sister."

"My name's Dean, and I like the smell of fresh sawed firewood."

"Hi. I'm Louise, and I like bringing in my garden."

"My name's Richard, and I like when you have to change the clocks because that's fun."

The door to the common room opened and David loped in, his oversized ball cap cranked on crooked, his bathrobe billowing out behind him.

"Great," Walczyk said under his breath. Kaley elbowed him, giving him a shush.

"David, good morning," Bruce said, extending his hand. David briefly shook it, said nothing, and plunked down in a chair next to Dean. "We're just introducing ourselves and saying something we like about the fall."

Walczyk braced himself for an outburst of profanity and unpleasantness. What he got was something unexpected: "I guess that I like that it gets dark earlier."

"Great," Bruce said. "I'd like to lead us in a group prayer, then we'll go on to our discussion for today."

The people in the room bowed their heads. Walczyk spied to make sure David did (he even removed his hat) before bowing his own head. "Heavenly Father, thank You for this blessed day and thank You for all You have given us. Thank You for the opportunity to worship with these people here today. Thank You for reuniting me with old brothers and sisters in Christ and for introducing me to new ones. Thank You for sending us your Son, Jesus, to spread the amazing word of Your love across the Earth. Please be with each and every one of us, both those in this room and those elsewhere, and let us feel the power of Your hand in our lives, today and every day. We pray to You in the awesome name of your son, Christ Jesus. Amen."

The room responded with a surprisingly enthusiastic "Amen." Walczyk looked up. "So, how was everyone's week?" Bruce asked.

There was a smattering of responses, most of them "okay" or "could be worse." Richard enthusiastically said that he'd had a good week because he made a new friend.

"Oh?" Bruce asked. "Who's your new friend?"

"Peter Walczyk," Richard said, pointing across the circle. Walczyk gave a wave, slightly embarrassed by being called Richard's new friend. Not that he disliked the guy, just that he didn't consider he had done anything to be worthy of being called a friend.

"Well, Peter, it's nice to see you here," Bruce said. "Mind if I ask where you're from?"

"Cole Island," Walczyk replied.

"It's beautiful down there," Bruce said. "My wife Elizabeth and I try to visit the island every summer."

"It is," Walczyk said, finding himself longing for Cole Island and Garry Olsen futzing about over him and dinners at the Barrelhead with his friends.

"Okay," Bruce said, standing. "Today, I want to talk a little about despair. What is despair?"

"Sadness," Penny answered almost immediately.

"Right," Bruce said, nodding, but not satisfied with the answer. "Who else? Who else can tell me what despair is?"

"It's when you just give up," David said.

"We're getting there," Bruce said, growing energized. "Anyone else?"

After a moment of people turning to look at each other around the circle, Kaley leaned forward. "Isn't it, like, a loss of hope?"

"Exactly, Kaley. Webster's defines despair as 'an utter loss of hope.' Now, who here has ever experienced despair, according to this definition?" Bruce raised his own hand to encourage the others. Slowly, everyone in the room raised their hand, in clusters of two or three to a time, no one wanting to go alone. The last in the circle was David, who casually slid his hand up.

"What are some ways we can combat despair?" Bruce asked.

"You mean like coping mechanisms?" Dean asked, clutching a leather-covered Bible in his hands.

"Right," Bruce said. "What are some coping mechanisms that we can use to combat despair?"

Several answers rang out from around the circle, ranging from taking a hot bath to indulging in a sweet snack.

"Good answers," Bruce encouraged. "But there's one really obvious answer that's waiting to be called out. Anyone?"

Again, more coping mechanisms were thrown into the circle: going shopping, curling up with a soft blanket, drawing, but none seemed to capture what Bruce was after. "Prayer?" Walczyk asked, the answer seeming painfully obvious to him, as this was church.

"Exactly! Why would we forget to turn to Our Father? The One who created us. The One who has said, time and again, that He would be there for us. Psalm forty-six, verses one through three tells us, 'God is our refuge and strength, a very present help in trouble. Therefore we will not fear, though the Earth should change and though the mountains slip into the heart of the sea; though its waters roar and foam, though the mountains quake at its swelling pride.' What's that telling us?"

"That the world can go to hell in a hand basket and God will still be there for us," David said.

"Exactly," Bruce said. "Things can be their bleakest ever. The Earth can literally rip itself apart, and we have nothing to fear, because God is our refuge and strength." Walczyk considered the verse a moment.

"This is just one example of God being there for us in our moment of need. I'm going to pass around a sheet with a collection of verses on it that deal with God's promise to care for us." Bruce reached behind him onto a small round table and picked up a stack of papers, passing it to his right, where Richard sat. "What say we take turns reading through this list?" Bruce suggested once the pages had been passed around.

As Walczyk skimmed the page, he was taken by the modern language in which the passages were written. There was no overabundance of "thee"s and "thou"s. It read less like spiritual Shakespeare and more like contemporary prose.

"Now, there's no pressure to read," Bruce said, "but the more you read the less you have to listen to me." There was a smattering of laughter. "Okay, who wants to start?"

There was a silence, then Louise half-raised her hand.

"Louise, great, go for it," Bruce said.

"'It is the Lord who goes before you. He will be with you; he will not leave you or forsake you. Do not fear or be dismayed.' Deuteronomy, chapter thirty-one, verse eight."

"Great. Next?"

"Psalm thirty four, seventeen," Dean said in his gravelly, New England accent. "'When the righteous cry for help, the Lord hears and delivers them out of all their troubles.'"

The pace picked up as the group went through the sheet, one by one reading verses from the Bible.

"Psalm three, verse three," David read. "'But you, O Lord, are a shield about me, my glory, and the lifter of my head.'"

"'Many are the sorrows of the wicked, but steadfast love surrounds the one who trusts in the Lord,'" Penny read. "Psalm thirty two, verse ten."

Rita read next: "Psalm forty-two, verse eleven: 'Why are you cast down, O my soul, and why are you in turmoil within me? Hope in God; for I shall again praise Him, my salvation and my God.'"

With a little help from Bruce, Richard read his verse, from Jeremiah twenty nine, verse eleven: 'For I know the plans I have for you, declares the Lord, plans for welfare and not for evil, to give you a future and a hope.'"

"'And I am convinced,'" Ken read, "'that nothing can ever separate us from God's love. Neither death nor life, neither angels nor demons, neither our fears for today or our worries about tomorrow – not even the powers of hell can separate us from God's love. No power in the sky above or in the earth below – indeed, nothing in all creation will ever be able to separate us from the love of God that is revealed in Christ Jesus our Lord.' Romans, chapter eight, verses thirty-eight through thirty-nine."

After a pause, Kaley read the next verse on the list: "Second Corinthians one, verses three and four: 'Blessed be the God and Father of our Lord Jesus Christ, the Father of mercies and God of all comfort, who comforts us in all our affliction, so that we may be able to comfort those who are in any affliction, with the comfort with which we ourselves are comforted by God.'"

Walczyk felt all eyes on him to read, even though he hadn't looked up from his page. Finally, feeling the silence closing in on him, he read. "John chapter sixteen, thirty-three: 'I have said these things to you, that in me you may have peace. In the world you will have tribulation. But take heart; I have overcome the world.'"

There was a smattering of murmurs through the room as the sheet was finished being read. "So," Bruce asked, "any thoughts?"

Again, the customary silence, then Ken spoke up: "I liked that one that Peter read."

The others chimed in that they, too, liked the verse.

"Which one was yours again, Peter?" Bruce asked.

"John sixteen, thirty-three," Walczyk answered.

"Okay," Bruce said, "let's talk about that one of for a couple minutes. 'I have said these things to you, that in me you may have peace. In the world you will have tribulation. But take heart; I have overcome the world.'" Now this is John recording the words of Jesus here. What is Jesus saying?"

Silence. David played with his ball cap. Patty pawed at the floor with her slipper-clad foot. "Anyone?" Bruce asked.

"Isn't Christ saying that he has told his disciples things so that they can have peace of mind?" Walczyk asked. "Peace in their heart? That, while they will face challenges and obstacles in the world, if they believe in Him, they can rest easy knowing that Jesus has conquered the world?" Walczyk felt completely and utterly foolish, having just spoken. He knew as much about the life of Christ and the teachings of the scripture as he did about splitting atoms and cloning sheep (or ex-wives). He braced himself to be completely corrected on his interpretation of the New Testament.

"Well put," Bruce said, smiling. "Peter's right. In the verses before this, Jesus has been speaking to his disciples, preparing them for what is to come. He has washed their feet, a significant act, and is telling them that he will soon be taken and put to death. He then tells them exactly what Peter said: that they are going to be challenged, but they can take heart in knowing that Christ, the man they have put their faith in, has overcome the world.

"So let's bring this back to coping with despair. How does this passage from the book of John help us deal with feelings of hopelessness and despair?"

"It tells us that if we, too, put our faith in Christ," Kaley said, "then we can take comfort in knowing that we have committed ourselves to someone so powerful He can overcome the world."

"Exactly. What a great friend to have!" Bruce stood, placing his paper on his chair. "This friend who has promised us aid when we need it, just for believing in Him and following His teachings. It's like the passage from Jeremiah that Richard read to us, where God Himself says, 'For I know the plans I have for you… plans for welfare and not for evil, to give you a future and a hope'. God has a plan, and He knows what that plan entails. *We* might not know it. That plan might involve some terrible obstacles, but God has planned for those obstacles. And this is not a plan for evil or malice. This is a plan for good! God only wants what is best for us!"

The group discussed a couple of the other verses on the photocopied sheet until it was time to wrap things up.

"Okay, we're going to close in prayer. No one has to pray aloud if they don't want to. It's totally optional. God hears the prayers on your heart just as he does the prayers on your lips. We'll just go around the circle and if we have something we need prayers for, just say it. I'll start us off with a general prayer and then I'll pass it to Richard. When you're done, or if you don't want to speak, just give a tap to the person next to you. And…" Bruce looked around the circle. "Kaley, when we're done, would you close for us?"

"Sure," she said, looking down.

Walczyk leaned over to Kaley and quietly asked, "We don't have to hold hands or anything, do we?"

"No," Kaley said, smiling. "Just be mindful and relax."

Walczyk clasped his hands together and looked up to Bruce, who was answering a question for Richard.

"Heavenly father, thank You for this time together here today where we can get together and worship Your amazing gifts that You have sent down to us. Thank You for the people in our lives, friends and family, and for having a master plan for us. We might not always understand that plan, and we might not always agree with where that plan is taking us, but we remain steadfast in our knowing that You have placed us on this path for our own good, not out of malice. Dear Lord, thank You for Your children gathered here today, for believers and for those seeking answers to questions. Thank You for giving us this institution of healing that we might learn to deal with our illnesses and learn how to take care of ourselves."

"Lord, thank you for my new friend Peter," Richard began after a pause. "Please help him find answers to what is making him sick and bring him happiness as he struggles with the stuff he struggles with. Lord, please bless my parents, and thank you for my doctors and nurses who take care of me."

"Dear Lord," Louise began, "thank you for my sister and her husband who take care of me. Lord, please continue to give me strength to fight this depression and help me get over my feelings of worthlessness and hopelessness and despair."

"Lord," Dean began, "Please continue to be there for my wife. She is headed down a sinful path and I don't think she'll see the light on her own. And Lord, please continue to work through my doctors in helping me stay on my meds and off the liquor."

"Lord, we're far from perfect, all of us," David prayed. "Me especially. Just please be patient with us and see the good in our hearts and help each of us get healthy so we can get out of here and get on with our real lives."

"Dear Lord… please help me learn to take care of myself so I can go home and take care of my babies." Elaine abruptly stopped, tears in her voice.

"Dear Lord, be with my wife," Ken said. "See that she is comfortable in our kids' house until I can come home and be with her. Please help me to make her understand that what happened to me is not her fault and that she don't need to blame herself for it."

Ken reached over and tapped Walczyk. He found himself unsure of what to say. "Help me. I'm lost. I don't know what to do. I've never faced anything like this before. I guess You would know better than anyone that I've never come to You for anything before. But I need something now. I need help getting through this. It says you promised to be there for us in our darkest hour. Well, I'm there now." Walczyk felt his eyes burning and tears seeping out. He sniffed and felt Kaley's hand reached out and take his. "Lord, thank you for what you have promised us and please help me to become a better person."

Walczyk squeezed Kaley's hand and she spoke: "Lord, as David said, we are none of us perfect. We can only strive to be better. And we will get better. Your plan for us is confusing, but You never promised that it would be a simple plan. Just that You had a plan for us, and that our own good was at the heart of that plan. Lord, be with our parents. Our wives. Our children and our friends. This treatment we are undergoing is as frightening and disconcerting to them as it is to us, and they need Your support and light. Almighty Father, we lift ourselves up to You, as well as our families and our friends, for consideration, love and prayer. In the name of Your son Jesus Christ, who made the ultimate sacrifice for our salvation, we pray to You today. Amen."

"Amen," Walczyk said with the rest of the group. He opened his eyes to find Kaley's hand still in his. "Thanks," he said to her, trying to stifle his emotions.

"It can be a moving experience, the first time." Kaley reached over to brush an errant tear from Walczyk's cheek. "But for someone who says he has never spoken to God before, you did well." Kaley squeezed Walczyk's hand and stood up. "Come on. I want you to meet Bruce."

As Walczyk crossed the room, a voice called out to him. "Yo, Peter!"

Walczyk turned. It was David. "Hey," Walczyk said coldly.

"Yeah," David said, his white ball cap was in his hands. His thin blonde hair was sticking up in different directions. "Look, about the other day. I ain't gonna make excuses for what I did. I'm just gonna say I'm sorry and that I hope we cool." David extended his hand.

Walczyk felt Kaley's eyes burning into the back of his head. Walczyk had never been pushed, shoved, or physically intimidated before in his life. And he didn't like his first experience with it. But he could either hold his grudge against David, and live in fear of him, or show him just a little of the respect he expected in return. Walczyk nodded at David. "Don't worry about it." Walczyk took David's hand and shook it, and found himself pulled in to a hug. Walczyk patted David on the back.

"So we cool?"

Walczyk smiled. "We cool."

Walczyk turned around and returned to Kaley's side as she walked across the room. "Look at you," she said. "First day of Sunday School and you're all Matthew five, thirty-nine."

"Matthew five, thirty-nine?"

"'But I tell you, do not resist a sinful person. If someone strikes you on the right cheek, turn to him the other also'."

Walczyk smiled. "You're just full of Biblical goodies, aren't you?"

She shot him a smile as they approached the table where Bruce was picking up his papers. "Hey, Bruce," Kaley called out. Bruce looked up from his work, saw Kaley, and his face lit up.

"Kaley, how are you?" he asked, accepting her hug. "How've you been doing?"

"I've been back on my meds for a week now," she said.

"That's great," Bruce said. "And your suicidal thoughts?"

She rolled her eyes. "Such a mistake."

"I agree. This world would be a much less cheery place without you."

She gestured to Walczyk. "Bruce, there's someone I want you

to meet."

Bruce's face lit up with a smile. "I'm Bruce Johnson. It's nice to meet you."

Walczyk smiled and extended his hand. "Peter Walczyk, and the pleasure's all mine, Bruce."

"My wife Liz and I really enjoy *Ordinary World*."

"*You* watch *Ordinary World*?" Walczyk asked, shocked.

"Don't miss a one," Bruce replied. "Though Ethan and the hooker... have to say I wasn't a fan of that plot twist." Bruce and Walczyk laughed.

"Would you believe me if I said that neither was I?" Walczyk asked.

"Careful, now," Kaley said. "I haven't even seen season two yet."

"Fine, but my silence has a price," Bruce said, holding his hand out. "Twenty bucks."

Kaley reached out and slapped Bruce's hand. "Peter checked in here on, what was it, Thursday or Friday?"

"I don't remember. I was pretty out of it when they brought me in."

"Are they making any progress finding out what's going on?" Bruce asked.

"Bipolar. I was on some meds that might have been aggravating the condition. Plus I wasn't exactly a happy camper to begin with, what with my personal life."

"Yeah, I read about all that. I'm so sorry. Is there any chance to reconcile the relationship?"

"Not really," Walczyk said. "Now, this plan God has for me – the obstacles He's put in my path – beats the hell out of me what the purpose is."

"It's like they say, He works in mysterious ways." Bruce countered. "The way I see it, God had a reason for putting you on your path. Taking you away from California, bringing you back to Maine, and even leading you to this hospital, it's all part of His purpose for you. Listen, do you have a Bible?"

"I must have one somewhere at home," Walczyk said, thinking about the question. If he still had his old Bible from his Sunday School days, he didn't know where it had gotten to. "I seem to remember referencing it when I was writing *R.U.R.*"

"Wait a minute, then," Bruce said, letting go of Walczyk's hand. He turned around and pawed through a book bag he'd brought with him. He turned around a moment later holding a paperback Bible. "Here. Take this."

"Bruce, I can't..."

"Yes, you can," he said. "You never know when you're going to find yourself in a dark place, needing an answer."

"Well, thank you," Walczyk said, stuffing the Bible under his arm.

Bruce reached out for Kaley, pulling her into a hug. "As always, a pleasure to see you, and I hope that next time I'm here, you're not."

"Thanks," she said, letting go of him. Bibles in hand, Walczyk and Kaley walked out of the common room.

CHAPTER EIGHTEEN
ALONE TIME

Walczyk lay on his bed for a moment, thinking about meeting Bruce and having actually gone to a religious service. The last time he could remember doing that was when he and Sara got married, and the involvement of clergy had more to do with tradition (and shutting the mothers up) than it did with his or Sara's personal religious beliefs. Walczyk reached over, grabbed *Dr. Jekyll and Mr. Hyde* from the nightstand, and got off his bed. He slid his slippers on and scuffled out into the hallway. He turned and started towards the quiet reading room, but stopped a couple of feet away from it. He turned around. Most of the patients were collected in the main hallway, laughing and talking and having a good time. Walczyk looked down at the book, with its picture of the man half in the dark, turned around, and headed back toward the group. Keeping his book with him, he sat down on the bench and opened it up, starting to read from where he remembered having last left off.

Before he could start, he was greeted by a couple of patients who had been in the morning worship service. "Good service this morning," Ken said to him. Walczyk was unsure if it was a question or a comment.

"It was," he agreed.

"I like Bruce," Dean said from across the hall. "He don't just preach at you. He makes you think."

Ever since Walczyk had left the worship group, he had indeed been thinking. About God. About His plan for Peter Henry Walczyk, and the entire notion that there was a purpose to his getting sick. He'd never put much stock in God. He found it too difficult to be a good person all the time, so he had given up on it years ago. It just became too difficult to juggle being a Christian with partying, being a filmmaker, drinking, having sex, and using whatever profanity he felt like using. He couldn't deny, nor did he ever, that there *had* to be a divine hand at work in the creation of the galaxy. He acknowledged scientific refutations of "intelligent design" like dinosaurs and evolution, but could never get beyond the fact that life was just too perfect to be a mixing of chemicals. But here he was, on a path laid out for him by God, intersected by a cuckoo's nest in central Maine. And somehow, it was making sense to him. His religious contemplation was interrupted the familiar voice of Richard. "Hey, Peter!"

"Hey, Richard. What's up?"

"Nothing. Whatcha doing?"

"Reading," Walczyk said, not looking up from his book.

"Whatcha reading?"

Walczyk held the book up, then after a few seconds of silence, announced the title: "*Dr. Jekyll and Mr. Hyde.*"

"Is it good?"

"So far."

Richard sidled down the bench to sit closer to Walczyk, putting his arm around him. "What's it about?"

Walczyk closed his thumb in the paperback and looked up at Richard. "It's a story about a man with a monster inside of him." That much, Walczyk thought, should be known to anyone.

"Is it a good monster or a bad monster?"

"A bad one."

"What's the monster's name?"

"Mr. Hyde."

Richard screwed his face up. "That's a stupid name for a monster."

"Hey, Richard," a voice called behind Walczyk. He turned around and saw Kaley standing there, tugging on her elbow-length fingerless black gloves. "Remember what we talked about? You have to give people space."

Richard's face fell, and for the first time since he'd known him, Walczyk felt a little bad for him. Kaley hadn't been cruel about it. In fact, she was very careful in talking with Richard, as if afraid to piss off a six foot tall, three hundred pound eight-year-old.

"I'm sorry," Richard said, standing up. He was hanging his head low, giving his thick back somewhat of a hump.

"Don't be sorry," Walczyk told him. "Just let me read for a while, then I've got a surprise for you."

Richard's face lit up. "A surprise?"

"Yeah. You and me and Kaley."

"The Cool Kids," Richard said, getting up. He turned back to Walczyk. "What's the surprise?"

"Now, if he told you," Kaley started, "it wouldn't be a surprise, would it?"

Richard took off down the corridor, telling everyone that Walczyk had a surprise for him. "He's autistic," Kaley said, sliding down to Richard's former spot. "So the social graces aren't necessarily his bread and butter, but he's a sweet kid. Well, a sweet kid who's almost forty."

Walczyk closed his book. "I gather you know Richard well."

"You could say that. We've been bumping into each other up in here and downstairs in the out-patient program for years now. He just can't take care of himself. He belongs in a group home, but can't get into one."

"Well, you have a good way with him."

"Believe it or not, he's been there for me, too."

Kaley opened her copy of *Dracula* and began reading Walczyk followed suit, looking for his page in *Jekyll and Hyde*. As he read, he felt Kaley's body leaning against him. "By the way," she whispered, "I'm glad to see you've started socializing. It'll go a long way in getting you discharged sooner."

"Well, I guess it beats spending the afternoon in my room, banging my head off the–"

A screaming from down the hall echoed out into the hallway. Everybody turned.

Loud, frightened screams were coming from one of the patients. It was David, still in his bathrobe and pajamas. He was in the clutches of the ever-so-charming Roger and Terry, a large, burly, bald-headed man Kaley had pointed out to him earlier as one of the nicer nurses. It was a very disturbing scene, Walczyk thought, watching from down the hall. David broke one arm free and made to punch Roger in the face, but the other nurse quickly grabbed it and forced it back down.

"YOU'RE NOT FUCKING TAKING ME DOWN THERE!"

By now, all eyes were on David, who was being lifted off the floor by the two nurses. Hope darted behind the nurses' desk and unlocked a cabinet. Walczyk kept his attention on the scene in the hall. David was thrashing with all his might to get free of his two captors, and he was giving them quite the struggle. The orderlies, both men of considerable size, were fighting with all they had to keep David from busting loose.

"Let me through!" Hope yelled, pushing her way through the crowd. Then Walczyk saw it. The deciding factor in this wrestling match. It wouldn't be Terry throwing a right across David's jaw that took him down. It wouldn't be Roger with a sleeper hold. It would be Hope with a Mickey in a needle. Roger made eye-contact with Hope, nodded slightly, and maneuvered David around, giving his backside to Hope. Hope yanked his pajamas down, stabbed him in the rear with the needle, and pushed the plunger. David screamed, struggled briefly, then went limp in the arms of Terry. Sandy, one of the other nurses, appeared with a wheel chair, and David was loaded into the chair and taken down the hall.

"What the hell was that?" Walczyk asked no one in particular.

The chatter that evening in the cafeteria was focused on the afternoon's episode in the hall with David. The staff must've been worried about people imitating David's little stunt, because the patients were all marched down to the cafeteria for supper in one very strictly managed group by Roger and Terry. Kaley convinced Walczyk to go all in with the whole socialization thing, and they sat at the big table with the majority of the other patients. The entire table was abuzz discussing David's earlier breakdown.

"What do you think set him off?" Elaine asked, poking at her pig-in-a-blanket with her fork.

"I heard he was talking on the phone and they told him he had to quiet down," Ken said, his mouth full.

"No," Dean said, picking his teeth with his fork. "He got

pissed because they wouldn't let him go have a smoke."

The others at the table weighed in on the incident, each one sharing their opinion as "the God's honest truth." Walczyk tried tuning it out, but with voices all around him chiming in with their theories, and no book to escape into, it was virtually impossible. The chatter continued upstairs after supper. The entire hallway was abuzz with excitement as the rumor mill continued to churn. Richard was loving it, parroting back whatever people told him. Around seven, as the gossip machine continued to grind out half-truths, speculation, and pure bullshit, Theresa clamped down on the entire conversation, suggesting that everyone either change the subject or go to bed and miss the Sunday night movie, which would be starting at seven-thirty.

Never before had Walczyk been so thankful for Nurse Theresa and her shoddy spray tan. He found himself growing weary of the constant rehashing of David's outburst. What good was it doing to go over the entire incident over and over again? What purpose did it serve? What was the point? The only purpose Walczyk could find for all of it was that it kept everyone entertained. No one was bitching about cigarettes or ex-husbands or not getting weekend passes. Everyone was fixated on one thing: the take-down of Bathrobe David. And as much as he tried, Walczyk just couldn't get into it. He couldn't get excited about one patient's tantrum. It didn't fill the needs he had. It didn't patch the holes in his life. It was just a sick man who had a bad turn and lost his temper.

Finally, around six-thirty, Richard bounded over to Walczyk, Kaley in tow. "You said you had a surprise for me," Richard said. "What is it?"

Walczyk smiled. As troubled as Richard was, he had a mind like a steel trap when it came to certain things. Walczyk got up from the bench, sliding his book into his back pocket.

"Okay, Richard. You have Kaley take you down to small common room, and I'll be right there."

"How'd I get roped into this?" Kaley asked. "I was minding my own business."

"Because you are a sweet young woman who likes everyone around you," Walczyk said to her. As Kaley was dragged away, Walczyk approached the front desk. "Good evening," he said to the nurse on duty, who happened to be Mary.

"Good evening, Peter," Mary said. "How are you feeling

tonight?"

"A little tired of the rumor mill, but otherwise quite well, thanks. And yourself?"

She smiled. "Nothing a little sleep won't help. What can I do for you?"

"That box of Legos back there with my name on them. I kind of promised Richard that we could play with them for a while. If that's okay."

"So that's the surprise," Mary said, standing up. She walked into a back room and looked over a collection of plastic tote cases. Finally, she exclaimed "Aha!" and the sound of one being popped open came from the back room. A moment later, she came out, carrying the Lego box, which had a Post-It note affixed to the front of it with "Peter" written on it. Walczyk reached out for the box, but Mary pulled it back. She had a devilish grin on her face. "You have to answer me a question first."

"Okay," Walczyk replied cautiously.

"Is Ethan the father of Danielle's baby?"

Walczyk gave her a look. He couldn't believe *that's* what she wanted to ask him. That *that* was what she was holding his Legos hostage over. "You're kidding."

"The hell I am," she said, hugging the box to her chest. "I've been dying to find out who that baby's father is. And since you were admitted, it's been *killing* me. I have to know. Is Ethan the father? Or is it that nasty Brad Stone?"

Walczyk saw an opportunity. "My last night here, I want to order out for pizza."

"I will *buy* your pizza if you tell me."

"No," Walczyk said, shaking his head. "Not just for me. I want to order out for pizza for the entire unit – patients and staff."

She laughed. "You're not serious."

"Dead serious. I want to throw a party for the ward. I want pizza and soda and chips for everyone."

Mary was beaming. "Well, it's been done it before. We'll just need to check with the doctors and make sure no one's allergic to anything."

"Okay," Walczyk said, then leaned in confidentially. "Ethan is the father."

"I knew it!" Mary jumped up and down. "Holy shit, I *knew* it!"

"Now that can't go anywhere, you understand? Not even my best friend Hannah knows that one."

"Of course." She slid the Legos across the desk. "One more question. Though it's more like a favor." She pulled her cell phone from her pocket and flashed him a broad smile.

"I don't know," Walczyk said, really not wanting pictures of him in a psychiatric hospital popping up on Facebook,. Or TMZ. Or Paparraz-Eye. But, the more he thought about it, the more he didn't care. So what if he was in a psychiatric hospital. He had a mental illness, where else should he be?

"Fine, but *please* don't put this on your Facebook page until after I'm discharged."

"Deal," she said, bubbling over with joy. She stepped out from behind the main desk, putting her arm around Walczyk. "Smile!" she called out, and flashed two pictures.

"And remember, you can't even tell your friends what I told you about the show. That was in confidence, and as a patient, I have my rights."

"Oh, don't worry, Peter," she giggled, examining the two photographs on her phone.

"See you in a bit, Mary," Walczyk said, picking up the box of Legos. He couldn't believe what he'd just said. Not about the series, and not about the pictures. He could give two shits if someone knew the goods on the show, and, for all he knew, the world already knew he was in a psychiatric hospital. He was thinking about the pizza party he'd just promised to put together. He never planned on throwing a party for the whole wing. He never planned on making any friends. He planned on getting diagnosed, getting help, and checking out. Wham, bam, thank you ma'am. But here he was, finding himself drawn to these people and their stories. Their own personal hells. The unique monkeys on all their backs. He needed to get to know these people. He owed them that much.

Richard had certainly enjoyed his surprise. As he assembled the Legos, squabbling with Kaley over how to assemble the X-Wing according to the detailed instructions booklet, Walczyk scanned through the channels of the archaic television in the corner. The Dirigo Psychiatric Hospital did not get, or had blocked out, the Paparazz-Eye Network. They did get E!, however, and sure enough, the banner "Peter Walczyk Checks Into Psychiatric Hospital" scrolled across the bottom of the screen with what scant few details they knew about his treatment. Nowhere was the picture of himself with Mary though. She'd held off posting it to her Facebook this long.

About an hour after he first started tearing bricks out of the box, Richard called for Walczyk and Kaley to come look. The X-Wing fighter was assembled, exactly like the photo on the front of the box. And in the cockpit was a little Lego Luke Skywalker figurine, clutching his lightsaber. Richard zoomed the space ship around the air in front of him, supplying the noises of the laser blasts and the proton torpedo explosions. Kaley walked over to Walczyk and sat down on the couch next to him. For the longest time, they just stared at the TV, commenting on the reality show tripe that was being broadcast and read the gossip headlines at the bottom of the screen.

"You surprise me, Peter Walczyk."

"How's that, Kaley Richardson?"

"Because you say you're not a Christian."

"I say that because I'm not."

"Do you believe in Christ?"

"I'm not sure. It's a lot to swallow."

"But you believe in God."

"Again, a big story to buy into. But… this can't all be a cosmic accident."

"Then I'll take that as a yes."

"That works for me. Now why are you surprised?"

"Because for a man who tells me he's not a Christian, you have a very Christian attitude about you."

"Get out of here," Walczyk said, pushing her aside.

She leaned into him. "You love Richard, despite his faults. You've cast aside your own grandeur and haven't asked for favor one from the staff since you got here. But the biggest thing you did is you learned to forgive."

"Forgive who?"

"Well, there's David. And your wife. And it's a while coming still, but I think you're beginning to forgive yourself for whatever sins you blame yourself for." Walczyk said nothing, staring blankly at the television. "How much have you actually read out of that thing?" She asked, tapping the cover of *Jekyll and Hyde*.

He laughed. "Not a lot."

She laughed with him, tossing her book on the floor. "Then

you're doing better than I am."

"I don't read much," Walczyk said.

She took the book from him. "Then spread out and try to stay awake."

Walczyk looked at her, curiously. She nodded at him. He put his feet up on her lap and lay back on the couch. She cleared her throat and opened the book, leafing through the dozen or so forewords by various literary geniuses before beginning with the first chapter, "The Story of the Door."

By the time Stevenson was ready to reveal the secret connection between Dr. Henry Jekyll and Mr. Edward Hyde, Theresa showed up, coldly asking Walczyk to sit up first, before telling them that it was bedtime. Richard handed Walczyk the Lego X-Wing, which he hated to break apart but had to in order to fit it in the box. Kaley suggested that Richard would enjoy putting it back together at a later date. Walczyk gave the box to Theresa and walked down the corridor with Kaley. As she turned to go into her room, Walczyk reached out to her and put his hand on her shoulder. She turned to look at him.

"What?" she asked.

"Would you do me a favor?" Walczyk asked.

"Of course," Kaley replied.

"Tonight. When you pray... would you pray for me too?"

She smiled. "I've prayed for you since I first met you, Walczyk."

They stared at each other for a long time. Walczyk realized she had the most amazing bright blue eyes. A scar graced her chin. He wondered where that came from, but that was a discussion for another time. "Well, good night," he said.

"Yeah. Sleep well." Kaley turned and walked into her room.

Walczyk continued down the hall towards his room. Richard was already in bed when he walked in. "Hi, Peter," he said as Walczyk walked by the bed.

"Hey, Richard."

"Thanks for letting me play with your Legos."

"Any time."

Richard sat up in bed. "You mean–?"

"I mean you can play with them sometime tomorrow, yes. But right now, we both need to get some sleep."

Walczyk stripped down to his shorts and slid into the stiff sheets of his bed. His only wish was that the hospital had thicker blankets to drape over the beds. He half thought of asking his parents to bring him some of his own blankets the next time they came to visit, but brushed the idea away. He wouldn't be here that long.

Walczyk reached into his nightstand and pulled out the portable radio April had brought him. He popped the ear buds into his ears and was about to switch the thing on when something stopped him.

Gently, he removed the ear buds, and he placed the radio back in his nightstand drawer. Not sure if he was doing it right, or if it even mattered, he began to pray silently.

Dear Lord, thank You for giving me today. Thank You for putting people like Kaley and Richard in my life. Thank You for my family. Too often, I seem to take them for granted, or worse, I see being with them as a chore to be done. But they have stood by me as I struggled to conquer this thing I've been diagnosed with. Thank You for Hannah and April and Vic. Lord, I hope I've done this right. But, as Bruce said, You hear the prayer in our hearts as well as the prayer on our lips. So I pray to You tonight. Amen.

Walczyk lay there, reflecting on the prayer he'd just offered up, and was asleep long before he could think of getting his radio from the nightstand.

CHAPTER NINETEEN
JUST ANOTHER MANIC MONDAY

Walczyk was slightly encouraged by the fact that his lithium no longer tasted horrible. Bupropion (the generic form of Wellbutrin), thankfully, didn't have an aftertaste at all; it was a coated pill that went down easily. Walczyk spent breakfast in somewhat of a daze. He couldn't put his finger on it, but there was something different about him. He wasn't aware of its source, but he was certainly feeling more relaxed. More at peace with himself. Kaley suggested that it might be God working in his life, easing him of his burdens. He didn't dismiss the notion, but he didn't comment on it either. However, an idea did strike him, suddenly, as he caught his reflection in a window behind Kaley's head. As the residents of Three North marched back to their ward from breakfast, Walczyk approached Emily. "I have a favor I need to ask."

"Sure, Peter, what is it?"

"The stuff my assistant brought, that you guys have to keep. In there, they brought me a beard trimmer, a razor and some shaving cream, right?"

"Right," Emily said. "But you can't use them without a staff member's supervision."

"Well, if you've got anyone who's not busy and doesn't mind

the sight of a man in his undershirt, I'd love to spend the next forty-five minutes with them," Walczyk said with a smile.

A half hour later, Walczyk stood in the bathroom with Hope, who was wearing her Buzz Lightyear scrubs and standing behind him, the electric beard trimmer in hand. Walczyk tried to block her out, not out of malice, but so that he could imagine himself in his own bathroom, cleaning himself up.

"Why do you want to do this again?" Hope asked.

Walczyk ran a hand over the thick growth of hair on his face. "Because I'm tired of looking like a sick person." Walczyk peeled his shirt off and scratched his chest. Walczyk could tell that Richard hadn't showered yet, as there were plenty of clean towels on the shelves. He held his hand out. "Trimmers."

"Trimmers," Hope said, placing the beard trimmer in his hand. Walczyk snapped it on. The trimmer emitted a low, rhythmic hum. Walczyk tipped it up, at an angle and began to carve chunks of hair off his face.

"You know you're doing me a huge favor," he said, one eye closed as he sized up his sideburns, making sure they were even.

"Mind if I ask you a question?"

"Is it about me or my show?"

"Your show," she meekly replied.

Walczyk laughed. "Go for it."

"Why didn't Ethan ever tell Kara that he was having the panic attacks?"

Walczyk thought, switching off the beard trimmer, a mess of errant hairs decorating both the sink and his face. He picked his T-shirt up from the floor, wiped the trimmer down, then unplugged it. He held his hand out again.

"Shave gel," he said.

Hope took the can of shaving gel from the plastic Target bag she'd put the shaving kit in.

"Shave gel," she said.

"I don't know if you know this," he said, wetting his face, "but having something wrong like depression, panic attacks, or even a mental illness can seem damned near impossible to deal with. Not just because you have a hard time dealing with it yourself. No, it's the fear that telling someone else – be it a friend, a lover, a relative – because that person *will* look at you differently forever. They'll treat you differently forever. They'll think of you differently. Forever. They might not mean to; they might fight the urge, but in the end, your mother or your wife or your best friend is going see you and think, 'I wonder if he's in one of his moods today.'" Walczyk washed the excess foam from his hands. "Does that make any sense?"

Hope looked at him in the mirror, looking like she was on the verge of crying. "It makes perfect sense," she said, opening the package and removing the razor. "So, expecting any guests today?"

"Just my parents and April," Walczyk said, starting at his left sideburn and running the razor down his throat. He ran it under hot water and shook it off, and started in again. The hot blade felt so good against his skin. He rinsed it off in the sink and went back to work, going over the same spot again and again until it felt smooth to the touch, filling the sink with a grayish-green sludge of tiny, chopped-off hairs and spent shave gel. Occasionally, he would spot Emily or one of the day nurses in the mirror as well. He was struck by the incongruity of performing a normally solitary task in front of an audience of women clad in scrubs.

"So what made you want to become a nurse in a psychiatric hospital?" Walczyk asked, stretching his upper lip out and shaving under his nose.

"I wanted to help people," Hope said, handing Walczyk a towel as he put the razor down. His face was covered in stray hairs, and several red spots where he'd cut himself, but he was rather impressed with the work he'd done.

Hope smiled at him in the mirror. "Not bad."

"Thank you," Walczyk said, rinsing the razor off and handing it back to Hope. She picked up the can of shaving cream and left, shutting the door behind her. Walczyk slid his pants down, stepped out of his shorts and got into the shower. He turned the water on as hot as it would go and let it drizzle down over his face. He reached up and touched his face. It was completely smooth. Walczyk pumped some soap from the dispenser and washed his face, hair, chest, and underarms. He finished and dried off, then shut the door almost completely, giving himself some privacy to dress in the room. He returned to the bathroom and wiped down the fogged up mirror, revealing something he hadn't seen since he left Hollywood so many months ago: Peter Walczyk.

After the morning meeting, which had been about the warning

signs that you're on a downward spiral, Walczyk sat out in the corridor, receiving plenty of compliments on his shaving job. Richard kept asking to touch his face, repeating Walczyk's remark that it was "smooth as a baby's behind." Kaley caught up with him on his way to Dr. Lentz's office, eyeing him curiously.

"Why'd you do that?"

"Guess I'm just tired of looking like I'm a sick person. Like it?"

They stopped outside the door. She evaluated the shave before responding. "Not really." She smiled and continued down the hall, towards the quiet room.

Upon entering the doctor's office, Lentz clapped his hands together, exclaiming, "Look at you!" Dr. Lentz exclaimed as Walczyk walked in through the door. "I like the shave, though, if you don't mind my saying, I'm fairly certain your left sideburn is a half centimeter lower than your right." Walczyk reached up to see if he could detect the difference by touch. "So, how was your weekend?"

"Good."

"Your weekend planning: did you achieve your goals?"

"Most of them."

"That's all we can ask for." Dr. Lentz leant forward and had a sip of tea from his ever-present tan-and-brown travel mug. "Are you writing again?"

"Going to be."

"Mind if I inquire as to what the project is?"

"That *Night of the Living Dead* remake I was talking about last time. I think I'm going to give it another try."

"How does the thought of that make you feel?"

Walczyk thought about it a moment before replying, "Good. It's nice to feel productive again."

"And what about *Ordinary World*?"

Walczyk shook his head.

"Are you going to quit?"

"Most likely."

"Supposing you stay, what will you be doing?"

"Mostly I'll oversee the writing, probably write the series finale myself. Otherwise, it's Ian's show."

"Are you sad to leave the series?"

"Not really," he replied without a thought.

"How much of this has to do with dealing with Ella and Sara?"

"None of it. I'd begun to lose interest in the series long before Ella and Sara."

"Hmmm," Dr. Lentz murmured, scratching his chin. He was dressed, once again, in a collared shirt and tie beneath a thick, camel-colored sweater and what looked to be the same pair of brown corduroys he'd worn Friday. Today he was wearing a pair of suede clog shoes instead of sandals. "I've heard you're starting to make some friends."

"Yeah. Richard's not a bad guy once you get to know him."

"No, he's not. And what about Kaley?"

"She's been a good friend," he replied after taking a moment to think. "I can't imagine the guilt of having my sister find me trying to kill myself."

"Clearly a difficult moment in her life. What did you think of Bruce Johnson and his Sunday morning worship?"

Walczyk grinned. "You don't miss a trick, do you?" Lentz winked. "Yeah, Bruce was interesting. I don't know how much of it I buy into."

"But?"

"But..." *But what*? Why was he so reluctant to admit to Dr. Lentz – to anyone – that he'd found some comfort in thinking that there was a God, and that God had a plan for him, and that no matter how rough that plan got, He was there for Walczyk? "But he did get me thinking."

"Not such a bad thing. So, tell me, do you have a plan for today?"

"I'd like to start writing again. My folks are coming later on this evening." Walczyk paused. "That, and I probably ought to call my wife. Tell her what's going on."

"You don't think she's heard by now?" Walczyk shrugged. "I hope you don't mind, but I kept my ears open over the weekend."

"What's the story?"

"The media know little more than what your agent released to the them: they know that you're in a psychiatric hospital here in Maine for undisclosed reasons. TMZ, Paparazz-Eye, even *People* and *Entertainment Weekly*, their websites have made no mention as to this particular hospital. No one knows you're being treated for bipolar disorder and no one knows about your harming yourself physically."

Something about this media black-out didn't sit right with Walczyk, however. "I wonder why the paps aren't being more aggressive."

"Oh, they are. We're just keeping the wolves at the gate, so to speak."

"Oh, well thank you. And sorry for the inconvenience."

"You're not our first high profile patient and I doubt you'll be our last. But, since time is precious, let's shift gears, shall we? Have you noticed any side effects from your medications?"

"None that I can think of. Tastes like ass, but I'm getting used to that."

"Yes, I'm told that lithium does have a nasty taste to it. Any increase in thirst?"

"A little."

"Give it time. I suggest keeping a bottle of water with you at all times for a while. Which, logically, will lead to increased urination, so don't let that throw you. How about dizziness? Muscle weakness? Swelling of the mouth, face, lips or tongue?"

"No. It seems to be working. I feel great. I'm feeling creative, social, optimistic. I've got energy I haven't had in ages, and I think it's safe to say I'm finally happy. I don't see why I'd need to be here much longer."

"While I'm glad to hear that you're feeling better," Dr. Lentz said, "Though I doubt the lithium has built up a significant level in your bloodstream yet to be proving effective. Rather, I think you're entering your next cycle of mania."

Walczyk was floored. "What?"

"Peter, you've been on the drug for four days now. Believe me, it's not uncommon to feel better in that period of time. Many patients report that their medication works quickly. But in all reality it could take up to two weeks to build up a sufficient level."

"You mean I'm going to be here two weeks?"

"Perhaps, though that's a–"

Walczyk shot to his feet. "Well, that's bullshit!"

"How so?" Lentz calmly asked.

"No," Walczyk said, shaking his head. "No, no, no, no, NO! I've done everything you guys have asked of me. I wanted to be left alone to read and wait this thing out. You all said no, I had to be social and socialize. So I did! I left my room and I got out there. I made friends! I take my nasty meds and I eat the nasty food and you tell me I'm not ready to go? Tell me what else I could have done."

"Peter, please sit down." The voice was firm, but calm.

Walczyk stared at the man, filled with fury and rage. He felt he'd been lied to. Misled. Betrayed. "So that's the way it works, huh? I do what you want, play by your rules, and you keep me longer?" Walczyk remained standing, never taking his eyes off Dr. Lentz.

The doctor continued in that same firm, calm voice. "Peter, I am sorry if you were under the assumption that you'd be leaving today. If I did anything, or said anything, to make you believe that, I do apologize. But the facts are these: you had a mental breakdown. You are being taken off a drug that has poisoned you and introduced to two new drugs that could possibly have a similar effect on you. On top of that, you have exhibited signs of self-abuse when under extreme stress. Now, while I do not believe these to be part of some suicidal ideation, they are self-harming behaviors. If I am to release you from this hospital, I must be assured that the medications you are taking are not harming you.

"Of course, as you are aware, you have checked into this hospital under your own authority, and as such, can discharge yourself, against medical orders, at any time, if you do not feel you are being fairly treated. Either way you want to have it, you will sit down and calm yourself."

The calm, collected voice was gone. This was not a request. It was an order. Walczyk dropped back into his chair.

"Peter." The tone calm again. "I am willing to chalk this outburst up to disappointment in your current circumstances and not as a symptom of a dangerous hypomanic episode. However, should you have another outburst like that, or should you decide to take your aggressions out on anyone or anything, you may be sedated for the safety of the other patients and yourself. Am I clear?"

Walczyk nodded.

"No, I want you to say it."

"Clear." Walczyk said, feeling numb. He was going to cry. That was inevitable. But he was sure as hell not going to give Dr. Lentz the satisfaction of seeing him broken. He swallowed the hard lump in his throat and blinked away the tears growing in the corners of his eyes. *Don't do it*, he told himself. *Not here.*

Then it just happened: Walczyk broke down, crying. Hard,

racking sobs. He tried speaking, but nothing intelligible came from him. Dr. Lentz offered a box of tissues, but Walczyk did not take it. There was nothing Dr. Lentz had that he needed.

"Because it's shitty thing to do, that's why!"

At Macy's Department Store in the Bangor Mall, April angrily shifted through a rack of clearance-priced shirts. Behind her, she noticed an older woman behind her shoot a nasty glare at her. She didn't care. Had old Gertrude just heard what Elias had just suggested, she'd have responded in kind, perhaps brandishing her cane at the man.

"*April, be reasonable,*" Eli's voice pleaded over the phone.

"I am being reasonable. He's going to be out of the hospital soon. He's going to need me here."

"*He's got to learn to live on his own. More importantly, you've got to learn to live on your own. You two have been shacked up together so long you're probably married under common law.*"

"Funny, Eli. Very funny."

"*I'm serious. You work together, your play together, you have the same friends, you have the same meals. You grocery shop together. You make sure he's taking care of himself, he makes sure you've got clean towels. You're the ultimate odd couple!*"

"So what if we are? He needs me."

"*He's a grown man! If he needs someone to cut the crusts off his sandwiches and remind him to send his mother a birthday card, then he can get a wife for that. There's plenty of fish in the sea.*"

"That's not all I do," April said, growing angrier and angrier with Walczyk's agent and supposed friend.

"*That's right. You read the contents of my e-mails to him, which he ignores. You nag him to do the things I'm asking him to do, which he ignores. You repeat, verbatim, the things I ask him to check up on, which he ignores. You're the assistant to a man who has given up on the will to work.*"

"You know, Elias, if you're trying to make me feel good about myself, you're doing a lousy damned job of it."

Tired of the old woman's disapproving scowls, April moved across the department toward intimate apparel.

"*April, I'm not trying to make you feel like shit. But you need to realize that you're being wasted in Maine. You've turned into his house maid. April, don't you want more?*"

"Of course, I want more. But for the time being, this is where I need to be."

"Your loyalty to him is charming, but it's striking me as a bit out-of-character for you, April."

"What do you mean?"

"I mean the April Donovan I met five years ago wouldn't have stood still and let her heels cool while her boss decided to drop off the map. She'd have kicked his ass into gear and gotten him going, or she'd have gotten going herself."

And suddenly, April found herself feeling that Eli was absolutely right. She was April Donovan, the woman who told studio heads that their movies were lousy and nailed major stars for taking easy roles and getting bad botox treatments. She'd once been a force to be reckoned with, but now what was she? The girl who went to town for Diet Coke and eggs because Walczyk and his friends wanted to have omelets for supper. "Okay, fine. What's the offer?" she asked.

"Remember when Ian suggested you come work for him?"

"I think that was pretty much a ploy to bed me."

"And it worked, didn't it?"

"Screw you, Eli."

"Relax, April, relax. Well, what would you say if I said I could do you one better on Ian's offer? And no sex required."

"You?"

"No. Burt Schueller."

April dropped the clothes she was carrying. "As in Burt Schueller your *boss*?"

"The same. Seems his assistant, Nicole, is stepping down soon. Don't know why. Just that he told me the other day he wants you to replace her."

April's paused. "But Eli, I don't have enough experience to–"

"I know that, Sweetie. But if Burt felt that way, he wouldn't have asked for you."

April took a deep breath. This was a big step. The personal assistant to the head of one of the most powerful and influential talent agencies in Hollywood. She loved the idea of it. But she hated the idea of leaving Walczyk. He'd brought her up in the industry, taken her by the hand and shown her a whole new world. He taught her a lot about being a person. How to sweet talk people. How to charm people. How to treat people like human beings. She would forever be grateful for that.

"I won't leave him while he's sick."

"*I told Burt that and he understands. The position isn't even open until around Thanksgiving. That should give Walczyk plenty of time to get out of the hospital. So?*"

"So," she sighed, "I guess Burt's got his girl."

Eli's little celebration on the other end of the line was interrupted by a beep. April pulled the phone away from her face. It was Henry Walczyk calling. "Eli, I gotta take this. It's Walczyk's dad."

"*Well, congratulations, April Donovan,*" Eli said. "*I'm proud of you.*"

"Thanks," she said, feeling like a traitor for even thinking of leaving right now. She tapped a button on the iPhone's display and switched the call over.

"Hey, Henry, what's the good news?"

It was not good news.

April stormed up the stairs, taking them two at a time. She reached the door to the ward, pulled on it, and it didn't give. Only then did she remember that the doors were electronically locked. She cursed and pressed the intercom button.

"How can I help you?"

"April Donovan, here for Peter Walczyk."

The door buzzed and clicked and April was able to pull it open. She strode into the ward, looking around frantically.

"Can I help you?" one of the duty nurses asked, an older woman in daisy-patterned scrubs.

"I'm here to see Peter Walczyk," April repeated, still scanning the ward.

"Well, our normal visiting hours are from seven to–"

"Look, I'm April Donovan and I want Peter Walczyk. If you can't do that, get me someone who can make it happen."

"Did you say April Donovan?" an accented voice called out to her. She turned. That voice belonged to a giant of a man.

"Yes," she said, suddenly putting the huge man in front of her to the description given to her by Henry Walczyk. "Dr. Lentz?"

He held out a large mitt of a hand to her. She took it. "Yes," he said. "Henry Walczyk told me you'd be stopping in." Lentz threw a glance over his shoulder. "It's all right, Sandy. I asked her here." They started down the hall together.

"What the hell's going on?" April asked, panicked. "I get a call from Henry saying Walczyk's gone off the deep end again."

Lentz indicated his office door, and followed April in. "I wouldn't use the term 'gone off the deep end,' but he *has* grown quite agitated, yes."

"Well, what set him off?"

"I'm did, I'm afraid," Lentz said, sitting at his desk. "Inadvertently, of course."

"What'd you say to him?"

"We were discussing his discharge. He was under the impression it was sooner, rather than later."

"'Sooner rather than later?'"

"Sooner, as in today or tomorrow, rather than later, as in a week or so."

"Well, where did he get the idea he was going to be released right away?"

"Your guess is as good as mine. He probably thinks he's cured. He knows what he has, he has the medication to control it, and the knowledge to combat it. On top of all that, he's able to be left unsupervised for periods of time and we've not had to keep him sedated, like some of the other patients."

"Where is he now?" April asked.

"In his room, resting."

"Can I go see him?"

"Please," Lentz said, rising. April left the little office and went down the hall to room six, where she found Walczyk lying on his side, curled up in a ball, staring at the wall.

"Boss?"

At first, there was no reply. No reaction. Then, softly, he spoke. "They're not going to let me out." The rain beating down against his window matched his mood perfectly.

"Yes, they will," she said, sitting at the edge of his bed. "I'll make them. But all in due time." She caressed his arm. "This is not going to be as easy as you thought, though. You can't just take a pill, say a prayer, and expect to wake up cured." Walczyk sniffled, and April kissed his forehead. "When did you shave?" she asked.

"This morning."

"Why?"

"I felt better."

"And you don't anymore?"

"I'm pissed."

"At Dr. Lentz."

"At myself. I should've known it wouldn't be this easy."

"Boss, it's going to take time. Dr. Lentz says the meds are just now starting to build up levels in your blood. If they let you out of here and you tweak out again, if you hurt someone, or yourself... well, no one wants that." Walczyk snuffed loudly. April ran a hand over his cheek, drying the collected tears from his cheek. "Listen, it's almost lunch time. Why don't I go to the cafeteria with you, we get some of that oh-so-yummy cafeteria food you've been bragging about, then after lunch, maybe you can work on *Night* some more. Maybe take me through what you've got so far so I can tell Eli what you're up to. How's that sound?"

Walczyk sat up, wiping his face. "I feel like a damned fool."

"Why?"

"Carrying on like this. Making you come all the way down here. God, Dad. What he's got to be going through."

"Your father is fine. Don't be worrying about the rest of us. These hospitals, they're nice, because part of your prescription is to be totally narcissistic."

Walczyk reached out for April. She held him in her arms, caressing the back of his head, which no longer showed signs of swelling. She wanted to hold on to him like this forever.

But she knew she couldn't.

Hannah Cooper stood in the corner of the cafeteria, watching the mass of students chow down. They were so oblivious to everything that was going on. So unaware that, while they chatted about what they did over the weekend, and who slept with who at such-and-such's party, people were on the brink of collapse. She chided herself for that thought, reminding herself that Peter was in the care of professionals, and that they wouldn't let anything bad happen to him. Nevertheless, he was her friend, and he was suffering, and there wasn't a damned thing she could do about it while she was on lunch duty.

"You look like hell," Cameron Burke observed as he stepped up beside her.

"Thank you," she said, not impressed with his attempt at

brevity, and returned her attention to the lunch room.

"You hear about Lyndsay Hartman?"

"What about her?"

"Stella's period two creative writing class, she turns in this rather... erotic short story about herself and Jason Wood."

"Captain of the boy's basketball team?"

"Yeah," Cameron said, shaking his head and chuckling to himself.

"Great," Hannah groused. "Now we get to listen to Stella piss and moan all week about how we shouldn't be wasting our time teaching creative writing."

"Whoa," Burke said, moving to stand in front of Hannah. He looked her up and down before asking, "Hannah, what's going on?"

"I'm just sick of all the crap that goes on around here."

"This is about Peter Walczyk, isn't it?" She said nothing. "I told you that you shouldn't have come in today," Cameron said, reaching out and putting a hand on her shoulder. "How is he?"

"I don't know," Hannah said in a hushed tone.

"What's wrong?"

"Henry told me that he had some kind of melt down this morning when he found out he wasn't getting discharged right away."

"Oh, no," Burke sighed.

She could not imagine going through that kind of experience: being held, pretty much against your will, in a hospital where, at least on a superficial level, you're one of the few "sane" people. "I'm sorry I'm being so nasty, Cameron," she said, patting his arm. With a false cheer, she asked, "So, how's your day been?"

"Well, period one was barely awake. Period two, now, is convinced that Ishmael and Queequeg are 'gay for each other.'"

"Well, look at the text. There *are* some pretty intense homoerotic scenes in that book. Really intense."

"Well, I'm well aware of that, Miss Cooper, but I can't exactly–"

"And graphic."

"Moving on," Cameron said, "period three felt it unnecessary to do the assigned reading, and period four... José Lopez thought that 'creative writing' was passing in a synopsis of the movie *The Fugitive* with all the names changed."

"Creative indeed," Hannah said, giving perhaps her first smile all day. "So, who killed Dr. Richard Kimble's wife in José's version?"

"It's Professor Robert Kimbrough," Cameron clarified. "And it wasn't the professor, it was the one-legged man that killed his wife." She laughed, albeit weakly. "So, you going to see Peter tonight?

"I don't know. Depends on what April reports back. If he's still agitated–"

"Go see him. He needs to know his friends still love him. That's the most important thing to him right now: that the real world still exists, and that it wants him back, and that all of this is just temporary."

"Cameron, you speak as if you've been through this."

"My sister Megan has what doctors call avoidant personality disorder. She's a shut-in. Afraid of what others will think of her. She's tried to kill herself twice now, so I've been down the road you're on. Those hospitals, no matter how nice they are, they're still–"

"I know," Hannah said. "It's so hard seeing him in there. Pajama clad and kept on a schedule like a little kid. Meal time. Morning group. Play time. I wouldn't be surprised if they had a nap time."

"Not at Dirigo," Cameron joked.

"Why don't you come along? He likes you, Cameron. He'd be pleased to see you."

"I'm flattered," Cameron said, turning back around, "but I try to stay away from that place as much as possible now."

Hannah glanced at her watch. "Ten minutes."

"Why do we run lunch for forty minutes? The kids are fed and cleaned up in twenty-five."

"So that they can use the other fifteen minutes to get into trouble," Henry Walczyk said, approaching them.

"Henry," Cameron greeted.

"Cameron," Henry greeted back, then turned to Hannah. "April's helped calm him down."

"So should I still go with you to see him tonight?"

"Absolutely," Henry said.

"I just didn't know, given everything that–"

"What happened," Henry said cautiously, "just goes to show that he needs us more now than ever."

After lunch, Walczyk assured April he'd be all right. He was going to take it easy that afternoon, maybe do some writing, and definitely take a nap. April promised to return that evening with Walczyk's parents. After she left, he walked down the hall to the main reception desk. Hope was doing a crossword puzzle in the newspaper.

"How're you feeling?" she asked, genuinely concerned.

"Foolish," Walczyk said. "I haven't thrown a tantrum like that since I was six."

"Don't worry about it. It's understandable. It's not like your brain isn't being flooded with brand-new chemicals or anything. Stop being so hard on yourself, Peter."

"Still," Walczyk said. "Is it possible that I could talk to Dr. Lentz? Just sometime before he goes home?"

Hope smiled. "I'll see what I can do."

"So what's on the agenda for this afternoon?" Walczyk asked.

"It's pretty chill," she said. "At one-thirty, Emily's doing a workshop on scrapbooking your emotions in the small community room, and I think they're watching a *Battlestar Galactica* marathon in the big room. Gym at three. Other than that, there's not much going on until dinner time."

Walczyk thanked Hope and went to his room, retrieving his notebook and a couple of pens, and walked down to the small community room, after poking his head in to confirm his suspicions that it was the original, Lorne Green *Battlestar Galactica* that was running in the big room. Walczyk sat down at the table with his notebook and pen and began to reread the last page or so of the treatment, trying to remember where he was in Barbra's journey. The morning felt like a dream. Like an out-of-body experience. That wasn't him who threw that fit in Dr. Lentz's office. It was a dream. It *had* to have been a dream. He wouldn't have behaved like that, not in public. Not in a doctor's office. So much of it was surreal. The screaming. The raw, ugly rage he felt towards Dr. Lentz. Crying in his bed like a child. April having to come in and calm him down. Six months ago he was supervising the production of a $2.5 million-per-episode television series for arguably the leading cable network producing original drama today, also serving as director, executive producer, and the head of the writing department. And what was he doing now? Crying in his bed, being cradled by his assistant. Playing Legos with the mentally ill. Dreaming about getting back to a life of playing video games and watching TV by his own schedule, not somebody else's.

Something had to change.

"I can see you're deep in thought. I'll come back," Kaley's voice called out from behind him. He turned around. She stood in the doorway, rail thin, dressed entirely in black with her fingerless black gloves stretching up to her elbows.

"No, stay," Walczyk said, throwing his pen down. "It's more like *lost* in thought anyway."

Kaley pulled out a chair and plunked down next to him at the table. "Still *Night of the Living Dead*?" she asked, poking a finger at the notebook.

"It's just *Night*."

"Ah. Rough morning?"

"Heard about that, did you?"

"Need to talk about it?"

"I probably should," he said.

"But you don't want to." She reached out and grabbed the notebook, flipping to the back page. "That's cool." She began to sketch on the blank paper.

"I lost my shit with Lentz," he finally said.

"I heard."

"And so, once again, I have become the scandalous story on the lips of the public."

"No, I mean *I heard*. I was in the office next door with my doctor, Dr. Cullins. They really need to soundproof the walls in this place."

"So what's everyone saying?"

"They're wondering if David gets out of solitary today." She looked up over the notebook at him. "Sorry, friend. Being taken down with a hypo in the ass by a nurse in front of almost the entire ward will *always* trump getting mad at a doctor as far as the gossip circle's concerned."

Walczyk smirked. "I guess I thought I did something bigger than I did."

"Walczyk, you're not the first person to lose their shit with a doctor because they found out they weren't getting out when they thought they were." She cocked her head to the side, continuing to sketch. "Just about every patient who sets foot on this ward goes through that after their third or fourth day."

"But I feel fine," Walczyk said. "Well, I did before this

morning."

"I got a newsflash for you, Slick. After you get out of here, you're still going to be a broken man. It's gonna be a little worse, actually."

"How can it get any worse? Right now, I feel like the only normal person amidst a sea of crazies."

"Well, once you get out there, you'll feel like the only crazy amidst a sea of normal people." She craned her neck again, furiously sketching away at the notebook.

"What the hell are you doing, drawing me?"

"Don't look!" she snapped, hiding the notebook from him. "Just sit still and keep talking to me."

"Okay, but now that I'm ordered to talk to you, I don't know what to say."

"Isn't that always the case?"

"I feel like such an idiot," Walczyk confessed after a moment, sitting perfectly still.

"Well, you should."

"Why's that?"

"I don't know. I just think we should all feel like idiots. Keeps the ego at bay."

"I know a couple of studio heads who could stand with a little of that."

"So are you done?" she asked, still sketching.

"With what?"

"The show? Not that I follow the gossip factory or anything, but from what I've heard on TV—"

"My agent announced that I was stepping back for a while." He looked into her blue eyes, and realized someone needed to hear the truth. And that Kaley was the one person who wouldn't judge him for what he was about to announce. "But yes, I am leaving the show."

Walczyk didn't know if he expected her to shriek "No!," or say "It's about time," or just spout some sage-like advice. But she did none of that. She simply put the notebook on the table, face-down, and slid it over to him. Walczyk picked it up and examined the page she'd been working on. Staring up at him from the notebook was a haunting sketch of himself, half bathed in light, looking a lot like the cover on his *Dr. Jekyll and Mr. Hyde* book. One side of him, the dark side, wasn't twisted and grotesque like Mr. Hyde was on the cover of the book. It was, instead, wearing a look of weariness and defeat. The world had gotten the best of him. On the other side of the picture, the light side of his face displayed a look of barely restrained excitability: wide eyes, a broad smile, and a creased forehead. There was almost a manic quality about the face. Walczyk looked at the sketch for the longest time.

"This is incredible," Walczyk said, still unable to take his eyes off of the abstract portrait.

"Meh," she said, waving the compliment off with her hand, "if I could have my stuff, I might have done better."

"You're an artist?"

"Yeah. Oils mostly, though I do wield a mean pastel, if I may say so."

"Why won't they let you have your art supplies?"

"Oh, *they* have no problem with it. Hell, *they* encourage it. It's my mother." She spat the word.

"Why wouldn't she want you to be able to work on your art in here?"

"Because she's pissed at me. Said it was irresponsible for letting my little brother find me like he did. She thinks I should be punished for messing him up."

"That hardly sounds fair."

"She's raising two kids on her own and holding down three jobs at the same time. 'Fair' can't afford to be a word in Darlene Richardson's vocabulary."

Before Walczyk could speak, Emily came sweeping into the common room, her arms loaded with supplies. Walczyk offered to help, taking a stack of magazines from the top of the stack and setting them down on the long table at the back of the room.

"How are you doing?" Emily asked.

"Better," Walczyk said, standing back as Emily set down the remaining supplies: a stack of those black-and-white covered school composition notebooks, a stack of tan art paper, and two shoeboxes, one filled with children's' safety scissors, the other with glue sticks.

"Sticking around for my workshop?" Emily asked.

"Scrapbooking my emotions?" Walczyk asked. Emily nodded.

"What do you say?" Kaley asked Walczyk.

"No thanks," Walczyk said, picking up his notebook and closing it.

"Come on," Emily said. "It'll be fun. I'm sure you can find plenty of stuff to use for your scrapbook."

"I'm sure I can" Walczyk reached out and held up a *People* magazine. On the cover was a photo of himself, in a suit, and Sara, in that revealing little red dress that drove him absolutely wild. The photo was torn in half. Embarrassed, Emily took the magazine from Walczyk, who turned and left the common room with Kaley.

"So what're you going to do now?" Kaley asked. "Surely you're not going to go watch *Battlestar Galactica*."

"No, I've got a phone call to make. Catch you in a bit?"

"Sure. Later." Kaley took off down the hall, towards the small quiet room at the end of the corridor.

Walczyk turned toward the main desk, and sat down at one of the phones. He pulled a slip of paper out of his pocket – the 800-number April had given him to make his long-distance phone calls through. He dialed the number, listened to the instructions, and entered the PIN number written on the slip of paper. He then dialed, from memory, the phone number. After two rings, "You self-absorbed tosser!" greeted him, followed by a constant stream of profanity, some of which Walczyk didn't even understand. Once the cursing had stopped, Ian Maeder barked, "Four months! Four bloody months, two mental breakdowns, and I hear nothing from you!"

"I know," Walczyk began. "I know."

"My God, Walczyk. Are you okay?" In the dozen or so years that Walczyk had known Ian Maeder, he'd never heard that particular quality in Ian's voice: concern.

"Ian, I'm–"

"I know, you're okay. In hospital, but okay."

"No, that's just it, Ian. I'm *not* okay. You're right. I am in a hospital. A psychiatric hospital, and I don't know when I'm getting out. I'm far from okay."

"What a relief," Ian said.

"What? You're relieved to hear that I'm in a mental hospital, or that I don't know when they'll let me out?"

"No. I'm relieved at the sound of your voice, Mate."

Ian and Walczyk discussed Walczyk's reluctance to invite his friends and family to share in his misery, his absolute ineptitude at keeping in touch, and his new psychiatric diagnosis. Ian shared tales of bedding starlets and signing a deal with Twentieth Century Fox to star in an adaptation of 1980s TV series *The Fall Guy*. After about twenty minutes, the inevitable came up: "So, I've got to know, are you coming back to *Ordinary World* or am I stuck with it?"

"No, I'm not," Walczyk said. "I just... I can't do it right now. I can't handle all of that. I'm sorry, Ian, I know I owe you better, but–"

"Walz, it's all right. The show will go on without you. Although, I'd consider it a personal favor to me if you stayed on as a writer. At least sketch the season, maybe do the finale. I think it would be a good way to give yourself some time to process this whole bipolar thing, yet keep your hand in the cookie jar."

Walczyk caught a flicker out of the corner of his eye. He turned to see several patients waiting at the reception desk. He turned back.

"Ian, I hate to do this, but I've got to go. There are people waiting to use the phone."

"Before you go," Ian said, "I just want to tell you that I love you. You're my best friend and I want so much for you to be well. And I know it's difficult, but I want you to know there are so many people who love you and care about you. You're one of the most genuine people I have ever met, and I've never had a friend like you. Know that I'm always here for you. Whatever you need, I'm here."

Walczyk wiped a tear from his eye. "I love you too, Mate."

He hung up the phone, apologized to those waiting to use the phone, and returned to his room. He laid down on his bed, picked up his book, and finished it. He held it in his hand, looking at the cover, and thinking about why his father had given him this particular book. And once again, he concluded, that his father was indeed a very wise man.

CHAPTER TWENTY
ONE WEEK

<u>**TUESDAY**</u>

Walczyk's parents had returned to the hospital Monday evening, as they had promised, with Hannah and April along for the ride. Before they ended their all-too-short visit, Walczyk confirmed that he would be leaving *Ordinary World* as a show runner, but would stay on to supervise the writing of what would be the series' final season. He would discuss his decision with Ian on Tuesday, then announce his intentions to HBO and the production staff once he was out of the hospital and back on Cole Island.

Having had a long nap Monday afternoon after finishing the book, Walczyk was more than rested when he awoke around five o'clock on Tuesday morning. He was not at all surprised to see it was still raining.

As he showered, Walczyk promised himself that today was going to be a better day. During an early evening meeting with Dr. Lentz, Walczyk had apologized for his meltdown, The doctor assured him, as Kaley had, that it wasn't out of the norm for patients to have both high expectations of discharge and to grow upset when those expectations came crashing down around them. Lentz promised that he would forget about the matter, and he encouraged Walczyk to concentrate, not on getting out, but on getting better.

His liquid soap shower finished, Walczyk pulled on his jeans and a clean T-shirt, slipped into his slippers, and quietly crept out of the room, so as not to wake Richard. With his notebook and pen in hand, Walczyk quietly walked down to the smaller of the two quiet rooms, where Dean was already awake, watching the morning news.

"Morning, Peter," Dean said not looking away from the TV.

"Morning, Dean," Walczyk said, sitting down at the long table in the back of the room.

"TV ain't gonna bother you, is it?"

"Not at all. Thanks for asking."

Walczyk flipped through the notebook until he found the page he'd left off on with his treatment. He worked for about an hour, going back and scratching out a good chunk of material he'd already composed. By the time the call came through for breakfast, Walczyk was confident that he had a satisfying conclusion to the second act of his film, having just shown that the children locked in the basement of the farm house were full-fledged zombies.

After breakfast, which he ate at the big table with the majority of the patients, Walczyk settled back into the common room, his pen on fire as he began to sketch out the final third of the film, pitting Barbra and her new-found savior, Ben, against bleak circumstances. At the nine o'clock meeting, Walczyk's mind was more focused on finishing the treatment than it was on the matter at hand: five steps to change any habit.

"We've got one quick announcement to make," Emily said, as cheerily as ever as she wrapped up the discussion. "Richard is going home tomorrow morning."

Walczyk spun around in his chair, looking behind him at Richard, who was shaking Ken's hand. He couldn't believe it. He didn't know why he couldn't believe it, couldn't put his finger on it. It was just an impossible notion to grasp: Richard was going home tomorrow.

"Because, quite frankly, there's not much more we can do for him here," Dr. Lentz explained, easing into his chair for his Tuesday morning meeting with Walczyk. "I can't get into it any further. But, bear in mind, it's natural to feel jealous about this. You want very much to–"

"That's just it, Doctor, I'm not jealous. I'm happy for him. It's just that I don't... the man can't take care of himself. His mind–"

"I'm sorry. I can't discuss it. Doctor/patient confidentiality."

"Oh," Walczyk said. "Well, I *am* happy for him."

"Are you really?"

"No. But I think that's just because I've gotten accustomed to seeing his big cheery face bouncing around." The rest of their session was rather unproductive, with Dr. Lentz constantly urging Walczyk to drop the subject of Richard and focus on his own feelings.

The rest of the day dragged on for Walczyk, so much so that he didn't even care that *The Empire Strikes Back* was going to show in the big TV room that evening. He spent the afternoon on the phone with Ian, outlining his intentions for his involvement in the final season of *Ordinary World*. After speaking with Ian, Walczyk called Eli.

"Walz, how's the hospital treating you?" Eli asked.

"Well enough," he answered. "How are things in L.A.?"

"Couldn't be better," Eli said. "Brandt Talbot just got arrested."

"What for this time?" Walczyk remembered Brandt only from April's description of him and his television work.

"Excessive speed. Tried to outrun three photographers on the Santa Monica freeway by driving like a maniac."

"When will they ever learn? If you're going to run away from the paparazzi, run slow, not fast."

"Well, not everyone bee-lines it for Maine when they decide to ditch the press."

"Worked, didn't it?"

"That it did," Eli conceded. "What's this I hear that you're shutting down *Ordinary World*?"

"How the hell?" It never ceased to amaze Walczyk just how quickly news spread in Hollywood. "I just told Ian that not twenty minutes ago."

"And in twenty minutes, he told someone, who texted someone, who leaked it to Paparazz-Eye. Now it's all over their main page, complete with a picture of you and some goth chick in a Motörhead T-shirt."

Kaley.

After demanding that Eli get a handle on the paparazzi situation outside of the hospital, the conversation turned to personal matters, with Eli making sure that Walczyk was okay, asking when he would be released, and what not. While Eli was commending Walczyk on his work on *Night,* Kaley appeared from around the corner.

"What's up?" Walczyk asked, his hand over the mouth piece.

"We're going down to the gym. Interested?"

"Sure," Walczyk said, a twinge of guilt at his friend's impending introduction to the world press. He returned his attention to the phone. "Listen, Eli, I've got to be going. We're going down to the gym."

"You're giving me the heave-ho over the gym?"

"Outside of meals, it's the only time of the day I get off the ward. I've got to take it when I can get it."

"Well, take care of yourself, then."

"You too," Walczyk said, hanging up the phone.

Walczyk continually tried bringing up the subject of the TMZ photograph with Kaley as they sat on the sidelines, watching a game of pick-up basketball, but couldn't find an appropriate way to tell a suicidal cutter that pictures of her were being posted on the internet.

Dr. Lentz, it seemed, had no problem at all discussing the matter with either of them. After gym, Kaley and Walczyk were summoned to his office, where news of the photo's existence had made it to the doctor's attention, courtesy of his partner, Jeffrey, who happened to be a lawyer. Walczyk got his first look at the photograph, shot through a telephoto lens from some distance away. Kaley, it turns out, was unconcerned with the presence of the photographers outside the hospital, and only mildly irritated that she was being referred to as the "Mystery Goth" on the TMZ and Paparazz-Eye webpages.

Dr. Lentz, on the other hand, was livid, and demanded increased security patrols around the hospital. The local police found themselves unable to help, even after April had gotten in touch with a state senator she'd heard Garry Olsen discuss often at the Bronze Lantern.

"Thankfully," April said that evening, as she, Walczyk's parents, Walczyk and Kaley met in Walczyk and Richard's room, "the photo doesn't say too much. Just that you're in an institution. No one seems to care who Kaley is, no offense."

"None taken," she softly replied. While Kaley had been assertive and vocal during their meeting with Dr. Lentz, she'd become curiously quiet once April had shown up with Walczyk's parents.

Walczyk's father stood. "April, isn't there anything we can do to stop this nonsense?"

"The hospital identified the location of the photos as the reading room at the end of the corridor," April said. "Curtains will be drawn in that room for the remainder of Walczyk's stay. I'd suggest you both keep the curtains in your rooms drawn as well."

"Just what I didn't want," Walczyk groaned.

"What's that?" his mother asked.

"For *this* to happen. For my being here to impact the others."

"Don't get upset," his father cautioned him, placing a hand on his son's arm. "We'll take care of this."

"The Bangor PD won't do anything?" his mother asked.

"Dr. Lentz's partner, Jeffrey Turner, is an attorney. He's going over the books with a fine-tooth comb, but it looks as though Bangor PD's hands might be tied."

Walczyk found himself, now more than ever, hoping he would soon be released from this mad house.

WEDNESDAY

"So how are you feeling today?" Dr. Lentz asked early Wednesday morning.

"Aggravated," Walczyk replied.

"Understandably so," Dr. Lentz remarked. "If it will make you feel any better, Jeffrey found a loophole and three paparazzi were taken away last night. Two for trespass and one... well, it seems he fell out of a tree."

Walczyk laughed. "Dr. Lentz, I am sorry for all of this craziness."

"Don't fret about it. Besides, I feel we shan't be besieged by them for long."

"Oh? Did the hospital get a restraining order?"

"Not quite."

"Are the police going to intervene?"

"No."

"Are you sending Theresa out there with poisoned coffee?"

"No, we're releasing you."

"What?"

"We're–"

"Is it because of what's happening?"

"Peter, you're being released because I feel you are well enough to go back to life outside of the hospital. I don't care if the entire Associated Press lands outside of this institution – if I did not feel you were fit to be released, you would not be released."

"Believe me, I'm not trying to argue. I just figured, after what happened Monday–"

"Well, you figured wrong. I'm confident that you can return to normal life, or as normal as life gets for you celebrity types, that is. Don't mistake me – you will still struggle. You have plenty of healing to do: plenty of coping and plenty of soul searching. But those are things you can accomplish on your own, outside of Dirigo, and through monthly follow-up appointments" Dr. Lentz said. "Now, we need to prepare you for your upcoming discharge. Your body seems to be metabolizing lithium nicely. There are no new side effects?"

"Just that I'm thirsty all the time."

"To be expected, I'm afraid. Now, I want to run some further blood work this afternoon. Then, if everything seems to be in order, I think you should expect to be out of here Friday afternoon."

Walczyk felt his entire body lighten. He couldn't believe it. He literally could not believe what he had just heard. Not forty-eight hours ago, he'd been told he was going nowhere. Now, he was told he was going home. It made no sense to him.

"Friday?" he repeated, not trusting what he'd heard.

"Friday," Dr. Lentz said, smiling. "But, mind you, that's contingent on a number of things."

"Like the blood work," Walczyk said, his chest thumping.

"Like the blood work," Dr. Lentz repeated. "And the manifestation of any side effects, which you do need to report immediately. But, yes, I see no reason you can't be discharged on Friday. You're managing your mood swings relatively well. As well as can be expected, given your unique set of circumstances. Your lithium..."

Walczyk listened to little else of what Dr. Lentz had to say. He tried. He earnestly tried, but it was just impossible. He was going home. Friday. He was going home Friday.

"You look noticeably happier," Kaley said, sitting down next to Walczyk at lunch. He'd opted for one of the quieter side tables today, as he had brought his notebook with him. "All the paparazzi in the world spontaneously combust or something?"

"Not quite," Walczyk began, putting his pen down. "Though I guess one did fall out of a tree last night."

"Good for him," Kaley said with a nod. "So when did Lentz tell you that you were getting discharged?"

Walczyk looked at Kaley, stunned. Was he really being that transparent about the whole thing? "How'd you know?"

"I've seen that face before. On other people and in the mirror. Remember, this is my third trip to the rodeo. So? When's he springing you?"

"Friday," Walczyk said, beaming.

"Then can I prepare you for two things that will inevitably happen to you?"

"Sure."

"One: the time is going to drag. Thursday is never going to end for you."

"Great. What's number two?"

"*Never* forget that you own this disease."

Walczyk furrowed his brow. "What do you mean, 'own this disease?'"

"I mean don't forget that you control it. You can't let it control you, your life, or your relationships, because the second you do, you're screwed. It'll run your life. Remember: you're not a bipolar person, Peter Walczyk. You're a person *with* bipolar. Don't ever forget that."

Walczyk thought about that for a moment. Owning a disease. He'd never thought of it like that, but she was absolutely right. If he let bipolar disorder dictate how he led his life, how he enjoyed things, how he maintained his relationships with his family and friends, he would be its victim. It would hold him down with its cloven hoof. And he imagined it would only bring him misery.

"Well," he said, changing the subject, "it's going to be lonely in my room, what with Richard leaving and all."

Kaley patted his arm. "Oh, they'll get you a new roommate. There's such a shortage of rooms in these places right now. I almost wound up back at TAMC."

"TAMC?"

"The Aroostook Medical Center in Fort Fairfield. It's a nice hospital, but it's a quite a drive to get there."

"I'll say," Walczyk said, imagining a map of Maine, with Bangor at its center and Fort Fairfield, nestled near the top of the state. And forever and a day from Cole Island.

After lunch, Walczyk and Kaley returned to Walczyk's room to find Richard and two individuals who were clearly his parents, packing his things into a little blue duffle bag.

"You two have got to be Peter and Kaley," Richard's mother jovially called out. When they confirmed that they were, the woman, a short, beefy person with a face that never stopped smiling, wrapped them both in a big hug, squeezing them. "Thank you so much for being so good to my little boy," she said as she hugged them. Finally, she let them go, and wiped at her eyes with a wadded up ball of Kleenex.

"So, Richard, where are you going?" Kaley asked.

"Oh, there's this nice place in Presque Isle that's not too far from where Momma and Daddy live and I'm going to live there with some other people who are a little slow like me."

"It's a group home," Richard's father said in a rough, scratchy voice. "It's a sort of supervised living place. It'll be good for Richie. He'll have to take care of himself there."

"And that's what I want," Richard said, pulling a pile of dirty laundry out from under the bed and shoving it into his duffle bag.

"God, I hope they teach him how to sort his clothes," his father said, chuckling. Walczyk sat on his bed and flipped through *'Salem's Lot*, while Kaley nosed through his notebook, no doubt reading his progress on *Night*.

"Well, that just about does it," Richard announced after about fifteen minutes.

"Okay," his father said, taking Richard's bag and handing him a wool hunting jacket similar in design to the one he himself was wearing. "We'll be down in the lobby when you're done with Peter and Kaley."

"Thank you again," Richard's mother said, then disappeared down the hall with his father. Walczyk followed Kaley's lead and stood.

"You guys are the best," Richard said, smiling. "I'm going to miss you."

"I'm going to miss you, too," Walczyk said.

Richard turned to Kaley. There were tears in both their eyes.

She reached up and held onto the gentle giant, her arms barely reaching around him. "You listen to what the people in charge of your group home tell you, okay?"

"I will, Kaley."

"And don't let them tell you you're not smart enough."

"They won't."

"And I hope I don't ever see you again."

"I hope I don't never see you again, too," Richard said, giving her one more hug before waving goodbye and disappearing out the door and down the hall.

Kaley dropped into her chair, fighting valiantly not to cry. Walczyk reached out, taking her hand, and gave it a squeeze. "Dear Lord," Kaley said softly. "Please look out for Richard and bless him as he makes his way in Your world. His path is truly a unique one, and it is one that I know You will be with him on. Teach him reliance on others when he needs it, and independence when he requires it."

After a silence, Walczyk spoke. "Lord, you place people in our lives for different reasons. Mysterious reasons. Richard Francis Daigle was placed in my life for one purpose: to teach me to love those different than I am. Please guide him and let him serve as a light and a teacher to another fortunate soul. In Jesus's name we pray, Amen."

Walczyk and Kaley sat in silence, Walczyk on his bed, Kaley at the desk, for a long time, not doing anything but studying the floor. Eventually, Susan arrived at the door. "Kaley, Dr. Cullins is ready to see you."

Kaley got up, wiped her eyes, and left the room without a word. Walczyk had tried starting 'Salem's Lot, but could not concentrate. It was such a bitter-sweet day: Richard was gone, and Walczyk himself was going to be leaving soon. Walczyk finally stood up, and walked down to the main desk, where he spoke with Emily. She'd been apprised of Walczyk's proposed pizza party and informed Walczyk that it had been run by Dr. Lentz, Dr. Berenbaum and Dr. Cullins, and they had no problem with it. They'd just held back announcing it to the patients so as not to get any hopes up.

Once Kaley was out of her meeting with Dr. Cullins, he flagged her down and put her to work.

"Take my notebook and go around and ask everyone – and I mean everyone – what kind of pizza they like."

"What kind of pizza they like?" she replied.

"Yeah. Keep it simple, but, at the same time, make sure they're getting what they want."

"Exactly why do you want to know all this?" Kaley asked. "Script research?"

"No. Just… just tell them that Three-North won't be eating at the cafeteria tonight."

While Kaley ran around collecting information, Walczyk called April and asked if she could do two huge favors. First, he asked her to pick up an order from Pat's in Orono and deliver them to the ward at five o'clock, just in time for supper. Second, he asked her to keep a secret. He couldn't handle it. He had to tell somebody.

"They're discharging me Friday," he said in a hushed tone, looking around to make sure no one was listening while he spoke.

"Oh, my God, Boss! That's terrific!"

Walczyk swore April to secrecy again, and she confirmed that his parents would be coming up as soon as school got out, and that Hannah would be with them. Vic sent his best, but an emergency at the Barrelhead kept him from making it up. Walczyk said he'd call Vic later on, after the party and the visiting, and let him know what was going on.

By the time he'd finished with April, Kaley was back with the pizza order. Walczyk sifted through the immaculately written list and figured out how many pizzas they'd need, still not telling Kaley exactly what he was up to. He called April again and gave her his order, told her which credit card to use, repeated that the pizzas had to be there at five o'clock.

"What are you doing all this for?" Kaley asked when Walczyk had finished with April and hung up.

"Because I want to bring a little fun to this place." He turned and looked at her, seeing if his answer passed muster.

"Sounds good to me."

At four o'clock, Mary informed the patients that there was going to be a pizza party, which everyone kind of guessed, given Kaley's pizza survey earlier. However, the cafeteria was still open to anyone who didn't wish to have pizza. Everyone except for poor, wheelchair-bound Patty elected to partake of the pizza. At Walczyk's request, his name was not mentioned in conjunction with the surprise. Walczyk wanted this to be about the patients getting to enjoy themselves, not about the patients getting to owe Walczyk a favor. At a quarter to five, April showed up with the first part of the order. The smell of pizza instantly permeated the ward. Four trips later, with two attempts by Dean to go help April bring up the pizzas and assorted sodas, ice, cups, plates, and napkins, the big common room was set up.

"So what's it like, being Walczyk's assistant?" Kaley asked April after everyone had picked up their first round of pizza. "Is he a real pain in the ass?"

"Actually, he's rather easy to work for, compared to horror stories I've heard about other, unnamed reality TV stars. Now, that having been said, the last couple of months *have* been something I never thought to experience as a personal assistant."

"How so?" Kaley asked.

"Well, frankly, who expects to go on a manic, cross-country escape from reality with their boss, living out of hotels."

"Must've been awkward. You know, living out of a motel room with him."

"Surprisingly, it wasn't," April said.

"And you two aren't–?"

April broke into her loud, annoying laugh. "Oh, God, no!"

"Sorry," Kaley quickly said, a wave of meekness drifting over her.

"Nothing to be sorry about," April asked. "I might have asked the same question about you two. You know, if you weren't in a hospital."

"Me and Walczyk?" Kaley asked, pointing to herself. She shook her head. "No, I'd never do that to him."

"Why would you say that?"

"It's just… I don't play well with others."

"I can't believe you started without us!" Hannah cried out from behind them. Walczyk and April turned around to see Walczyk's parents and Hannah standing in the doorway, smiling. Walczyk rushed to his parents, hugging them tightly.

"You're early," Walczyk said.

"No, it's seven o'clock," Henry said.

Walczyk looked around. The "party" was still going, people munching on pizza and socializing. But the clock on the wall said seven.

Walczyk turned to Kaley, who had looked up from her conversation with April. "Kaley, you met my folks earlier–"

"Hello, Kaley," Walczyk's mother said. "How are you doing today?"

"Fine, thanks, Mrs. Walczyk."

"Please. Diane."

Kaley nodded.

"And this young woman," Walczyk said, walking past his mother, "is Hannah. Han, this is my friend Kaley."

Hannah smiled and took Kaley's hand. "Hello, Kaley. Nice to meet another friend of Peter's."

"He doesn't make you call him 'Walczyk?'"

"He's tried," Hannah said, smiling, "but I won't indulge him."

Smiles and handshakes and greetings were exchanged. Walczyk urged everyone to go grab a piece of pizza.

"Don't you have something to tell your parents?" April asked. Walczyk shot her a dirty look.

"What, Peter?" his mother asked.

"Dad, you might want to take the day off from school Friday..."

Diane clasped her hands to her mouth, a smile showing from either side.

"You mean–?" Hannah began.

Walczyk smiled, giving a slight nod. Henry reached out and grabbed his son by the face, planting a kiss on his forehead. "I'm so proud of you," he said.

"Dad, it's nothing."

"Bullshit it's nothing," Henry said, plainly surprising Hannah and Walczyk's mother with his choice of language. "Peter, you've been through a lot. And you've learned to cope with a lot. Don't discount this."

"Where's Richard?" Hannah asked.

"His family picked him up today," Walczyk said. "I thought I told you about that."

"Wow," Hannah observed. "Everyone's getting out."

"Yeah," Kaley said, solemnly.

"You told us that Richard was being released," his mother said. "But nothing about it being today."

"Where's his family from again?" his father asked.

"Caribou," Kaley said. "But they're moving Richard into a group home in Presque Isle."

"That'll be good for him," Walczyk commented. "That way his family can visit him there, but he'll have some independence."

Gradually, the other patients left the common room, leaving only the Walczyks, April, Hannah and Kaley in the room.

"So, Kaley, where are you from?" Walczyk's mother asked, before adding, "If you don't mind me asking?"

"Millinocket."

His mother made the connection that Millinocket wasn't too far away. April and Hannah began packing up the party mess, and Walczyk sat back, enjoying the scene. His friends, new and old, and his parents. He truly was blessed.

"Excuse me," a voice said from the doorway. Walczyk turned to see David, looking heavily medicated, clutching the doorway. "I heard there was a pizza party."

"And there are still several slices left," Hannah said, walking toward the door. "Do you need some help getting to the table?"

David reached out and took Hannah's arm, while April brought the box they'd collected the remaining slices in over to the table.

Kaley rose to her feet. "David, are you okay?"

"They doped me up pretty good, Kaley," he said, tucking a napkin into his t-shirt neck. "Whose all these people?"

"This is my family," Walczyk said, and introduced everyone while David ate.

"I gotta apologize to you, man," David started to say. "I was so out of line the other day when I–"

Walczyk smiled at David. "You already apologized. Remember? We cool."

Walczyk held his fist out, which David slowly bumped with his own. "We cool."

"There you are, David," Mary said, scrambling into the room. "You shouldn't have wandered out of your room."

"Rita told me there was a pizza party," David said weakly.

"And it's not a pizza party unless everyone gets some," Hannah said.

David continued eating away at a cold slice of pepperoni. "Well, can someone come get me when he's ready to leave?" Mary asked. "He can't be walking around on his own right now."

"Will do, Mary," Kaley said.

Through conversation, they learned that David had been diagnosed with borderline personality disorder. He'd also tried to kill himself after he went off his medication. After eating a second slice of pizza, David said he needed to get some sleep, and April fetched one of the nurses, which happened to be Terry, the bald man Walczyk remembered seeing take David. Before he left, David apologized again for assaulting Walczyk, was reminded that they were cool, and told Hannah that she had "very pretty eyes."

"What was he apologizing to you for?" Mum asked after he'd been escorted from the room.

"It's nothing," Walczyk said, looking out the door. "We cool."

THURSDAY

Kaley had promised him that Thursday would be the start of an unending, hectic day, and she wasn't lying. After breakfast, Walczyk and April had a very info-heavy meeting with Dr. Lentz, who gave Walczyk a bulky folder with information on bipolar disorder and his medications, phone numbers for the hospital, and a list of recommended psychiatric doctors on and around Cole Island that he should consult with for further treatment.

"Why can't I just continue seeing you?" Walczyk said. "I like you. You're honest, no-nonsense, and you're the only doctor I ever met who wears sandals in October."

"Because," Dr. Lentz said, smiling at his footwear, "I only see people who are sick."

After his meeting with Dr. Lentz, Walczyk was whisked away by Emily, who gave him another large folder, containing information on dealing with depression, coping skills, and even a handful of weekend planners, with the word "weekend" scratched out and the word "daily" written in over. April was given explicit directions that Walczyk needed to do one every day. After he'd finished with Emily, Walczyk called home to tell his parents not to drive all the way back to Bangor that night, instead giving them a window of ten-thirty to two for his discharge on Friday.

April departed shortly after the meetings with the staff were over, and Walczyk returned to his room for some writing. Several beats into the third act of his treatment, there was a knock at the door. It was

Susan, accompanied by a very nervous looking couple in their late forties and a very skinny, very pale young man with large glasses, who was staggering along, held up by his father.

"How's it going, Peter?"

"Not bad, Susan. How are you?"

"Good. Peter, this is Zack. Zack, this is Peter. He'll be your roommate for a day or so."

"Okay," Walczyk said. "Hey, Zack. How's it going?"

Zack mumbled something incoherent and was eased down onto his bed.

"Take your time," Susan quietly told Zack's parents. Seeing Walczyk collecting his notebook, she shook her head and mouthed the word "stay" to him, and slipped out down the corridor.

Walczyk looked across the room, feeling like he was invading some sacred family rite. He watched the father, wearing a sport coat and wrinkled Dockers, standing helpless. He watched the mother, in brown pants and a matching floral turtleneck, holding Zack's hand, caressing it. What should he say? Apparently Susan thought he should say something, as she had asked him to stay put.

"So, Zack," Walczyk said, desperate to find some kind of common ground with the boy. He glanced at Zack's shirt, noticing the emblem of the New England Patriots on the front. "Pat's fan, eh?"

Zack looked up, weakly. Walczyk suspected that even if he wanted to speak, the meds were preventing it. At a loss as to what to say to this poor kid that would make him feel any better about what was going on, Walczyk sat at his desk and began to write.

"So, Peter," the father said from across the room, "what's this place like?"

Walczyk shrugged. "It's not a bad hospital. Personally, I think they could have a few more programs for us during the day. But it's very well-run. Not that I have any frame of reference, of course." The father cracked a very weak smile. "Where are you folks from?"

"Jay," the mother said, still sitting on the bed, her arm around her son.

"Wow, that's quite a trip," Walczyk commented.

The father nodded. "You?"

"Cole Island."

"That's quite a trip in itself." The father paced around the room. Walczyk sat back down and tried to write.

"How are they with visitors?" the mother asked. "The nurse who checked us in said that visiting hours were just from seven to eight every night."

"I've had people in and out of here all week," Walczyk said. "Parents. Friends. They're pretty good about letting people in as long as it's not distracting the others. Are you folks going to stay in town?"

"We'd like to. Is there anything nearby?"

Walczyk gave them the lowdown on the Birch Point Inn, and even promised to have April check into getting them a room. Walczyk learned that their names were Brian and Kathryn English, and that Zack had been experiencing extreme paranoia. Bill stopped by the room on his way and informed Walczyk it was lunch time. Walczyk wished them well and said he'd be around if they had any more questions.

After lunch, Kaley talked him into going to Sandy's creative self-expression class in the common room. In front of each chair was an eleven-by-fourteen piece of canvas. In the center of the table, a large pile of oil paints and canvases. Walczyk and Kaley sat down at the far end of the table.

"Is there a theme?" Walczyk asked, taking a couple of brushes from a shoebox of paint brushes.

Sandy tied on an apron. "Just express yourself."

Walczyk thought that was the general point of art, but didn't quibble. He grabbed a pencil and stared at his board. All around the table, people had already begun sketching out their ideas for paintings. He tried to come up with a design, but everything seemed too heavy handed. A pair of hands, bound by a long string of film, each frame bearing Sara's face. Himself blindfolded by film, each frame bearing either Sara's or Ella's face. He was considering sketching out the drawing Kaley had made for him the other day, then inspiration hit him. He began drawing, fast and furious, as others around the table began squirting oil paints out onto their plastic pallets.

"What is it?" Kaley whispered, leaning over.

"The beginnings of a painting," he replied, cryptic. "What about you?"

Kaley showed Walczyk the canvas. On it was a picture of a skinny woman in black, painting a picture of a skinny woman in black, painting a picture of a skinny woman in black. Infinite regression. Hannah would no doubt have had a *Star Trek* trivia tidbit or something about the concept. The intriguing thing about the Kaleys within the painting was that each one was different. The skinny t-shirt clad Kaley was painting a Kaley in a black dress. Black dress Kaley was painting a Kaley dressed like a school girl. From there, Kaley hadn't sketched any more Kaleys. "Well? What do you think?"

"Ambitious," was all Walczyk could come up with. He really liked the concept, and could see there was a great deal of artistic talent in this young woman.

Kaley took back her canvas and laid it down. "I get the feeling I'll have plenty of time to work on it," she said with a glimmer of woe in her voice, then leaned forward and began collecting paints.

At the end of the hour, Kaley had finished the first Kaley and the room she was in, and had started the second Kaley, the black dress one in the first painting. She plopped her brushes into a cut-off milk jug filled with purple water and many other paint brushes. "Well, what'd you accomplish, Mr. Famous Hollywood Produc-*or*?"

She craned her neck over and Walczyk held up his painting. In it, a faceless man stood in front of a living room soundstage. The man had no face, but in each hand he held two masks: one a sad face, the other smiling fiercely, clearly manic. Both masks resembled Walczyk.

"Interesting," Sandy said, looking over Walczyk's shoulder. "Very interesting." Walczyk picked up a paint brush and signed the painting, down in the corner, and slid it over to Kaley.

"There. Now we each have an artistic expression of my bipolarity."

"Thanks," Kaley said. "Mind signing a certificate of authenticity so I can sell it on e-Bay?"

After they'd cleaned up, Walczyk and Kaley walked the ward for a while, discussing "the real world."

"So, what's the first thing you're going to do when you get home?"

"Go into a room – any room – and shut the door. Maybe even lock it."

"You think April will let you get away with a locked door?" Kaley asked.

"April's going to be letting me get away with quite a bit for quite a while," Walczyk laughed. "But seriously, the first thing I want to do when I get home... I just want life to get going again."

"I hear you there," she said. "It's all *Walczyk Interrupted* right now. Don't expect it to come back right away. It'll take time. A week or two. You'll be lucky, though."

"How so?"

"You live with someone. Last time they let me out, since I cut and am suicidal, I had to stay with someone who could keep an eye on me. So here I am, having just left my abusive douche bag boyfriend before checking in, looking for friends who are safe to be with and will let me crash on their couch for a night or two, because I was *not* going back to my Mom's place. So asking to sleep on people's couches, when I had an entire apartment of my own... it was a little humiliating. Well, I promised them a month of not staying alone. They got two weeks. I just couldn't take it. But you, you're all set, because you've got April living right there. Well, that and you're not suicidal or a cutter."

"Don't be so sure," Walczyk said, and he explained his desire to die to Kaley, and how he had kept it from Dr. Lentz. "I just figured, if I told him that, he'd never let me out."

"You're not now, are you?" Kaley asked, dead serious.

Walczyk shook his head. "No."

Kaley took Walczyk's face in her hands. "Promise me you're not."

"Kaley–"

"Promise me!"

Walczyk looked into her blue eyes. She was serious. Concern and panic were in her eyes as she stared wide-eyed at him.

"I promise you, I want to do nothing but live."

Kaley's eyes scanned his for a moment, no doubt looking for signs of deceit. Apparently satisfied, Kaley let go of Walczyk's hands and regained her composure.

"Think you'll ever be up Millinocket way?"

"Depends," Walczyk said.

"You've got grandparents in Patten, your mother said."

"My Grandmother Walczyk, yes. And I need to visit her sometime. I haven't seen Gram in years."

"You've been home for almost four months and you've not seen your grandmother? I'd beat you if they wouldn't throw me in isolation for it!"

Walczyk and Kaley spent the rest of the afternoon chatting with the other patients out in the hallway. Most of them congratulated Walczyk on his good news, which was announced in the morning meeting. Rita said Walczyk hadn't really been there an awful long time. Ken bemoaned the fact that they wouldn't be seeing "that cute little blonde with the mouth like a sailor" any more. Most of them wondered if, when Walczyk said he'd be "going home," he meant Los Angeles or Cole Island.

At four, Walczyk broke off from the group and retired to the quiet room. The curtains were still drawn. He settled into one of the tables and began to sketch out some more of *Night*'s final act. He respected the shock of the original *Night of the Living Dead*'s hero, Ben, being shot down by the angry mob at the end, mistaken for another zombie. He wanted to give his version a similar shock, but was at a loss as to how to do it. Unable to resolve his ending after forty-five long, quiet minutes, Walczyk packed his things up and returned to his room. He entered quietly, trying not to wake Zack. However, as he put his notebook in his desk drawer, he realized his new roommate was awake.

"What's going on?" Zack asked, feebly.

"Just putting my stuff back. I'll be gone in a second."

"No. Please, don't rush off." He still looked extremely medicated.

"Okay," Walczyk said, sitting down on his own bed. "Do you remember meeting me this morning?"

"No," Zack said, shaking his head.

"I'm not surprised. You were pretty stoned. How are you feeling?"

"Confused."

"That'll pass," Walczyk said. "Is there anything I can do to help you out?"

"You wouldn't help me get to the bathroom, would you? I've got to take a whiz."

Walczyk got up and walked over to the bed, pulling Zack to his feet. He wondered if he should've called a nurse to do this, but wagered that if he let Zack fall, Zack wouldn't remember it. Walczyk snapped the bathroom light on and led Zack to the toilet.

"If I were you, I'd sit down. We're not proud people here at Dirigo, so no one'll think anything weird of you."

Walczyk stepped just outside the door and let Zack do his business. Once he heard the toilet flush, he turned back around, helping the young man up from the toilet and holding him steady while he washed up, then returned him to his bed.

"Thanks," Zack said, flopping back down in his bed.

"If you don't mind me asking," Walczyk said, sitting down at the foot of Zack's bed, "how old are you?"

"Eighteen," he replied.

"College freshman?" Walczyk asked, hoping this was the case. It wasn't.

"High school senior."

Walczyk studied the poor young man. There was barely anything to him. Walczyk doubted it was some kind of eating disorder, mainly because everything about Zack was small, from his frame to his build to his height. No, this was just a tiny little guy, probably about five-eight, five-nine.

"Mind if I ask what's wrong?"

Slowly, Zack spoke: "I just can't shake this bad mood I'm in. I'm so sad. All the time. And... and I know it's not real... but I get this feeling that someone's out to get me."

Walczyk had a good idea where this was going. "That bad mood... what'd you do to take care of it?"

"I emptied the medicine cabinet."

"Damn."

Walczyk learned there was no girlfriend and not many friends awaiting young Mr. English outside the walls of the Dirigo Psychiatric Hospital. At five o'clock, Kaley stopped by to let Walczyk know that it was supper time. Walczyk introduced Zack to Kaley, who gave a quick "hello" before heading out to supper.

The baked ziti served up in the cafeteria was certainly no match for the fresh, piping hot Pat's pizzas they'd had the previous night. Seated at the large table, Walczyk listened as Dean told a couple of dirty jokes (before being silenced by Roger the Man Nurse) and answered questions about what he was going to do upon being discharged. Again, Dean had a couple of off-color suggestions, which amused everyone but Roger, who circled even more closely to the table thereafter. Walczyk even entertained a few questions about his career, but he refused to divulge any secrets about the upcoming season of *Ordinary World*.

"So, do you think you'll get back together with your wife?" Rita asked.

Walczyk shook his head. "No, that boat's sailed."

"Yeah, to the Lesbos Islands," Dean said, wheezing with

laughter. Roger promptly warned him that one more off-color remark and he'd be taking his meals alone.

After dinner, Walczyk sat in on part of the evening movie, *The Empire Strikes Back,* before retiring, once again, to the quiet room with his notebook, hoping and praying that an answer to this screen would treatment come to him. Eventually it did, and almost two hours later, Walczyk put down his pen and leaned back in his chair, his hands behind his head. He'd done it. In less than a week, he'd banged out a treatment to a movie he never wanted to make. And what was more, he was now very interested in working on this film. He wasn't a huge fan of the last shot, but at least it was an ending. An ending to have an ending. He took a deep breath and smiled. He felt almost human.

"Tell me you've finally finished that damned treatment," Kaley said behind him. He turned to smile at her.

"She's done," he said, closing the notebook and writing the word "*Night*" across the front of it.

"So, where do you go from here?"

Walczyk considered the question. "You mean in life or in regards to the movie?"

Kaley smiled. "Either/or."

"From here," Walczyk said, putting his pens neatly on the cover of the notebook, "I sit down with the treatment and give it one more revision, like you'd revise a short story. I put a little more flesh on the bones. Layer in a few more details. Then I do the first draft of the screenplay. That's where I put in the dialogue, introduce new characters or remove unnecessary ones. From there, it's a seemingly endless stream of rewrites and revisions… incorporating studio notes, incorporating producer notes."

"Then you make it?"

"Then Marathon's director of choice makes it. I've decided that I'm not directing this time out."

"So tell me the truth: is it any good?"

"Right now? Probably not. I basically retold the original movie from memory, twisting here and there to accommodate all of my own characters. But in my second pass, I'll change things up. Maybe make the man be the one in shock and make the girl this kick-ass commando type."

"Yeah, there's enough wimpy women in movies. Makes us look bad."

Not long after their discussion of strong women in film had begun, Mary stopped by. "It's almost nine," she said.

"Okay," Walczyk said, getting up from the table.

"Did you get your treatment done?" she asked.

"Yep."

"Congratulations. And congratulations on going home tomorrow."

"Thanks."

"Did Dr. Lentz tell you that you won't be getting a sleeping pill tonight?"

"I was made aware," Walczyk said. "Ought to be fun, doing it the old fashioned way."

"I'm sure you'll fade right off," she said. "Why don't you both come on down. I can give you your meds."

As they walked, Mary interrogated Walczyk about his newly-finished treatment.

"So what's your movie about?"

"Ever see *Night of the Living Dead*?"

"No."

"Okay. Basically the dead are rising, as zombies, and attacking the living. The movie focuses on a group of people holed up in…" An idea hit him. Walczyk quickly opened his notebook and scribbled in the margins of the last page, *It's the little girl who comes out of the house as a zombie.* "Sorry," Walczyk said, closing the notebook. "They hole up in an old farm house and fight to survive."

"Sounds scary," Mary said.

"It *is* a horror movie," Kaley commented.

Mary got buzzed behind the nurse's station by Theresa, who did not give a greeting to either Kaley or Walczyk. The two patients walked around the corner, where a metal gate covered the little window. The gate came up, and Mary removed a little paper portion cup with pills in it and handed them, with a cup of water, over to Kaley. Kaley stepped aside and took her meds while Walczyk was given his. Both of them had to open their mouths and lift their tongues, proving they'd not "cheeked" or "tongued" their meds. Mary shut the metal gate and met Kaley and Walczyk on the other side of the nurse's station.

"Well, if I don't see you again," she said, extending a hand across the station desk, "take care of yourself."

Walczyk and Kaley started back down the hall. In front of Walczyk's door, Kaley stopped and put her hand on Walczyk's arm. "I'm going to ask you to do something tomorrow, and I need you to promise you'll do it."

"Sure," he said. "What is it?"

"Don't say goodbye."

"What?"

She shook her head slowly as she spoke. "I just... I can't. I don't do goodbyes well at all. Please. Just leave tomorrow."

They looked at each other for a long time. Walczyk wasn't ready to say goodbye to her. He guessed he'd have never really been ready to say goodbye to his new friend. His friend who had taught him so much. Introduced him to so much. Understood him so well, because she had been there herself.

"Well, I'd better get going," she said. Kaley put her arms around Walczyk and held onto him for a moment, then stood up on her tiptoes and kissed his cheek. "We good?"

Walczyk felt his eyes getting wet. "We good."

Kaley let go of him and proceeded down the hall to her room. Walczyk watched until she disappeared into her room, then turned and entered his own room. He'd meant to pack during the day, but never did. He realized that he couldn't have packed anyway, since he had no suitcase to put anything into. He imagined April would take no time at all sucking his personal belongings from the institutional wardrobe tomorrow morning when she showed up. Dr. Lentz hadn't given him a time frame as to when he could check out, so Walczyk erred on the side of being early.

In his room, Zack was asleep. Walczyk puttered around, taking his clothes from the closet and stacking them neatly on his desk and leaving his dirty clothes in a pile at the bottom of the wardrobe. He emptied the desk out, leaving the portable radio on his pillow. He stacked the desk's contents, two paperback novels, his notebook, five black pens, and the Bible Bruce had given him.

Walczyk stripped out of his clothes and slid into the stiff sheets for the last time. Ever since he was a kid, he had taken note of doing things "for the last time." "This is the last time I'll eat lunch at Cole Island Elementary School." "This is the last time I'll have class at Cole Island Junior High." "This is the last time I'll make out with Hannah at Cole Island High." He didn't know where it came from, but he always did it. He marked unpleasant occasions that way, too. "This could be the last time I'll see Grampie Walczyk." "This is the last time I'll work with this great cast." Even before he had fled from California, as she cried, begging for forgiveness, he had thought to himself, "This is the last time I'll see my wife." But the last time he'd slip into this bed was certainly a happy occasion. He shifted until he was comfortable, lay still, and prayed.

Dear Lord, thank You for being there for me. Thank You for my friends and my family and the love they give me. Thank You for my friend Kaley. Please be with her and give her peace of mind and spirit as she struggles with the confusion that comes with her illness. Lord, I ask You to watch over the patients in this hospital. I know I can't ask You to take their illnesses away completely, so, please, just help them be able to live with them; to own them. Finally, Lord, please see me quietly, peacefully, and swiftly through this night. In Jesus' name I pray, Amen."

Two hours passed and Walczyk hadn't so much as begun to feel drowsy. His mind rolled the past week over and over. It felt like such an absurd dream. The fact that he was in a mental hospital. It didn't feel real. Like he was having some sort of wacky dream, except that all of the details were so real to him. Everything was so vivid.

He shook his head, trying to clear these thoughts from his mind, like some kind of mental Etch A Sketch. One thing was absolutely sure to him, however: he was going to need some chemical aid if he was expected to get to sleep.

He slipped into his wind pants, which were at the bottom of a stack of clothes on his desk, and padded down the hall to the nurse's station, where he had the pleasure of having his final encounter with Spray Tan Theresa.

"I can't sleep."

"And you are?"

As if she doesn't know by now, he thought to himself. "Peter Walczyk."

"Peter Walczyk," she repeatedly murmured, scanning through the list on her clipboard. Finding it, she said, "Yeah, I don't have you down for anything. Sorry."

Walczyk felt the urge to argue his case. It was torture, lying in that room, listening to the hours tick away in his mind. But he'd learned that arguing with Theresa was like fighting for peace: an exercise in futility. Walczyk walked into the common room and snapped on the TV, settling in. However, he only got three channels into his survey of Bangor's late-night cable TV offerings when a figure stepped in front of the TV, shutting it off.

"No TV after bedtime." It was Roger. Charming, empathetic, understanding Roger. He held his hand out for the remote.

"Well, I can't sleep," Walczyk said. "And I can't have a pill and I can't watch TV. Any suggestions?"

"Try harder," was Roger's helpful tip.

Walczyk muttered some nastiness under his breath as he was escorted from the room. He continued back towards his room, and got the distinct impression he was being followed. He turned around upon reaching the door, to see Roger standing there, watching him.

"Look, are we going to be destroying any sense of order if I take a book and go down to the quiet room? If I read in my room, the light will wake up my roommate."

Roger looked completely put out. His head cocked back (Walczyk still couldn't figure out why he carried himself like that), Roger frowned. "You're supposed to be in bed. Asleep."

"And, believe me, I would *love* to be passing the time in an unconscious state of being, but that's proving to be impossible. I've tried for two hours now to get to sleep, to no avail."

Roger's mind spun around these facts, Walczyk could tell by the frown on his face changing shape and size. Finally, he threw his hands up. "Whatever. I don't care. But if I have to come down there just once to tell you to keep it down, it's back to your room and lights out." Roger turned and stormed away while Walczyk tried to figure out how much noise he would be able to make alone in a room with only a notebook.

But, not one to tempt providence, Walczyk grabbed the entire stack of books on his desk, a couple of pens, and quietly slid down the hallway toward the quiet room.

He sat on the couch in the corner, his copy of *Jekyll and Hyde* in hand. He knew the story had been adapted for film and television dozens of time, with famous actors in the dual title role and with bizarre twists to the entire transformation process. But one thing he was never quite sure of was whether or not the transformation had ever been a psychological one instead of a chemical one. He considered a

Henry Jekyll afflicted with bipolar disorder. And he does something dreadful while in a manic phase. So he takes a chemical, possibly prescribed, to extricate the manic side of his personality, thus leaving him calm and rational. But the drug turns him into a purely manic entity, who gives himself an identity, Edward Hyde, and wreaks havoc on New York, raping and pillaging and even murdering. Jekyll consults with a friend, Lanyon, about what he has done, and the two scientists try to create some sort of cure.

The door opened to the quiet room and Roger looked in, skeptical of Walczyk's intentions.

"Last warning: keep this door open!" he barked, then turned and left, leaving the door open behind him. Walczyk wondered, thinking of both Roger and Theresa, why a person would take up a position in a psychiatric hospital if that person disliked dealing with people, especially people with delicate needs.

Walczyk returned his thoughts to the *Jekyll and Hyde* idea, taking notes as he went along. In the end, he decided that Jekyll has to realize he needs that other side in him. To complete him. So simply extricating it can't be enough. He needs to dominate it.

Walczyk tore the paper from his notebook and tossed it into a trash can, half expecting Roger to come racing in and complain that he was being too loud. It was crap. All of it. Walczyk then stared at the blank page, lost in thought. Soon enough, he numbered the page one through ten. Under one, he began writing, small. By the time he'd finished, he'd plotted out ten episodes for the fourth season of *Ordinary World* in pencil, resolving the pregnancy/paternity plot line once and for all and actually putting Ethan and Danielle together in some sort of romantic relationship.

"Can't sleep?" a friendly voice asked from behind him. He turned to see Mary poking her head into the room.

"Not a wink," Walczyk said. "But I *was* warned this would happen."

"Yeah, it's pretty common," she said, walking into the room. "Whatcha working on?"

He gave her a smile. "Nothing you want to know about."

"Come on... try me."

"It's the outline for the final season of *Ordinary World*."

"The *final* season?"

"Yeah, but it hasn't been announced yet, so please try to keep that under your hat."

"Why would you cancel the show? You're on top right now!"

"And that's the perfect place to go out. Besides, *Ordinary World* has always been the story of a young Peter Walczyk and his journey to discover who he is in this world. Well, Peter – Ethan – has found that answer. It should end there before everyone involved loses sight of what we set out to do."

"But it's such a good show," she pled.

Walczyk opted not to debate that point with the only member of the night staff who could stand being around patients. "And there will be others. What they'll be like, I don't know."

"Well, good luck," she said, putting a hand on his shoulder. "And again, it was a pleasure to meet you."

"Likewise," Walczyk said, getting up. After Mary had left, he tossed the notebook onto the table. There was no heaviness in his eyes. There was no weariness. Just a feeling that there was something to be accomplished, he just had to find it.

Walczyk looked through the books he'd brought with him. He'd already read *Jekyll and Hyde*, and he knew that if he started *'Salem's Lot*, the other book delivered to him by his family, he'd never get it finished. He never read at home, for some odd reason. There was the stack of paperwork Dr. Lentz had given him, but three o'clock in the morning was too early (or too late) to be sifting through medical jargon. He'd give them to April to read and keep track of. At the bottom of the stack was the Bible given to him by Bruce. He picked the book up, such a daunting volume of history and belief and faith. He'd never read the Bible cover-to-cover before. He'd used it as a research aid, when he wanted one of his characters to say something profound. He'd used it quite a bit when he wrote for Harry Domin for *R.U.R.*, making the man who took the role of God into his own hands a great quoter of scripture. Walczyk sat down on the couch with the Bible. He didn't remember who told him this, but he remembered that if you pray on an issue and then open the Bible, the answer will be on those two pages somewhere. He found it hard to fathom that this book, no doubt printed in China or Malaysia or Pittsburgh, was some sort of a three age-old Magic 8 Ball. Nevertheless, he pressed the volume's spine against this forehead and thought to himself, *Lord, what will I do if I ever hit rock bottom again?* He thumbed through the thin, crinkly pages, then stopped. Tucked between two particular pages was a folded sheet of notebook paper. Walczyk pulled it out and read.

Walczyk,

If you're like me (and I suspect you are), you face your problems alone and admit your defeat alone. I ask that you consider reaching out to someone, be it your wonderful friends Hannah and Vic, your steadfast assistant and friend April or your wonderful parents. But that's the easiest thing to do, isn't it, to bottle everything up inside so that it doesn't bother you or affect the lives of those you love? I tried it that way, and it almost got me killed. You tried it that way, and it gave you a concussion. I think it's about time we both changed the way we go about living this thing called life.

There's a verse in the book of Ecclesiastes that Bruce shared with me. I think it applies to your situation as much as it applies to mine: "Two are better than one, because they have a good return for their work: If one falls down, his friend can help him up. But pity the man who falls and has no one to help him up!" (4: 8-10)

As you explore your own personal relationship with God, please know that it's not God's way to reach down from heaven and cure you with a magical touch. He won't take away your pain or give you a perfect life. Because that would be too easy. And that's not how God works. Your pain and misery have put you on a path, like Bruce talked about. I truly think your path is to take care of others who have been cursed with this disease. Not as a nurse or a doctor, but somehow, I know you were put on this path to educate and provide solace for other people who suffer with bipolar disorder.

I sincerely hope that we meet again, under better circumstances. When (if?) I get out of here, I'd be honored to be your friend. 201-0626, if you ever need it.

Love, Kaley

Walczyk replaced the letter and continued to flip through his Bible, to the passage from Ecclesiastes that Kaley had quoted and read the verse again, aloud. As he flipped through the Bible, he stumbled upon another passage that his Grammie Reynolds always used to read to him. He sprawled out on the couch and began to read:

There is a time for everything, and a season for
every activity under the heavens:
A time to be born and a time to die,
A time to plant and a time to uproot,
A time to kill and a time to heal,
A time to tear down and a time to build,
A time to weep and a time to laugh,
A time to mourn and a time to dance,
A time to scatter stones and a time to gather them,
A time to embrace and a time to refrain from embracing,
A time to search and a time to give up,
A time to keep and a time to throw away,
A time to tear and a time to mend,
A time to be silent and a time to speak,
A time to love and a time to hate,
A time for war and a time for peace.

An hour later, Walczyk found Mary hovering over him. "I think it's finally time for bed," she said softly. Walczyk rose, collected his things, and let her usher him back to his room, where he quickly passed out.

FRIDAY

"Up and at 'em, Pete!"

Walczyk bolted up in bed, shaken from his slumber by the booming voice. Standing in the doorway, smiling, was Susan, hands on wind pants-clad hips. She smiled at Walczyk.

"Come on, Pete. Don't want to miss your last breakfast here, do you?"

Walczyk would've gladly traded the yellow egg-substitute and shriveled up sausages for another hour of sleep, but as he crawled out from under his scant few hours of sleep, the import of the statement "your last breakfast here" struck him: it was discharge day!

Walczyk leaped from his bed, still in his clothes from last night, and peeled his shirt off, changing it for a clean one on his dresser. He slid on his grey hoodie and started across the room. Zack was lying there, eyes wide open.

"Come on," Walczyk said, giving Zack's mattress a little shake. "I don't have a lot of time, and there's a lot I need to tell you."

In the cafeteria, Walczyk sat at one of the tables off to the side with Zack. Across the room, he noticed Kaley, sitting with the ever-silent Patty, neither one talking.

"So what do they make you do?" Zack asked, his hand shaking as he raised his spoon full of Cheerios to his mouth.

"Whatever you want. Well, whatever you want within reason. I learned last night that the no TV after lights-out rule is strictly enforced." Walczyk recommended the quiet room as *the* room to read and write and work on other noiseless pursuits. He told Zack that Emily was a sweet person, albeit a little over-eager, and that Rick was cool to hang around with. He warned Zack to steer clear of Roger and Theresa at night, but to take Susan and her drill-sergeant attitude with a grain of salt, because underneath her gruff exterior she was a good person. "It's important not to lose touch with the outside world," Walczyk warned. "The phone's there. Use it. Now I've heard back from my assistant. Your parents are all set at the Birch Point Inn for at least a week. It's a good place, not far from here, so they'll be able to come visit you often. Cherish those visits, Zack, because they'll be your only link to the outside world."

On their way back up to Three-North, Walczyk explained the purpose of the morning meeting, and stressed that the information given out in them was generally useful. He urged Zack to stick around after group on Sunday for Sunday Worship, if for no other reason than just to be inspired by the positive energy that Bruce Johnson exuded. Zack seemed heartened that there was such a service. Settled back in to the ward, Walczyk gave Zack a tour, pointing out such curiosities as the isolation room and the infirmary, where Walczyk had a date to have one more blood draw before he left.

At nine, Walczyk checked in on his discharge. It would most likely be around noon, he was told, so he gave April a heads-up call. His parents were taking her to return her rental car then everyone was coming to the hospital. Walczyk then attended his last morning meeting, again giving Kaley a wide berth, though he did catch her giving him fleeting glimpses. He shot her a smile and she smiled back before returning her attention to the discussion Emily was conducting on how to be your own best friend. After morning group, Zack was called away to meet with Dr. Lentz. Walczyk wandered around the ward, finally landing in the small common room, where Patty was sitting in her wheelchair, staring at the television. A Three Stooges short was playing.

"Do you like the Stooges?" Walczyk asked. She said nothing. "I think the Shemp ones are actually pretty good. A different kind of humor than the Curly shorts, but still funny. Now the Joe Besser ones... don't get me started. Those barely deserve the name of–"

From the wheelchair, a squeal came. Walczyk turned in disbelief, watching as Patty burst out laughing. The on-screen slapstick violence continued, and Patty continued laughing. Walczyk laughed along with her, and the two patients enjoyed a half hour with the Three Stooges. After the Stooges, though, it was like a switch was flipped, and Patty was suddenly quiet again. Walczyk couldn't blame her; he'd never found *Hogan's Heroes* worth laughing at.

At ten-thirty, Walczyk was called to the front desk, where his family and April had were waiting. They walked down to his room, armed with a suitcase, and began packing up Walczyk's belongings. Susan gave Walczyk the okay to lace up and put on his sneakers and around eleven-thirty, just as April was beginning to complain about the length of time the entire discharge was taking, Dr. Lentz arrived at the front desk.

"I understand you're rather anxious to get going," Lentz said. "I don't blame you. The trip to Cole Island is quite a lengthy one." Dr. Lentz signed some papers, had Walczyk sign some pages, and explained the medication schedule to Walczyk, his parents, and April. "Well, that should just about do it," Dr. Lentz said, extending that huge hand of his. Walczyk reached out and took it. "It was a pleasure working with you, Peter. Should you have any questions, my numbers are with the materials I gave you."

"Thank you, Doctor," Walczyk said. "I mean it. Thank you."

"You're quite welcome, Mr. Walczyk." Dr. Lentz smiled.

Walczyk turned for the door and was just about out when Lentz called back to him.

"Hold on a minute!"

Walczyk's stomach lurched. There was a look of terror on his parents' faces. April looked like she was ready to commit a crime. Walczyk turned back. Dr. Lentz was holding the X-Wing Lego kit that Hannah had brought Walczyk.

"Thanks," Walczyk said, once he was able to breathe again. He reached out and grabbed the box, turned, and muttered to everyone, "Let's get the hell out of here. Before they really do change their mind."

Stepping out the front door, Walczyk felt like he was back in Hollywood. Photographers shouted his name. Flash bulbs went off in his face. He could clearly see his parents were bothered by this. He made himself focus not on the media circus outside of Dirigo, but on the sky. It so bright to him. The air was still chilly, and the clouds threatened to rain again, but Walczyk could have cared less. He couldn't believe it had been a week since he'd breathed fresh air. Since he'd seen the sky clearly. Since he'd been outside. He turned around and looked at the hospital one last time, swearing he could see Kaley looking out the window of the small quiet room.

Hospital security created a corridor for Walczyk and his family and escorted them to their car, which was parked right in front of the hospital. Once the doors were shut, his father cautiously took off. Walczyk stared out the window. The sky seemed so bright to him.

"Are you okay, Peter?" his mother asked, putting her hand on his shoulder as they settled into the back seat.

He smiled. "Couldn't be better, Mum."

CHAPTER TWENTY-ONE
MEANWHILE, BACK ON COLE ISLAND...

"Now they're all green," Hannah said hesitantly, sitting on the floor with Dexter in her lap.

Vic cursed loudly, yanking the cables from the back of the television. The picture on the screen blinked out.

"Now they're all gone," Hannah said.

Vic glowered at her from over the top of the television. "Are you trying to help?"

"Yes!"

Vic checked the colors of the cables against the back of the Blu-ray player. "Really. I couldn't tell." He plugged all the cords back in.

"Now they're all yellow."

Vic unplugged the cables from the back of the player. "It's a Blu-ray player. You'd think I could hook it up just fine."

"One would think."

"You know, I really need an HDMI cable for this," Vic said.

"Can't you get one at the hardware?"

"I highly doubt that Marley's has HDMI cables."

"They might." Hannah stood, Dexter still glued to her side. She'd developed a tight bond with the dog, taking care of it for Peter and April all week. Being with Dexter made her wish all the more that Garry Olsen allowed pets in her apartment.

Vic threw the string of cables down on the floor. "Then give them a call and check."

Without comment, Hannah left the room. She crossed the hall into Walczyk's office, where another TV hung from the wall, awaiting Vic's delicate touch. She pulled out her cell phone, looked up the number, and dialed.

"Marley's Hardware. Chester speaking."

"Hi, Chester, this is Hannah Cooper. I'm calling to see if you have something called an HDMI cable."

There was a long silence. "What the hell's a HME cable?"

"*HDMI*," she stressed. "It's for hooking up a Blu-ray player."

"Oh, movies? Try Salinger's." The line went dead.

"Helpful," she said, frowning. In the two days leading up to Walczyk's imminent return home, Hannah and Vic had taken up the task of taking care of all the neglected tasks around the house that Walczyk had never gotten around to in the mania leading up to his hospitalization. Hannah had spent her out-of-school time the past two days getting the kitchen cleaned and organized, which included unpacking the pots and pans that were still in their boxes from the ill-fated trip to Bangor a month ago. *Apparently,* she thought, *April's not much of an at-home cook.* Vic had seen to the electronics, knowing that the TVs in Walczyk's bedroom and office had yet to be hooked up. He had run coaxial cable through the house, mounted the bedroom and office flat-screens according to April's specific instructions, and was now in the process of hooking up the Blu-ray players to the TVs.

Hannah returned to Walczyk's bedroom. The TV was back on. The picture was crystal clear. "Nice, but it's in black-and-white."

"Damn it!" He yanked the cords out again, making the screen go blank.

"I could call Henry in Bangor and have them–"

"We're not going to bother the Walczyks right now. Andrew is going to Portland this weekend. I'll have him make a run to Best Buy down there." Vic went back to work, cursing and plugging in cables. It had been Vic's idea to get the house put together as a welcome home surprise for Peter. Hannah had considered a party, but Vic had said, rightfully so, suggested that a houseful of people making a fuss over Walczyk might just send him back to Dirigo.

"What do you want for lunch?"

"Where are you going? The Moondoggy or Mama Rosa's?"

"I figured the Moondoggy."

"Then a cheese steak, hold the mushrooms."

"Fries?"

"Home cuts, please."

"Soda?"

"A Bud."

"I'm not buying beer in the middle of a school day. People will talk."

"Fine, then... *root* beer. O'Mallory's"

"O'Mallory's?"

"That kind they have in the glass bottle." Vic pulled his wallet from his back pocket, but Hannah held her hand up.

"Nope. You treated when we went to Bangor. It's my turn. Need anything else in town?"

"Should we get him a card? You know... for getting out of the hospital?"

"Like a get-well card?"

"Well, it wouldn't be a graduation card, would it?"

Hannah shrugged. "Point taken. No, I think we're all right on the cards front. Besides, have you seen the stack on his desk?"

On Walczyk's desk in his office were stacks of cards, with return addresses from Maine to California, and names on those return addresses like "Favreau" and "Eastwood." One card, Hannah assumed, was from Richard Dreyfuss, who she had learned through her internet research also had bipolar disorder. In all, there must have been well over a hundred get well cards. She recognized almost all of the Maine addresses, with postmarks from Patten (Henry's mother), Orrington (Max Leavitt lived in Orrington with his partner, an engineer named Micah), Boothbay Harbor (Hannah couldn't figure that one out), and a large pile from Cole Island, addressed simply to "Peter Walczyk, The Old Merry Place, Cole Island ME." Postmaster Staples must've had a field day stamping all of those cards as "improperly addressed."

"Well, we ought to get him something," Vic said. "I mean, he's coming home. We should be doing something."

Hannah put a hand on Vic's shoulder. "I have a feeling he's going to want to go straight to bed as soon as he gets home."

It was nearly four o'clock before Henry Walczyk pulled onto Walker Bridge, the last leg of the journey home. Peter had slept most of the way home, leaned up against his mother's shoulder. In the front seat, April was on her phone, keeping everyone at the house apprised as to their progress and keeping Henry awake.

"I think you should take Monday off," April said while sending a text message to Eli. "You've been through hell and you deserve a three-day weekend at home."

"Thank you, April," Diane said from the back seat, softly. "I've been trying to get him to realize that all week."

"There are things that need tending to," Henry said. "I'm not taking Monday off. I've already taken quite a bit of time off as it stands."

"The school will survive for one more day," Diane said, putting her hand on Henry's arm. "This weekend's going to be big for Peter. His father should be around."

"Big weekend?" Henry asked. "What do you have planned?"

"Nothing special. I just think it'd be nice if everyone were around." Diane leaned forward, poking him in the shoulder. "And you, Mr. Walczyk, need your rest."

"How about this, I'll go in at noon."

"It's a start," April said.

"Are the kids planning anything for tonight?" Diane asked, checking to make sure Walczyk was still sleeping.

"Absolutely not," April said, finishing her text message. "Vic is hooking up some electronic equipment that the boss has been putting off – TVs and the like – and Hannah took my credit card to Ferguson's and stocked the kitchen. There's no reason Walczyk should have to leave the house for a couple days."

"You really think that's healthy?" Henry asked. "Letting him hole up like that?"

"Everyone's going to want to make a fuss over him being home," April said. "And we all know how he feels about big fusses."

"They will give him his space, won't they?" Diane asked, stroking Peter's hair. "The press, I mean. They know he's been through a lot."

"According to Vic's Uncle Donny," April said, "a couple of photographers had been staking out the house, but no one's been on the property besides Vic and Hannah."

"Ugh, those photographers," Diane groaned. "Why can't they just leave him alone?"

"He's a celebrity fresh out of rehab," April said. "The tabloids will want pictures of him looking bad."

"Such a disgusting job," Diane muttered, "taking pictures of people at their worst."

"As to his medication," April said, taking a drink of the now cold coffee that was sitting in the center console. "Dr. Lentz said he called in the prescription to Arbo's before we left the hospital and gave us enough sample packets to get him through tonight and tomorrow morning. I'll run into town tomorrow and pick them up." April's phone vibrated. She checked text message on the screen. "Text from Hannah," April reported. "Asking if they should be at the house when we get home."

"Of course they should," Henry said. "They're family."

"Of course they should," Walczyk heard his father say, miles away. "They're family." Walczyk slowly came back to the land of the living, feeling the shift in terrain beneath his father's Lincoln that told him they were off the bridge and back on terra firma. He'd considered lying there, pretending to be asleep, enjoying the few moments he wasn't being fussed over. Since he'd left the hospital, someone had been continuously questioning if he was okay, if he was comfortable or if he was feeling all right. But he knew he had to get up and face the world, as much as he didn't want to. Slowly, he sat up, opening his eyes for the first time since they'd passed the Newport exit, southbound on I-95.

"Feeling better?" his mother asked, smoothing down his hair.

"I feel like I've been asleep for a hundred years."

"They didn't dope you up again, did they?" his father asked.

"No," April said from the front seat. "It's good old fashioned fatigue finally catching up with him."

"Want anything in town?" Walczyk's father asked.

"No," Walczyk said, shaking his head. "I just want to go home."

The trip from town to his own little spot on the Back Nine seemed to take forever. But eventually, the car pulled into 2575 Island Road. The house looked beautiful. Everything seemed to glow with familiarity. The sun was starting to set on the water behind the house, casting an orange glow onto everything. Walczyk got out of the car and walked around it, stretching his legs. It felt good, after almost two hours in the back seat of his parents' compact car, to be up and about again.

The front door of his house opened, and Hannah and Dexter came bounding out, down the stairs and along the path, Hannah with her arms spread wide. Walczyk smiled and took her in his arms, holding tightly to her. Dexter jumped at the back of his leg. Walczyk heard Hannah sniffling, telling him that she was, or had been, crying. He couldn't blame her. He was choking back his own emotions. Walczyk took her face in his hands, wiping away the tears, and kissed her gently. "Thank you," he whispered. Behind her, Vic had made his way down the pathway and was shaking hands with Walczyk's father and hugging his mother.

"So," Hannah asked, carefully letting go of Walczyk, "how've you been holding up?"

"I survived it," Walczyk said, enjoying the wide smile on her face. "And I think I may have learned a thing or two."

"That's all that matters."

"And one of those things," Walczyk said, walking towards Vic, "is how much I missed this guy!"

Vic picked Walczyk up off the ground in a bear hug, holding tightly to him. "You okay?" Vic whispered into Walczyk's ear.

"I am now," Walczyk whispered back.

The inside of the house looked wonderful, considering Walczyk remembered having left it in a great state of disarray. Hannah proudly displayed off her domestic work, opening cupboards and showing off the fridge, which was stuffed with healthy meal choices.

"So," Vic asked Walczyk, pulling out his cell phone. "Hungry?"

Walczyk put his suitcase down on the living room floor. "Thought you'd never ask." He started for the door and only turned back when he noticed he was alone.

"Well?" Walczyk said. "You guys coming?"

"Peter, Vic offered to have supper sent over from the restaurant," his mother explained.

"The hell he is. Guys, I haven't been in a restaurant for over a week now. I gotta get back into my routine. I need to be around people again. Hear dinner conversation that's not centered on which nurses are sneaking smoke breaks and which patients are 'supposably' faking their illnesses to get out of legal matters."

Everyone exchanged looks, but it was Hannah who made the first move, collecting her fleece jacket from a chair at the kitchen table and putting it on. "You heard the man, people," she said. "Let's go."

"So this guy's tweaking right the hell out, thrashing and swearing. I think he even took a swing at one of the orderlies, who, believe me, deserved it. So they've got him by the arms and he starts lashing out with the feet. He's just gone apeshit!"

"Peter," his mother scolded.

"Sorry, Mum, but that's the clinical word for it: 'apeshit.' This guy had gone absolutely berserk."

"So how'd they take him down?" Vic eagerly asked.

"Remember that skinny little nurse? Hope?"

"The redheaded one?" Hannah asked.

"The same," Walczyk replied.

Vic's eyes widened. "No way."

"She charges through the ward, whips the protective tip off a hypo, and jabs him right in the ass. Down he went and into the padded room for two days."

"That's awful," Hannah said.

"That probably saved him from being kicked out of the hospital and not getting the treatment he obviously needed," Walczyk reflected.

"Did you know this boy well?" his father asked.

"Yeah," Walczyk said, turning to Hannah. "Remember the guy at the pizza party you helped out, the one in the bathrobe?"

"Yeah," Hannah said, a look of realization crossing her face. "That was–?"

Walczyk smiled. "That was David."

Walczyk's mother was shocked. "That little thing in the baseball cap?"

"A chemical imbalance can do strange things to you," Walczyk said.

Vic picked up his empty bottle from the table. "I'm going for a refill. Walz, you want a rum and Coke?"

Diane cleared her throat, looking directly at Vic.

April was not as subtle: "Absolutely not!"

"No," Walczyk said, chuckling. "I have to be careful from now on. Dr. Lentz warned me that lithium dehydrates the system."

"He also said that mood stabilizers don't mix well with mood-altering chemicals like alcohol," April chimed in.

"Oh, sorry," Vic said, dropping his head. "I never thought about that."

"Look, it doesn't mean you guys can't," Walczyk said.

Walczyk's father slowly slid his chair away from the table, rubbing his stomach. "So, Peter, tell me, what was the hardest part of being in there?"

Walczyk thought a moment. "I guess I'd have to say feeling like a sane man in an asylum."

"What do you mean by that?" Hannah asked.

"Well, after the meds they gave me in Augusta wore off and my mood stabilized, I didn't feel like there was anything wrong with me. I was regular old me, maybe a bit more restrained. But I felt like I was the only normal person in a nut house with a bunch of sick people."

"But you *were* sick," Mum said. "You still are."

"Oh, I realize that. Nevertheless, I still felt like there was nothing wrong with me. And being told I couldn't leave on Monday, that only compounded it. Now I see it was the solution to my problem, and I'm glad I went. But... there were moments when I felt I was never going to get out of there. That I'd be trapped in there with those people forever."

"God," Vic shuddered.

"It must've been scary," Walczyk's mother added.

"Incredibly," Walczyk said.

"So, tell me this," Hannah said, finishing her iced tea. "Was there a best part about being in there?"

"A 'best part?'" Vic asked. "Hannah, it was a nut house!"

Things around the table grew quiet. Walczyk saw Vic sit back down in his chair, not taking his eyes from the wall behind Hannah. Walczyk thought a bit on this one. What was the best part about being in there? The joy the other patients took away from the pizza party? Seeing David apologize for pushing him out of his chair? Meeting Kaley? "Learning that I'm never alone."

"You have your mother and me," his father said, taking his son's hand.

"Always," his mother added.

"I know that," he said, giving his father's hand a squeeze. "But I mean that God is always there for me. Not just when I need Him, but always."

At the bar, a loud, raucous laugh broke out. Everyone turned to see Uncle Donny holding court over Stumpy McGillicuddy and Gibby Perkins, no doubt sharing an absolutely filthy, tasteless joke.

"Well, it's about that time," Walczyk's father said, taking his napkin from his lap and reaching for his wallet.

"Oh, no," Vic said, rising to push Henry's wallet back. "Knock that off, Henry. Not tonight. This is my treat."

"Victor," Walczyk's mother began. "Please. Let us–"

"No," Vic firmly said. "Just kiss your son and get to bed. Tomorrow morning's going to come quicker than you want it to."

"Well," Mum said, kissing Vic on the cheek and hugging him. "Thank you, Victor. For everything."

"We're just a phone call away," his father said, pulling Walczyk close to him and hugging him tightly. "I love you," he said, kissing his son's cheek.

"I love you, too," Walczyk said, holding tight to his father for a moment before letting him go.

"Breakfast tomorrow? Your place?" his mother asked.

"Better make it brunch," April said. "Because we're sleeping in tomorrow. But rest assured, I'll have everyone up and clothed by eleven."

"Well, I'm letting myself in at ten, so don't panic if you wake up to the smell of bacon cooking."

"I don't think anyone has ever panicked at waking up to the smell of cooking bacon," Walczyk said, pulling his mother close and hugging her long and hard. "I love you, Mum."

"I love you, Peter," she said, kissing her son.

As he watched his parents walk out of the Barrelhead, hand in hand, Walczyk thought back on Kaley and her mother, and realized what great parents he had.

"So, tell me," Vic said as he and Hannah slid around the table, moving closer to Walczyk. "What was the hardest thing to deal with on the mental ward?"

"Aside from learning to call it a *psychiatric hospital*," Walczyk said. "I'd have to answer that it was having you guys around,"

Walczyk said. "You came. You visited." He looked at April. "You rescued me from temper tantrums. You were always there, and I love each one of you for that. But in a way, you weren't there. You were someone else. You weren't April, or Vic, or Hannah, swinging by the house to visit Walczyk. You were Vic and Hannah and April, coming into a psychiatric hospital to visit Peter."

Vic looked to the bar, holding his empty bottle up, and quickly changed the subject. "I heard Dougie Olsen almost got picked up for a pot."

"Again?" Hannah said, disgusted.

"Sure enough. Uncle Donny told me. He was driving home the other night and..."

Walczyk sat back in his chair and watched as Vic animatedly told his story, Hannah listened intently, and April dug out her iPhone, texting away, probably to Eli or someone else on the West Coast. And he smiled.

It was nice to be home again.

CHAPTER TWENTY-TWO
A SLOW RETURN TO NORMALCY

Dr. Lentz had warned him before his release that the "return to normalcy" would be a slow one – that it would be a bumpy road with many obstacles in the way. But if he stayed positive, asked for help when he needed it, and accepted recovery as a challenge, he would persevere. However, the good doctor failed to mention that while the obstacles he faced in his everyday life would not change, the people that filled his life *would*. And in drastic ways.

Over the weeks following his discharge from Dirigo, Walczyk soon began to realize that everyone in his life, from friends to family to passersby in the community were all behaving differently around him, each in their own quirky little way. He was convinced this wasn't some paranoid delusion, brought on by an over-abundance of medication in his system like last time. No, this time, he was positive, beyond a shadow of a doubt, that he was being "handled" by his family and friends.

Hannah was very attentive. Almost *too* attentive. She was always at his side, coming to his house around dinner time every night, bringing papers to grade and projects to work on while spending time with him. Making good on a promise he made her one night over the phone while in Dirigo, Walczyk began showing Hannah the rough cuts of season three of *Ordinary World*, which she gobbled up two a night for a week. But he knew it was more than just *Ordinary World* that was compelling her to make the eight-mile bike ride from town out to the Back Nine. There was something else.

"How are you feeling?" she asked one Saturday night, bringing their weekly *Star Trek* marathon to Walczyk's house. Hannah had taken to sleeping on the couch over the weekends, vocal about saying she felt April deserved some time alone with Vic. The end result was that Walczyk couldn't help but feel smothered by her.

"Fine," he replied, not drawing his attention from the implausible story of the crew of the *Enterprise* searching for Spock's surgically removed brain.

"No, *how are you doing?*" she restated, as she always did when Walczyk half-heartedly gave her an answer.

"*Fine*," he restated. "A little down, but I'm dealing."

Hannah reached out, remote in hand, and paused the DVD. She got up from the couch and sat down on the ottoman in front of Walczyk's leather armchair and gently asked, "Is everything okay?"

"Hannah," he responded, growing weary of the constant second-guessing of his emotional state, "I am fine."

"Because we can call Dr. Lentz. Maybe get you back to Dirigo – just to see him, not to check in."

"Dr. Lentz can't see me. He only deals with in-patient cases."

"Then we can find you someone around here. Robert Williams is a new doctor in town. He's good, I hear."

"I'm not seeing any more general practitioners. Besides, April's finding me someone out-of-town."

"Good," Hannah said, relaxing a tiny bit. "But still, if you're depressed, then your body's trying to tell you something. Are you having bad dreams?"

"No, I'm not," he said, humoring her.

"Trouble sleeping?"

"Nope."

"What about concentration. Dr. Lentz said you might have trouble concentrating."

"I *have* been having a hard time keeping my mind focused lately," Walczyk truthfully admitted. "But I'm telling you, Hannah – I am fine!"

"But you're depressed."

"Yes and when I see my doctor, whenever April gets that going, I'll tell him, and they'll no doubt put me on something to take care of it."

Hannah reached out and grabbed his wrists in her tiny, pale hands. "You're not suicidal, are you?"

"No, I'm not."

"How about your... private function?"

"My what?"

"You know... your private function... your..." she groped for the word, finally finding it: "...potency."

"Wouldn't know," he said, a bit put off by such an intimate question, even from a former lover like Hannah. "I haven't really felt the urge."

"They say that's a warning sign in itself," she suggested. "Peter, it's okay, you know. You can talk to me about this. We're friends. We've been there and we've certainly *done that*. Nothing's off limits."

Walczyk smiled. As annoying, frustrating, invasive, and smothering as she was, Hannah was all heart. "I promise you, when my inability to perform becomes an issue, you and I will sit down and discuss it like two rational adults."

Walczyk's parents were equally attentive, arriving nightly at six forty-five (on the dot) for their nightly seventy-five-minute visit with Walczyk and whoever else was at the house, usually Hannah and April. Walczyk enjoyed the company of his parents, and felt a closer bond to them given what he'd experienced in Dirigo, but the visitations felt almost... artificial, as though they were visiting just to check up on him. The only exceptions to his parents' visitation schedule were Friday night, when Walczyk and April were invited over for the revival of Friday night dinner, and Saturday night, when Hannah would commandeer the house for her *Star Trek* marathons. As much as Walczyk was growing to dislike the pomp and ceremony his mother had placed on what used to be a casual Friday night dinner with family, he did find that he was no longer dreading these get-togethers. Discussing this with April, he had come to realize that perhaps his enjoyment in the dinners stemmed from not having to hide anything from his family – they finally knew he had been feeling useless and hopeless. He wasn't absolutely sure if it was part of some divine plan or just the result of the lithium taking effect, but there was a definite sense of hope within him.

As for feeling useless, well, that was another story. On top of doting on him and constantly popping in, his mother had begun to wander about the house during her visits, sometimes disappearing for sizeable chunks of time. Walczyk and April would later discover that the woman had been a busy little beaver, helping herself to laundry that needed folding. More than once, the sound of running water in the kitchen drove April from one of her animated discussions with Walczyk's father about the current political climate into the kitchen, where his mother was doing dishes.

To top it all off, Walczyk awoke one morning to discover his mother had called his phone. He'd never heard it go off, but when he reached over for it before getting up for the three hundredth time to go to the bathroom, he noticed a missed call from his mother's cell phone. He dialed her back, worried, as his mother seldom used her cell phone. The phone rang in his ear... then his mother's ring tone, "Ode to Joy," sounded from downstairs. Another ring in his ear. More "Ode to Joy" downstairs. Clad only in his underwear, Walczyk slipped out of bed and quickly made his way down the stairs, to discover that the ringing was coming from the living room. Walczyk found his mother passed out on his couch, her cell phone on the coffee table and Dexter curled up beside the couch. The Weather Channel, muted, was on the TV. A quick inspection of the downstairs made it apparent that she'd been cleaning: the bathroom smelled of fresh cleanser, the stove was sparkling, and there was a trash bag filled with damp, Windex-soaked paper towels by the door.

While his mother had become obsessive in her keeping of Walczyk's house, his father had turned his attention to Walczyk's schedule. Much like April, his father had become insistent that Walczyk start setting goals for himself, and frequently checked in with him to see what he was working on and what progress he was making on his projects. His father had been a huge proponent of Walczyk's continued work on *Night*, even offering to read what had been written, despite his inexperience in analyzing a professional screenplay.

When not drilling him about the movie, or encouraging Walczyk to find a new project, Walczyk's father was pushing his son to adopt some physical activities, offering to go for walks with him in the evening while he was over visiting. Already noticing an increase in his appetite (and his waist line), Walczyk took his father up on the offer. The nightly walks were a chance to get away from April and his mother, who would invariably be "politely debating" the upkeep of the house while Hannah tried playing peace keeper. There was no conversation on these little sojourns, rather chunks of dialog interspersed with silence and the sounds of the world around them.

"So, do you have a plan?" his father asked him.

"A plan?"

"Yeah. For life. The future. Next week. Anything."

"I plan on going for a walk with my Dad and maybe watching some TV."

The crickets chirped and the waves crashed against the shore around them.

"What about *Night*? Is it in any shape for me to read?"

"Not really."

"Are you still working on it?"

"A little."

They walked for a while, listening to nature around them.

"April says you've got to find a doctor somewhere so you can keep getting your meds filled."

"I do."

"Have you called anyone?"

"She's on it."

"Peter, I remember Dr. Lentz saying that *you* should be the one to make those calls."

"April handles my business affairs. She'll deal with it."

"But April's not the one who needs someone to talk to."

"Have you seen her lately? She could use some lithium herself."

The surf filled the awkward silence that had cascaded down upon them as their stroll continued.

"Your sister is planning on coming home for Christmas."

"She said."

"That should be fun."

"Yeah."

His father turned to him suddenly. "Peter, are you all right?"

"Yeah, Dad. Why?"

His father seemed to relax a little. "Just checking." They walked in silence some more. "If you weren't all right, you know you can – "

"I'd tell you," Walczyk said, the ghost of a smile on his face.

April was back to her overbearing, albeit caring self, taking charge of Walczyk's life and demanding to make changes to his world. It was as though nothing had changed at all. Except that gone were all unhealthy foods and drinks from the home. Bottles of Absolut vodka and Captain Morgan's spiced rum were replaced with a water cooler pumping out ice cold water. Walczyk's favorite snacks, Trix cereal and pork rinds, vanished, baby carrots and a great quantities of Greek yogurt, in various flavors in their place. Meals were eaten at home, or at his parents' house, except for the two times a week April allowed them to dine out at one of the Island's eateries.

Over and done with was the staying up all night watching movies or playing video games. Lights out in the Old Merry Place was eleven o'clock. Walczyk half-suspected that April would remain up for an hour or two, creeping up the stairs stealthily to make sure he was asleep, and not sitting up in bed, playing video games on his laptop or working. April's big thing, though, was seeing that Walczyk resume his social activities. She cited Dr. Lentz, Dr. Phil, and a plethora of other television "doctors" on this one – Walczyk needed to start getting out of the house and into public settings again. If he didn't, she warned him, then he'd never be able to take care of himself.

"No. Not that. I can't do it," Walczyk said, fidgeting in the passenger seat outside the bookstore, just shy of a week after his release from Dirigo.

"Yes, you can," April said, looking for a place to park. "Besides, you've got to."

"I don't know… I don't want a scene."

"There's not going to be a scene." April deftly slid the Jeep into a spot along the sidewalk.

Walczyk turned to April. "Trust me. There's going to be a scene." April leaped from the Jeep, collected their laptop bags from the back seat and walked around the vehicle. Walczyk was still sitting inside. She rapped on the glass.

"Come on, you wuss!"

There was no getting out of this. Walczyk had been dreading this moment since before he left Dirigo. He *knew* it was going to be a scene. But April was right. Partially. The longer he put it off, the bigger it would be. Reluctantly, Walczyk opened the door and slunk out of the Jeep, taking his laptop bag from April, and together they walked inside the Bronze Lantern.

It was a welcoming sight, the familiar stack of books. The smell of the Island Roast coffee. The sight of Garry Olsen scrambling about the store. "God, I hope he doesn't spot me," Walczyk said, looking around the store. Walczyk and April made their way past the magazine stacks and walked into the café of the Bronze Lantern. Everything was as it had been when he left. The same odd assortment of tatty chairs along the back wall. The long, gouged wooden camp table set up in the corner, covered in books and magazines. The same odd assortment of mismatched tables dotting the main floor. And Ol' Yeller, reading a rumpled newspaper in the corner by the camp table. Walczyk had April order him a mint hot chocolate and made his way to the back table to settle in.

"See you're back," Ol' Yeller said in his usual clipped fashion.

"Yeah, I'm back," Walczyk said.

"Good," the loafer said before returning his full attention to the *USA Today* he was tearing apart.

"Garry must know you're back in town," April said, sliding a mug of mint-smelling hot chocolate across the table to Walczyk. "The girl at the register said she's under strict orders not to charge us for drinks."

Walczyk smiled and started up his laptop. Pulling his hand-written pages from Dirigo out of his laptop bag, he set to work, typing it out. About twenty minutes into his work, a hand landed on his shoulder. He spun around quickly, his ear buds dropping from his ears. It was the red, cherubic face of Garry Olsen, smiling down at him.

As Walczyk stood to greet Garry, the entrepreneur picked him up in a large bear hug. "Welcome back, Peter, m'boy! How're you doing?"

Walczyk was winded when Garry finally let him go. "Not bad, Garry."

"What was it like there? In the cuckoo's nest?"

"Nothing like you see in the movies or on TV," Walczyk said, picking up his drink. "It was a very nice place. A caring staff – well, most of them – and a modern facility."

"No one tried to bite you or anything, did they?"

Walczyk laughed politely. "No. It wasn't like that. Most of us were in there for depression. Many of us were suicidal."

"Huh."

Walczyk debated going into any depth with Garry, but he remembered what Kaley said to him on that last day: *Own the disease, don't let it own you.* "I was diagnosed with bipolar disorder," Walczyk said. Garry looked mildly surprised. "It's a disorder where–"

"I'll be damned. Amanda was diagnosed with it in the eighties."

"Your wife?" Walczyk asked, shocked.

"I didn't think they diagnosed it anymore." Garry said. "Well, you see Amanda. I guess there's life after bipolar. Don't you worry. You're in good company."

"Thanks, Garry," Walczyk said.

"Mr. Olsen to the front registers, please. Mr. Olsen to the front registers."

Garry looked up at the ceiling, as if it would tell him what the problem was, then back down at Walczyk. "Well, they always need me somewhere. Take care, Peter. Good seeing you back!" And with that, Garry was off for the front registers. Walczyk sat back down, catching April's smile.

"What?"

"Nothing."

"No, what?" Walczyk asked.

"I said it's nothing. It's just–"

"What?"

"He likes you."

"What, Garry? He just likes having a celebrity in the place."

"You're not that big a celebrity," Ol' Yeller grumbled.

Fuming, April shot to her feet. Walczyk reached his hand out, grasping hers and squeezing. April got the message and sat back down. After chilling out for a few moments, she asked, "Have you talked to Sara yet?"

"I don't know what I'd say," was Walczyk's exasperated response.

"Why not just say 'hello' and see where it goes?"

"Because…" Walczyk began, looking for a reason why not to call her. But none came to him. Truth was, ever since he'd had that dream about her, he'd wanted to talk to her. But he couldn't tell if it was just a desire to talk to a friend, or if it was that he was still sexually attracted to his estranged wife. Either way, something told him calling her wasn't such a good idea.

It was Vic, however, who had changed the most in his attitude. Walczyk had looked forward to having Vic around, as he was always relaxed and calm about everything. While he was staying at the Dirigo Psychiatric Hospital, Walczyk had found Vic's visit, and the improvised Mick-a-Palooza, to be extremely reassuring. However, in the days following his release, Walczyk began to notice that Vic was slowly drawing *away* from him. While Hannah had practically established the living room as a second residence, and his parents were becoming evening fixtures at the house, Vic almost seemed to be ignoring Walczyk. And this was awkward for Walczyk, as Vic was often over visiting with April. But instead of visiting in the living room, where Walczyk could enjoy his company too, Vic would show up and he and April would immediately take off for her room to do whatever they did in April's room.

And while things had been a bit off with Vic since that first night back, when the three friends and Walczyk's parents went out for dinner at the Barrelhead, it was the Wednesday after Walczyk's discharge that he first noticed that Vic avoiding him. Early that afternoon, April and Walczyk had stopped by the restaurant for lunch. Everyone was happy to see him. Uncle Donny picked him up off the floor with a big hug and there were kisses from just about every waitress in the house. Even Andrew, who rarely left his kitchen, came out to give his best wishes. Vic, however, was painfully absent from Walczyk's return to the Barrelhead. And while he did make his customary appearances during their meal, it was as though his attentions were almost aimed only at April. What conversation he did have with Walczyk, greeting him and asking how he was and commenting on the Patriots, was thin and cardboard; it only bore the shape and appearance of conversation, lacking the depth that made it a relished part of Walczyk's life.

"What the hell was up with him?" Walczyk asked later that night, as he and April worked in tandem on their supper: hot roast beef sandwiches with sautéed vegetables and provolone cheese.

"What the hell was up with who?" April asked, dicing mushrooms on a plastic cutting board.

"Your boyfriend." Walczyk snapped.

"Vic? What do you mean 'what's up with him?'"

"I mean he barely spoke to me today."

April rolled her eyes. "He spoke to you. He told you about the produce order being late, and the–"

"Stuff he'd talk to the MacPherson's about. He didn't share one iota of town gossip. Nothing about Gibby Perkins' old lady, or that new guy from Boothbay Harbor that Ingrid is seeing."

"Well, I, for one, am glad he decided not to discuss that slut," April said haughtily, dumping the mushrooms into a frying pan of oil and stirring them as they sizzled. "She turns my stomach."

"You're not using olive oil?" Walczyk observed, changing the subject.

"No, I don't care for it," April said. "You know that." She allowed another small dollop of sunflower oil in the pan, then capped the bottle and slid it across the counter. "Now, what makes you think that Vic is ignoring you?"

"Well, he's spent more time slobbering over you and ordering that new busboy back to work than he did talking to me."

"You made it abundantly clear that you don't want to be made a big deal of in public. Frankly, I'm surprised you let Donny and the staff fuss all over you like they did."

Perhaps, he thought, as he added the chopped up peppers and onions to the frying pan, he was being silly. After all, he *had* asked his friends not to fuss over him now that he was home.

But in the five days since he'd made that simple, rational request, he found April trying to force him back into his life as if nothing had happened, Hannah virtually moving in, his parents micro-managing his affairs, and his best friend nowhere to be found. But without one of his best friends a part of his life, Walczyk began to wonder if he should have stayed at Dirigo.

CHAPTER TWENTY-THREE
INTOLERANCE

"I just don't know what to do with you!" Henry Walczyk looked across his desk at the students gathered in his office.

"I just don't see the big deal, Mr. Walczyk," Taylor Hodges said, seeming entirely earnest.

Henry rose up behind his desk, crossing his arms and looking down at the rogue's Gallery of film nuts assembled before him. "The big deal, Mr. Hodges, is that when Coach Conklin found you and your 'film crew' in the boy's locker room after school yesterday evening, you were filming smut!"

"Sir, I wrote that scene," Sasha Connary said, raising her hand, "and it was *not* smut."

"And I watched the video tape, Ms. Connary. You had two students in the boys' locker room, naked, making out in the shower!"

"Sir, that's far from smut," Taylor countered. "And, technically, they weren't naked!"

"Your actress," he barked, pointing a finger across the room to Heather Urquhart, who was looking thoroughly ashamed of herself, "wasn't wearing a shirt, Mr. Hodges! She was in a shower in her cheering skirt and a bra! And your actor," he said, now pointing at

Patrick Forgue beside her, "was in his undershorts! I shudder to imagine where the scene was going from there."

"Well, sir," Sasha Connary quietly said, proffering an opened copy of the movie's screenplay, "if you'd read to scene fourteen–"

"You will turn in all video you've shot on school property to me," Henry ordered, cutting Sasha off. "You will leave any equipment you have borrowed, acquired, or appropriated from the school with me." There was a groan from the group. "You are all expected to report to Coach Conklin Monday after school to begin serving two weeks' detention."

"Two weeks?" Taylor screamed, leaping to his feet.

"Would four work better for you, Mr. Hodges?" Henry asked, picking up the digital video tape from the corner of his desk. "How about an in-house suspension?"

A hushed, collective whisper of "Shut up, Taylor!" hissed through the room.

Taylor looked around, seeing all eyes on him and sank back into his chair. "Two weeks is very generous, sir. Thank you."

"I'm so glad we agree. Taylor and Sasha, stay here. The rest of you, get back to class."

The students quietly filed out of the room, Sasha and Taylor remaining front-and-center in the three chairs line up opposite of Henry's desk.

"I hope you appreciate just what I've just done here," Henry said, sitting down opposite them.

"Yeah, you ruined my damned movie," Taylor grumbled.

"That was not my intention," Henry said softly.

"Bullshit," Taylor cursed.

Henry remembered to pick his battles and let the profanity go. "Taylor, what I saw on that tape is not the kind of thing this school can serve as a soundstage for. Do not get me wrong: I appreciate what you are trying doing here. I do. I recognize that not all students are athletes, nor are they interested in becoming such. And there has been a sizeable interest in an afterschool film club here for many years. But with material like this, I'm afraid I have to forbid you from–"

"You can't shut us down!" Taylor seemed to be on the verge of tears as he protested loudly.

"May I finish?" Henry asked, exercising great calm. Red-faced, Taylor sunk back into his seat and sullenly nodded. "As I was saying, I have to forbid you from shooting on campus. I just can't have violent and/or sexually explicit material being shot on school property. The school board, the community, Mrs. Lyons, they'd have a field day and I'd be out of here in no time. But there's nothing I can do or say that will shut your production down for good."

"Well, sir," Sasha meekly said, "that *is* what it looks like you're doing now."

Henry was tired of bouncing off the brick wall constructed in his path. He needed to get through to these kids that what they wanted to do was just not feasible. Then he glanced across the room at a picture on the wall. A photograph, in black and white, of his son, his wild, eager eyes staring through the bars of a clapper board. *Intolerance* was the name of the production scribbled on the clapper in white chalk.

And it came to him. "You two, you're are fans of my son's work, right?" Slowly, the three nodded and murmured affirmatives. "Even when he was a student at this school, I knew he would make an incredible filmmaker. His freshman year, he made an impressive film–"

"*Crabapple Pie*," Sasha said, perking up. "It was about a witch who poisoned a pie and gave it to her bullied daughter as a birthday present, to kill off one of the students picking on her. He and Miss Cooper wrote it."

"Yes," Henry said, impressed. "*Crabapple Pie* won the 'Best in Show' award that year, beating out many upperclassmen movies. The following year, he wrote and directed *The Boat*. Another 'Best in Show' winner."

"They all were... *Crabapple Pie*, *The Boat*, and *About a Girl*," Taylor said, "but they were pretty safe films, too."

"Arguably," Henry said. "But the same can't be said for his senior entry."

"There was no senior year film from your son in the festival," Sasha said. "I always found that odd."

"Indeed, it *was* odd," Henry said. "But there *was* a senior year entry by Peter in the school film festival. *Intolerance*."

"*Intolerance*?" Taylor asked.

Sasha shook her head, trying no doubt to reconcile things in her logical mind. "But, sir, there *was* no entry from Peter that year. The winning film that year was–"

"*Glory Ball*," Taylor recited, making no effort to hide the disdain in his voice. "A documentary about the school's championship-winning football team."

"You're right," Henry said, impressed by their knowledge of the school's film festival winners. "*Glory Ball* was the winner in 1996."

"My sister showed it to me," Sasha said. "It was nothing more than a propaganda film cut together by some cheerleaders."

"And a very popular one," Henry said. "At least amongst Coach Conklin and the football team."

"The same could be said for Sasha's sister," Taylor remarked, receiving a glare from Henry and an elbow in the ribs from Sasha.

"How did it win 'Best in Show' over this lost *Intolerance* film?" Sasha asked.

"Simply put, it won because *Intolerance* was disqualified from competition."

"Disqualified from competition?" Sasha repeated.

Henry shook his head, remembering it all too well. "You see, there was never any faculty supervision for the film festival. The movies were made in spare time, outside of school hours. Once or twice, kids would use the school as a set. Teenagers invariably make movies set in schools. But then there was my son, and Miss Cooper, and Max Leavitt."

"Who's Max Leavitt?" Sasha asked.

"One of Peter's closest friends when he was in school here. He and Max would spend hours upon hours putting off their homework, hatching ideas for a series of short ten-minute films, only a couple of which ever got made. *The World Hates Peter and Max*, as Peter called it. The gist of every short was the same: bad things happen to the boys. In my favorite one, Peter and Max played a cutthroat game of *Monopoly* and Max lost – and was forced to become Peter's indentured servant and was put through a menial series of assignments and chores, solely for Peter's amusement.

"Max came out his junior year. Mind you, this was the nineties. It was a different world back then, not that it's gotten much better now. Max's coming out garnered much grief for him and his family. For the most part, though, that trouble didn't come from his fellow classmates – only a small handful of them were outwardly hostile towards him about his sexuality. The trouble… that came from the adults; the community at large. And thus, *Intolerance* was born."

"What was it about?" Taylor asked softly.

"It's been years since I've seen the film. Not since after I re-watched it following the Spirit Week Film Festival in 1996. But it went something like this: two men meet at a gym and become good friends. They hang out all the time. Watch movies together. Go jogging together. Drink together. That sort of thing. Well, their friendship grows into something else.

"Someone in town – an officious little woman the type of which I'm sure you'd recognize – finds out about this and goes berserk. She holds a town meeting to run them out of town. The town is sickened and horrified by what is going on within their moral town.

"Then, one night, a storm hits. It starts to rain. There's thunder and lightning. The power is knocked out. Some of the townspeople decide God is punishing them for allowing these men to live in sin together. They form a mob and decide to storm the house the men now share together and demand they leave town that night, for the sake of humanity and whatnot. The mob arrives at the house, and there is an altercation. Max's character is beaten by a group of townspeople when he demands they leave his home. A torch gets knocked down and the house is set ablaze. Convinced they have no place in this world, the two men go back inside the burning house. And no one stops them. The end."

Sasha and Taylor stared wide-eyed at Henry, each wearing a look of shock greater than the one before them, with Taylor being the most blown away.

"Oh, my God. That's–" Sasha began.

"Unforgivable," Taylor whispered.

"How so?" Henry asked, still envisioning the final shot of that burning house in the rain.

"This Max guy pours his heart out about how he feels, living in a town that hates him, and gets told his story is 'unfit'. You ask me how that's unforgivable?"

Henry held up a hand to placate Taylor. "Oh, I quite agree with you, Taylor. It was unforgivable to censor that film."

"Yet you did just that," Taylor said. "Just like you're doing now."

"Taylor," Sasha began. "Our movie and that one, they're not in the same league."

"But they're both being censored for controversial content,"

Taylor said. "So what happened to your son's movie?"

"He knew it would never get shown if it were officially entered. So Peter submitted it disguised as of his *The World Hates...* shorts.

"Son of a bitch," Taylor whispered, smiling.

"Watch your language," Henry warned. "But, that *was* the general consensus when the faculty, Superintendant Williams, who was new to the district, members of the school board, and several parents saw *Intolerance* at that year's Spirit Week. They were *furious*. Not just with Max and Hannah and Peter, but with me."

"You?" Sasha asked.

"I was the director's father," Henry said. "Furthermore, I was his principal. I should've known what he was up to."

"There's no way you could've known," Taylor said.

"Do you think that really mattered to people like Madelyn Qualey and Belinda Neeson and Stella Lyons?"

"Is this the suspension Peter talked about in his 2001 interview with *Rolling Stone*?" Taylor asked. "The one that he said shaped his career?"

"I don't know if it shaped his career, but it created a rift between us that almost never closed," Henry said softly. "The school board and Superintendant Williams demanded that they be punished. All three of them. I made a case for Hannah – Miss Cooper – and Max, that they weren't involved in sneaking the movie into the playlist. No one cared. They wrote it. They produced it. They were in it. They were responsible."

"You suspended your own son and two of his friends for making a freaking *movie*?" Taylor said incredulously.

"One week," Henry said. He felt sick to his stomach just thinking about it. "For one week, Hannah Cooper, Maxwell Leavitt, and Peter Walczyk were forbidden to set foot in Cole Island High School. Their assignments were sent home to their parents, and they were to think about the horrible thing they had done."

"It still bothers you even now, doesn't it?" Sasha asked, leaning forward.

"Every time I see students like yourselves," Henry admitted, "students with real talent, being stifled because of a closed-minded community... Can I give you a piece of free advice?"

"Please," Taylor said softly.

"Find somewhere else to shoot your movie. That way, I can't say a word about its content." He gave them a moment to digest this before rising. "Now get back to class."

The three students rose and headed for the door. Taylor stopped, and turned.

"Yes, Taylor?" Henry asked.

"If you don't mind, can you tell your son I hope he's doing better?"

Henry felt a smile tug at the corners of his cheeks. "You think a lot of Peter, don't you?" Henry asked.

"He's an incredible writer and director, sir. I can't imagine movies without him. I'm just sorry that he's had to put up with so much crap from the press. Just tell him... tell him I hope he's all right."

Henry reached across the desk and picked up the red-covered script. "Do you mind if I show this to him?"

Taylor was silent a moment, staring wide-eyed at Henry. Finally, he smiled. "Please."

"Go on, now. You've missed enough class for one day."

Taylor filed out of the office. Henry flipped the script open and started reading a random page. A smile crept across his face. Despite what he was supposed to think, the script was actually quite good.

April shut the refrigerator door, pressing a bottle of water to her forehead, which was still glistening with sweat from her morning jog. Yet another jog that Walczyk had missed. The plan had been for Walczyk to join April on her morning jog, in an attempt to add the suggested structure to his days. However, he was still having difficulty sleeping without help, and had refused to go on sleeping pills, so April took pity on him and let him sleep in.

Dexter bounded around the corner, skidding to a halt. His little paws were still having a hard time navigating the slick wooden floor. April looked down at the white and tan beagle, who cocked his head in one direction and then the other, regarding her hopefully.

April was going to Augusta with Vic, and while she wanted to take Dexter with her, she did not want to become one of those monsters who lug their dogs all over creation, only to leave them locked up in their cars, panting for air and starving for attention.

"Sorry, Buddy, but Mumma's going on a trip with Uncle Vic" she told him. Dexter sat, tongue sliding in and out of his mouth, the illusion of a smile spread across his canine features. "You get to play with Walczyk today!" she cheered, glad that no one in Los Angeles could hear her talking baby talk to a dog. "Let's go take a shower! That'll cheer you up."

April had learned, way back in the days of the Meadowbrook Motel that she couldn't shower alone. Not with Dexter around. No sooner would she step into the stream of water than Dexter would sense this, know he was missing out on something really important, and absolutely *need* to be part of the scene. She discovered that it was easier, although a bit off-putting in the beginning, to simply bring the dog into the bathroom with her. She opened the bathroom door and patted her right leg, inviting the dog to come in with her. Once in there, he sat in the corner, tail swishing across the hardwood as she undressed and stepped into the shower.

The water, refreshingly cool on her skin, cascaded over her, wetting the tips of her blonde hair, which she noted was in need of trimming. She poked her head out the shower door, checking on Dexter. The dog was shaking his head furiously, one of April's bras clenched between his teeth. The white plastic hamper lie overturned on the floor, dirty laundry spilling out of it. *Aah, Dexter, the bra-sniffing dog,* she mused as she pulled her head back into the shower and finished washing up. She stepped out to find Dexter pouncing on her bra's foam-lined cups, denting one in. He then turned his attention to the other. The foam, however, would reform, restoring the first cup to its proper shape by the time he'd sunken the second cup. He would play this game back and forth until either he was quick enough to crush both cups or he'd have the bra taken away from him.

In this instance, the game ended with April bending over for the bra. "Give me that, you little pervert," she said, scratching under the dog's jaw with her hand before dressing.

April's phone rang on the counter across the room. April finished fastening her bra and reached over, picking up the phone. The caller ID read "Schueller Agency." She smiled, wondering why Eli was awake so early in the morning on the West Coast.

"Eli, you sexy fruit," she instantly said upon answering the phone. "What's up?"

However, it was not Elias Gaul calling.

Tears dribbled down Danielle's cheeks as she pushed,

screaming in agony as the doctor checked out everything below. Ethan held her hand, urging her to squeeze it when she needed to. Another contraction, and –

Walczyk hit pause on the remote, freezing the image, and reached across his bed for his notebook, scribbling a few notes into it. He resumed playback of the disc, and after a few more pushes, the canned sound of a baby crying filled the soundtrack. More than a few glances back and forth between Ethan and the newly minted mom and the screen faded to black and a slow, bluesy rendition of the Guns 'N Roses classic "Sweet Child O' Mine" by Eric Clapton began to play over the end credits. All in all, the episode – the eighth in the season's ten-episode run – hadn't been as dismal as he'd previously envisioned it to be. After all, it was the last episode that Walczyk had directed and written by himself for the series, entrusting the remaining two episodes to another director, Nathan Anderson. The episode's direction was rather lackluster, with a lot of static shots and inconsistent blocking. It was also weak in the story department, but there was little that could be done editorially, short of calling everyone back for a reshoot, which he knew the studio wouldn't go for. The shortcomings of his last ever episode of *Ordinary World* would have to be left alone, a notion which Walczyk did not relish. He felt it was lazy to present a story knowing there were problems with it, but he also knew that pieces of writing are like onions – they can make you cry and are impossible to peel just a little away from.

He'd just spun up episode 309, the first of two from recurring director (and recurring guest star) Jonathan Frakes. As he watched the opening credits for the umpteenth million time in his life, the names of the cast and crew forming out of falling raindrops against the Seattle cityscape, there was a knock at his bedroom door.

"Come in," he said, feeling nothing as his "created by" credit came up. April came in, hair damp, wearing her favorite red puffy vest and some dark blue jeans.

"Boss, it's almost noon. What are you doing still in bed?"

Walczyk pointed at the TV with the remote, pausing the video. A smile grew across April's face. "You're finally watching the season."

"Episode nine."

"Color me impressed. Though you could've used a jog this morning," she added, always giving him the needles about something.

"Coulda, shoulda, woulda," Walczyk said, tossing the remote down onto the bed. "What's up today?"

"Going to Augusta with Vic."

"Visiting John?" Walczyk asked. John Gordon had been moved into a nursing home by Vic and Andrew after he almost killed himself in a grease fire over ten years ago. Since then, Vic made a once a week trip to Augusta to visit his father, whose condition Vic told Walczyk was declining rapidly. Vic would always liken the odds of his father actually recognizing him to those of a craps game – you either throw a seven, or you don't. Since they'd begun their romance, April had been going with Vic to the nursing home, lending moral support, spending some quality time with Vic, and trying to get to know the man who raised Vic, Andrew and Angie on his own. Walczyk was always invited, but even before he himself spent time in an institution, he couldn't bear the notion of visiting a nursing home. All of those haunted-looking people tooling around in wheelchairs, wearing pajamas two sizes too big for them, with their empty eyes, drooling and gaping out into nothingness, no idea of who or where they were. These were the living dead as far as Walczyk was concerned, not the zombies that Marathon wanted to see on the big screen.

"How is he?" Walczyk asked. "Vic's not saying much about him lately."

"He's…" she thought carefully before finishing that statement. "He's not so well. I had to spend most of our last visit in the hall because he thought I was his ex-wife and he wouldn't stop cursing at me."

"April–" Walczyk said, getting out of bed.

"I know," she said, warding him off with a hand, "it's just how the disease makes his mind work. It's just… I hate seeing what it's doing to Vic and Andrew. These guys are supposed to be becoming their father's new best friends at this stage in their lives. But instead, they're having to hide their girlfriends from him and–"

"You're a girlfriend?" Walczyk said mischievously. April smiled in spite of herself.

"Oh, shut up!" she said, changing the subject. "Did you call the doctor in Augusta?"

"What doctor?"

"Dr. Woodward," April huffed. "The doctor we found for you online. Seriously, Walz, you need to call her. You're almost out of lithium."

"Can't you call?" Walczyk asked, pulling a T-shirt over his head.

"I've tried. Her office won't talk to me."

"You piss them off already?"

"No," she said. "They want *you* to set up the appointment."

Walczyk huffed. So much of this hospital stuff was stuff that the doctors insisted Walczyk do himself. No one understood that Walczyk didn't ask April to do these things for him because he was incapable of doing them, but because it was her function, as his assistant, to do them. "Fine," he said, grabbing his cell phone. "What's the number?"

"It's on the marker board on the fridge. And it's programmed into your phone. When you call, tell them you're just about out of lithium and that you need to see them ASAP."

"Okay," Walczyk said.

"And have your pill bottles with you when you call in case they ask the names and dosages of the drugs you're on."

"Gotcha."

April started for the door and turned. "You plan on going outside today?"

"Not really."

"Would you? Dexter will need to go out later. Maybe go for a walk with him? He doesn't enjoy watching TV as much as you do."

"I'll strongly consider it."

"What time did you wake up this morning?"

"Around ten-thirty."

This didn't seem to please her in the least bit. "Next week we're getting you up at nine. No excuses. You need to get back to normal with your sleep."

"April, I never got up at nine!"

"And that's not normal," April snapped. She was striking Walczyk as bossier than ever today. Something was off with her, he felt. He'd have to discuss it with her, but he wasn't going to open that can of worms just now. "Oh, and one more thing–"

Walczyk knew perfectly well what this "one more thing" was, but decided to hear her out, if for no other reason than he didn't want to antagonize the woman who was giving him his meds. "What's that, April?"

"I really think you should–"

"–start seeing a psychiatrist, I know," Walczyk finished. April had been on his back since the morning after he'd been discharged from Dirigo to see a psychiatrist as well as a medication management specialist. April, Hannah and his parents in fact. He suspected she'd have been on his case to see one during their ride back from Bangor to Cole Island if he'd been awake at all for any of the one hundred sixteen mile drive back home. He was growing increasingly aware of April's attempts to make him more self-reliant lately – leaving him alone nights while sleeping over at Vic's apartment, urging him to start structuring his day on his own, and, of course, pushing him to get back to work on *Night*, which she felt he'd made a respectable start on. But the shrink thing, that was her driving ambition it seemed.

"No," she replied, crossing her arms. "Actually, I was going to say I think you should call Sara."

"I'd rather start seeing a psychiatrist," Walczyk said, searching the bed for his notepad and pen.

"Clever," April said.

"Why the hell does everyone want me to call Sara?"

"I don't know about *everyone else*, but personally, she's driving me nuts. Forever calling me to see how you're doing. Asking personal questions."

"You're my assistant," he reminded her. "You deal with my contacts from the public at large."

"Public at large? That's how you refer to your wife now?"

"*Estranged* wife," he stressed, collecting his pens and his notebook. "And I could call her *much* worse."

"So, what are you going to do?"

"Well, first I'm going to evacuate my bladder. Then I'm going to have some Honey Comb and watch these last two episodes, then probably evacuate my bladder again," Walczyk said. "Is that enough structure?"

"It's a start," she said, moving for the door. "Get you anything in Augusta?"

"Yeah," Walczyk said, stepping into his slippers.

"What's that?" April asked, turning in the doorway.

"Answers."

"Answers?"

"Yeah. Specifically, why my best friend is avoiding me."

"Again with the avoiding?" April shifted her stance, moving her weight from one foot to the other. Her tell. Everyone had their tell. Ian rubbed his nose. Sara always gave too much eye contact. Hannah, well, Hannah always stared through you at the wall behind you. April's was a bit more subtle, but still easily detectible to the trained eye. April shifted her weight from one foot to the other. She also tended to repeat the last couple of words of a sentence. It was so obvious. "Boss, we've been through this. Vic's just been busy. He's not–"

"April," Walczyk said, his shoulders dropping. "Don't play these bullshit games with me. You know something's up. Vic has been avoiding me like the plague. If it's something I did–"

"You didn't do anything," she said, shifting her weight from one foot to the other. "And Vic isn't ignoring you. He's just been... distracted. Believe me, if he had a beef with you, he'd have told me by now. Look, are you sure this just isn't related to the depression? Or the bipolar? Dr. Lentz did say that–"

"Don't blame this on my sick mind," Walczyk said. "I'm sure if you asked Hannah, she'd come up with the same conclusion. Vic is avoiding me. And on the odd occasion we are in the same room together, he's, I don't know, stand-offish with me. The conversation rarely strays from the weather or the Red Sox. Which is telling in itself, since Vic knows I can't stand baseball."

"There you go," April said, pointing a finger at him. "'My sick mind.' Walczyk, when you say shit like that, it makes things so difficult."

"Sorry," Walczyk said, feeling guilty. "I didn't know my being sick made everyone so uncomfortable."

April rolled her eyes. "There you go again. Boss, if you insist on playing the victim, you're going to get treated like one."

"So Vic thinks I'm acting like a victim."

"No! He thinks you're acting like an invalid!"

The words stung Walczyk. He heard them come out of April's mouth, but it was surely Vic speaking. *An invalid.*

"Look, I've got to get going. Now when I get back, the three of us – you, me, and Vic – are going to sit down and talk this out. Like we should have from the get-go."

"Drive safely," Walczyk said, putting on a false cheer. April put her hands on Walczyk's shoulders, stepped up on her tiptoes, and gave Walczyk a kiss on the cheek.

"Thanks," she said, stepping back. "Now you get on that damned phone. Dr. Woodward or Sara, I don't care who. But someone has to get a phone call from you today!"

She headed out the door and down the stairs, calling out behind her, "And if you're having cereal for breakfast, please don't have it for lunch too!"

Once April was gone, an instant loneliness descended upon Walczyk. He'd felt alone for some time now as far as April and Vic were concerned. Walczyk felt there had been a distance from Vic ever since he returned to Cole Island, and lately that distance had seeped into his relationship with April, too. He'd wondered if she wanted out. After all, as his mother reminded him not long ago, she was hired to be the assistant of one of Hollywood's golden boys, not some mentally ill guy from southern Maine.

Walczyk opened his closet door and stared blankly at the clothes within. As he wondered whether or not he wanted to wear his navy blue Dr. Zoidberg T-shirt or his black *Dracula* one, his phone rang. Seeing who was calling on the display screen, he answered with, "Hey, Dad. What's up?"

"I'll never get used to that," his father said.

"What?"

"This caller ID. You know who I am before I even get to say 'hello.' I don't like it."

"Sorry. What's shaking?"

"Nothing. Do you have lunch plans?"

"Mum's coming over around noon probably. But she does that every day."

"Think you could ask her for a rain check? I'd like you to come down to the school and have lunch with me. I've got something I want to discuss with you."

"Sure," Walczyk said, thrown. "I was just about to hop into the shower."

"Okay. Good. First lunch starts at 11:30."

The line went dead after that tidbit of information. Like April, his father was never one to end a call with "See you later" or "Goodbye" even. Walczyk got up, went back to the closet, and pulled out the *Dracula* shirt. He had a feeling this was going to be an interesting afternoon.

Forty-five minutes later, Walczyk stepped into Cole Island High School, suddenly wondering if this was such a good idea. He felt very self conscious, walking through the halls, people turning to stare as he passed by. Walczyk poked his head inside the main office looking for his father and, after a great deal of interrogation about his health and how he was treated in the "mental hospital," he thankfully caught his father walking by.

"Peter," his father said, clapping a hand on his son's shoulder. "Just in time." His father led them out of the office and down the hallway, toward the cafeteria. As the two Walczyks walked through the hallway, students all around them pointed and whispered.

"Peter Walczyk, what a welcome surprise," a familiar voice called out from behind them. Walczyk turned to see his old English teacher, Stella Lyons, standing there, arms opened wide.

"Stella, how've you been?" Walczyk asked, his voice laced with an artificial airiness as he stepped forward, stooped down, and hugged the old woman.

"Fair to middling," she said, bearing the same fake courtesy in her tone. "And you? I understand you've had some health troubles lately. Thank God you're mending. How are you faring?"

"I'm breathing, productive, and happy," Walczyk said, honestly. "There's little more I can ask for."

"So glad to hear it," Stella said, her demeanor changing suddenly. "Well, I don't have time to stick around and chat. Do take care of yourself, Peter." Stella grunted in her principal's direction before waddling on down the hall. Walczyk and his father continued their way to the cafeteria.

"Did you just hug Stella Lyons?" his father asked in a hushed tone.

"Peter hugged Stella?" Hannah asked, coming up behind them and joining them in line. "I don't believe it."

"Believe it, kid. I've returned to the darkest depths of schmoozing," Walczyk said, wiping at his arms.

"So what brings you to the cafeteria today? April forbid you from having cereal for breakfast *and* lunch?" Hannah asked.

Walczyk gave her a short, forced laugh. "Actually, I was thinking of re-enrolling. I hear that one of the English teachers is a real hottie."

"Stop it," she said, reddening as she looked around to make

sure they weren't overheard.

"So," his father asked, "how has your day gone, Hannah?"

"Surprisingly good. Third period actually seemed prepared for their *Silas Marner* quiz."

"Thank goodness for small miracles," Walczyk said, stepping up to the lunch window. On the other side, wearing matching plastic aprons, were the Donnelly twins, Donna and Deanna. Four years in high school and Peter could never tell them apart. He'd just adopted the clever habit of calling both of them "Dee."

Donna (or was it Deanna?) looked up from her steam table. "Peter Walczyk! How are you doing, honey?"

"Oh, I'm doing okay, thanks. How are you doing, Dee?"

"You know, same old, same old. What can I get you today?"

The cook's steam table held a mixture of some kind of curly pasta mixed in with tomatoes and onions, something that looked suspiciously like Campbell's chicken noodle soup, and a large rectangular sheet of golden brown pepperoni pizza. Things hadn't changed much in this cafeteria since his days of standing in line fifteen years ago.

"I'll have the macaroni and tomatoes, please," Walczyk finally said.

Donna (or Deanna) filled the tray with a generous portion said, then looked up, and smiled. "Sorry to hear about your being sick."

"Thanks," Walczyk said, awkwardly, taking his tray.

"Didn't you buy the old Merry place?"

"I did. Figured if I didn't act now, there wouldn't be a decent space left to buy when I was in the market for a summer home."

"Well, you take care, sweetie," she said, and Walczyk moved down the line, saying hello to the other "Dee" before moving to the milk cooler.

Letting his father take the lead, Walczyk was led to a table in the corner, by the flag. This was, in his day, where the shop kids always sat for lunch. His father and Hannah sat down, and Walczyk put his tray on the table and plopped down in his seat. He felt every eye in the cafeteria on him as he sat down at one of the low-rise cafeteria tables with his father and Hannah, wondering if he'd gotten fatter or if kids had gotten smaller. He dug in, the simple mixture of macaroni and stewed tomatoes still as delicious as it had been all those years go. Looking up, he noticed he was being watched by one group of students in particular. "What's up with those kids?" Walczyk finally asked, pointing with his fork over Hannah's shoulder.

"Who?" Hannah asked. "Taylor Hodges and his friends?"

"If he's the one with the big ears and the bowl haircut, then yeah, Taylor and company," Walczyk said.

"They're the business I want to discuss," the principal said.

"How's that?" Walczyk asked, his mouth full.

"They are the school's current filmmakers," his father said, folding the little cardboard spout of his milk back in before putting the empty cardboard carton on his tray. "I think it's safe to say that the two of you, along with Max Leavitt and a couple others, were the driving force behind filmmaking at this school during your time here."

"And, if I remember correctly, we were also the death of that particular after-school activity, too," Walczyk said bluntly. "Well, with the help of a certain venom-spewing poison dwarf. Well, she and a father-for-a-principal who had no compunctions about suspending his own son just for making a controversial little movie."

"Been holding that in a while?" Dad asked.

"There's just some things you don't say during an Emmy Award acceptance speech," Walczyk said.

"Look, both of you, I never told you how much I hated having to suspend you two. If I had it to do over again, I think I might have–"

"No, Dad, I'm glad you suspended me," Walczyk said.

"You are?" Hannah asked. "Frankly, I could've used a little less drama my final three months here."

"Yeah. I learned a lot from that experience. What battles to fight and what battles to pass on. That sometimes, as a filmmaker, you answer to a higher authority. And that sometimes, the mythos surrounding a controversial film can make more of an impact than the film itself might have."

His father smiled. "Does that mean you've forgiven me?"

"Hell, no," Walczyk said, smirking.

"Over the years, unofficial film clubs have sprouted up, none of them school sanctioned. Headed up by different cliques of students, with various levels of talent. Most of these were amateur stunt reels, like that *Jackass* show or someone making music videos out of footage of kids drinking, doing drugs and flashing gang signs at parties. Trifling things with no artistic merit, but troublesome enough that when I came across them, I had to confiscate them and call parents in."

"Then why not just sanction a film club, appoint a faculty advisor, and supervise what they're doing?" Walczyk asked.

"Because certain members of the community have found ways to encourage the school board to take preventative measures."

Hannah put her fork down. "Peter, these kids... I've seen some of their work in my class. They're incredibly talented kids."

Walczyk's father reached into a manila envelope he'd been carrying and removed what looked to be a screenplay. He slid it across the table to Walczyk and Hannah. "What's this?" Walczyk asked. He picked up the red-covered script, opening it up and looking over a couple of scenes. The formatting was spot-on. The dialogue sharp and the scene descriptions mercifully brief, but informative. Walczyk turned to the inside cover, reading the title page aloud. *"Coach Conklin.* As in our Coach Conklin?"

"Coach Conklin as in Frank is not amused," his father said a wry smile crossing his face. "Hell, he's screaming for the heads of all involved."

Walczyk smiled, liking the material that much more. He flipped to the inside cover and read aloud: "Written by Taylor J. Hodges and Sasha Connary. Directed by Taylor J. Hodges." Walczyk looked up at his father, then Hannah. "This is by those film kids?" His father's nod spoke volumes. Walczyk returned to the script, opening up to a bookmarked passage. The scene, set in an empty locker room, burst to life with two characters, a cheerleader and her football player boyfriend, making love in the showers, tearing away clothes with wild abandon. While in the throes of their passion, a figure approached. A figure wearing a clear plastic rain poncho over a varsity jacket crept up behind them, murdering them and leaving their bloodied, half-naked bodies in the steamy shower. As he turned away, the name on the jacket became clear – Coach Conklin.

When he was done, Walczyk looked up at his father. "The story's a bit amateurish, but so is half of the stuff April sends across my desk." He looked back at the script again, his smile growing. "Actually, I take it back. This is better than some of the stuff that comes across my desk. Pretty damned good, in fact." He closed the script and rolled it up in his hands. "So, you need me to help them? Like fund it or something?"

"No, nothing like that. I think making it on their own will be an invaluable learning experience. I'm just thinking that Taylor might benefit from a little sage advice from his idol."

"Idol?"

"This kid worships you, Peter," his father said. Hannah was nodding in agreement by the time Walczyk turned to look at her. "I'm not talking an internship or anything big. Just sit down with the kid sometime. Talk to him about his script."

"Look, if you want me to dissuade him from making a violent, edgy film–"

"I have no say in his film, editorially. It's not a school project. There are certain things I can't allow him to shoot on school property, but if he finds a way to shoot it away from the school, what can I do?"

"Then what do you want? You're not saving this kid from Frank Conklin and Stella Lyons because you have a big heart and a lot of regrets over having shit-canned a controversial film in the past."

"Watch your language," his father said. "And no, I'm not. Let's just say I'd like to see my son involved in something that demands more of him than just putting dialogue to an outline of a movie he never wanted to write in the first place or looking at videos of episodes of a TV show he wants nothing more to do with. I'd like to see him help someone else and, in the process, himself."

"I'm not starting some after-school club for misfit filmmakers now," Walczyk stressed, rolling the *Coach Conklin* script up. "Can you picture me, twenty or so film club wannabes, and Hannah as a faculty advisor hunkered down in the library, going over what makes a good film?"

"I never expected you to go that far," his father said. "And, honestly, I don't think that would be such a good idea."

"Why not?" Hannah asked. "This school has no outlet for the creative arts. Not since the theatre department was torpedoed following the disaster that was the Class of 2005's senior variety show."

"Peter's just barely out of the hospital, Hannah. He's not up to something like that. Given time, I might be able to get behind him reorganizing the Masquers. But for now–"

"For now," Walczyk said, "I think I've been strong-armed into mentoring the *next* Peter Walczyk."

"You need to start spending some time with Walczyk," April said, reaching for her blue towel as she stepped out of Vic's shower, water trickling down her back.

"I do?" Vic asked, quickly and a tad defensively, as he dried himself with his favorite orange towel. "I sat and talked with you guys for about five or ten minutes the other day when you came into the restaurant."

"Vic," April said, sliding the towel down her legs, "that's not *time*. And that certainly wasn't with him. It was with me. He just happened to be in the booth with me."

"April," Vic protested, "I spend time with Walczyk."

"When's the last time you were over at the house?"

He thought. "I was over just Monday night."

"You showed up at ten, barely said three words to him and came into my room."

"Look, if you'd rather me not come over, I won't."

"I'd rather you acknowledge your sick friend who needs your support right now" April said, grabbing her clothes from on top of the clothes dryer that sat in the far corner of the bathroom. "Look, Vic, I don't want to nag–"

"Then don't."

"It's just that he said something to me this morning."

"What?"

"He said that you haven't been around as much lately. His feelings were obviously hurt."

Vic quietly pulled a pair of clean boxers from the clothes dryer. "April, it's just–"

"I'm trying not to chastise you, Victor. I'm just saying that your best friend feels like he's losing touch with you."

"April, that's bullshit. He's not losing touch with me."

"I'm not saying you are or you aren't. I'm just saying that right now, in his current mindset, that's how he sees it." She saw Vic roll his eyes as he slid his boxers up. "Vic… I'm serious."

"I know you are."

"He's fragile right now. He's readjusting to life. He feels a lot of pressure on himself to be better."

"I'm not telling him to be better."

"I never said you were."

Vic pulled on his pants. "I do think he's got something more important than me to focus on right now."

"Like what?"

"Like getting better. April, he's been through hell. He's

changed. He's a different person. He's not the guy who dragged you here to Cole Island. Hell, he's not the guy who married Sara. And that bipolar basket case is *certainly* not the guy I grew–"

The crack was deafening. After she'd done it, April couldn't believe she'd hit Vic. She did not believe in violence. She had never hit anyone before in her life. The red imprint of her hand remained on Vic's face, however, remained as proof that she just had.

"What was that for?" he screamed, putting a hand to his cheek.

"You piece of shit," April muttered, pulling her T-shirt down over her head. She snatched her hoodie from on top of the dryer and headed out of the bathroom.

"Where are you going?" Vic called out, following April as she stormed towards the front door.

"I'm going home!"

Vic's shoulders sagged. "April!"

"No," she said, sliding her sneakers on. "You don't want me in your bed tonight."

Vic exhaled loudly, sighing. "Come on, April. I didn't mean it!"

She zipped her hoodie. "You certainly *did* mean it, Victor John Gordon. And it makes me sick to my stomach that you said it!"

"Babe, I've been under a lot of stress lately."

"And I haven't? *Babe?*"

"You don't understand. This whole bipolar thing… it's not easy for me to deal with."

"Oh," she said. "It's hard for you? Vic, I'm sorry. I never realized, I guess, because it's been such a picnic for Hannah and me and Henry and Diane. And Walczyk… wow, it's been his excuse to finally get away from it all!"

"April!"

"Vic, don't call me until you have something intelligent to say to me."

She slid the glass patio door open and stepped out into the light drizzle. Barefoot, Vic followed her out onto the deck.

"April, I'm sorry!"

"You said that," she called out, not looking back.

"Look, what do you want from me? I said something stupid. Something… nasty. Unforgivable. And I'm sorry about it."

She quickly turned. "Sorry because you feel like shit about it?"

Vic's eyes avoided hers, staring at the dark, damp grass instead. She climbed a couple of stairs, the drizzle trickling down her face. She looked into Vic's piercing blue eyes, she saw remorse. "Come back inside?" he asked. "It's really crappy outside right now."

She considered it. She did not want to leave things like this. She didn't believe in going to bed angry. She didn't believe in driving away angry, though she often did it. And she didn't want to be alone tonight, which is what she'd be if she took off.

Bipolar basket case.

The phrase stuck in her head. It rang loud every time she looked at him, standing there like a scolded child. But she couldn't forgive it.

"It's really crappy inside right now, too," April said, and continued to go down the stairs toward the Jeep.

CHAPTER TWENTY-FOUR
THE BLAME GAME

"What makes you think your father is up to anything?" Diane Walczyk asked from the stove, where she tended two grilled cheese sandwiches. Lately, Peter had been a touch paranoid about things, especially where his friend Vic was concerned. He'd been feeling a lot of anxiety about abandonment as well.

"Because something's up and I know I'm not paranoid," Peter said, fishing the two liter bottle of Diet Coke out of the fridge. He noted the label. "Caffeine free, Mum?"

"I read this article online about bipolar disorder and food," she said, inching the sandwiches around the inside of the fry pan. "It said that sugary foods like chocolate or those silly breakfast cereals you like, or foods with a lot of caffeine, can actually make you quite manicky."

"And just how's that a bad thing?" Peter quipped. Lately, he'd seemed to be slipping back into a depressive state. April said he was sleeping a lot more. Henry had told her that he heard from Hannah that Peter was becoming cranky and argumentative, being especially harsh on April and even snapping at Hannah for misplacing some absurdly overpriced remote control. This all worried Diane, as Dr. Lentz had never mentioned rising anger when he briefed them on what to expect.

She made a mental note that, after Peter left, she'd have to do some internet research on anger issues connected with bipolar disorder. Diane had marked the decline in Walczyk's mood in the journal she'd been keeping on the family computer, notating his highs and lows, trying to find some discernable pattern to all of it. So far, there was none.

"Well, we want you in a happy medium," she said, flipping the sandwiches again over the low heat of the gas stovetop. "Besides, Dr. Lentz did say that a good diet was one of the keys to equilibrium."

She removed the frying pan from the fire and brought the sandwiches to the table, sliding one of them from the frying pan onto Peter's plate.

"Thank you," he said. He bowed his head, saying a quick silent prayer, then looked back up, taking a drink from his soda. "I was wondering if you could take me to Augusta."

"Of course," she answered, a bit surprised. He must have wanted to get off the island; he hadn't been off Cole Island since his time at the Dirigo Psychiatric Hospital. This was a good sign, as far as she was concerned. "What did you have in mind? Finally decide on a doctor?"

"Not quite," Walczyk said, reaching for the bag of chips at the center of the table. "I need to get a car."

"A car," she said warily, putting down her sandwich.

"Yeah. I was looking at the new Ford Fusion online."

"Okay," she slowly said. "We can discuss it."

Peter looked up at her a moment, studying her. "Uh, Mum, there's nothing to discuss. I'm getting a car."

"Peter, isn't this a little hasty?" He shifted in his chair, his temper bubbling beneath the surface. "I'm not trying to tell you what to do – you're a grown man, after all. But I'm just worried that–"

"That what?" he asked, sounding a touch agitated.

"Well, honestly, that you're doing this in an attempt to make yourself feel better!"

"I'm doing this," he said, clearly controlling himself, "because I need a car. You have a fit whenever I borrow April's Jeep, and I can't get Vic to talk to me, let alone borrow his truck. Mum, I can't be footbound for the rest of my life. I need a car."

"Peter, you can always borrow our car," she said, feeling nervous. *Is this a sign of the way things are going to be now?* she asked herself. *Filling with fear and nervousness every time I disagree with my son?*

"What's so wrong with me getting my own car?" he asked. "It's not like I can't afford it."

"I know," she said, hoping to calm him down. "It's not that. It's just... it's a big purchase. And you're just mentioning it today."

"You mean your little network of spies hasn't reported back to you that I've been talking about getting a car since I got back home."

"Peter, that's not fair," she said, feeling guilty for employing Hannah and April to keep her apprised about her son's health condition. "But in all truth, I *do* have to rely on April and Hannah to tell me how you're doing, because you don't tell me anything."

"How I'm doing," Peter said. "I'll tell you how I'm doing. I'm miserable. I can't write. I can't read. I can't watch TV. I have *zero* time alone any more. I've got Hannah living on the couch, smothering the hell out of me. April's ordering me around like a drill sergeant. I've got Vic... well, I *had* Vic acting like nothing had changed. And then there's you and Dad, always–" Peter stopped, stared at her a moment, then returned to his meal, taking a drink.

"'Me and Dad always' what?" Diane ventured.

"Nothing. Forget it. I'm just being cruel. It's... you're right, it's just the depression."

They returned to their lunch, quietly eating their sandwiches and drinking their iced teas. The extent of their conversation for the remainder of the meal was requests to pass the bag of chips back and forth across the table. It was driving Diane mad. She hated the awkward silence. After lunch had been finished and they'd stared at every wall in the kitchen, Diane picked up the dishes and put them in the sink. She pulled out a plastic dish pan and filled it with water and soap, and began washing the dishes. Peter eventually got up and reached inside the drawer under the counter, pulling out a dish wiper.

"Uh, uh," she said, preemptively. "Wash your hands first." She didn't know if her stopping him would set him off again, or if it would simply wash over him. Peter put the towel down on the counter and gave her a look, half rolling his eyes, half smiling. *He's trying*, she realized. *He is trying to climb out from under this darkness.* She smiled back at him, and then threw the dish cloth into the pan. "To heck with it. Let's leave them." She pulled out his chair at the table, and he sat. She sat down beside him. The silence consumed them again, but it was not as uncomfortable this time. The lonesome cooing of one o'clock being struck on the loon clock Henry's mother had given her as a birthday present broke the silence. She wrapped her hands around her son's right arm, and leaned in, placing her head on his shoulder.

"I think it's my fault," she said softly.

After a moment, she could feel Peter looking down at her. "What do you mean, 'your fault?' Mum, I'm just in a lousy mood. It's nothing that anyone–"

"No, not the bad moods," she said. She contemplated ending the conversation, knew it was time she said it to someone. "I have to tell you something."

"What?" Peter asked, taking her hand and giving it a squeeze.

"As you know, I had two miscarriages before I had Melanie. During my pregnancies with you and Melanie, I took a hormone called Provera, on the suggestion of my doctor, who believed it would prevent miscarriage. As you are probably unaware, Provera is no longer used for this purpose, since it has the potential to cause birth defects, especially cleft palate. When you were a toddler, I wondered if the hormone might have caused your hyperactivity and mood swings, but it didn't seem to affect Melanie that way. Then you were diagnosed with bipolar disorder–"

"–and you started questioning Provera again," Peter finished.

"Yes. Peter, if it was something I took when I was pregnant with you–"

Peter reached out and took his mother's hand, squeezing it. "Mum, I seriously doubt that Provera caused my bipolar disorder. April has done a lot of research on her own, and what she's found leads me to believe it's not something you develop, so much as something you inherit."

"Inherit? But no one else in the family has bipolar disorder."

"That we know of. But there's Aunt Harriet's family. I'm not trying being funny here, but there's something off with all of them: Leah the kleptomaniac, Christopher the moody unemployed artist, Maggie the sex addict… any one of them, or perhaps all three of them, could be diagnosed bipolar. And then there's Robert."

"My God, Robert." Diane had never considered Robert Aaron. Not as proof that bipolar disorder could be inherited. But looking at Robert in context, it all made perfect sense. Diane's nephew Robert was a depressed young man. His parents, her Cousin Harriet's daughter

Elyse and her husband John, never used the word 'depression;' Robert was just 'sick.' Robert's 'sickness' would grow so severe that he have to would drop out of school for periods of time, being home schooled by his mother. By some small miracle, Robert graduated high school and had started attending the University of Maine's Presque Isle campus, but couldn't cut it. His 'sickness' had grown too severe, and he dropped out, moving back home after an abysmal first semester. Late one cold February morning, Robert was found by the local sheriff, frozen to death, having gone for a swim in nearby Lake Conlin. Robert Aaron was nineteen.

"And that's just your side of the family. What about Dad's uncle Mickey? The one who ran away from home when he was fifteen?"

"Yes," Diane said, seeing the pieces of the puzzle tumble into place in her mind's eye. "Last anyone in the family had heard from Mickey was 1981, and he was going by the name Michael Wallace. Now that you bring it up, I've always wondered about your aunt Catherine and Uncle Stewart sometimes."

"So, you see," Peter said, smiling, "it's not your fault."

"No," Diane said, thinking it over. "I guess it's not."

"You don't sound relieved."

"Well, I'm not. Not completely."

"Why not?"

"I don't know," she replied, honestly. "Maybe part of me wanted it to be my fault."

"Why would you want that?"

"Well, if it was my fault, then it was nothing anyone else did wrong. If I were to blame for it, then there was a reason for it, and it was not just a fluke. If I was the reason you had bipolar, then it's not God's fault.

"Mum, listen to me," Peter said, looking her in the eyes. "My illness is *no one's* fault. Do you understand me? Prenatal drugs or family histories or divine intervention – it doesn't matter. What's done is done. I can't spend the rest of my life playing 'what if?' with this. I've got a sickness. Fact. I'm going to learn to live with this. Fact. I'm not going to waste my time trying to assign blame or figure out why I have it. I've got enough to do, trying to learn to live with it, to worry about the cause."

"When did you grow up?" Diane asked, admiring her son's

bravery and resolve.

"I think it was somewhere in between making movies and marrying a lesbian."

"You're right," she laughed. "It's not my fault. Not with all those crazy uncles and aunts." She and Peter laughed long and hard about that, finally falling into a bemused silence.

"Whatcha thinking about?" Peter asked after a while, looking into her eyes. The same hazel eyes she had.

"I had never before been as scared as I was when I found out you had this illness. Not when your Grandmother Reynolds's M.S. progressed to the point where she no longer remembered her family. Not when your aunt Lynn was diagnosed with breast cancer. Not even when *I* had been diagnosed. It was scary, and troubling, to see my mother and sister suffer like they did, and it was life changing to know that there was cancer growing within me. It tested my faith, but you know what, it also strengthened it somehow; God would see us all through, whether it meant they lived here on Earth with us or with Him up in Heaven.

"But your illness... how do they put it? 'This time it's personal?' Some unseen force was messing with my baby boy, and I sure as hell wasn't going to sit back and take it." She saw a smile cross Peter's face. "I'll tell you, I questioned whether or not God was testing me. Perhaps He was. Life, after all, is a series of tests."

"Maybe He's testing both of us," Peter said.

"Could be," his mother said smiling at him.

"Someday we'll figure out why, I guess. For now, I just have to take it on faith that there *is* a reason."

"Maybe it's so you can write about your ordeal. Share it with others who don't have the love and support that you have."

"You really think someone's going to read a book about a screenwriter with bipolar disorder?"

He was such a brave boy. Here he was, his entire life falling apart at his fingertips, first losing his wife, then receiving such a life-changing diagnosis, and he was taking it all in stride, with an almost calm wisdom about him. "So, what time do you want to leave for Augusta tomorrow?" she asked.

Vic's main problem was that $15,334.71 and $29,043.32 did not even closely equal $54,765.63.

"Son of a bitch," he cursed, throwing the calculator across the desk in the cramped little office wedged between the freezer and the back wall of the Barrelhead's back room.

"Problems, Chief?"

Vic looked up. Ingrid was standing over him, her curly, dirty blonde hair piled on top of her head and held in place with a couple of number two pencils.

"Nothing a good bottle of gin can't handle," he said, pushing away from the desk. "What's up?"

"The schedule's a mess."

Vic swore, winding his pen across the desk after the calculator.

"Don't get bent out of shape. I think I fixed it."

"How's that?" he asked, leaning back in his rolling office chair.

"Well, you scheduled McKenzie to open on Thursday, but she can't open Thursdays–"

"–because her grandmother can't watch Ricardo," Vic suddenly remembered.

"Which is fine, Vic, because Amy *can* work Thursday mornings."

"Do it," Vic said.

"Except that puts Amy at forty-one hours for the week."

"And she doesn't want to work forty-one?"

"April said something about keeping everyone under thirty-five hours so that we don't upset the–"

"April's not here anymore," Vic said. "After breaks, that'll put Amy at what? Thirty-eight hours? Fine. We'll take care of it next week."

Ingrid sat on the corner of Vic's desk. "Where did Miss Congeniality go?"

"She's not here anymore," he repeated. "What time is it?"

"Four-thirty."

Vic looked up at Ingrid. As bleary and worn down and washed out as he felt, Ingrid was just the opposite. She'd been there since ten in the morning, and her blue eye shadow and dark red lipstick were still impeccable. If she was feeling any fatigue, it wasn't showing, either in her posture or under her eyes. And her attitude... she was a real trooper.

"I suppose it's too early to get a drink," Vic ventured.

"Uh, you told me to make sure you don't drink on the job anymore."

"Why would I do a stupid thing like that?"

"Because it's unprofessional."

"I got a big mouth."

"And an even bigger heart," she said, rubbing his weary neck. "A shame it's broken right now."

"Oh, no," Vic said, standing up from his chair, moving away from her soft hands.

"What?"

"You don't get to hit on me if I don't get to have a drink."

"You saying you need a drink to handle me hitting on you?"

"I'm saying I need a drink to keep from falling for your hitting on me."

She thought about it. "Vic, that makes absolutely no sense."

"Then a drink won't hurt."

"What happened?"

"You don't want to hear about me and April."

"Yes, I do."

"No, you really don't."

"What happened, Vic?"

He plopped back down in his chair, and gestured for her to come in. She stepped forward another foot, and the door to the office swung shut behind her. Ingrid sat on the corner of the desk.

"Something very stupid was said," Vic said after a silent moment, not looking up at Ingrid.

"It generally is during a break-up."

"But this something stupid was the *reason* for the break-up."

"Oh," she said, nodding, as if understanding exactly what had happened.

"Something I..." He never finished the thought. Instead, he smacked himself in the forehead.

"Hey!" she cried out, reaching forward to grab Vic's hand. Once she'd stopped it from inflicting any more damage upon himself, she continued to hold his hand. "Don't do that. You'll give yourself a headache!"

Vic didn't want to repeat it. It was bad enough he kept thinking it, but to say it again, that would mean that it really happened. That he'd really said it. That he'd really felt that way. "You know

Walczyk's been sick."

"He's been in that mental hospital in Bangor, yeah."

"*Psychiatric hospital.* Well, that night I went to visit him in there, all he's talking about is bipolar this and manic depressive that. Then he gets pissed at me for saying that Brad Folmer was a head case."

"Well, Brad Folmer *was* a head case," Ingrid confirmed.

"I know! But it's like I can't say anything around either of them anymore without offending him or pissing her off. So screw it."

Ingrid was quiet. She just continued holding his hand. "Care for some friendly advice?"

"From you? Always."

"I think you're making too much out of this. There was this one time I was talking about Casey German and I called her a 'loopy dyke' to Jen Provencher. Then months go by and I don't hear from Casey. She used to e-mail me every week. Call every other. And suddenly nothing. Time wore on and we stopped talking each other. I had been the maid of honor at her freaking lesbian wedding, and now we weren't even speaking. I felt so guilty for calling her that. Then, finally, one day, I find out that her Dad died in a car wreck. I so felt awful. So I screwed up my courage and texted her and just said that I was sorry about her Dad. Within a minute, the phone rings. It's Casey. We talked and cried and laughed and cried some more for almost three hours. And you wanna know the kicker? It'd never even gotten back to her that I'd called her a loopy dyke. Almost a year of not talking to one of my best girlfriends from high school, all because I felt guilty about something I said and never even meant."

"So you're saying–?"

"I'm saying, Victor John, that you really shouldn't wait for something else bad to happen to Peter Walczyk before you make things right."

Vic smiled, bowed his head, and kissed Ingrid's hand. He looked up into those heavily made-up blue eyes and saw the warm soul that so many people on this stupid podunk island never saw in Ingrid Connary.

A knock at the door shook him out of his reverie. "Come in," he called out, letting go of Ingrid's hand. It was his brother, Andrew.

"What's up, Andrew?"

"You've got a visitor out front."

"Is it April?"

"Nope," Andrew said, turned, and left the office. Not all that strange. Andrew was never big on conversation. Which was curious, considering he was seeing a girl who was paid to flap her gums on TV for the greater Southern Maine and New Hampshire viewing region.

"I'll let you go," Ingrid said. "Besides I have to go tell McKenzie that everything's taken care of with the schedule."

"Yeah," Vic said, standing. "Tell her I'm sorry about the screw up, and that I'll make sure it doesn't happen again."

"You're such a good boss," Ingrid said, smiling.

"And don't you forget it," Vic replied. Ingrid puckered her red lips and Vic leaned forward, kissing her quickly. She smiled, spun on her heel, and left the office.

What the hell are you doing, Vic? He asked himself as he stepped out of the office, shutting the door behind him before.

In the dining room, standing by the front door, was Diane Walczyk. Vic's throat instantly tightened. Diane had never come in alone, and he doubted she had come in for the daily special. He forced a smile onto his face and crossed the room.

"Diane," he called out. "How've you been?"

"Fine," she said, curtly. "Is there somewhere we can talk?"

"Sure," he said, indicating the table by the front window, looking down over the beach. Diane followed Vic over and sat, facing the window. Vic slid into the booth opposite her. "What's wrong? Is it Peter?" She opened her mouth to speak and stopped. She chewed at her bottom lip, just like Walczyk did when he was lost in thought. "Diane, is something wrong with Peter?" he repeated.

"Yes," she snapped, then, as if she was taken aback by her own ferocity, breathed in deeply and continued in a softer tone. "He's miserable, Vic."

Vic felt himself short of breath. He drew in deeply, restoring air to his lungs. "Miserable?"

"Yes."

"Why's that?"

"Because his best friend wants nothing to do with him."

"Diane, I…"

"No. You've been silent this long, hearing me out another five minutes isn't going to kill you. That boy is miserable because he's been diagnosed with a life-altering illness and his best friend is nowhere to be seen."

"Diane–"

"I'm not finished," she said. "He's struggling to get through the days. To make sense of it all. His life is over and he's finding himself creating a brand-new life. The press is speculating that he's either faking the whole diagnosis to explain his running away from Sara and Hollywood, or they're wagering on when he'll crack up and go on some stupid manic spree. He needs his friends now more than ever. Most of his Hollywood friends, they're gone. Either upset over how he handled the entire *Ordinary World* thing or afraid of the manic-depression. Here, he's just got you and April and Hannah. Or should I say April and Hannah."

"It's not–"

"I know this is difficult for you. How do you think his father and I feel? He's *not* the same person he was. The 'old' Peter Walczyk stayed in that institution and a new one came out, and that new one takes a lot of getting used to. But you *have* to give him a chance, Vic. You can't just turn your back on him because he's different."

"Diane, I can't say anything around him, or anyone else it seems, without offending them somehow. After you left his coming home party, I referred to Dirigo as a 'nut house'. I didn't know if he was going to get up and leave or tell me what I could do with myself. And anytime anyone says 'mental hospital,' he comes back with–"

"Psychiatric hospital," Diane finished. "I know. He's just... he's sensitive about it still."

"I know. So I let it go. I figured the best thing to do was to give it some time. He's got more important things to worry about than me anyways. When he gets better, he can come find me, and we'll pick up where we left off."

"Vic, you can't put a friendship on pause just because something bad happens to one of the people. Imagine something bad happened in your family. What if–"

"Diane, I lost my temper with April and I called him a bipolar basket case. Believe me, you don't want me around your son! He's too fragile, and I'm too stupid."

"Vic, you're not–"

"No. I'll do it again. I know I will. It's the last thing I want, but I know damned well what'll happen. I'll let my guard down, say something without thinking, and put my foot in my mouth again. I promise you."

"Vic, what do you think Peter would say if he heard what you just said? That you're staying away because you don't want to say something stupid and offend him? That you're staying away from him because he doesn't need to deal with you right now?"

"He'd probably say *I'm* the basket case."

"Exactly. He knows he's overly sensitive right now. And he's working hard not to be. And he knows it's weird. You saw him wandering around that psychiatric hospital in his pajamas, for Heaven's sake. How do you think that makes *him* feel?"

Vic couldn't bear to look at her. He studied the top of the table. It needed to be sanded and refinished soon. "Victor," she said, taking his hand in hers. He looked up. "You're miserable too. I can tell. It's eating you up inside."

"I'm just tired. Now that April and I are... I've got books to balance and math's not my strong suit."

"I can help you fix your books," Diane offered. "But I can't fix your friendship. Only you can fix that."

"I'm sorry, Diane," Vic said, resisting the urge to get up and walk out of the restaurant. "I just don't think that I'm what Peter needs right now. He needs friends he can rely on."

"I'm sorry to hear that, because I *know* he relies on you. He loves you. And it's destroying him to think that this illness has ruined your friendship. He thinks it's his fault, you know?"

Having said her piece, Diane got up, gave Vic's hand a squeeze, and walked out the door.

It was time for that drink.

"They're driving me batshit crazy, Kaley," Walczyk complained one night during what April had designated on his schedule as "phone call time." Kaley Richardson had just been released from Dirigo herself a week ago and had immediately established contact with Walczyk.

"So just what are these miserable sods doing that is so wicked and evil?"

"They're not being mean. It's just... they're smothering me."

"They'll do that," she said between puffs. He never knew she was a smoker, not that she could've indulged her habit in the hospital. "They think they're helping."

"Exactly. Like April. It's like she's hell bent on scheduling me every second of every day."

"Remember what Emily told you: structure is good," Kaley reminded him.

"I agree. *Some* structure can be the difference between having achievable goals throughout the day to strive towards and wallowing in the ether. But, Kaley, things are getting way out of hand." Walczyk reached out to the desk and snagged a pink sheet of paper from on top. "Here we are. Today's edition of April's daily schedule for me. She tacks up copies in every room of the house and revises them throughout the day as things change. This is the version 3.0."

"A bit OCD, I guess," Kaley said.

"You think? She's scheduled my morning shower. Nine forty-five, 'Personal Hygiene,' right between the nine o'clock walk I never join her on and 'Writing I' at ten. And she's even put a goal for my writing: eight and a quarter pages a day."

"That doesn't sound too bad."

"Kaley, that's almost three feature-length scripts in a month. Hell, they don't work at that pace in television!"

"Okay, I'm starting to see what you mean."

"No, you're not. You haven't heard the worst of it. I've been *granted* a half hour's worth of open time to do as I please. And the rest of the day's broken up into writing, social time with my friends and my mother, and an hour called *wind down* that's really just getting into my pjs, brushing my teeth, saying my prayers, and getting into bed."

"Don't tell me she tucks you in!"

"I'm being serious here, Kaley. All that time at Dirigo – the place that was preaching all this structure and whatnot – and things weren't this outlined."

"What about your other friend? Your ex-girlfriend. What's her name? Heather? Do you see her much?"

"Hannah? Oh, she's moved in."

"Oh," Kaley said, her voice laced with curiosity. "Managed to put things back together, have you?"

"Nothing like that," Walczyk said. "Thursdays through Sundays she camps out in my living room. She says it's to give April some time with Vic."

"Your assistant is dating your best friend?"

"I honestly don't know anymore."

"You don't know if they're dating?"

"I don't know if he's my best friend."

"Pulling away, is he?"

"Yeah," Walczyk said warily. "Is that common?"

"Oh, yeah."

"Anything I should worry about? My mother suggested that dealing with my having bipolar is extra hard on him because of his father."

"What's wrong with his father?"

"He has Alzheimer's."

"Damn," she muttered.

"Vic literally watched his father fall to pieces. Mum says that it's kind of like that all over again. Another person he cares about with a mental illness."

"Still," Kaley said, "that's no excuse for letting someone fall out of your life like Vic is with you. If he can't handle it, he owes it to you to tell you as much. It's selfish for him to just cut you out of his life."

"Sounds like you've been there," Walczyk said.

"More than a couple of times. Hell, I'm going through it right now."

"How so?"

"When I got out of the hospital, I didn't have anyone to pick me up. Dr. Lentz actually had to get me a cab. That's when I decided that Millinocket was no longer home."

"That was nice of him," Walczyk remarked.

"That's Dr. Lentz," Kaley said.

"Where was your mother?"

"Home."

"And she didn't come get you?"

"You remember how I told you how my brother found me?"

"Yeah," Walczyk said, recalling the mental image of Kaley locked in a running car in her garage.

"Well, since then, Blake's been messed up. He doesn't sleep good at night. Has bad dreams. And he wouldn't get into that car. She had to trade it in for a new one."

"Wow," was all Walczyk could say.

"Well, she said that's it. She's done risking his health for mine. I've had my chance – many chances – and I blew them all. She said she'd be damned if she was going to waste any more time and money on me, now that she's got another 'fucked up kid' to worry about."

Walczyk could feel his face grow red hot. He took a moment or two to chill out. Nothing he wanted say about Kaley's mother needed to be spoken aloud, let alone to her. When he finally felt calm, he asked, "So what are you doing now?"

"I'm living in Newport, actually?"

"Newport?"

"I've got a cousin there who got me a job at the Four Seasons. It's this little diner in town, which isn't far from home. I had some money saved up, so I was able to put down my first month's rent at this skeevy little place. It's not much; a bedroom and a kitchen, but it's better than a sidewalk and a cardboard box."

"Exactly," Walczyk said, knowing that Kaley was working very hard to stay positive right now. "Is there anything you need?"

The line was silent for a moment. Finally, Kaley's voice came back. "I don't need money."

"Okay," Walczyk said, not a fan of people who force their money onto others. His friendship with Kaley was relatively new, but it was a deep-running one. He hoped she knew that if she ever did have a need, she only had to ask.

"Plans for the future?" Kaley asked after another moment's silence.

"I decided to end my TV show."

"I heard that on the radio," she said. "Good for you. You said weren't happy with it anyway, right?"

"Not really."

"Any other projects? What about that movie you were working on at Dirigo? The *Night of the Living Dead* thing?"

"*Night* is stalled for now," Walczyk said. "I've got zero creative energy right now."

"That's depression for you," she commiserated. "Don't force it. I don't know how it is with writing movies, but when I'm depressed, I really can't get a decent painting off the ground."

"I was afraid it was the lithium," Walczyk said. "A lot of the material I've read says it saps your creativity."

"It can. I've never felt it, though."

"So how's the job going for you?"

"Eh," she muttered. "It's a greasy spoon in a truck stop town.

You do the math."

"Sorry to hear that," Walczyk said, suddenly feeling very fortunate. After all, he had enough money saved up that he didn't have to worry about going to work for quite some time now. On top of that, the work for which he got paid allowed him to sit around the house, in his underwear if he so chose, pecking away at his laptop, with every expectation of the first draft being horrible. He never had to worry about where his next paycheck was coming from, how he would be paying for the expensive medications that Dr. Lentz put him on, or if he'd have enough money to cover rent and bills.

"Could be worse, I suppose." There were more sounds of smoking from the other end of the line. "I could have to be a stripper, or a hooker, or work at one of those telemarketing places."

"Those are the worst," Walczyk laughed, remembering with great detail the three and a half months he worked for ComKey, a phone sales contractor that basically called people offering them things they didn't need. The job, which he'd hastily taken after dropping out of Hofstra, having felt he'd learned all he needed to, was the last straw before Walczyk pitched his idea to Ian that they move to L.A. He'd argued to Ian that if they couldn't afford housing in Los Angeles, at least life on the streets would be warmer than it was in New York. Walczyk stuck it out three months, earning enough moving capital to get himself off the east coast and onto the west.

"I've heard horror stories," Kaley said.

"I've *lived* horror stories. You've not really lived until you've been told what you can go do with yourself in four different languages."

"Sounds like a fight with my mother."

"Your mother speaks four different languages?"

"No, but get enough coffee brandy into her and she sure sounds it," she laughed.

There was a knock at Walczyk's bedroom door. "Yeah," he called out, knowing who it was already. The door opened, casting light from the hallway into the darkened room. It was Hannah.

"Oh, hey, there you are," she said, forever an abysmal liar. "Just wondering what you were up to."

"Taking to Kaley," he said, his hand over his phone.

"Oh, Kaley," Hannah said, excitedly. "Tell her I said hello." And with that, Hannah spun on her heel and left the room, leaving the door open. As difficult as she had it, Walczyk found he envied Kaley in one respect: she could lie down on her bed and talk to her friend in peace and quiet without constantly being checked up on.

"She left my door open," Walczyk muttered, continuing to stare at the wedge of orange light piercing the darkness of his bedroom.

"Who?"

"Hannah. She came up to check on me and left my door open. Like they do at Dirigo. I'm telling you, Kaley, I can't take it anymore. They're driving me crazy. The ones who talk to me and the one who won't."

"Well, in their defense, you *are* already crazy. It's a short drive." Walczyk managed a polite chuckle. "Seriously, Walczyk, I'm willing to bet they're just looking out for your best interests. I mean, it's obvious that they want to help. Let them. You're always complaining that Vic isn't around anymore. Be thankful they've stuck by you."

"I suppose you're right," Walczyk said grudgingly. "It's just that it's hard to be thankful for over-attentive friends when I can't even go to the bathroom without being interrupted mid-stream by knocks on the door, making sure everything was okay."

"I'm sure you're exaggerating."

"Give it three minutes. There will be another knock at the door."

"As fun as that sounds," Kaley said, "I've got to get going. I'm close to going over on my minutes for the month and can't afford the overages."

"Well, Kid, thanks for calling."

"Promised you I would," she said. "I'll be praying for you."

Walczyk smiled at the notion of prayer advice from a Goth girl with scar-ridden forearms. "Take care of yourself. If you need anything, you know the number."

"Thanks," she said. "Keep in touch, Mr. Famous Hollywood Produc-*or*."

Walczyk closed his phone and tossed it on the mattress. He flopped back down onto his bed, and had just gotten comfortable when a light rapping came from his doorframe. *Three minutes.* He sat up. It was April.

"Sorry to interrupt, Boss."

"It's okay. I was just lying down."

"Stomach still bothering you?"

"It's like I've got opening night jitters all the time."

"I was in a depression support chat room earlier today. It's not that uncommon with the cocktail you're on. Listen, you want to come downstairs for a minute."

"Why?" Walczyk asked, sitting up. "What's up?"

"Just… come down stairs."

Walczyk got up, sliding his phone in his pocket. He followed April down the short hallway toward the stairs that led to the living room below. As Walczyk stepped down on to the stairs, he saw the surprise. Sitting on the couch was Vic Gordon.

CHAPTER TWENTY-FIVE
CASSANDRA

Hannah was nowhere to be seen when Walczyk got to the foot of the stairs. April stood uneasily by, fidgeting, her fingers twiddling behind her back, like she had done on the few occasions when Walczyk had seen her nervous.

"Hey," Walczyk said.

"Hey," Vic replied.

"Well, then," April said quickly. "I'm gonna go call Eli and..." She never finished the thought, instead quickly leaving the room.

"Peter, we have to talk."

"We sure do," Walczyk said, sitting in his recliner. He looked over at his friend on the couch. Vic looked awful. He was sporting a thick five o'clock shadow from a couple days ago. His eyes were ringed with dark circles, and his hair was simply combed down, not styled as usual. Walczyk also thought he detected the smell of alcohol on Vic. "What's up?"

Vic looked down at the floor a moment, running his hand through his hair. "Your mom came into the restaurant this afternoon."

Walczyk sat forward in his chair, that antsy feeling already agitating his stomach having doubled. He opened his mouth to speak, but Vic held up a hand.

"She's a hell of a woman," Vic said genuinely. "Both your parents are great people. Raised you and Mel to be fine, upstanding people. People who… well, people who know how to take care of their friends." Vic ran his hand over his face, scratching his beard growth, thinking.

"Vic, you don't…"

"Yes, I do," Vic said, his voice hoarse and cracking.

Walczyk got up from his chair and sat on the couch next to Vic, putting an arm around his friend's shoulder. "Tell you what; let's forget about the past three weeks. Tonight can be the first night you've been over since I got back."

Vic looked up, tears swimming in his eyes. "I wish I could. I've ruined so much, Peter."

"Like what?"

"Our friendship, for one."

"It takes a lot more than not talking to me for a couple of weeks to ruin our friendship."

"And what I had with April."

"Can I tell you a secret about April?" Walczyk asked confidentially.

"What's that?"

"Doesn't matter who she's with… could be the hottest young actor in Hollywood or the most devoted restaurant owner on the east coast, eventually she'll get into a huge fight with him over something stupid."

"She left me because I called you a bipolar basket case," Vic blurted out.

"And, my friend, you were quite right." They laughed. "Look, April's been under a lot of stress lately. She's getting twice as many calls from L.A. She's keeping Hannah from wearing me out with all her Hannah stuff, and making sure that my parents are kept up to speed on every little change in my metabolic readings."

"I think she's got more going on than that," Vic said. "I just can't put my finger on it. You got anything to drink around here?"

"No," Walczyk said, "April was pretty thorough in declaring this a dry house."

"All for the better," Vic said, sitting back. He picked a plastic steering wheel up from the coffee table and offered it to Walczyk. "*Mario Kart?*"

The two men played video game go-kart racing for an hour or so before, at the end of one of their games, as the animated characters made their victory laps, Vic said, "I'm sorry I've been staying away. It's just... I'm having some trouble too and I didn't want to bother you with it."

"What's the matter? Is it your Dad? Is he okay?"

"He's fine," Vic said. "It's not him. It's... it's my mother."

Vic *never* talked about his mother, not to say how he missed her or to say how he hated her. It was just something he never brought up, and something that no one else ever brought up. So Vic's doing so now was pretty surprising, to say the least.

"What's going on?" Walczyk asked, proceeding carefully.

"You remember her. Crazy. Always getting wound up over those get-rich quick schemes she'd hatch up when she was up all night drinking coffee and popping diet pills."

"Public dish washers," Walczyk said, remembering one of her hair-brained schemes to have coin-operated dish washers for housewives to bring their dirty dishes to.

"Living rooms for rent," Vic said.

Walczyk fought the urge to laugh. "And how'd that other one go? The one with the kitchens?"

"Oh, yeah, coin-operated kitchens. Come in on your lunch hour, pop your TV dinner into the oven, and dump seventy-five cents in quarters into the thing. Forty-five minutes into your half-hour lunch break, a toasty warm Salisbury steak TV dinner. She had a thing for coin-op monstrosities, didn't she?"

"She sure did."

"You know she barely slept?" Vic shook his head. "I just don't know. I don't think she was on drugs. She wasn't a drunk. Just acted like it sometimes."

"I remember her wandering around the house naked once when I was over."

"Yeah, she pulled that one often," Vic said, embarrassed still. "She said her clothes restricted her 'various thought processes.'"

"Don't know if you ever knew, but I told Mum and Dad about it. That's why I stopped coming to visit until after she left."

"Wish they'd have banned me from my house too." Vic chuckled. "Damn it, Walz... she did some wacky shit." Walczyk simply nodded. "She wanted to tattoo Angie and me, you know. With our addresses, so that if we ever got lost, no one would have any reason for not knowing where we belonged. Went so far as to write it out in black Sharpie on our backs before Dad caught her."

Walczyk had always heard that Cassandra Gordon was not a stable woman, but never had any real reasoning behind the statement; it was just something people said about the woman. But this address tattoo thing... there was something very familiar about it. Walczyk knew he'd never heard the story before, because it shocked and stunned him. Yet, something felt *very* familiar about the whole thing. The same for the coin-op schemes. Roaming the house naked in front of the kids.

"Uncle Donny came over one night not long ago," Vic said. "You were still in the hospital. I think it was after mental hospit – sorry, *psychiatric* hospital Mick-a-Palooza. Said we had to talk. So we sat down with a bottle of scotch and destroyed the thing, talking about the old days. About Ma and all the crazy shit she did as a kid and all the crazy shit she did as a grown woman. And we talked about you and all the crazy shit *you* did as a kid, and the crazy shit *you* were doing now." Vic grew silent. Walczyk sat patiently, waiting. He knew Vic had something to say, and wasn't going to rush it. He had Vic back – he'd wait until Judgment Day for Vic to tell his story if he had to. "My mother was sick," Vic said softly. "I guess I always knew it. Angie knew it. Hell, even Andrew knew it, and he was still a baby practically. There was a lot of crazy scheming in that house, Peter, but there was also a lot of crying in that house. I guess we figured she was just sad because Dad was always yelling at her, telling her to behave herself. 'For the kids,' I remember him telling her on more than one occasion. 'Just do it for the kids.' Uncle Donny says she'd cheat on Dad a lot, and then she'd come home, cry, he'd tell her to pull it together 'for the kids,' and she'd hit him. But you know Dad – he'd never hit a woman; he just took it. She'd come up with a vending machine that sold things like eggs and steaks and fresh produce, get all wound up about the thing, draw up plans, whatever; then she'd take them to Dad. He'd be nice about it, but say that they didn't have the money to make the prototype. He'd shoot her down, and she'd head right back to the drawing boards, coming up with her rentable living rooms or her swimming pools filled with soap so that you could take a bath with your friends while having fun. Then, it's like she'd run out of steam. She'd just crash. Then the tears would start. Then another chorus of 'do it for the kids' would start. Then we'd stay at Uncle Donny's for a week or two because 'mommy was sick,' as Angie would tell Andrew. I talked to Angie not long after Donny came over. She knew something was wrong. I guess I always knew it, too… I just never put it together until that night Uncle Donny came over. He thinks Mum had bipolar disorder, Peter." Tears were sliding down Vic's face. He wiped them, seemingly furious that they were coming. "It was just too much for me to handle. I didn't want you to turn out like..."

Bipolar basket case.

Walczyk reached out and put his arms around Vic, pulling him tightly to him. Vic cried. Walczyk patted him on the back, fighting to hold back his own emotions. It suddenly made so much sense to him: why would Vic want a bipolar best friend when it was a bipolar mother that had torn his family apart.

"Sorry," Vic said, pulling back, wiping his wet face on his sleeve.

"Vic, there's nothing to be sorry about," Walczyk said, reaching out and taking Vic's hand. He gave it a squeeze, then let go.

"No, I *have* to be sorry. I *am* sorry. I should never have ignored you like that. I abandoned you when you needed me most."

"Hmmm," Walczyk said, considering that statement. "You wouldn't happen to be quoting one Diane Walczyk there, would you?"

Vic smiled, still wiping his eyes. "She was pretty pissed when she showed up today. Scared me. I haven't seen her that mad in a long time."

Walczyk shrugged. "What can I say? Mumma don't let no one mess with her baby."

"I guess not." Vic picked up his wheel-shaped Wii controller and restarted the video game.

"So, mind if I get a little bit nosy? After all, I've been out of the loop for a while."

"Go ahead and get a lot bit nosy," Walczyk replied, picking up his controller.

"What's the deal with you and Sara?"

Walczyk felt the air leave his lungs temporarily. It'd been a long time since he'd spoken to anyone about Sara. Probably not since he was in Dirigo, being grilled by doctors and Kaley had he opened up about her.

"Truth be told, Vic, I don't know." Vic looked at him blankly. "I know, I know," Walczyk said preemptively, "but I just *don't* know.

I'm so torn over this."

"It's okay," Vic said. "There's no one single way to handle these things. I mean, your divorce – if it leads to… *that*–"

"Oh, it's leading to *that*," Walczyk confirmed.

"Well, it's different than my folks' divorce or any other divorce out there. And I guess what I was trying to ask is this: are you okay with the idea of getting divorced from Sara?"

"I don't see any other option," Walczyk said. "She's got Ella now."

"And what if Ella wasn't in the picture anymore?"

"Huh," Walczyk grunted. "You know, I honestly never considered that."

"Never?"

"Never. It's always been a given that Ella would be in the picture, blocking me from recovering what was left of the marriage. I've never asked myself what I would do if she weren't there, in the way."

"Well, what *would* you do?"

Walczyk imagined, for a moment, an alternate reality where he'd stayed in Los Angeles and worked things out. Where he didn't know who Sara had cheated with; just that she had cheated. Somehow, he found it easier to face her infidelity when there was a big dark spot over the face of 'the other person.' He saw nights of screaming and yelling and crying. He saw apologies and promises and forgiveness. He saw himself and Sara putting it all back together, the press having no idea what was going on. He saw a new life forming for them, a life where they were both more honest with each other. A life where they allowed each other to have their own faults. A life that surely couldn't exist in the real world.

"I don't see it going any other way," Walczyk said. "I lied to her about my health and she lied to me about our marriage." He shook his head, letting that perfect life he'd just concocted for himself scatter in the wind and dissolve like the little fluffy seeds of a dandelion flower.

Vic sat up straight. "Lied about your health? You mean you never told her–?"

"Not a thing." Walczyk began to see just how much he'd never shared with anyone. "Things with Sara and I hadn't been good for a while. She was forever complaining about my mood swings. I was forever complaining about her never being around. And when she was around, she was complaining about my moods, about how I'd either be so dark and sullen or excitable and hyper. 'Like a kid on crack, this one' she would tell anyone who would listen." He laughed. "Had I known what was going on with me... with her... things might have turned out quite different. I might have been able to tell her how I was feeling, and she might have been able to accept that, and want to help me through it." Walczyk tossed the Wii wheel onto the couch. "I don't know. It's just..."

Walczyk never finished the thought. A moment or two later, Vic leaned forward, putting his hand on his friend's knee. "Just remember, my friend, it takes *two* to make a lousy marriage."

CHAPTER TWENTY-SIX
THE LAP OF LUXURY

"What color are you interested in?" Vic asked as he, Walczyk, and Hannah trudged across the sizeable lot at Stanley Motors in Augusta ("Slippery Stan's," as Vic said his father used to call the dealership). Walczyk honestly had never thought about color. It turned out that he, unlike most men, was flat-out uninterested when it came to automobiles. Sara had picked out his silver Jaguar, which April forced him to remember was a Jaguar XF Portfolio, so he wouldn't sound like a rube when asked by the press what he was driving. This time around, it wasn't the driver (or the driver's wife, or the driver's assistant) that was going to pick the car; it was the car that was going to pick the driver. Walczyk had faith that he'd know which car he wanted when he saw it.

However, he *did* know that he didn't want another Jaguar. Not that he didn't like the car – he loved that car. It handled beautifully, had all the right additional accessories, and was easy to squeeze into a small parking spot. But it was also a reminder of a life he'd left behind. A life he'd never have again, even if he returned to Los Angeles. He had, for a millisecond, considered getting a Jeep, like April's, but wanted something a little different. He was sure, however, that he didn't want a Jeep, nor a pick-up truck. He enjoyed Vic's enough, but always felt carsick when riding so high up off the ground, even when he was at the wheel.

"Something dark," Walczyk threw out there. "Black, maybe a dark red."

"There's a maroon van," Hannah said from the back seat, pointing out the window over Walczyk's shoulder.

"Old ladies drive maroon," Vic commented.

"April's Jeep is maroon," Hannah mentioned.

"As I said, old ladies drive maroon," Vic shot Walczyk a smirk.

"Vic, be nice," Hannah said. "That's our friend you're talking about."

Vic looked to Walczyk, who shrugged. He certainly didn't want to get in the middle of that fight. But at the same time, he felt uneasy saying it was okay to make fun of April. Hannah was right: she *was* their friend, and when Vic was in a disagreement with an ex, he could get nasty. "How about this," Walczyk hesitantly suggested, "we just don't mention her at all. That way no one feels censored, and no one feels that friends are being slighted."

Vic looked over to Hannah, who nodded. "Deal," he said. "No old lady talk."

"Peter, I thought your mother was going to take you car shopping," Hannah observed as they continued their winding trail up and down aisles of cars and trucks and SUVs.

"That was the original plan," Walczyk said. "But you know Mum and things that have moving parts. She thought Vic might be better equipped to help me make a good decision."

"So," Vic asked as they turned a corner, "are we buying new or used?"

"Really haven't decided," Walczyk said. "Probably new." This statement stoked Vic's excitement.

"Peter," Hannah said, "there's nothing wrong with buying a nice, used car."

"I know." He turned to Vic. "And you, remember – I'm not going to buy some extravagant midlife-crisis mobile just to let it rust up from the rock salt all winter."

"A very wise decision," Hannah said.

"But you can afford it. If I were you, I'd get another Jag."

"I don't want another Jag, Vic. Besides, I don't want to spend too much. Who knows how long Eli will let me stay here in hiding before he finds an excuse to drag me back to L.A."

"You'd really let him drag you away?" Hannah asked.

"*Let* him? No. But something will come up. I know it will. I have every confidence that I'll end up being cajoled into returning for the final season of *Ordinary World*. There's no way in hell Ian will let me write from here in peace and quiet."

"That's stupid," Vic assessed. "It's just writing."

"Yeah," Hannah chimed in. "Can't you do it just as easily from your balcony as some stuffy writers' room?"

"One would think so, yes," Walczyk said. "But it's hard to have a crew when the captain isn't on the bridge. Imagine the *Enterprise* is going into battle against the Romulans and Kirk isn't on the ship."

"Oh, like in episode sixty-four, 'The Tholian Web?'"

"'The Tholian Web?'" Vic asked, turning in his seat.

"Don't ask," Walczyk warned him. But it was too late.

"One of the few good third season episodes," Hannah began, eagerly. "Kirk is supposedly killed when the U.S.S. *Defiant* vanishes into nothingness, with Kirk aboard."

"I warned you," Walczyk said under his breath.

"With Kirk gone, Spock is given command, but the crew doesn't take well to that scenario at all. Dr. McCoy–"

Vic looked back at her. "Hannah, what does this sidetrack into 1960's kitsch have to do with anything we're talking about?"

"It means," Hannah said, sounding very much the teacher, "that just because you have a replacement lined up, the writing staff won't necessarily like him."

"It's Ian. He's charming, handsome, and British. Hell, they like him more than they like me." Then Walczyk stopped, grabbing Vic's arm. "Hold up, guys."

Vic stopped the truck and Walczyk hopped out, his modest entourage following him over to a sporty-looking car with a dark blue paint job. Having seen the car, Vic whistled through his teeth.

"Is this a good one?" Walczyk asked.

"Are you kidding?" Vic asked. "The CTS-V Coupe? This puppy's got a blown 6.2 and puts out five hundred fifty-six horsepower…" Vic looked up from the window sticker. "Think you can get me one too?"

"Okay, Vic, tell me something I'll understand."

"Okay… it'll go from zero to sixty in four seconds. And the twin 4-lobe rotor keeps it quiet."

Walczyk smiled. That was all he needed to know, that Vic was happy with the car. Vic was always his automotive litmus test. He didn't understand half of the stuff that Vic had just rattled off to him, but he understood that Vic understood it, and that was good enough for him. Plus it was pretty freaking cool car.

Forty-five minutes later, none of that mattered, as Walczyk drove off the lot, the proud owner of a 2014 Cadillac CTS-V Coupe. Vic parked his truck at the Walmart down the road from the dealership and they took turns driving the car around the far end of the parking lot, revving it up, squawking the tires, and making general nuisances of themselves. Hannah was initially too intimidated by the price tag of the car to dare get behind the wheel, but eventually, Walczyk insisted she climb into the driver's seat. While she would not speak while driving the car, let alone take her hands away from ten and two on the steering wheel, or look away from the field of vision afforded by the windshield, she did crack a smile her third or fourth time around the lot, eventually daring to drive the car around other vehicles.

"Well?" Walczyk thought.

"It's daunting," was all she said as she got out of the car after fifteen minutes of tooling around the parking lot.

"It's not supposed to be daunting," Walczyk said. "It's supposed to be fun."

"I hardly consider $50,000 'fun.'"

"Fifty thousand?" Vic screamed from the back seat. "Walz, you got screwed! I could've gotten you out of there for forty-six-five."

"Not everything is about wheedling the dealer down to what you feel like paying," Walczyk said, getting behind the wheel. "Besides, Kelly might have been offended if you'd tried to talk her down."

"Kelly?" Vic asked.

"Our salesperson."

"You remember her name?"

"Of course I remember her name."

"He should," Hannah said. "He just gave her fifty thousand dollars."

Walczyk shook his head, laughing. "Hannah, the money isn't

an issue."

"Of course it isn't," Vic said from the back seat. "Though I bet old Kelly's eyes lit up when she got a peek inside your bank account."

"Will you stop it?" Walczyk shifted the car into drive and took off through the Walmart lot, looking for the exit back onto Civic Center Drive. "I do not want to sleep with the car dealer."

"I should hope not," Hannah said. "You're not even a single man yet."

"*Yet*? You finally getting a divorce?" Vic asked, surprised.

"Most likely."

"That's what I get for missing staff meetings," Vic said, reaching forward to clamp Walczyk on the shoulder with his hand. Hannah quickly spun around, removing Vic's hand. "What the hell, Han?"

"He's driving! Don't distract him!"

"Yeah," Walczyk growled, "because your wrenching his hand from my person, that's not distracting."

The radio came booming on, an annoying rap song with plenty of bass and far too little aesthetic quality. Walczyk tapped a button on the radio, skipping to the next channel. Chamber music. He left it on a moment, allowing Hannah time to enjoy it before changing it.

"Hey, I liked that," she said.

"So did I," Walczyk said, "but chamber music has a certain soporific effect on me."

"What the hell's a 'soap opera effect?'" Vic asked.

"*Soporific*," Hannah clarified. "It means sleep-inducing."

"Oh," Vic said, enlightened. "Like that opera shit we're listening to."

"Exactly," Walczyk said, feeling his stomach rumble. "Who's hungry?" Vic and Hannah agreed that they could use something to eat. "Okay, then. Where to?"

"Depends," Vic said. "Are we eating in the car?"

When April stepped into the Barrelhead, she felt a vibe. An off vibe. The customers grew quiet. The waitresses sneered at her as she walked by. And she could've sworn that Ingrid Connary turned around and walked right back into the kitchen, sending one of the bus boys out with the platter of food she was bringing to customers.

All the better, she thought. This needed to be a quick trip anyhow. April walked over to the bar, but couldn't find Vic's Uncle Donny anywhere. "Donny?" she called out.

She heard a loud crack, some cursing, and Donny stood, rubbing the back of his head, a clipboard in his free hand.

"April, honey," he said, lighting up when he saw her. "How've you been, sweetheart?"

"Fine," she said, feeling a smile grow on her face. "And you?"

"Oh, you know, each day is its own adventure," Donny said, putting the clipboard down on the bar. "You know Vic ain't here. He's in–"

"–in Augusta with Walczyk and Hannah, getting Walczyk a new car. Yeah, I know."

"Yeah," Donny said. "Picked a hell of a time to leave, too. On a Saturday."

"I imagine it was the only time Hannah could go, given her school schedule. Besides, it doesn't look too busy."

"Oh, it ain't the customers. The place full of customers I can handle. Makes the time go quicker. No, I mean the girls don't want to be here. So they get pissy and bitchy and take it out on me and Andrew."

"What about Ingrid? I thought Vic made her wait staff captain or some stupid thing."

"He did, but are you kidding? me She's the worst of the whole lot. Thinks just because she's..." Donny caught himself, lamely replying, "... because she's been here longest, she deserves special treatment." April didn't buy it. She wasn't surprised. It was Vic's *modus operandi*, after all: date a girl, break up with a girl, go back to Ingrid, rinse and repeat. It was just a matter of time before Vic took solace between the sheets of Ingrid Connary's bed again.

"In this economy, you think they'd know that a round of firings shuts up whiny employees pretty quickly."

"Oh, I agree with you, honey. But Vic'd never fire any of 'em. Thinks too much of 'em. Even the lousy ones."

"That's why you don't get too close to people you do business with," April said. "You end up getting burned in the end."

"The *end* is right where he's gonna get burned. You know he still ain't got the books done for September?"

"You're kidding," April said. She'd worked most of August and September getting Vic's books caught up, drawing up spreadsheets to track money spent and money brought in, calculating the restaurant's actual earnings and, more importantly, if it was actually making a profit. She'd tried to show Ingrid how to do this, as a good faith effort to bury any hatchets that existed between them, but Ingrid's mind was more on her fingernails and her glittery pen than on learning how to help Vic out.

"I'd like to help, but…" April was truly tempted to go into the office and straighten things out. But all that would do is buy Vic another month off the hook with his responsibilities.

"I know," Donny said. "They ain't exactly happy to see you."

"I noticed that."

"Well, you know women. They're protective with Vic. Like you are with Peter. And, in their minds, you screwed with Vic and broke his heart–"

"Me? He's the one who–!"

"I know," Donny said. "He told me all about the whole basket case thing, and I told him he was an idiot."

"Smart man," April said, meeting Donny's warm, grey eyes.

"I try," he said casually. "Listen, why don't you sit down? I'll get you something to drink and a sandwich or something. If I tell him it's for me, the girls probably won't mess with it too bad neither."

"No. I'd like to, Donny, but I just stopped by for this." She reached into her pocket, pulling out a copper-colored key. She carefully put it down on the bar, sliding it over to Donny. "Can you see that…?"

"Sure," he said. "You know, it's a shame you two kids can't work this out. I mean, him and Peter are talking again and all."

April thought about it. She'd like nothing more than to fix things with Vic Gordon. When he wasn't loathing himself or behaving like an idiot, he was a decent guy. Always generous to a fault. And if you were Vic Gordon's friend, you had twenty-four hour-a-day counseling service.

If you were Vic Gordon's friend.

"I just don't see it happening, Donny. I'm sorry."

"S'okay. I know it happens. Happened to me three times before I give up on proposing to 'em."

April appreciated Donny's ability to take a sad situation like being divorced three times and turn it into an anecdote to be tossed off lightly. "Well, I've got Dexter in the car. I should be going."

Donny stepped out from behind the bar, his arms opened wide.

April smiled, walking over to him, and taking the hug. The large, soft man held tightly to her, squeezing her just the right amount. In that moment, April felt loved. For the first time in a while, she felt wanted. She breathed in Donny's Old Spice and apple pipe tobacco. Finally feeling herself on the verge of an emotional scene, she let go of him.

"You take care of yourself, darling," Donny said, kissing her lightly on the forehead. April turned around, ignoring the spiteful waitresses and the prying eyes of their wait team captain from behind the swinging kitchen doors, and walked out of Victor Gordon's life.

"Do you really need to drive like you're a maniac?" Hannah asked, gripping the passenger side door with white-knuckled fright. Peter had behaved himself most of the ride back to Cole Island, but once they hit Wiscasset, he'd begun to throw caution to the wind, increasing his speed, taking corners sharply, and deriving great satisfaction in the squawking of his tires. Of course, it didn't help that Vic was egging him on from his truck.

Why must boys be boys? Hannah wondered as they passed the sign informing them of the twenty-five mile-per-hour speed limit entering Boothbay Harbor.

"Aren't you going to slow down?" Hannah asked, wrenching her neck back to see the back of the speed limit sign.

"I did," Walczyk said. Hannah leaned over and looked at the speedometer. Technically, he had slowed down, from seventy-five miles-per-hour to fifty-five, but Hannah still found herself uneasy with their speed.

"Things seem pretty good between you and Vic," she said, trying to take her mind off the road race.

"Yeah," Walczyk said, noncommittally. "It's nice to have him around again. Didn't feel right with him gone."

"But does that mean we have to sacrifice April now?"

"I shouldn't think so," Walczyk said, swerving around Vic and honking his horn.

"Because I like April," Hannah said.

"Me too. She's the best."

"And I'd hate for things to be weird for her hanging around us just because of her and Vic's separation."

"I'm sure she'll be able to handle it. She's used to dealing with situations like that all the time."

"Really?"

"Sure," Walczyk said, finally slowing down as he entered downtown Boothbay. "Everyone in Hollywood has dated someone else in Hollywood. So when we take meetings, there's always some elephant in the room. You just learn to ignore it and stick to business at hand."

"So when you get back to L.A. and you take a meeting and Sara happens to be there–"

"We'll smile, hug, give each other the requisite kiss on the cheek, and get on with business."

"Right," Hannah said, having a hard time picturing Peter acting so blasé about being reunited with his ex-wife. "'Requisite kiss on the cheek.' Have you even talked to her yet?"

"Nope," Walczyk said, switching the radio back on. He selected the chamber music station that Hannah had liked so much, no doubt trying to change the subject.

Hannah reached out and jabbed at the radio, but instead of turning it off, she switched the station over to a very crude talk program, where the on-air personality was placing bets as to how many times some in-studio idiot could take having people break wind in his face. Hannah gave Walczyk a disgusted look. He reached out and turned the radio off.

"Better?" he asked, and then made a farting noise with his mouth.

"Sometimes it's hard to believe you're thirty-five."

"Because I make fart sounds?"

"No, because you're going to stand back and let two of your best friends – people who love you and have gone through hell with you – fight with each other."

"I know Vic, and I know April, and if neither of them wants to patch this up, it ain't getting patched up."

"If this doesn't get patched up, you know what's coming next."

"Ingrid Connary."

"Exactly. And I've watched him rebound a lot more than you have over the years, Peter. If that woman's not already sowing the seeds of a rekindling, she's looking for her moment. I'm telling you, she'll have him in her thrall faster than you can say Cole Island Bourbon Burger."

"So Vic gets back together with Ingrid. What's the big deal?"

"He gets together with Ingrid, and he starts to change. Her tendrils sink into him and she rewrites his brain. He'll start drinking a lot more. Staying out all night. Ignoring the restaurant. The last time he was with Ingrid, after Staci Langdon, Andrew actually called me at the school and asked if I'd go in and tend to the books. This went on for four months."

"Until–?"

"Until I pumped myself up, got really angry with him, and swore a lot."

"You swore? What'd you say?"

"It's not important."

"Yes, I think it is," Peter said, the sight of Walker Bridge coming into view ahead of him.

Hannah sighed. "Damn, a few hells, the 'S-word'... the 'F-word'–"

"The 'C-word?'"

"Certainly not!"

"How about the 'K-word?'"

"What's the 'K-word'?"

"I don't know. Ask Mum. She claims I used it once when I was in high school. How about the 'B-word'?" Hannah's lips said nothing, but her silence told it all. "Wow, Han," Walczyk said. "I'm impressed. You must've gotten quite pissed off in order to talk about Ingrid like that."

"I was."

"And–?" Walczyk began.

"And it turns out Ingrid was outside the office, listening to the whole thing."

"No!"

"I still remember that horrible day. Ingrid showed up at the school to pick up her little sister. She asked if we could talk a minute. I figured it was about a vocabulary test that Sasha had done poorly on. No such luck. She asked me, flat out, 'Hannah, why did you call me a bitch?'" Hannah whispered the word, looking like she was going to cry. "Well, I got sick. I felt a cold wave of terror come over me. I thought I was going to wretch right then and there. I felt about three inches tall."

"What'd you say?"

"I told her that I... *did* call her a... the 'B-word.'" Peter laughed. "Well, she was being one!" Hannah cried out in her own defense.

"What happened next?"

"And then I let go on her. I told her I hated the effect she was having on Vic. What being with her would turn him into whenever they would start dating. I said that if she really loved Vic, then she needed to encourage him to take better care of himself. That they needed to chill out on the boozing and the pot and that he needed to be reminded he was running his father's business."

"Then what? She hit you?"

"Not exactly."

"What happened?

"She hugged me."

"Ingrid Connary *hugged* you?"

"And she cried. And she said it was hard and that she was sorry and that it must've taken a lot of courage for me to say the things I said, both to Vic and to her. And ever since then, she's been very warm with me. Friendlier. She chats with me when I see her in the stores around town. She makes a point to come stop by my table at the Barrelhead, even if she's not my waitress."

"So you tamed the bully by standing up to her."

"Yeah." She'd never thought of it in those terms, but he was right. Ingrid had always been a bully, intimidating her at school and around town. Bossing people around like she did with Vic; making Hannah feel about four feet tall when she would talk to her. And with a simple, albeit hateful, five-letter word, Hannah had turned the tables forever. She stood up to the bully. Maybe, she thought, she should call Stella Lyons the "B-Word."

"You're sure," Eli said over the phone, no doubt trying not to sound overly anxious.

"I'm sure," April said, not feeling all that happy with herself as she sat in her Jeep outside of the Bronze Lantern.

"All right. I'll tell Burt and we'll start to draw up the papers. Welcome to the Schueller Agency, April Donovan."

"Sounds good."

"What's wrong, April?"

"Wrong?"

"You don't sound like you just made the next leap forward in your career."

"Well, it's just... how the hell do I tell Walczyk?"

Walczyk hit "Save" and leaned back at his desk, putting his hands triumphantly behind his head. He'd done it. He'd managed, despite the seemingly best intentions of everyone in his life, to finish his first draft of a film he really didn't want to make. Six figures in his bank account for his work, regardless of whether or not it was any good or not, was not a bad thing. He'd give it a day or two to gestate before going over it, giving it a quick polish. Surely his use of the military was not exactly up-to-spec, but he didn't care. He'd shoot off the scenes he needed some military enlightenment on to the namesake for the character of "Soldier #1," his friend-in-the-know, Drake McBreairty, and then, after Hannah's promised read-through, it would be e-mailed to Anthony Severance.

Walczyk closed the lid of his laptop and got up from his chair, his legs sore and a little bit numb from sitting so long. He rubbed his thighs and reached over to his bed, pulling on the jeans that lay amidst the pile of unmade bedding. He never slept in a made bed. Not if he could help it. Walczyk slid on, appropriately enough, his *Night of the Living Dead* T-shirt and stepped into his sneakers. As he skipped down the stairs, he dialed up his phone.

"Hannah?"

"Peter, what's up?"

"I just finished *Night.*"

"Congratulations!"

"Get dressed. nothing fancy. I'm taking everyone out to celebrate at the Barrelhead."

"Peter, I–"

"Nothing fancy, Han. Just a top and some bottoms. And shoes, Vic's really picky about people wearing shoes in the restaurant.

"I'd love to, but–"

"Great. Give me fifteen and we'll be over."

"'We?'"

"You, me, April and Vic."

"How are you going to get April and Vic under the same roof?"

"Leave that to me."

He hung up before Hannah could say anything else – like "no" – and walked through the living room, toward April's bedroom. He rapped on the doorframe.

"Yello," April called out from the bathroom.

"April, comb your hair and grab your coat!"

"What the hell for?" she asked as she left the bathroom, clad only in a white towel, and walked into her bedroom, shutting the door in Walczyk's face.

"Because *Night* is done-zo and this *night* is still young! We're going into town, we're picking Hannah up, and we're going to the Barrelhead, where everyone – and I mean *everyone* – will have a glass of champagne to celebrate one hundred seven pages of flesh-eating, zombie-killing, little kids covered in blood and gore wholesome family entertainment."

"We don't carry champagne," Vic called out from the couch, where he played on the PlayStation. Walczyk jumped and turned around.

"Shit. Sorry, Vic, didn't see you there. You're so–"

"Quiet" Kind of have to be, with Ilsa the Sound Nazi in the other room."

"I heard that, ass hat!" April growled from behind the bedroom door.

"You knew Vic was here?" Walczyk asked the bedroom door.

"Ass Hat better not be here to see me," April warned.

"You wanna talk about asses, there, Princess? Yours could win the first place blue ribbon at the 4H County Fair for that–"

"Vic! April! Please. Can't you two make an effort to iron things out, for the sanity of the gang?"

Vic shrugged. "Hey, I've tried, Walz, I've *tried*. She'll have none of it."

"What are you pissed about?"

The bedroom door gave no reply.

"Fine. Vic, what's she still pissed about?"

"Oh, that I called you a 'bipolar basket case' forever and a day ago."

"She knows you and I talked about that, right?"

He shook his head, his eyes not leaving the TV. "I told her that you were okay with it and that–"

"I wouldn't say I'm 'okay' with it."

"Well, then, that you understand where I was coming from."

"Better."

"And that you know I didn't mean it."

"Exactly."

"And that all is forgiven."

"As should be whatever's lurking in the atmosphere between you and my assistant."

The bedroom door opened and April came out, wearing her dowdiest house coat, a towel wrapped around her hair. Ignoring Vic, April approached Walczyk. "Is he going to be here long?"

"I didn't even know he was here until–" Walczyk's phone rang. He looked at the screen. "It's Hannah. Please hold off on killing each other 'til I'm done talking to her." April gave an exasperated "all right" with her face and Vic shot Walczyk a thumbs-up. "Hey, Han, we're just about ready. April's gotta dress and we'll be right–"

"Peter, I've been thinking about it. Maybe it's not such a great idea."

"Why not?"

"Because it's a school night."

"And you have to be in by eight on a school night?"

"And I don't think I can take it."

"A drink?"

"No, not a drink."

"Going out – literally five minutes from your place – for an hour on a school night?"

"No."

"Then what?"

"I can't take Vic and April. They're driving me crazy."

"Well, lucky for you, I have a pill for that."

"Seriously, Peter. Maybe this weekend. Three of us. I promise."

Walczyk felt the air begin to hiss out of the balloon. "Fine. I guess."

"I'm sorry. And I'm so proud of you for getting the screenplay written."

"Thanks."

"And I look forward to reading it."

"Thank you."

"Well, good night!"

"Night, Han."

She ended the call and Walczyk replaced his phone in his pocket. "I doubt either of you want to go out for a drink with me."

"I don't want to go out if he's going," April began, "and I don't want you drinking, so I guess the answer to that is 'no.'"

More air left the balloon.

April walked over to the fridge, pulled out a humungous bottle of water, and retired to her room. On the way, she called out, "Vic's got to be gone and you've got to be in bed by nine, by the way."

"Vic can take a hint," Vic yelled across the room, and shut the TV off. He stormed off to the entry way and put on his shoes.

"Vic," Walczyk said softly, "I'll talk to her, but I know April – you're going to have to meet her more than half way."

"I'm not kowtowing to some stuck-up Hollywood witch."

"I heard that, Ass Hat!" April screamed from her bedroom.

"I said *witch*, you nosy bitch!"

"Hey," Walczyk snapped. "I don't give a damn what's going on between the two of you, you're not using language like that to her in front of me. Deal?"

"Sorry," Vic said.

"Apologize to her," Walczyk said.

"Sorry!" he screamed through the wall. No reply came.

"See? I apologize and she just ignores me."

"No, she accepted your apology."

"How can you tell?"

"Because if she hadn't, she'd be out here, nails raking across your face."

Vic clamped his hand on Walczyk's shoulder. "Night, Buddy. And congrats on the script thing. I bet it'll be a kick-ass movie!"

"Thanks, Vic," Walczyk said, and opened the door for his friend to leave. The balloon was limp and impotent, no more desire left in it. Walczyk opened the fridge and grabbed a two-liter bottle of Diet Coke and started for the stairs.

"That better not be a two-liter of Diet Coke," April called out. "Not before bed."

Walczyk really wished April would make up with Vic, if for no other reason than he could have his life back.

CHAPTER TWENTY-SEVEN
FULL HOUSE

A muffled howl of excitement shook April from her deep sleep. She reached over and pulled the alarm clock closer. It read a quarter past one. April slid out of bed, the static charge building between her body and the sheets, reminding her why silk sheets were such a nuisance. She pulled on some flannel pants and a tank top, stepped into her slippers, and ventured out in search of the son of a bitch who had woken her up. The continued combination of profanity, repeating instrumental music, and over-exaggerated sound effects gave April the answer she needed before she even traveled the short journey from her bedroom to the living room: there was a *Mario Kart* tournament raging in the living room of 2575 Island Road.

Vic, his bare feet up on the coffee table, sat in a wooden kitchen chair, cursing at the TV while Dougie Olsen, beached out in Walczyk's favorite armchair, guffawed loudly, dented beer cans encircling him. At Dougie's feet, Dexter slurped hungrily at a bowl of cereal. They were like children, playing that stupid machine. Little children, wasting their nights with video games and massive amounts of sugared cereal. On the couch, Walczyk sat at one end, his head cocked back, snoring. At the other, her feet across his lap, was Dougie's unfortunate fiancée, Mia. Vic's current plaything, Ingrid, was nowhere to be seen.

April slipped wordlessly in front of the television and pressed a button on its side, shutting it off. Groans and complaints swelled from the two individuals who were still awake.

"What the hell!" Vic cried out. "I was in the lead!"

"Correct," April said. "You *were*. Do you have any idea what time it is?" No one replied. "Anyone?" Again, no response. April looked over to the couch. "Walczyk, what time is it?" He said nothing, snoring away. "Mia, how about you?" Mia did not twitch. "Well, I do know what time it is. It's a quarter past one! That means it's time for you," she said, grabbing Vic's wrist and pulling, "and your merry band of freeloaders to get the hell out. You've played enough *Mario Kart* for one night."

"You know, I never really noticed before just how bitchy you can be," Vic said, standing up, letting the Wii controller slide out of his lap and onto the floor.

"Goes to show you just how observant you can be," she said. "Doug, would you wake your girlfriend and go home?"

"Sure," Dougie muttered, stepping over Walczyk's legs to jostle the petite young girl's shoulders. "Babe, come on. Wake up."

"A word?" April asked Vic, heading for the kitchen.

Vic obliged, carrying a handful of empty beer cans with him. He dumped them into the sink, making a loud clattering sound as he did. "What's up?"

"This has got to end."

"What?"

"Don't play dumb with me, Vic. You know what. Walczyk has rules in place so that he doesn't relapse. If he doesn't get his sleep, he goes manic and does something stupid, or he gets depressed and tries something again. We might not be so lucky next time."

"He's not going to kill himself because he didn't get a good night's sleep. You're just saying that to make me look like shit."

"Have you seen yourself lately?" she asked. "I don't have to work that hard."

"Keep talking smack about me, April," Vic said, trying to sound menacing. "One of these days, I'm going to let *you* have it."

"Just tell me when so I can mark it in my calendar. 'Useless things to do today: alphabetize my CD collection, organize the magazines in Walczyk's bathroom, get told off by Vic Gordon, pick my nose–'"

"That's about all you're doing these days anyhow," Vic said. "'Useless things'. When was the last time you did anything of any consequence?"

"I don't know, maybe when I got the books for your little diner in order? I hear you're doing them now. That must be interesting. Give the IRS my regards."

"You know, I don't know what's up with you. First you nag me to come spend more time with him. Something, I admit, I needed to do. But now that I'm doing just that, you're still bitching at me."

"I meant spend some time with Walczyk," April stressed. "Not drag Dougie Olsen and that bunch of miscreants in here until all hours of the morning to play Walczyk's Wii and lounge around on Walczyk's furniture and eat all of Walczyk's food."

"I'll have you know we brought our own food and beer this time," Vic insisted.

"That's another thing! You don't need to be drinking in front of him. In case you don't remember–"

"I know, I know, he can't drink anymore. But he said that doesn't mean what we shouldn't. He's the one that told me I could bring the beer over, so back down, April."

She shook her head. "What happened to Vic Gordon?"

"He's standing right here."

"No, I'm talking about the Vic Gordon who thought it was a great idea to bring Walczyk some home cooking while he was in the hospital. The Vic Gordon who didn't want to be alone after his friend got sick. The Vic Gordon who cried when he saw what had happened to his best friend. Because I don't see him anymore. All I see is a beer-drinking, pot-smoking, video game-playing halfwit who, if he's not careful, is going to lose everything he has."

"You know what," Vic said, turning around, "screw this. I don't need to take your shit anymore. You're not my boss and you're not my girlfriend." Vic returned to the living room. "Doug, come on!"

Dougie picked up the lifeless form of Mia and nodded in April's direction. "Good night, April," he said.

"Night, Dougie," she said, following the trio to the front door and shutting it behind them. She returned to the living room, clicking on a light. "Walczyk," she called out. There was no response. "Walczyk." Nothing. "Walczyk!"

"Mwaah!" Walczyk lurched forward, as if out of some catatonic state. He looked around him, surprised by his surroundings. He looked up at April. "Where are–?"

"Where are the Lost Boys? I just sent them packing."

"What time is it?" he asked, getting to his feet slowly, tugging his shirt down over his stomach.

"It's almost one thirty in the morning."

"Oh," Walczyk said, heading for the stairs.

"Not so fast," April said. Walczyk turned to her.

"What?"

"Lithium?"

Walczyk obediently trotted over to the kitchen after April. She pulled his purple pill-minder from the cupboard and opened up the Wednesday PM compartment, shaking out two round pills. Walczyk opened the fridge, poured himself a small glass of iced tea, and took the pills from April. She turned around to return the pill-minder to the cupboard when she heard two faint, distinctive tapping sounds. Turning back around, she found Walczyk was bending over, picking the two lithium tablets up off the floor. As he stood back up, April noticed his hand was shaking.

"What's that?"

"What's what?" he asked, blowing on the yellowish pills before popping them into his mouth.

"Your hand. It's shaking."

"Yeah," he replied, his mouth full of iced tea. He swallowed, and then promptly took a second gulp of the tea before adding, "It's been doing that lately."

"And felt you didn't need to tell me?"

"You've been preoccupied," he said, putting the empty glass in the sink.

"What makes you think I'm preoccupied?"

"Well, everything with Vic–"

"Vic Gordon and I are *never* going to get in the way of your health. Get that straight right now, friend. Now how long have you had that tremor in your hand?"

"I don't remember." April could tell that he was telling the truth; he *didn't* remember when the shakes had started.

"I doubt you've called that doctor I found for you."

"I forgot."

"Because you're not sleeping well."

"Because–"

"Because Vic is over every night playing video games with his little entourage, keeping you up until all hours of the morning."

"April–"

"To bed, mister," she said, pointing at the stairs. "You've got an early day tomorrow. We're going for a walk after breakfast."

"Come on," he whined.

"Look at yourself," she hissed, poking him in his growing stomach. "You're already putting on weight."

"Dr. Lentz warned me that would happen," he said, tugging self-consciously at his shirt hem.

"Well he didn't say you had to accept getting fat. Starting tomorrow we walk every morning. We nip this in the bud now; you won't be putting on any weight. Understood?"

"Understood," he said, sulking. He started for the stairs.

"Walczyk," she said, feeling like shit. He turned around. "I'm not trying to be a pain in the ass here. Really, I'm not. I just don't want you getting into any bad patterns. I want you to get better, so you can come back to Los Angeles with me."

"Go back to L.A. with you?" Walczyk asked. "When are you going back to L.A.?"

She'd never meant to bring Schueller's offer up. Not yet.

"Eventually," she said, evasively. "Now go to bed. I'll see you in the morning. Nine o'clock."

"Fine," he said, ascending the stairs. "Night, April."

"Night, Boss," she said, and returned to her room. She shut the door behind her and peeled off her robe, sliding back between the silky sheets of her bed. She honestly didn't know if Walczyk could survive on his own, without her. And that made the pit of her stomach roil.

The patrons of the Bronze Lantern café were hunched over laptops and notebooks, pecking and scribbling away at the projects unfolding before them.

"Everywhere I turn lately, someone's writing something."

Hannah Cooper looked up from her notepad. Vic stood over her, a smile on his face and a take-out cup of coffee in his hand.

"They call it Peter Walczyk fever," Hannah said. "Careful, though, it's contagious."

"Don't worry about me. I'm immune."

Hannah smirked. "Hey, the next great American novel could be itching to burst from your fingertips and you'd never know it."

"The only things I have to write about are crazy ex-girlfriends, the goings-on at an inherited restaurant, and life with my bipolar celebrity best friend."

"A story I'd like to hear more of," Hannah said. "Especially the part about the handsome young restaurateur who is plagued by a jilted high-powered personal assistant hell bent on exacting her own, twisted brand of justice."

"What about the celebrity best friend?" Vic asked, sipping at the paper coffee cup in his hand.

"Can't put all of it in one novel," she replied. "You have to save something for the sequel."

Vic laughed. "And what's the small-town school marm writing about? Murder? Political intrigue? Or is it one of those Sluttyquin romances?"

"Right now it's the life story of an empty sheet of paper," Hannah replied with a frown.

"Well, I better leave you to it," Vic said. "Don't want to be responsible for snuffing out a literary masterpiece before it's even escaped the pen."

"No! Sit!"

Vic obliged her, pulling out a chair opposite her at the small wooden table and sat. "So what are you writing about? Or, at least, *trying* to write about?"

"I don't know yet." She sighed. "I've been telling my kids at school that they need to start writing more. We need to focus on encouraging kids to use their computers for something more than Facebook and Skype."

"What's a Skype?" Vic asked.

Hannah smiled. "But when it comes to taking my own advice, I seem to be failing miserably. You know, I've not written, at least written for fun, in years?"

"You're asking a guy who hasn't written a story since Mrs. Robinson's high school English class if not writing for fun in years is shocking?"

"Well, for an English teacher, it's sad. Cameron Burke writes a novella every summer."

"That as long as a book?"

"No. A novella is usually about 40,000 words."

"Holy shit!"

"After graduating college, I used to participate in NaNoWriMo."

"Is that some kind of grad school sorority?"

She smiled. "No. It's short for National Novel Writing Month."

"Not that short," he muttered. "So have you written a novel?"

"I've written first drafts for two novels," Hannah said sheepishly. "But I never got very far with them."

"Really?" Vic asked, fascinated. "What were they about?"

"Nothing," she said dismissively.

"Come on," he coaxed. "What lurid stories have come from your finger tips?"

"One of them was about a teacher living in frontier times trying to teach adults to read and write."

"Fascinating," Vic said sarcastically.

"Hence why I dropped it. There was no conflict, except for the locals not wanting to learn to read or write and the teacher thinking they should."

"And the other one?"

Hannah leaned forward confidentially, she said, "This doesn't leave this table, all right?"

Vic leaned in, curiosity piqued. "Deal."

She drew a deep breath, locking eyes with Vic. "It was a thriller about this girl who kidnapped her old high school boyfriend, who is now a famous musician, and made him answer for breaking her heart."

"Oh," Vic said, no doubt making all the appropriate connections between her fictional musician and a certain best friend who, also, happened to break a girl's heart after high school before running off to become famous. "Did this musician happen to have a charming, intelligent, roguishly good looking best friend?"

"His best friend was a rogue," Hannah said, smiling. "Remember, you promised."

Vic held a finger to his lips. "Not a word." He rose from his chair. "Well, I'll leave you to it. I've got my own books to work on."

She cocked an eyebrow. "I take it you're doing the restaurant's books?"

"Well, when April quit the relationship, she kind of quit the restaurant. Believe me, it's better than letting Ingrid do them."

"I see," Hannah said, sipping at her coffee. "And after the books? How do you plan to spend your Sunday?"

"I'm going to go back home, throw on a DVD, and pass out with a beer in my hand."

"Any idea what movie?"

"Probably something James Bond. Definitely something Sean Connery. Most likely *You Only Live Twice*."

Hannah searched her brain. "Is that the one in the Alps with Telly Savalas?"

"No, that's *On Her Majesty's Secret Service* with George Lazenby," Vic corrected. "And that one only gets watched when I'm especially lonely for an especially sexy girl I watched it with about ten years ago.

Hannah blushed, knowing exactly who Vic was talking about. "And what about Ingrid?" Vic gave her a quizzical look. "You two are back on, aren't you?"

"Word travels fast," Vic retorted. "Yeah, we're back on."

"I imagine April's taking that well."

"I wouldn't know," Vic said curtly.

"Unfortunately, I would. She called in quite a huff this morning. Said she banned you from the house."

"Something like that."

"And you two got into a screaming match."

"I wouldn't call it 'screaming.' We didn't wake Walczyk up."

"And that she feels bad for calling you a... how'd she put it? A 'beer-drinking, pot-smoking, video game-playing halfwit.'"

"Wow, some memory that girl has on her."

"She feels awful about it."

"She didn't act it."

"Nonetheless it's true."

"Good. She should feel bad. I'm not a pot-smoking halfwit."

"But you've been smoking pot with Dougie and his friends quite often as of late."

"Yes, *Mom*, I have."

"Not a judgment call," Hannah said. "Just an observation."

"Well, she's been her own barrel of fun lately, too. Did she go on about how she's been a control freak and that she's the one who ended things, not me? Doubt it. And did she say anything about how she's blown this whole basket case thing completely out of proportion?"

"Yeah, she likes clinging to that one," Hannah said, trying to stay out of Vic and April's not-so-private little war.

"Tell me something, Han," Vic said, finishing his coffee. "What are you doing down here? I mean, you live just upstairs. Why come all the way down here to write?"

"Dishes. House work. *Star Trek VI*. Napping. Calling my mother."

"Dishes, house work, *Star Trek VI*, napping, and calling your mother," he repeated, searching for a connection.

After letting him ponder the list for a moment, she replied, "What are things that distract me from writing?"

"Aah," Vic replied, rising from the table. "If you talk to Peter, tell him I'll figure out a way for us to hang out."

"Okay."

"And if you see April–"

"I'll say hello," Hannah sternly finished.

Vic smiled, leaned down to kiss Hannah on the top of the head, and walked out into the October afternoon. Hannah tried returning to her writing, but it kept gnawing at her. This feud that was growing between Vic and April. April was forever denigrating Vic to her, failing to take into consideration that she was bashing a man whom Hannah considered a very dear friend. And this was growing thin. On the other hand, it was also growing thin to hear Vic play this innocent act, as though April was a rampaging bull and he was the innocent matador. The innocent matador who kept throwing darts at the angry beast. Then there was herself, the red cape; held out by one party for protection, trampled through by the other with nary a thought. Frankly, she was growing tired of it, but she did not bring it up with Peter. As much as she needed to get it all off her chest, she was not going to burden him with it. No doubt April and Vic were trying to drag him into their little fight as well. So she told herself that she'd put up with it, but she didn't know how much longer she could do that. The entire black hole of dislike was beginning to collapse in on itself, and when it did, Hannah knew it would drag everything – and everyone – around it in without prejudice.

"Okay," Walczyk's mother called from the kitchen. Walczyk and his father got up from their comfortable perches in the living room, where they were watching some legal justice being dispensed by a posse headed up by a character actor Walczyk couldn't quite place on the westerns channel.

"What're we having?" Walczyk asked.

"You got me," his father replied ahead of him.

"Spaghetti," was the answer from the seemingly omniscient cook in the kitchen. "And we're eating in here tonight.

It had been ages since Walczyk was over for a meal that was not on a Friday night. But lately, with the hectic pace his friends were setting for him, he felt it important to spend some time away from everyone. To that regard, he invited himself over for Sunday night dinner. He felt awkward asking April if he could go alone to this dinner, as April always ate with him when he visited his parents. Given the mood she was in when he let her know, this wasn't a problem. She was still sore about Vic's all-night video game spree, and she was taking it out on anyone she could. She'd informed Hannah that she needn't sleep on the couch any more, as she didn't need "time off" to go stay with Vic. With that wounded puppy look on her face, Walczyk quickly told Hannah she could spend as many weekends on the couch as she wanted to. Only once he'd said it, he regretted it, both because Hannah's time at the house was becoming stifling, and because he hated lying to her.

"Henry, leave some sausage for everyone else," Mum scolded as Dad ladled the thick homemade sauce over his pasta.

"Just simmer down, now," he said, popping one last chunk of sausage on top of his plate. He passed the ladle to Walczyk.

After Walczyk had gotten his portion and sat down, his mother followed suit, a smaller portion of spaghetti but two thick slices of garlic toast on her plate. "Peter, will you say grace?" she asked, just as his father was about to scoop that first forkful of pasta into his mouth. Without a word, he quietly put his fork down.

Walczyk bowed his head. "Lord, thank You for the blessings You have bestowed upon us. Thank You for this food and more importantly, thank you for the family we share it with. Thank You for absent friends and family members. In Jesus's name we pray, Amen."

A chorus of *Amen*s rang out around the table. Henry picked up his fork, already twirled with spaghetti, and enjoyed that first bite.

"So, Peter," his mother asked. "How's the car running?"

"Fine," he said. "It's real nice. You'll have to take her out for a spin after supper."

"Absolutely not," she said. "That's your car. I don't need to be driving it."

"Well, I do," his father said. "Wanna take her into town after supper for some ice cream?"

"Ice cream? From where?" Mum asked.

"Does Guy Martin still serve ice cream year-round?" Walczyk asked.

"He sure does," his father replied, spooling up another forkful of spaghetti.

"Hard serve," his mother said. It was a known fact that the one thing that drove Diane Walczyk absolutely ravenous was ice cream. Not hard ice cream, from a scoop, but soft serve ice cream, from a machine. Her lust for "dairy cream" was known over sixteen counties, from the very tip of Aroostook county to the bowels of York county.

"Ice cream's ice cream," Walczyk said, knowing this would inspire some kind of debate or show of indignation from his mother. Deep down, he *hoped* it would. His mother's ice cream mania was one of his favorite things about the woman.

"Maybe in California," she muttered, taking a bite from her toast.

"So, Peter, what'd you do today?" Dad asked.

"Well, I went into town and wrote for a while."

"Oh?" Mum asked, interested. "Your *Night of the Living Dead* thing?"

"Yeah, to no avail." He was still unable to make any headway on the project. Every scene he turned out was worse than the last. He saved none of it to his computer.

"Can't make Marathon's notes work?"

"Not really," Walczyk said, covering his mouth as he spoke. He swallowed. "I did start plotting out the final season of *Ordinary World*, so it wasn't a total loss."

"Wow," his mother said before taking a drink of water.

"How's that going?" Dad asked.

"Not bad," Walczyk said, stabbing a meatball with his fork. "I've got the first five episodes pretty much sketched out."

"Now, isn't this work your writing staff does together?" Walczyk's mother asked.

"Yeah," Walczyk said. "But since I'm not going to be there, I figured I'd just give them my ideas and let them run with them."

"So, if they don't like how you end it–?"

"Tough crap," he said bluntly. "I get final say story-wise. Ian promised me that when I made him show runner."

"And how is Ian?" Walczyk's mother asked.

"He's good," Walczyk said, sifting through his latest conversation with the Brit, seeing if there was anything worth relating that didn't have to do with sleeping with starlets. "Oh, he's getting a new house."

"Good for him," his mother said. She'd always liked "that boy," as she called him. "Such a well-mannered young man. Not at all like the sex-fiend they have made him out to be in those trashy gossip magazines." *If you only knew, Mother, if you only knew...*

"What do you hear from Sara?" his father asked.

"The sound of crickets," Walczyk said, then changed the subject. "But I did hear from Garry Olsen at the bookstore said that old Fitzie Fitzgerald's not doing so well."

"No, he's not, poor old Fitzie," his father said, shaking his head. "Cameron Burke said he saw him playing Bingo at Garry's last Saturday. Poor old man just has no idea what's going on anymore."

"That's terrible," Mum said. "Someone should take care of him. Put him in a home or something."

"Who?" his father asked. "He's only got one kid, and they don't speak."

"Vic never got around to telling me what exactly was wrong with Fitzie," Walczyk admitted.

"Alzheimer's," Dad said, and then returned to his supper.

Since before Walczyk was admitted to Dirigo, he'd feared losing his mind. He lived in utter dread of being in a state of being where he could no longer take care of himself. Where his family and friends were doting on him, seeing to his every need: that his meals were served, that his meds were given, that his ass was wiped. It was a humiliating thought, he felt. But one that he couldn't shake.

After supper, his mother ordered him out of the kitchen with his father. The two men retired to the living room, where an episode of *Wagon Train* was playing.

"You all right?" his father finally asked after the two sat and watched about half the episode.

"Yeah," Walczyk said. "Why?"

"You've been awful quiet."

"I'm just thinking about Fitzie Fitzgerald."

Henry reached out with the remote and shut the TV off. "Something's bothering you, and it's not Fitzie Fitzgerald. What's up?"

"It's nothing," Walczyk said, not wanting to get into it. "You'll just think me an ingrate."

"Because you don't want your friends around anymore?"

Walczyk turned to his father. The old man's powers of mind reading were baffling. Instead of feigning ignorance, Walczyk instead sat back and unloaded. "Kind of."

"I can–"

"You see, Dad, between Hannah virtually moving in and joining April in doting on me like an invalid and Vic bringing people by at all hours of the night, that sort of thing–"

"Then there's your mother and me, always swinging by," his father offered.

"Dad, you and Mum are welcome at my place any–"

"–at any time, I know, Peter. I know. But–?"

"But, there are times I'd just like to be left alone. I have no 'me' time. Every minute is scheduled by April, filled by Vic, and followed up on by Hannah. Don't get me wrong; they're my friends, and I love them, but... if something doesn't give soon, I don't know what I'm going to do."

"Then you better address the issue," Dad said. "And sooner, rather than later. Before you do something you didn't know you were going to do."

"I know, I know," Walczyk said.

His father laughed. "Having Vic and April, split up, under the same roof together can't be all that fun either."

"It's awful. They're always fighting and picking on each other. And now that they're split up, it's worse. Always trash-talking the other to me, trying to get me to choose sides."

"What's Hannah have to say about all this?"

"She's too busy making sure their fighting isn't upsetting me to register an opinion."

His father laughed. "Sounds like you do need to get away from it all."

"God, that'd be nice," Walczyk said, at his wit's end about the whole situation.

"Then go for it," his father suggested.

"Yeah, right."

"You've got the money."

"I do."

"You've got the time."

"In spades."

"So go on a trip."

"But Hannah would want to come along and make sure I was all right. And Vic would want to bring Dougie and Mia and Ingrid. And April would have every second of it planned out, from how long it took to unpack and disinfect the room to giving us sixty-two minutes to be seated, order, and eat at the restaurant."

"Then don't invite any of them."

"They'd never let me get away with it," Walczyk said. "I'm like Fitzie Fitzgerald. I need someone to take care of me."

And the thought really, really bothered him.

With Hadley "Fitzie" Fitzgerald on his mind, Walczyk drove back to his place from his parents' house. It was a short trip normally, four or five minutes. But tonight, Walczyk decided to drive through town. He knew April wouldn't be home, as she'd gone out with Hannah and Cameron Burke to see a movie at the Nickelodeon in Portland, and that Vic, unless business at the Barrelhead had been lousy tonight, would be hard at it with Donny, Ingrid and the crew at the restaurant. That meant only one thing: Walczyk was going to have the house to himself for the first time since coming home from Bangor. To celebrate the occasion, Walczyk look "the long way" home, taking a tour through time to snag a pint of Ben & Jerry's from Ferguson's Market. He was going to crack open the ice cream – a verboten food under the new regime at his house – and sit down to his treatment for *Night*, which he hadn't gotten to put his full concentration into yet, and pray he could make sense of Marathon's notes for it.

As he drove into his yard, however, Walczyk's plans melted away like so much ice cream. The yard was filled with vehicles. And only one of them he recognized. On the porch, Dexter miserably sat by the door, looking very eager to get inside. Walczyk opened the front door and loud, coarse laughter flooded through the house. As he turned the corner into the living room, a disturbing scene unfurled: everyone had a beer in their hand, including three girls Walczyk didn't even know. The TV was on, but no one was watching it. The stereo was blaring, but no one could hear it over their own personal scenes. Ingrid was sprawled out in his armchair, legs dangling over the arm. On top of her, exploring her mouth with his tongue, was Vic. On the couch, Mia was passed out, a beer barely held in her hand. And standing on the coffee table in dirty sneakers was Dougie Olsen, a beer in one hand and Walczyk's Academy Award, which he'd no doubt snagged from the high shelf over the couch, in the other.

"There's just a few people I want to thank," he announced, waving the trophy around. "First, of course–"

"WHAT THE HELL, VIC?"

"Walczyk!" Vic called out, bolting up right, causing Ingrid to momentarily lose her balance atop him. "Welcome home, Peter. What's shaking?"

"Give me that," Walczyk snapped, snapping the Oscar from Dougie's hand. He stormed up, ignoring Vic's further calls to stay and have a beer, and slammed his bedroom door. Then his father's words hit him, and he opened his closet door.

The sting across Vic's face pulled him out of his sleep, shaking him. He looked up and saw the blurry outline of April Donovan standing over him, Pissed-Off Look number forty-seven plastered across her face.

"What the hell'd you hit me for?" he asked, rubbing his face.

"Because anything else would've left a blood stain on the chair."

"What do you want?"

"Oh, nothing important. Just... *where is Walczyk?*"

Vic thought hard. Had Peter come in? Did he show up? It had been weird that he'd not been around when Vic showed up with Dougie and his crew. They were going to surprise Walczyk with the new *Call of Duty* game for the PS3, but he never showed up.

No! Wait a minute! He *did* show up. "Yeah, he's upstairs," Vic said. "He stopped and said 'hey' and whatnot before going upstairs."

"When I get back down here," April said, looking around at the passed-out forms of Dougie, Mia, Ingrid and the Ingrid's friends, "this room better be empty."

"I'll go, I'll go," he groaned, pinned to the chair under the dead weight of Ingrid.

"No. *You'll* stay, because you and I are going to have a long-overdue talk about the rules at Rancho Walczyk."

April climbed the stairs and Vic shook Ingrid, trying to wake her.

"Babe," Vic softly said. "Ingrid, get up. We've got to go."

"*VIC!*"

That did not sound good. Hurriedly, Vic tried waking Ingrid. When she would not stir, he slid her off his lap, sending her crashing to the floor.

"What the–?"

April stormed down the stairs, Pissed-Off Look number seventeen on her face.

"Where the hell is Walczyk?"

CHAPTER TWENTY-EIGHT
THREE DAYS AND TWO NIGHTS

He didn't care if he'd ever be found. He hated them. All of them. He bet they wouldn't even come looking for him.

Peter strolled through the green, crackly woods behind his house, his backpack getting heavy. He'd packed everything he would need for his journey: Pop-Tarts, a sheet to sleep under, a pair of clean underwear, a stack of paper and a pencil, a water bottle filled with orange juice, and his two favorite He-Man figures, Battle Armor He-Man and Hordak.

He knew this part of the woods like the back of his hand. He'd traveled it with Vic and Hannah many times when they'd go for nature hikes. Up ahead of him, "The Mountain" sat, looking back at him. The Mountain was a giant round rock with moss growing all over it. Part of it had been broken away, and it made a perfect look-out for He-Man and his forces when he and Vic would recreate the kingdom of Eternia in the woods. A few yards from the Mountain were the rotted, crumbly remains of an old picnic table, probably put there by the Dennisons, who used to live in the house just out of the woods from here. Wanting a break, Peter sat on a wobbly rock in front of the Mountain and took a look at the old red picnic table, which was falling apart even worse than it was last summer when he, Vic, and Hannah had come down here. Vic had promised to tell them what sex was. Hannah said she already knew what it was, but the boys were skeptical. She was too much of a goody two-shoes to know about something naughty like sex.

Peter popped the cap from his plastic water bottle and gave it a squeeze, emptying the last of the orange juice into his mouth. He hoped he'd find a spring or a clean pond as he passed along the shore. He put the water bottle back into his backpack. He was just about to zip the backpack up when something caught his eye, sticking out from the stack of paper he'd brought with him. He pulled it out of his backpack and saw what it was: it was a picture of himself and his sister Melanie, with Mom and Dad behind them. It was the real picture he and Melanie had painted on the rock down by the shore. Peter felt bad that they hated him; that he hated them. *Honestly, I am disgusted with you!* But that's the way it was. *You let me down, Peter.* He knew it was his fault. *It's going to be a long time until we can trust you again.* He didn't care if he was grounded. He wished he had been. That way, he could at least stay home.

I am disappointed in you.

That was the worst part of it. He pulled his knees to his chest and cried, hard and loud, until there were no more tears and no more sobs left in him. His stomach was burning, probably from the orange juice. His stomach always burned when he drank too much orange juice.

Peter got to his feet, jumping to the ground from the wobbly rock. As soon as his feet hit the ground, a sharp pain jumped through his foot, moving deep into his heel. A scream blew from his mouth, and more tears came to his sore, red eyes. He looked down, slowly picking his foot up. As he did, a part of the picnic table came up with him. The broken, faded piece of red wood was stuck to his foot! Another scream bellowed out. He carefully backed up, sitting back on the wobbly rock. He picked his leg with the hurt foot up carefully, the pain growing the longer he kept it in the air. He grabbed the piece of wood, ready to push it away from his foot.

"Peter, don't do that!"

He turned around, seeing his father jogging through the woods toward him, worried.

"Dad." It was neither a question, nor a statement.

"Don't touch it," Dad said, rushing around the Mountain. He knelt down, gently pushing Peter's hand away from his leg. "This might hurt a little," his father warned him. Then, with super-strong strength, his father broke the old, crumbly wood up, until none of it remained around his foot.

"That's about all we can do here," Dad said, pushing Peter's legs together and picking him up, giving a little grunt. "You okay?"

"It still hurts," Peter replied.

"It should. It looks like the nail went into your foot."

A cold shiver flooded through Peter, and his stomach felt sick. "Why did you come find me?"

Dad looked down at him. "Because I was scared. I was afraid you'd leave your mother and me for good."

"But what about–"

"But nothing. What happened in town happened. No one got hurt. Vic's dad and your mother and I just have to pay for a new window, that's all."

"You mean you don't hate me?"

"Peter, I'm your father. There are things you have done that I don't like. There will be things you are going to do that I won't like. But don't you ever think, for a minute, I don't love you."

"Why?"

"Because you're my son. You're a part of me, and a part of your mother. It's impossible for me not to love you."

Walczyk wasn't sure why he remembered that story just now. Maybe it was because, since he was a young man, running away from his problems had been his default mode. *No, that wasn't it.* The memory of being held in his father's arms, carried out of those woods, and taken to the Island's medical center made him realize it wasn't about running away. It was about having someone to run *to*. People who cared about him and forgave his mistakes; people who sacrificed of themselves to ensure his well being. Walczyk shook off the nostalgia, taking a chug of his Diet Coke, and rubbed his bleary eyes.

There was a great serenity to the Maine highway system. In the summer, the trees, running a straight line up the median strip from Augusta to I-95's terminus in Houlton, were a gorgeous reminder as to why people flocked to the modest wilderness state. In the winter, snow blanketed the earth and the trees, giving everything in view a grayish pallor. On a cloudy day, a person might almost think they'd lost all perception of color, if not for the bright yellow lines blazing up from the pavement. Walczyk preferred the fall look of I-95, with leaves of gold and red and brown dotting the sides of the road, bare branches showing on the trees. It reminded him of the narrow, winding road that led into Grampie and Grammie Walczyk's house, eight miles out from a small, modest northern Maine town called Patten. There, too, walls of trees lined the road, broken up here or there by a house or an empty lot. He wasn't sure if it was the solitude, or the breathtaking sight of those brightly colored leaves falling from the birch and poplar trees, but he felt a wave of calm fall over him as he drove, no real destination in mind.

It was hours yet until sunrise, and the highway stretched on and on and on ahead of Walczyk. Bear McCreary's percussion-heavy score for *R.U.R.* rumbled across the speakers of the car, booming loudly. Time melted away with each orchestral chord; his anxiety shattered with every booming thud. Walczyk started to relax around the time he passed the northbound Augusta exit on I-95.

He considered pulling off and catching some sleep when his leg pulsated. He reached down, cupping his left thigh. His silenced cell phone was vibrating again. This was the sixth time. He was tempted to let April – and he knew it *was* April – leave her message at the tone. However, he also dreaded having to listen to those messages once he decided to pull his head out of the sand and admit that he was, most likely, taking off, half cocked, on some damned fool manic adventure. The notion that he was behaving irrationally wasn't lost on him, even in his current mindset. He probably *was* manic, but he no longer cared.

The vibration ceased and Walczyk exhaled. Round six, over and done. He reached over and turned the music back on, leaning back in his seat. Then the vibration started again. The deviation from the norm threw Walczyk; April's other calls were spaced about twenty minutes apart, but call number seven landed before call six had a chance to finish leaving its angry message.

April meant business.

Walczyk tapped his iPod, silencing the music, and answered his phone. "Peter Walczyk," he said casually.

Where there should have been profanity and threats and more profanity, there was only a frustrated scream.

"Hey, April. What's up?"

"You son of a… you rat… you… *YOU!*"

His first reaction was to enjoy her flustered state of existence, but some level of maturity kept the laughter at bay. Of course she was scared, he rationalized. Even if she didn't realize that she'd helped drive him to it.

"Listen, April... let me–"

"*Shut. Up.*"

There was a great rustling and talking in the background. Another frustrated scream, this one Walczyk imagined was aimed at Vic. Finally, more jostling, and a warmer, friendlier voice came on the line: "Peter, its Hannah."

"I know the sound of your voice, Han."

"Where are you?" Instantly, Hannah's voice had increased in intensity. He no longer found it amusing that everyone was freaking out over his exodus from Cole Island.

"In the car."

"Pull over."

Walczyk flicked his blinker on, only realizing as he slowed and pulled off onto the shoulder that he was the only car on the road and that his turn signal was completely unnecessary.

"There," he said, pulled over. "I'm in the breakdown lane."

"Good," Hannah said. "Now where the hell are you?"

"I needed some air," he said. He was pretty sure Hannah would take that as a flippant response, but he was being absolutely serious with her – he *was* out for fresh air. "I'm on the highway."

"The highway?" Hannah repeated, sounding horror struck. "What's on the highway?"

"I don't know," he said. "I just... I need some time."

"Time?" Behind her, a chorus of voices erupted in discussion and debate. Walczyk sighed. This was not something he was going to be able to do over the phone.

"Hannah?" There was no response. "Hannah?" Still no response.

Finally, when it came, the response wasn't from Hannah. "Walz, its Vic. Dude, look, if this is about your Emmy and the coffee table–"

"It was my Oscar, and it's not about my Oscar, or the coffee table."

"And I'm so sorry about dragging Dougie and those guys into your place. I never meant for anything–"

"It's not entirely about Dougie Olsen and Ingrid and the

others."

"Then what's it all about?"

"Put me on speaker." Walczyk envisioned April and Vic fighting over the phone while Hannah stood back.

"You're on," Hannah yelled, always feeling the need to do so when on speaker phone.

"Good. Now, in response to Vic's question, it's about me."

"You?" Hannah asked, her voice betraying her nervousness.

"Yes, me. It's about me needing some time alone."

"You don't have a wife, a job, or anything to do! How much alone time do you need?" April asked, having calmed down considerably from her earlier, monosyllabic grunts.

He took a breath, a bit anxious about what he was about to do. These three people had turned their own lives upside down to ensure his own happiness and mental health. And he was about to give them hell for it. "Let me clarify, then. By 'alone time,' I mean time where I don't have half-hourly room checks to make sure I'm still alive. By 'alone time,' I mean not having my living room turned into a hostel for wayward, albeit well meaning friends. By 'alone time,' I mean not being forced to go to the Bronze Lantern or Mama Rosa's or my parents' house when I've spent more than a day at home, having to play referee between feuding friends, or incessantly being asked to talk about my feelings." Things were quiet back on Cole Island for a moment, as the three of them digested what they'd just heard. "I just want things to go back to the way they were. Before Dirigo."

"But, Peter, they can't," Hannah said. "You're not the same person."

"Yes, I am," Walczyk stressed.

"No, you're not," Hannah insisted. "You're different. You're–"

"Don't you dare say *sick*!"

"Okay," Hannah back-pedaled, "I won't say *sick*."

"I would," April snapped.

"See, it's shit like *that*," Vic cut in, "that makes him want to leave here in the first place. You've always got to have the little remark. The little quip. The–"

"I think you've got the *little* part all taken care of, my friend," April said.

"Now wait just a damned–"

"Shut up!" Walczyk screamed. Once the din had died down, he continued. "This isn't helping, all this selfishness and backbiting! I can't take it! Two of my best friends hate each other, and the third one is working overtime to make me *not* notice it. This lifestyle just isn't working for me. I need to be left alone."

"Last time you needed to be left alone, you hopped in your car and took off across the country," April remarked. "I'm beginning to notice a pattern."

"That's right. Treat him like crap. He'll come right back home," Vic said.

"Will you two stop it?" Hannah pleaded. "You're driving him crazy!" Then Hannah caught the last word she'd used, and freaked out, a series of squeals and gasps coming across the phone. "Oh, my God, Peter, I'm so sorry. I never meant to–"

"No, Hannah, crazy's an accurate word," Walczyk said. "But I don't know if I'd use it to describe myself or you guys."

"Look, Walz, I understand that stuff's gotten out of control," Vic said. "Between me never being around then bringing Dougie and the gang over all the time, and Hannah's moving in, and April's being a b–"

"Brusque," Hannah delicately said. "April's being *brusque*."

"Look," April said, "Just come back and we'll deal with it."

"You want me to come back? Fine. Hannah: turn my living room back into a living room and not the island's premiere sleepover destination. April: let me decide when I go to the bathroom and when I make my phone calls and when to nap and when to pull an all-nighter. And, Vic: fix this bullshit with you and April. I'm not saying get back together, but at least try to be civil."

"Fine," the three each said in their own way.

"Good," Walczyk said, shifting the car back into drive and flicking on the left turn signal. "I'll see you all in two or three days."

"What?" echoed over the phone in three different pitches.

"I'll be home in two or three days," Walczyk clarified.

"Where are you going?" April asked.

"Oh, no... I tell you that," Walczyk said, "and I'll have a certain maroon Jeep Liberty tracking me down."

"I could just activate the GPS in your phone," April said.

"You're making that up," Walczyk said. "You can't do that."

"Try me."

"Are you manic?" Hannah asked.

"Probably," he admitted.

"I'm cancelling your credit cards," April threatened.

"You seriously think I don't have credit cards you're unaware of?"

April cursed. After five years, he knew how she thought. Truth be told, though, there wasn't another credit card. If she called his bluff, he was going to be sleeping in his car or trying to get a hotel room and food for three days and two nights on $800 cash.

"I think it's a good idea," Vic finally said, breaking his silence.

"What?" the girls asked accusatorily.

"I think it's a good idea. He's right, guys: we're smothering the hell out of him. All of us. He needs to recharge."

"Let him recharge here, then," Hannah said. "I'll go back to my place and you can go back to yours. It'll just be April and Peter."

"Three days. Two nights–"

"Not counting tonight," April verified.

"Not counting tonight. Just a little recharge, then I'll be home," Walczyk said.

"But where are you?" Hannah pleaded.

"In-state," he offered. "Nothing north of Bangor or south of Portland."

"Thanks for all that, Walz, but there *is* nothing north of Bangor or south of Portland," Vic said.

"Will you quit playing games with us?" April pleaded. "Just tell us where you're going. You have my word we won't come tracking you down."

"I'll tell someone," Walczyk said, an idea popping into his head. "But I won't tell you who."

"That's useful," April groused.

"This person will keep their mouth shut about the entire thing, unless I'm not home in three days. Then that person will go to you and tell you where I am. Happy?"

"Are you kidding?" April spat.

"We're happy," Hannah quickly said.

"Sounds like a damned fine plan," Vic commended.

"Okay, then. I'll never get... well, where I'm going... if I don't get back on the road. Take care of each other. And my house. And I'm serious... things have to change when I get home. Okay?"

The three conveyed their understanding.

"Love you all," Walczyk said, shutting off his cell phone and tossing it onto the passenger's seat of his car, where a Mason jar filled with Nerds candy lay. He picked up the jar, screwed off the lid, and shook out a mouthful of the tangy candies into his mouth before getting back on the road.

It felt like hours had passed when the GPS announced, "Exit 157 – Palmyra/Newport – on your right in five miles." Walczyk was flipping through songs on his iPod, not really in the mood for anything that was on there. Walczyk pulled off the highway and made a circuit through town, noticing that there were far more chain restaurants than last time he'd been to Newport. He knew that finding a decent looking hotel that didn't have "No" illuminated next to its "Vacancy" sign would be a tall order this time of year, as hunting season had brought a lot of traffic to the area. Finally, tucked away from the rest of the commotion that was Newport, was the Pine Barrens Motor Inn.

The Pine Barrens was a rather nice little motel, no doubt due to its management by the Trudells, the lovely elderly couple that greeted Walczyk at the front desk. Martin, a wispy-haired man with a slender build and red buffalo plaid shirt, no doubt tended to the bills and handled routine maintenance. Jeannie, with her snow white hair and her diligently plucked, pencil-thin eyebrows, most likely decorated and cleaned the rooms, and made sure that Martin did the bills, tended to the motel's maintenance, and kept out of the box of After Eight mint chocolates tucked beneath the reception desk. Those, she'd told him during Walczyk's check in, were for the pillows, and Martin knew full well he couldn't be eating candies on account of his sugar.

The décor of the room was tasteful, almost homey, which was a pleasant surprise after seeing the radioactive yellow buildings that made up the Pine Barrens Motor Inn. Walczyk had hoped to check into one of the two luxury cabins that sat a short distance from the motel itself, but he was told that the cabins were being rented by a large party of hunters who had called to reserve them back in June. Martin grumbled something about the possibility of the cabins being free tomorrow if the hunters didn't keep the volume on their television sets down. Walczyk was pleased with the room he had rented, however. The walls were white stucco that had to have been either recently painted or bleached, because they were pristine. The round table in the corner, by the front window, was more than enough room to set up his laptop and the stack of scripts he had to go through. The sparkling condition of the bathroom, which offered a rather large bathtub, helped Walczyk decide that he would be safe not picking up the core elements of April's "clean hotel" kit at the local Walmart.

Walczyk dropped his computer bag in a chair by the table, kicked off his shoes, and hung his blue hooded sweatshirt on the coat rack by the bathroom. He'd been debating whether or not he wanted to unpack into the three long dresser drawers, but finding *12 Angry Men* on Turner Classic Movies convinced him to leave his suitcase right by the dresser and have a lay down on the firm, standard issue hotel mattress.

Before he knew what happened, Henry Fonda's impassioned pleas turned into one of Basil Rathbone's brilliant deductions, as *12 Angry Men* had become *Terror By Night*, one of those Universal's *Sherlock Holmes* pictures from the 1940s. Walczyk gave himself a full-body stretch, feeling his tight muscles tugging against the ends of his body, and eventually rolled over, dropping his feet to the floor. The sun had already risen over Newport, which let him know it was somewhere in the neighborhood of eleven o'clock.

In many ways, it had been a long eight months. Los Angeles, TV and film production, his "Hollywood friends," and even Sara, were becoming memories to him. What did it smell like on *Ordinary World*'s soundstages? Was the Thursday special at Domingo's the chicken tomato basil melt or the sable and white fish? He found he was even beginning to forget the layout of his house in Laurel Canyon. His *old* house, he corrected himself, then tried plotting the place in his head. The mental blueprint he was sketching started out with bold, black lines, but as he sketched the interior of the two-story he'd shared with Sara for five years, plus the two he lived there alone, he found the bold lines either turning grey, or disappearing all together.

Walczyk contemplated heading out for breakfast, and one look out the window at the downpour of fat, almost white raindrops almost convinced him otherwise, but the rumbling in his stomach told him that it was time to head out and meet Newport properly.

"*Walczyk*," she stressed, growing weary of Sanjay's butchering of names. "Peter Walczyk. You might have heard of him."

"No, I have not," Sanjay said.

"Doesn't really matter," April said. "The point is, he's got bipolar disorder and is on the run from his friends and family."

"Miss Donovan, this really is a matter for the police–"

"The police don't want to do shit, Sanjay. They don't think he's a threat to himself or to others. They don't have the authority to track him down. And they don't consider him missing for another fifteen hours and twenty-three minutes."

"But we are just his credit card company, Mrs. Dominic–"

"*Donovan!*"

"Donovan. What do you expect us to do?"

"Trace his charges. Let us know where he – " Hannah's phone began to ring out in the kitchen. "Hold the line," April barked, watching intently as Hannah looked at the display.

"It's Henry," Hannah announced, looking at the ringing phone.

"Well, answer it!" April demanded, then returned her attention to her own iPhone. "Take it easy, Sanjay," April said, ending the call.

"Good morning, Henry," Hannah said, trying to sound calm. "How are you?"

April looked over at the couch, where Vic was being ever-so useful, passed out. She wanted to walk over and crank his head to the side, to stop his snoring, but restrained herself. She knew it would take more than wrenching Vic's head around to make her feel better.

"You do?" Hannah asked. "I see."

"See what?"

"I'll tell her. Thank you so much, Henry. I can't promise I'll be in top form, but I'll be at school. Buh-bye." Hannah closed her phone.

"Well? What's he say?"

"Peter is safe and sound."

"Where?"

"He wouldn't say."

"You mean they know where he is and they're not going after him?"

"Nope," Hannah said, pouring herself a cup of coffee.

"Why the hell not?"

"Because Henry says he needs to get away from all of us for a while. Himself and Diane included."

"And they're okay with that?"

"Henry says he indirectly suggested it," Hannah said, going over to the fridge for the milk.

"So I'm supposed to just drop this?"

"Exactly. He promised Peter would be home Thursday morning. Henry said he just needs some time."

"Time he can have… when he gets back here."

"What'd I miss?" Vic asked, stretching on the couch, yawning.

"He's dead," April said. "They found his body on the side of the highway. Zombies on bath salts ate his face off."

"April!" Hannah shrieked. "That's horrible!"

April didn't know how much more of this she could take. Now that they couldn't smother Walczyk, Hannah and Vic were doing a good job of smothering the hell out of her.

"*Hannah,*" Vic said, redirecting his question, "what's new?"

"I just talked to Henry. Seems Peter called them before he even left Cole Island last night. Told them he'd keep in touch, but that he had to get away for a while." Hannah returned to the coffee, bringing a cup to Vic.

"You going to school today?" Vic asked.

"Yeah," she unenthusiastically replied.

"You two might as well go back into town," April said to Vic. "We've got it under control. Go home. Sleep. You've had a hard night, sweetheart."

"You know, you catch more flies with honey than you do with being a bitch," Vic snapped, sitting up.

There was a huge crash in the kitchen. April turned quickly, to see Hannah holding the handle of a coffee cup in her hand. The remainder, and the coffee that was once in it, was scattered across the table. "Will you two get over yourselves and shut the hell up?"

Hannah was shaking with fury. April had never seen her like this before. Vic brushed past April, putting his hands on Hannah's shoulders.

"Sweetie, what's–?"

"Shut up! Shut up, shut up, shut up, shut up… *SHUT UP!*"

"I think we broke Hannah," April whispered.

Hannah slowly turned her gaze to April. There was almost fury in those green eyes. April swallowed. It wasn't that she was afraid Hannah would physically hurt her. Then again, maybe she *would*; she didn't know her *that* well, after all. But she didn't need to feel responsible for another Cole Islander losing their gourd this year. Realizing she was holding her hands up in surrender, April slowly lowered them to her sides.

"It's never occurred to you two that *this* is what drove Peter to run away from home, has it?" Hannah asked angrily.

"This?" Vic asked back, waggling his finger back and forth between himself and April.

"Yes, *this*," she said sarcastically, copying Vic's finger waggling. "This non-stop infighting and bickering and snapping and sniping and name-calling and pissing and moaning!"

April didn't know what to say. She certainly was not getting along with Vic at the moment, not since he'd shown his true colors, abandoned his friend, and called him a basket case. But that was between Vic and herself. What the hell did that have to do with Peter?

"Now just hold up a second, little girl," Vic said, stepping forward. "If I remember correctly, he didn't run away because he was sick of listening to me and April fight–"

"April and me," April corrected.

"There you go again!" Vic screamed, spinning around to point his finger at April. "Can't you just shut the hell up for one single minute?"

"I'd keep quiet if you had a proper mastery of the English language."

"You think you're so smart."

"I have a masters in communication and English from UCLA. What've you got? A restaurant?"

"April!" Hannah hissed.

"No, Han, that's okay," Vic said, headed for the door. "Let her have her little jokes and her smug superiority. They're all she'll ever have in this life until she learns how to be anything but a frigid bitch!"

Vic stormed off, slamming the door behind him. April felt Hannah's accusatory gaze fall on her. "What?"she asked, innocently. "He's always shown complete ignorance for *me* versus *I*. As an English teacher and his friend, I'd think you would appreciate me trying to educate him."

"Don't you mean 'appreciate *my* trying to educate him?'"

April felt her face redden. "Whatever."

The bell hanging from the door tinkled and, a moment later, Vic reappeared from around the corner.

"Back for round two?" April asked.

"No. I just need you to move your Jeep so I can get out."

The Four Seasons came highly recommended by Martin and Jeannie as *the* place to go for good cooking, and one of the few without a national chain standing behind them. Around noon, Walczyk pulled into the parking lot of the little restaurant, tucked away from the hustle and bustle of Oxbow Road. The rain falling from the dark purple clouds overhead had turned from a steady patter to an intermittent drizzle.

The Four Seasons was one of those smallish places with the fancy gold, red and black hand-painted lettering on the front window and white vinyl siding in serious need of a pressure washing.

The interior, however, was a clean, neat, cozy little place, with just enough knick-knacks and tchotkes in its décor to make it homey. While pleasant enough, the waitresses were exactly as he'd expected: a collection of harried moms in their mid-thirties to early forties, feverishly rushing around in embroidered white polo shirts, blue aprons, and black pants, doing far more work than they needed to get their jobs done. Nervous or stressed out waitresses always bothered Walczyk. They made him feel like he was popping in on them at an inopportune time.

Walczyk was amused by the fact that his asking for a table near an electrical outlet plunged the hostess, LaVerna, into a fervor nothing in Dirigo could have prepared him for. Having pulled the hood of his blue hooded sweatshirt back, Walczyk removed his laptop from his shoulder slightly wet shoulder bag and plugged it in. Having ordered a Diet Coke without consulting the menu as to whether the Four Seasons offered Coke or Pepsi products, he started up his laptop and opened the *Night* screenplay, which he hadn't so much as looked at since sending his first draft to Anthony Severance a week ago. It turned out that Hannah's expertise on critiquing screenplays didn't go beyond spelling and grammar, and once Walczyk explained that grammar meant nothing in a screenplay, she simply commented that it was "good." He began absent-mindedly skimming it, fixing a word here or there, and changing a character's name. Walczyk was fond of a cast list that featured names of people he knew in real life. "Little Easter eggs," he called it when talking with Jarvis Willingham of *Entertainment Weekly*. Walczyk's big decision, however, was that the first notable change he was going to make to his draft was to reinstate the entirety of the piece's title, *Night of the Living Dead*. To his tastes, *Night* sounded too much like a something out of the *Twilight* series.

A slender young woman in black denim jeans and a long-sleeved white T-shirt approached the table, her jet black hair pulled back into a ponytail. "Good morning," she said without looking up from her order-taking notepad. "My name's Kaley and I'll be taking care of you this – "

Walczyk looked up, smiling. "Good morning, Kaley."

Kaley Richardson's jaw dropped when she saw Peter Walczyk sitting at her table.

"Walczyk?" she asked as she stood there, staring at him dumbly.

"In the crazy flesh," he said, smiling. He rose from the table and wrapped his arms around Kaley, holding her long and tight. "How've you been, Kid?" he asked her softly.

"Shitty," she said with her typical bluntness.

"Well, sit down and we'll talk about it." He let go of her and sat back down.

"What the hell are you doing here?" she asked, sitting down across the table from him.

"You heard how it was going last time we talked. I just... I need a break from it all." Walczyk picked up the menu that Kaley had been carrying under her arm. "Figured I'd come to a place where nobody knows your name."

"You knew I worked here," she said, eyeing him suspiciously.

"I knew you were a waitress in Newport, but I didn't know where. Honestly, I planned on calling you later in the day and doing this like a normal human being, not like some demented stalker."

"But you're not some demented stalker," Kaley said.

"As far as you know."

She smiled. It was rare that Kaley Richardson smiled, at least to Walczyk's knowing, so he considered it special when she shared that facial expression. "So are you off your meds already?"

"No," he said, pulling his plastic pill-minder from his pea coat's inside pocket. "I've got enough here to get me through Saturday."

"Good. Because, honestly, for a second there, I thought–"

"That I was in mega-manic mode?"

She cast her eyes down to the table. "Yeah," she murmured.

"It's not entirely impossible that I'm not, but things just got too tense at home."

"Hannah still smothering you?"

"Yeah."

"April still micro-managing your life?"

"Oh, yeah."

"Vic still ignoring you?"

"Vic actually came through. The whole bipolar thing was just tweaking him out because his mom was bipolar."

"Wow." she asked.

"You could say that. Yeah, she abandoned her family when Vic was seven."

"That's rough."

"It was." Walczyk took in deep breath

"Kaley!" LaVerna shrieked from across the restaurant. "Decaf on four!"

"Shit," Kaley said under her breath, scrambling to her feet. "I'll be back. Must be the Hendersons. Cute old couple. The biggest pains in the ass I've ever waited on. Can I get you a drink?"

"I told the screaming meanie I wanted a Diet Coke." Walczyk answered.

"LaVerna? Yeah, I better bring it. She'll be all day, by the time she's done meddling in everyone else's orders."

"Hey, Kaley, any chance you have any limes?"

"I don't know. I can check. I'll give you a minute to look over the menu." And with that Kaley vanished into the cluster of tables at the center of the restaurant.

As Walczyk flipped through the menu, he wondered how she did it. He was already several weeks out of Dirigo and was still barely able to fix himself a meal, let alone plan a day for himself that didn't involve long naps and lots of television. But here was Kaley, same diagnosis, yet she was running around a crowded restaurant, taking orders, and pouring coffee. Then the answer came to him: he had the luxury of sitting around all day, doing nothing, with only a handful of people to bother. Kaley *had* to find a way to do it in order to keep afloat. Furthermore, not only did Kaley work in order to keep afloat financially, but the work no doubt gave her something to focus on other than her traumatized little brother, her unforgiving mother, her string of abusive ex-boyfriends, and the myriad of crisscrossing scars hidden under those long sleeves of hers.

Walczyk had barely enough time to get back into *Night* when Kaley returned to the table, sliding a lime-less Diet Coke across the table. "Sorry," she said. "Our specials today are a two piece fried chicken dinner with your choice of potato, coleslaw or veggie – we have corn, steamed broccoli, or peas and carrots with pearl onions – and a homemade roll for $8.99; our famous Bunyan Burger, which is a quarter pound of Angus that comes with cheese, onions, pickles, tomatoes, lettuce, mayo and ketchup. You get fries or homemade chips, and coleslaw for $7.99. And, of course, the reason all the old folks show up here: the All-You-Can-Eat fish and chips, with homemade chips or fries, coleslaw, our signature tartar sauce on the side, and a homemade roll also for $9.99. Today's soups are creamy chicken noodle, tomato parmesan, and New England clam chowder. For dessert–"

Walczyk held up a hand, seeing her face turning slightly purple. "You eat the food here, right?"

"Yeah," she replied cautiously. "Why?"

Walczyk closed the menu and slid it across the table to her. "Tell me what's good."

"Um, I don't know," she said, fidgeting on the spot. "The chicken parm sandwich is really good. Buzzy makes it with a real chicken breast, not that frozen crap."

"Okay, so, we've got the Buzzy's chicken parm sandwich. There's got to be more tasty stuff than that. What's your absolute favorite thing to order?"

Embarrassed, she squeaked out, "The mac and cheese."

"You work in a restaurant and get mac and cheese?"

"It isn't the stuff from a box. It's a five cheese macaroni and cheese. I think its sharp cheddar, Romano, Gouda, and Asiago."

"You said its five cheeses. That's only four."

"Oh, and parmesan. And they put some green leafy stuff for decoration and sprinkle it with some Cayenne pepper."

"And that's your favorite? The five cheese mac?"

She suddenly looked nervous. "It's not fancy, I know, but–"

"I'll have the five cheese mac and cheese. Can I get a side of fries with that?"

"Of course. Do you want those regular, loaded with cheese and bacon, or poutine?"

"Poutine?" It sounded to him like a dirty word.

"They don't do poutine on Cole Island?"

"If they do, they hide it from me."

She gave a slight laugh. "It's just fries with mozzarella cheese and gravy."

"Let's go all out, then. Poutiney my fries."

"*Poutine*. Do you want those right now, or when your meal comes?"

"Well, I haven't eaten since Cole Island."

"Did you take your morning meds?"

"Not yet," Walczyk said, feeling like a child caught not following directions at school.

"Then you're getting your fries now. Lithium on an empty stomach does no one any favors. Take your meds and I'll go put your order in."

"Will do," Walczyk said, fishing his pill-minder out of his pocket again. He popped open the "Monday AM" compartment and shook out two four hundred and fifty milligram Lithium pills and the small white Wellbutrin. He popped the meds into his mouth and washed them down quickly with his Diet Coke, then pulled out his phone and, with a few taps to the screen, his e-mail inbox came up. He had five new messages: four from Eli (marked "Urgent") and one from Anthony Severance, one of the development honchos at Marathon, entitled "Your First Draft." He opened Anthony's e-mail first, actually feeling a slight flutter in his stomach. This was, after all, the first piece of real work he'd done since being released from Dirigo – if it was a flop, chances were it would be the beginning of the end for his career as a writer in Hollywood. The e-mail, thankfully, was standard studio exec fare: equal parts ass kissing, name dropping, and constructive criticism, followed by about ten pages of intricate notes, all basically following under one of two categories: "More Violence and T&A" or "Less Character Development."

He scrolled back, looking at the e-mails from Eli. Surprisingly, only three of the messages pertained to work. The last one, entitled "Urgent: Ketchup," was actually a personal correspondence, in which Eli got caught up with Walczyk, asking how he was doing and telling him that his domestic partner, Mark Stern, finally popped the question, after *only* four years together. Eli said he and Mark wanted Walczyk to come to Los Angeles and be a part of the ceremony in the spring, but Eli said that he understood if that arrangement would be difficult.

Walczyk thought about the situation a moment, closing out of his e-mail. He knew he should go to Los Angeles for Eli's wedding, but even thinking about returning to the West Coast made his chest tighten. He knew he should take part in the celebration of Eli and Mark's love, but the notion of being in the same town as Sara shortened Walczyk's breath. He knew he couldn't avoid L.A. forever, but the idea of bumping into Sara at a wedding still filled him with dread.

Thankfully, Walczyk had very little time to consider reestablishing contact with Sara, as Kaley arrived at his table, a steaming plate of fries and gravy and cheese in her hand.

"Be careful," she said, setting the plate down. "That is some *extremely* hot poutine."

"Thank you," Walczyk said, examining the culinary creation before him. "This looks great."

"Tell me," Kaley said, indicating Walczyk's laptop at the far edge of the table. "Are you getting internet in here? I've never been able to, but my laptop's also kind of old."

"I don't know. I only use my laptop to write, since I can do my e-mailing and whatnot from my phone."

"Oh," Kaley said, looking around the restaurant before sitting.

Walczyk stabbed at the mound of fries, lancing a pair of crinkle cuts and, seeing the gravy making an escape from the fry to the table, cupped his hand under the forkful and stuffed it into his mouth. Once the intense sensation of the hot fries and hot cheese and hot gravy was gone, he was pleasantly surprised to discover that it tasted like what one would expect fries smothered in gravy and cheese to taste like. The mozzarella was very subtle, almost overpowered by the rich brown gravy.

"Well?" she asked, snagging one of the rather drier fries from the edge of the plate.

"Not bad," he honestly replied. "I think I'll see if Vic can do something like this at the Barrelhead." He pulled another forkful up from the plate, blowing on it before putting it into his mouth.

"So what are you working on?" Kaley asked. "*Night?*"

"Well," Walczyk said, covering his full mouth with his hand to block Kaley's view of him chewing poutine. "*Trying to.* Dealing with this Anthony Severance dill hole at Marathon is like talking to a brick wall. I just can't get anything of any sense out of him."

"For instance?"

"For instance, I just got an e-mail back regarding my draft with a laundry list of changes he wanted made."

"Good changes?"

Walczyk pulled the e-mail back up on his cell phone and read. "Well, one note says that the male lead should be 'written in the voice of an ethnic persuasion that would make him seem menacing at first glance.' Perhaps South African or Iraqi."

"That's awful!"

Walczyk smirked. "Apparently he never saw the original movie."

"Why do you say that?"

"Because the lead male is an African American man." She laughed, snagging another fry from his plate and dabbing it in gravy. "Then there's this one: 'While it is a great twist that neither Ben nor Barbra survives to the end of the picture, it also, unfortunately, closes the book on a possible sequel featuring this identifiable cast.'"

"I'm sorry, Walczyk, but that makes no damned sense."

Walczyk shrugged. "Now you see my problem."

Kaley looked across the restaurant. Walczyk followed her gaze. Two old people, no doubt the Hendersons, were looking around for Kaley. "Well, duty calls," she said, getting up.

"When do you get off work?" Walczyk asked.

"Two. Why?"

"If you get bored, swing by the Pine Barrens. That's where I'm staying. Number six."

"I'll seriously consider it," she said, giving her classic half-smile and walked away, across the restaurant, to the Hendersons.

CHAPTER TWENTY-NINE
PATIENCE

"No, I'm not telling you," Henry said, briskly walking down the hall. Hannah found it difficult to keep up. Her fatigue played into it, no doubt, but she also knew that Henry was avoiding her. It happened that, from time to time, Henry would try to avoid her. When the afterschool theater program was dismantled, he avoided her for a week by conducting most of his business in the men's room. And judging from his route, she knew that was where he was headed. Summoning every ounce of energy she had available to her (which wasn't a whole awful lot), she overtook him, blocking his path as he headed for the doorway to the men's room.

"Oh, no. You're not using a urinal to keep me away this time," she said. "I've got Vic calling me every half hour wanting to know if I've found out where Peter is. Then I've got April on the quarter hour. Please, Henry. We're not going to go after him. We just want to know where he is. We want to know if he's okay."

"Well, then, that's easy," Henry said. "He's fine. He's healthy, has his meds, and has settled into a motel. Now, if you'll excuse me…"

Henry ducked under Hannah's arm, disappearing into the bathroom.

"You can't avoid me, Henry Walczyk! I'll just wait here until you come out!"

A toilet flushing was the only response Hannah received from within the bathroom. In the hall, the bell rang, sounding fifth period. Students rushed past her. She did not budge. She was going to get her answer, *damn it*. What she couldn't understand why was Henry being so dodgy about this; so playful about knowing where Peter was. Surely he had to be worried, as his son was not entirely mentally sound. It pained her to think of Peter in that way, but it was the truth: he was not fit to be on his own right now.

"Excuse me, Miss Cooper," Brad Stone said out of nowhere. She looked over, noticed that her arm was blocking the exit of the bathroom, and pulled her arm down.

"Sorry, Brad."

"Is everything–?"

"Get to class, Brad," she said curtly. Brad nodded and disappeared down the corridor into the throng of students rushing to their fifth period classes.

"Miss Cooper, what's up?"

Hannah turned around again and found Taylor Hodges standing behind her, looking at her with confusion on his face.

"Nothing, Taylor. Don't you have somewhere to be?"

"Yeah, but you're kind of blocking the way."

Hannah rolled her eyes and stepped back. Taylor started through the doorway when inspiration hit her.

"Wait!" she cried out, grabbing Taylor by the shoulder and dragging him out of the bathroom.

"Uh, Miss Cooper, not that I mind or anything, but I think this might be crossing a line."

"The line must be drawn here," she said.

"Are you going to let me use the bathroom or should I just go sneak into the teacher's bathroom around the corner?"

"You better not be sneaking into the teacher's bathroom," Hannah warned, then wondered why Henry hadn't snuck into that bathroom himself. Hannah spied Taylor's notebook in his arms, and tugged it away.

"Hey!" he protested. She flipped through, past crudely drawn pictures of naked cartoon characters and the repeated name of senior Lyndsay Howard. She finally found a sheet of blank paper and tore it out. She shoved the notebook back at Taylor and held out her hand.

"Do you have a pen?"

"What?"

"A pen, Taylor. You know, an writing implement full of ink? To write with?"

Clearly put out, he reached into his pocket and fished one out. Hannah clicked it furiously and scribbled a note on it. She folded the note up and pressed it into Taylor's hand, along with the pen. "Now go in there. Look under the stalls. A pair of brown oxfords."

"Principal Walczyk?"

"Yeah. Him. I want you to–"

"No, I mean Principal Walczyk," Taylor said, pointing. "He's trying to get out."

Hannah spun around. Henry stood in the doorway, the playfulness gone from his face. "Taylor, get to class. Miss Cooper, walk with me."

Taylor quickly ducked into the bathroom while Hannah walked slowly down the hall beside Henry. They went in into the main office, to the back, and through the door with "Henry M. Walczyk, Principal" stenciled onto the glass. Inside, Henry indicated a seat across from his and Hannah sat. He shut the door.

"This has got to stop, Hannah," he said, moving across the room for the chair behind his desk. "You are just going to drive him further away. All three of you. I know your motives are good, but you *need* to give him some air."

"Tell me if I'm out of line, Henry," Hannah began, her stomach jittery at the thought of what she was about to say, "but you and Diane are just as bad as we are."

"I know," Henry said. "He said as much last night. And we've already talked. We need to let go. We need to let our adult son live his life."

"Henry, we want him to live his life too. We just–"

"Hannah, you have moved into his living room. You clock his every movement. Vic practically sits on the toilet and reads a magazine while Peter showers. And April... well, I've just spoken with April."

"How? You were in the bathroom."

Henry pulled his cell phone out of his pocket. "Twenty-seven text messages. In the past hour. All from April. This has to stop. The three of you have become so obsessive in your taking care of him that you're going to drive him right off this island for good."

"Henry, he won't leave Cole Island just because–"

"When his wife left him, he drove cross-country. What do you think he'll do when the only other people he trusts become too much to bear?"

"Canada?" she asked, realizing how flippant the response was as soon as she'd said it.

"Very well could be," Henry said. "My point is this: he's a grown man. If he wants to sit around the house and watch television until the mood to write strikes him, let him do it. It's worked for him for years. If he wants to be alone on a Saturday night instead of going out to some community event, let him. He's never been an overly social person. You know that. None of us Walczyks are. Am I making myself clear?"

"Perfectly," she nodded, flashing back to the scolding she took in this office fifteen years ago when she was suspended from school for her part in producing *Intolerance*.

"Good. Now you'd better get back to your class. I can't promise you Stella hasn't found out they're unsupervised and has taken over."

Hannah smiled weakly. She got up and started for the door.

"Oh, and Hannah," Henry called out. She turned around.

"Yes?"

"Thank you."

"For what? You just said we're making him miserable."

"But you're loving him, and he does need that right now."

Hannah smiled and waved goodbye, feeling great affection for the man as she left his office, and truly wondering if Stella had taken over her classroom yet.

"Come on, April... just one quick photo. A candid. Anything. That's all we want." Mike Trevor was rushing down the sidewalk beside her, camera slung around his neck. Mike was one of the few paparazzi who had relocated to Cole Island over the summer to land the perfect picture of Walczyk.

"Sweetie, I couldn't help you, even if I wanted to," April said, hoping her brisk pace would soon deter the chubby photographer from following her.

"What? Is he not on Cole Island or something?"

April tried not to screw her face up in confusion. "What the hell gives you that kind of idea?"

"Well, no one's seen him in a couple days. He hasn't left the house, he's not been into the Bronze Lantern or the Barrelhead, and those are his two favorite spots. No one's seen him at his parents' house, and–"

"I thought we had an understanding," April snarled, backing Mike into the side of Lando and Auggie's Pet Shop. "Remember the deal, Dipshit? I play ball with you, let you guys get some shots of Walczyk so you can eat, and in return, you stay away from the parents and the friends!"

"Well, April, that deal expired when Walczyk stopped showing up."

"Let me be clear," April said, encroaching closer into Mike's personal space, but very careful not to physically touch the man. "Henry and Diane Walczyk's house is not a location of interest for you people. Neither is Hannah Cooper's apartment. Stay away from them. And the school."

"The Sheriff's made it abundantly clear that we're not allowed near the school, though I don't necessarily think that's legal."

"It doesn't have to be legal to be effective," April said. "Who's over by the Walczyk house anyway? Is it Harry and that sketchy guy with the yellow teeth, Jensen?" Mike eyed her, seriously put out. But after a few minutes of playing stare-down with April, he nodded. "Thanks, Mike," April said, backing away. Mike straightened up and made a cursory check of his camera, which had not been touched, and started down the sidewalk. April had been careful not to touch any part of Mike, for fear that she would become the next big story. She could see it now: "Walczyk Assistant Roughs Up Photogs" would be the banner streaming across the bottom of the screen on the entertainment channels.

She pulled open the doors and stepped into the Bronze Lantern, which was rather busy for a Monday. The air in the bookstore smelled of fresh mulled cider, which must've been the week's beverage special. She shot a polite wave to Dougie Olsen, who called her name from across the room, and got in line for her coffee. She'd have gone to Been's, but, honestly, they always made their double-double a bit too sweet for her taste and there was no inside section open to the public.

"Large, double sugar, double soy," April called out. Before she'd arrived on Cole Island back in May or June (she was unable to remember which anymore), the standard fare at the Bronze Lantern was cream, skim milk, or an assortment of powdered non-dairy creamers in colorful little packets. Within a month, however, April had convinced Garry that the island's lactose intolerant customers would prefer their Island Roast with an alternative to dairy. She then gave Garry five dollars to purchase his first container of soy milk, and the sales of coffee doubled in a month. Garry insisted on giving April ten dollars back – sales doubled, her investment's return doubled. Grudgingly, and with a lot of fighting, she took it, but turned around and spent it on magazines in the store. When Walczyk asked what the point of going through all that rigmarole over a stupid four dollar cup of coffee, April said that she'd be damned if she didn't get things the way she wanted them, even if they were just staying on the Island for a few weeks.

The brown and gold and red leaves floating down to the ground from the maple trees across the street in front of the now closed Cole Island Tans reminded April that it was more than just a few weeks that she'd spent on Cole Island. She sat back and drank her coffee, still wondering where Walczyk was, but put at ease by Henry's voice mail that he and Diane knew where their son was. Listening to Henry speak, she couldn't believe the actions he described were hers. She had no idea she'd gotten to be so controlling; that her little spats with Vic were so upsetting to Walczyk. She was so accustomed to pushing herself, and it felt weird now not to be. Her life had grown uncomplicated now that her only job was to take care of Walczyk. She'd begun to feel she was in a rut before he was admitted to the hospital – living in some strange, twisted kind of domestic partnership with her boss, fixing meals alongside him, doing the dishes with him, and becoming a part of his parents' routine.

It had to end.

This was not April Donovan. She loved these things. She loved these people, even Vic, who was an incredible pain in the ass. But April wanted to be more. She wanted to be a player. She wanted to call the shots. That wasn't going to happen running laundry orders and picking up roast beef from Ferguson's Market.

April pulled her phone from her jacket pocket and tapped a few buttons on the screen.

"*Schueller Agency, this is Nicole.*"

"Hello, Nicole. April Donovan for Burt Schueller."

"*And this is in regards to–?*"

"It is in regards to April Donovan returning a call from Mr. Schueller."

"I understand that, but this call is in regards to–?"

"That April Donovan is returning his call is all he needs to hear from you. Now make it happen."

There were a few stunned moments of silence on the line before April heard Nicole say, *"Hold for Mr. Schueller."*

April smiled. She still had it.

"April?" Burt Schueller's voice rasped from the other end of the line.

"Hello, Mr. Schueller," April said, feeling herself smile.

"Well, what do you say. Kiddo?"

"I say I'm in, Mr. Schueller."

"Then cut out all this *Mr. Schueller* shit. And welcome aboard."

Walczyk re-awoke around four in the afternoon, cursing himself for being so lazy. Three hours had elapsed since he'd gotten back to the Pine Barrens from his lunch at the Four Seasons, and he'd gotten nothing done, either on Severance's *Night* notes or some other, more worthwhile project. As he now reread his work and considered Severance's notes, however, he found his passion for the project fading, reminding him once again that he had initially been opposed to being involved with a remake of one of the best horror films ever made. All Walczyk had done, really, was lift elements from other classic horror movies, like Sam Raimi's *The Evil Dead* and that memorable final scene from Phillip Kaufman's 1978 remake of *Invasion of the Body Snatchers*, tweak them and pawn them off as his own, patting himself on the back for his ingenuity.

Walczyk rose from his bed and padded into the bathroom. After doing his business, he went to the sink to wash up. It was there that he really saw himself for the first time in a while. He was starting to look just like he had when he was admitted to the Dirigo Hospital: bleary eyed and unshaven. Walczyk returned to the table by the window and sat down to his laptop. He pointed and clicked a couple of times with his mouse, pulling up his e-mail inbox. The one new message, from Hannah, simply read "I'm sorry." He smiled and cached the e-mail alongside all of the other messages sent by her in a special folder labeled *Han*. Browsing the net, he learned from paparazz-eye.com of a gang brawl had at a nightclub in L.A., purportedly instigated by the posses of two prominent rap artists Walczyk had never heard of before. The site was still running their "Where in the World Is Peter Walczyk?" sidebar, with a photo of Walczyk leaving the Barrelhead dated a week ago. Walczyk wanted to say his meal had been chicken cacciatore. TMZ, meanwhile, was running some front-page pseudo-Walczyk news, sort of: a video of Sara on *The Tonight Show* as part of a press junket for the new series she was shooting for NBC. According to Eli, Ian, and Garry Olsen, when asked how Walczyk was doing, all Sara said was, "I can't comment on his health at the time."

Of course you can't, Walczyk thought. He'd not talked to Sara since she called to inform him that she was filing for divorce. Walczyk closed the cover of his laptop, turned the television on, and watched the last half hour of one of *The Omen* sequels before the phone rang. He reached over and grabbed it and looked at the caller ID. He sighed. At the fourth ring, he slid his finger across the screen and placed the phone to his ear. "Hello?" he answered, not fully understanding why he decided to act as if he didn't know who was calling.

"Peter?" The voice sounded surprised, despite having called him.

"Hey, Sara. How's it going?"

"Fine," she said uncharacteristically softly. "How are you?"

He settled back onto the bed and lied to her: "Things are good."

"And how are you feeling?" Sara asked after a moment.

"Fine," Walczyk said, again lying. "I'm feeling fine."

"So the depression's gone?"

"Not necessarily."

"How's that?"

"It's more like it's at bay than anything."

"And... the other thing?"

Walczyk seemed to know where she was going and after she struggled for a moment, he relieved her of the burden of saying the word. "The suicidal thoughts have subsided."

There was a relieved exhale in L.A. "Peter, I never, never thought that... well, I mean... I can't believe you wanted to kill yourself."

"I didn't actually *want* to kill myself," Walczyk explained.

"But April said you were thinking about–"

"I was. But it's more like I felt it was the only solution to everything I was feeling. I was hiding so much of this stuff inside me, keeping it bottled up so I didn't worry my folks. April, Hannah and Vic. You keep something dark like that bottled up inside of you, it's got to come out sometime, somehow. You must know how that feels." As soon as he'd said it, he felt like an ass. "I'm sorry. That was a dig."

"Peter, it's okay. God knows you've earned it."

"No, it's not. I didn't mean that–"

"Peter!" she loudly said, shutting him up. "It's fine. And, well, you're right. It was hell keeping all of that inside. Sleeping in our bed with you, keeping this secret. It tore me apart. But... well, the truth is, Ella's not something I think I can quit. I know you must think it terrible, considering the man you've become. That I'm a horrible–"

"'The man I've become?'"

"Well... you know."

"No, I don't."

"It's... well, April told Eli you found God in the hospital."

It was Walczyk's turn to laugh. "When you put it that way, you make it sound like I should still be in there."

"You know what I mean. That you've... I don't know... found a greater meaning to life."

"Sara, that doesn't make me perfect. I'm still flawed, disobedient, and sinful; I use bad language, don't love others as I should and I barely open my Bible. I'm no paragon of perfection."

"So I'm just going to ask one more question on the subject, then we'll drop it, okay?"

"Ask away," he said, dreading the upcoming question. Considering the source, it could be *anything*.

"How do you know?"

"'Know?'"

"That... that God is real."

He smiled. "Because I'm alive."

"I like that."

"So, what are you working on?"

"The pilot I was doing with Neil Patrick Harris got a thirteen-episode commitment from NBC as a mid-season replacement, and the movie I started shooting after you left, *Tar Paper*, opened last weekend. I was on *The Tonight Show*."

"Congratulations! That's great!"

"Thanks."

"What's the pilot called?"

"*Night Out*. I think you'd like the general premise. The entire season takes place over one night out on the town for a group of friends and the morning after that night out. But the events of that night are told in reverse order, starting with the morning after and, eventually, if we make it, the season finale will be the start of the night out on the town."

"Interesting," Walczyk said, curious about the script.

"So what are you working on? Eli says you wrote a remake of *Night of the Living Dead* when you were in the mental hospital."

"*Psychiatric* hospital," Walczyk corrected, starting to feel like a pompous ass every time he corrected people on that. "But, yeah. Marathon asked me before the breakdown if I'd work on it. I kept putting them off. Then I found myself with tons of time and nothing to do but feel sorry for myself."

"So, in a *psychiatric* hospital, fresh off a desire to end your own life and God knows what else, you manage to write an entire treatment for a horror movie for a major studio? No doubt a new one for your floor."

"I don't know. Could be many of their patients have delusions that they're penning the next great movie, or the next great American novel."

"But none of them have an Academy Award waiting for them at home."

Walczyk shrugged. "You got me there." The line went silent. The first time he'd spoken with Sara since his mad rush out of Los Angeles, the conversation was brief and rather one-sided: he'd hung up on her after she told him she wanted a divorce. But this time around, things felt different. It was still uncomfortable as hell, and all he really wanted to do was throw the phone out the window, curl up in a ball on the floor, and bang his head against the wall for old time's sake, but everyone, from Dr. Lentz on down to his mother, were rooting for him to talk with Sara. About what, no one ever said. "So, I'm guessing you still want to get that divorce?"

This was *not* what Walczyk had intended to say. On the other end of the line, Sara was silent again. Walczyk was unsure if she was thinking it over or just stunned that he'd asked. "Yes, I do," she finally said, her voice wavering.

"You're sure we can't work this through," Walczyk said for the first time since he'd run off in May. "Because once we go through with this—"

"I'm positive," she said after another pained silence. "Ella and I... we might not be forever. There's no telling anymore. But I am sure of one thing: I can't string you along any more. Is it what you want?"

It was Walczyk's turn to take a few seconds in replying. He was confident that he could never resume his relationship with Sara. The trust was gone, and without trust and mutual understanding, he saw nothing to build their marriage upon. Plus he'd been ditched for another woman. Open about same-sex couples as he was, this one stung like a bastard. At the same time, though, he really didn't want to say goodbye to one of his best friends. The woman who knew so much about him; who shared so much with him. "It's what I want," Walczyk said, forcing his emotions deep down within him. "It's what we need."

"I want you to know something, Peter."

"What's that?"

"We can dissolve our marriage... but we can't ever erase our friendship."

Damn, I hoped you weren't going to go there. From the internet counseling he'd gotten through another chat room visitor to bipolarchat.com, he was supposed to make a clean break of it. To let go the past and focus on the future. But at the same time, he really didn't want to let go of Sara. He was probably not supposed to feel this way, but he *did* still love her, on some level, and couldn't bear the thought of erasing her from his life.

"I truly hope not."

"Well, I think it's time I ask the big question."

"Shoot."

"The *psychiatric* hospital... what was it like?"

For the next hour and a half, Walczyk somewhat reluctantly relived his entire stay at the Dirigo Hospital, from his very confusing first moments, waking up under the haze of Lorazepam to his final moments with Kaley in the hallway, to stepping out the doors of the hospital and into a bright, sunny fall day, his mother holding his hand and his father smiling as he was photographed from every angle. When he was done, he simply fell silent. He just wanted to take another nap. A nap that would last through this whole divorce process.

"Wow," Sara breathed after a moment or two. "That's…" Words seemed to fail her.

"Intense is my word of choice."

"Peter, you need to write that down. *All* of it. Before you lose the detail. Before it becomes a memory."

"It's been suggested before."

"By your mother, no doubt."

Walczyk smiled. "Yeah."

"How is she?"

Walczyk wished she hadn't asked. His parents were *his* parents. They weren't her in-laws anymore. It was only fair. After all, he didn't ask about her parents. "She's good," he finally said. "Adjusting. There's a lot going on over there."

And, of course…"And Henry?" There was a note of longing in her voice as she asked. Sara had been very drawn to his father, from the moment she met him. She'd been quite vocal about what a handsome, upstanding, decent man he was.

"Henry's good," Walczyk said. "Though I've noticed that, since my discharge, he's been much more affectionate."

"Of course he has – he almost lost you. Of course he's going to remind you that he loves you."

There was a knock at the door. Walczyk got up off the bed, with a few too many grunts for his own taste, and crossed to the door. Checking the peep hole, he saw Kaley standing outside the room, looking around in the dark.

"Listen, Sara, someone's at the door–"

"Really?" she asked with tantalized curiosity.

"It's just Kaley."

More tantalized curiosity. "The girl from the hospital?"

"Yeah."

"Well, let her in! I'll talk to you in a couple days, okay?"

"Sounds good." Walczyk lied getting up and opening the door. Kaley meekly stepped in. "I'll tell Eli to get the ball rolling on those divorce papers and–"

"Sweetie, there's no rush."

"Sara, if this is going to work… you can't call me 'sweetie' anymore."

She was remarkably silent. When she spoke, she sounded a little hurt. "Sure thing… Peter. But yeah, the divorce; we might as well get it over and done with so we can move on with our lives." Walczyk flashed Kaley a quick smile. She sat down on the foot of the bed. "Take care of yourself."

"You, too," she said, before adding, "And remember, I love you."

I love you? You break my heart, destroy my faith in society, and send me into a nosedive that ends with me spending a week in a psychiatric hospital and you say I love you? He calmed himself. He reminded himself that this was typical Sara Collins: to put on a front, like nothing was happening, while turmoil and agony roiled behind it. He took a deep breath and spoke: "Have a nice day, Sara."

She was taken aback by this, but said nothing. "Bye, Peter."

Walczyk took the phone from his ear, tapping the big red button to end the call and crashed down onto the bed.

"Breathe," Kaley coached him from her chair by the window. "Breathe in…"

He breathed in slowly.

"And out…"

He exhaled through his nose slowly. She coached him through the cycle a few more times, until the urge to have the world's greatest panic attack had left him. Once he had resumed a normal pattern of breath, he turned to look at Kaley, the hood of her black sweatshirt pulled up over her red-streaked hair. "How was work?"

"Miserable," she said. "Best tip I got all day was yours." She pulled a folded fifty dollar bill out of her hoodie pocket and placed it on the dresser in front of her. "I can't take that."

"Yes, you can," he said, reaching out for the bill.

"No, I can't," she said. "Friends don't tip friends."

"Are you kidding? Friends tip friends even better than they do strangers."

"Walczyk, I sincerely appreciate it, I can't accept it. Thank you all the same."

"Kaley…"

"Walczyk…"

He pushed the money on her. She looked down into her hand, pondering what next to do. Finally, she looked up, pushing a lock of red-dyed hair out of her eyes. "Fine, but I get to take you out tonight, get your mind of the former missus. Dinner. Maybe a drink."

Walczyk wasted no time giving his response. "I could use one right about now."

"'Stay open year-round, Vic,'" Vic mocked, watching the minutes tick by on the clock over his desk, unfinished ledgers in front of him. "'It'll be great for your repeat customers and it'll foster some community pride!'" Famous last words. "My ass it will."

Then the silence was broken by the jingling of the bell on the front door. Vic scrambled from his seat and dashed through the empty kitchen. He looked in the dining room. There was no one there.

"False alarm," Uncle Donny said from his post behind the bar, the remaining minutes of Final Jeopardy playing out on the TV behind the bar. Not even Stumpy McGillicuddy or Gibby Perkins had graced the Barrelhead with their presence tonight.

"Thanks for nothing, April," Vic said, crossing to the door and flipping the closed sign. He turned around to the audience watching him: Donny, Chelsea and McKenzie. "I'm calling it. Clean up and head out, guys. Sorry."

Without a word, the two waitresses began breaking down the dining room for the evening.

Had this been the summer, he would have been absolutely crushed not having his brother around for a weekend, but this was October. And a Monday. Andrew was in Portland, visiting his girlfriend, a curvy, rather gothic looking girl named Miranda Albright, who, like Walczyk, also directed for television. Miranda was the director of the noon, six and eleven o'clock newscasts for the local NBC affiliate, WCSH. It had been months since Andrew had seen his hard-working girlfriend and long-distance things were getting strained. Tired of hearing Andrew complain about never seeing Miranda, Vic decided to send him off to get it out of his system. He would return from his four-day weekend rested, relaxed, and hopefully well laid.

Uncle Donny pulled on his well-worn, well-loved Boston Red Sox hat and screwed it down onto his head, almost obscuring his silver grey hair, and grabbed his coat from the railroad spike that he kept it on. "You sure you're gonna be okay here, Kid?"

"Fine," Vic said, smiling. Thirty-four years old, and he still liked being called "Kid" by his Uncle Donny. He picked up the grey plastic tub and headed for the kitchen.

Behind him, he heard a rap on the door and Donny call out to the person coming in, "Sorry, Hon, but we're closing up. Mama Rosa's stays open until one on the–"

Then Donny paused. Vic turned to see April Donovan standing on the other side of the glass door, her hair dancing around in the wind behind her.

"April?" Vic asked, coldly.

"Holy shit!" Donny cried out, unlocking the door. "April, sorry Sweetie, didn't recognize you!"

April smiled at Donny, cocking her head to the side. "It's okay, Donny. I'm not looking for a meal. Just a friend."

Vic noticed Donny slip out the front door, rather stealthily for such a large man.

"How've you been?" April asked, walking over to Vic.

"Busy," Vic lied. Complaining had not been what he wanted to do, should he see April again. "Hear anything from Walczyk?"

"He's okay. We know where he is. Well, *Henry* knows where he is. They're asking us to leave him be," April said. There was a very substantial pause that filled the restaurant. Softly in the background, Carly Simon sang through the Muzak system and an occasional mop bucket banged against the walls between the dining room and the kitchen.

"How've you been?" Vic asked, putting the Rubbermaid tub down on a table.

"Good," April replied, her voice uncharacteristically soft.

"Good," Vic replied. "Good." He stared at her for a few moments before spotting the bar, spotless, and got a notion. "Drink?"

A huge exhale burst from April's red lips and her eyes rolled into the back of her head. "I would *love* one." She made her way over to the bar and took a seat.

"What'll you have?" Vic asked from behind the bar.

"Shit, I don't know. Surprise me. Nothing too froo-froo."

"Nothing too froo-froo," Vic said, smirking. He threw a bottle of Captain Morgan's into the air, caught it and poured it like a pro. However, he did drop a bottle of gin he'd been deftly juggling, knocking over one of the two glasses he was concocting the drink in. "Shit," he spat at no one in particular, reaching for a rag. "So no specifics from Henry?"

"Just that Walczyk's okay and that he'll come home by Wednesday, or Henry's allowed to turn me loose and tell me where he's hiding."

"Guess we did kind of overdo it there," Vic conceded, grabbing a towel out from under the bar and wiping up the spilt drink.

"You think?" April asked. "I'm surprised he didn't go back to L.A. after the smothering and mothering we've been giving him."

"I think it was more than the smothering and mothering," Vic said.

"Like what?"

"Hannah was in earlier," he said, returning to the drink he was preparing. "Seems we've gotten a little out of control with our fighting."

"She told me it was more than a *little*," April said, locking eyes with him.

"There," Vic said, piercing a slice of lime with a cocktail umbrella. "Try that."

"What is it?" April asked.

"Try it," Vic insisted, wiping down the bar. April took a sip from the pinkish drink. A smile broke out across her face.

"Mmmm…"

"Good?" Vic asked.

"Damned good!"

"You had doubts?"

April took another sip. "What is it? It's like a Long Island Iced Tea, but with something different in it."

"It's a *Cole Island* Iced Tea."

She laughed. "And what, pray tell, is in a Cole Island Iced Tea?"

"Most of the same stuff as the Long Island: Tanqueray, vodka – the cheap stuff they bottle in Lewiston, nothing fancy – Captain Morgan's, Cuervo gold, triple sec, sweet and sour mix, *Diet* Coke, a dash of cranberry juice, and a lime instead of a lemon."

She shook her head, enjoying the drink. "Victor, you never cease to amaze me."

"So what's up?" he asked. "If April Donovan wants a drink, she doesn't need to head out on a cold night, all dolled up, with just the right amount of make-up on, smelling as good as she did that night in Bangor."

"She does when there's a prohibition going on at home."

"I find it unlikely that you left the Walczyk home completely dry."

"Okay, then. I didn't want to drink alone."

"Fair enough."

"That and I guess I'm just curious."

"About–?"

"How much you really hate me."

"April, I don't hate you," Vic said surprised. Hate was far from what he was feeling as he sat there, enjoying a mildly sweet drink with a mildly sweet girl.

"Why not? I would."

Vic knew that when April was in one of her self-deprecating moods, there was no getting her out of it. She would have to emerge from under the funk on her own. So, he opted to change tactics. "You're being awful hard on yourself. What's going on?"

Thought lines creased her brow for a moment or two before she blurted out, "I got a job offer in Los Angeles."

"April, that's great," Vic said, raising his own glass in a toast. She half-heartedly clinked glasses with him. "That *is* good news, isn't it?"

"The best. The founder of the agency Eli works at, Burt Schueller... he needs a new executive assistant. And, it turns out, he wants me."

"April, that's wonderful!" Vic said. "What's Walz say about losing you?"

"Nothing," April said slowly, avoiding Vic's eyes. "He doesn't know yet."

"Why not?"

"Because..." she trailed off, not finishing her sentence.

"Because you don't want to hurt him?"

She nodded.

"Because you don't want to walk out on him after everything he's done for you?"

Her eyes glassed over as she took a hefty toke from her drink.

"Because you don't want to leave him alone in that house after what's happened to him?"

Tears spilled down her cheeks, plopping down onto the wooden bar. Vic reached across the table, wiping tears from her cheeks. He felt her face smile as she reached up and took his hand, squeezing it. "Shit," she muttered under her breath.

"What?" Vic asked, passing her a napkin.

"I'm crying like a simpleton."

"I wouldn't liken these to simpleton's tears," Vic said, trying to meet her eyes with his. They both laughed and finished their drinks in silence, appreciating the other's company.

"I shouldn't keep you," she said, picking up her purse.

"You shouldn't drive home," Vic said, grabbing her arm as she got up.

"Vic, it was one drink. I think I can handle a Cole Island Iced Tea."

"I wager you can, too," Vic said. "But it seems we're back to the point where I need an excuse to drive you home."

She finally gave Vic her bright blue eyes, which were still glassy from her brief tears. "You really think that'd be such a good idea?"

"Probably not," Vic said, letting go of her. "But, damn, would it feel good at the time."

She stepped close to him, grasping his biceps and stepping up on her tip-toes, kissing him gently. "You are one of the last true gentlemen, Victor Gordon," she said, and turned around, grabbing her purse, and heading for the door.

Long after she'd left, Vic still stood, leaning on the bar, staring at the door. He had half a dozen solid reasons why he had to stay put and not run off into the rainy night. Excuses all of them. He thought about going home to that apartment alone tonight, with Andrew out of town, and getting plowed. But that thought was just damned depressing. Then he remembered April lying there beneath him, those lips smiling, those fingers playing with the hair on his chest. The rhythmic sound of her breath as she slept, a metronome to synch his own breathing with. The taste of her skin. The smell of her hair. It all came flooding back to him in one crashing wave. Suddenly what was two weeks ago seemed like two minutes ago. Aware of the tricks his brain and his mind's eye were playing on him, he quickly shut the torrent of images down, cramming his eyes shut and rubbing them furiously.

He couldn't tell how long he'd stood leaning on the bar, his arm falling asleep. Finally, he gave up on seeing that door open, and returned to the books.

It was all for the better.

Slippery's was a little bar located not too far off the beaten path. The interior of the bar was rather standard fare: the front door opened up on a long, hardwood bar, with a string of locals and truckers bellied up. A quartet of waitresses in their late thirties to early forties, wearing tight blue jeans and tighter black t-shirts, flitted about the place, playfully engaging the locals in conversation and doing a good job at looking comfortable with the advances of the folks that were from out of town. Walczyk had no doubts that he'd be getting called "Sugar" or "Sweetie" by whichever waitress he got by the end of the evening. The menus, photocopied from an original and laminated in what looked to be clear Contact shelf paper, were left in fours at every table.

Walczyk put his menu back, turning to Kaley, who had yet to pull her black hood down. Now that she was out of work, gone were was long-sleeve polo shirt and back were her trademark long, fingerless gloves, which Walczyk knew hid the multitude of sins scarring her pale white forearms. "You're from around here," he said to her, "tell me what's good here."

"Are you kidding?" Kaley asked.

"About what?"

"This is the first time I've ever set foot inside this place."

"Then why'd you–?"

That thought was never finished, as a buxom woman in her forties wearing heavy eye make-up and a wash of glitter on her neck and chest stopped by the table.

"Evening," she said. "My name's Vivian and I'll be taking care of you. What would you like to drink?"

Walczyk looked at Kaley. They'd discussed the fact that they were going to a bar briefly on the ride over, but never whether or not they'd be drinking. He didn't know if Kaley was a teetotaler, a heavy drinker, or something in between, given her medications and her psychiatric condition. Kaley's order, however, answered Walczyk's question quickly: "I'd like a Coke."

"Okay," Vivian said before turning to Walczyk. "And you, Sugar?"

"I'll have a Diet Coke with a wedge of lime."

"Sure thing. Look over your menus and I'll be back."

"So what're you thinking about our little hamlet here?" Kaley asked once Vivian had left them.

"I like it. Very quaint. Very cozy. Almost like a landlocked Cole Island."

"I don't know about landlocked."

"This place isn't on the water."

"The middle of this place *is* water."

"The middle?"

"The town surrounds Sebasticook Lake."

"Hmmm… I did not know that."

"See? They say you learn something new every day."

"They do indeed."

"So, Walczyk, tell me: are you feeling any better since the last time we saw each other?"

"I didn't seem fine at the diner this morning?" Walczyk asked.

"I meant since the hospital," she said softly.

"Things are getting better," Walczyk said. "The depression comes and goes."

"How about the situation with your friends back home?"

"They're the reason why I'm here."

"Drove you out of your house, did they?"

It was remarkable how she had the answers to her own questions. "But I guess it just goes to show that they care, so I can't complain."

"If you could, what would be your biggest complaint?"

"Well, most of the time, regardless of if I'm feeling like shit or like a million bucks, I can't make myself sit down to write."

"When you *can* write, how's that going? What happened with that movie treatment you wrote in Dirigo?"

"Shitty. The studio wants a dumbed down movie with lots of unnecessary nudity and a long list of plot points I have to incorporate."

"Sounds to me like you can't just aim your head at the blank screen, write, and please Hollywood."

"Far from it. I worked almost three weeks on that first draft and I virtually have to start over from scratch for the studio."

"That's a lot of work and misery for a movie you don't want to do. Which leads me to my next question: why the hell are you doing it?"

"At the time, in the institution, it seemed like a good idea. Now–"

"Now what?"

"Now I'm being told I'm 'thinking too hard' on this by one the studio chiefs."

"Judging from the movies of yours that I've seen, you don't strike me as someone who settles for cookie cutter, formulaic crap."

Walczyk leaned forward. "I didn't know you were familiar with my work."

"You're Peter Walczyk. How *can't* I be?"

"You're such an expert on the genius that is Peter Walczyk, how do you explain *Speed Dating* or *The Reset Button*."

"First of all, 'genius' is your word, not mine. Secondly, yes, they're crap, but at least they're *original* crap."

"Thank you," he said, following it quickly with, "I think."

Vivian arrived with the drinks, curiously regarding him as she delivered the sodas, making a particular point out of noting the lime wedge in Walczyk's Diet Coke.

"Any food for you two?" Vivian asked.

"Honestly, we haven't even looked at the menu yet."

"No rush," she said, smiling at him. She winked and left.

"I think Vivian likes you," Kaley said.

"I think Vivian's old enough to be my mother," Walczyk said.

"So, what'll we drink to?" Kaley asked, raising her glass.

"I don't know," Walczyk replied. "Sanity?"

"Friendship?" Kaley suggested.

"Divorce."

"There we go," she said. "To divorce."

They clinked glasses and drank, then turned to their menus. Walczyk saw a smattering of sandwiches and deep fried specialties, everything with its own quirky name. "Anything float your boat?"

"The Heart Attack Basket," Kaley said dryly. Walczyk looked around the menu, finally finding said delicacy: seasoned chicken fingers with a combination of French fries, mozzarella sticks, jalapeño poppers and onion rings.

"Better you than me," Walczyk said. "My old gut could never handle that."

"Listen to you and this 'old man' bullshit," she ribbed.

Kaley was certainly different out of the hospital: she was a bit bolder, a bit brasher. Walczyk liked this; it was an attractive quality for her to possess, given all she had to be meek and shy about.

Vivian returned to the table, notepad in hand. "Okay, honey, what can I get you?" she asked Kaley.

"I'll take the Heart Attack Basket," she said, reading it from the menu.

"Brave girl," Vivian said. "Dipping sauces?"

"Marinara for the cheese sticks, ranch for the chicken and just ketchup for the rest. And when that comes, can you bring me three salad plates?"

"Salad plates?"

"You know. Those ones that are bigger than a saucer, but smaller than–"

"I know what they are, Hun." Vivian kept any further questions to herself and made a note of Kaley's request, speaking aloud as she wrote. She then turned to Walczyk, giving him the eyes all over again.

"And for you, Sweetie?"

"I'll have the Chick-chick-chicken burger basket. Light on the mayo, no tomato."

"Okay."

"And those fries… can I get those with no salt on them, please?"

"No salt," she repeated aloud as she made a note. "Anything else?"

Walczyk looked to Kaley before telling Vivian, "That should do it." He closed his menu, collected Kaley's, and put them back in their place, between the Heinz 57 and the sugar.

In the background, the juke box kicked on and some country music began playing. At the far end of Slippery's, away from the bar, was a pool table, a dart board, and a wide-open space that no doubt served as a dance floor on the weekends or for parties. He found himself hoping Kaley didn't want to dance.

"Are you sure you've never been here before?" Walczyk asked.

"Positive," Kaley replied. "Why?"

"Because that big guy over there is staring at you," he said, looking in the general direction of the bar. Kaley's craned her neck, saw who Walczyk was talking about, and shrank back in her seat, her demeanor suddenly changed. "The guy in the Smythe Construction T-shirt sitting next to the one in the blue Patriots jersey?"

"Yeah. Do you know them?" he asked, already knowing the

answer.

"I know the one on the right. Sadly."

"And he is…?"

"Steve Ashland. It's not bad enough he and his buddy over there are bad-tipping regulars at the restaurant, but Steve and I went to high school together back at Stearns."

"The tone of your voice says that Steve Ashland's not the kind of guy you'd appreciate me inviting over for a drink and some get-to-know-you conversation."

"Not necessarily," she said. "Not only have I heard he's turned into a wicked drunk, but… well, let's just say there's history."

"History?"

"History," she said, offering nothing more.

"History as in…?"

"History as in didn't you once say you dated this German girl who lifted your wallet one night after some very disappointing sex?"

Walczyk had forgotten that he'd shared that particular story, about a fling he had at the University of Maine with a German grad student named Greta.

"I just want to know what he's like, that's all."

"Why? Can't we just forget about Steve Ashland?" she asked.

"No, we can't."

"Why the hell not?"

"Cause he's on his way over," Walczyk observed.

Steve Ashland was a tall guy. His pronounced belly was made even more prominent by the tucked-in dirty T-shirt he wore. Walczyk noticed a faint aroma of sawdust as he neared their table. Steve pointed a finger in Kaley's direction, and asked, "People at the Four Seasons know you're at another place?"

She smiled, turning red. "It's allowed."

"How've you been?" he asked, not seeming impolite at all to Walczyk.

"Not bad. Not looking forward to the double I have to work Thursday."

"Thursday? Me and Ron will have to stop on by and keep you company for a while."

It *was* apparent, however, that this Steve Ashland guy was still taken with little Kaley Richardson.

"You been up home lately?" he asked, having finished his beer and put the bottle down in front of Walczyk.

"Not really," she said diplomatically. "You?"

"I head up every other weekend," he replied casually. "Hang out with what guys are still in town. Get a little drinking done. Catch up with the family and all. Speaking of, I ran into your mom at the Hannaford in town."

Walczyk saw Kaley tense up, surely not wanting to hear that Steve was told by Kaley's mother about her daughter. "Yeah," she said uneasily. "So, I don't think I ever asked at the restaurant, but what are you doing in town anyways?"

For the next fifteen minutes, Steve spat out a stream of residential construction technical jargon and redneck bullshit, slowing down long enough to order his next beer.

"Now I never thought I should ask this at the restaurant because people's always around, but since it's just us, I figured what the hell: I heard a rumor you was at some nut house in the county. Tried to kill yourself or some shit?"

Kaley took a deep breath and looked ready to speak when Walczyk made his move. He reached out, taking her hand in his, and caressed the top of it with his thumb. "Actually, she came to visit me."

Steve turned. "Who are you?"

"Peter Walczyk."

He rolled the name around a bit before remembering it. "No shit. That movie guy that lives on the coast?"

"That'd be me."

"You're the one with the lesbian wife."

Walczyk loved how it always came back to that with people. "Yep."

"The one who just got out of the nut house."

Sudden revealing who he was wasn't such a brilliant idea to Walczyk. "Well, it was a *psychiatric hospital*," he qualified. "And, yes, I–"

"Yeah, Peter just got released," Kaley said, giving his hand a squeeze. "And I was there visiting him for a week."

"Where'd you meet a movie writer, Kale?"

"Well–"

"We ran into each other over the summer on Cole Island. She was vacationing and I–"

"You were… working on… something," Kaley lied.

Walczyk supplied a fake laugh. "Yeah, I'll be damned if I remember what it was."

"So I figured I owed it to him to visit, since Newport's not far from Bangor." For a moment, Walczyk saw affection in Kaley Richardson's eyes.

"That's pretty cool of you," Steve said. The rest of their conversation was pleasant enough, though Steve had reigned in some of his charm as the beers stopped coming. Walczyk noticed that Steve kept glancing at Walczyk and Kaley's hands clenched together. It was finally Vivian, with their meals, that broke things up. Kaley gave Steve a half-hearted hug, deftly avoided a kiss, and told him it was nice seeing him again. Steve half-heartedly told Walczyk it was nice to meet him and went along his merry way, back to the bar, where he began animatedly talking with his friend Ron, throwing his thumb over his shoulder in Walczyk's direction.

"Thank you," Kaley said after Vivian had left the table. "Sorry to drag you into that." She slowly extracted her hand from Walczyk's.

"Hey," he said, smirking as he stabbed at the French fries on his plate with his fork, "always happy to be the pretend boyfriend." Walczyk took a few fries, nibbling away at them as he looked over at Kaley. She was sorting out her food on the three salad plates, just as he figured she would when she asked for them when placing her order. "So we've torn my life apart," Walczyk said, taking a bite from the steak. "Let's give yours a whirl."

"Let's not," she flatly said, removing the last fry from the onion ring side of her plate and dropping it onto the plate.

"Okay," Walczyk said.

They ate in silence for a bit before Kaley spoke. "When I was sixteen, my mother pulled me out of school."

Walczyk put down his chicken. "Why?"

"She sick of getting phone calls from the school telling her to come pick me up."

"What'd you do?"

She shrugged. "Well, my biggest offense was that I liked to pick fights when I was depressed. It let me get the rage and the unhappiness out. When I was manic I'd use the girl's bathroom as a smoke house; cigarettes, weed. Not because I liked it; just because I knew I could get away with it"

"So you got pulled out of school by your mother for smoking

in the girl's room?"

"Well, that and because she thought the other girls were encouraging me to do this." Kaley pulled the tops of her gloves back, and for the first time, Walczyk saw that her pale forearms were a mosaic of crisscrossing welts. While the majority of them years old, others looked somewhat recent.

"My God," Walczyk said, reaching hesitantly out to take Kaley's thin arm in his hand. It felt so cold and rigid. He resisted the urge to reach out with a finger and trace the scars. He let go of her hand and she promptly pulled her glove back up over her forearm, hiding the pain away. "Can I ask you a frank question about that?"

"Because the pain reminds me I'm alive." Walczyk looked at her curiously. Apparently she'd been posed this question many times before. "It's hard for someone who hasn't cut to understand, so don't worry if you don't get it."

Walczyk instinctively rubbed the back of his head. "Oh, I get it." He took a drink. "So what happened after you were taken out of school?"

"I got homeschooled until I was seventeen, then she let me take night classes and get my GED. They offered to let me to march with my class. I said screw that."

"How was the home schooling?" Walczyk asked, remembering all too well the homeschooling he received from his mother when he was suspended senior year.

"It sucked. Everyone in town thought I quit school because was pregnant. I got the worst looks from people when they'd see me in town. Like I was some degenerate."

Walczyk took a bite of his chicken burger while and he and Kaley continued talking, swapping manic stories and laughing at one another's folly. Kaley confessed that during one manic high, while being homeschooled, she posed nude for a friend's photography project, seductively draping herself over gravestones in the cemetery. Walczyk confessed that once, in what he now identified as a state of heightened mania, he shaved his head. "Well, part of my head. Seems I missed some spots. Ian had a field day with that. He called me 'Patchy' for a month."

Kaley finished the last of her French fries, and looked up at him. "This has been fun."

"We need to do this more often," Walczyk commented, putting

his flatware on this empty plate. "Not to come off as creepy or needy, but I need someone like you in my life."

"What," Kaley asked. "someone to remind you that you don't have it so bad after all?"

"Someone to remind me that I'm not alone. That mental illness has a face; that it's not just a clinical diagnosis."

"So, I'm the poster girl for mental illness now, am I?"

He laughed. "You do it well, Kaley Richardson."

"Thank you." She snagged a fry from his plate and snacked on it. "How are you doing in your journey with Christ?"

Walczyk looked around the bar a second. "You sure this is the place to talk about this?"

"He's here with us right now, so why not?"

"But we're in a seedy little dive bar."

"You forget, I'm talking about a guy who used to hang around with hookers and murderers."

"Point taken," Walczyk said with a shrug. "What was the question again?"

"I asked how your journey with Christ is going."

"It's going."

"Are you going to church?"

"Once in a while I'll go with Mum, if I feel up to facing the town."

"Curious about your transformation, are they?"

"Holy crap do they ask a lot of questions. Mum says it's all out of love, but sometimes I wonder if there's just a bit of morbid curiosity mixed in there."

"That's okay, Walczyk. Traditional church isn't for everyone. Hey, I rarely go."

"Why's that?"

"The questions… the judgment… the looks," she rattled off.

"Something I did get out of it is this Bible verse that the minister gave one Sunday. Philippians 4:13–"

"'For I can do everything through Christ, who gives me strength,'" Kaley recited. "So you're studying the Bible Bruce gave you?"

"Not a lot," Walczyk said, feeling the shame of not doing as he was instructed as a child in Sunday School all over again. "But I have been praying." His prayers had been conversations with God, as he liked to tell his mother when she would ask. He was sure to thank God for the blessings he had bestowed upon him, like a strong family and friends network to make sure he was okay (even when those friends and family were stifling the hell out of him). He thanked God for each day he had, and had even begun thanking Him for the talents he had been given. He prayed for resolution with things with Sara, and that they could at least maintain some fragment of a friendship, so that she would not be totally lost to him, despite his fears of seeing her again in the flesh.

"Good," Kaley said, seeming satisfied. "Do you feel yourself benefiting from a relationship with Jesus?"

"Well, I have a lot more to talk about with my mother," he remarked with a smile. "But, yeah, I do find myself benefiting from my relationship with Him. I know now that, when things get their darkest, when I've lost all hope, I'm not alone. I have someone there for me, twenty-four/seven/three-sixty-five."

"But you've always got your friends," Kaley remarked. "Vic, Hannah, April, me."

"But there's… this sounds funny, I know, but there's no fear of waking God up with my problems."

"That's good," Kaley said. "Remembering that you can rely on Him is a very important lesson."

The conversation came to an abrupt end when Vivian returned to the table to collect the plates.

"Refills on your drinks?"

"Please," Walczyk said. "And can we see a dessert menu?"

"Sure thing, Sugar," she said, flitting away.

"I've got to tell you something that you're not going to like, Peter Walczyk."

"What's that?"

"As much fun as this has been, and as much as I want to be a part of your life, it's high time you move along home. You don't belong here."

"I know," he said softly. "I just had to get out of that house, though. Those people–"

"Your family and friends," she stated.

"My family and friends, they were suffocating me."

"And now they know that," she said, "and I'm sure that you've taught them their lesson. But you can't keep running away from your problems. At some point, you need to stand up to them; meet them head-on."

"I know," Walczyk simply nodded. He knew that she was absolutely right. He had to face his demons, his friends, and get on with his life. But first, he wanted to make his parents and friends sweat it out just a little bit longer.

CHAPTER THIRTY
NEW BUSINESS

Walczyk was surprised when he pulled into his door yard. There was only one extra vehicle in the there – his mother's. There were no Chevy Silverados. No bicycles. No one rushed from the house, screaming and swearing, waving fingers and brandishing fists. As he lugged his suitcase up the front stairs, he heard laughter coming from within the house. Laughter that grew exponentially louder as he pushed the front door open. He wheeled his suitcase down the hall, the general din of happy noise turning into recognizable voices. His mother and April. As he neared the living room, those voices coalesced into actual, structured sentences.

"...So by the end of the day, it had gotten around the entire school that Henry had taken pictures of me in the bathtub."

"Oh, my God," April gasped. "You must've been *mortified*."

"April, I'm Peter Walczyk's mother; I'd left mortified a *long* time ago."

"What did you do?"

"First of all, we made Peter tell his bus driver that his father had, in fact, *not* been taking pictures of me in any part of the house. Then Henry had to go around, like a one-man fire brigade, putting out every single fire that Peter started. He had to tell the elementary school principal that Peter was making things up. He had to tell the middle school principal that Peter was making things up. He had to make the rounds on the phone with the school board and the superintendant, assuring all of them that rumors of his photographic proclivities had been greatly exaggerated. And it took him three weeks to convince Stella Lyons that there had never been any bathtub pictures. To this day, though, every time that poisonous little woman sees me in town, she gives me the evil eye, as though she thinks she knows something."

"That's awful," April said, laughing. "What'd you do to punish Peter?"

She shrugged. "I don't remember." She looked up at Walczyk. "What *did* we do to you?"

April turned suddenly, seeing Walczyk over her shoulder. He, too, shrugged. "I honestly don't remember, but I imagine it must've included no He-Man for a long time."

"Sounds like you got off easy," April said, getting up. She walked over to the coffee table and picked up his mother's cup. "Another decaf, Diane?"

"I'd like to, April, but I really should get going," Mum said. As she passed her son, she reached out, giving him a kiss on the cheek. "Are you and April up for supper with the folks tonight?"

"Sounds good," Walczyk said. Something wasn't right with this picture. The army wasn't here. Hannah wasn't crying, Vic wasn't antagonizing April, and his parents weren't frowning worriedly at him. Kaley's voice popped into his mind, asking him if that's what he wanted. To be punished. To be told what he could and couldn't do. *Certainly not,* he answered the voice in his head. "Where's Dad?"

"School," his mother said, as though the answer were painfully obvious.

"Aah. What about Hannah and Vic?"

"Vic's got a truck coming in this morning and he won't let anyone unload it without him. And Hannah's also at school," April stated.

"Well, I'll see you later on," Mum said to April. She stopped to give Walczyk one more kiss on the cheek before she walked out of the house. Walczyk slowly turned to April, who had one of those soap-dispensing sponge brushes, scrubbing out the coffee cups. He took a piece of biscotti from the plate on the kitchen table and bit into the tough, dry cookie.

"Don't do that," April said, still washing dishes. "They're almond, and you don't–"

"I don't like almond," Walczyk said, disposing of the rest of the biscotti in the kitchen trash can. "So, what's new?"

"Let's see…" April said, placing the coffee cups in the drying rack. "Vic finally fired that Phil kid."

"I take it you two are talking again."

"Let's just say we made peace and leave it at that."

"Okay," Walczyk said, opening the fridge, disappointed to discover that it was empty. But, he reminded himself, it doesn't just fill itself. "How's Hannah?"

"Calming down," April said, matter-of-factly. There was a distance about her. But it wasn't the kind of distance that she would put up when she was pissed about something. This was different. New. Walczyk didn't like it.

"Well," Walczyk said, stretching. "I think I'll make us up a shopping list and head into town, if you want to–"

"Sit down." April's demeanor had changed quicker than any of his bipolar moods. Walczyk didn't pretend not to hear her, shutting the refrigerator door. He walked across the kitchen to the table and pulled out a wooden chair and sat. April took the plate of biscotti away, putting the pieces into a Tupperware container and sealing it up before sitting herself. She just looked at him for a long time. The emotion behind the mask of a face she wore was inscrutable. The silence between them was deafening. The hum of the overhead light numbing.

"Look, I know, I screwed up," Walczyk said. "I talked about it with Kaley. I've got this really good thing going on, with you guys and the family. I know that you love me and want to protect me and make sure that I'm taking care of myself. But I've got to start telling you guys what *I* need. And what I need is a little freedom. Some room to move without explaining myself to anyone. A night at home alone, without a grand parade of activity and a chorus line of people wandering in and out of the place. I need things to start to return to normal around here. The way they were before I got so screwed up."

"Sounds good," she said. "But that's not what we need to talk about."

"Oh. What then?" he asked, warily.

April opened her mouth to speak several times, each time only exhaling and keeping her thoughts to herself. Finally, she spoke: "I'm going back to L.A."

"That's cool. You deserve some time off."

"No, Boss, I…" She shook her head. "Peter, I'm leaving."

Walczyk's chest tightened, as though he'd just been kicked in the ribs. The air whooshed from his lungs. The room began to spin. He fought hard to maintain control, but it was going to happen. He got up from the table, staggering down the hall for the front door, his vision blurring. He made it as far as the front steps when he dropped to his knees, wheezing. His head was filling with air. It felt like it was going to explode. He fought for every breath, only to have it taken away with a wheezing exhale.

A pair of arms wrapped around him. They were April's. He let her pull him into her lap and just lie there on the porch. He continued to fight for air as she caressed his temples, stroking his hair, shushing him, telling him it would be all right. Then another face appeared. The photographer who was always camped out across the road.

"My God, is he okay?"

"It's nothing," April's voice said from miles and miles away. "He's fine."

"He doesn't look fine."

"*He's fine*," she stressed. "And if anything to the contrary appears on the internet–"

"Hey, I can't report this – I'm part of the story now," he said, holding his hands up.

"Get me up," Walczyk said weakly, reaching out to the photographer. The man pulled, bringing Walczyk to his feet, and helped him over to the porch swing.

"Thank you, Mike," April said, settling onto the swing beside Walczyk. "And *please*, nothing about this."

"Depends," Mike said, looking at them with a smirk on his face.

"On what?" Walczyk weakly said.

"Let me know next time you're headed for the Bronze Lantern? A candid of you two walking in would be great."

Walczyk and April looked at each other, then Walczyk turned back to the photographer. "Sure," he said, shaking his head.

The silence after Mike left was long, but comfortable. April had leaned her head against Walczyk's shoulder.

"So you're leaving," Walczyk said, breaking the silence.

"When did you decide this?"

"I've been thinking about it for a while, now," April replied. "And, honestly, I've been torn. The best thing for you has been coming back here and living with your family and friends, letting them help take care of you. But at the same time, I've felt like I've been held back." Walczyk opened his mouth to speak, but she silenced him with a look. "It's nothing you did, or said. It's not your sickness or what happened with me and Vic or anything like that. It's just... well, I love you, and I don't want to leave you. But Boss, this isn't the place for me. I belong back there. Eli made me realize that when I went to home in September. I'll never be content being your roommate.

"But you're probably asking yourself when I really knew I was leaving. Four weeks ago. You were in the hospital. Your father had called me and told me you were having a bad day. What he didn't know was that before he'd called, I'd been on the phone with Eli. Word in the office was that Nicole, Burt's personal assistant, and–"

"Burt wants you to come to work for him," Walczyk said.

"Yeah," April said, smiling nervously. "Burt called me himself a day or so before you left for Newport and offered me the job."

"He told me this would happen," Walczyk said, numb.

"He did?"

"Three years ago. The Schueller Agency holiday party. We were having some very old scotch that Paul Newman had given him years ago. We were watching you dance with some hot young actor. I don't remember who. Could've been that shirtless werewolf guy from *Phases*, could've been Zac Efron. Doesn't matter who. This... this smile came over Burt's face. Lit him right up. More than the scotch was doing. He put a hand on my shoulder and said, 'Peter, that's one hell of a girl you got there. You had better be careful, because one day I will steal her away from you'." Walczyk looked at April, smiling. "And now he has, and I couldn't be happier." April took Walczyk's sleeve and dried her tears. "I'm so proud of you, April."

"Then you're not mad at me?"

"Not at all. You're right – this isn't your place. You need to move on. On to bigger and better things. You need it, and I think I need it. You know what I learned in Newport?"

"What?"

"That I can take care of myself, if I lean *just a little* on my family and my friends. And I've got plenty of them around here."

"So you're not disappointed in me?"

"For being offered a better job where you get to do more than make my lemon Jell-O? Hell, no!"

"And I'm not abandoning you?"

"April, in all truth, I never planned for you to stay here this long. I figured you'd get sick of Maine, or me, and take off after a couple of months. Truth is, you haven't been my assistant for a long time now. You've been my wife. My housekeeper. My best friend." Walczyk took a deep breath. "And, it gives me no pleasure to do this, but I have to." Walczyk leaned forward and kissed April. "You're fired."

"According to April, Walczyk seems to think they'll like it," Vic insisted, stirring the gravy in a little sauce pan over by the stove.

"And I seem to think these are people who have been sharing a large order of French fries for at least twelve years now. They're not going to want us smearing mozzarella cheese and gravy all over their routine."

"No, *poutine*," Vic said as Andrew lifted the fry basket from the hot oil. After Andrew had finished shaking the excess oil from the fries, Vic snuck his hand into the basket and snagged a handful of French fries before Andrew transferred them to a plate.

"Hey! If you want your own fries to experiment with, make them yourself. Don't steal them from the MacPhersons."

"But this is easier," Vic said quickly dropping the fries onto a small plate and reaching for the bag of mozzarella cheese he'd set out on the counter. He reached in and pulled out a handful of cheese, sprinkling it over the hot fries.

"Now, look at this!" Andrew complained. "I'm not serving that! Your hands aren't even clean!"

"I washed them before I started!"

"But you're contaminating everything. You've touched fries, now you're touching cheese. You're getting fry oil in the cheese bag. Cross-contamination, Big Brother!"

"Oh, shut up! You're just afraid to try anything new." Vic poured the gravy over the fries.

"Order up!" Andrew screamed into the dining room, adding a sprig of parsley to the plate. Any chef worth his salt would not bother garnishing French fries, but Andrew knew that the MacPhersons thought it was fancy, and that extra touches like that were what kept the locals coming back, if only for French fries.

The swinging café doors pushed open and Ingrid came through. She avoided Vic's eye, instead taking the steaming plate. "Table four?"

"Table four," Andrew said, not looking at the slip Ingrid had brought. It was Alec and Mary Caroline McPherson.

"Ingrid," Vic said, holding out the plate of poutine he'd made. "This, too. Tell them it's something new we're trying. It's on the house."

Ingrid coldly turned around and walked into the dining room, leaving Vic holding his small plate of fries and gravy.

"Didn't take it well, did she," Andrew asked, wiping down his counter.

"No, she didn't," Vic said thoughtfully. "I don't get it, Andrew. It's not like I told her I was leaving her for April, or any another woman."

"No, you told her you were leaving her for *no* woman."

"Yeah!"

"No!" Andrew crossed over to the counter where Vic had been working and starting wiping up stray shreds of mozzarella. "Bad move, Vic."

"How's that?" he asked picking up one of the steaming hot fries with his fingers and gingerly putting it in his mouth.

"You left Ingrid for no one. In her mind, that's the equivalent of saying that you'd be better off alone."

"Really?"

"Really," Andrew said. "If you'd left her for April, at least she'd have had some other girl to call a 'bitch' behind her back. But with no one, Ingrid's got no one to blame–"

"But herself," Vic said, nodding. He smiled at his little brother, clamping a hand on his shoulder. "How'd you get so smart, Andrew?"

"By watching your mistakes."

Vic laughed. "Well, you've had lots of opportunities then."

Ingrid's head appeared over the doors. "Walczyk's here!" she shouted, then disappeared.

Vic turned to Andrew. "I'd have been better off telling her I was leaving her for Walczyk!"

"Perhaps," Andrew said. Vic stepped out of the way as

Chelsea slid into the kitchen and gave Andrew an order.

"Hey, Vic," she said, sliding tightly past him and out the kitchen door. Vic followed her out the door with his eyes.

"Don't even think it," Andrew said, looking over the slip. "That's a mess of beans you don't want to be cleaning up."

"I was just–"

"*Go*! I've got work to do." Andrew looked at the slip. "What the hell's a 'putty melt.'"

"I'll send her back in."

"You'll keep away from her. She's our second-best waitress, penmanship aside. We don't need you pissing her off too."

Vic held his hands up in surrender, turned, and walked out the kitchen door. In the dining room, at his usual table, number seventeen, Walczyk sat alone, setting his laptop up.

"Walz!" Vic cried out. Walczyk looked up, saw his friend, and rose to give him a big hug. "Great to have you back," Vic told his friend, thumping his back.

"Good to be back," Walczyk said. "Sorry I had to be such a dink about leaving."

"Hey, forget it. There were bad calls on both sides."

"Both sides?"

"Fine! Bad calls on my side. But it's all water under the bridge, right?"

"Of course," Walczyk said, beaming.

"Good. Then sit down."

Walczyk sat. Table seventeen was in Ingrid's section which explained why there was no silverware set up and no glass of water.

"It would seem my waitress doesn't like me anymore," Walczyk said as he opened up his laptop.

"No, it's not you."

"Yeah, I figured it wasn't me. I'm not the one who broke up with her."

"How the hell'd you find out about that? I just broke up with her last night."

"When Karen brought me to my table, she warned me to be careful of Ingrid; that she might be 'in a mood.' Something about getting dumped last night by the boss."

Vic slumped into the booth. "Yeah, guess I *am* responsible for your crabby waitress."

"Oh, she's not been crabby. She's not been unpleasant in the least. She's just not been by."

Vic smiled. "That's my Ingrid: don't let personal issues get in the way of treating everyone with that Barrelhead five-star customer service." He sighed, craning his head around to see Walczyk's screen. "Whatcha working on? *Night of the Living Dead*?"

"Nope," Walczyk said, proudly. "I've washed my hands of that thing. I submitted my first draft to Marathon from Newport this morning with a letter to Anthony Severance. They can like it or they can lump it."

"Good for you," Vic said, patting Walczyk on the arm. "So what's the new project?"

"We'll know when I figure out what it is I have to say."

"I think you should do a movie about a guy who's gonna lose his Dad's restaurant to the bank and to save it, the waitresses all have this bikini carwash."

"You see, Vic, it's ideas like that one right there that get you banned from my house and make you Enemy Number One in your own restaurant."

"Look," Vic said, "it was pretty stupid of me to be dragging those guys over there all the time."

"Hey, it's not like I was an invalid stuck in the corner, his mouth wired shut. It was nice having company."

"Even if it was Dougie Olsen and his entourage?"

"Hey, they're not all that bad. I just don't want them playing with my Oscar or my Emmys."

"Yeah, well, it's because of Oscar and Emmy that I've given up on Mary Jane," Vic said.

Walczyk put his hand on Vic's shoulder. "Glad to hear it. Now, tell me the truth, did you guys smoke up in my house."

"No. Truthfully. We never smoked up in your house."

"Tell me you didn't have sex with Ingrid in my house."

Vic shook his head. "I didn't have full-on sex with Ingrid in your house."

"*Full-on* sex?"

"We might have fooled around a little, but pants stayed on."

Walczyk took a deep breath. "Listen, I'm getting a new couch. You want the old one?"

"Shut up," Vic said, punching Walczyk in the arm.

"Now tell me you're going to ease up on the drinking."

"I'm going to ease up on the drinking."

"And, please, tell me you'll make a good, honest effort to be civil with April. No using Hannah and me as sounding boards to vent your frustrations."

"We've already sorted that one out," Vic said, offering his hand. Walczyk took it and they shook.

"So what *did* happen with Ingrid? You didn't wake up at my place this morning, so you're not back on April's good side."

"I'm not on any side of April at the moment, and that might be the safest place to be," Vic said. "As for Ingrid, I told her it wasn't working."

"Okay."

"That I was tired of repeating the same, meaningless relationship with her over and over when there were only two things we had in common."

"Sex and what?"

"Sex and this restaurant," Vic said. "She asked if it was April. I lied and said no. She said she didn't believe me; that there had to be someone. She asked if it was anyone here. If it was anyone in town. Hell, she asked if it was Hannah."

"Insecure much?" Walczyk commented.

"I finally assured her that there was no other woman," Vic said. "That I just couldn't bear another meaningless go-round with her. That I was getting too old for that."

"Well done, Victor"

"Then she tried to stab me."

"What?"

Vic pulled up his shirt, showing Walczyk the trail of red Sharpie marker slashes from his nipple to his belly button. "And that's just what bled through my shirt."

"She attacked you!"

"With a Sharpie."

"And you didn't fire her?"

"There was three pair of scissors, a letter opener, and a fork on my desk. I'm counting my blessings and leaving things as they stand." Growing tired of waiting for Ingrid to either show up or show up and tell them both to go to hell, Vic looked over his shoulder toward the waitress station and called out, "Chelsea!"

A soft, stern "Vic!" came from the kitchen as Chelsea, all smiles, walked over to the table.

"Good morning, Mr. Walczyk."

"'Walczyk' is just fine."

"It seems Ingrid won't be waiting on us today," Vic said.

"Yeah, she said you could go to hell," Chelsea said. "She also said to tell Walczyk she's sorry she trashed his place all those times."

"That Ingrid... so sweet," Walczyk said. "Tell her thanks for me?"

"Sure. Can I start you off with a beverage?"

"Sure. Could I get a Diet Coke?"

"And I'll take a root beer," Vic said. Chelsea made notes. "Walz, you know what you want?"

"The patty melt looks awful good."

"I just don't see what the problem is," Cameron Burke said, settling into his chair beside Hannah Cooper. Hannah despised these teachers' meetings. She understood the need for the faculty to be on-board with what was going on the school, and what Henry was planning in the way of upcoming events. She had no problem with that. But every teachers' meeting ended the same way – in an argument of some kind between at least one other teacher and Stella Lyons. Henry would decide that they'd discussed the matter enough for one day, adjourn the meeting, and be cornered by Stella. But today, Hannah's mind was only half on the meeting. The other half was on the situation back at Walczyk's place. She'd not been around all weekend, though she did call April yesterday afternoon, to see what was going on.

"Apparently Vic and April are back on civil terms," Hannah told Henry.

"Peter told me as much this morning when I called him after period two," Henry confirmed.

"How's he doing?"

"He's much more relaxed," Henry said. "You should stop by. It's time. He'd like to see you."

"Survived his little trip out of town, eh?" Cameron asked, having been filled in over lunch the past couple of days with the details.

"I'm just glad that you four are friends again," Henry said. "I, for one, was worried he'd end up moving in with us."

"Well, now that the 'Where Is Peter Walczyk?' crisis is over," Stella Lyons groused from down the table, "I'd like to get on with the meeting. I've better things to do than follow Hollywood gossip."

"Stella's right," Henry said through gritted teeth, "we should be getting on with the meeting. Anyone know where JoAnn Benes is?"

"I witnessed her getting in to her car as soon as the last bell rang," Stella said innocently.

"Yeah," Roberta Palmer, the librarian, confirmed. "I figured she told you. The hospital in Augusta changed her chemotherapy day to Wednesdays."

"That's right," Hannah said, remembering JoAnn telling her such. JoAnn, who taught history at the school, wasn't much older than her and had been diagnosed with breast cancer over the summer. She'd opted to try chemotherapy over a double mastectomy.

"But she never told Henry," Stella stressed, shaking her head and tut-tutting under her breath. "That kind of thing is just inexcusable."

"I'll talk with her," he reassured Stella. Hannah had very little faith in the notion that this *talk* would be severe and punitive.

The meeting progressed rather smoothly. Almost too smoothly, Hannah feared. Jack Duncan, vice principal and the business teacher, re-voiced his concern for the need of new computers in the computer lab, as the current ones were woefully out of date, and growing slower and slower. Stella griped that computers were the least of the concerns the business department should be worrying over, but Henry quickly glossed over that and addressed the issue of dress code. After a detailed run-down of students who should be ashamed of themselves from Stella, Henry stressed that the faculty *did* need to start clamping down on the student dress code. Stella blithely remarked that a few of the teachers, both present and absent, should also consider what image they're putting forth before arriving at school.

"Finally, on a much lighter note," Henry said, "Cameron Burke has some exciting news for us."

"Well," Cameron said, sorting through his papers, "I was thinking it's high time we give the old drama program another try."

There was a mostly positive buzz coming from around the table. Stella's mouth curled down and Coach Conklin sat stiff as a statue.

"What a great idea," Mrs. Palmer said.

"What's the play?" Jack Duncan asked.

"*The Importance of Being Earnest*," Cameron said.

"A classic," Mitch Duffy, the calculus teacher, said.

"Never heard of it," Dylan Scott, the biology teacher said. "What's it about?"

"It's about this guy who—"

"I wouldn't get my heart set on it," Stella said, looking up from her interlaced hands. "I don't think the school board would be interested in sinking money into a project that has, in the past, failed to generate either the revenue or the positive response from the community that high school basketball does."

"But there's the beauty of it, Stella – we won't be spending school money. In fact, we'll be making use of equipment we've already put good money into. I'm setting it modern day, so the kids will wear their own clothes, we'll be using a minimal set. As to what money we will need, I have an ideas for fundraising."

"Legal, I hope," Stella sniped. Hannah felt her blood rising in her veins. It was bad enough this woman was so bitterly opposed to change that she shot down any original idea sent her way, but now she was going to shoot down ideas that could make the school money, give the students not interested in bouncing balls around an activity to entertain them, and promote school pride. An activity that would somehow raise its own expense money.

"Perfectly," Cameron said, rolling his eyes. "I plan on seeking out a group of community sponsors; individuals who–"

"Now I get it," Stella said. "Henry Walczyk's boy wants a theater program at the school, so he pulls Daddy's strings, takes in a few meetings with some of our more impressionable faculty members, some of which I have to question the depth and breadth of those relationships, and he throws a little money around so he can–"

"Oh, will you *shut up*!"

Hannah felt her cheeks burning as the faculty, one by one, turned to stare at her, perched between Cameron and Henry.

Stella rose from her chair, hands in front of her on the table. "Excuse me, young lady?"

"I said *shut up*. As in stop talking."

Cameron's hand was on her arm immediately. "Hannah…"

She shook his arm off, quickly looking past him to Henry, who, while concerned, was not making a move to do anything. "I'm

sick of it, Stella. Sick of it. In one sentence, you tore down four people
– three of them in this room. Co-workers of yours. You accused the
principal of being a puppet–"

"I never–"

"You accused Mr. Burke of being a push-over."

"Well, if he is–"

"And you insinuated that... well, that Peter Walczyk and I
share more than just a friendship."

"If that's what you want to call it."

"Stella, that's enough!" This time it was Henry standing, red-
faced, hands on the table.

Jack Duncan stood. "Why don't we adjourn for the day? Next
week? Same time, same place?"

"Different fight," Dylan muttered under his breath beside
Hannah as the teachers filed out of the room. Eventually, the library
held only Henry, who seemed to have calmed himself; Stella, who was
still leaning on the table; Cameron, who looked helpless to stop any of
the insanity that had just erupted; and Hannah, who still stood, hands
balled into fists, breathing loudly.

"Cameron, you should go," Henry said softly. Cameron said
nothing, scooped up his belongings in his arms, and slid from the room
without another word. Henry took a deep breath and began. "Let me
just say–"

"That was *completely* out of line, young woman!" Stella
growled.

"*Let me just say,*" Henry reiterated, "that this feud between the
two of you ends tonight. I don't care if you hate each other. I don't care
if you disagree on curriculum, on teaching styles, or on whom it is or
isn't appropriate to be friends with – all of this in-fighting *will* end
before we leave this room, or so help me God, I *will* bring the
superintendant in on it."

"Jim Williams has more important things on his plate than to
worry about which teacher is *shtupping* the principal's son."

"And *that*," Hannah barked, pointing a finger at the woman,
"will be the last time you discuss my friendship with Peter Walczyk
inside this school! Do you understand me, Stella?"

"Please," Stella said, turning to Henry. "We're getting all
agitated... over what?"

"Over ignorance," Hannah said. "And intolerance. You have

spit enough venom and hatred and bile around this school to pull it down to the ground floor. You strut about here as if you own the place, telling teachers how they will teach their classes, what they will teach, and when they will teach it. And it's not just the English department. You've pushed Dylan Scott around for wanting to teach sex-ed to seniors. Eighteen-year-old kids! You've complained to the school board because you heard that JoAnn discussed her breast cancer with some *female* students. And let's not forget about the yearly threats to remove Henry Walczyk from his position because he supports the arts. You know, Stella, there's a lot of talk about bullies in the schools lately, and I think they're right: bullies *are* insidious creatures that gnaw away at the weaker people around them to feel better about themselves. But they're not just the students."

Stella picked up her tote bag and started for the door. She turned, looking at them. "Seven months from now, when this little play thing blows up in everyone's face, tell me I was wrong. Tell me I was wrong about all of it."

The library door slammed shut behind Stella. Hannah breathed in and felt her legs give out from beneath her. She collapsed into her chair, Henry quickly grabbing her arm.

"You all right?"

"My God, Henry, what have I done?"

April's legs burned as she pushed herself past the McNabb house. She'd run almost four miles now and she was feeling it. She'd not been out for a jog in ages, and it certainly felt it as she pumped her legs just that much harder. She'd promised herself she'd stop for a rest at Henry and Diane's before turning around and starting the trip home.

The tan Lexus belonging to Garry Olsen's wife, Amanda, whizzed by, tooting its horn. April threw an arm up in the air, not sure if Amanda had even seen her wave.

As April wondered what would change in her life next, her iPhone began to ring. She reached down the front of her sports bra and slid the device out, looking at the screen. It was Eli. She slowed her pace to a jog and answered. "Eli, what's shaking?"

"Just what I want to know!"

"Just a second," she looked around, and then sat on the grass in front of Jimmy McNabb's house. "What's wrong?"

"Anthony Severance isn't happy about that e-mail."

"What e-mail?"

"Walczyk didn't tell you?"

"Eli, Walczyk fired me."

"But that was a joke, wasn't it?"

"I don't know. He hasn't talked to me about any projects lately."

"Do me a favor?"

"Sure."

"Go find him and see what he's thinking."

"Why? What's happened?"

"Paparazz-Eye is reporting that Peter just told Anthony Severance what he could go do with himself and Night.*"*

"That would work out just fine for me," Walczyk said, looking at his schedule April had prepared for him on the computer. "One o'clock, Tuesday the twenty-fifth. Great."

"How do you stand on your meds?" the receptionist at Dr. Woodward's office in Augusta asked.

"I've got a week's supply left."

"You've cut it a little too close. We can't prescribe without seeing you, but Dirigo should be able to authorize a refill to get you through until you see us."

"Great," Walczyk said. "Thanks so much."

"No problem. See you on the twenty-fifth at one. Have a nice day, Mr. Walczyk."

"You too," Walczyk said, taking the phone away from his head and ended the call.

He sifted through the phone's contact list, which was still filled with the names and numbers of many famous people. But there was only one "Lentz" in the list. Walczyk tapped a button and the number dialed up. Downstairs, he heard the front door open and April call out, "Boss?"

"Up here," he called out into the hallway from his office before returning his attention to the phone.

"Thank you for calling the Dirigo Psychiatric Hospital," an automated message began. Walczyk listened closely to see if he could put a face to the voice, but ultimately could not. *"If this is a life-threatening emergency, please hang up and dial 9-1-1. If you know the extension of the person you are dialing, press '0' now. Otherwise,*

please listen to the following options. For–"

Walczyk pulled the phone from his ear and pressed '0'. He had no sooner put the phone back to his ear when April, dressed for running in her red sports bra and black running shorts, appeared in the doorway, hanging from the frame, exhausted. Walczyk stood, sliding the rolling office chair across the room to her, as he keyed in the extension number April had put on his list of medical phone numbers.

"Who are you talking to?" she asked.

"Dirigo," Walczyk said quietly, then returned his attention to the phone. In his ear, Dr. Lentz's voice mail kicked in.

"You have reached Dr. Jonathan Lentz," Lentz's British accent intoned. *"Please leave a message at the tone, including your name, making sure to spell any difficult names, a phone number where you can be reached, and a brief message, and I will make every effort to return your call promptly."*

At the beep, Walczyk spoke: "Hello, Dr. Lentz. This is Peter Walczyk." Walczyk then spelled out his last name and provided his phone number. "I'm calling because I've just now gotten an appointment to see a doctor locally, a Dr. Cheryl Woodward in Augusta, but my medication will run out before I see her. I'm taking Lithium and Wellbutrin. The pharmacy information should be in my file. Thank you and hope to hear from you soon." His not-so-brief message left, Walczyk hung up. "You look beat," he said, taking a glance at April, who was no doubt stuck to the leather chair.

"I *am* beat," she said. "Your mother wasn't home and you were on the phone. I had to run back here from Jim McNabb's."

"But weren't you out for your daily run anyway?"

"Yeah, but I had to double-time it," she said, panting. "Make sure you were all right."

"I'm fine," Walczyk said, opening the small two-drawer filing cabinet under his desk and filing away the medical fact sheet. "Why wouldn't I be?"

"I got a call from Eli," she said grimly. Walczyk returned to his desk and clicked a few buttons on his mouse, clearing away the files on his computer desktop.

"Is this about the Paparazz-Eye thing?" Walczyk asked.

"Yes."

"Yeah, well, Severance must be pissed at me and wants to make me look bad. The e-mail Paparazz-Eye is running is *not* the e-mail I sent a few days ago from Newport."

Walczyk returned to his laptop, clicked a few buttons, and pulled up the e-mail:

```
To: Anthony Severance
From: Peter walczyk
Subject: Current Status of "Night"

Dear Anthony:

I shall make this brief, as you no doubt
have   other   matters   to   attend   to.
Unfortunately,  I  will  not  be  able  to
continue working on "Night" for you. I have
delivered what I consider to be a quality
script,  and  I  feel  that  incorporating the
notes  provided  to  me  by  the  studio  would
only  take  away  from  the  integrity  of  the
screenplay.

I  apologize  for  the  inconvenience  of  this
move, but feel it is one I must make. I wish
you  the  best  of  luck  with  "Night"  and  hope
that  we  can  work  together  on  another  project
in the future.

Sincerely,
Peter walczyk
```

"*What he can go do with himself?* I'd like to know where he got that," April groused, having read the e-mail over Walczyk's shoulder.

"It's easy. He's an executive, and executives like Anthony Severance think they're a better writer than anyone out there with a pen and paper; a better director than anyone sitting behind a camera with headphones and a furrowed brow. His ideas were gold, in his book, and me saying that I felt they would hurt the integrity of my work... well, I kind of asked for it."

April stood back up, gingerly. "Well, I'm going to take a shower. Try not to piss off any more studio executives until I'm clean and presentable."

"I can't make any promises," Walczyk said, returning to his cell phone.

"What've you got planned today?" she asked. Walczyk noticed – and respected – that she was being very careful to sound like she was asking a question instead of implying that he should be doing something.

"Well, Dirigo and Woodward's office are called. The twenty-fifth at one, by the way."

"Look at you! You want me to come along?"

"Actually, I thought I'd ask Dad."

April smiled. "That's a very good idea. He'd love it."

"I've got to finish up my outline for the last season and then I'm e-mailing that whole thing off to Ian."

"The final season, in a nutshell," she said. "One of the most sought-after e-mails in Hollywood."

"Yeah. Don't tell Hannah. She's finding it hard enough not telling Cameron Burke what happened in season three."

"Deal," April said, a satisfied smile on her face. She turned, limped out the door and down the stairs. Walczyk flipped over a stack of papers on his desk and took a red pen in his hand. At the top of his "Things to Do Today" list, he crossed off "Call Dr.Woodward's office for appointment." All that was left now was "Make Appointment with Taylor."

Walczyk picked up his phone and dialed the number outright instead of sifting through his contacts.

"Cole Island High School," the voice of his father's secretary, Martina, called out.

"Yes, this is Peter Walczyk calling for Henry Walczyk."

"Peter, how are you doing, Honey?"

"Much better," he said, smiling. "Thanks for asking."

CHAPTER THIRTY-ONE
DATE NIGHT

April kicked the front door open, laden with a dozen or so plastic bags. She waddled through the front hallway and into the kitchen, depositing the bags unceremoniously all over on the floor. She looked over at the couch, where Vic was lying, watching TV.

"What the hell are you doing?" April asked, sorting through one of the grocery bags and putting its contents away.

"Waiting for you," Vic replied, sitting up. "We have a date, remember?"

"First off, it's not a date. It's a civil get-together. Second, you're an hour early." She looked into the living room. "What are you–?" Her question was answered when she saw the screen. With a running time code at the top of the screen and a "Property of Walz-Ian Productions" stamp at the bottom of the screen, she knew exactly what it was: the upcoming third season of *Ordinary World*. "What the hell are you doing watching those?" she demanded, storming into the living room and collecting the invaluable discs which had been strewn about.

"Walczyk told me to look through them. Wanted to know what I thought." April was a bit miffed. Even she hadn't been given access to those episodes yet. "Frankly, the ending to episode four needs some serious work, maybe a reshoot. There's no drama to it whatsoever.

Now episode five, that one's not too bad. A bit redundant in the Ethan/Kara department, but Hugh Laurie as Danielle's father, that makes up for it."

April gave a half-hearted smile and turned around, continuing to put the groceries away. Vic entered the kitchen area and helped pick up some of the bags up, placing them on the kitchen table.

"So, how've you been?" Vic asked.

"Fine," April replied.

"Okay, I'm gonna ask that again, and this time don't give me the bullshit answer you need to give yourself. How have you been?"

April turned around, hands balled into fists. "You wanna know how I'm doing, Vic? I'm lousy, that's how I'm doing."

"Why?"

"Because I'm suddenly the villain of the piece."

"'The villain of the piece?'"

"I'm abandoning poor, sick Walczyk in his most desperate hour to go follow my own, selfish whims and desires."

"Who said that? Diane? Because she's been getting pretty mouthy lately, if you ask me."

April laughed, shaking her head. "No, no one said anything. It's… it's what the voice in my head has had playing on a loop for the past couple of weeks. Ever since Burt Schueller offered me that damned job."

"You *do* want the job, don't you?"

"Of course I want the job! Are you kidding? I've wanted that job since… well, since before I knew there were jobs like that."

"Really?"

"Oh, yeah. My mom and I would watch a movie, I never wanted to be the hero, or the main bad guy. I wanted to be the right-hand man."

"Really? I always pictured you wanting to be the number one bad guy; you're more Darth Vader than Grand Moff Tarkin."

"Who said I'm not Darth Vader?"

"But you said you're the henchman–"

"That's right. But Darth Vader was the right hand of the Emperor."

"Touché," Vic said, raising his eyebrows.

She nodded in appreciation, then returned to the kitchen to finish putting the groceries away. "So, where do you want to have our little get-together?"

"You mean our *civil* get-together? What's wrong with right here?" Vic asked.

"Vic, nothing hinky's going to happen tonight, you know."

"Who said anything about 'hinky?' Nothing will happen that you don't want to happen."

She thought a moment before replying, "Fine. But no funny business."

"I'll be completely serious," Vic said, moving his hand across his mouth to wipe away his smile.

"Oh, God, I'm in trouble," April said, reaching up into the cupboard for a couple of wine glasses.

"Wine?" Vic asked. "I thought the Old Merry Place was a dry house."

"I figured what the hell, it's a special occasion," April said, going down the hall. Vic followed her, glasses in hand. April rooted around through her closet, and finally stepped back, carrying a bundled up towel. She slowly peeled away the pink towel, revealing a bottle. Vic smiled, nodding in her direction, and followed her back into the kitchen, where she retrieved a cork screw from the utility drawer and uncorked the bottle.

"Question," Vic said.

"Answer," she replied, pouring Vic a glass.

"If there's to be no booze in Walczyk's house, why is there a cork screw in the utility drawer?"

She poured herself a glass and tossed the cork screw back into the drawer. She raised her glass. "To a new friendship."

"No," Vic said. "To an *old* friendship, take two."

April smiled and the two clinked their classes and drank.

"Mmmm," he said, looking at the label. "What is this?"

"It's a bottle Walczyk had been saving from his wedding. A gift. It's called 'Screaming Eagle Cabernet Sauvignon.' From the Napa Valley."

"It's exquisite," Vic said, pouring a little more. "I should look into seeing if we can get a bottle or two for the restaurant. You know, for special occasions."

"I'd hold off on that," April said. "This bottle alone cost $1,500."

Vic coughed, wine dribbling out of his mouth. April dashed to the sideboard and got some paper towel, not surprised by such a Vic's reaction to learning the price of the wine he was drinking. "$1,500... April, you don't drink that for just any occasion. Where'd this come from?"

"Walz said to get rid of it. I can't think of a better way. I think it was a gift from Chuck Lorre."

"Well, thank you, Chuck," Vic said, and then took another sip. "Now, tell me something: why do you keep talking about going back to L.A. like it'll be some great relief? I thought you liked it here."

"I do," April said, setting her glass down and continuing to put the groceries away.

"Then what's the big draw to L.A.?"

"What's the draw?" she asked. "The draw is, in L.A., I was a power player. A shark. One of Hollywood's most successful and feared personal assistants. But here, I'm not intimidating studio execs or organizing meetings with Oscar-winners. I'm playing nursemaid to an out-of-work writer, making sure he calls his doctor to get his meds on time. Shit, I used to know big people, Vic. Walz and I used to go to Jon Favreau's house to grill! I used to smoke cigars with Christopher Nolan. And now who do I know? Garry Olsen. Dr. Lentz. And Mr. Restaurant Big Shot, Victor Gordon."

"Whoa, hold on, now," Vic said. "Take all the pot shots at yourself you want, but leave me out of it. I'm more than happy with my lot in life."

"You are, aren't you? You really don't want anything else out of life. Is *this* really the man you want to be for the rest of your life?"

"Maybe not for the rest of my life, but for now, yeah. I've got it pretty damned good: a steady job at a successful restaurant and a roof over my head and food on my table. That's a hell of a lot more than some folks can say these days. So, yes, I guess I *am* happy with my life."

"How I envy you," she said, amazed by the simplicity of it all. She turned to him and asked, "Another glass?"

"Whoa! Whoa! Back it up there!" Walczyk cried out, pausing the video.

"What?" Hannah asked, looking down at him on the floor, slightly more than a tinge of annoyance in her voice.

"Who are those two guys?"

"Captain Kirk and Mr. Spock," Hannah explained.

"The hell they are!"

"What are you talking about?"

"That is *not* William Shatner and Leonard Nimoy."

"Oh, God, Peter, not again," she pleaded.

"But seriously. Who are these two? That one on the left, he doesn't even have pointed ears!"

Hannah got up and grabbed the remote from Walczyk's hand. He slapped at her hands, but eventually let her steal the remote. She resumed the episode. As the fight went on between the stunt doubles vaguely dressed like Kirk and Spock, Hannah snipped, "And I doubt your show has any faults."

"Of course it does," he said. "But on my show, unlike *Star Trek*, when Danielle and Kara get into a fight, you can always tell, stunt double or no, that it's Danielle and Kara, and not a Mexican who only looks like Kara when shot from behind."

"I don't remember them having a fight," she said, searching her memory.

"Aah, but they will," he teased, having just outlined the scene this morning.

Hannah bounced into a seated position, pausing the DVD and looking down at her friend, propped up against the couch. "Kara and Danielle throw down?" Walczyk had shown Hannah the as-yet-unaired season three of *Ordinary World*, but had refused to share plot details from his season four outline.

Walczyk shrugged, confident that Hannah had just lost all interest in whether or not Kirk was able to get the rest of his crew to beam up from the paradise farm planet that coincidentally looked like the Santa Ynez Valley in Southern California.

"Why?" she asked excitedly. "What happens?"

"If I were to tell you," Walczyk teased, taking the remote from the couch and resuming the episode, "we'd never learn where these mysterious spore plants came from."

She jumped down off the couch, cozying up next to Walczyk. "At least tell me, when does it happen? Who starts it?"

"If I were Starfleet, I'd evacuate the planet, and then use some kind of futuristic space DDT to kill the plants."

Hannah leaned her head against his shoulder, swaying gently against him. "It was Danielle, wasn't it?"

"You'll just have to wait," he said to her. "Ian and I haven't even *discussed* season four yet. I don't want to commit to anything I can't pay off."

"Fine," she said, pouting. "I'll just break into your house and raid your laptop."

"Please do. A sexy red-headed stalker caught breaking into my house? That will make my bipolar announcement seem mundane."

"Like you'll talk about it with the press."

"Hey, when the right reporter comes along, from the right news organization, with the right agenda, I most certainly will. I've got nothing to hide."

"That's very brave of you," she said, hugging his arm as she leaned against him.

"So tell me about this film club kid Dad wants me working with," he said, watching Kirk, Spock, and McCoy have their charming final thought moment on the bridge of the *Enterprise*.

"Taylor's a pretty good kid. Actually, he reminds me a lot of you. He's got this sharp, astute wit about him. As far as he's concerned, there are no limits; no lines that can't be crossed. He'll fight you, tooth and nail, to tell you why he should do a project his way. Granted, his arguments aren't always strong, or logical, but Peter, the results this kid comes up with. He can find a way to incorporate *any* assignment into something that matches his interests."

"For instance," Walczyk posited.

"For instance, he did a forty-minute video in which he depicted the Boston Tea Party in real time, like an episode of *24*." She leaned up against the couch beside Walczyk. "Did you finish going over his script?"

"Yeah," Walczyk said. "It's not bad. I mean, it's nothing I'd put into production at a studio, but as far as high school movies go, the beginning, middle, and end all flow into each other seamlessly." She smiled at him. He noticed. "What?"

"Nothing. It's just—"

"What?" he said, a smile creeping across his face.

"Well… I hear your name, and I don't think about the man winning an Academy Award for something he wrote. I think about us sharing a sleeping bag, drunk, on the beach. I don't think about the guy who calls people like James Spader and Natalie Portman and Ian Maeder friends; I think about the boy who told me that night we first made love that he was going to be famous some day. My only regret is that I never told you until now just how very, very proud of you I am."

"That's okay," he said. "I never said goodbye to you. I think we're even."

She laughed silently. "I always felt so bad for you."

"Why's that?" Walczyk asked, curious.

She looked down at the floor, absentmindedly tracing a random swirl into the dull wood. "Because in another city, another state, in a bigger school, you could have done amazing things."

He smiled at her. "I like to think that I *did* do some amazing things."

"You did, but–"

"Any artist worth their salt, be they a writer, director, actor, painter, singer, whatever, creates a toolbox. A place where they store every bit of their life that they can: kissing a grandmother's forehead one last time before she dies; impressing a girl at Walmart with your ability to improvise prop comedy in the plumbing department; hitting your best friend for stealing your toys at recess, all of that is in there. Then you exploit it, use it. That final kiss becomes Jackson saying goodbye to Laren."

"That was a heartbreaking episode," Hannah said softly.

"But if I'd been at another school, in another state, Stella Lyons wouldn't have gotten my movie banned for 'glorifying the gays,' I'd have never gone to Hofstra at the same time Ian did, and I'd have never had a friend to drag to California with me. The point is–"

"–that the toolbox would have different things in it."

"Hell, for all we know, the kid that went to that fancy high school of yours is now sorting sneakers at a Foot Locker in Riverside Iowa."

"So you're telling me that you have no regrets?"

"Oh, I have regrets. Just none about where I came from."

"Now *that's* the way to live," she said, getting up from the floor. "Be right back. Gotta pee." Hannah silently slid, barefoot, across the shiny wood floor.

It was a comfortable little apartment, Walczyk thought as he looked around the tiny one bedroom 'inefficiency' apartment, as Hannah called it. Built entirely out of proportion, Walczyk couldn't understand the intentions of whoever laid out the box-shaped space above the Bronze Lantern Book Store. Probably Garry Olsen himself.

The narrow kitchen that the apartment opened up into had just enough room for a piece of a counter, a four foot tall under-the-counter refrigerator, a stove, two six-foot adjustable shelves, and a three foot square table that folded up into the wall. The kitchen, with its pastel green appliances, reminded Walczyk very much of that dive he and Ian first lived in back in Hempstead, New York. Barely enough room to eat a meal, let alone cook one. The bathroom, which was off the end of the kitchen, was actually considerably larger than the kitchen, but was by no means luxurious. It did have a bathtub, though, and Hannah confessed that it was that convenience that had sold her on the space. The remainder of the apartment was a large open space looking down over Main Street. He could just imagine watching the Fourth of July parade from the living room, or seeing the perpetually drunk Carl Tanner drive his rusted-out red Chevy truck right through the large display window of the Misfit Toys Christmas Shoppe. Whereas Walczyk would have been content to get a fold-away sofa bed and tuck his made bed back into the couch when company came over, Hannah had a neatly made twin bed in the far corner.

In the remaining two-thirds of the relatively large living room, she'd set up three large bookshelves, all containing her favorite books, with everything from *Anne of Green Gables* and *Little Women* to *Carrie* ("It spoke to me," she always said, defending the choice) and a dog eared copy of the novelization of *Star Trek II: The Wrath of Khan*, a gift inscribed by her Grandpa Allen. A dinged-up nineteen-inch TV, modest by even his parents' standards, sat on top of an old school desk that had to have been salvaged from a trash pile in the basement of the high school. Tucked away inside the cubby space under the wooden desktop was a DVD player and a small collection of movies, most of them *Star Trek* titles, lavish remakes of the great historical novels, or the entire series (so far) of *Ordinary World*. End tables sandwiched a long, anorexic looking couch that was covered in maroon fabric. On the wall above the couch was the framed autographed photo of the cast of *Ordinary World* that he'd sent her one Christmas a few years ago. Framed photos of Walczyk, Hannah, and Vic at Walker Beach, her parents in front of their new home in Belfast, Hannah and her college roommate, Paula Copeland, and another shot of Hannah, Vic, and Walczyk, about ten or eleven, in Halloween costumes, filled the remaining wall space.

Walczyk laughed out loud, staring at that picture. Hannah and her mother had shopped through all three of the Island's thrift stores looking for clothes to make a hippie costume out of, finally sewing a seam down the sides of a patchwork quilt her mother had made for her as a child. With her hair in pigtails, a sad looking bouquet of daisies and dandelions in her hand, and a peace sign painted on her cheek, she had shown up at the Walczyk house, where she'd be joining Vic and the Walczyks for Trick or Treat. Walczyk had been obsessing since June, wanting the perfect Halloween costume. Finding a paint-stained pair of coveralls in his grandfather's barn during their summer sojourn to Patten, he decided to make his own proton pack and be a Ghostbuster. And Vic had his boxed Spider-Man costume, one of those plastic jumpsuit affairs with the asthma-inducing plastic mask, and changed at the house, having just chosen the disguise from the meager assortment of dusty *Dukes of Hazzard* and Strawberry Shortcake boxed costumes remaining on the shelves at Arbo's Drug Store the night before.

"Remember how the crotch split out of that Spider-Man costume when Vic got into the car?" Hannah asked, leaning over Walczyk's shoulder.

"I remember him crying like a baby until Dad patched it back up with Duct tape," he said, turning around. "And I remember Mum safety-pinning that red towel into his shirt so he'd have a cape."

"Well, she felt Spider-Man needed a cape. Do you remember your sister in that green sequined flapper dress?"

They both burst out laughing, remembering all too well. "I remember Henry coming close to a stroke when he saw her come down the hall spilling out the top of that old dance school outfit."

"Oh, God, yes," Walczyk said.

"Your father was mortified."

"And thus began the first of many inappropriate fantasies about my sister that Vic would have."

"His first true love," she cooed.

Laughing, Walczyk walked back to the couch and sat down on the floor in front of it.

"Interested in seeing the *Star Trek* where Spock goes into heat?"

"Saw it."

"When?"

"You made me watch it in high school when we were dating."

"That was fifteen years ago!"

"And I still remember it," Walczyk said. "Spock goes into heat, throws some soup at the wall, and gets tricked into thinking he killed Shatner."

"All right, then. How about the one," she said, flipping through the boxed set, "where they land on the Nazi planet."

"Space Nazis?" he said with a groan.

"Or the gangster planet."

"Space gangsters?" he remarked with equal disdain.

"Ooh," she said, holding a disc up, "Apollo and Mount Olympus!"

"Han, I thought the entire point of the *Enterprise*'s mission was to explore strange, new worlds, not just the Paramount back lot."

She replaced the disc in its case. "So, no *Star Trek* of any kind?"

"I'm afraid four's my limit. And the limit for any sane human being," he said. "Unless you want to break out some booze."

"Not on your life, buddy," she said, putting away the plastic DVD case. "How about a game?"

"Clue?"

"Kind of pointless with just two people."

"*Monopoly*?"

"You always cheat."

"Hiding money under the board for a rainy day isn't cheating."

"Yes, it is!"

"Hey, nowhere in the rules does it say I have to disclose my full earnings to my opponents."

"You cheat," she repeated.

"Fine. What about Uno?"

"Don't have it."

"TV?"

"I don't have cable, and I don't have an HD antenna."

"Wait a minute," Walczyk said. "You don't have cable?"

"Right," she said.

"But you said religiously watched *Ordinary World*."

"I do."

"How?"

She pointed over to the laptop set up on a small, wooden café table in the corner.

Walczyk smirked. "But HBO doesn't stream episodes online without a subscription."

She avoided his eye as she replied, "No, they don't."

"Which means you're illegally downloading episodes and watching them?"

"Well, technically, Cameron's downloading them and burning them to a disc for me."

"Bootleg DVDs! Even better!"

She cringed at the look on his face. "Peter, I just can't rationalize the cost of cable for one show, even if it's yours. I'm just a school teacher, after all."

He shook his head, milking the moment. "You won't spend your money for it, but you'll take it out of my pocket to watch it on your computer."

"Peter," she pleaded, hurrying across the room to him, "I'm sorry. I didn't know it would hurt..." The light bulb went on. "Hold up a second. I've used your laptop. You have a massive music collection on there."

"That I do."

"And you once said that you barely own twenty CDs."

"Another accurate statement."

"Explain that," she demanded, her hands on her hips.

"Simple: I'm a hypocrite."

"Another accurate statement," she parroted back moving across the room and picked her guitar up from its stand in front of one of the windows which overlooked the darkened town.

"I can't believe you still have that thing. When did you get that, Christmas 1990?"

"1994, my sixteenth birthday. And not only do I still have it," she said, plucking a string or two, tuning the instrument. "But I've finally learned to play it."

Walczyk sat up, smiling. Next to the sound of a piano on a scoring stage, a gently played acoustic guitar in an intimate setting was his favorite musical sound. "Kevin Booker teach you?"

"Kevin and his family moved to Rhode Island in '07."

"But he was the only teacher in town. How'd you learn?"

"Promise you won't laugh?"

He shook his head. "I never promise not to laugh. Who taught you, huh? Does Dwayne McGraw have a secret talent?"

"Absolutely not!" she said, disgusted. "If you must know, it was Willard McIntyre."

"Willard McIntyre?" Walczyk laughed. "He's what, ninety-four?"

"Ninety-one," she corrected, "and a beautiful player."

"Does Violet back him up on the banjo?"

"If you must know, Violet passed away four years ago."

"Oh. Well, as they said in those old westerns Henry loves to watch, are you just gonna pluck that thing, or are you gonna play something?"

Hannah smiled proudly, and adjusted her position on the pillow, tugging her skirt back down over her knees, and picked a song from her repertoire.

As she played, Walczyk stole a pillow from the couch and sprawled out on the floor, the image of them sitting here in her apartment on a Friday night stuck in his head. He had to use it somehow. Maybe the series finale. A woman in a red striped skirt and a white cashmere sweater sits on an overstuffed purple pillow, playing a guitar. The man, jeans and a T-shirt, lies there, listening, a stupid grin plastered across his face. As his mind tried to figure out how to work it into the episode, Hannah's silky sweet voice sang, her fingers slowly, but skillfully, turning six metal strings and a wooden box into a source of beautiful folk music as he drifted off to sleep on the rug.

Four hours, a $1,500 bottle of wine and the better part of a gallon of cheap vodka later, Vic and April were cuddled up on the couch together. A huge stack of DVDs and Blu-rays lie spread out across the floor. The empty box of what used to be a large pepperoni from Mama Rosa's had been kicked into a corner. On the TV, the volume very low, was Kevin Smith's *Chasing Amy*, April's favorite "drunk movie." She lay curled up against him, her head on his chest, her eyes shut.

"What are we going to do, Vic?" she slurred.

He slid his hand over hers, fingers interlacing. "We'll do what all doomed romances do."

"Kill ourselves?"

"Are you kidding? I don't trust you enough to have faith that you'll do me first. No, I meant we'll just have to make the best of whatever time we've got left, and then decide before you leave if we'll stay exclusive."

"Exclusive," April repeated. "That'd mean no Ingrid Connary, you know."

"Yeah, I think the Vic and Ingrid romance has used up its ninth life."

"Good. I always thought you could do better."

"Like who?"

"Oh, I don't know."

"What? You?"

"Well," she said, smiling broadly, sliding Vic's hand back over her stomach and holding it there.

"What are you thinking about?" Vic asked after the movie had ended and April had shut the TV off.

"Bran."

"As in the flake?"

"As in the Wellington. Brandon Chester Wellington III."

"Brandon Chester Wellington III," Vic repeated, amused. "Sounds like one of those preppie guys in the pink polo shirts and white dress pants who sling sweaters over their shoulders."

"Well, Bran *did* look good in pink. But we were living in Arizona, my mother and I. It was plaid shorts and sockless loafers year-round."

"Eesh," Vic said, squirming. "Sockless loafers in Arizona. You must've wished he'd wear his socks when he got into bed with you."

"What about you?" April said.

"Pee."

"What?"

"I was thinking that I had to pee. But now I'm thinking about this Bran Wellington. Was he the one? The one you fell in love with first?"

"Yeah," she said, snuggling tighter against Vic. "Bran was a good guy. Always made me feel like a lady."

"Good. Because I'd hate to have to track him and his sockless loafers down and exact bloody vengeance."

"What about you? What girl made you feel like a man? And *do not* say Ingrid."

"No, not Ingrid."

"Hannah?"

Vic bolted upright. "How the hell'd you know about Hannah?"

"Vic," April said, sitting up to join him, "I knew about you and Hannah before we showed up at the restaurant after meeting on the beach."

"Walczyk's got a big mouth," Vic said.

"He does. So if it's not Ingrid, and it's not Hannah, then who?"

"Gillian Nicholson."

"Who?"

"Gillian Nicholson," Vic said. "A few years after we all graduated, Dougie Olsen and I were sharing this little apartment down on Bennoch Road. And Dougie was just starting to date Mia. I was working at the restaurant, but not running it. Dad hadn't... Well, anyway, this girl comes in with her family. She's this hoity-toity priss of a girl, nicely dressed, well-mannered. Donny catches me checking her out and dares me to go wait on her. So I snag some menus and take off for the table. The old man of the family's kind of a jerk, and the mother's a complete lush. But this girl, she keeps making eyes at me when no one's looking. While I'm passing out the deserts, I feel her hand slide into my pocket. I check it out later – it's a piece of paper with a phone number on it. It's her hotel room at the Spruce Nettle. Well, Donny gives me a couple beers from the bar, we meet up and have a good time. They stayed two weeks on the Island. Near the end of it, Doug says we should have this big ass party and invite her along with half the Island. She shows up, and we have a great time. One thing leads to another, and... well, you know."

"Just how the hell did sleeping with some dirty girl masquerading as a priss make you a man?"

"Because it was the first."

"A girl like that? Likely."

"No, it was because my first."

"Even *more* unlikely."

"Not *that* first. One night she invited me out to dinner at DeLancie's with her family. I met her father, her mother, and her little brother, a spoiled rotten little shit. It was the first time I'd ever gotten dressed up for a dinner, the prom aside. It was the first time I went through the whole 'meeting the father' bit, and it was the first time I was in a position to pull a chair out for a woman. It's like *Titanic*: I was the lower-class guy and she was the rich lady who–"

"I swear, if you say she made you feel like the king of the world, I'm going to lose it."

"I was going to say she was the rich lady who made working-class me feel like a real gentleman, if only for a night."

"Drunk as I am right now, that was a rather touching story, Vic."

"Thank you." He kissed her and lay back down on the couch, spooned up beside her under the quilt.

"You are aware this really sucks!"

"It sure does. I have to pee and don't want to get up."

"No, I mean having to leave Walczyk alone. He thinks he's ready. He says he is. But I just don't know. I think–"

"April, you'll never be leaving him alone. Not here." April leaned up to kiss Vic, but suddenly groaned, doubled over, and pulled away. Confused and concerned, Vic turned to April. "What is it?"

She flew to her feet, hands clutching her stomach. She tore off through the living room, down the hall. Vic and Dexter bounded after her. "April?"

Hearing April throw up, Vic stopped, turned around, and walked into the kitchen, where he took a bottle of water from the fridge before going into bathroom. There, he found April on the floor, propped up against the bathtub. He handed her the bottle of water, ordering her to drink it, and wet a washcloth under the tap with cool water. Vic pressed the cloth to her red face.

"How's that?" he asked, taking a seat on the floor beside April. "Feel better?"

"No," she groaned, taking a large drink of water.

"What's wrong? You gonna be sick again?"

"No. It's just… now, on top of a raging headache and an upset stomach and puke taste in my mouth, I still have to decide what to do about L.A."

"No, you don't," Vic countered.

"Yes, I do," April said wearily. "I don't know if I'm coming or going."

"I suspect you know what you're going to do," Vic answered, sliding down to the floor beside April. "I think you've known all along what you want to do, and that's what's making you so sick. Well, that and fifteen hundred dollar wine with a cheap vodka chaser."

Tears welled up in April's eyes and she buried her face in Vic's chest, sobbing. Dexter wandered into the bathroom and curled up on the mat by the tub, resting his head against April's hip as she fell asleep in Vic's arms.

No one in either Walczyk's house or Hannah's apartment was an early riser the following morning. It was Walczyk who finally broke the ice, texting April from Hannah's couch around 10:45 to see if she was interested in seeing just how late Costigan's would serve breakfast. He wanted to eat before his 12:30 with Taylor Hodges, the high school Hitchcock.

An hour later, Walczyk and Hannah walked from Main Street to Commerce Street, where they found Vic and April nestled in a corner booth, sitting rather close together.

"Good morning, friends," Walczyk said, unslinging his book bag and sliding into the booth.

"Good morning to you too, Boss," April said. "Hannah, how's it going?"

"Not bad at all," she remarked. "Fatigue aside. Vic, what's up?"

"Oh, not a lot," he said, sipping at his coffee. "Hope you don't mind April and I ordered already. We didn't know how long it'd take you to get presentable."

"So, *April and you*" Walczyk said, eyeing them. "Are we to assume you two are back together now?"

"I wouldn't call it that," April remarked.

"Friends with benefits?" Hannah asked.

"We're opting not to define it," Vic said. "It is what it is."

"Don't tell me you've made rules governing how this 'it is what it is' works out," Walczyk groaned.

"No, we didn't write down rules," April said petulantly. "We might have agreed on a few key principles, but nothing written in stone."

"Just rules of thumb, really," Vic added. "Suggestions."

"So she's free to have Hannah hook her up with Eggy Robinson?" Walczyk asked.

"Who the hell's Eggy Robinson?" April inquired.

"Another time," Hannah said, looking nauseous.

"And Vic, that leaves you in the clear to start back up with Ingrid," Walczyk teased.

"Ingrid and I are as the dodo is," Vic stated.

"The sex lives of our friends now discussed," Hannah said,

"what have you got up your sleeve? You said it was 'absolutely imperative' that we get together this morning."

"Well, if it's not official yet, it is now: April's leaving us."

"What?" Hannah cried out. She elbowed Walczyk. "Peter, you never said anything!" She turned to April. "Where are you going? When? Why?"

"That leaves who, what, and how," Vic retorted.

"I've taken a job with Burt Schueller, the founder of the talent agency that represents Walczyk. I'm returning to Los Angeles the second week of November to take over for Burt's current executive assistant."

Hannah reached across the table. "April, that's wonderful!"

"I'm proud of her," Walczyk said. "Burt Schueller is a very discriminating man, and I'm sure that if he's decided to poach my assistant, he's got a damned good idea as to just how talented she is." April nodded her thanks in Walczyk's direction. "So, this woman I've spent five years of my life answering to is leaving me. I need you guys, her friends in Maine, to help me plan her going away party."

"Peter," Hannah said in hushed tones, "shouldn't this be a surprise?"

"Oh, no," April said. "I don't do surprises."

"Yeah," Walczyk confirmed. "She sucks at them. She always figures it out three weeks ahead of time, and either makes other plans, throwing the entire party into disarray, or she gets really obnoxious about knowing the secret. Either way, she ends up miserable because she knew it was a surprise and angry because no one hid it well enough."

The waitress, a pretty teenage girl with a name tag reading "Logan," arrived at the table, a platter balanced somehow on her hand. "Cinnamon pancakes?" she asked. Vic raised his hand and she set the plate down in front of him. "The fruit and yogurt parfait must belong to you, then," she said, placing a large sundae glass filled with a blend of yogurt, fruit, and granola in front of April. She turned her attention to Hannah and Walczyk. "Are you having anything this morning, Miss Cooper?"

"Still serving breakfast?" Hannah asked.

"Until one," Logan replied.

"Excellent. Can I get the Belgian waffles?" Hannah asked, closing up her menu and handing it to Logan. "With strawberries and a cup of coffee?"

"Sure thing, Miss Cooper. And for you, Mr. Walczyk?"

"Plain old 'Walczyk' is just fine," he clarified, having not opened his menu. "Just... oh, I don't know... three eggs, over hard. Side of salsa. Toast. Sausage links and hash browns. Oh, and corned beef hash. A side of that, please"

"He'll have *two* eggs and hash browns. No corned beef hash." April corrected. Logan looked from April to Walczyk. "Guess Mother has spoken. Two eggs. But when the meal comes, I'd like a large glass of milk–"

"–with ice in it," the others chimed in. With a curious expression on her face, Logan scribbled down the specifics and left the table.

"What the hell was that?" Walczyk said, turning on April as soon as Logan was gone. "'He'll have two eggs...' Who do think you are now?"

"Your friend," April said. "Look at you, Boss. You've already put on, what, ten pounds?"

"Lentz said weight gain was to be expected from the meds."

"That doesn't mean you have to sit there and get fat. *That's* why I'm pushing you to exercise more. To make better choices in what you eat. It's bad enough you've got to deal with bipolar disorder, I don't want you facing diabetes, heart disease, or obesity on top of it."

"Why don't we get back to the party?" a very uncomfortable Hannah suggested. Vic sounded his agreement, digging into his pancakes.

"Suits me," Walczyk said. "I figured we'd drag April in on this one, since she'll be doing most of the organizing and purchasing."

"What makes you think that?" April asked. She turned to the group, adding, "What he's failed to mention is that when I told him about this a week ago, he fired me."

"Peter!" Hannah hissed.

"Well, what was he to do?" Vic asked. "She was a turncoat. A risk. She could expose his entire web of bullshit and lies."

"Still could," April said. "But, Walz, I figured I *would* be organizing this party, so I've already made some preliminary plans." She fished out her iPhone and started tapping the on-screen buttons. "God knows what kind of mess it would turn out to be if I left it in your care."

"That's my girl," Walczyk said. "Now, I do have just one suggestion. I figured it'd be cost-effective and convenient for all if we had the party at the Barrelhead."

"We are not having it at the Barrelhead!" April barked out, the volume of her voice startling an elderly couple who sat finishing up their coffee at the table behind them.

"You wanna lower your voice?" Walczyk chastised. "You're scaring the Fishers."

Lowering her voice, she continued with her point. "Where's the joy in it for Vic, having a party for your lover–"

"Lover, is it?" Vic asked, grinning.

"Go to hell," she countered. "What fun is it to have a party for *a friend* when you have to supervise the restaurant she's having it in?"

"I do take time off from work, you know," Vic reminded her.

"So, Vic," Hannah asked, changing the subject, "how are the pancakes?"

"A complete frigging mystery."

"I beg your pardon?" she asked as Walczyk and April looked at Vic, puzzled.

"These pancakes… how they're made… it boggles my mind."

"Here we go again with the pancakes," April said, rolling her eyes.

Vic ignored her sarcasm, thrusting his fork in Walczyk's direction. "Walz, you think it could be a tablespoon of cinnamon to every cup of batter?"

Walczyk grinned, and ate the piece of pancake dangling from the fork. "I have no idea what you're talking about. I'm no cook. An eater, yes," he said, stabbing another piece of Vic's pancake with the fork, "but no cook."

"Look, can we get back to my party?" April growled, her fruit and yogurt parfait untouched in front of her. "So the Barrelhead is out. What's next?"

Vic passed a fork over to April. "You think *two* tablespoons of cinnamon for every cup of batter?"

"Why does she get to decide the Barrelhead's out?" Hannah pouted. "Just because it's her party. Personally, I think it would make more sense to have it at the Barrelhead. Friendship and loyalty aside, it's the best food on the island."

"That," Walczyk said to April, "and I'm fairly certain that if you sleep with the one of the owners, you might be able to get us a deal." April was not impressed.

"We could always do the Moondoggy," Vic suggested, smirking. "Guy could play 'Happy Birthday' on his ukulele."

"The place is already dressed like a party from hell," April quipped.

"Oh," Vic said, excited, "and we could all order the Peter Walczyk Celebrity Special."

"I'm a jerk," Walczyk said. "We all know that. But even *I* wouldn't force everyone to pretend to enjoy a ham, turkey and corned beef sandwich with ketchup, spicy and regular mustard, provolone cheese, pickles, lettuce, onion rings, and ranch dressing on blueberry rye bread."

"Either Guy really is touched in the head or he just hates Walczyk," April said.

"Guy Martin hates no one," Hannah said. "He's just... well–"

"Touched in the head," Walczyk suggested.

"Hannah," Vic said, cutting off another piece of pancake, "you try this." Vic passed the fork with a piece of pancake pierced on its tip to Hannah.

"What exactly is it you're looking for?" Hannah asked.

"Cinnamon to batter ratio."

Hannah ate it. Swallowed it. Considered it. Furrowed her brow. Frowned. Licked the inside of her mouth. "I have no idea, Vic. But I can tell that they're using Splenda instead of sugar."

"How the hell could you tell that from one taste?" Vic asked, baffled.

"I asked Kristy for the recipe a couple of months ago," Hannah said, smiling.

Vic frowned and took a sullen bite of his pancakes. "So where are we with restaurants? Just the Barrelhead and the Moondoggy?"

"What about DeLancie's?" Hannah asked.

"I hate seafood," Walczyk replied.

April asked, "What's that Red Sky at Night place down on Bleaker?"

"Seafood," Vic said. "Weezie's?"

"We're *not* doing it at Weezie's," April demanded. "Damn party would have to wrap up before one in the afternoon, or Weezie would kick us all out.

"What about that Escobar place down on Belfast Road?" Walczyk asked. "They used to do half-decent Mexican."

"Eight years ago they did," Hannah said, frowning. "Now they do half-decent seafood."

"Well, damn, does anyone in this town do anything that's not seafood?" April asked.

"On an Island off the coast of Maine?" Vic countered.

"Weezie's," Walczyk suggested.

"The Moondoggy," Hannah supplied.

"The Barrelhead," Vic offered.

"What about that Figaro's down on Broccoli? That one near the school?" April asked, hopeful.

"Amazing food," Walczyk said, excited.

"The *best* breadsticks," Vic added. "They've got this buttery garlic spread I've been trying to decipher for years."

"Then why not have the party there?" April asked.

"They're closed for the off-season," Vic said.

"They are? Since when?" Walczyk asked.

"I don't know," Vic said. "Ninety-seven? Ninety-eight? You really should have stuck around; you'd know these things."

"Now I know why we always loaded up the car and headed across to Portland for birthdays and anniversaries." Logan returned to the table with Walczyk's platter of food and Hannah's waffles.

"So, why the ice in the milk?" she asked, topping off the delivery of food with Walczyk's iced milk.

"Don't ask," April said. "Long, disgusting story."

"Okay," Logan said warily, backing away from the table.

"Honestly, guys," April said, finally attacking her parfait. "Don't worry about it. It doesn't need to be fancy. Just friends, the folks, and some good food. Hell, I'd settle for a home cooked food and some of that wine in the box."

"There's a notion," Vic agreed.

"Don't go making it easy for us," Hannah said, poking at Vic.

"No, you're getting a proper party," Walczyk informed her, "like it or not."

"Besides, what else do we have to do?" Vic asked, still tasting his breakfast carefully, making notes on a napkin.

Two teenagers walked up to the table, both looking every bit the kind of film student Walczyk would have expected to see at

Hofstra. The young man reminded Walczyk of himself, sporting a wrinkled *Citizen Kane* T-short and baggy cargo pants; the young woman looked like Ingrid Connary, if Ingrid dressed like Hannah did. She wore a baggy sweater and a long skirt, with black stretch pants under it.

"Sorry, but no autographs, kids," April said, holding her arm out like a linebacker.

Hannah looked up. "April, it's all right. I know them. Taylor, Sasha, what's up?"

"Taylor Hodges and Sasha Connary?" Walczyk asked, turning to face them.

"Yes, sir," Sasha said. Taylor simply nodded eagerly.

"Well, gents and ladies… and April," Walczyk said, rising from his seat, "my twelve-thirty is here, so we're going to go find ourselves a table. In another establishment. April, can you ask Logan to box that up for me?"

"What do I look like, your assistant?"

Walczyk gave her a smile and got up, taking his coat from the back of the chair and slinging his book bag over his shoulder. "See you guys in a bit. And good luck with the party planning." Walczyk threw a hand on Taylor's shoulder, guiding him toward the door.

"Well, now that *he's* gone," April said softly, "I've got another party I want to discuss…"

Taylor, Sasha, and Peter Walczyk found a nice, out of the way table at the Bronze Lantern just a block over and settled in. Taylor ordered a coffee and a bagel with cream cheese for himself, a soy latte with extra foam for Sasha, and a hot chocolate with a mint tea bag for his guest, who looked the table over and commented, "You guys are really drinking coffee?"

"Why wouldn't we?" Sasha asked incredulously.

"You're what, fifteen?"

"Sixteen," Taylor replied, a tad more defensively than he'd wished.

"And I'll be seventeen in August," Sasha added.

"Look, Mr. Walczyk–"

"Actually, Taylor, I prefer just 'Walczyk.'"

"Sorry," Taylor said, already kicking himself for messing up in his meeting with the famous director. "Walczyk, I didn't mean to drag you away from your friends. If I'd known, we could have rescheduled for–"

"Relax. I've spent more than enough time with that bunch since I got out of Dirigo."

He brought it up! Taylor shot a glance at Sasha, unable to believe that Walczyk brought up the mental institution. "How was that whole thing, if you don't mind my asking?"

"I don't mind at all," Walczyk said. "It was… unique. You've never really lived life until you've taken a liquid hand soap-only shower in a psychiatric institution."

Taylor wanted to laugh, but held it in. "So, did you get a chance to read some of my script?"

"*Our* script," Sasha chided.

"Fine. *Our* script."

"Oh, I read the whole thing," Walczyk said matter-of-factly.

"Really?" Sasha blurted out with him.

"Three times," Walczyk said, fishing it out of his book bag. "Very impressive, for a sixteen-year-old and a sixteen-year-old-going-on-seventeen-year-old."

"Thank you," Taylor said, finding it hard to breathe.

"That means a lot," Sasha coolly added.

Taylor noticed that Walczyk's copy of *Coach Conklin* was littered with red markings. He knew he had to have every one of those notes. Sasha quickly began scrambling through her bag, retrieving a pen and a notebook.

Sasha leaned forward in her chair. "Your father said you were interested in discussing it with us."

"That I am," Walczyk said. "But you need to understand, as it is in show business, everything I say is blunt and to the point. But remember, it's not about you–"

"'It's about the story,'" Sasha said. "You said that to Judy McNamara in your June 2009 interview in *American Screenwriter* magazine."

"Impressive memory, Sasha," Walczyk said, opening the script. "Now that we're on the same page, one of the bigger things that struck me was your lead, Morgan. Right off, he's in love with the cheerleader."

"Monica," Taylor answered.

"Yeah, you've got to change one of the names. You don't want to have two M's for your leads. Doesn't seem it, but it could get confusing. Personally, I'd change Monica. Morgan's more uncommon for a guy; more memorable." Sasha scribbled the note into her notebook while Taylor tried his damnedest to look casual drinking his coffee. "You've got lots of shit to fix in here that's technical, and I know if you see where I've marked it, you'll understand. Small stuff; the language you use in describing things to the reader. Things you need to include in your descriptions and stuff you need to forget about. But you'll learn about that the more screenplays you read. I want you to check out a book called *How NOT to Write a Screenplay*. It was written by a professional script reader, Denny Martin Flynn, and uses copious examples from actual film scripts. Anyone who wants to write a script needs to own a copy."

Sasha continued scribbling notes down at a furious pace while Taylor just sat back and soaked it in. He couldn't believe it – he was taking a meeting with Peter Walczyk! This was nothing short of incredible. He hoped Sasha was appreciating just how rare an experience this was.

"Now, let's talk character," Walczyk said.

Sasha turned a page in her notebook, not looking up.

"Take Morgan. He's a shy guy who learns to step up and confront his fears – i.e. the coach – in order to save the day and get the girl. I like that. The best horror pictures are the ones with the unlikely heroes. Just look at *Fright Night*, *Gremlins*, or *Halloween*. But there are points in the script where he's just too confident, too sure of himself. This is a guy who is out of his element lifting a baseball bat, let alone attacking someone with it." Walczyk turned the opened screenplay so he could read it. "Yeah, you had this part on page eighty-one where he *confidently* swings the bat and takes out one of the jocks. Almost anyone can pick up a baseball bat and take out a guy. I think it'd be more interesting to see him pick up the bat and *not* be able to take the jock out on the first try. Make a scene of it. Then, in the end, he manages to subdue the guy using his brains. Have you seen *Goldfinger*?"

"Of course," Taylor said, putting down his coffee. "1964. Sean Connery, Honor Blackman and Gert Frobe, directed by Guy Hamilton."

"Well, guess we know what you're an expert in," Walczyk said, grinning. "Anyhow, in the end, when Bond and the giant bad guy are locked in the bowels of Fort Knox... it's a suspenseful fight because there's no way Bond can take this guy out; the henchman's just too damned big. If Bond had *confidently* cold-cocked the henchman, then gone about disarming the nuke, it would've been a boring, unbelievable scene. Not to mention shorter and less suspenseful. But the henchman is stronger than Bond. Outmatches him in every aspect except one: Bond's a fricking genius. He adapts to his surroundings and, eventually, figures out how to electrocute the bad guy, then disarm the bomb with only 007 seconds left on the timer. See?"

"Yeah," Taylor said, madly trying to keep up with Walczyk. He was in awe of the amount of knowledge that Walczyk had; that he was just *giving away* to him. It was overwhelming.

"So, in that scene," Sasha said, rewriting aloud, "Morgan and the jock fight. Morgan swings at the jock. The jock grabs the baseball bat and shakes it, throwing Morgan off. Kicks Morgan a little. Then Morgan–"

"Morgan takes a pen out of his pocket and jabs the jock in the Achilles tendon," Taylor said, feeling on fire.

"Exactly, guys! That's Morgan assessing the situation, and not only using his smarts, but his own weapons, to subdue the bad guy. And that pen through the Achilles is much more painful, I would imagine, than getting socked in the stomach with a Louisville Slugger."

With Walczyk's guidance, Taylor and Sasha broke down the other four or five main characters, paying particular attention to the coach. Walczyk suggested that he rename the titular villain to Coach *Kramer* to avoid any complaints from the real Frank Conklin. After they discussed character, they broke the linear plot of the story down, discussed ebb and flow, and established beats. Finally, Walczyk discussed some of what he'd seen in the footage confiscated by his father, honestly but fairly critiquing the camera work.

"You know this means you'll have to go over every frame of footage you've shot and figure out what you can keep and what you need to reshoot," Walczyk warned. "I've talked to Dad. You can have it back, but you can't use it. I'll need your word on that before I hand the tapes over."

"Of course," Sasha said, finally sounding excited.

"You've got my word," Taylor replied, never having expected to get those dailies back. Walczyk reached into his book bag and pulled out a handful of digital video tapes, passing them over to Sasha, who carefully placed them in her book bag.

"Thank you," she said.

"You've got good instincts, both of you," Walczyk said, finishing his drink. "You guys really understand character, which is a plus, and you understand suspense. That puts you light years ahead of some of the people I've worked with. Better still, you know how to take critique. I'm thinking you should give lessons to a certain studio head who's trying to start something in the trades with me."

"I read about that," Sasha said. "That's totally unfair."

"More like totally bullshit," Taylor said. "I mean, what's the point of asking someone's advice if you're just going to get offended when they give it?"

"Thank you," Walczyk said. "You've restored my faith in humanity."

"No, thank you," Taylor said

"So, I've yakked enough. Do either of you have any questions?" Walczyk asked.

"Just one," Sasha said, closing her notebook. "Why'd you agree to talk to us about the script? You must have better things to do."

"I initially read your script as a favor to my father, who was desperate for his son to find something to fill his time with. But as I looked at it, I found myself intrigued and impressed with it." Taylor reddened. "That, and it's not like I'm working right now."

"I've got a question, Walczyk," Taylor said.

"Shoot."

"It's about *Night*? Your draft of the script... how'd it come out?"

"Eh," Walczyk said after thinking it over. "Okay I guess. I mean, it's rather cookie cutter."

"I'd love to see it sometime," Sasha commented.

"Yeah," Taylor added. "Even if it *is* only a what-if now."

"Give me your e-mail addresses, I'll send it over. Who knows, we could end up collaborating on it."

Taylor's stomach knotted up. "You want *me* to look at your stuff?"

"You two are the demographic I'd be shooting for. If you think it's lousy, then it's lousy."

Taylor stared at him a moment or two, unable to comprehend

what he was being asked. Using a napkin Walczyk slid across the table, Taylor gave Walczyk his e-mail address. When he was finished, he passed the napkin to Sasha, who wrote her e-mail down in immaculate lettering.

"Great. So, I'll give that book to Hannah… to Miss Cooper. The Denny Martin Flynn one."

"No, that's okay. I'm sure I can just have Garry Olsen order a copy for me," Taylor said.

"No, I want to make sure you get it. It's *the* bible for screenwriters in my opinion. Besides, I always keep two on hand."

"Well, thank you," Sasha said, offering her hand to Walczyk.

"You're welcome," Walczyk said, rising. "Now, if you don't mind, I'm going to rejoin my friends." As Walczyk left, Taylor and Sasha sat back a moment, contemplating what had just gone down.

They had just taken a meeting with Peter Walczyk.

CHAPTER THIRTY-TWO
THE SELF-IMPROVEMENT OF PETER WALCZYK

"Together again?" Henry Walczyk asked, leafing through the dog-eared issue of *People* magazine in Dr. Woodward's waiting room. "But she said at dinner Friday night–"

"I know, *I know*," Peter said, throwing his hands up in the air. "I don't see this ending well, either. She's going to Los Angeles in November come hell or high water and he'll never leave Cole Island. That gives them about four weeks to really mess this up, putting Hannah and me right back in the middle."

"Come on, Peter," Henry said. "That's not entirely fair. They *could* make a go of it."

"Dad, Vic's not going to up and move to L.A., no matter how many times he says, 'Y'know, Walz, I could do it!' And April's not going to give up this job, no matter how many times she says, 'Boss, I'm really not looking forward to this.' I'm afraid a happy ending here is just not in the cards."

"When did you become a skeptic?"

"I don't know. When did you become a hopeless romantic?"

Henry had to concede that one. Peter was right: he was behaving very much like a hopeless romantic and very little like the stern, unflinching realist he knew himself to be. Maybe it was taking

April under his wing, being a father figure to a young woman who had never had one. Or maybe it was Vic, a young man who he'd always felt a strong affinity for. Maybe his feelings for these two kids were clouding his judgment.

"So, are you nervous about seeing this new doctor?" Henry asked his son, finding the article about some celebrity chef named Aurora Naples and her recently unearthed sex tape to be exploitive.

"Nervous? About what?" his son replied, a little on edge. Over the past couple of days, Peter had been sinking from a content, if somewhat manic state to a more depressive, argumentative state. Henry figured this was in part due to the news about April leaving, but he also knew that his son's moods shifted without any cause or rationale. He did seem more stable today than he'd been the past couple of days.

Henry picked up another magazine, an issue of a publication called *NAMI Advocate*. There was a picture of a young woman on the cover, the world behind her a blur. He soon learned, through his reading, that this young woman, Sylvia Davies, was a former child star who had a mental breakdown at fifteen and was subsequently diagnosed with bipolar disorder herself. Henry couldn't fathom dealing with a burden like bipolar disorder at such a young age. For that matter, he couldn't fathom having to deal with it at Peter's age. Or any age, for that matter.

"Peter?" a voice called out. Henry looked up and saw a nurse standing in the doorway, looking at a clipboard. Beside him, Peter rose, tossing a celebrity gossip magazine with himself on the cover onto the coffee table.

Henry stood with his son. "You sure you don't–?"

"I'm thirty-five, Dad. I can see the doctor on my own."

"Okay," Henry said, suddenly feeling absolutely helpless. "I'll be here when you get back."

"Why don't you go sit in the car? Nap?"

"Nah," Henry said, waving a hand. "I'm fine right here." Peter gave his father's shoulder a squeeze and followed the woman with the red glasses through the door. This was harder than watching Dr. Hill pull that nail out of Peter's foot when he was only eight.

"For starters, let's not pretend you're *not* who you are," Cheryl Woodward said, reaching out to him with her hand. "It's a pleasure to meet you. You've got me dying to see the new season of *Ordinary*

World."

"Glad to hear it," Walczyk said, feeling at ease. "And the pleasure's all mine, Dr. Woodward."

"Cheryl," she corrected. "And do you prefer *Peter*? *Pete*?"

"Actually, I prefer 'Walczyk,' but you can use 'Peter' if you think it's more professional."

"'Walczyk' works just fine for me. I haven't gotten your files from your previous doctor yet, so bear with me if some of this seems repetitive and tedious."

"No worries," Walczyk said.

"Now, you told our receptionist when you called that you've been diagnosed type II bipolar disorder, correct?"

"Yes."

"And that you were diagnosed at..." she read from her notes, "...at the Dirigo Psychiatric Hospital in Bangor."

"Right."

"Good. Let's start with a little personal history. When and where were you born?"

"November 9, 1977," Walczyk said. "Maine General."

Walczyk filled Cheryl in on the particulars of his life, from his childhood illnesses to his history of running away from his problems, from Hannah to Hofstra to ditching his wife in L.A.

"So, tell me, why'd you return to Maine?"

"I really don't know," Walczyk said.

"If you had to take a guess..."

"I guess I felt everything falling apart. Things weren't so good between Sara and me. I was unhappy with *Ordinary World*–"

"Really? But it's so popular."

"Not for me."

"Understood," she said. "Continue."

"If I really think about it... I guess I knew I was in trouble." She nodded and wrote. "And I didn't want to fall apart out there."

"Regression is a coping mechanism," Cheryl said. "But I think you're more of a guy who runs from personally challenging situations rather than one who regresses to cope with them. It's basic your fight-or-flight response, and you're choosing flight. Nothing wrong in that. But you do have to face the music at some point."

"I think I have. I mean, I've managed to repair my friendship with Hannah; she's one of my closest friends now. And Sara and I are talking. We've agreed to a divorce. She's been very supportive of me."

"That's good. What happened when you ran away to Newport after your discharge? When you got home?"

"My friends got the hint," he said, smiling. "They've chilled out since."

"These friends you keep mentioning, their opinions mean a lot to you."

"They do. These guys saved my life. They *are* my life."

"It's good to have a strong social network like that... people you can rely on in a jam. Now let's shift gears and talk about things leading up to your diagnosis."

For the next twenty-five minutes, Walczyk walked Cheryl through the chain of events leading up to his hospitalization at Dirigo, how his time there went, and anything Dr. Lentz had given him for information. They moved onto Walczyk's medications, all of which Cheryl seemed to approve of, as she nodded and gave the occasional "good."

"Any side effects from the meds?"

"My hands shake," Walczyk said, exchanging one sheet of paper for the other. "When I'm holding things, carrying things–"

"Everything winds up on the floor," she said, nodding. She scribbled a note onto a small notepad. "What else?"

"Actually, now that you mention discontent south of the border..."

"Diarrhea can be a side effect of lithium," she said, navigating a window on her computer. "What else is on that list of yours?"

"I'm having a lot of trouble concentrating and remembering things. I'll go to the store and have to call home to see what it was I was sent for."

"Still feeling kinda crappy? Depressed?"

"Yeah."

"On a scale of one to ten, one being the lowest of lows and ten being intensely high, where would you rate your depression?"

"Well, when I feel it, it's at, I don't know, a five or a six."

"So nothing to sneeze at. What do you mean 'when you feel it?'"

"Well, my moods have been swinging. I'll have times – sometimes stretches of days – where I feel fine. Then I'll just sink into this... this blackness. I'll feel useless."

"Are you feeling suicidal?"

"Not really."

"'Not really' isn't good enough. *Are you feeling suicidal?*"

"Sometimes I still get hopeless, but it's not like I'm planning anything or fantasizing about it. I just... fail to see the point in it all. Like I'll never be normal again."

"Well, can I share a little secret of the trade with you?"

"Sure."

"Normal's overrated," she said frankly. Walczyk went through his list of other side effects he was feeling, everything from his increased appetite and weight gain, to which Dr. Woodward simply suggested that he learn some self control, to increased thirst, which he told her Dr. Lentz warned him about.

"The good news is, most of these side effects are treatable. The bad news is that some of them aren't. I'm going to put you on a drug called Propranolol. It's a beta blocker and should help with the anxiety and the tremors. Drink more fluids is all I can tell you for the dry mouth, and start watching what you eat, because your weight can get out of control *very* fast if you're not careful. Being faithful with taking your meds as prescribed should clear up the diarrhea." She put her notepad down.

"That just about does it, Walczyk. It's been a pleasure meeting you. Confidentiality is one of our primary concerns here, so if you prefer, the office can refer to you by another name while you're in the public areas."

"'Peter' is just fine out there. Paparazz-Eye probably has it on their website that I'm here anyway."

Cheryl Woodward rose from her chair. "I look forward to seeing you again in a month. I'll call your meds in to the pharmacy on Cole Island that you gave me. If you ever find yourself in a dangerous situation, don't call me; call 911 or a friend or family member. Sounds like you have a very strong network of friends surrounding you, so I'm not too concerned there. You have the office number; if you need anything, don't hesitate to call."

"I won't. Thanks so much, Cheryl," Walczyk said, leaving the office, feeling he finally had a new lease on life.

"So, you liked her?" Walczyk's father asked in between bites of his mushroom and Swiss burger. As children, Walczyk and Melanie used to love coming with their parents to Whistler's, a fantastic out-of-the-way burger place in Augusta. Whistler's had an entire menu of just hamburgers. Over the years since he'd last been to Whistler's, Walczyk noticed they had sprinkled in some chicken and veggie items, but for his money, the only real reason to set foot inside Whistler's was for their patty melt, which still tasted the same after all these years.

"Yeah, I liked her," Walczyk said. "Blunt, but she knows her stuff."

"Good," his Dad said. "I was reading in one of the waiting room magazines. Learned quite a bit about this organization called NAMI."

"The National Alliance on Mental Illness? Yeah. April came across them in some of her online research. They're all about breaking down the stigma behind mental illness."

"It's funny you should see Dr. Woodward this week. The magazine said that this week is Mental Illness Awareness Week."

"We get a week?" Walczyk asked, smiling. "Don't tell Mum. She'll make a giant lithium pill-shaped cake."

His father did something he was doing more of lately: he laughed. "I don't know. I think she's handling all this rather well. I was afraid she'd become a wreck. Don't get me wrong, she's a strong woman, but she's just dealing with depression and mental illness from every angle it seems."

Walczyk stopped eating. "What other angle is there?"

"Well, there's me and my depression," his father began.

"You have depression?" Walczyk asked, the words feeling foreign coming out of his mouth.

"Yeah," his father replied. "Surprised?"

"Kind of, yeah. I mean, I know depression, bipolar and mental illness run in both the Walczyk and Reynolds families; Mum helped me plot that out. But that's the distant relations. I never figured anyone close–"

"Sorry," his father said, taking a sip of his Coke. "I didn't mean to freak you out."

"No, no, I'm glad you told me. I am. It's just... well... you're supposed to be infallible."

"I wish it worked like that. But it doesn't, and about three times a year, I get down."

"How down?"

"*Down.*"

"Ever miss any school because of it?"

"Two days this spring, before you moved back here."

"Are you taking anything?"

"Paxil."

"Who do you see?"

"Andrew Tang at the medical center."

"Good. If you were going to say Sherman Cottle–" Walczyk took a drink. "So all of this tracing depression through the family tree and all these talks with Dr. Lentz and this never came up?"

"You're upset."

"Kind of, yeah! All this talk about honesty and being forthright, that only applies to me?"

"It probably doesn't help, but we did tell Dr. Lentz about it. We just didn't want to burden you with it."

"Burden me, dad! *Burden me*! Do you know how much better I'd have felt if I'd known I wasn't the only one who dealt with this shit!"

"Peter, I'm sorry," Walczyk's father sighed. "Your mother and I, we never thought–"

"I know," Walczyk said, now possessing an inkling of what his parents must've felt when he came out about his own mental illness. He had to remind himself that Henry Walczyk came from both a generation and a family of men who did not discuss depression and certainly did not say that they suffered from a mental illness; they just got "down in the dumps," or were "moody." "I'm sorry, Dad. You just threw me, that's all. But from now on… we're depression buddies, okay?"

"What's a depression buddy?"

"Kind of like those breast cancer buddies you see on the news: we keep each other in check. Let's say one of us starts to slide, we're honor bound to call the other and say that we're feeling like crap. That person then goes to work figuring out things to do: movies to watch, walks to take, anything that will help the other guy through that depression. We can share scripture, we can talk, or we can just sit in silence. We can smoke those cheap-ass cigars you and April smoke. You know, I don't think I've ever smoked with you before."

"It's a deal," Dad said. Walczyk noticed his father's eyes were glassy, but said nothing about it.

"So your depression, I'm guessing it's related to the seasons."

"The time changes, basically. Oh, and Christmas."

"And we're coming up on a time change."

"And no doubt after that time change, once my body starts to adjust to it, I'll begin to drop off."

"We should plan a preemptive strike against the depression. First week of November, maybe we should go up to that hunting camp on Upper Shin Pond. You know, the one Grampie Walczyk helped build."

"Vince Griffith's old place?"

"Yeah. We go up there, do some fishing."

"Peter, fishing season will be over."

"Then we could hunt."

"Two depressives in a cabin filled with guns?"

"We could bring Vic," Walczyk suggested. "God knows he could use the break from it all."

"Okay. Three depressives in a cabin filled with guns."

"Vic's not depressed."

"You need to learn to pay attention, son; Vic is very depressed."

Walczyk thought about that statement. His father did seem to be right: Vic did have "down" spells. Walczyk just attributed it to the circumstances of Vic's life: the shame of a bipolar mother that abandoned him, his father having Alzheimer's, the restaurant, Ingrid, April... Walczyk could see how it would all add up over time, and how it could mask some depression. "Okay, no guns. Instead, we make a big trip of it. You, me, Mum, the dogs, Vic and Hannah. Veteran's Day weekend. I mean, Vic and Hannah don't have to know about the depression."

"Hannah already knows," Henry said.

"Hannah knows! Wow! Who didn't you tell, Duane McGraw?"

"You're making too much out of this."

"No, making too much out of this would be to storm out of here. Making just enough out of it would be to get slightly indignant, let you pay the check, then take you to over to Best Buy and *make* you let me buy you a new TV."

"For the one hundredth time, we don't need a new TV set."

"First off, they're not called 'sets' anymore. Second, you *do* need a new one. Because the Blu-ray player I'm getting you for Christmas won't hook up to – nor will it look good on – your decrepit standard definition screen."

"Why do you feel the need to burden us with all this new technology? Your mother will have a panic attack just trying to change the channels."

"Are you telling me she's got a psychological disorder too?"

"Nothing other than a healthy fear of technology."

CHAPTER THIRTY-THREE
LOOSE ENDS

April was less than impressed with Merlin's Beard, Cole Island's "premiere" costume rental shop. April found her trip to the shop with Vic to be essentially discouraging, given the rather tatty look to some of the rental pieces. Along for the ride, Vic was able to point out what year several of the items had made their way into the shop, including a particularly ratty looking combination of a furry jumpsuit (quite possibly an old Cole Island Jaguar mascot costume donated by the school) and a cheap looking Chewbacca mask. This half-assed, homemade *Star Wars* costume was tagged "Giant Hairy Space Ape." Then there was the leather cat suit with the generous portions of duct tape inside holding the crotch together. Just touching the hanger of that particular outfit, "Super Hero Pussy Cat," made April feel like soaking her body in lye to remove the rampant diseases no doubt making their way up the hanger and onto other costumes.

There had been one advantage, however, to perusing the racks at Merlin's Beard: she was able to gather ideas as to what the gang would like to dress up as for their Halloween excursion, wherever that may be. Hitting the internet, April found a couple of websites for local costume shops over in Augusta and the surrounding area. However, from what she saw from the photos she'd requested, they weren't that far ahead of Cole Island's costume shop.

After tirelessly gathering everyone's thoughts and opinions in a manner that struck Walczyk as a bit over-the-top, even for April, she broadened her search parameters and finally settled on a costume supplier. She gathered Hannah and Walczyk and met with them at the Barrelhead around eight one evening, right after the dinner rush had cleared up, and presented results to everyone.

"Let me begin by saying that I won't be using those smallpox-ridden blankets that are being passed off as costumes down at Merlin's Crotch for our Halloween outing."

"Actually, April," Hannah cut in, "it's Merlin's *Beard*."

"Whatever," April snipped. "I know you are all partial to those lice-infested felt and polyester trappings, but I will not be squeezing my own personal business into anything like that. Instead, I'll be ordering from the Starburst Masquerade Company, one of the better costume shops in L.A. These will be a little pricey, but I know a girl who knows a guy and can ship our costumes to us for a nominal charge if we order by Tuesday."

"Now, before you launch into your sales pitch for your recycled movie and music video costumes," Vic said, "I was thinking we just go the simple, cheap route. I've always liked making my own costume. I think it entails a certain level of craftsmanship."

"Vic, sweetie," April said, in a tone almost passing as gentle, "You know what homemade costumes tend to look like?"

"Crap?" Vic cautiously replied.

"Worse. They tend to look like homemade costumes."

"Well, we don't need the original curtains dress from *Gone With the Wind*," Hannah said.

"Yeah," Vic piped in. "We can go as pimps and hos!"

The look of sheer disgust that crossed Hannah's face made its way down the table to April, who inhaled deeply, no doubt wondering how to phrase her reply so as not to be too harsh on her lover. "Have you ever seen a real pimp, Vic?"

"Yeah. They have loud suits and big hats with feathers in them, like the greeter at the Walmart over in Auburn."

"No, no they don't. How about a real prostitute? A 'ho'? Ever see one?"

"Well, he *has* been off and on with Ingrid more than a light switch," Walczyk snickered. Hannah elbowed him, barely stifling a laugh.

"No, April," Vic hissed at his friend, "I've never seen a real hooker, either. Just strippers."

"Excuse me," Walczyk growled, rising up in his chair. "I'll thank you not to put strippers down."

"Come on, Walz, you know I didn't mean Sara," Vic said, leaning back in his chair.

"I never assumed you meant Sara. She was a *burlesque dancer*, not a stripper."

"I thought the Kitty Kat Girls were strippers," Hannah said.

Walczyk smiled. "Where would you get that silly idea? No, the Kitty Kat Girls are more like a modern-day interpretation of a burlesque show. Sexy little outfits. Singing and choreography. A few–"

"So they're musical strippers," Vic said.

"No, there's not!"

"Why?" Hannah asked.

"Because the outfits stay on."

Vic put his glass down. "Then what's the point?"

"Can we cease discussing my wife, the Kitty Kat Girls, strippers, pimps and hos, and get back to Halloween?" Walczyk asked.

"Hear, hear!" Hannah called out.

"So, April, what do you think?" Walczyk asked.

After much ridicule and debate, they narrowed it down to five possible themes: former Presidents of the United States as zombies, the Three Stooges (but including Shemp to make four stooges), Hannah's vote for the cast of *Star Trek* (with herself as Spock), Greek gods and goddesses (which Vic admitted he suggested just an excuse to get April to wear a bed sheet), and famous figures in film. Stuck at an impasse, they turned to the internet for their answer. And there it was, at the top of the third page of costumes that they stumbled upon four outfits that absolutely astonished them.

"You think…?" Hannah asked, pointing to the one she'd no doubt be wearing.

"I hope," Vic said, winking at her.

"The men's costumes don't look comfortable," April said.

Vic cocked his head sideways, looking at the costumes from another angle. "I'm sure they're fine."

"Besides, it's Halloween," Walczyk said. "And we'll only be

in them for, what, five or six hours tops?"

"Well, I'm in," Hannah said.

"I want that one," Vic said, pointing to the costume on the left, "or I'm not doing it."

"I get the one on the right," Walczyk called out.

"I'll get the credit card," April said, happy to have Halloween solved.

Walczyk felt his chest tighten. A soft gasp was forced out through his purple lips as his entire body stiffened. The sensation crawled from his feet up, coursing piggyback on his blood as it flowed throughout his entire body. He had only been in for the briefest of moments – three, four seconds at most – but the sensation awakened his body. When he opened his clenched-shut eyes, the entire world seemed brighter. The blue sky floating overhead was electric with energy, the clouds sharply off-setting it. The salty smell of the fresh air filled his nostrils. His head felt light. The tide continued to sneak up on him, kissing his toes, the tops of his feet, eventually even his entire foot.

"Peter! What the hell are you doing?"

He turned around. Assembled along the wooden railing up by the road were a series of local onlookers and paparazzi, pointing and yammering away. Running across the beach towards him was Vic Gordon, a spray of sand kicking up behind him.

"Vic, it's okay!" Walczyk screamed out across the beach, waving him off. Vic either didn't hear or didn't care, because he continued running across the sand toward the shore. Walczyk climbed up the shore, picking his socks and sneakers up along the way. His pants were still rolled up around his calves.

"What the hell do you think you're doing?" Vic asked, panic stricken, grabbing Walczyk by the shoulders.

"Cold water restart," Walczyk said plainly.

"A what?"

"A cold water restart. It's something I learned about in a depression support chat room."

"And this 'cold water reset' thing's supposed to help you how?"

"'Restart,'" Walczyk corrected. "Sometimes, we get so overloaded and bogged down with the details of the world that we just need to restart. Like a computer; sometimes it just gets to running so slowly and it just needs to be rebooted. So you push that power button until it shuts down, then you count to five, and restart it. That's all I'm doing."

"Dude, you're not a computer!"

"In a way I am. The human body is really just a complex, bio-mechanical machine. The brain is its organic CPU. The hands, they're the mouse and keyboard. The eyes are the monitor. The–"

"I get it. We're all computers. But this computer," Vic said, thumping his chest, "just got scared shitless when that crazy, Goth mortician chick from the funeral home came running into the Barrelhead and said you were walking into the ocean."

"Oh, shit," Walczyk said, finally putting together why he had an audience down on the beach.

"Yeah."

"It's okay," he screamed to the crowd assembled on the side of the road looking down at the beach. "I'm not trying to kill myself! I'm just meditating! You can go about your business!"

He'd noticed that many of the onlookers had pulled out cell phones and were either taking pictures or recording the entire incident. Remembering Robert Downey Jr.'s advice to him that ignoring them is always the best option, Walczyk turned around and walked back to Vic. "You wanna try it?"

"What?"

"The cold water restart. Reboot your system. God knows you could use it."

"Even if I thought this crazy yoga shit worked–"

"It's not yoga. I'm not sure it's anything. I just found this guy in the chat room talking about it. He said it's like the polar bear guys who go swimming in the middle of the winter. The rush they get from jumping into that cold water just revitalizes them."

"You really believe this."

"I really believe this. Vic, I feel so energized right now."

"You're manic. Your mother's charts show it... you're trending upwards towards another manic spell."

"Why do I bother trying to tell you guys otherwise?" Walczyk said, shaking his head.

"We've got proof!"

"You've got medically refuted charts made by a woman who is

assuming my mental status and plotting it on a line graph."

"Can't you accept that maybe you're not the best judge of your own mindset? That's the bitch of this disease. What I've read tells me that–"

"You're reading?"

"Just some blogs and websites written by people with it and people who live with people who have it. No big deal. Just some shit April sent my way."

"Really," Walczyk said, impressed. "What'd you learn?"

"That you guys aren't always in full awareness of what you're up to. You could be talking a mile a minute, and really, you're thinking you're going so slow."

"Vic–"

"Dude, just stop. For a second, and look at it from my point of view. You're walking into the Atlantic Ocean – with your clothes on – in October. Tell me that's not a little suspect."

"That's not a little suspect."

"What?"

Walczyk smiled. "It's a *lot* suspect. And I'm aware of that. That's why I left that note on the windshield of my car saying exactly what I was up to and that I was not a danger to myself."

"You expect people to read notes on windshields?"

"So you still think I'm being irrational?" Walczyk asked.

"Well," Vic said, clearly thinking it over. "You're actually kind of making sense. A little." Vic paused for a moment. "So, those polar bear dudes... they *do* get revitalized by jumping into that freezing water?" Walczyk nodded. "Well, Hannah did say she was reading where some people get this electro-shock therapy to treat their bipolar or something."

Walczyk held his hand out. "Wanna give it a try?"

Vic looked from Walczyk's bare, sand-covered feet up to his face. Walczyk felt him made eye-contact. Normally, Walczyk avoided eye contact. It made him uncomfortable. He always felt that prolonged eye contact would give people access to the inner-most recesses of his soul. But this was Vic, and if Vic wanted to look into his soul, he'd let him. Walczyk met Vic's gaze and studied his friend's blue eyes, seeing past Vic's defenses, into *his* soul. He was looking into the eyes of someone who loved him very much. Someone who wanted very badly to understand and care for him. Someone who was willing to give anything.

"I must be out of my frigging mind," Vic grumbled, sliding his shoes off and placing them in the sand and slid his socks off, placing them safely inside his shoes.

"Ready?" Walczyk said.

"Ready," Vic said, nervously. Together, the two grown men walked into the Atlantic Ocean. Vic howled as the water ebbed up over his feet. The agonized smile on his face was priceless. He whooped and hollered as the waves came and went, bringing new levels of coldness to every course.

"Well?" Walczyk screamed over the surf.

"You're freaking crazy," Vic hollered back. "But I love you."

He gave Walczyk's hand a squeeze, and the two men stood in silence as the waves splashed around them for a good five minutes, until Vic told Walczyk it was time to go: his lips were turning blue. Walczyk noticed the same effect on Vic, and they sat on the beach, letting their feet dry before dressing them.

"So how are things at the restaurant?"

"Not bad," Vic said.

"Considering the fact that your head waitress hates your guts," Walczyk said.

"Actually, I think we might have ironed some of that out."

"How?"

"I gave Elijah ten bucks to lock us in the walk-in cooler and not to let us out until I texted him the password."

"And you thought a cold water restart was confusing."

"Hey, it worked," Vic said. "It forced us to be in the same room and to listen to each other. She told me she was hurt by what I did. I told her I was sorry. She said I was a child for not being able to pick which woman I wanted. I said I was sorry. She said that under no circumstances would we ever get back together again."

"I swear, if you said you were sorry–"

Vic laughed. "No, that time I told her I agreed with her. And that she was going to have to hold me to that promise. And she said I'd have to hold her to hers. Then we shook on it. No hug. A nice solid handshake. Then I tried to text Elijah."

"*Tried?*"

"Seems a cell signal can't get through the walls of our walk-in. It was forty-five minutes before Andrew forced Elijah to open the door so I could give the check to the seafood delivery guy."

"A flawless plan," Walczyk said. "Congratulations, Vic. I'm proud of you. That wasn't an easy thing to do."

"No, but it was a necessary thing to do."

The men sat in silence a moment before Vic asked, frankly, "Think it'd be in poor taste to bring a date to April's going-away party?"

"April, you certainly have a lot of…"

"Shit?"

"Actually, 'stuff' was where I was going with that," Hannah said. "But yeah, you certainly have a lot of stuff. Didn't you only come to Maine with ten days worth of clothes?"

"Initially. But, remember, I've been back to Los Angeles, spent a week in Bangor having packed nothing. And then there's that little vintage shop on Commerce Street–"

"Ooh, the one between the Dusty Tome and New Worlds bookstores and across the street from Costigan's?" Hannah asked.

"That's the one."

"I love that place," Hannah said. "Things Past."

"That's right. Things Past." April gave the room a quick glance. "Yep. It certainly is a lot of shit."

"But it's sortable… shit," Hannah cheerily remarked. "I say we break it down into categories: clothes, books, music and movies, mementos, and stuff you don't want anymore."

"Listen to you," April said, smiling.

"I love organizing. I know, I know, it's very nerdy of me. But I love it. It was one of my favorite parts of college, packing and unpacking my stuff every fall and spring when I'd arrive at Bates and when I'd leave. I think it's been eight or nine years since I've moved."

"That's an eternity in one place to me," April said, pulling open the drawers and beginning to pack away her underwear.

"No, that's not how you want to do it," Hannah said. "Suppose your luggage gets lost again. Just one piece of it. Do you really want to be left with only a suitcase of bras and panties?"

"No," April said warily.

"Of course you don't. So pack outfits. Fill each suitcase with at least one complete change of clothes: underwear, socks, a top and bottom. Now specialty things, like dresses and bathing suits, sprinkle them throughout."

Hannah began emptying the closet while April laid out a series of suitcases, loading each with a week's worth of clothes. She hated to admit it, but Hannah was right: this was the smarter way to pack. That was one of the things she was going to miss most about Hannah Cooper, her crazy, silly logic. The girl was flighty and twitchy and naïve, but damn it, she was also brilliant and loyal and all heart.

Once they'd finished packing the clothes, down to the last odd sock and a bikini bottom with no coordinating top, the suitcases were wheeled out of the room. A week's worth of clothing was left in the dresser for April to work her way through. Then they went about packing up April's DVD collection, the paltry few CDs she'd acquired, and her books and screenplays, which were numerous. Those were packed in boxes that Hannah got from Ferguson's Market, where Old Man Ferguson himself was sorry to hear that April was leaving town.

"So how'd that thing with you and the old battle ax at the school turn out?" April asked, dropping a stack of unread screenplays into one of her boxes. "Last I heard, you told her what to go do with herself."

"Stella? Well, it's still up in the air. She's sickeningly polite when she sees me in the halls, which is her way of saying a big eff-you to me without making a scene."

"She's old. Let a mouse loose in her classroom and let it scare her to death."

"April!" Hannah gasped.

"Too cruel?"

"Indeed," Hannah said. "That poor mouse wouldn't stand a chance."

After all of the books had been packed away, they moved on to mementos. From the walls, April plucked almost all of the photographs she'd framed and hung, including shots of herself, Vic, Hannah and Walczyk in Bangor celebrating her return to Maine, and a shot of herself with Vic and Dexter at the beach.

"Oh, God," April gasped.

"What is it?" Hannah asked, holding a collection of loose sheets of paper, folders, and knick-knacks from April's desk across the hall.

"Dexter." April's heart sank. She'd never given a single thought to the fact that she wouldn't be taking her baby with her.

"Peter will take care of him. I'll promise that," Hannah pledged.

"I'm not worried about that. He'll be perfect for Peter. Give him some routine. But, no, I was just realizing that I've got to give him up."

"You could always get another dog when you get to L.A. Or maybe you could bring Dexter with you. They fly pets now."

"No, I don't want him pining away in some cargo hold."

"You could get him classified as a 'comfort dog' and bring him in first class with you."

"Comfort dog?"

"Yeah. People with nervous disorders and such, they get special permission to have their pets with them in stores, on busses, and in hotels. The experts claim the animals calm the people down and keep them on an even keel."

"That's the most ridiculous pile of nonsense I've ever heard," April said, disgusted. "If I ever hear of Walczyk declaring Dexter a comfort dog—"

A couple of hours later, April's bedroom was a ghost of its former self. The television hung from the wall above the dresser still, and April was taking none of her bedding or towels with her. On her desk there was a small white box with a bright red bow on it.

"What's that box? Shouldn't that have gone in with mementos?" Hannah asked.

"What's it say on it?" April asked, busying herself with the troublesome zipper on one of her suitcases.

Hannah walked over to the box and picked it up. "April, what's this?" she warily asked. "It's got my name on it."

"I don't know," April said, turning around as she stuffed unneeded bedding into one of her infamous vacuum sealed bags. Hannah lifted the lid. Inside, attached to a miniature model of the starship *Enterprise* was a large key. Upon closer inspection, Hannah saw that it was a car key.

"April," Hannah asked, cautiously, "why is the key to your Jeep in this box with my name on it?"

April turned around and handed a folder to Hannah. She opened it. Inside was all of the paperwork to the Jeep, which had April's name and Peter's name on the title.

"You're not—"

April put her arm around Hannah. "Congratulations. One trip to city hall with me tomorrow and you're the proud owner of a 2012 Jeep Liberty."

Hannah dropped the box in horror. "No. You can't."

"I can," April said, picking the box back up. "And I want to."

"But this is *your* car."

"But I can't take it with me. I can't drive it back to California alone."

"Take Peter with you."

"Like he'd go."

"Take Vic!"

"As if he'd take the time off. Look, Hannah, I discussed it with Peter. We both want you to have it. You need it."

Hannah felt her throat start to choke up. She tried to speak, but the words failed her. She threw herself at April, wrapping her arms around her. April patted her back, holding her tight.

"I love you," Hannah sobbed.

"Careful," April said. "The last person who said that to me, I ran out on."

"And the last person *I* said that to ran out on *me*." Hannah pulled herself together. "Thank you so much, April. This is–"

"–depressing," April said, looking around the empty room.

"I know," Hannah said, inspecting the *Enterprise* key ring. "It is the hardest part of moving, having to say goodbye."

The silverware had been polished: the good, gold silverware that belonged to Grammie Walczyk, not the regular Walmart-issue stuff they usually used. Moisture beaded up on the outside of the wine goblets, ice cold water inside them. The dishes, which Walczyk did not know whether they were real china or just some handed-down blue-patterned plates, were laid out carefully. A nice white linen tablecloth had been laid on the table, and place cards had been left in each plate, telling the guests where to sit.

"I see Diane has been watching Martha Stewart again," Vic cracked, fidgeting with his tie.

"Ssh," Walczyk's father hissed. "She's been on pins and needles lately about April leaving and Peter living in the house alone. One wrong remark and she's liable to break down crying, and none of us want that."

"Yeah. Remember the time we teased her about *The Waltons*?" Walczyk asked.

"Oh, God," Dad said, shaking his head.

"What's this about *The Waltons*?" Vic asked.

"Well," Walczyk said, taking off his jacket and hanging it on the back of the chair in front of the name card that read *Peter* in fine calligraphy. "One night – and, honestly, for no reason – Dad, Sis and I started teasing Mum about her wanting to watch *The Waltons* over some stupid movie. It went on relentlessly until she went into her room and cried."

"Surely not one of our finest hours," Dad remarked to Vic. "So, Vic, how's your father doing?"

"He has his days," Vic said, looking a little unprepared for the question. "This week, thankfully, was a good one. He recognized April when she came to say goodbye to him, but I don't think he grasped that she wouldn't be coming back."

"That's a shame," Walczyk's father said, frowning.

"And just what's going on over here?" Hannah said, looking lovely in a rather sleek little black dress that Walczyk suspected once belonged to April. "Three handsome men standing together, murmuring amongst themselves. Sounds like a recipe for trouble, if you ask me."

"You want trouble?" Walczyk's father asked. "I've got trouble: Stella Lyons is still fuming about how you treated her at the teachers' meeting."

"Oh, no," Hannah said, her posture slumping.

"Are you kidding?" Walczyk cried out. "That was two weeks ago!"

"On the plus side, though, morale amongst the rest of the staff has never been so high."

"I noticed the same thing at the Barrelhead when I broke up with Ingrid," Vic observed. "People love drama."

"Drama's all well and good, as long as it's put on by a director and staged in an auditorium," Hannah complained. "Henry, I don't know what to do."

"Invite her down to the shore for a cold water restart," Vic said. "It did wonders for me."

"A cold water restart?" Walczyk's father asked.

Walczyk left Vic to explain the concept to Hannah and his

father. He was curious as to where April had gotten off to. He poked his head in the kitchen.

"You seen April?" Walczyk asked his mother.

"No, I haven't," she said, wearing a flour-covered apron over a nice, wine-colored dinner dress. "If you find her, steer her towards the dining room. Dinner's almost ready."

Amused that his mother chose *dinner* over *supper* for once in her life, Walczyk checked the living room, where he found Cocoa and Brownie passed out on the couch, Dexter on the floor in front of them. He glanced outside, suspecting that she might have reverted to form and taken up smoking in her stressful, final days on Cole Island, but she was on neither porch. As he went to check the bathroom, he noticed his bedroom door was ajar. He poked his head in. Sitting back to him on the bed was April, her hair elegantly piled on top of her head.

"You okay?" Walczyk gently asked.

"Fine," she lied, following her response with a sniff.

"What's up?" Walczyk asked, walking towards the bed.

"I hate this," she said, looking up at him. Her eyes were puffy and red. The last time he'd seen her like this, they were sitting on the steps of his home in Laurel Canyon, on a Sunday morning, mere minutes away from disaster striking.

"I know. It's not easy."

"They're just so... I have a mother. A strong, protective woman, who never let anything bad happen to her kid, aside from letting them grow up without a father. I had grandparents, Pop Pop and my Bubbe Rosa. That's it. My mother was an only child and I was an only child. My father was out of the picture. I had relatives, but there was never really family. Then I met your parents at the *Aaron Lawrence* premiere, and all of that changed. Your Dad... he's so Ward Cleaver, so Mike Brady. The Dad who would love you when you screwed up, who would stand up for you, and who would tell you he loved you at the end of the day." She sniffed again. "We came back here, and I looked forward to getting to know him better. But I never figured I'd fall in love with him. Or your mother. Or your friends. And now, here I am, torn about pursuing a career I've always wanted, because I can't get Vic Gordon and Hannah Cooper and Henry and Diane Walczyk, or their brilliant son, off my mind and out of my heart."

The call for dinner came booming down the hallway. Walczyk

gave his hand to April and together they walked out of Walczyk's childhood bedroom, out into the hall, and into adult life.

The last of the roast chicken lay on a serving platter: a drumstick, two shriveled wings. The glass casserole dish of stuffing was empty, and the same could be said for the bowl of mashed potatoes at the center of the table. Around the table, belts were loosened and ties undone. April leaned back in her chair, rubbing her stomach. Walczyk reached across the table, snagging the remnants of Hannah's water glass, fielding disgusted looks from everyone gathered around him.

"Diane, that was excellent," Vic said, breaking the silence. "Thank you so much."

"Well, I know it's just the first of many such get-togethers, but Henry and I wanted to say goodbye to April the way we welcomed her to Cole Island."

"You certainly did," April said, reaching out to take Walczyk's mother's hand.

"Yes, thank you," Hannah said. "I had no right to eat this well."

"Oh, we'll be paying for it," Vic said to Hannah beside him. "I volunteered us to do clean-up duty so the Walczyks and April could relax together in the living room."

"Did you, now?" Hannah asked flatly. "Thank you so much, Victor. What a gentlemanly thing to have done."

"Vic, I told you, just leave it. Henry and I can get it later on."

"No, Diane, I'm just giving Vic a hard time," Hannah said, rising to her feet. "It's the least I can do."

"You know, Walczyk," April said, "six months ago, when you dragged me here, I half wondered if you were losing your mind."

"Turns out I was," Walczyk joked.

"I found something on the internet that I wanted to share with you," she said to Walczyk. "Proverbs 27:17, and yes, I looked up a Bible verse. It says, 'As iron sharpens iron, so a friend sharpens a friend.' Well, you've certainly sharpened me, Peter Walczyk. From a gawky, overanxious mass of nerves and anger into a competent, confident, eager woman. There is no university course that could have done that; no on-the-job training. Only living by your side for five years."

Walczyk reached over and took her hand, fighting back the

tears. He gave it a squeeze.

As they ate desert, Walczyk's mother's famous apple streusel pizza, a dish for which she'd ciphered out the recipe over many trips to the Portland Pizza Hut buffet during her cancer treatments. Vic shared his Uncle Donny's latest tale about Gibby Perkins and his "old lady." In the latest episode, Gibby's old lady had left him for good and had "taken up" with the town Postmaster, the portly, grumpy Conrad D. Staples.

"Does he still insist you address him as *Postmaster*?" Walczyk asked.

"Sure does," his father replied.

"And speaking of *Postmaster* Staples," April said, "something came in the mail today."

"What?" Walczyk asked, grinning.

"Oh, we'll find out Saturday night," she said with a smile.

"What's Saturday night?" Walczyk's mother asked.

"We didn't tell you?" Walczyk countered.

"Tell us what?" his father nervously asked.

"We're headed to Portland," Hannah said, smiling broadly.

"There's this night club that Andrew told us about," Vic continued, "It's called Asylum, and they're having this all-out, balls-to-the-wall Halloween party."

"You'll have to pardon his description of the party," Hannah said, scowling in Vic's direction.

"Asylum?" Walczyk's father asked.

"I know," Walczyk said. "Rather fitting, don't you think?"

"Quite. How many of you are going?"

"Just the four of us."

"And what are you going as?" Walczyk's mother asked.

"That, *mi madre*, is what the Spanish-speaking world calls '*uno surpriso*.'"

CHAPTER THIRTY-FOUR
SUITING UP

"The things we do for love," Vic said, leaning back in his chair on Walczyk's balcony, a cigar clamped between his teeth. Despite Walczyk's insistence, he was not going to put on his mask until the last minute.

"So it *is* love?" Walczyk smirked, teasing his friend as he, too, puffed away at a stogie and tugged at his costume. "Given her plans to return to L.A., that's got to suck."

"Don't go delving into relationships that don't exist, Peter," Vic warned, shooting Walczyk a look.

"Sorry."

"You know, I've known you for about thirty years now. I stood with you at your wedding. I'm by your side during your divorce. I've watched you go to hell and back and, for some strange reason, I've never asked."

"Asked what, Vic?"

"What the hell is it with you and Halloween?"

Walczyk laughed, almost choking on cigar smoke. "What's the matter, Vic? Feeling a little self-conscious in your black tights?"

"Just a smidge," Vic said, demonstrating with his thumb and forefinger the miniscule amount a *smidge* stood for.

"Remember when we used to go Trick or Treating? The magic of that night, as we got dressed up as someone – or something – else and burst out onto the streets of Cole Island, as He-Man, the Incredible Hulk, a Transformer or even a G.I. Joe?"

"I remember the cheap-ass costumes my old man used to buy me at Arbo's," Vic complained. "Remember how the crotch would always split out of the damned thing before we hit our first house?"

"I remember you crying like a baby when they would."

"Oh, well. I suppose those costumes weren't designed to be worn over snowsuits." Vic picked up his beer and took a sip.

"Damn," Walczyk muttered, feeling his mouth salivate.

"Sorry," Vic said, stashing the beer out of sight.

"No, it's fine. I just… I wish that I could have a beer with my buddy again."

"I didn't think you even liked beer."

"I don't."

"Then what–"

"It's the *act* of drinking the beer. The relaxed air that surrounds two friends having an alcoholic beverage together. Beer. Scotch. Rum and Coke. I just… our Mick-a-Paloozas were special to me, Vic. The fried chicken, the bad movies and especially the drinking 'til we were barely coherent."

"Tell me again, what is it that keeps you from drinking, Walz? April? Hannah? Your folks?"

"All of the above," he joked. "No, it's not that I *can't*. It's more like I shouldn't. Something to do with the meds in my system and how my body processes them. You want details, ask April. She knows all about it and probably has charts to illustrate the point."

"Okay," Vic said, laughing as he stubbed out his cigar. "So, how have you been feeling?"

"Fine," Walczyk said.

"Cool," Vic said, standing up and adjusting his belt.

"Why do I get the feeling you're up to something?"

"No, nothing like that. I just… Well, what with all this April craziness, we haven't really talked much. But things are good, right?"

"Things are very good, thanks," Walczyk said, smoothing out the front of his costume.

Vic put a hand on Walczyk's shoulder. "You know if anything comes up, day or night…"

"I know."

"Good," Vic said, getting up and grabbing his mask. "Let's go finish suiting up."

"Explain to me again," Hannah asked, putting on her make-up, "Why'd you want me to come over here to get dressed?"

"Because it's something girls do, getting ready for a big night out together," April said, pacing around the bathroom behind Hannah, Dexter watching the entire show with fascination.

Hannah frowned, adjusting her black wig. "I'm not buying it, April."

"Fine! I wanted to make sure you wore the costume."

"April, I told you I liked it," Hannah said, defending herself. "It's just that it's a little smaller than it looked in the picture."

"You want to switch?" April asked, exasperated.

"No, I'm fine," Hannah said, tugging her skirt down in the back.

"Good," April said, picking up a tube of red make-up from the bathroom counter. "Because you're still wearing that ratty bathrobe."

"I'll take it off when we're ready to go."

"Damned right you will." April finished the last touches of her face paint. "So, you dated Vic *and* Walczyk, right?"

"Yeah, Peter for a year and a half and almost three with Vic, counting high school and after high school," Hannah replied, curious. "Why?"

"Because I need to ask you something. You know, as someone in the know; someone who's been there."

"I'm sorry, April, but I don't gossip about my relationships."

"Oh, no! That's not what I mean," April said quickly. "But can you tell me how you knew?"

"'Knew?' Knew what?" Hannah dragged the word out, filling the silence, as she gave her wig a final spray.

"That it was serious?"

"Well, the first time with Vic, I don't think that it was serious." She shrugged. "It was high school romance. Kissing under the bleachers and word of it being *official* spreading through the school by town crier. It was just hormones. But the second time I dated Vic... the second time it was a serious relationship."

"But how'd you know it was serious?" April pressed, checking her own make-up in the mirror behind Hannah, who was fussing with her headpiece.

"Toilet paper," Hannah called out, and April passed her a roll, which she balled up in clumps and shoved down the front of her costume. "I didn't know it was at the time. It was just... an evolution. Like your hair growing, or water evaporating. It was so gradual, so subtle. There was no one moment, just the culmination of many, many moments."

"But there had to be a moment," April said, passing Hannah her boots as she sat down on the edge of the tub.

"For as open and forthcoming a person as Victor Gordon is, he's also a very private person. So don't go discussing our little conversation with him, okay?"

"Deal. But he lets you see what he wants you to see," April said, nodding. She was guilty of living like that. Surviving like that. "But what told you that you guys were serious?"

"When he told me about John. Mind you, back then, no one knew about him. It was something they were keeping hush-hush, so as not to make poor John a topic of gossip around the Island." Hannah finished placing her toilet paper, fluffing her chest up a bit before turning to April. "Now I've got a question for you."

"Shoot."

"Just where am I supposed to keep my cell phone in this thing?"

A loud knock on the door let April and Hannah know it was show time. Hannah headed to the door, but April's arm on hers stopped her.

"What?"

"It's time," April said, holding her hand out. Reluctantly, Hannah loosened the tie to her robe and took it off.

"Damn," April said. "You look quite nice in that."

Hannah's cheeks reddened. April pushed her out the bathroom door and down the hall, to the living room, where Walczyk was texting. He turned around, a blue body suit with red shorts and a large "S" emblazoned across his chest, which was clearly being given rippled definition by the plastic insert under suit. A red cape flapped behind him.

"The things we do for truth, justice, and the Canadian way," Walczyk said. "You about ready up there?" he yelled up towards his bedroom.

"Nice to see you, Superman," Hannah said, stepping out from behind April. April noticed Walczyk's eyes travel up from the floor, past the shiny red boots, the blue skirt with its silver stars, the red bustier, and the gold tiara in her now-black hair.

"Likewise, Wonder Woman," he said, bowing slightly to her. "Where's your lasso of truth?"

"Here," Vic said, in a husky voice, stepping down the stairs from Walczyk's room to the living room, cloaked head to toe in black body armor, a large bat spread across his chest, and piercing white eyes staring out from his sculpted cowl.

"Thank you, Batman. Room in that utility belt for this?" She held up her cell phone.

"Do I have any special powers?" April asked, a giant inflatable hammer in her hands as she stood in the doorway to the living room, dressed in a purple tuxedo with sinister clown make-up sloppily drawn across her face.

"Are you kidding? The Joker's the Clown Prince of Crime," Vic informed her. "He's Batman's arch-nemesis. But I thought you decided on going as Catwoman."

"Remember that girl who knows a guy? Seems 'the guy' sent the wrong costume."

"Explains the generous cut," Walczyk commented on April's baggy costume.

"Um," Hannah began, looking the group over, "how the heck are we all supposed to get into the Jeep in these ridiculous things?"

Hannah walked down the stairs of Henry and Diane Walczyk's house quickly, her hands holding her skimpy blue skirt tightly against her bottom. Walczyk knew his Hannah, and knew that she was dreading Monday morning, when she had to show up in school and face his father. It was humiliating enough that Walczyk had paraded them through his living room like they were all seven again, modeling their costumes for his parents before heading out.

"That was completely humiliating," Hannah grumbled as the Justice League of Cole Island made their way back to Hannah's new Jeep (which April was still driving).

"You're humiliated," April groused. "You at least knew something about your character. I couldn't tell them jack about the

Joker."

"And whose fault is that for not doing their internet research?" Vic chided.

"At least your mothers didn't accuse you of stuffing your tights," Walczyk complained. But, for all their humiliations at the hands of Walczyk's parents, there was one saving grace: his mother's legendary candy apples, made for her "special, grown-up" trick-or-treaters.

As they joked about stopping at Jim and Agnes McNabb's to Trick or Treat, the muffled sound of Vic's cell phone came from the plastic utility belt of his Batman costume. The closeable compartments of that utility belt had proved to be the perfect place to keep the car keys and four cell phones. One by one, Vic opened the compartments on the belt, finally finding his own ringing phone. Having learned on the way over to Walczyk's house that it was impossible to hear a cell phone through the thick headpiece of his costume, Vic switched the phone to speaker mode.

"Hello," Vic called out as they made it to the edge of the driveway.

"Victor? It's Andrew. S'up?"

"Just getting underway. What do you need?"

"Vic, you're not going in there tonight," April growled, then turned to the cell phone. "He's not coming in there, Andrew!"

"I won't keep him long, April, I promise," Andrew said through the phone. *"But we blew a fuse and the restaurant's pitch black."*

"So go flip the breaker," Vic growled, looking a little frustrated.

"I would, but the fuse box is in your office. And you didn't leave me the key."

Vic punched the dashboard. "Damn it, Andrew. Why is it I can't have one night? One night! That's it!"

"Because you won't give me a key to the office."

The silence following Andrew's feeble joke was heavy and deafening. Finally, Vic sighed and said, "We'll be there in ten. And I'm leaving my cell phone there."

"You're my hero, Victor," Andrew said, ending the call.

"You don't know the half of it, Baby Brother," Vic said, flipping his phone shut and putting it back into his utility belt.

"You know you work too much," Hannah said from the back seat, putting a hand on Vic's plasticized shoulder armor.

Vic turned back to her as much as he could, and said, "This from the woman who gives herself fourteen days off during the summer, then calls herself lazy the rest of the time."

"Hey, you've got a staff of people to delegate responsibility to. I've got the team of me, myself, and I," Hannah said defensively.

"What staff? I've got one waitress with dyslexia, one with bad handwriting, and a chief executive whatever-the-hell-we're-calling-her with delusions of self-entitlement because we used to sleep together."

"Whose fault is that?" April sniped.

Vic ignored her. "I've got a team of stoned busboys Wonder Woman there couldn't even find in her heart to pass through school. And then there's my dear brother, who can carve a gargoyle out of an onion but can't even fix a blown pilot light."

"Look, can we not talk about the restaurant?" April groaned. "I'm one more imbecilic restaurant emergency away from siphoning the gas out of this Jeep myself, burning the place down and taking you to L.A. with me."

"If you do, just warn me first," Vic said. "I want to make sure the insurance policy's paid up."

As they pulled into the Barrelhead's parking lot, it was clear that this was the wrong night to have a pilot light go out. The parking lot was filled with cars, but there wasn't a sign of life inside the darkened building.

"Holy shit," April said as Vic pulled up to the front steps. "Looks like he blew more than just a pilot light."

Fumbling at his seat belt through his rubberized gloves, Vic grumbled, "They'll be 'til midnight serving all these people." He continued fidgeting with his seat belt.

"Walczyk," April said, pushing Vic back into his seat. "Why don't you take the keys in to Andrew? Vic's never make it out of the Jeep dressed in that."

"I'm not going in there alone," he protested, drawing attention to the red Speedo he was wearing over his tight, blue tights. "Not like this."

"I'll go with you," Hannah said, reaching up front for the keys April had just removed from the utility belt.

"Well, guess we'll be right back," Walczyk said, not savoring the idea of parading through a crowded restaurant in spandex tights that were only padded in the chest. He hopped out of the vehicle, went around, and opened Hannah's door, helping her out.

"Cold?" he asked as they headed through the parking lot, noticing her hands had immediately clamped down on her bottom.

"I wish I had a cape," she grumbled.

"Wonder Woman's cape, when she did have one, generally fell around the small of her back," Walczyk volunteered.

"Why don't women in these comics ever wear pants and shirts?"

"Because a woman flying overhead in pants and a shirt is boring. A woman flying overhead in a star-studded bathing suit, however, that's exciting."

"I suppose," she said, freeing a hand to grasp the railing as the ascended the stairs to the restaurant.

"Lieutenant Uhura on *Star Trek* didn't wear much more."

"No, she didn't," Hannah said, opening the door. "But that was a fleet-wide women's uniform policy."

"And that makes it better?" Walczyk asked, pushing the front door open. The restaurant was dark. He crept in slowly.

"Andrew?" Hannah called out, grabbing Walczyk's arm.

"Donny?" Walczyk said, expecting Andrew and Vic's foul-mouthed uncle/bartender to call out with some playful, albeit insulting, reply.

There was no reply. "Hello?" he called, confused that no one belonging to the army of cars in the parking lot was replying. "Anyone?"

Walczyk's eyes flashed white, as the sudden flash of light overpowered his eyes.

"*SURPRISE!*"

CHAPTER THIRTY-FIVE
SUPER FRIENDS

As his vision cleared, Walczyk saw that the Barrelhead was decorated in a mixture of Halloween and birthday decorations and filled beyond capacity with people. Walczyk stood rooted to the floor, still not putting together everything before him. Andrew and the staff, the room full of cheering people, and even old Donny Sullivan, were dressed in Halloween costumes.

"Oh, I'm sorry," Hannah said, still hugging his arm, "Did you *really* want to drive all the way to Portland?"

"This…" he whispered under the roar, shaking his head. "Hannah, this–"

"–was a *bitch* to plan!" April said behind him. He turned around quickly, and another flash of light blinded him. When his vision cleared, he saw April holding up her digital camera. "But that picture, that'll make it worth it." She reached out and gave him a big hug, kissing his cheek. "Happy Birthday, Boss!"

Λ heavy arm fell across his shoulder. He turned to see an uncharacteristically smiling Batman, looking at him. "And you better enjoy this, Buddy, because I've missed too many of your birthdays of yours to throw you a lousy one."

"Thank you," he said, patting his friend's back with several loud, plastic-thumping smacks.

"So," Hannah said, stepping up next to him, "what do you think?"

"I think someone wanted me to have that costume birthday party I always wanted." Walczyk pulled her into a big hug, picking her up off the floor.

"Peter! Put-me-down!" she squealed, beating her wrists against his shoulders. "My skirt!"

He slowly put her back down. She smoothed her hands down over the back of her skirt again. "So you approve?"

"I..." he said, spotting Uncle Donny serving up beers at the bar, wearing Tom Brady's New England Patriots jersey and black paint under his eyes, "I think that it's incredible. Thank you."

"I hope you like it," she said. "Because as I told April earlier, this is the last time I'm baring my bottom to the whole town."

"Hannah," he said, gazing into those sharp, perfect green eyes, "It's perfect. Thank you."

"Young man, unhand her!" a familiar voice snapped in an even more familiar tone. Hannah and Walczyk turned around quickly, surprised. Taylor Hodges and Sasha Connary were standing in front of them. Sasha, wearing a rubber bald cap, was dressed unmistakably as Principal Henry Walczyk, while it was Taylor who stole the show, dressed as Stella Lyons. Walczyk shook his head, grinning.

"I will pay you real money to drive over to my father's house right now in those get-ups," Walczyk said.

"Oh, he'll see them when we wear them to school on Halloween," Taylor said, adjusting his fake, floppy breasts. "After all, Mrs. Lyons has yet to ban Halloween at Cole Island High."

Hannah, clearly catching Taylor's eyes giving her the once-over, casually crossed her arms and asked, "Now just how did you guys get in here? The Barrelhead's closed."

"Door's not locked," Taylor said through a playful sneer.

"Don't worry," Sasha said, tugging on Taylor's arm, "we're not staying."

"You dressed up just for this?" Walczyk asked.

"Not that it wouldn't have been worth it," Taylor said, struggling to make eye contact. "but Lyndsay Howard's parents are out of town for the weekend and she's throwing this–"

"La la la," Hannah sang out, fingers in her ears.

"What the hell are you doing?" Taylor asked, cocking his head to one side.

"Language," Hannah snapped reflexively.

"I think," Walczyk said, "she means that if we don't know about it, we're not responsible for saying anything."

"Fair enough," Sasha said.

"But we did want two things before we left," Taylor said, reaching into his coat.

"I'm afraid to ask," Hannah said.

Taylor pulled a digital camera from his pocket. "Think we can get proof we *were* here?"

Walczyk shook his head, impressed by the kid's tenacity. "Sure, but if it winds up on paparazz-eye.com, I want half of what you sold it for."

Taylor turned to Hannah. "Would you, Miss Cooper?"

"Sure," she said. The junior faculty of Cole Island High crowded in around Walczyk as Hannah set the shot. "Ready?"

They all called out "Walczyk" and the camera flashed. Taylor stepped in beside Hannah to check the picture. "Nice. Thanks, Walczyk."

"You're welcome, Taylor," Walczyk said with a nod.

"And there's this," Taylor said, pulling something else out of his inside coat pocket.

Walczyk fingered the package, guessing it was a DVD. "If I'm supposed to autograph this..." Walczyk said, tearing the paper from it. He looked down at the package, and his jaw fell open. "Oh, my God..."

"What?" Hannah asked, moving closer to look over his shoulder.

"How'd you guys...?" Walczyk asked.

"A little research and an evening on Sasha's computer."

"Peter, what is it?" Hannah asked.

He handed the DVD to Hannah. She gasped. The cover read, *The Early Films of Peter Walczyk*. Walczyk looked at Taylor and Sasha. "*Crabapple Pie, The Boat, About a Girl...* and *Intolerance*? How the hell did you get your hands on this?"

"Let's just say you're not the only filmmaker with connections," Sasha said.

"And it didn't hurt that we knew your father has copies of all your stuff in his office," Taylor added.

"This is incredible. Thank you so much. You have no idea how much this means to me. No idea."

"You've been our inspiration," Taylor said. "Not just as a celebrity from our town, but as a student filmmaker who challenged the *status quo*."

"Still," Walczyk said, moved, "you really didn't have to do this."

"Yes, we did," Taylor said, offering Walczyk his hand. Walczyk took it and shook it.

"And we should leave it at that and take off before we *do* get into trouble," Sasha said, tugging on the fake Stella's coat.

Taylor held up his camera. "Picture, Miss Cooper?"

"You're pushing it, Taylor," Hannah said, knowing such a photo would be her downfall once it started circulating amongst the student body.

"Honestly, Taylor. Sasha. Thank you." Walczyk extended his hand, which Taylor took. "This is…"

"It's my pleasure. Happy birthday, Walczyk!"

Mini-Henry and Mini-Stella headed for the door. Walczyk was still looking at the DVD. "I don't believe this."

"Believe it," Hannah said. "You're a hero to them. One without tights and a cape."

"And you'll always be the Amazon in a short skirt with the fake boobs and shiny blue panties. At least to Taylor," Walczyk sneered.

"I wish I'd been drunk when they saw me. At least that way, I wouldn't remember."

"Let's rectify that now, " he said, taking her by the arm and leading her across the restaurant, which looked strange with all the tables cleared away to make a dance floor."

"Oh, no," she said, tugging on Superman's cape. "I still remember the nightmare that was the last time we got drunk together."

"Nightmare? That was one of my favorite nights alone with you."

"Peter, we almost–"

"Hey, get the hell outta the way! Let 'em through, you buncha savages!" The bellow came from behind the bar. The crowd dispersed, and Walczyk saw Vic's Uncle Donny signaling them toward the bar.

"No one stands on line on their birthday," he spat out in his thick, almost indecipherable Boston accent. "How you doing?" he asked, leaning across the counter to give Walczyk his hand.

"Great, Donny. You?"

"Couldn't complain if I'd wanted to," he said, grabbing a glass. "Rum and Coke?"

"And a Kamikaze for my beautiful friend here," Walczyk said, pointing to Hannah.

"No, I'm fine," Hannah protested, "and so's he."

"Han–"

"You shouldn't be drinking. Not on your meds. Not with April nearby."

"Bullshit!" Donny said, shoving a oh-so familiar looking rum and Coke across the bar. "It's Mr. Hollywood's birthday. You're drinkin'."

"Peter, I've got a bad feeling about this."

Walczyk picked the drink up. The sweet aroma of the rum played with his nose, taking him back to better times. "Han, I checked the bipolar chat rooms and message boards. If I behave and pace myself, I should be fine."

Hannah bit at her bottom lip, thinking it over. "Fine, but not a word to April, or she'll kill us both."

Walczyk turned to Donny. "She'll take a Kamikaze."

"I don't know about no friggin' Kamikaze," Donny said. "Never made one."

"How about a pear martini?" Hannah asked over the loud, booming music.

"Maybe," he said, confident in his uncertainty. "Lige," he called over to Elijah, the busboy who was helping tend bar. "Get out back. I think Andrew's got a can of fruit cocktail out there. I need it for Barbarella-over-here's pear martini!"

Elijah gave Donny a quizzical glance, and took off before he could get told again.

"Donny, I'm not Barbarella. I'm–"

Walczyk put a hand on her shoulder. "You really think it's going to matter?" She laughed. Walczyk spied Vic and April across the room, holding one another tightly, dancing. "It's weird."

"What's that? Seeing Batman and the Joker bumping-and-grinding?" Hannah asked.

"More like… this is it."

"*This is it?*"

"For this old gang of ours. April leaves in a week."

Hannah rested her head on Walczyk's shoulder. "Are you going be okay with that?"

"Do I have a choice in the matter?" Walczyk asked. "I think I'll be okay with it."

"Good," Hannah said.

From behind them, Donny announced, "One fruity pear martini!" They turned around and Donny proudly slid a large glass of clear liquid (probably vodka) with fruit cocktail in the bottom across the bar towards Hannah. She regarded the drink curiously, then politely smiled and thanked him. passed Walczyk his rum and Coke. Instinctively, Walczyk reached for his wallet, tucked into his red shorts.

"Oh, no! Batman's orders. Superman don't pay for no drinks," Donny said, crossing his arms. "And neither do none of the other superhero pals." He paused, following that up with, "Excepts for him." Donny pointed across the room at Cameron Burke, who was wearing a clearly homemade (but *well* homemade) Starfleet uniform. "Dr. Spock pays double."

"Donny, be nice," Hannah pleaded.

"Fine, but only because you're looking the best I've ever seen you," he said, leaning across the bar, lips puckered. Hannah nervously gave him the side of her face, which he kissed softly.

"Thank you, sweetheart," Donny said.

As they left the bar, a man dressed as a prostitute slapped Walczyk on the back and screamed "Happy Birthday, Walter!" before he and a woman dressed as a pimp slipped off into the bathroom.

"Where the hell did you get my guests, Han? Craigslist? Hang a poster at the Y? Take out an ad in *Uncle Henry's Swap or Sell It Guide?*"

Hannah took a sip of her drink, screwed her face up, and left it on a nearby table.

"What's wrong?"

"Tonight, we learn that fruit cocktail and vodka does not a pear martini make."

"Makes sense. Chicken and rice without the chicken would be–"

"Bland," she said, taking his rum and coke and taking a sip.

She tipped her head side to side, evaluating it. She took another sip, repeating the procedure. Finally, she looked up to Walczyk. "If there was nothing else, I might be able to enjoy this."

"Why don't we find Victor and April and toss back a few Johnnie Walkers."

As the evening progressed, with dancing, a birthday cake depicting the Hollywood sign sinking just off the coast of Walker beach, and a lot of drinking, Walczyk found himself impressed. It couldn't have been easy for Vic and Hannah to come up with this many people to come to a birthday party for him, as he'd been gone fifteen years and only a handful of his old classmates were still around. Beyond his classmates, though, he saw some of the locals he'd gotten to know. Tyler Salinger, a dead ringer for Johnny Depp's Captain Jack Sparrow, was having an animated discussion with Harry Hayes, Cole Island High's history teacher, who was dressed as Ghandi. Even Garry Olsen was in attendance with his wife Amanda, looking smart as Gomez and Morticia Addams.

As Walczyk staggered across the room to compliment Dougie Olsen on his one-eyed cowboy costume, possibly Marshall Rooster Cogburn from *True Grit*, a familiar voice called out to him: "There you are, Peter."

Walczyk turned around and found himself looking Sara right in the face. Not thinking, he reached out, grabbed her by the shoulders, and kissed her, hard. The strong taste of vodka filled his mouth. He knew Sara didn't drink vodka, but didn't care at the moment. The tongue sliding over his felt different. *Must've been all that time apart*, he told himself, and continued the embrace, inhaling deeply. The aroma of her body wash was gone, replaced with what he could only describe as stripper perfume. Then it hit him.

What was Sara doing in Maine?

Walczyk gently pushed Sara back from him. He looked her up and down. That shiny jet-black hair. Those bright red streaks. Those full, red lips and that eyeliner mole on her upper lip. It *had* to be Sara. But how? She was in Los Angeles right now. And why would she be on Cole Island? She was with Ella now. She didn't love him anymore.

He reached forward to touch her face, his hand brushing through her black bangs. A lock of dirty blonde hair crept out from under her hair. He stepped back. *How? Why?* Walczyk picked his heavy head back up, and scanned Sara's face. It was all wrong. Her eyebrows were thicker. Her nose was upturned. Her chin had a cleft. But it was the eyes that convinced him he had been seeing things. This new Sara's eyes were an almost oceanic blue, not the warm brown he'd been so accustomed to. And with a change of the dance lighting, suddenly Sara was gone.

Ingrid Connary was standing in front of him, holding his hands, looking pretty wasted.

"Peter? What's wrong?" Ingrid asked, looking concerned and confused. Walczyk opened his mouth to speak, but the rising urge to throw up crept up his esophagus, preempting that notion.

"Now *that* was nice," Vic said, bending down to pull on the black undershirt of his costume. "Though I thought we agreed to never let that happen again. Not that I'm complaining."

April worked her fingers behind her back to fasten her lime green bra. "We did."

Still panting, April turned her back to Vic, who handed her the purple dress pants of her costume. "No, it'll no doubt make things just that much more awkward a couple weeks down the road."

They dressed in silence. When they finished, Vic helped her pull on the purple tailcoat that finished off her ensemble. "You know I don't want you to leave."

"You're assuming I want to," she said.

"Then don't go."

"Vic–"

"No, seriously. Don't go. Stay here. We can–"

"We can what? Run the restaurant together? You'd fire me in a week. Move in together? You'd throw me out in a month. Get engaged? Vic, I'd never wish that kind of hell upon you."

"You always put yourself across as some unforgivable bitch," Vic said. "But do you want to know a secret? You're not. Not even close. Beneath that diamond encrusted exterior – which *isn't* invulnerable, I'll have you know – there's a heart, and it beats loud and strong. There's passion in there. Passion for your friends. Passion for your job. Passion for–"

"For you?"

"I'd like to think so, yeah."

"Vic, I learned long ago not to let my shields down for

anyone."

"'Shields?' Have you been watching *Star Trek* with Hannah again?"

"I've always enjoyed *Star Trek*."

"Then, at the risk of lowering your shields, can you answer me just one question? Is this at least hard for you? Leaving?"

"Of course it is! Vic, I've loved my time here. I've loved getting to know Henry and Diane, Hannah and, yes, even you. I'm so thankful, so... grateful that Walczyk is finally returning to something resembling happy. I think he needs to be out of the spotlight for a while."

"And you? What do you need, April Donovan?"

"I need to get the hell out of here!" she screamed suddenly, louder than she'd planned.

He stepped toward her. "Why is it so damned important that you get out of here?"

She shoved him back. "Because I'm falling in love with you, you idiot!"

"In love? With me?"

She shook her head, seething. "Don't. Don't even pretend you're in love with me."

"Who's pretending? I'm mad about you. Nuts. I've been wondering how the restaurant would survive if I followed you to–"

"This place would fold in a week if you left," April said firmly.

"Same conclusion I keep coming to," Vic replied. "So you're afraid of falling in love with me. Why? What's so wrong with being in love?"

"What's so wrong with being in love," she slowly began, "is that it scares the hell out of me."

"What about it scares the hell out of you?"

April took a deep breath. "Vic, we've been drinking. We just had some amazing sex. We're not thinking clearly. It's Walczyk's birthday. We're here to celebrate." She took his hands in hers, pulling him close to her. "Can we talk about this later?"

"Every time I try to talk to you about this, you ask if we can wait till later."

"And I'm asking again. If you love me, and we know you do, can it wait?"

Vic thought long and hard about it. He wanted to get things cleared up. It was driving him nuts – they *did* love each other. And yet April wanted to end all of that and run back to California. To a life without him. And she was so damned unwilling to talk about it. "Fine," he finally said, breaking the silence. "Tomorrow. Ten o'clock. Just you and me. Costigan's. Cinnamon pancakes and we talk."

April smiled. "Can we make it closer to eleven? I–"

"Ten," he replied firmly.

"Ten it is," she said, wrapping her arms around his neck. She stepped up on her tiptoes and kissed him. She still tasted like birthday cake and Guinness. And he never wanted to stop tasting it.

The first of November shared her cool breeze with Walczyk as he sat a few hundred feet from the water, watching the cold, black waves lap the shore in rhythmical surges. His feet buried in the cold, clammy, wet sand stretching up from the water, he stared out across the dark sky. The street lights lining Walker Bridge stretched across the dark ocean, pointing away from Cole Island.

Los Angeles was a great city. Things didn't shut down at ten o'clock. A person could go days without being recognized, provided that person wasn't being followed by photographers. And, most importantly, there were more than three dining establishments that stayed open year-round. And none of them shared a name with the surf shop next door. But for all the glitter and glamour that life in the fast lane offered, with its fancy cars and exotic girls and legendary landmarks, there was a lot that L.A. didn't offer. A lot that Walczyk had right here on Cole Island. There were Jeeps you could pull the top off on a hot day, honest women you could fall in love with just by staring into their eyes, not down at their cleavage, and the serenity of the places that witnessed you growing up. For all of Hollywood's hustle and bustle and endless nights, it was this moment, wrapping him in silence as he sat alone on a beach, staring up at familiar stars, that reminded Peter Walczyk of a bit of profound wisdom his Grampie Walczyk once shared with him: the grass is greener on the other side of the fence.

"Penny for your thoughts?" Hannah's voice called out behind him, slipping unobtrusively into the melody of crashing waves and distant cars that were the soundtrack of his evening. He turned to see Hannah walking towards him, her red boots in her hands.

"And a quarter for your mind," Walczyk said, smiling at the in-joke that neither could remember the origins of. Hannah dropped the boots by the large, jagged, oblong rock that Walczyk was leaning up against and sat down beside him.

"You okay?"

"I'm fine. How's Ingrid?"

"Telling anyone who'll listen that you almost threw up on her."

Walczyk chucked a broken clam shell across the sand, into the water. "What are the odds, Han?"

"That Ingrid would dress up for your Halloween-slash-Birthday party as a Kitty Kat Girl?"

"No, that Ingrid would dress up for my Halloween-slash-Birthday party as *my* Kitty Kat Girl."

Their laughter filled the empty night air, and as it subsided, the waves cut back in, and they sat in silence, shoulder to shoulder, embracing the company of each other.

"You know, I miss her."

Hannah picked her head up, looking at Walczyk. "If you don't mind my finally asking, what happened?"

"It's really an age-old story, Han. Boy meets girl. Boy marries girl. Boy gets depressed and goes all *non-communicado*. Boy lets girl down. Girl meets another girl. Girl moves on."

"So she *did* get together with Ella." He nodded. "Is she happy now?"

"Seems it. From what I keep hearing from Eli and Ian and some of the other L.A. friends we share, they're amazing together. They've got all the disgusting, saccharine couple shit going on. They finish each other's sentences. They take turns deciding who washes and who dries when they do dishes. Both of them are a size two."

A pocket of that comfortable, pleasant silence settled over them, Hannah's head finding its way back against Walczyk's shoulder. A torrent of images, much like the recaps that preceded episodes of *Ordinary World*, trickled through his mind. He remembered dancing with Hannah at the Junior prom. Agonizing over loving his best friend's girlfriend. A midnight skinny dip, Hannah's idea. He remembered the day Vic broke up with Hannah, leaving Walczyk to bounce between two good friends. There were the red and gold blasts that lit Hannah's face as he leaned over and kissed her beneath the

Fourth of July fireworks display on Walker Beach. There was the morning after the big Class of 1996 graduation party at the Lambert camp, with Hannah wrapped in his arms, sound asleep. With forty-three days left before they had to head off to colleges in different directions, Hannah told Walczyk she loved him. He repaid her by racing across Walker Bridge, leaving a note on his parents' kitchen table and a package with "Han" in big letters left in the mailbox of 178 Matagamon Lane. He remembered watching Cole Island shrink away from his rear view mirror as he crossed the bridge. He left behind true love. He left commitment. He'd made a big mistake.

"I suppose now's as good a time as any to say I'm sorry I treated you like I did."

"Now, that wasn't so hard," Hannah said, still staring out at the ocean. "And to think it only took you, what, fifteen years?"

"What can I say? I'm a fast learner."

Walczyk lay back down on the sand. After a while, Hannah asked him, "So, what's it like? Being bipolar?"

Eventually, he answered her. "It's like... like I'm cracking up." Hannah sat in silence, her hand continually caressing Walczyk's spandex-clad arm. "I'll wake up feeling like the happiest idiot on the planet, walking on sunshine and pissing out excitement. And then something in my brain flips a switch and it all goes dark."

"You black out?" If she was trying to mask the concern in her voice, she failed.

"No. I just... it's like that book Dad gave me. *Dr. Jekyll and Mr. Hyde.* We're never sure why the change happens; only that it's an uncontrollable chemical imbalance."

"But Jekyll took something that started it all. What about you? Did you take something? A drug? Acid? Meth?"

"No, no, no," he said, shaking his head. He took a moment to compose his thoughts. "Nothing like that. But Henry Jekyll, he's chilling out. Hanging with his friend Utterson. Then Utterson leaves, and with the flip of a switch, or whatever, Jekyll... it's like he was never there. No memory of the joy his friend brought him. Completely unable to even remember what happy *felt* like." He felt Hannah's hand slide down his arm, clutching his hand. Her fingers interlaced with his. "All that's left, standing there, in that exact spot, in those exact clothes, scowling at the world with dead eyes and such... such blackness in his head, is Edward Hyde." The salty tang of tears sent a signal from his parched lips to his brain.

Hannah stared directly into his hazel eyes and asked, with an unsure voice, "And what does Mr. Hyde do?"

"Sometimes, he just stays hidden in the house. Sometimes, he burns his bridges. Sometimes, he gets blasted out of his mind. Almost always, he just counts the time."

Either she had nothing to say, or she had to figure out just how to say what was on her mind, because another period of silence enveloped them, this one less comfortable than the last.

"You're a writer. A very good one. The industry thinks that. Your fans think that. Myself, Vic, April, your parents... we all feel that way. But you don't sit down to a blank screen knowing that Ethan is going to end up back with Kara, right?"

"No. I have no idea if Ethan and Kara would ever, *could* ever reconcile."

"But somehow they did. How did you learn that it was what they needed to do?"

"I don't know. I just let the story unfold."

"One thing I've heard you say over and over since you got back here, aside from your cracks about my *Star Trek* obsession or your extreme distaste for reality television, is that you don't know what you're supposed to be doing next."

"And I don't. I'm losing my passion for my work, Han. Even at its height, *Ordinary World* was more of a chore than it is a delight. That's why I cancelled it."

"How about this: you told me that when you write, you don't plan ahead. You just let the story unfold; let the characters take you where they need to go. Why don't you take your own advice? Put Peter Walczyk on a blank page, just write for him, and see where he goes."

"Fine, but if he ends up on a reality show, it's your ass on the line."

She gave him a smile. "Fair enough."

Walczyk looked out over the water, rippling quietly under a rising sun that still gave them no heat. The town behind them was waking up. Weezie was no doubt warming up her griddle. Been's was putting on the first seven pots of coffee that would last them probably forty-five minutes, if they were lucky. Every single senior citizen, healthy or otherwise, was waking up, seeing no sense in wasting daylight, their days busy with games of Bingo at the Bronze Lantern, lining up in front of the post office, and complaining about the President, regardless of which guy they voted for. The smell of fresh baked bread from the Sisters' Bakery across the street from Hannah's apartment was now permeating the neighborhood. And somewhere deep within the inner recesses of the Barrelhead, Vic and April laid passed out together, no doubt naked and sweaty.

"Come on," Walczyk said, slowly getting to his feet. "We've got to walk back to your place, and I'd rather not parade through town in a dirty Superman costume when everyone and their uncle will be out."

"That's some smart thinking." Hannah reached up, grabbing Walczyk's hand, and pulled herself to her feet.

"I kinda liked the wig," Walczyk said. "What happened to it?"

"I think I stuffed it into Garry Olsen's car," she said, picking up her red boots. "I'll have to call him later and make sure that was his tan Lexus."

As they reached the foot of the steps leading to the side of the road, Hannah grabbed for Walczyk's shoulder, wiped her feet as clean as she could get them, and slid her glossy red boots back on.

"It's a sure sign Hannah Cooper has been drinking when she can't remember which car she put her wig in," Walczyk quipped.

They walked up the steep stairs to the main road in silence. As they started towards town, Hannah chirped, "I've got an idea!"

"I'm almost too afraid to ask."

"Let's *run* back to my place. First one there gets the bed."

"You? Running? In that skirt and those boots? I'd let you win just to enjoy the view."

"Shut up," she said. "You're running too. You need to establish an exercise routine, and I'm going to help you." She let go of him and tore off down the road, amber hair flowing behind her, sand-coated blue panties screaming "good morning" to the world as her skirt flapped in the breeze. As wise a woman as she was, Hannah Cooper was even wiser for never having lost her sense of childish adventure. Walczyk admired that as he leisurely walked down the road, enjoying the notion that any motorist or townsperson out and about would have to question their own sanity as they saw Wonder Woman running towards Main Street with Superman following close behind her. Then again, it was Cole Island, and anyone passing such a sight would laugh, shake their head, and say, "Oh, that's just that Walczyk boy. He'll be going places someday. He'll be doing things some day."

And he did go to those places, and he did do those things. He'd surpassed everyone's estimation of what he was capable of, primarily his own. And now, on the other side of his career peak, all he wanted to do was live out his days in the Old Merry Place, in seclusion from the media, plunk away at a screenplay or maybe even a novel, and enjoy the fact that, contrary to another well-known adage, he *could* go home again. And for the first time in a long time, he was happy to be himself – just Walczyk.

ACKNOWLEGMENTS

Books don't write themselves. At least, this one didn't. The publication of *Walczyk* was a team effort and I just want to thank that team for their tireless devotion to the project and to me.

First and foremost, I have to thank Deborah Coolong. My mother, the editor. If there anyone who knows the ins and outs of Cole Island as well as I do, it's my Mum. You have been with me on this journey since the beginning, encouraging me, revising, rewriting, and forgiving my use of the "F-word." Thank you for believing in me.

Nathan Anderson. You never once asked for a page before I was ready to share it, yet you've supported this project and shown a keen interest in it from the beginning. How you spent four years reading paperbacks at the book store while I wrote downstairs, I'll never know.

Tyler Costigan. You encouraged me to try National Novel Writing Month (NaNoWriMo) back in June of 2009, a time when I felt I had very little to live for. Now, four years later, I realize just how much I *do* have to live for.

Hannah Cyrus. Your nitpicking over "em dashes" (or are they "en dashes?") and comma placement helped turn what could just as easily been a whimsical side project into a published novel. (And please note that the question mark is *inside* the quotation marks.)

Douglas Esper. My go-to guy in the field of self-publication. We barely know one another, Doug, yet you showed a keen interest and great pride in my work.

Mandy Fahey. The eagerness with which you devoured this book showed me that it was, in fact, readable. Your support, encouragement and motivation were invaluable.

Blake Johnson. Self-pub guru and cover model. You showed me the ropes, gave me advice from your own experience in self-publication, and never gave up hope that either of us would be published.

Bruce Johnson. You have been my spiritual guide and a true friend. It was an honor to get to place you in Walczyk's world and let him benefit from your generosity and love.

Logan Tripp. Your professionalism and patience brought life to Walczyk (the person and the book) in a way I never could have. Beyond that, your enthusiasm for this project has been so invigorating!

Finally, the ability to write did not come by me accidentally. I truly believe I was destined to have bipolar disorder, and that I was destined to write about it. That is part of the plan He has for me. Thank you, Lord, for giving me these talents, and letting me figure out how to use them, both to spread Your word and to just tell a story.

I'm leaving a lot of people out, I know, but know that you've all earned yourselves a special place, not only in my heart, but as welcomed guests of Cole Island.

Tellis K. Coolong
August 22, 2013

Made in the USA
Lexington, KY
18 June 2014